ANTARCTICA

Kim Stanley Robinson was born in 1952 and, after travelling and working around the world, has now settled in his beloved California. He is widely regarded as the finest science fiction writer working today, noted as much for the verisimilitude of his characters as the meticulously researched hard science basis of his work. He has won just about every major sf award there is to win and is the author of the massively successful and lavishly praised *Mars* series.

'The land looks like a fairytale.'

ROALD AMUNDSEN

Voyager

ANTARCTICA

Kim Stanley Robinson

HarperCollins*Publishers*

Voyager
An Imprint of HarperCollins*Publishers*
77–85 Fulham Palace Road,
Hammersmith, London w6 8jb

The *Voyager* World Wide Web site address is
http://www.harpercollins.co.uk/voyager

Published by HarperCollins*Publishers* 1998
1 3 5 7 9 8 6 4 2

Copyright © Kim Stanley Robinson 1997

The Author asserts the moral right to
be identified as the author of this work

A catalogue record for this book
is available from the British Library

ISBN 0 00 225393 3

Set Aldus

Printed and bound in Great Britain by
Caledonian International Book Manufacturing Ltd, Glasgow

Contents

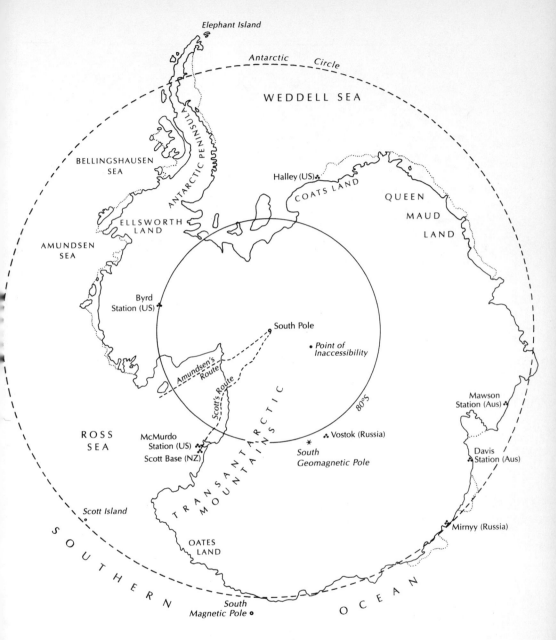

Antarctica

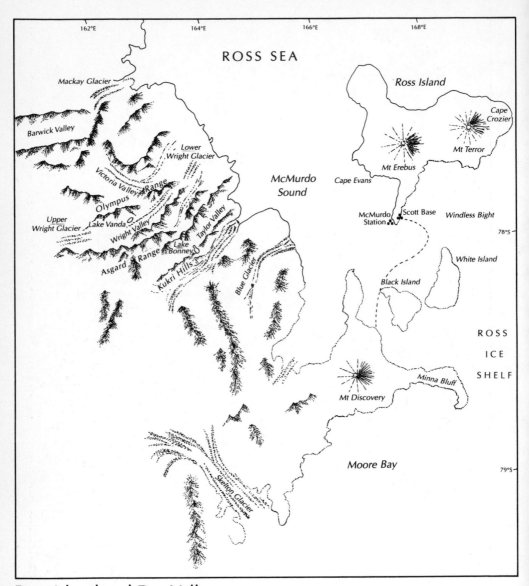

Ross Island and Dry Valleys

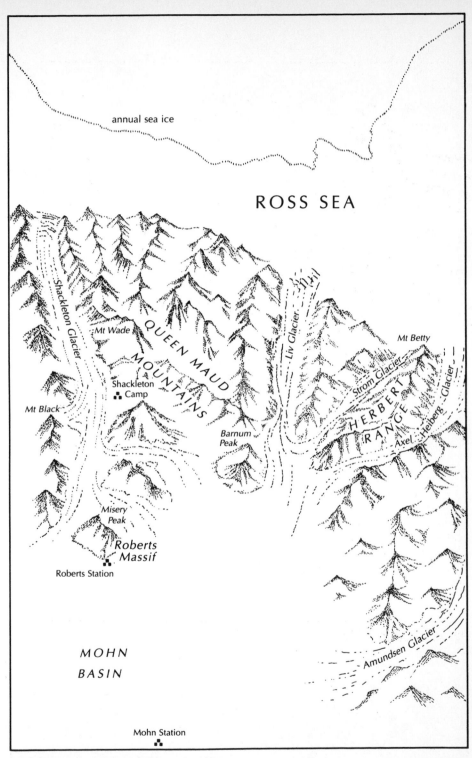

The Queen Maud Mountains

CHAPTER ONE

Ice Planet

First you fall in love with Antarctica, and then it breaks your heart.

Breaks it first in all the usual sorry ways of the world, sure – as for instance when you go down to the ice to do something unusual and exciting and romantic, only to find that your job there is in fact more tedious than anything you have ever done, janitorial in its best moments but usually much less interesting than that. Or when you discover that McMurdo, the place to which you are confined by the strictest of company regulations, resembles an island of service stations clustered around the off-ramp of a freeway long since abandoned. Or, worse yet, when you meet a woman, and start something with her, and go with her on vacation to New Zealand, and travel around South Island with her, the first woman you ever really loved; and then after a brief off-season you return to McMurdo and your reunion with her only to have her dump you on arrival as if your Kiwi idyll had never happened. Or when you see her around town soon after that, trolling with the best of them; or when you find out that some people are calling you 'the Sandwich', in reference to the ice women's old joke that bringing a boyfriend to Antarctica is like bringing a sandwich to a smorgasbord. Now that's heartbreak for you.

But then the place has its own specifically Antarctic heartbreaks as well, more impersonal than the worldly kinds, cleaner, purer, colder. As for instance when you are up on the polar plateau in late winter, having taken an offer to get out of town without a second thought, no matter the warnings about the boredom of the job, for how bad could it be compared to General Field Assistant? And so there you are riding in the enclosed cab of a giant transport vehicle, still thinking about that girlfriend, ten thousand feet above sea level, in the dark of the long night; and as you sit there looking out of the cab windows, the sky gradually lightens to the day's one hour of twilight, shifting in invisible stages from a star-cluttered black pool to a dome of glowing

1

indigo lying close overhead; and in that pure transparent indigo floats the thinnest new moon imaginable, a mere sliver of a crescent, which nevertheless illuminates very clearly the great ocean of ice rolling to the horizon in all directions, the moonlight glittering on the snow, gleaming on the ice, and all of it tinted the same vivid indigo as the sky; everything still and motionless; the clarity of the light unlike anything you've ever seen, like nothing on Earth, and you all alone in it, the only witness, the sole inhabitant of the planet it seems; and the uncanny beauty of the scene rises in you and clamps your chest tight, and your heart breaks then simply because it is squeezed so hard, because the world is so spacious and pure and beautiful, and because moments like this one are so transient – impossible to imagine before-hand, impossible to remember afterward, and never to be returned to, never ever. That's heartbreak as well, yes – happening at the very same moment you realize you've fallen in love with the place, despite all.

Or so it all happened to the young man looking out of the windows of the lead vehicle of that spring's South Pole Overland Traverse train – the Sandwich, as he had been called for the last few weeks, also the Earl of Sandwich, the Earl, the Duke of Earl (with appropriate vocal riff), and the Duke; and then, because these variations seemed to be running thin, and appeared also to touch something of a sore spot, he was once again referred to by the nicknames he had received in Antarctica the year before: Extra Large, which was the size announced prominently on the front of his tan Carhartt overalls; and then of course Extra; and then just plain X. 'Hey, X, they need you to shovel snow off the coms roof, get over there!'
    After the sandwich variations he had been very happy to return to this earlier name, a name that anyway seemed to express his mood and situation – the alienated, anonymous, might-as-well-be-illiterate-and-signing-his-name-with-a-mark General Field Assistant, the Good For Anything, The Man With No Name. It was the name he used himself – 'Hey, Ron, this is X, I'm on the coms roof, the snow is gone. What next? Over.' – thus naming himself in classic Erik Erikson style, to indicate his rebirth and seizure of his own life destiny. And so X returned to general usage, and became again his one and only name. Call me X. He was X.

The SPOT train rolled majestically over the polar cap, ten vehicles in a row, moving at about twenty kilometres an hour – not bad, considering the terrain. X's lead vehicle crunched smoothly along, running over the tracks of previous SPOT trains, tracks that were in places higher than the surrounding snow, as the wind etched the softer drifts away. The other tractors were partly visible out of the little back window of the high cab, looking like the earthmovers that in fact had been their design ancestors. Other than that, nothing but the polar plateau itself. A circular plain of whiteness, the same in all directions, the various broad undulations obscure in the starlight, obvious in the track of reflected moonlight.

As the people who had warned him had said, there was nothing for him to do. The train of vehicles was on automatic pilot, navigating by GPS, and nothing was likely to malfunction. If something did X was not to do anything about it; the other tractors would manoeuvre around any total breakdowns, and a crew of mechanics would be flown out later to take care of it. No − X was there, he had decided, because somebody up in the world had had the vague feeling that if there was a train of tractors rolling from McMurdo to the South Pole, then there ought to be a human being along. Nothing more rational than that. In effect he was a good luck charm; he was the rabbit's foot hanging from the rear view mirror. Which was silly. But in his two seasons on the ice X had performed a great number of silly tasks, and he had begun to understand that there was very little that was rational about anyone's presence in Antarctica. The rational reasons were all just rationales for an underlying irrationality, which was the desire *to be down here*. And why that desire? This was the question, this was the mystery. X now supposed that it was a different mix of motives for every person down there − explore, expand, escape, evaporate − and then under those, perhaps something else, something basic and very much the same for all − like Mallory's explanation for trying to climb Everest: because it's there. Because it's there! That's reason enough!

And so here he was. Alone on the Antarctic polar plateau, driving across a frozen cake of ice two miles thick and a continent wide, a cake that held ninety-five percent of the world's fresh water, etc. Of course it had sounded exciting when it was first mentioned to him, no matter the warnings. Now that he was here, he saw what people had meant when they said it was boring, but it was interesting too − boring in an interesting way, so to speak. Like operating a freight lift that no one ever used, or being stuck in a cinema showing a dim print of *Scott of the Antarctic* on a continuous loop. There was not even any weather; X travelled under the alien southern constellations with never a cloud to be seen. The twilight hour, which grew several minutes longer every day, only occasionally revealed winds, winds unfelt and unheard inside the cab, perceptible to X only as moving waves of snow seen flowing over the white ground.

Once or twice he considered gearing up and going outside to

cross-country ski beside the tractor; this was officially forbidden, but he had been told it was one of the main forms of entertainment for SPOT train conductors. X was a terrible athlete, however; his last adolescent sprout had taken him to six feet ten inches tall, and in that growth he had lost all co-ordination. He had tried to learn cross-country skiing on the prescribed routes around McMurdo, and had made a little progress; and sometimes it was a tempting idea to break the monotony; but then he considered that if he fell and twisted an ankle, or stunned himself, the SPOT tractors would continue to grind mindlessly on, leaving him behind trying to catch up, and no doubt failing.

He decided to pass on going outside. Monotony was not such a bad thing. Besides there would be some crevasse fields to be negotiated, even up here on the plateau, where the ice was often smooth and solid for miles at a time. Although it was true that the Army Corps of Engineers had mitigated all crevasses they didn't care to outflank, meaning they had blown them to smithereens, then bulldozed giant causeways across the resulting ice-cube fields. This process had created some dramatic passages on the Skelton Glacier, which rose from the Ross Sea to the polar plateau in less than thirty kilometres, and was therefore pretty severely crevassed in places; so much so that the Skelton had not been the preferred route for SPOT; the first trains had crossed the Ross Ice Shelf and ascended the Leverett Glacier, a gentler incline much farther to the south. But soon after SPOT had become operational, and quickly indispensable for the construction of the new Pole station, the Ross Ice Shelf had begun to break apart and float away, except for where it was anchored between Ross Island and the mainland. The Skelton route could make use of this remnant portion of the shelf, and so every year the Corps of Engineers re-established it, and off they went. X's night-time ascent of the Skelton, through the spectacular peaks of the Royal Society Range, had been the most exciting part of his trip by far, crunching up causeway after causeway of crushed ice concrete, with serac fields like dim, shattered Manhattans passing to right and left.

But that had been many days ago, and since reaching the polar plateau there had not been much excitement of any sort. The fuel depots they passed were automated and robotic; the vehicles stopped one by one next to squat green bladders, were filled up and then moved on. If any new crevasses had opened up across the road since the last passing of a train, the lead vehicle's pulse radar would detect it, and the navigation system would take appropriate action, either veering around the problem area or stopping and waiting for instructions. Nothing of that sort actually happened.

But he had been warned it would be this way, and was ready for it.

Besides, it was not that much different from all the rest of the mindless work that Ron liked to inflict on his GFAs; and here X was free of Ron. And he wasn't going to run into anyone he didn't want to, either. So he was content. He slept a lot. He made big breakfasts, and lunches, and dinners. He watched movies. He read books; he was a voracious reader, and now he could sit before the screen and read book after book, or portions of them, tracking cross-references through the ether like any other obsessive young gypsy scholar. He made sure to stop reading and look out of the windows at the great ice plain during the twilights bracketing noon, twilights that grew longer and brighter every day. Though he did not experience again anything quite as overwhelming as the indigo twilight of the crescent moon, he did see many beautiful pre-dawn skies. The quality of light during these hours was impossible to get used to, vibrant and velvet beyond description, rich and transparent, a perpetual reminder that he was on the polar cap of a big planet.

Then one night he got some weather. The stars were obscured to the south, the rising moon did not rise on schedule, though clearly it had to be up there, no doubt shining on the top of the clouds and, yes, making them glow just a little, so that now he could see them rushing north and over him, like a blanket pulled over the world; no stars, now, but a dim, cloudy rushing overhead; and then through the thick insulation of the cab he could for once hear the wind, whistling over and under and around his tractor. He could even feel the tractor rock just a tiny bit on its massive shock absorbers. A storm! Perhaps even a superstorm!

Then the moon appeared briefly through a gap, nearly a half moon now, full of mystery and foreboding, flying fast over the clouds, then gone again. Black shapes flicked through the clouds like bats. X blinked and rubbed his eyes, sure that he was seeing things.

A light tap on the roof of his vehicle. 'What the hell?' X croaked. He had almost forgotten how to talk.

Then his windscreen was being covered by a sheet of what looked like black plastic. Side windows and back window also. X could see gloved fingers working at the edges of the plastic, reaching down from above to tape the sheets in place. Then he could see nothing but the inside of the cab.

'What the hell!' he shouted, and ran to the door, which resembled a meat-locker door in both appearance and function. He turned the big handle and pushed out. It didn't move. It wouldn't move. There were no locks on these tractor doors, but now this one wouldn't open.

'What-the-*hell*,' X said again, his heart pounding. 'HEY!' he shouted at the roof of the vehicle. 'Let me out!' But with the vehicle's insulation there was no way he would be heard. Besides, even if he were . . .

He ran down the narrow low stairs leading from the cab into the vehicle's freight room. On one side of the big compartment were two big loading doors that opened outward, but when he twisted the latch locks down, and turned the handles and pushed out, these doors too remained stubbornly in place. They were not as insulated as the cab doors, and when he pushed out on them hard, a long crack of windy darkness appeared between them. He put an eye to the thin gap, and felt the chill immediately: fifty degrees below zero out there, and a hard wind. There was a plastic bar crossing the gap just below eye level holding the doors shut. 'Hey!' he bellowed out of the crack. 'Let me out! What are you doing?'

No answer. His face was freezing. He pulled back and blinked, staring at the crack. The bar was welded or glued or otherwise bonded across the doors, locking them in place. No doubt it was the same up there on the outside of the cab door.

He recalled the emergency hatch in the roof of the cab, there in case the vehicle fell through sea ice or got corked in a crevasse, so that the occupants had to make their escape upward. X had thought it a pretty silly precaution, but now he ran back and pulled that handle around to the open position, a very stiff handle indeed, and shoved up. It wouldn't go. Stuck. He was trapped inside, and the windscreen and cab windows were covered. All in about two minutes. Ludicrous but true.

He thought over the situation while putting on the layers of his outdoor clothing: thick smartfabric pants and coat, insulated Carhartt overalls, heavy parka, gloves and mittens. He would need it all outside, if he could get outside, but now he began to overheat terribly. Sweating, he turned on the radio and clicked it to the McMurdo coms band. 'Hello McMurdo, McMurdo, this is SPOT number 103, SPOT calling Mac Town do you read me? Over, over.' While he waited for a reply he went to one of the closets of the cab and pulled a brand new hacksaw from a tool chest.

'SPOT 103, through the miracle of radio technology you have once again manipulated invisible vibrations in the ether to reach Mac Coms. Hey, X, how are you out there? Over.'

'Not good, Randi, I think I'm being hijacked!'

'Say again, X, I did not copy your last message, over.'

'I *said* I am being *hijacked*. Over!'

'Hey, X, lot of static here, sounded like you said say *Hi to Jack*, but Jack's out in the field – tell me what you mean, if that's what you said, over.'

'*Hi*-JACKED. Someone's locked me in the cab here and taped over the windows! Over!'

'X, did you say hijacked? Tell me what you mean by hijacked, over.'

'What I mean is that I'm in a storm up here and just now some—somebody landed on my roof and covered my windows on the outside with black plastic, and none of my doors will open, something's been done to them on the outside to keep them from opening! So I'm going to go back and try to cut through a bar holding the back doors together, but I thought I'd better call you first, in case, to tell you what's happening! Also to ask if you can see anything unusual about my train in any satellite images you have of it! Over!'

'We'll have to check about the satellite images, X, I don't know who is getting those, if anyone. Just stay put and we'll see what we can do. Don't do anything rash, over.'

'Yeah yeah yeah,' X muttered, and pushed the transmit button: 'Listen, Randi, I'm going to go to the back doors and see if they'll open, be right back to tell you about it, over!'

He went to the back and shoved out on the doors again. Again they stopped, but this time he fitted the hacksaw into the crack over the bar and began to saw like a maniac. Some kind of hardened plastic, apparently, and the doors impeded the saw. By the time he had cut through the bar he was sweating profusely, and when he flung the doors open the air crashed over him like a wave of liquid nitrogen. 'Ow!' he said, his throat chilling with every inhalation. He pulled his parka hood up, and held onto the door and leaned out into the wind, his eyes tearing so that he could barely see.

But he had a door open. He was no longer trapped. He leaned out to look; the next vehicle in the line was following as if nothing had happened. It was like being in a train of mechanical elephants. No one in sight, nothing to be seen. Rumbling engines, squeaks of giant tractor wheels over the dry snow, the whistle and shriek of the wind; nothing else; but a gust of fear blew through him on the wind, and he shivered convulsively. He needed more clothes. Back up in the cab he could hear Randi's voice, a clear Midwestern twang that cut through static like nothing else: 'Mac Coms calling SPOT 103, answer me, X, what's happening out there? Weather says you're in a Condition One out there, so be careful! They also said their satellite photos do not penetrate the cloud layer in any way useful to you. Answer me, X, please, over!'

Instead he dropped down the steps and onto the hard-packed snow beside the vehicle. It squeaked underfoot. 'Shit.' He ran forward and leapt onto the ladder steps that were inset into the lower body of the cab. Black plastic on the windows, sure enough. 'Shit!' He tore at it, and the freezing wind helped pull the sheet away from the metal and plastic; he held onto the sheet with a desperate clench, so that he would have evidence that he had not hallucinated the whole incident. Then he hesitated, irrationally afraid of jumping down wrong somehow and screwing up, as in his ski fantasy. But surely in the state he was in, he could run a lot faster than the tractors were moving; and it was too cold to stay where he was: the wind was barrelling right through his clothes and his flesh too, rattling his bones together like castanets. So he leapt down, and landed solidly, and as his tractor lumbered past he ran out of the line of the treadmarks to be able to see back the length of the train. It looked short. He counted to be sure, pointing at each tractor in turn; while he did his vehicle got a bit ahead of him, and when he noticed that he ran like a lunatic back to the side of the thing, and leapt up and in, panting hard, frightened, frozen right to the core. There were only nine vehicles now.

High rapid beeping came from her crevasse detector, and Valerie Kenning stopped skiing and leaned on her ski poles. She was well ahead of the rest of her group, and with a check over her shoulder to make sure they were coming on okay, she stabbed her poles deeper in the dry snow of the Windless Bight, causing a last little surge of heat in the pole handles, and took the pulse radar console out of its parka pocket and looked at the screen, thumbing the buttons to get a complete read on the terrain. A *beepbeepbeep*; there was a fairly big crevasse ahead. They were entering the pressure zone where the Ross Ice Shelf used to push around the point of Cape Crozier, and though the pressure was gone the buckling was still there, causing many crevasses.

She approached this one slowly and got a visual sighting: a slight slump lining the snow. She would have noticed it, but there were many others that were invisible. Thus her love for the crevasse detector, like a baseball catcher's love for his mask. Now she used it to check the crevasse for a usable snowbridge. The music of the beeps played up and down – higher and faster over thin snow, lower and slower over the thicker bits. In one broad region to her left, snow filled the crevasse with a thickness and density that would have held a Hagglunds. So Val unclipped from her sledge harness, plucked her poles out of the snow and skied slowly across, shoving one ski pole down ahead of her in the old-fashioned test, more for luck than anything else; by now she trusted the radar as much as any other machine she used.

She recrossed the bridge, snapped back into her sledge, pulled it across the crevasse, and stood waiting for the others, chilling down as she did. While she waited she checked her GPS to scout their route through the crevasses ahead. A bit of a maze. The three members of the 1911 journey to Cape Crozier, the so-called 'Worst Journey In The World', had taken a week of desperate hauling to pass through this region; but with GPS and the latest ice maps, Val's group of twenty-four would thread a course in only a day, or two if Arnold slowed them too much.

There were only two days to go before the springtime return of the sun to Cape Crozier, and at this hour of the morning Mount Erebus's upper slopes were bathed in a vibrant pink alpenglow, which reflected down onto the blue snow of the shadowed slopes beneath it, creating all kinds of lavender and mauve tints. Meanwhile the twilit sky was pinwheeling slowly through its bright but sunless array of pastels: broad swathes of blues, purples, pinks, even moments of green; as Val slowly cooled down she had a good look around, enjoying the moment of peace that would soon be shattered by the arrival of the pack. A guide's chances to enjoy the landscapes she travelled through came a lot less frequently than Val would have liked.

Then the pack was on her and she was back at work, making sure they all got across the snowbridge without accident, chatting with the perpetual cheerfulness that was her professional demeanour, pointing out the alpenglow on Erebus, which was turning the steam cloud at its summit into a mass of pink candyfloss thirteen thousand feet above them. This diverted them while they waited for Arnold. It was too cold to wait comfortably for long, however, and many of them obviously had been sweating, despite Val's repeated warnings against doing so. But even with the latest smartfabrics in their outfits these folks were not skilful enough at thermostatting to avoid it. They had overheated as they skied and their sweat had wicked outward through several layers whose polymer microstructures were more or less permeable depending on how hot they got, the moisture passing through highly heated fabric freely until it was shoved right out of the surface of their parkas, where it immediately froze. Her twenty-four waiting clients looked like a grove of flocked Christmas trees, shedding snow with every move.

Eventually a pure white Arnold reached them and crossed the snow-bridge, and without giving him much of a chance for rest they were off again through the crevasse maze. Although they were crossing the Windless Bight, a strong breeze struck them in the face. Val waited for Arnold, who was puffing like a horse, his steamy breath freezing and falling in front of him as white dust. He shook his head at her; though she could see nothing of his face under his goggles and ski-mask (which he ought to have pulled up, sweating as he was) she could tell he was grinning. 'Those guys,' he said, with the intonation the group used to mean Wilson, Bowers and Cherry-Garrard, the three members of the original Crozier journey. 'They were *crazy*.'

'And what does that make us?'

Arnold laughed wildly. 'That makes us *stupid*.'

black sky
white sea

Ice everywhere, under a starry sky. Dark white ground, flowing underfoot. A white mountain puncturing the black sky, mantled by ice, dim in the light. An ice planet, too far from its sun to support life; its sun one of the brighter stars overhead, perhaps. Snow ticking by like sand, too cold to adhere to anything. Titan, perhaps, or Triton, or Pluto. No chance of life.

But there, at the foot of black cliffs falling into white ice, a faint electric crackle. Look closer: there – the source of the sound. A clump of black things, bunched in a mass. Moving awkwardly. Black pears in white tie. The ones on the windward side of the mass slip around to the back; they've taken their turn in the wind, and can now cycle through the mass and warm back up. They huddle for warmth, sharing in turn the burden of taking the brunt of the icy wind. Aliens.

Actually Emperor penguins, of course. Some of them waddled away from the newcomers on the scene, looking exactly like the animated penguins in *Mary Poppins*. They slipped through black cracks in the ice, diving into the comparative warmth of the −2°C water, metamorphosing from fish-birds to bird-fish, as in an Escher drawing.

The penguins were the reason Val's group was there. Not that her clients were interested in the penguins, but Edward Wilson had been. In 1911 he had wondered if their embryos would reveal a missing link in evolution, believing as he did that penguins were primitive birds in evolutionary terms. This idea was wrong, but there was no way to find that out except to examine some Emperor penguin eggs, which were laid in the middle of the Antarctic winter. Robert Scott's second expedition to Antarctica was wintering at Cape Evans on the other side of Ross Island, waiting for the spring, when they would begin their attempt to reach the South Pole. Wilson had convinced his friend Scott to allow him to take Birdie Bowers and Apsley Cherry-Garrard on a trip around the south side of the island, to collect some Emperor penguin eggs for the sake of science.

Val thought it strange that Scott had allowed the three men to go, given that they might very well have perished and thus jeopardized Scott's chances of reaching the Pole. But that was Scott for you. He had made a lot of strange decisions. And so Wilson and Bowers and Cherry-Garrard had manhauled two heavy sledges around the island, in their usual style: without skis or snowshoes, wearing wool and canvas clothing, sleeping in reindeer-skin sleeping bags, in canvas tents; hauling their way through the thick drifts of the Windless Bight in continuous darkness, in temperatures between minus forty and minus seventy-five degrees Fahrenheit, the coldest temperatures that had ever been experienced by humans for that length of time. And thirty-six days later they had staggered back into the Cape Evans hut, with three intact Emperor penguin eggs; and the misery and wonder they had experienced en route, recounted so wonderfully in Cherry-Garrard's book, had made them part of history for ever, as the men who had made the Worst Journey In The World.

Now Val's group was in a photo frenzy around the penguins, and the professional film crew they had along unpacked their equipment and took a lot of film. The penguins eyed them warily, and increased the volume of their collective squawking. The newest generation of Emperors were still little furballs, in great danger of being snatched by skuas wheeling overhead, the skuas trying some test dives and then skating back on the hard wind to the Adélie penguin rookery at the north end of the cape. As always, Cape Crozier was windy.

Val's clients finished their photography, and then were not inclined to stay and observe the Emperors any longer; the wind was too biting. Even dressed in what Arnold called spacesuits, a wind like this one cut into you. So they quickly regathered around Val. George told her they were hoping that they would still have time in the brief twilight to climb Igloo Spur and look for the circle of rocks that Wilson, Bowers, and Cherry-Garrard had left behind.

'Sure,' Val said, and led them to the usual campsite at the foot of Igloo Spur, and told them to go on up and have a look while there was still some twilight left. She would set up a security tent and then follow. George Tremont, the leader of the expedition, which was not just another Footsteps re-enactment but a special affair, went into conference with Arnold, his producer, and the cinematographer and camera crew. They had to decide if they should film this moment as the true live hunt for the rock circle, or else find it today and then film a hunt tomorrow, in a little re-enactment of their own.

Val had very little patience for this kind of thing. Her GPS had the co-ordinates for the 'Wilson Rock Hut', as the Kiwi maps called it, and so they could have hiked up the spur and found the thing immediately. But no; this was not to be done. George and the rest wanted to film a finding of the rock igloo without mechanical aid. They seemed to assume that their telecast's audience would be so ignorant that they would not immediately wonder why GPS was not being used. Val doubted this notion but kept her thoughts to herself and concentrated on setting up one of the big team tents, looking up once or twice at the gang tramping up the ridge, with their cameras but without GPS. It was pure theatre.

After she had the tent up and the sledges securely anchored, she hiked up the spine of the lava ridge. About five hundred feet over the sea ice the ridge levelled off, and fell and rose a few times before joining the massive flank of Mount Terror, Erebus's little brother. As she had expected, she found her group still hunting for the rock hut, scattered everywhere over the ridge. In the dim tail-end of the twilight this kind of wandering around could be dangerous; Cape Crozier was big and complicated, its multiple lava ridges separating lots of tilted and crevassed ice slopes running down onto the sea ice. When Mear and Swan had re-enacted the Worst Journey for the first time, in 1986, they had lost their own tent in the darkness for a matter of some hours, and if they hadn't stumbled across it again they would have died.

But now the wandering had to be allowed; this was the good stuff, the treasure hunt. The camera operators were hopping around trying to stay out of each other's views, getting every moment of it on their supersensitive film; it would be more visible on screen than it was to the naked eye. And everyone had a personal GPS beeper in their parka anyway, so that if someone did disappear, Val could pull out the finder unit and track them down. So it was safe enough.

The searchers, however, were beginning to look like a troupe of mimes doing impressions of Cold Discouragement. The truth was that the rock igloo that the three explorers had left behind was only knee-high at its highest point, and both it and the plaque put there by the Kiwis had been buried in the last decade's heavy snowfalls; though most of the snow here had been swept to sea by the winds, enough had adhered in the black rubble to make the whole ridge a dense stippling of black and white, hard to read in the growing darkness. Every large white patch on the broad ridge looked more or less like a knee-high rock circle, and so did the black patches too.

So hither and yon Val's clients wandered, calling out to each other at every pile of stone or snow. Several were trying to read their copies of *The Worst Journey In The World* by flashlight, to see if the text could direct them. Val heard some complaining about the vagueness of Cherry-Garrard's descriptions, which was not very generous given that young Cherry had been terribly near-sighted and had not been able to wear his thick glasses because they kept frosting up, so that among the other remarkable aspects of the Worst Journey was the fact that one of the three travellers, and the one who ended up telling their tale, had been functionally blind. A kind of Homer and Ishmael.

Val sat on a waist-high rock next to a couple of the film crew, who had given up filming for the moment and were plugging their gloves into a battery heater and then clasping chocolate bars in the hope of thawing them a bit before eating. They were laughing at George, who was now consulting a copy of Sir Edmund Hillary's book *No Latitude For Error*, which recounted the first discovery of the rock hut, forty-six years after it had been built. Hillary and his companions had been out testing the modified farm tractors they would later drive up Skelton Glacier to the South Pole, and once at Cape Crozier they had wandered around like Val's companions were now, with their own copy of Cherry-Garrard's book and nothing more; essentially theirs had been the experience Val's companions were now trying to reproduce, for at that time Cherry-Garrard's description of the site was the only guide anyone could have, with no GPS or anything else to help. So Hillary and his companions had argued over Cherry's book line by line, just like Val's group was doing now, only in genuine rather than faked frustration, until Hillary himself had located the hut.

His book's account of the discovery, however, also proved to have a certain vagueness to it, as if the canny mountaineer had not wanted to reveal an exact route. Although he had said, as George was proclaiming now, that the hut was right on the line of the ridge, and in a saddle. 'As *windy* and *inhospitable* a location as could be *imagined!*' George read in an angry shout.

'We should be filming this,' Geena noted.

'Elka's getting it,' Elliot said calmly.

Sir Edmund was proving as little help as Cherry-Garrard. It occurred to Val that someone could also look up the relevant passages in Mear and Swan's *In the Footsteps of Scott*, for those first re-enactors, the unknowing instigators of an entire genre of adventure travel, had also relocated the hut in the pre-GPS era, and had published a good photo of it in their book. But it was a coffee-table book, Val recalled, and probably no one had wanted to carry the weight. Anyway, no book was going to help them on this dark, wild ridge.

Elliot echoed her thought: 'A classic case of the map not being the territory.'

'Although a map would help. I don't think they're gonna find it without GPS.'

'Has to be here somewhere. They'll trip over it eventually.'

'It's too dark now.'

And the wind was beginning to hurt. People were beginning to crab around with their backs to the wind no matter which way they were going. It was loud, too, the wind moaning and keening dramatically over the broken rock.

'I'll give you even odds they find it.'

'Taken.'

'I can't believe they camped in such an exposed place.'

'They wanted to be close to the penguins.'

'Yeah, but still.'

Indeed, Val thought. She would never have set a camp here on the ridge; it was one of the last places on Cape Crozier she would have chosen. And Wilson had known it was exposed to the wind; his diary made that clear. But he had decided to risk it anyway, because he too had been concerned about losing their camp in the darkness, and he had wanted it to be where they could find it at the end of their trips out to look for penguins. Fair enough, but there were other places that would have been relocatable in the dark. Putting it up here had almost cost them their lives. Oddly, Cherry-Garrard had claimed in his book that the hut had been located on the lee side of the ridge, thus protected from direct blasts; he had also explained that later aerodynamic science of which Wilson could not have been aware had revealed that the immediate lee of a ridge was a zone of vacuum pull upward, which is what had yanked their roof off when the wind reached force ten. But since the shelter actually was right on the spine of the ridge, as Hillary had noted (Val was pretty sure she could see it down in the saddle below her, a big hump of snow among other big humps of snow) it was hard to know what Cherry had been getting at – either making excuses for Wilson's bad judgement, or else so blind he truly hadn't known where they had been.

'It certainly looks like another stupid move to be chalked up against the Scott expedition,' Elliot said.

'Infectious,' Geena suggested. 'A regional thing.'

'Below the fortieth latitude south,' Elliot intoned, 'there is no law. Below the fiftieth, no God. And below the sixtieth, no common sense.'

'And below the seventieth,' Geena added, 'no intelligence whatsoever.'

There was little Val could say to contradict them. After all, here were a couple of dozen people staggering around in a frigid wind, just to the left, the right, the before and the beyond of an oval rock wall that any of them could have found after a ten second consultation with their GPS. One of them was actually tripping over the end of the shelter at this very moment!

But Val said nothing.

It got colder.

'These Footstep things,' Geena complained. 'Want some hot chocolate?'

'I like them,' Elliot said, taking the thermos from her. 'You get to add historical footage to the usual stuff, it's great.'

'Be careful, it's hot.'

'I worked for Footsteps Unlimited for a while. Popularly known as FU, because that's what the clients were most likely to say to each other after they got back.'

'Ha ha.'

'I also freelanced for Classic Expeditions of the Past Revisited, which its guides called Stupid Expeditions of the Past Revisited, because the trip designers always chose the very worst trips in history, sometimes with the original gear and food.'

'You're kidding.'

'No. But you'll notice they're out of business now.'

'Masochistic travel – a new genre, still under-appreciated.'

'It'll catch on. All travel is masochistic. People will do anything. I shot Hannibal's crossing of the Alps, elephants included – Marco Polo, Italy to China by camel – Scott's walk to the Pole – Napoleon's retreat from Moscow.' He pulled up his facemask and drank from the thermos. 'That one was colder than this.'

'Wow. I shot a gig with Condemned To Repeat It once, where we followed Stanley's hunt for Livingstone. People said it was more dangerous to do now than it was then.'

'Condemned To Repeat It?'

'You know – those who know history too well are condemned to repeat it.'

'Ah yeah. But some of those old trips are unrepeatable no matter what, because they were impossible in the first place.'

'Sure. I heard Shackleton's boat journey was a total disaster.'

Val's stomach tightened. She had guided that one herself, and did not want to talk or think about it. Now she saw Elliot making a gesture with his thumb up her way, to warn Geena. That's the guide right there, shhhh, don't mention it! God. What a thing to be known for. Val had guided every Footsteps expedition in Antarctica, from Mawson's death march to Borchgrevinck's mad winter ship, even fictional expeditions like the one in Poe's 'Message Found In A Bottle' (including the whirlpool at the end), or in Le Guin's 'Sur' (the latter of which ended with an emotional meeting with the author, the women thanking her for the idea and also making many detailed suggestions for logistical additions to the text, all of which Le Guin promised to insert the next time she revised it) – all these *very* difficult trips guided, practically every early expedition in Antarctica re-enacted—and what was she remembered for? The fiasco, of course . . .

Suddenly there were wild shouts from down the ridge. George and Anne-Marie were standing next to the snowy hump Val had picked out as the likely site.

'Show time,' Elliot declared, and hefted his camera pack. 'I hope this baby stays warm enough to keep its focus.'

George had Elliot and Geena and the other camera operators shoot him and Anne-Marie re-enacting the rediscovery of the hut, their shouts thin compared to the happy triumph of the originals. Then they tromped back down to the dining tent and ate the happiest meal they had had so far, while Val set up the rest of the sleeping tents. After that they slept through the long dark hours of the night, snug in their ultrawarm sleeping bags, on their perfectly insulated mattress pads. By the first glow of twilight on the next day they were all back on the ridge and working around the mound, some of them carefully clearing ice and snow away from the stacked rocks with hot-air blowers and miniature jackhammer-like tools, the others building a little wooden shelter just up the ridge; for they were there to undo the work of Edmund Hillary, so to speak, and return all of the belongings of Wilson's group that Hillary and his companions had found and taken away.

The rock shelter itself was a small oval of rough stacked stones, many of them about as heavy as a single person could lift. The old boys had been strong. The wall at its highest was three or four rocks tall. The interior would have been about eight feet by five. The old boys had been small. They had put one of their two sledges over the long axis of the oval, then stretched their green Willesden canvas sheet over the sledge, and laid the sheet as far over the ground as it would go, and loaded rocks onto this big valance, and rocks and snow blocks onto the roof itself, until they judged the shelter to be as strong as they could make it. Bombproof; or so they had thought. A small hole in the lee wall had served as their door, and they had set up their single Scott tent just outside this entryway, to give them more shelter while affording the tent some protection from the wind, Val assumed; Wilson's reason for setting the tent when they had the rock shelter had never been clear to her. Anyway, the shelter had been pretty damned strong, she could see; the wind that destroyed it had not managed to pull the canvas out of its setting, but had instead torn it to shreds right in its place. As she had on her previous visits, Val kneeled and dug into the snow plastering the chinks in the wall, and found fragments of the canvas still there in the wall, more white than green. 'Wow.'

And looking at the frayed canvas shreds, Val again felt a little frisson of feeling for the three men. It was like looking at the gear in the little museum in Zermatt that Whymper's party had used in the first ascent of the Matterhorn: rope like clothesline, shoes – light leather things, with carpenter's nails hammered into the soles . . . Those old Brits had conquered the world using bad Boy Scout equipment. Like this frayed white canvas fragment between her fingers. A real piece of the past.

Not that they didn't have a great number of other, larger, real pieces of the past, there with them now to return to the site. For Wilson and his comrades had left in a hurry. The storm that had struck them had first blown their tent away, and then blown the canvas roof off their shelter; after that they had lain in their sleeping bags in a thickening drift of snow for two days, the temperatures in the minus fifties, the wind-chill factor beyond imagining – singing hymns in the dark to pass the time, although with their tent gone they were doomed, with no chance at all of getting back to Cape Evans alive. So when the wind had abated enough to allow them to stand, and they had got up and wandered around in the dark, and miraculously found their tent at the foot of the ridge, stuck between two boulders like a folded umbrella, they had carried it to their shattered camp and packed what they could find into one sledge and left immediately, in a desperate retreat for their lives. Thus began the third and worst stage of the Worst Journey, when they had hauled the sledge asleep in their traces, and slept in sleeping bags that had become nothing more than bags of ice-cubes, which were nevertheless warmer than the air outside.

So when Hillary and his men had come on the site forty-six years later, they had found a lot of gear scattered about. They had collected it all and put it in their farm tractors, and taken it back with them to Scott Base at the other end of Ross Island; eventually it was all taken back to New Zealand, where the items were distributed to a number of Kiwi museums. Cherry-Garrard, still alive at the time, had written from England to approve this recovery and disposal of the gear, although since it had already been done when he was asked about it, he might very well have felt there was little else he could say. Val suspected that he had been the kind of person who would not complain about something when it could make no difference; and he certainly wanted his two long-dead comrades remembered as much as possible – not realizing that his book was so much greater a memorial to them than any objects in museums, that it would end up inspiring many people every year to return to Cape Crozier itself. And yet find there at the site only the emptied rock shell.

George Tremont had at some point come to feel that this removal of gear from the site had been a grave mistake. George was a Kiwi, and during a season's film work at Scott Base, which included a few visits to Cape Crozier, he had become convinced that all the objects taken from the site – 'looted', he would say privately after a few glasses of warm Drambers, 'vandalized; *plundered*' – ought to be returned and replaced. In other places around the globe one had these kind of inspired ideas in the bar and then sobered up the next day and dismissed them. But there was something about Antarctica that fuelled obsessions, that created all manner of *idées fixes* which then took over whole careers and lives. The ice blink, some called it. Roger Swan, for instance, sitting in a college film theatre watching *Scott of the Antarctic*, had thereafter devoted his life to repeating Scott's journey, an unlikely enough reaction one would have thought to a tale of continuous grim suffering; but the idea had obsessed him, and the Footsteps movement had been born.

And George had become the same way about the Cape Crozier artefacts. He had laboured for ten years to argue all the relevant authorities over to his side – ten full years, like a bureaucratic *Iliad* and *Odyssey* combined, involving New Zealand's Antarctic Heritage Trust (which George had joined and become president of before announcing his plan), the Historic Sites Management Committee of the Ross Dependency Research Committee, the New Zealand Antarctic Society, the Antarctic Treaty committee concerned with historic sites, the UN's

World Heritage Site Committee, and scores of other societies, government agencies, university departments and museum boards all over the world. The agreement of the Canterbury Museum in Christchurch had been the critical battle won, as they were in possession of the majority of the artefacts; this agreement had taken the advocacy of the Prince of Wales himself, but after that convincing everyone else had become progressively easier, as there grew more and more muscle to bring to bear on any little Kiwi museum that did not want to part with its relic of the holy crusade. Even Sir Edmund Hillary had eventually written a letter in support of the idea of returning the objects to the site, turning out to be as agreeable as Cherry-Garrard had been earlier. So in the end George had got all of the items donated back, and had also obtained permission to build a small wooden shelter to hold them, located nearby ('but out of photo range', Elliot noted), and modelled on the old meteorological instrument shelter standing on Windvane Hill over the Cape Evans hut, on the other side of the island.

The new shelter had been built in Christchurch and then disassembled for transport to the site, so now, even in the cold and dark and wind, it only took a few hours to reassemble it. When it was finished, and its footing securely anchored by piles of stones similar to the piles in the rock oval itself, the happy group tromped back down to camp, and began hauling up the sledges full of the old items.

Val helped to pull these sledges up the slope, feeling peculiar as she did so. All these items pulled up this very ridge by the three men who had first come here; then hauled away by Hillary, the first man to climb Everest, half a century later... Now up they went again, with Elliot and Geena and several other camera operators recording every step, and Arnold and George and Anne-Marie all shouting frantically for various angles and so on. That part was awful, really. But something about the feel of the load, tugging hard at her harness ... Then one of the people hauling slipped, and for a second it looked as if the lead sledge might slide back down and hit the following one. George and Arnold and several others (especially the people hauling the second sledge) shrieked in panic. Ridiculous, really. Still, there was something about it ... They looked like pilgrims. Perhaps, Val thought, there was always something ridiculous about a pilgrimage, something self-conscious and theatrical. Maybe that didn't matter.

Eventually they got all the holy relics safely on the ridge. George and his assistants went to work installing the pieces in the display shelter. The shelter did indeed look like a larger version of the wooden box on Windvane Hill, and when the items were installed, glass would protect them. A fair number of visitors would then get to see these things here at the site; not as many as would have seen them in the Kiwi museums, true, but it would mean more to those who did see them. So George had argued, for ten long years, and now Val could see his point. And in the boom market of wilderness adventure travel, re-enacting the trip called The Worst Journey In The World was always going to be popular. So a good number of people would see this in the long run.

When they had finished Val walked over with the rest to take a look. It was a nice display. Most of the items had been left unlabelled, as they were self-explanatory. The spindly wooden sledge they had left on the rock hut, stripped to the grain and bleached by its first stay out here, was now placed next to the shelter in a kind of cradle of rock. Then under the roof and behind the glass of the shelter itself, were a pick-axe, a blubber stove, a tin of salt, a hurricane lamp with a spare glass, a tea towel, a canvas bag, a thermos flask, several little corked bottles of chemicals, a bulb atomizer, a magnifying glass, several micro-scope slides, seven thermometers (three Fahrenheit, one Celsius, one minimum reading, two oral); a lead weight on a string, five eye drop-pers, a pair of tweezers, thirty-five sample tubes, all corked; a skewer, a bottle of alcohol, two enamel dishes, four pencils, a glass syringe, four envelopes with *Terra Nova* printed on them; six plain envelopes, some perforated stickers, three rolls of Kodak film marked 'To be developed before May 1st 1911', two tubes of magnesium powder for a Agfa camera flash; and then, along with the letters from Cherry-Garrard and Hillary concerning the disposition of the artefacts, repro-ductions of the two photographs that had been taken of the three explorers by Herbert Ponting, one before they took off, and the famous one after they got back, in which they were sitting at the big table inside the Cape Evans hut. Lastly, in George's finest coup of all, they had the shells of the three penguin eggs that Cherry-Garrard had donated to the uncaring keepers at the Museum of Natural History in England; George had tracked them down in a specimen drawer in Edinburgh University, and now they were in the display too.

The camera pros were checking out the old film and flash powder, oohing and ahhing. It certainly did seem that these objects served to make the three travellers more real to the imagination. There was so much of it – and this was just the stuff they had left behind!

'They sure travelled heavy, didn't they?'

'Wilson was interested in a lot of things.'

'And back when there was such a thing as amateur science.'

'Hey, unpack your bag and tack it up and it'd look just like this.'

'I don't know – a tea towel? Seven thermometers? A chemistry set?'

George was now wandering around the ridge, looking at the new structure from all the angles he could. Mercifully the wind had died for the moment, so that people could pull up their ski-masks. Val saw that George was stuffed with a contentment beyond happiness; serious, as in the midst of a religious ritual. This was his moment, and it had actually come off. Elliot and some other camera-people were still filming, but everyone had forgotten them. As George passed by Arnold said, 'It's beautiful, George! It's a great idea! The people who make it here will really appreciate this.'

The little smile on George's face was angelic.

Then he was busy organizing the start of the dedication ceremony he had worked up. While they did that, Val took a closer look at the two photos of the three explorers. After they had survived the hurricane on this ridge, and were given back their lives by the miraculous recovery of their tent, their struggle home had been a nightmare beyond anything a Footsteps expedition could reproduce, thank God. But they had made it back. And Ponting had taken this photo within an hour of their return, after they had cut their frozen outer clothing off them and thawed them a bit over the stove. Wilson looked straight out at posterity, grim, shattered, knowing full well that he had escaped leading his friends to death by sheer luck alone. That he would just months later walk south with Scott to the Pole was amazing.

Cherry-Garrard also looked into the camera. He had suffered from depression much of the rest of his life, and in this photo he appeared crazed already, driven out of his mind by the extremities of the journey. Although possibly that was just his near-sightedness. But no; such naked looks, from both him and Wilson; that was not just astigmatism. Ponting had caught their souls on film, caught their souls in the act of slipping back into their bodies, abashed at having taken off prematurely for the afterworld.

And then there between them was Birdie Bowers, knocking back a mug as if just back from a walk down to the corner shop – looking if anything more refreshed and rested than he had in the departure photo. Bowers! Henry Robert Bowers, God bless him, his beak of a nose profiled like a parrot's; Birdie Bowers of the Antarctic, who never got cold, never got tired, never got discouraged; Bowers the Optimist, whose only fault appeared to have been an optimism so extreme that it sometimes made his companions want to strangle him. After the hurricane had relented, for instance, he had wanted to make one last visit to the penguins before retreating. And back at Cape Evans he had given a lecture explaining how perfect their Boy Scout equipment was, so perfect that it could not possibly be improved upon in any regard; this from a man wearing a canvas jacket and hat rather than a parka. And when he had been caught with some of their ponies on an ice floe that broke away from the ice shelf, he had refused to save himself until he could save the nags as well. And on the fatal trek to the Pole he had pulled the hardest of all, even deprived of his skis, and had cheerfully done most of the camp work as the other men slowly lost strength and died around him. And never a word of complaint, not right to his death; rather the opposite.

It must have taken a lot, Val thought darkly as she looked at the photo, to kill Birdie Bowers off. She felt an affinity for that little man, she treasured his memory in particular of all the old boys; because Val was an optimist herself. Or at least people often accused her of it. And indeed she did try to make the best of things. It seemed to her that that was the way one should behave – it was how her mother and grandmother, both dead now, had taught her to behave, by precept and example. And on adult reflection, she approved of the lesson fully. Making the best of things was what courage meant, in her opinion; that was right action in the face of life. And how hard it was, given how dark her thoughts had become, and how dismal everything sometimes appeared to her; how against the grain of her temperament it had become. But she kept at it anyway, as an act of the will. And all it did was get her laughed at, and most of what she said continually discounted or put down, as if being optimistic was a matter of a somewhat obtuse intelligence, or at best the luck of biochemistry, rather than a policy that had to be maintained, sometimes in the midst of the blackest moods imaginable.

No; the Birdie Bowers of this world were only regarded as fools. And the world being what it was, Val supposed that there was some truth in it. Why be optimistic, how be optimistic, when there was so much wrong with so much? In a world coming apart it had to be a kind of stupidity. But still Val held to it, stubbornly, just barely. Without even thinking she would say the thing that took the most positive slant on the matter, and get laughed at, and grit her teeth and try to live up to that slant. Such an attitude was an asset for any mountain guide, of course, or should have been. But the way it was received was one of the things that was beginning to turn her into burnt toast. It took an *effort* to be optimistic, it was a *moral position*. But no one understood that.

'Those guys,' Arnold said, looking over her shoulder at the old photos. 'They really were crazy.'

'Yes. They were.'

Then George was hustling them all around to their various stations, becoming more manic as time passed; for the sun was soon to come up, and they would not be able to film a second take of that. Happily the sky was clear, and the horizon to the north-east a straight line of startling clarity: shiny ice below, pale blue sky above.

With most of the group gathered in a little knot next to the rock hut, George began by reading the climactic passage from Cherry-Garrard's book, when the storm had ripped away their tent and hut roof, and left them apparently with only a few more hours to live. Val, uneasy at hearing this passage that struck right to the heart of what she had been thinking, moved back up the ridge beyond the new structure, where she could just hear George's voice, a reedy tenor wavering on the freshening wind: '"Gradually the situation got more desperate . . . There was more snow coming through the walls . . . our pyjama jackets were stuffed between the roof and the rocks over the door."' George read in a sing-song like a preacher, and though Val could only catch a phrase here and there over the sound of the wind, Cherry's King James cadences were obvious. '"Bowers . . . up and out of his bag continually, stopping up holes, pressing against bits of roof . . . he was magnificent . . . And then it went . . . The uproar of it all was indescribable."'

Val bent her head, trying to imagine the scene; the thunder of the wind lashing the canvas to shreds, the rocks falling in, the snow pouring onto them, the means of return blown away.

'"The next I knew was Bowers's head across Bill's body. *We're all right!* he yelled, and we answered in the affirmative. Despite the fact that we knew we only said so because we knew we were all wrong, this statement was helpful."'

Val turned away abruptly and walked up the ridge, feeling a sudden increase in her strange pain. Who *were* these men? The clients she guided were not like that; and she was not like that either. Could people change so much, century by century?

'"Birdie and Bill sang quite a lot of songs and hymns,"' she heard George exclaim. This was the cue for the music, George going a bit over the top in his enthusiasm. But everyone there began to sing except for Val and the film crew, anchored by a quartet of professionals from Wellington. They sang a version of the Tallis Canon, adapted by Benjamin Britten to fit some hymn verses written by Joseph Addison. The sky overhead was now fully light, a pure transparent pale blue, shading to a bright white over the north-eastern horizon, where the sun was about to make its reappearance. They could see for many miles over the white sea ice covering the Ross Sea, clotted with icebergs from the old shelf, so that in the growing light the plain turned pewter and shaved silver, a mirror jumble. The quartet took off in the parts of the canon, somehow weaving together the words of the old hymn, George conducting them with great sweeps of his hands:

'The spacious firmament on high,
With all the blue ethereal sky,
And spangled heavens, a shining frame,
Their great Original proclaim.

Soon as the evening shades prevail
The Moon takes up the wondrous tale,
And nightly to the listening Earth
Repeats the story of her birth;

Whilst all the stars that round her burn,
And all the planets in their turn,
Confirm the tidings as they roll,
And spread the truth from pole to pole.'

And as they sang the last line the sun cracked the horizon to the north-east, the incredible shard of light fountaining over the sea ice and the immense bergs caught in it, illuminating the scene with a blinding glare, the great world itself turning all to light, in a space spacious beyond words. The little group around the rock hut cheered, they hugged each other, they hugged George, and shook his hand, and clapped him on the back, all cameras forgotten; but Elliot and Geena kept filming.

God knew what the three explorers would have made of it. They had lain there in the midwinter darkness exposed to the hurricane for two more days without food and with very little sleep, before the wind dropped and they could go out and look for the tent, and find it. 'Our lives had been taken away and given back to us,' as Cherry wrote. So that this was not an inappropriate site for a spring celebration, now that Val thought of it; the return of the sun, the rebirth, the gift of life.

So she went down to the others less reluctantly than she might have, got them all back off the ridge to the team tent, and joined the celebratory meal; and when a toast was offered to the old boys she said 'Hear hear' gladly, and with feeling; with too much feeling, really. For those three men were her saints, in a way – the patron saints of all stupid pointless expeditions into the wilderness, the Three Silly Men to match the Three Wise Men, silly men who yet remained gracious in the face of death. Who had made it back to Cape Evans alive, and thus turned all the stupid false stories of their Victorian youth into one stupid true story, transforming Tennyson to steel. The Worst Journey in the World! And now this memorializing group had done a proper homage to that best journey in Antarctic history, and made a shrine to craziness and decency that was, in some way she didn't fully understand, something Val could believe in. Her own brand of religion. She proposed another toast, throat tightening as she did: 'To Birdie Bowers, the optimist!' And they cried 'Hear hear' and drank hot chocolate, and Elliot, of all people, teasing her she supposed, cried out, 'We're all right! We're all right!'

And so they were, for the moment. Though of course the return home would be a pain in the ass.

Then later, when she was back up on the ridge cleaning the site of any stray debris (canister top, foil paper, etc.) Val got a call from Randi on her little wrist radio. 'Hey, Val, this is the voice of the south coming to you again through the miracle of shaped and directed radio waves, do you read, over?'

'I read you, Randi. What's going on?'

'Did you hear what happened to your sandwich?'

'Don't call him that, what happened?'

'Your ex, then. He's out with the SPOT train, you know, and he just called in a while ago – he's been hijacked!'

'What?'

'He's been hijacked. Someone locked him in the lead vehicle during a Condition One, and when he got out there were only nine vehicles instead of ten! Plundered by ice pirates!'

'Who the hell would do that!'

'Ice pirates!' Randi laughed. 'Who knows. But isn't that funny it happened to X?'

'No! Why would that be funny?'

'Well, because it's okay! I mean he's okay, and now he's finally had the big adventure he came down here looking for!'

'Maybe,' Val said darkly. Feeling bad about what she had done to X was another reason she was toast.

'Oh come on,' Randi was saying, 'he'll love it. That's the kind of dreamer he is.'

'Maybe.'

CHAPTER TWO

Science in the Capital

Wade Norton had just solved the last movement of Tchaikovsky's Fifth Symphony when his boss, Senator Phil Chase, called. It was late on a very hot September evening in Washington DC, part of a heat wave in fact, the temperature 115°F with humidity near a hundred percent, the roar of the city outside the window damped down as all parts of the metropolis went into Turkish bath mode, stewing as they waited out the latest EWE, or extreme weather event. Torrential floods, blistering droughts, record highs and lows, earthquakes, tornadoes, hurricanes, assorted other superstorms; this year, like all the last several years, had seen everything.

Wade had been sitting before his overmatched air conditioning unit, conducting the Fifth for a few hours. He had been working on this version during his snippets of spare time for eight months, studying the score and recording bar by bar, struggling especially with the finale, using the latest Maestro program to manipulate all possible aspects of pitch, tempo, dynamics, colour, intonation, vibrato and so forth, all down at the level of the individual soundwaves on the oscilloconductor, working mostly with synthetically generated sound but occasionally with the instruments in a base performance recorded for Maestro by the Vienna Philharmonic. And now he had the version he wanted. And it had been no easy thing, because the last movement was, as Brahms had noted to Tchaikovsky after hearing a performance in Hamburg, somewhat of a mess structurally. In his usual insecure way Tchaikovsky had immediately agreed with Brahms, and it had taken him a couple of months to rally and decide that it was not his Fifth that was deficient but Brahms himself, whose music Tchaikovsky said was 'the pedestal without the statue', a riposte which still made Wade smile, and had even given him a clue to conducting the Fifth, which was to treat it as a statue without a pedestal, floating in the air like a tone poem, the beauty of each component passage different in kind from the other

26

passages; then turn the variously awkward junctures as best he could, exploiting things the Maestro could do that living orchestras would find hard. The home conducting subculture was of course mostly uninterested in these overplayed warhorses of the concert hall, exactly the material from which computer conducting had freed them; and indeed Wade was coming to this piece from several years' work on unrecorded music in the opuses of D'Indy, Poulenc and Martinu; but recently there had been movements, obviously related, to explore both 'sensuous surface' and the neglected warhorses, and Wade felt that this performance he had put together was perhaps good enough to justify sending it out, at least to the Tchaikovsky crowd, the finale of the Fifth being somewhat in the nature of Fermat's last theorem, to which his version might be the Wiles proof.

But there was the phone beeping. And of course it was Phil, Senator Philip Krishna Chase of California, his boss and friend, calling from the other side of the world and uncertain of the time difference as always. Phil had two years before lost the chair of the Senate Foreign Relations Committee, and was often spoken of as passé following the Republican retaking of both Senate and House that year; he had seldom been in Washington since (not that he had been here all that often before), and he appeared intent on proving that as the great telesenator he could do his job while on a more-or-less permanent junket/global pilgrimage (depending on who was characterizing it). The pundits were convinced he was wrong, and there were weekly calls for Phil to get back to his job and put his nose to the grindstone like everyone else, etc.; and back home in California Chase had the highest negatives and the highest positives ever recorded. But he had won his last re-election by twenty-three percent, and as Phil often said, California had led telecommuting from the very beginning, even before the technology was there, and most Californians were proud of their senator's work among the many troubled overcrowded starved flooded and drought-stricken countries of the developing world which Phil made his special-ity – proud also of the breakthroughs he had made in telecommuting itself, working the Senate from all over the world and introducing legislation to make it even easier for people to do likewise on their jobs. So with his power base secure Chase continued to walk and paraglide around the world, pitching in to help local relief work and employee-owned eco-businesses, and doing his Washington work by phone, fax, proxy, an active staff, and the occasional spaceplane blitz on the capital.

So Wade was used to punching the button on the phone and hearing 'Wade! Wade! Time to work!'

'Hi Phil.' Wade hit *save* on the Maestro and reached for a notepad.

Typically these conversations would last for half an hour to an hour, and include a dozen commands, two dozen suggestions, and three dozen reflections; he took notes so he would not forget anything in the deluge. 'Where are you tonight?'

'It's morning, Wade, it's tomorrow where you are, and I'm in Pakistan, walking up to the sixteenth tee, five under handicap and shooting with the wind all the way home, but let's get to the point, Wade. I hear that you are the staff expert on Antarctica.'

'Antarctica?'

Phil had a wild laugh; it was said to have won him his first election. 'Yes, John tells me you had to work it up as part of your Southern Club studies.'

'Yes, but that was just an overview.'

'I know, I have it right here onscreen. "Complications Attendant on the Non-renewal of the Antarctic Treaty, An Overview." By WN.'

'Yes.' Wade had researched the Antarctic Treaty System (a complex of treaties, protocols and agreements) the previous year, when Senator Winston, Phil's replacement as Chair, had directed his majority on the Foreign Relations Committee to vote to sit on the ratification of the Treaty's scheduled renewal, which had been in negotiation the previous three years. It had seemed clear to Wade that the blockage of the ratification, aside from being part of a general strategy of obstruction of the President on all fronts, had to do with Senator Winston's ongoing battle with the Southern Club, and for that matter with the Southern hemisphere in general, home in Winston's mind of all ungodly sloth and indolence. Also the renegotiated Treaty continued to contain the bans on oil, mineral and other resource extraction that it had had since the 1991 environmental protocol had been attached; of course Wall Street had been unhappy about that, as it did not fit with their ongoing campaign to dismantle all remaining global environmental regulations and any other constraints to the full exercise of the free market, etc.

All part of the ordinary contemporary political battlefield, in other words; and interesting in that respect; but the idea that Wade was therefore an expert on Antarctica was laughable, as Phil was proving at this very moment. Wade had learned what he had needed to know the way one crams for a test, and afterward retained the usual portion of knowledge from such efforts. Antarctica! as he and the staff had often proclaimed at that time – the highest, coldest, driest, iciest, windiest, and least significant of the continents!

Through Chase's last chuckles he said, 'I didn't learn that much about it, Phil. I like my ice in bloody marys.'

'You're very wise in your modesty, Wade. Here, wait a second while I make this drive. Ooh. But you're my staff expert on the place, Wade, and there's been some things come up in the last month that I want you to look into for me. It appears the absence of a ratified treaty is beginning to wreak some havoc down there, and if we can find out anything that we could use against Winston, naturally it would be a good thing. Of course I'd go myself to have a look around, it sounds great, but I have – ah come on! – business in Kashmir that can't wait.'

'What have you heard?' Wade asked cautiously.

'Well, some funny stuff has been going on down there. I've got friends who've been telling me about it, and it looks funny to me. Something going on down there. Get the NSF rep on site to give you a full report, I'm not sure I've heard it all yet anyway. But if we can get something to use against Winston and his gang, it would be good. That guy is really beginning to get on my nerves, just between you and me—'

'And the rest of humanity.'

'—screwed the population planning, the foreign aid, the debt-for-nature, the UN payments, really this guy has to be stopped, he's like *leading* the Götterdämmerung. He's riding all four horses at once, that's why he's so bowlegged. We've got to see if we can find some kind of crowbar to whap him on the knees a little, straighten those legs up, so to speak, and send him packing. I swear I cannot understand why the American people elect guys like him, it's absurd. Congress from one party and President from the other, they do it more often than not, what can they be thinking? All it does is make it impossible to do anything!'

'That's the point. That's what they're hoping for.'

'But why hope for gridlock? No one likes to see it in traffic.'

'They're hoping that if the government can't do anything, then history will stop happening and things will always stay just like they are right now.'

'What's so great about right now!'

'Not much, but they figure it can only get worse. It's a damage control strategy. They can see just as clearly as anyone that the globalized economy means they're all headed for the sweatshop.'

'True, that's what I say all the time, but there are better ways to deal with it than gridlock in Washington!'

'Are you sure?'

'Sure I'm sure! There sure as hell should be anyway.'

'Should be. But right now the voters have to go with what they have. Stop history and hang on. Hope for the best.'

'Well, I find that very sad. They're waiting for something, Wade. They're waiting for us pick up the ball and run with it.'

'From out of the gridlock.'

'Exactly! So okay, that's what we're doing here now, that's why

29

you've got to go to Antarctica. I'll send you what I've got on the situation so you can read it on your way.'

'On my way?'

'Yeah. There's National Transport Safety Board people going down, you can join them.'

Wade had written on his notepad *To Do:* and under that, *Break Gridlock*, and under that, *Go To Antarctica*. He stared at the page, at a loss.

Phil laughed again. 'What's the matter, Wade, don't you like the cold?'

'Not that much.' In fact Wade had grown up in Hemet, California, and he began to shiver when the temperature dropped below eighty. Even with the global warming he considered Washington a cool place.

'Well, I hear it's not that cold down there anyway.'

'In Antarctica?'

'It's spring down there, right?'

'Early spring. Actually two weeks away. The coldest time of year there, as I recall.'

'See, you are my expert! Ah, ha ha ha! You'll get used to it. Hold on a sec, Wade, I'm going to putt.'

Chase often relaxed from his humanitarian efforts by playing in working foursomes, with the other players telecommuting like himself so that they played in semi-detached realities, and did not converse a great deal; but this time Wade could hear a lot of banter in the background, and guessed this was a more social round. It was possible Pakistan did not have as many telegolfers as the States, where the courses routinely had fax machines next to the ball cleaners. 'So, Wade, go down there and find out what's going on and how we can use it. There's a flight leaving from LA for Auckland tonight.'

'Tonight?'

'Do we have a bad connection, Wade?'

'No.'

'All right then, get to it and let me focus on this next drive. I envy you this opportunity, Wade, and I'll make it down there next time, so I want you to learn everything so you can tell me where to go. And I'll want a daily report, you can tell me everything and it'll be almost like I'm there, you'll be my eyes and ears like you always are in DC, only this will be more fun for both of us. We'll talk soon, I have to visualize this drive now, 'bye.'

He grew up near Redlands, California, in a region still covered by orange and lemon groves, and avocado orchards. But the inexorable metastasizing of Los Angeles rolled over his home when he was a boy, and he watched mute and uncomprehending as over the years of his childhood and youth the groves were cut down and replaced by freeways, malls, condominium complexes and gated suburban communities. And when he went off to Berkeley to go to college, and began to think about what had happened to his childhood home, it made him mad.

He transferred to Humboldt State to study forestry. He hiked, he learned to climb, he learned ice craft. He moved to Alaska for a year. He went back down into the world to go to law school, to learn environmental law in order better to fight for the wildernesses he had come to love, wildernesses that were everywhere being overrun by the insane proliferation of human beings and their excesses. He saw more clearly every day that the big slogan-ideas like democracy, free markets, technological advancement, scientific objectivity, and progress in history, were all myths on the same level as the feudal divine right of kings: self-serving alibis that a minority of rich powerful people were using to control the world. Modern society, like all the societies before it, ever since Sumer and Babylon, was a giant fake, a pyramid scheme in which the wealth of the world funnelled up to the rich; and their natural environment was laid waste to bulk the obscenely huge bank balances of people who lived on private islands in the Caribbean.

He got his law degree and took a job with the Wilderness Defense Club's big office in Washington DC, figuring that to make the biggest impact he had to be in the heart of the heart of the beast, doing battle over the big laws. The WDC was one of the biggest environmentalist groups in the world, and its Washington office had won several of the most important victories for the environmental movement in the last decade. They were a tough, smart gang of committed lawyers. They made it seem like more than a rearguard action; they worked fourteen-hour days and then talked through the Georgetown parties all night long.

He joined them and fought the good fight. They won some and lost some. He developed some diseases of civilization: he drank a bit too much, he smoked cigars sometimes, he couldn't seem to stay in relationships for more than a year; the women he connected with wanted more than policy, and many of them were not much interested in spending their precious vacation time ice-climbing in the Yukon or on Baffin Island. There seemed no one quite on his wavelength, even in the WDC. They were all neurotic; and so was he. The discrepancy between his beliefs and his life was nearly too much to bear.

31

Then he was assigned to work on the latest shameless assault on wilderness, co-ordinated by the timber lobby and the US Forest Service, that implacable enemy of wilderness in general and forests in particular – a plan to inventory all federal lands and assess what could be opened up to new logging, now that all the land previously opened to logging had been clear-cut. The Forest Service claimed that all future logging would be done according to their new integrated forest management plan, and that this plan was ecologically sound, and that therefore many previously unlogged regions could be opened up to the newly enlightened 'selective cut' timber industry. The timber lobby went at the Congress, which as always was the best that money could buy, campaign finance reform having once again mutated into campaign finance recomplication; and timber had the relevant subcommittees sewn up, and the chances of stopping them looked poor indeed. But all the big environmental groups opposed the opening of the new land, which amounted in the Forest Service's first proposal to some hundred million acres scattered all over the United States, and they pooled their resources to fight the plan in the courts.

So he worked sixteen-hour days, now, and eighteen-hour days, engaged in the fight of his life, consumed by it. Nothing else mattered. They had to defeat this proposal.

Then another factor intervened. The President had visited Alaska's North Slope, and now he was in favour of establishing the wilderness and wildlife refuge that had been proposed so long ago, there on the shores of the Arctic Ocean, which would in effect lock up a large oil and gas reserve. Oil prices were getting higher since the Siberian field's troubles and the general rapid depletion of all the world's known supergiant fields, and the President's proposal was controversial, but in the capital the machinations of the various players ground it into the equation; and all that wildlife out on the open tundra was very photogenic, and very far away; and all the memberships of all the big environmental groups supported the idea of the park enthusiastically. The President's staff entered into the negotiation process, and they and the Congressional staff and the big environmental groups and the timber lobby and the oil lobby all had their say, and in the end a compromise was worked out: the Arctic slope would become a national park, with a special provision for oil extraction in case of national emergency; and to balance this 'concession to wilderness', ninety percent of the hundred million acres were to be opened up to the new 'environmental logging'. And the environmentalist groups all went along with it.

He had opposed this compromise every step of the way. But the process was a lot bigger than he was. Indeed the Wilderness Defense Club was one of the major supporters of the compromise, having advocated the Arctic slope park for decades. So not only did his superiors in the organization not listen to his protests, he was on the contrary assigned to go back to California and make sure that the local grass-roots organizations in Humboldt County and the Sierra foothills did not challenge the new logging plan in the courts, so that the entire compromise package would be able to go ahead as planned without impediments that possibly would derail the whole delicate agreement.

So he went back to California; but as a private citizen, having quit the Wilderness Defense Club in rage and disgust. He had no job, he had no home. He spent most of a year living off his savings and climbing the great granite walls of Yosemite, which was cheap entertainment compared to some. His home was the ledge on the Lost Arrow Wall called the Jefferson Airport. His diseases of civilization got a bit worse. He told all his climbing partners about his experience in Washington DC, told the story of the Arctic compromise sell-out again and again, bitter and ranting. But each retelling only made him feel angrier.

Then one group of climbers based in Tuolumne took him with them on a long winter ski trip down the length of the Muir Trail, stopping to dig up caches of food and climbing rope, to make winter ascents of the best of the peaks they passed. It was a wild trip, his companions wild men. And one night when they were camped at a low enough altitude to make them comfortable with burning wood for a campfire, they sat around the flames into the depth of the night, telling stories. And he told his DC story again, and they laughed at him. You should have known, they told him. Reform will never work. It's just another form of collaboration.

But you have to do something! he protested.

Of course, they said. But you have to do something that works. And nothing works but direct action.

Direct action?

They looked at him over the firelight, their eyes glittering.

Over the remainder of the trip he learned what they meant. They were part of a group they laughingly called *ecotage internationale*. It was not a public group with any formal organization of any kind; that was just an invitation to repression. That was the mistake Earthfirst! had made, they said; publish a newsletter and go public and you only made it easier for the powers that be to sic the FBI on you, like an insane police Rottweiler going for your throat. Or even worse, the private security forces of the timber and mining industries, which were counter-insurgency-type organizations trained by the CIA or by Third World secret services, silent and deadly.

No. It was crucial to stay underground, unknown, unheard of,

33

unorganized, unrecognized. They had no name. They had cryptographers working the internet for them, they had ecotage experts working on methodologies. Anonymity was crucial. They had no management, no lawyers, no war chest, no public relations. They did have members, however; several thousand of them, as far as anyone could tell, grouped in clandestine and nearly independent cells. No infiltration was happening because no one knew to infiltrate them. They were very, very careful about whom they told about the group. Nevertheless it was a growing group, because the condition of the Earth was worsening right before their eyes, and as a result radical environmentalism was attracting more people to it.

And they thought he might be interested.

For the first time in over ten years, a knot in his stomach began to untie a bit. Near the end of his trip, up on the Diamond Mesa south of Forester Pass, they spent one short, silvery winter afternoon moving shards of granite into a goldsworthy, as they called it, a new work of environmental art, created to welcome him into the fold of *ecotage internationale*; essentially a little thigh-high Stonehenge in the Sierras, with a centre stone symbolizing his location in the group; his and everyone else's. They all were at the centre of the world, they said; and they danced round the stones in the sunset, howling, drumming on their pots, drinking whisky and throwing rocks at the moon.

The next morning they knocked over the stones and moved on. And the next spring two of that clandestine group drove by his Berkeley apartment one night and asked him to join them on an expedition. They drove up into the Sierra foothills, where environmental forestry was being extensively practised. Even environmental forestry needed some logging roads, however, and a new network was being cut into the land north of Highway 80. Private security police were protecting it, as had become standard practice. But it was the dark of the moon, and the road system was at that vulnerable point where it had been surveyed and marked out with plastic flags and spray paint, but not yet cut and 'dozed.

So they drove to the end of a dirt road, into an obscure car camping site, and they got out and jogged into the bush. The Sierra foothills are very tough to hike cross-country in, especially at night, but his companions had a route worked out, and they came down a slope onto the planned course of the new road, and began to sneak around like primeval hunters, using night glasses and running like silent maniacs once or twice to avoid patrols; and they pulled up stakes, and cut down flags, and sprayed graffiti dissolvers on the painted tree trunks; and in that one night, three weeks' work by the logging company was wiped out.

Of course the logging company could repeat the work, his companions told him in the dawn ride back down to the Bay Area. No doubt they would. But their costs would rise. Logging was only profitable at the margin, and the bean-counters on Wall Street would look at the P&L statements and logging wouldn't look as good to them, wouldn't get the same kind of investment. The megacorporations that owned the logging companies might get disenchanted and sell; like the loggers they were only extraction companies anyway, they strip-mined their subsidiaries' resources and then they were redundant; and it could be that the megacorporation executives considered the forests of the world basically extracted already, at least in their most profitable phases. So that they might lose interest, and it all might collapse back to a need-for-wood basis, rather than a need for liquidated assets.

And there were other ecoteurs out there, pouring sugar into gas tanks, cutting ditches, rolling boulders onto roads, introducing computer viruses; all invisible, non-violent, non-organized, non-publicized. Never hurt anybody, never brag, never talk at all. Ego radical or eco radical. Let the Greenpeace-style organizations do the PR work, play to the media and do theatre for the Earth; that was important too, but it wasn't their job. What they did was done at night, by people, mostly men, who wanted to *do something* to save the world, who wanted also those nights of adrenalin terror and accomplishment. It was somewhat like the Brits who had created the crop circles at the end of the last century, doing something beautiful in the wild night to combat the meaninglessness of modern civilization. But this was better yet. This was resistance to the mindless evil of the world's economic regime.

So he had found his cause. It made him calmer. He got a relatively low-paying job in a Berkeley law firm, spending his time fighting SLAPPs, or Strategic Lawsuits Against Public Participation, and arguing social issues for the residual progressive culture in the area, and also for the poor, because really it was the poor who bore the brunt of the environmental collapse. And then he did everything he could to erase his environmentalist past. He got less neurotic, less guilty. He gave up cigars. When he worked he worked, he did his best, he did pro bono; but then when he wasn't working, he relaxed. He said 'Fuck it' and went out for a run. He climbed on vacations, in the Arctic and elsewhere around the world. It used jet fuel but what the hell. No martyrdom of virtue any more, just fight the good fight. He saw the Himalayas, in a series of glorious treks. And a few times a year he went out with friends he never otherwise saw or talked to, except on Telegraph Avenue, on certain holidays; and they went through intensities of ecotage that made the rest of life seem like a pale dream.

Eventually, he recruited some climbing friends to the movement himself. He began to pay attention to the *Federal Register* and other sources of public information, to plan ecotage raids of his own. He did more and more of them; and no one knew.

And then on one of his vacations, he joined an adventure travel group in a climb of Mount Vinson, the highest peak in Antarctica. Like the Himalayas, it was an overwhelming experience for him; the purest wilderness he had ever seen. He came home in love with the place. Life in Berkeley seemed harder to bear after that, somehow. He still drank a bit too much. He started cigars again, occasionally. He fell in and out of relationships, sometimes painfully, sometimes perfunctorily. He was thirty-four years old.

Reading the news became a kind of self-flagellation. Things looked so dire. The world's population was over ten billion and the Dow Jones average was over ten thousand. Global average temperatures were ten degrees higher than a century before, and extreme weather events were a weekly occurrence, causing untold destruction and suffering. About four billion people had no access to electricity, while at the same time whole bioregions were already collapsing; and still the ruthless extraction of the world's natural resources continued apace. One of his eco friends with experience in the markets laughed blackly one night as he railed at this destruction, and explained to him what was happening. Say a company owned a forest that it had harvested selectively for generations, delivering its shareholders a consistent ten percent return. Meanwhile the world financial markets were offering bonds with a fifteen percent return. Lumber prices dropped, and the company's returns dropped, so the traders dropped it and its shares plummeted, so the shareholders were angry. The management, on the edge of collapse, decided to clear-cut the forest and invest the profits from that lumber sale immediately into bonds that yielded a higher return than the forest had. In effect the money that the forest represented was more valuable than the forest itself, because long-term value had collapsed to net present value; and so the forest was liquidated, and more money entered the great money balloon. And so the inexorable logic of Götterdämmerung capitalism demolished the world to increase the net present values of companies in trouble. And all of them were in trouble.

His friend stared at him, laughed at the no doubt sick look on his face, lifted his hands; that's the way things were. That was the explanation for the Götterdämmerung; not suicidal murderers in high places, but simply the logic of the system.

He had walked home through the smog and traffic noise, unaware of any of it. Seeing the world in his mind's eye, all falling apart.

Then one day he was reading the news again, helplessly, using print newspapers picked up in coffee houses so that his reading could not

36

be monitored by any hypothetical surveillance, and he came across a long article on the current situation in Antarctica. The Senate's hold-up of the renewal of the Antarctic Treaty was causing a circling for advantage among the Treaty nations; and some southern hemisphere nations, never party to the Antarctic Treaty, had seen this happening and recently formed a consortium called the Southern Club Antarctic Group, to begin oil explorations all over Antarctica. They were going to do it there too. The last pure wilderness on Earth.

When he walked out of the coffee house he went to the university library to use a public monitor, with the knot back in his stomach, and the Berkeley noise and smog like some final conflagration. The last pure wilderness in the world, fouled and wrecked, and for nothing more than the hope of perhaps five more years of the world's oil consumption; and, more importantly, many billions of dollars.

He read up on the situation. The US Geological Survey estimated that Antarctica held perhaps fifty billion barrels of oil; only a couple more decades' worth, at current consumption rates. But at twenty dollars a barrel, that was a trillion dollars. Which was only a year of the US government's budget, and only a year of the world's military budgets; but more than enough to pay off all the debts that had the southern nations lashed to the harshest austerity programmes the World Bank and IMF could devise. He could see how the logic of the system might drive them to it.

He walked over to the house of one of his ecoteur friends, the one who had introduced him to the movement, and who co-ordinated a cell about the same size as his. Look, he said to his friend. Something's got to be done. There are no locals down there to defend the place. We need to do something a bit out of the ordinary this time. Something that might stop them for good.

CHAPTER THREE

In the Antarctic Grain

Within hours of his arrival at the South Pole, X was on a Herc back to McMurdo. His welcome at the Pole was wary at best; no doubt he was regarded as some kind of Jonah; and as there was a plane on the skiway waiting to take off, he was whisked onto it without seeing a thing of the celebrated new station. Ninety degrees south, 'bye 'bye.

Back in McMurdo he was taken directly from the Herc to the Chalet, where he was questioned intensively by the bosses of Antarctic Supply and Logistics and many National Science Foundation people, as well as investigators brought down especially from the north; a big meeting, to which X was able to contribute very little, and indeed after telling his story he was soon ignored by the others while they discussed a number of other odd incidents of which he had previously been unaware. The nature of some of these incidents made it clear that his trip as conductor of the SPOT train had not been anywhere near as straightforward as he had been led to believe, a fact which no one at the meeting noticed, of course. He was just part of the train's software, in an oversized package. A kind of organic robot.

In fact, he thought as he watched the others talk things over, his entire job as General Field Assistant was in effect to be doing the robot work that robots could not yet do. He had come to Antarctica to seek adventure and here he was stuck in Mac Town, shovelling snow, cleaning bathrooms, washing galley ovens, humping loads, yes even peeling potatoes. Every day a different mindless labour. Good For Anything indeed.

As if to illustrate this thought, he was excused from the meeting to answer a call from Ron to report to the heavy shop. There he found that a forklift operator had accidentally forked through a wall and struck the frame of some shelving in the next room, knocking it onto the floor along with all of its bins and cups and drawers full of nuts, bolts, screws, nails, clips, cotter pins, washers and other assorted small hardware, now all strewn on the floor in a big heap.

Ron came in and smiled cruelly. 'Clean this up, X.'

As head of Mac Town maintenance Ron was often X's boss; also president of the local chapter of the Why Be Normal Club, which in McMurdo was saying a lot. He was one of several old iceheads who had been around so long they thought they were secret master of McMurdo, and Ron was more correct in this opinion than most. But his charm for X, such as it was, had long since worn off.

'Yes, boss,' X said to the now-empty doorway. Clearly it was robot work of the worst sort, except that robots were still too stupid to distinguish between a nut and a bolt. So X sat down heavily on the chilled concrete floor and started sorting, trying to treat it like some kind of Zen exercise, but fuming more and more as the hours passed: it was not human work. And it did not help that at every meal break he shambled into the galley black-fingered and smelling of engine-grease and concrete floors, to contemplate over his meal the beakers at their round tables chatting away, completely oblivious to him. Of course there was no such thing as class in America, which was why the beakers here could be outfitted in red parkas with their names on their lapels, while the ASL folks generally wore tan Carhartt overalls with labels on the lapels that said Small, Medium, Large or Extra Large – pick your size! – and yet no one noticed this distinction or commented on it. The beakers wandered over to the galley from the Crary Lab, on their own schedules, clearly having the time of their lives; they were on fast career tracks by being down here doing whatever they were doing, mostly wandering the landscape and knocking off bits of it, as far as X could see, and then dating the bits. And this was their work; people paid them money for this; they had nice upper-middle-class homes and families and lives and careers, all from doing this kind of thing. This was how they earned their paycheques! While fraternizing with them in the same galley were people working for hourly wages, on seasonal contracts – lifting loads, freezing their butts, losing fingernails crushed under metal objects, running machinery, crawling in utilidors, gaining no career credits to speak of – all to keep the infrastructure and services going which allowed the beakers to gallivant about fishing or watching penguins, or deciding whether their bits of rock were old or really old.

So X fumed as he returned from the galley to his concrete floor and resumed sorting ironmongery. No, it was a class system, no doubt about it. Watching the scene in Mac Town, X's reading was finally beginning to coalesce for him; it was all beginning to fall into place. Back in the world the overwhelming flood of information clouded the certainty of any analysis; there was just so much of everything that any description of it might be true. But here they were living in a stripped-down microcosm, 'Little America' as one precursor base had been named; and X saw that it was the global class system in miniature, everything clearly laid out, and shockingly similar to accounts he had read of Tsarist Russia, not to mention pharaonic Egypt: a ruling caste and an underclass, aristocrats and serfs, with a few middlemen thrown in. The red parkas and tan Carhartts only colour-coded it, as if ASL and NSF knew all about it and knew also that they could shove it in people's faces and no one would protest, not in this the globally-downsized, post-revolutionary, massively-fortified stage of very late capitalism. The in-your-face effrontery of it made X even angrier, and as he continued to pluck up nuts and washers from the concrete and drop them in their proper bins, he fantasized images of slave revolts, Spartacus, general strikes – in short, *revolution*. Guillotines on Beeker Street!

Except with a little more thought – and sitting on that cold concrete, he had a lot of time for thought – the image of the guillotine made it clear how impossible these fantasies were. Not in the practical logistical sense, as the heavy shop could probably bang together a guillotine in a day – but in the problem of all the fraternizing, the small numbers, the close quarters, the common galley. The common work out on the ice. All that meant that he and the rest of the Carhartts met a lot of beakers at least briefly, and ninety percent of them were very nice people – or say eighty percent – or at least seventy-five – but wait, there he was going into beaker mode himself, got to watch out for that, it was catching – anyway, they were just people. Lucky to have good jobs, and often kind of eccentric, but nice – the young women very nice, in fact, and seldom at all stand-offish, nicer often than the ASL women in fact, counting on the red parka to protect them perhaps – but nice smiles, very friendly, and often very smart. But also quite often deeply spaced, in classic beaker absent-minded professor mode; all the ASL folks cherished their various stories of beaker spaciness, the latest going the rounds being the one about a beaker who had decided to end thumb fatigue on snowmobiles by tying the throttle lever tight to the handlebar and then starting the engine with a pull start while standing beside it, so that the snowmobile had taken off solo across the sea ice never to be seen again, no doubt ending up down on the bottom of the bay next to the motor tractor the Scott party had mishandled over the side of their ship, an early example of beaker incompetence–

Ron appeared in the door, breaking this train of thought with a rude snort. 'Still picking this shit up, X? You've been at it for three days now!'

'Yes.' Through clenched teeth.

'Well, now you're needed elsewhere. Get down to the helo pad real quick, you needed to be there ten minutes ago, and finish this off soon as you get back. *Du muss schon gegangen sein!*'

'Jawol, Herr Commandant.'

And suddenly he was down at the helo pad, earplugs in, then wedged in the back of a helo with a bunch of equipment, no view, no headset, feeling the thing chuntering over the sea ice to somewhere in the Dry Valleys – he didn't even know where. He was dropped with some equipment in brilliant low sunshine and frigid cold, in a brown shadow-crossed windy valley like a freeze-dried Nevada.

After the helo had dragonflied away and the vast windy silence had descended on him, a group of beakers hiked over to the pile of dropped gear, shook gloved hands with him and introduced themselves: an older man, Geoffrey Michelson, no doubt the principal investigator; and three somewhat younger men, one the group's mountaineer. X's boss for the day was a Kiwi named Graham Forbes. A grad student had fallen sick and been medevacked out, and so on this day Forbes needed some help writing down figures he would be reading off the landscape. It would make the work go a lot faster. He looked to the side as he told X about this, almost as if embarrassed, although otherwise he showed no sign of any emotion at all; on the contrary he exhibited what X had come to think of as the pure beaker style, consisting of a Spocklike objectivity and deadened affect so severe that it was an open question whether he would have been able to pass a Turing test.

So: writing down numbers. 'Fine,' X said. It had to beat picking nails off the floor.

And at first it did. Forbes wandered away from the other beakers, and X followed, and they got right to work. But it was a windy day, the katabatic wind falling off the polar ice cap and whistling down the dry valleys, making all outdoor work miserable indeed, especially if you were just sitting on the ground writing figures in a notebook. Forbes was doing fabric samples, he explained as he wandered around looking at the ground through a box. That meant measuring the compass orientation of fifty random elongated pebbles in a particular area. So he was looking at pebbles through the compass box and calling out '351 . . . 157 . . . 18 . . . 42 . . .' and so on endlessly, and X was writing the numbers down in columns of ten. Fine.

Over and over again they did this. As they worked and the day passed it got windier, and the chill factor went plummeting far below zero – down, down, down – into the minus forties, X reckoned, even perhaps the fifties. Between samples he tried first all the gloves in his daypack, then all the mittens, then all the mittens over the gloves, his cold hands so numbed inside the thick masses of cloth that he could scarcely grip a pencil, much less write legibly – nose and eyes running – his face getting so numb that he could barely answer the mountaineer's questions when he came by, barely even remember to conform to the mountaineer's protocol, which consisted of answering him by putting both hands on one's head and exclaiming 'I AM FINE, SIR!' The mountaineer had instituted this regime because in situations of severe cold, common sense was one of the first things to go, causing many a deeply hypothermic person to mutter 'I'm okay' and soon after fall like a block of ice and die. So they were supposed to remember something slightly out of the ordinary to show they had not done a Paul Revere (and gone a little light in the belfry), and thus when the mountaineer came by, grinning crazily and inquiring how they were, X and Forbes lifted their mittens onto their heads and replied 'I AM FINE, SIR,' when obviously any group that had to institute such a system was not fine at all, and needed to get to shelter as fast as possible. Not that there was any shelter. They were many miles from shelter of any kind, the beakers' camp being over in the next valley, and X's helo pick-up not scheduled for hours and hours. Of course they could have huddled in the sunny lee of a boulder and eaten chocolate bars for the caloric infusion of warmth; but no. This Forbes compassed pebble after pebble, section after section, doggedly oblivious to the frigid chill. Of course X had been out in bad cold before, exposed to the bitter winds through the gap just behind the cold workyards of Mac Town. He had been teamed there with old iceheads who sometimes worked on in the teeth of the coldest windy colds, as a kind of icehead rite or contest, punishing themselves to the limit and carrying on anyway, cursing brutally and muscling through everything with a tight, hunched, savage, cold efficiency, so that they could finally finish whatever it was they were doing and stagger down into the galley near dead, take their temperatures and get readings like ninety-three or ninety-two and say 'Yar' and 'Fuck' and thaw themselves out over giant hot meals, and mug after mug of hot coffee and hot chocolate, growling at the beaker girls and their icy hearts, or at friends who passed by, 'Grrrrrrrr, grrrrrrrr,' knowing that they were the iciest of iceheads, the hardest Antarcticans of all. Just growl and go, as the old Brit seamen had said. Grin and bear it. It was a real cold-macho thing.

But this guy Forbes wasn't like that. He seemed oblivious to the cold, and was certainly ignoring it; hunkering down a bit perhaps, pinched, focused on the work to the exclusion of all else; so focused that he might not notice if he precipitated and flashfroze in position, like the Tin Man in *The Wizard of Oz*: the Ice Beaker, still creaking his numbers through frozen jaws, intent on the rock under him to the point of crystallization and beyond. It was a scary thing to witness. X's hands were now so cold they felt like insufficiently microwaved steak from the freezer, soft at the edges but stiff underneath. His butt was cold and the ground was cold and the light slanting down the valley was cold in his eyes. The cold air rushed over him, each gust a bitter chill slap pushing into his cold lungs, and though X had to admit that the passage down his cold throat appeared to thaw the air to the point that his chest did not actually freeze from inside, still, as the cold had been filtered on its cold way down, his cold nose had frozen and his cold brain was a frigid white block of hard, cold clay, plunging further down the scale of coldness with every cold breath, colder and colder, down toward absolute zero, his cold thoughts numbly syruping from crystallizing synapse to frozen axon, every molecule of mind freezing slowly as it chilled in sad cold viscous thrall to helpless memories of his ice maiden's cold treatment of him, terrible freezer burn from her brutal, cold treatment that had frozen his heart forever. A bronze man in a bronze land. Absolute zero cold. Total frozen immobility. End of timespace. Very cold. Cold cold cold.

Finally the mountaineer came by and rescued X from his insane master for the day. 'His helo's coming soon,' he told Forbes, 'and we need to get back to camp.'

'All right.'

X got to his feet, a ten-part movement with lots of care necessary to balance all the frozen components. As they creaked back to the helo rendezvous he tried to concentrate on the figures he had written rather than his painful fingers. 'Looks like the average of this last fifty will be about a hundred or so,' he noted.

Forbes looked up from the ground which he was still inspecting, hunched forward as they walked. 'That's not what we do.'

He explained that the figures had to be run through a sophisticated analysis, which only then would tell one how randomly the pebbles had fallen. If there were patterns of a certain kind, then a stream had probably run over them and sorted them lengthwise to the flow, while a completely random orientation indicated deposit through the still water of a lake or pond.

'Ah,' X said, amazed at what beakers came up with. It was really quite beautiful. Not so beautiful as to justify freezing to death, of course – not unless you were very obsessive-compulsive – but then again so many beakers *were* obsessive-compulsive. It was practically the definition of the type. So that it could be said that Antarctica was an entire continent ruled by obsessive-compulsives – just like all the rest of them, now that he thought of it, but elsewhere not so cold-hardened by their obsessions. This Forbes was almost as bad as the mountaineers, who ran around the ice as ecstatic as dogs all the time, because these were just the kinds of dreadful conditions they craved and sought out all over the world; Antarctica gave them a continuous supply, so they loved Antarctica and were happy all the time, like Val. No, the beakers were more normal than that, even the cold-hardened ones like this guy. Just as normal and friendly and hard-working as anyone else. And the occasional high-handed snob – well, there were jerks in every job. Like Ron, for instance. No, jerks were scattered at every level up and down the hierarchy; but most people were not like that.

And so, no guillotines. No revolution; no strike. Obviously. X shook his head, trying to rid it of that whole train of thought, and said, 'What's your field? What are you guys studying?'

Forbes glanced at him, trying to judge the level of answer he should make. 'I'm a glaciologist. A glacial sedimentologist.'

This struck X as a bit fine; next he'd be saying that he was actually a lateral morainologist. But X let it pass.

'We're looking at sandstones in the Sirius group. They're at the centre of a controversy concerning the age of the big polar cap. The standard view had the polar cap being a stable feature about fourteen million years old, or older. But this group thinks the ice was mostly gone three million years ago, during a warm period in the Pliocene.'

'You don't agree?'

'No no, I think they have a good case. They've identified marine microfossils in Sirius rock that date from the Pliocene, and biostrat-ification is a well-established dating method. So there had to be liquid water, in places where now there's only ice. Now they're looking for other confirmation of this view, and so they've invited me to join them.'

'And as a glaciologist, you . . .'

'The Sirius group is fossil glacial till, that much is clear. So I'm looking for things that glacial sediment can tell us. How the sediment was laid, in what conditions – disconformities to show where things changed – that kind of thing.'

In cold slow motion, X considered it. 'Liquid water? Like sea level?'

'Possibly. The dry valleys that open onto the sea are paleofjords, that much is clear.'

'But aren't we really high here? You aren't saying that sea level was this high, are you?'

Forbes glanced at him again. 'No. The idea would be that these deposits were made when the land was much lower, and then the Transantarctics rose substantially.'

44

'This far up in the last three million years?' X asked. 'Isn't that kind of fast for mountain uplift?'

He had no idea, actually, but again Forbes glanced at him, eyebrows raised. 'I'm not a geomorphologist,' he said at last.

Now that was the pure beaker style. And the other scientists were closing on them, as they all approached the helo rendezvous from different directions, converging at a flat spot on the empty brown valley floor. This guy would not want to talk about the group's project to an amateur with the other members of the group there to hear; none of them liked to do that. So X shrugged and slouched down heavily in the lee of a rock. 'Neither am I,' he said to Forbes, sharply enough to get yet another surprised look.

Then the red dragon choppered out of the pale sky, and X was heloed back to Mac Town like a big side of frozen beef. And the next morning, still cold even after huddling all night in his thick blankets, he was back in the heavy shop on the floor, picking up nuts and bolts as if the Nevada freeze-drying had never happened. The pile of metal parts on the floor did not look any smaller than when he had started. X wondered if Ron might be dumping new junk on the pile at night, in one of his awful practical jokes. The pile would never end. It was the Good For Anything's nightmare job. He was Sisyphus; he was the Golem, made for dead work; he was Frankenstein's monster, big and misshapen and clumsy. Call me X. It was interesting how many flaws there were in screw threading, and how few washers were truly flat. But not really.

The heavy shop was nowhere near as bad, however, as running into Val. This painful event was unfortunately unavoidable, and happened time after time; Mac Town was just too small to avoid people. Even if he spent his off-hours skulking in the few spots where he knew Val did not go, he still ran into her; and each time it was as traumatic as ever, so that he would spend the rest of the day fulminating, sweating as he fantasized stinging denunciations and/or revenge scenarios, which often involved saving her from death and then walking disdainfully away – sad wastes of his mental time, as he knew even while he was in the midst of them. But he couldn't help it.

And he kept running into her. Usually it happened in the galley; he would go in feeling perfectly equable, empty as a gourd, and then there would be Val, sitting at one of the big round tables with her women friends, the usual gang, a group of gals who were loud, boisterous, confident, a bit intimidating to walk past, giving off the faint whiff of xenophobia that all groups exude when their esprit de corps is pitched just a bit too high – but a good crowd nevertheless, in fact admirable

45

in X's view, given the situation in America – no shopping anorexics here, but skilled and tough people, just the kind of women he was attracted to, and among them a fair number of his best friends in town – but with Val smack in the middle of them, the Queen of the Amazons, laughing at something and ignoring him. And another meal would turn to lead in his gut. He even tried spending the extra money to eat in the Erebus View, the private restaurant over the mini-mall on the docks (which did not have a view of Erebus, of course); but then she would appear there too, and it would be expensive lead in his gut. They seemed to be on the same eating wavelength, as they had been when they first started talking. It got to the point where X would rather go hungry than risk running into her. But of course he had to eat; he had a big appetite, and skipping meals only made him feel faint and irritable, so that he would rush down at midnight the moment the galley opened for mid rats, starving, and there she would be coming in from a late survival class at Happy Camper Camp, or an expedition or something, and he would go faint and feel like screaming Leave Me Alone! But of course it was just 'Oh hi', 'Oh hi', and he would be doomed to another desperate gulping meal, hands shaking from hunger, followed by a sweat-chilled, gut-twisted revenge fantasia, in his room or up on the peak of Ob Hill or on the floor of the heavy shop picking up nails.

And no one to talk to about it. This after all was the group of acquaintances who had just recently been calling him the Earl of Sandwich. And even when he ventured to say something about it to Joyce, the sole friend he trusted enough to talk to about such matters, she only gave him a look from across the great crevasse of gender, a very complicated look, which seemed to be saying among other things that he was a fool to get so involved with a beauty like Val in the first place.

Then, after more complicated looks, and some indirect mutterings, she finally said, 'Oh come on, X. Just grow up and get over it. Men have been dumping women just like this for generations. I've got no patience with guys who come down here and find the situation is somewhat altered and start moaning about it. So there's some buyer's market behaviour from some of the women, surprise surprise, but it's no excuse for all the whining I hear, all the accusations and remonstrations concerning us terrible, trolling ice women, and all from men who were doing the same kind of shit all their lives right up to the very moment they arrived in Mac Town.' She shook her head. 'Come on, X. Get real. If you wanted a *relationship* to go well,' stressing the word like it was an archaic silly concept to begin with, 'then why did you come to Antarctica?'

'Yeah yeah,' X said, and wandered back to the heavy shop, discouraged. Why indeed? Fingers picking up iron, without need for any help from the brain whatsoever: why indeed?

At this point he could barely remember. He could not recall what his pre-arrival image of Antarctica had been. A place of adventure, surely. A place where even the humble jobs that a GFA could expect would be transformed. But even that quick disillusionment had been as nothing compared to the experience with Val. Even if love were nothing more than a bourgeois fabrication, outdated in Mac Town along with everywhere else, it was strange how much it could still hurt; and strange how many men in McMurdo were wandering around even more bitter than he was, burned by trolling ice women and swearing never to have anything to do with them ever again. Which would last right up to the next time.

But even structures of feeling were a social construct, as Raymond Williams had made clear. And the structure of feeling down here was clearly skewed by the disparity in number between men and women; there were about nine hundred men in town, and three hundred women; and that was the explanation right there, along with the fact that everyone in town had tested negative for sexual diseases. No doubt X had been lucky to have got even an extra word from Val, him a lowly GFA and a fingie to boot when he had first met her, and her the beauty of the town and one of the best known of the mountaineers, veteran of expeditions that people talked about in tones of amazement. And even though the mountaineers were ASL employees too, and caught in the same seasonal contract trap as the Carhartts, their job was one of the glamour jobs for sure, with about the same social status as the beakers.

So it had been a mismatch from the start. She was the hotshot mountaineer who had climbed many of the world's highest peaks, and repeated Shackleton's impossible crossing of South Georgia Island; he was just a – he didn't know what. A gypsy scholar. An over-age college student, finished with college. He didn't even know why she had paid attention to him at all; except for his size, no doubt. As she was six foot four inches tall, and therefore considerably taller than most men, he would have stood out in that sense. Someone she had to look up to, ha. And then he could talk, a little; he was a reader of books; and she had known an awful lot about the history of Antarctic exploration, and had been an interesting talker herself. No, they had had some good conversations! So good that it was painful to remember that period, when he had gone down to the galley three times every day hoping to run into her, timing his meals to match what seemed to be the likeliest times to meet her. And then eating big meals together, both with big appetites, and talking at length about all manner of things. She had told him about some of her climbs, and her admiration for Ernest Shackleton, and her grandmother who had died a couple of years before; and he had told her about his reading, which in the absence of other leisure activities in McMurdo had become more voluminous than at any time of his life, even in college. He read mostly political philosophy and culture theory; that was what he liked; it was interesting, as he explained to her, to try to understand why the world was the way it was. And now in Antarctica, he said, he had begun to put together his reading and his life in a way that made sense; he was beginning to see patterns. In all the evenings he had with nothing else to do, he had begun to travel backwards in the history of philosophy, trying to track his analysis to its source. Everything that impressed him turned out to be based on something that had come earlier. So that he had read *The Götterdämmerung* and become a devotee of Frank Bailey, like any number of grad students around the world; then he had sought out Bailey's roots in prepostcapitalist theory, and so had read Deleuze and Speier, and become a neoleftist; then gone further back and read Jameson and Williams and then Sartre, and found it had all come from Sartre, and so become a Sartrean; then a Nietzschean, for really it all came from Nietzsche; and then he had read Marx and Engels, and become a Marxist. At that point he had recognized the retrograde pattern of his intellectual movement, and rather than go to the trouble of travelling further backward in the history of Western philosophy, which was soon going to lead him into the monstrosities of Kant and Hegel, he had simply skipped them all and gone right back to Heraclitus, becoming a confirmed student of that most Zenlike of the Greeks, a man whose extant body of work could be read in ten minutes, but then pondered over for the rest of one's life. Yes, now he planned to meditate on fragments of Heraclitus and never read philosophy again, but start paying attention to the world instead!

And Val had laughed at his foolery. It had seemed to entertain her, at the time. But if you could never step in the same river twice, as Heraclitus had famously said, then why did he keep on running into Val in the galley? And why was he stuck in this same moment of pain? And how could he get to his food without going through that pain? And why had she inflicted that pain on him in the first place?

He had thought they had been having a good time. That was what hurt. They had talked in the galley, and laughed; they had hiked up to Ob Hill together, and sneaked into the greenhouse; they had made out; they had made love; they had even gone to New Zealand together on vacation, which in the Mac Town structure of feeling was serious stuff indeed, a kind of commitment. And X had thought they had had a good time there, a really good time. Of course he had not been able to climb mountains at Val's level, that was impossible and scary even to contemplate, her casually pointing up at routes she had done that looked completely vertical or even distinctly overhung; when they had driven up to Mount Cook, for example, past the biggest, most turquoise lake imaginable, she had mentioned climbing Cook the last time she was there, and X had gazed up at that distant white spire, like something out of a dream, and stared at her open-mouthed until she had laughed. It's not that hard, she said, although it is crappy rock, Weetabix the Kiwis call it, which is a breakfast cereal; it cuts your hands all up and yet crumbles under your weight, actually last time we got avalanched up there, it was great . . .

X had listened and nodded, trying not to look frightened. And after many climbing stories from her, all terrifying, recounted as they hiked the steep trails in the area, he had confessed in turn that he had been pretty bad at sports, and at physical activity in general. Always a disappointment to his school's coaches, naturally, as he had always been big, and therefore looked promising. But after his last spurt of growth he had lumbered around 'like Frankenstein's monster', as he put it, which caused Val to look at him oddly; and she didn't offer any similar stories about herself. Apparently she had been quite a jock in school, when she had bothered. Good at volleyball in particular.

But X had been plagued by sports as by a curse in a fairy tale. In high school he had taken a swing at a pitch while the baseball coach was watching, and accidentally hit the ball 548 feet as later tape-measured by the coach; it had taken two years of baseball after that without X ever even hitting the ball again to convince the coach that that one shot had been a fluke. Then in the winters X had been talked onto the wrestling team, and had wrestled in the heavyweight division, and lost every match for three years, all by pin; and was also perhaps the only wrestler ever to be pinned by an opponent weighing a hundred pounds less than he did; no doubt also the only wrestler ever stupid enough to agree to such a no-win contest in the first place.

But worst of all had been basketball. He had caught the attention of the UCSD coach, who had talked him into joining the team, and trained him intensively for two years in hopes of making him their centre. But it hadn't worked. Everything about it had been against the grain, and although eventually X mastered some aspects of the game, he never could make the ball go through the hoop, despite hours of training by a coach who in every game chewed a white towel to ribbons. All that frustrated effort culminated somehow in a crucial grudge match against their archrivals the UC Santa Cruz Banana Slugs, a nightmarish affair in which everything X tried went wrong and everything the Banana Slug centre tried went perfectly, until there came a moment when X was fed a pass in the key and all his baffled frustration with sports surged into a single moment of rage, and he whirled around and leapt past his opponent, intending to slam dunk the ball right through the floorboards, but missed by a fraction and hammered the ball onto the back rim so that it shot up into the rafters of the building, lost to sight for seconds, and X's wrist hit the front rim wrong, and he came down on his ankle wrong, and in the agony of a double sprain he twisted and fell, not quickly but like some immense tree cut at ground level, turning and crashing to the floor with his whole body at once, a perfect faceplant, afterward watching stunned as his teammates and opponents gazelled over him in pursuit of the ball on its return from orbit. The college paper's sportswriter had called it the greatest missed shot in the history of basketball. And an existential moment for X, a bifurcation point in his life; for after that he had given up sports for good.

And Val had laughed at that story too. And instead of trying to take him up Mount Cook, or anything like it, she had driven him into the Southern Alps on the road from Christchurch over Arthur's Pass, and just short of Arthur's Pass she had parked the car at the Bealey Hotel, overlooking a wide grey gravel riverbed seamed by the many intertwining braids of a silvery river; and led him on a hike up the Bealey Spur, a green ridge rising over the braided riverbed, giving them a more and more spectacular view of it, and of the snow-capped mountains standing in all directions around them. A glorious walk it had been, with the whole world seemingly to themselves, no one else in it at all.

And then after lunch, on a kind of rock battlement near the high point of the spur, Val had leaned over and started unlacing a boot. And when X had understood why she was doing that, his heart had leaped in his chest. And though their lovemaking out in the sun on the mountaintop was wonderful, and though it was wonderful again to lie on yellow tufts of grass and watch Val walking around naked on the rock outcropping – just an animal checking things out, big and graceful, like an ibex become a woman in order to ravish him with her mountain glory – still, that moment when he saw her untying her boot, and understood why – that was the moment which later made his hands shake, which made him moan in his bed at the magnitude of his loss. Because after their vacation was done she had gone back to the States to take care of some business concerning her grandmother's empty place, and X had travelled some more, and visited home himself, and not seen her for the three months of the Antarctic off-season; and when they had both got back to Mac Town the following Winfly, she had dumped him. And without ever saying why. She had arrived two days before him and started up something immediately with one of the other mountaineers, he heard later; but obviously that wasn't

50

the whole story. No – she hadn't had the same kind of time in New Zealand that he had had, that was clear, or else she wouldn't have done it. He had racked his brains trying to remember anything he might have done wrong, in the wan hope of somehow making up for it.

And as he sat on the heavy shop floor, picking up nuts and bolts on automatic pilot, he racked his brains again, and cursed himself for talking to her about political philosophy, of all things. He cursed himself for making fun of his athletic career, what had he been thinking? To an obvious jock? And yet she had laughed at all that, she seemed to have been enjoying it. And the hike up Bealey Spur, looking around at those magnificent peaks, and the braided silver of the river below; he had done fine, he had enjoyed the climb and they had had a lot of fun. Of course at one particularly steep point in the trail, huffing and puffing, he had made some joke about being driven by such a hard taskmaster of a pro mountaineer, and her response had made it instantly clear that she didn't think that line of humour was funny at all; which made sense, and he had immediately apologized and backed off. So that couldn't have been it, could it? Just one little bad joke? And if that had been it, and getting dumped was the penalty for one misbegotten remark, what then did that say about her? It didn't make sense. She was a very easy-going person, she was always so cheerful, so casual. She never seemed worried about anything. Such fun, ah, God . . . he couldn't think of it, it hurt too much. And yet he thought of it all the time. Like pushing a sore tooth with your tongue. Yes, it still hurts, you fool. You idiot. But what, what, what had he done?

So his poor racked brain spun, and his fingers picked up screws, nails, nuts, bolts, washers and cotter pins and put them in their bins. And slowly, slowly, he gave up all hope of getting back with Val; and, returning to his other unhappy track of thought, he gave up all hope of revolution bringing down the heartless aristocracy of the world; and when he slunk into the galley, starving and cold, Val's gang laughed at their table, and the beaker girls smiled and passed him by, on the other side of an invisible spacetime discontinuity which was class.

After which, back to the heavy shop. The Sisyphean pile was of course as high as ever. This is work, X thought; this is what work is.

Ron appeared in the door. 'Shit, X, are you still doing this?'

X glared at him.

'Tell you what, X. I got a proposal for you. Something completely different. It'll still be work, hard work. But compared to this good for anything stuff you're doing, it'll be pure shits and giggles.'

Dulles to LAX, LAX to Auckland on the overnight, half-watching two half-movies, half-eating two half-meals; watching the face of a sleeping English nurse who worked in Australia, who had been very cheery until Wade had asked her about her job; three patients had died recently of melanoma; she slept dreaming of them, looking troubled. Wade wanted her for his nurse.

Later he woke to the insistent beep of his wristphone. 'Wade Norton,' he said blurrily into it.

'Wade, it's Phil. Where are you now?'

'Somewhere over the Pacific,' Wade said, trying not to wake up fully.

'What, you're not there yet?'

'You just told me about this what, I don't know.' Wade checked his watch, but could not remember what time zone it was keeping.

'Have you made it past the international date line? Or I am still calling you from tomorrow?'

'I don't know. I was asleep.'

'So was I, Wade. But then I woke up and turned on CNN, and saw Winston being interviewed, and I was so pissed off that I couldn't get back to sleep.'

'So you called me.'

'As always.'

Wade pulled his phone headset from his briefcase and put it on, then plugged it into his wrist.

'—he did today? It's not enough to block your Antarctic Treaty, and my debt-for-population reduction package – now he's making noises about the CO_2 joint implementation deal, knowing that any noise and the Chinese will throw a tantrum and run. Invasion of national sovereignty, he called it. We can't be paying for their trouble! As if global warming was their trouble! Didn't he notice Hurricane Velma? His own damn state about a hundred miles *skinnier* than it used to be, and him on CNN saying it's a Chinese problem? Where do they *find* these guys? They must be breaking the cloning laws down there, they keep electing the same guy over and over.'

'He's popular,' Wade said, leaning his head against the cool, smooth jet window.

'Yes but why, Wade, why? How do these people win elections? I have never understood why so many decent hardworking Americans will loyally, and you have to say even pigheadedly, continue to vote for people whose explicit declared project is to rip them off.'

'People don't see it that way,' Wade said, beginning to doze again.

'But it's so obvious! Cutting jobs, reducing wages, increasing hours, shaving benefits and retirements – all this downsizing is the downsizing of labour costs, meaning less of what companies make is given to the employees and more to the owners and shareholders. And this is the Republican programme! They advocate this transfer of profits! They write and pass the laws that allow it, and oppose the laws that try to stop it! So why do people vote for them, why? Nobody making less than about seventy grand a year should ever even think of voting for them! And even the people who make more should reconsider their priorities.'

'You're a true Democrat, Phil.' Though he had been a Green in his first term, and an independent in his second.

'That's true, but still, how do they do it?'

'They tell people it's Democrats ripping them off, with taxes. People see business paying them and government taking it away.'

'But business takes it away too! They take it first and they take more and then they run off with it! People are just squeaking by while their employers are zillionaires! At least if the government rips you off then they use the money to build roads and schools and airports and jails and all, they build the whole damn infrastructure! No, taxing and spending is good, that's what I say – tax big and spend big, I say that right on the floor of the Senate.'

'We know, Phil. We watch in the office and we weep.'

'Yes you do, because government is the people! The owners just take the money and build castles in Barbados. How can they justify that, how can they *sell* that programme?'

'Ideology is powerful.'

'I guess so. You must be right. Although I've never understood why you can't just look the situation in the face and see what's going on.'

'An imaginary relationship to a real situation.'

'*Very* imaginary. But we've got to be even more imaginative than they are, Phil. Our imaginations are stronger than theirs!'

'Maybe. They seem to have the upper hand right now.'

'Do you think so? Don't you think we're gaining on them?'

'Do you?'

'Sure I do! I know it looks slow. But there are lots of people out there sick of being downsized. Give them half a chance and they'll go for it. They don't want revolution, but if they see a reform process leading to a desirable goal then they'll walk away from these Götter-dämmerung cowboys and they'll all start up their own co-ops.'

'Capitalization trouble.'

'Yeah but it's legal, that's the thing. It's like a kind of progressive's loophole in the law. And there's so much of it happening already, under the radar. It's like there are two sides battling for which fork of the path history is gonna take.'

'Your teeter-totter teleology.'

53

'What's that? Sure, ecology's on our side. It's a good angel bad angel kind of thing. Co-opification versus the Götterdämmerung. But you know, everything going down in flames – ordinary people with kids can't possibly like that, can they, Wade? They'll have to choose co-opification.'

'You would think so.'

'We have to make sure. Oh, man. I'm getting tired. I think the nightcap has finally done its thing, Wade. I'm gonna crash I think. I'm in Kashmir, try not to call me in the middle of the night, okay? But give me another report when you get there.'

'I will. Good night, Phil.'

'Night night.'

Then he was waking up again under the light touch of a stewardess, and an hour later off the plane and through the airport and onto a smaller plane, and flying south to Christchurch, over the green hills of New Zealand's two islands. Then down onto a small town airport, and out waiting for luggage, in the late afternoon. His wristphone told him it was three days after Phil's call about Antarctica; but he had lost a day crossing the international date line. His internal clock appeared to be at about 4am.

He pushed his luggage on a cart through the carpark, out to the roundabout at the airport entrance, where his hotel was located. Just around the corner, he was told, was the US Antarctic Centre. So after checking in and taking his luggage to his room, he walked around to the Centre in a dreamlike state, to make his appointment for clothing issue.

Inside a big low building he sat on a long wooden bench with some other men checking in, and tried on an entire LL Bean catalogue of winter clothing, pouring cornucopiastically out of two big orange canvas bags packed specifically for him. The array of solar and piezo-electric gloves and mittens was particularly impressive, and he commented on it to one of the Kiwi helpers in the room. The man looked at his manifest and shrugged: 'You're going a lot of places.'

'Am I?'

'That's what it says.'

So Wade hefted his bags and shambled back to the hotel, then had dinner in the hotel restaurant. Every face there came straight out of Masterpiece Theatre, New Zealand now being considerably more British than the British. Back in his room he slept deeply, barely woke to his alarm; stared at his face in the bathroom mirror; goodbye to that world. He lugged his bags back to the Centre. It was dawn, and he and several other men changed into their extreme weather clothing.

'We'll cook in the plane,' an American commented, 'and if we go down this stuff won't keep us alive a single second longer.'

'Propitiating the gods,' a Kiwi official suggested.

The official herded them into a larger room, like an ultra-functional airport lounge, where they and their orange bags were sniffed eagerly by a big black dog on a leash. Then they were led out to an old bus, and driven across the airport tarmac to the side of a big green four-engined prop plane with the numbers '04' painted in white behind its nose. Wade followed the other passengers up tall steps and through a small oval door, into a dim interior.

He shuffled back into a big, poorly-lit cylindrical space, which was almost filled by the bladeless fuselage of a khaki helicopter. The walls were covered with things; on the floor against the walls, aluminium tubing supported red nylon webbing seats. The other passengers sat here and there, and Wade realized there were only going to be a dozen of them – half in black overalls and big red parkas, half in khaki pants and leather flyers' jackets. These latter were the Kiwi crew of the helicopter. Wade sat down next to them.

Overhead the space was filled by scores of pipes, lines, struts and canisters, many of them encased in grey canvas-covered insulation tubing, tied into place with what looked like very long shoelaces, and marked everywhere by stencilled numbers, acronyms, cryptic instructions and so forth; and all covered with a layer of dust. If it had been a film set the art director would have been accused of shamelessly camping it up: a flying machine of the previous century, how quaint! Except this one had to fly them for eight hours across an islandless stormy sea.

Uneasily, Wade jammed the foam earplugs he had been given into his ears, and got his webbing seatbelt fastened. Then the engines started, and even with the earplugs the roar was deafening. The dozen passengers were cast into a speechless world, a world of sign language, smiles, nods, thumbs up, and so on. A crew member wearing a jacket that proclaimed him part of the New York Air Guard checked them over, then climbed up a hatchway to the cockpit. They were moving; perhaps they were taking off. The other red-parkaed passengers drifted into books, or reverie; the Kiwi helicopter crew members got up and wandered about, finding flat places to lie down and go to sleep. This left the webbing seats around Wade empty, and he lay down as well. Hot air alternated with frigid blasts.

He managed to sleep for a while. When he woke up he stood and made his way forward, and established by hand signals with one of the crew that it was okay to go up the steps and into the cockpit. Up there it was a scene out of a World War Two film; two pilots up front, under a bank of small windows, in bright light; two officers behind them; a flight engineer to one side. Here it was just quiet enough to talk, and they chatted over the dull wash of the engines as they ate lunches out of brown paper bags, like school kids. They didn't look much older than school kids either.

'When was this plane built?' Wade asked the engineer.

'1960.'

'Metal fatigue?'

'All the moving parts get replaced. The fuselage itself is thick as a sewer main. These Hercs are tough. This one here spent fifteen years under the snow after it lost an engine and crashed. Then they dug it out and put on a new engine, and here it is.'

'Amazing.'

'Yeah. Although the Herc bringing in the new engine crashed and was totalled, so it was no net gain.'

'Oh.'

Wade returned to his seat. So these planes really were antiques. Technology from the previous century. Which sometimes crashed. He forced himself to go back to sleep.

When he woke again the interior of the plane was distinctly brighter. He pulled himself up and looked out of the porthole. White light blasted his eyes and he fell back, eyes running, and fumbled on sunglasses before looking out again.

Mountains; white mountains. Here and there the sheer face of a black cliff, but everything else covered in what looked like a coat of whipped cream, overspilling all the landscape. The creamy pure white of the snow was unlike anything he had ever seen – as if while he had slept the old Herc had skipped through hyperspace, and was now flying over another planet entirely. Ice World. A white waste of creamy snow, stretching out to fisheye horizons, with a blue-black sky above. Wade knelt on the webbing and pressed his nose to the cold glass, staring as the white mountains flowed under them, the speed of their passage not as great as the usual jet's passover, so that there was a kind of fluid slow motion quality to the changing angles of the black cliffs, all sliding by in the white noise of the Herc. Wow, Wade thought. Maybe it really will be different.

When he turned and sat down again, he noticed that one of the young New York Air Guardsmen was wandering around the plane with a flashlight in hand, pointing it up into the dim network of pipes and wires overhead, then going to the porthole in the rear door to look out intently at the left wing. He did this for a while, back and forth, back and forth. He wiped his brow; he was sweating. In fact he looked terrified. He was like a mime doing Deep Fear.

Wade looked around and saw that the New Zealander helicopter crew had also noticed the Air Guardsman. He leaned over to shout in the nearest Kiwi's ear.

'What's up?'

'–flaps aren't working,' in a very strong Kiwi accent. Fleps ahnt wuh-keen.

'A flap isn't working?'

'None of the flaps are working!'

Wade pulled back to stare, feeling his stomach shrink. The Kiwi pilot was grinning, and he nodded to show that Wade had heard right. Then he leaned toward Wade to add more.

'Wash them in Cheech – water freezes in there – won't move after that.'

'And so?' Wade shouted.

'–don't need flaps to land.'

'You don't?'

The man shook his head, then grinned at the Guardsman and shouted to Wade, 'I don't think he knows that!'

'No!'

Obviously he didn't. But Wade did. Or so a Kiwi helicopter pilot had told him. Not need flaps to land a plane? Wasn't that exactly what they were for? Certainly the Kiwis did not look worried. In fact they were watching the Air Guardsman sweat it out, and glancing at each other and grinning, then trying to look dead serious when the Guardsman walked by, then laughing hilariously – all this in pantomime, in the white noise of the howling engines. The Air Guardsman was oblivious to them, however, and he pinballed around the plane, tracing the big hydraulics lines that ran along the ceiling from the cockpit to the wings. Wade saw with a sinking heart that this was a machine run by the force of liquids pushed around in tubes. And the Air Guardsman was sweating bullets, he was literally wiping his brow, though it was freezing in their compartment. The Kiwis could barely contain their mirth when he turned their way. Wade watched it all with his mouth hanging open, wondering who to believe. He preferred to believe the helicopter crew, of course, but they were Kiwis, and who knew what they would do? Not need flaps to land?

Then another crew member came down the hatch, and gestured for them to belt up. Wade could not tell by his expression whether he was worried or not.

So Wade sat for a long time, in the roar which was like a kind of silence, waiting, trying to figure out how a plane could not need flaps. He had seen them curve out and down on a hundred landings, perhaps a thousand. It was like a duck landing. They were definitely part of the descent mechanism.

Finally the plane appeared to slow down. The pitch of the roar lowered; then abruptly it cut back to nearly nothing. Oh my God, Wade thought, his heart beginning to race – they've cut the engines. The crew members were rushing around the interior. One of them went to the door at the front and began to open it. *Opening the door? Were they bailing out?* The other passengers were standing up, and with fumbling fingers Wade unhooked his seatbelt and leaped to his feet.

The door opened. Brilliant white light poured into the plane, and a man in a T-shirt appeared in the doorway. Wade jumped at the sight, severely startled.

They were on the ground. He had felt no tilt forward in the plane, no touchdown on a runway. Actually they appeared to be on snow. A skiway. Apparently a landing made on skis, and without operating flaps, was a very gentle thing indeed.

Mildly stunned, Wade made his way to the open door. White snow everywhere. The airport consisted of four Hercs in a row, and a few lines of red buildings on wheels, with giant hitches at their front ends, like immense U-Haul trailers. It was intensely bright, and very cold; the man in the T-shirt was seriously underdressed. He waved Wade down the steps. 'Welcome to Antarctica!'

Hello, my friends. Thank you for joining me on this voyage across the bottom of the Earth. As you can see, I have nearly completed the flight south from New Zealand. Soon we will arrive on the frozen continent. As we approach our landing, we see that deep in the big notch in the continent called the Ross Sea, a magnificent volcano has risen from the sea floor. This volcano makes a triangular island seventy kilometres across, and it rises around four or five thousand metres from the seafloor. Every measurement of this volcano's height comes up with a different figure, a fact that confirms what the eye sees immediately, that the inner line of Erebus's form creates a knot of *lung-mai* or dragon arteries that is precisely contiguous with its outward form, so that we see it in all five dimensions at once. This sometimes makes ordinary calculations of its height difficult.

Now we have landed, my friends, and are being driven across the sea ice to McMurdo. The little town, as you see, is placed in a scooped out hollow on the tip of a long peninsula of the volcano island, an arm of lava that surged down off Erebus to the west not so very long ago, leaving a final lava cone at the very tip. How strong the dragon arteries of this island!

As we approach the tip of the peninsula and our landfall, let me recall for you the story of the first human landfall on Antarctica, which happened on January 24th 1895. When Borchgrevinck's expedition approached the Antarctic Peninsula, they were aware that all previous landings had been on islands offshore, and that no one had ever stepped on the actual land of the continent before. Borchgrevinck and his ship's captain were rowed toward the rocky beach by a sailor, and as they approached they saw their chance at history. Borchgrevinck began to move to the bow of the boat to climb out, and the ship's captain began to wrestle with him, claiming for some reason that he had the right to go first. The two men were wrestling still as the boat coasted up to the rocky beach, and seeing it the seaman rowing them leaped over the side into waist-deep water, and ran up to the shore ahead of the entangled officers. Thus he was the first human ever to step on Antarctica. What was his name? I can't remember.

On the slope of the town, now, we look back toward the airport on ice, and beyond it, across some fifty kilometres of the Ross Sea, to the mainland of the continent. It is a superb prospect. Over there mountains jump immediately out of the ocean: peaks taller than Fuji and Mont Blanc stand within twelve kilometres of the ocean, and the whole range, as you can see, is complex, multi-faceted, and deeply riven by glacial valleys, down which slanting beams of yellow sunlight glow. On certain days optical effects in the air create *fata morgana* in which the mountains appear five times as tall as they do now. Oh my, yes. This view from McMurdo is very strong, bringing into play simultaneously all the landscape's oppositions: *hsü-shih* or empty-full, *yin-hsien* or invisible-visible, *chin-yuan* or near-far, also finite-infinite. Thus naturally the fifth dimension, *li*, the emptiness before all spacetime, is strongly evoked as well; and also that value of a landscape that goes beyond all notions of beauty, its *i-ching* or density of soul, and its *shen-yun* or divine resonance.

Here in the town itself, the views are all *kao-yuan*, looking up; before anything else, therefore, I am going to walk up to the top of Observation Hill, the volcanic cone at the end of the peninsula, overlooking the town as you see.

Up here, as you see as I climb, the perspective changes to *p'ing-yan*, the level perspective from a nearby mountain which gives a view horizontally to distant mountains, shading into infinity. I like *p'ing-yan* very much.

The buildings below me comprise McMurdo Station, Ross Island. The town resembles one of the rusty mining towns of Mongolia. But this *shen-yuan* angle, looking down from above, is but one part of the picture. We will find soon enough that the seemingly haphazard and emptied village we look down on is actually inhabited by a civilization wielding all the latest in futuristic technology. It is a strange place, as you will see.

The peninsula, however; the island; the sea ice studded with icebergs; the distant mountain range, so far yet so clear: all beautiful.

As we descend to town, I want to remind you that this Ross Island is tangled deeply in the dragon arteries of history. It is the island both Robert Scott and Ernest Shackleton used as their base of operations. Therein lies a sad story. The first time they came down was in 1902, on the ship *Discovery*, in an expedition commanded by Scott. Shackleton was a junior officer, from the merchant marine rather than the navy, but a strong personality. Scott not so much so; withdrawn, and at first somewhat at a loss concerning what to do in this new land. People had stepped on the continent for the first time, as I said, only seven years before. In human terms, it was a blank slate. The geographical societies of imperial Europe had declared it the next great problem for their imperial-scientific study, and the geographical society in England convinced the British Admiralty that dedicating a ship to the exploration of this new continent would be a good thing strategically. Part of the normal course of the business of the empire. So in the same year that we in our country were fighting the Boxer Rebellion against the oppression of these British colonialists, other men in other offices in London, occupied with other arms of that world-spanning empire, agreed that a single badly-built boat, a clunker, a lemon, could certainly be spared for such an umpromising venture. In the same spirit they agreed to send Captain Robert Scott, who had been recommended to them for unknown reasons by the head of the Royal Geographical Society. And so two years later Scott and his men landed on Ross Island, and built the hut that you can see on the point at the other end of town – that little square building in the centre of the screen, badly exposed to the wind. We will visit it later.

Scott had not spent his two years of preparation very usefully, however, and once on Ross Island he had no very clear brief; just exploration and science, as far as his formal orders went. But geology and the other earth sciences were in their infancy as well, this has to be understood. Without *feng shui* they had no way to read the inner shape of the landscape, and without plate tectonics they had no real understanding of why the Earth looked the way it did, or what might have happened to it in the past. They thought mountains were the result of the Earth shrinking, and the overlarge crust then buckling in lines; or alternatively, perhaps they were the result of the Earth expanding, and lava mountains leaping up out of the resulting cracks. Wegener would soon articulate every schoolchild's notion that South America and Africa must once have been joined, but that idea was scoffed at for another half a century; the truth is they did not think there had been time for continental drift to have happened, for they were just beginning to come to grips with the tremendous age of the Earth. Lord Kelvin at that time maintained that the Earth, because it was still radioactive, could not be more than a few million years old. So all earth sciences in 1902 were a kind of taxonomy, gathering information in hopes it would help some later generation of scientists better to pierce the veil of the past.

This being the case, Scott's scientists took weather data, kept records, gathered rock samples, surveyed the territory, and tested methods of travel to see how they would work. Never had men worked in weather quite so cold as this; it averaged thirty degrees Centigrade colder than the Arctic, and the storms could be brutal, even then.

So they wandered around in short sledging trips away from Ross Island. Their sledging worked, except for in the Dry Valleys on the mainland immediately across from them, sledges being for travel over ice and snow. They did not know how to use the sledge dogs, however, to pull the sledges for them, and had brought along no one who could teach them; they thought they had, but the man didn't really know, and you cannot teach what you do not know. Nansen had learned from the Inuit how to do it, and crossed Greenland using the dogs, and

Amundsen learned from Nansen. It was not so hard; the dogs like it. It is only a matter of training and the right harnesses, and off they will go as if it were their destiny to pull humans across the ice – their first act of partnership perhaps, long ago when the whole world was ice.

But Scott never learned that about dogs. What he learned instead was the dogs' own pleasure in hauling. This is the critical point, my friends; this is the crux of the matter. Scott and his men discovered that even though manhauling wasn't as efficient as other methods, efficiency was not the highest value. Much more important was the act's own *shen-yun*, its divine resonance. And they found that it is a very satisfying thing to haul your home across the snow and ice of this world, setting camp after camp. It appeals to something very deep and fundamental in our collective unconscious. That there is a collective unconscious, my friends, never doubt; it may not be exactly as Carl Jung described it, but it exists most certainly, as the very structures of our brains. The human brain grew from about three hundred cubic millimetres to about fifteen hundred cubic millimetres during the time when we were living the lives of nomads, carrying our homes across the surface of this world; and much of that growth occurred in ice ages, my friends, ice ages when even China itself was a kind of Antarctica. And so the structure of our brain reflects that co-evolution, and even now, in landscapes of snow and ice such as those we are looking at, our brains fairly hum with the fullness of their complete structure, resonating under the impact of all the co-evolutionary forces that blew it up like a balloon.

And so Scott said damn the dogs, and damn the motor tractors, and damn the hot air balloon, and the Siberian ponies, which alas could not endure the cold; and even the skis, which in those days were like long planks, and which at first the British tried to use with only a single ski pole, so far out of touch were they with snow and their own bodies. None of that mattered; they had discovered the pleasure of hauling their homes with their own power alone, on foot. Quickly they learned to use two ski poles, and they stomped along on the skis as if they were on two long snowshoes, but only to float themselves better in their walking. It was walking on this Earth they had fallen in love with.

CHAPTER FOUR

Observation Hill

McMurdo's Chalet was in effect the Government House of
Antarctica, but the Americans didn't have Government Houses, so only
Sylvia Johnston thought of it that way. Sylvia was an American citizen
by way of a brief but useful marriage many years before; otherwise
she was English to the core, English in the way that only long-term
expats became.

She arrived at the Chalet (in fact a little American prefab 'chalet'
from the 1960s, and one of the oldest buildings in town) at 7am, as
she did every day of the week except Sundays. She poured a cup of
tea and went into her office. First up on the day's schedule was the
orientation meeting for W–003, the latest participant in the Artists
and Writers' Programme, this one a Chinese man named Ta Shu,
writer and journalist, with no equipment or office needs, which was a
relief. Sylvia had come to the National Science Foundation as a biologist, having spent many seasons studying skuas and petrels; she was
not much interested in the Woos.

Alan and Debbie and Joyce and Tom and Jan all filed in and sat
where they usually sat in these meetings. Soon thereafter they were
joined by Ta Shu, a short, wiry man with a grey goatee, and long grey
hair pulled into a ponytail; his face however only lightly lined, so that
Sylvia couldn't guess his age. She would check his file after the meeting.

He sat in the single empty chair at the table and nodded to them.
Sylvia asked them all to introduce themselves.

'I'm Debbie, from helicopter operations. I'll be scheduling all your
helo flights out of McMurdo.'

'I'm Joyce, from the Berg Field Centre, where you'll get all the gear
you need that you didn't bring along.'

'I'm Alan, head of the Crary Lab this year. I can show you the lab,
and help you work with the scientists based there, if you need to.'

'I'm Tom and I work with Alan.'

'I'm Jan, NSF's contact to the private contractors working down here.'

Sylvia went last: 'I'm Sylvia Johnston, the NSF representative this year. You've been allotted ten helo hours for your time down here, I see. You share hours with other people on your flight, so you may be able to be in the air a lot longer than ten hours, if you work it right. You'll need to go through the snowcraft course given by Search and Rescue before you're authorized to go out in the field. I see you're scheduled to join T–023, the 'In the Footsteps of Admundsen' expedition, which leaves a week from today. That's a good one, I've heard. Joyce will help get you outfitted for that, so you need to make an appointment with her office. Please feel free to use the map centre and the library all you want, and come to any of us with any questions you may have.' She went through a short stack of documents they needed him to fill out, describing each as she gave it to him. He nodded, eyes watching her brightly.

She concluded with the usual warning, delivered with a serious look and a raised finger: 'Now you must know that we are very pleased to host our artists and writers down here, but you have to understand that you will not be allowed to go off and meditate on your own.'

Ta Shu looked puzzled. 'This is what I do.'

'Pardon me?'

'I am a geomancer. A practitioner of *feng shui*. I often must sit alone. I come to meditate in several sacred Antarctic places, tell people what I observe. As I said in proposal to US Antarctic Program,' with a gesture at the pile of documents.

'I see. Well. In any case – nevertheless – you have to understand that you may have to do your meditation with someone else around, because we operate by the buddy system when in the field. Antarctica is a dangerous place.'

'Very true,' Ta Shu said, nodding deeply, as if there was more to it than she knew. 'I will accommodate myself. With many thanks for your help.'

After Ta Shu had left the office they sat in silence for a while, looking down at their papers. Somewhat irritably Sylvia said, 'All right, I didn't read all of his file. But what in the world are they doing sending down a geomancer?'

'Giving him a chance to meditate on his own,' Alan suggested.

Sylvia stared at him, and he raised both hands in defence: 'This guy's famous, really. He's broadcasting this trip back to a big audience in China. And he's been down here before in the Woo programme, about fifteen years ago. His name was Wu Li then. He's the one that wrote that book of really short poems?'

'That's this same man?' Sylvia had seen the book, one of those volumes that lay on the Crary lounge's coffee table for years at a time. People said the book's author had come down as a very long-winded poet, a kind of Chinese Walt Whitman, but after his visit to the ice he had gone silent, and this little chapbook published many years later had been the only poetry ever published by him again. About forty pages of poems, if you could call them that, all of them four words long; things like

> *blue sky*
> *white snow*

or

> *white cloud*
> *black rock.*

Sylvia, swamped by her massive daily influx of NSF paperwork, had always liked the brevity of these things.

'After that book he took up *feng shui*,' Alan said. 'He travels around the world and meditates in places to, you know, grasp their essence. He uses all the old Chinese methods, but apparently he's into modern science as well. A kind of quantum mechanical *feng shui*. We at Crary are very interested.'

'Oh come on.'

'No, he's very big, I'm telling you. He's *feng shui*ed half the sky-scrapers in east Asia. His fibrevideo audience for this trip will be huge.'

'So I suppose millions of people just saw me tell him not to go off and meditate in the field when that is the essence of his art.'

'In 3-D,' Joyce added.

Sylvia pursed her lips. She had tried on a TV facemask for the first time just the previous year, and she had found the three dimensional effect quite distinct, although somewhat shimmery and planar – quite beautiful, actually. Apparently people were trying various computer enhancements to render the images crystalline or kaleidoscoped or van Goghed or Rembrandted, whatever. No doubt many of Ta Shu's audience would be surfing these effects, trying a little of everything. Antarctica as Cézanne or Seurat or Maxfield Parrish, with Ta Shu's voice-over narration.

'I don't think he was wearing his video glasses,' Alan reassured her.

Sylvia paged through his file. He was sixty-one years old. 'Does it seem to any of you that the Woos have been getting stranger and stranger?'

65

'Compared to when?' Joyce said.

'Evolution of the arts,' Alan opined.

'Or they're running out of candidates.'

'Remember the sound artist?'

They smiled. This Woo had come down and learned to do vocal impressions of all the seals, penguins, skuas and whales in the McMurdo area, also the helicopters, ventilators, generators and winds, all then mixed together in his compositions. His farewell performance in the galley had been quite amazing, actually, an Antarctic symphony that put Vaughan Williams's to shame.

'Remember Jerry and Paul?'

'Who could forget,' Sylvia grumbled. Those two had been administrative trouble; a painter and photographer travelling together, with a penchant for taking off in borrowed vehicles. They had also suborned the New York Air Guard into flying two of the Hercs in tandem over the Transantarctics, to get video of one from the other. Randi had taken a position fix from Herc 02, then heard 04 on the air and said, 'Where are you, 04?' and 04 had given her exactly the same fix as 02, giggling like seven-year-olds.

'What about Leslie, she was just as bad.'

'True,' Sylvia said. Leslie was a photographer with an unerring instinct for the illicit and transgressive; her big coffee table book had made Antarctica look like 1930s Berlin. A scandal at the NSF home office, and she shuddered to think what it had done at ASL. Heads would certainly have rolled.

Having started, they recounted once more some of the litany of memorable Woos: the painter still working on a single canvas of Cape Royds after four trips down; the modeller who had shaped a working replica of Mount Erebus too heavy to fly out, so that it was still out there in the lumber yard; the novelist whose book had portrayed the NSF as fascist villains, explaining in his acknowledgements that the NSF had been nice to him but mean to his characters; the filmmaker who had slithered around on the sea ice living the life of a Weddell seal pup, including a traumatic unplanned killer whale attack (this movie was still popular at the video rental); the sculptor who had spent all his time making traditional snowmen in the streets of McMurdo; the eminent science writer who had not heard that his flight down had had to turn back just before the Point of Safe Return, so that after eight hours he had climbed out of the Herc back in Christchurch and looked around and said, 'Why all the trees?'

Then Paxman came in to announce Sylvia's next appointment, and they composed themselves a bit guiltily, as for the most part they had liked these Woos they had been laughing at. Compared to the scientists, who were often ambitious, tense and resentful of NSF's control over the purse-strings, the Woos were great comic relief, an endless string of court jesters. And it looked as if Ta Shu was going to fit right in.

Then her next appointment was in the room, a slender, good-looking, bemused man with black hair. After introducing her colleagues to him, Sylvia excused them; she needed to talk to him alone. Wade Norton, adviser to the Wandering Senator, on an unscheduled visit; this was not good.

Though obviously tired and disoriented, he was friendly in manner, and had focused on each of the others as they were introduced in a way that made Sylvia think he was fixing them in his memory. A man in his position would be greatly helped by a good memory for people. He seemed low-keyed; looked sympathetic; a good listener. Dapper still, despite the obvious hammering of the flight from Christchurch, and from Washington before that.

'How was your trip down?'

'It was interesting.'

Awkward pause.

'Well,' Sylvia said, gesturing out of the window at what could be seen of the town. Her window faced across a dry gulch and a pipeline to the blank side of the Crary Lab. 'Tell me what exactly you would like to accomplish down here, and we'll do our best to accommodate you.'

The man smiled and held up a palm: appeal for sympathy. 'Senator Chase used to be chairman of the Senate Foreign Relations Committee, as you know. Now the current committee majority is blocking the renewal of the Treaty. They've also noted that the new South Pole station is finished, at considerable expense, but that NSF has requested the same level of funding for the Antarctic Program for the next five-year budgetary period as for the period of construction. At the same time they're hearing all kinds of reports from down here, this recent, um, disappearance of a polar traverse freight vehicle? And trouble of various kinds. I think it would be fair to characterize the committee majority as becoming sceptical about the idea of NSF continuing to run the US Antarctic Program, rather than, I don't know, privatizing things even further than they have been. ASL in combination with a university group or whatever. This is the same majority that advocates privatizing USGS and the EPA, so who knows what they might suggest? Now, Senator Chase wants NSF in charge, but he needs to be able to support his support of NSF, so to speak. So he's sent me down to investigate the situation and make a report, particularly about these recent, um, troubles. I take it there's been some unusual activity.'

'Yes,' Sylvia said, feeling as if she should imitate the geomancer's knowing nod: more than you know, sir.

He watched her closely. 'Well – the Senator is curious about that. I think he's wondering if things happening down here might not be used to advantage to get the Treaty out of committee and back on the table. If he weren't in the middle of his Asia aid walk he'd be down here himself, because he's a big believer in the power of face-to-face. But he can't come now, so he's sent me. What he wants is more information to work with.'

Sylvia nodded cautiously. Many people came down claiming to be sympathetic allies, and they usually had their own agendas and were merely hoping to use the Antarctic situation somehow to push those agendas. That's more or less what this man had just said about Senator Chase. In any case it would be imprudent to reveal anything of a truly confidential nature to an outsider. Which he knew as well as she did. Therefore laying groundwork for later, perhaps.

In the meantime his visit much resembled yet another Distinguished Visitor outside committee budget review. Why did Antarctica cost so much? Why should American taxpayers pay for it? What was going on down here that was so valuable to ordinary Americans? Review boards and committees came down to ask these questions frequently, and often they were adversarial exchanges, in that they sometimes wanted to look like brilliant cost-cutters, while the Antarctic budget had already been pared to the bone at the same time that NSF had been asked to do more with it, in an environment where safety factors could not be scrimped. Visitors like this man could influence the people in Washington making the money decisions, so to a certain extent they held the purse-strings for NSF the way NSF held the purse-strings for the scientists down here – a thought which gave Sylvia new insight into the feelings the scientists must occasionally have toward her – an unpleasant mix of caution, hope, and fear.

But still, this one was claiming to be an ally, and she thought it was likely to be true. Like everyone she had heard a fair bit about Senator Chase, and though she did not think he was any longer a serious player in Washington, she admired a lot of what he had done.

'Since this is a continent for science,' Norton said now, 'NSF is in effect the government here, isn't that right?'

'Not exactly,' Sylvia said, though she had often thought of it in just those terms. 'There's SCAR, for instance, the Scientific Committee for Antarctic Research. They work under the auspices of the Antarctic Treaty nations, and do a lot to direct what kind of research is done here, and how it's done as well. In many respects they are as powerful as NSF.'

'Interesting,' he said. 'But do they have a budget? I mean, do they fund research?'

'No.'

He left his point unsaid: money was government, here as elsewhere.

She walked him over to the big wall map of Antarctica. 'Here are all the field camps deployed this year – the blue pins – and all the trekking groups, the green pins. And I've marked the location of all the non-Treaty camps that we're aware of as well, with the red pins.'

'Are these all that there are?'

'All that we can confirm,' she prevaricated.

He nodded, staring at the map. There were perhaps ten red pins, some around the Weddell Sea, some here in the Ross Sea region, some on the polar cap. 'And the yellow pins?'

'Those represent odd sightings on satellite photos, for the most part. Things or shapes, or mostly heat signals from the IR. We don't have the resources here to investigate all of these sightings, I must admit, and those we have looked into have not revealed anything on the ground. So we mark them, and look at especially interesting ones, but we don't know what they mean.'

'I see.'

He stared at the map, looking puzzled; perhaps at what he should do next. Sylvia suggested what was in effect a short version of the Distinguished Visitor tour, designed to show distinguished visitors exceptionally scenic places in the hope of making them Antarctic advocates when they went home. It very often worked like a charm. 'Perhaps the Dry Valleys, and South Pole Station of course, and up onto Mount Erebus,' pointing at the map.

'That would be great,' he said agreeably. 'But what about visiting these oil explorations? What they're doing complicates the Treaty ratification process a good deal. Can you tell me more about them, and perhaps arrange a meeting with one of them?'

Sylvia waggled a hand. 'We can ask, of course, to visit one of their stations. But we've done that already, and so far they've not answered. We could do a Greenpeace on them, I suppose, and drop in uninvited. But the diplomatic repercussions of that might be more than you want. The Southern Club Antarctic Group is a very mixed bag of countries.'

'Yes, I take your point. But how serious are they? Do we know how much oil might be out there, or how much methane hydrate?'

'There are estimates, but the drilling they're doing now is exploratory only, as I understand it.'

'But they're pretty sure oil is there.'

'Some oil. There are no supergiant fields, but a few suspected giant fields, and many smaller ones. The old USGS estimate is fifty to a hundred billion barrels. As compared to the eight billion that were under Alaska's North Slope, or the five million sequestered under the Arctic National Park. But spread around the continent inconveniently, you see. It's not certain that even in the current state of the global inventory it will be economically viable to mine them. You'd think the new photovoltaics would be supplanting the need for fossil fuels pretty effectively.'

'Capitalization troubles. Besides I've heard talk about how important the remaining oil is going to be for its non-fuel uses.'

'Yes, there is that.'

'Is there someone I could talk to who would know how realistic these estimates are? And can tell me more about the methane hydrates situation under the ice cap?'

Sylvia thought it over. 'Yes, there are several people, I suppose. Geoff Michelson would be good, I think. He's been coming down here for a long time and knows the geology of Antarctica very well. He's also very high up in SCAR, part of their policy-making echelon. So you could kill two birds with one scientist.'

'Where is he?'

'They're out in the Dry Valleys this season.' She pointed to the spot on the map. 'They're spending a very short time in the Barwick Valley, which is an SSSI, a Site of Special Scientific Interest. Essentially it's a valley closed to human presence, to keep it as free of contamination as possible. So theirs is an unusual visit. In fact we wouldn't be able to fly you in there, because overflights by helo are forbidden. You could perhaps walk in with one of the groups we have touring the Dry Valleys.'

He was frowning; not a hiker, perhaps. Or perhaps he was only thinking of the time he had.

'You'd like to talk to him quickly.'

'Yes.'

'Well.' Sylvia thought about it. 'We might be able to send you out with one of our mountaineers, if one is free. We could drop you at their helo rendezvous, and you could walk in with the mountaineer.'

'That would be great.'

Sylvia called Joyce. 'Joyce, is there a mountaineer free to take Mr. Norton out to S–375 in the Barwick Valley? They'll just need a day or two there?' She looked at Wade, who was nodding confirmation. 'Okay, that's fine. When does the Amundsen leave? Yes, we can get them back in time for that. Thanks, Joyce.'

She hung up.

Norton said, 'What are these trekking groups about? Don't they infringe on the Treaty as well?'

70

'Well, the Treaty promised free access to everyone. Not that NSF encouraged tourism before, of course. But it's a matter of coping with the reality in the field. On the one hand there were more and more private adventure travel companies bringing expeditions down here, flying them in little old planes from Chile into Patriot Hills and other private camps. Then they were skiing or hiking or climbing about. And the Russians were coming down to the Dry Valleys in old Arctic icebreakers and dropping off big groups. Really, they were going everywhere. And the environment down here is very delicate because of the cold; a campsite that leaves behind refuse or human waste will have it here for centuries. You can still find all the depots of the first expeditions down here, it's quite amazing. But it's an archaeological site when Amundsen or Scott's people did it, whereas when it's an expedition from last week, it's just trash. So that was a problem which NSF was helpless to prevent, because no one owns Antarctica, as you know.'

Norton nodded. 'It's a bizarre situation.'

'Yes. And with Congress asking NSF to run a full programme down here on a smaller and smaller budget, it's become quite difficult. The Pole Station had to be finished for it to be occupied at all, and everything else was pinched by that effort. So about ten years ago NSF decided to try a plan whereby we offered carefully designed trekking expeditions through our own private contractor for services, ASL. That way the expeditions could be kept to certain areas and routes, and kept also to very high standards of cleanliness and environmental accountability. We even added a certain amount of data collection to some of the treks, modelling them on the Earthwatch expeditions. So we gave it a try, and our operation here is so big compared to any of the private firms that had been coming down, that the expeditions we offered could be that much better.'

'So you can offer better tours, and presumably at less expense.'

'Well, we charge top rates. But the expeditions are better in every way. And cleaner.'

'And has this in fact cut off the proliferation of small companies?'

'Yes, it's worked very well. We have to offer the same kind of small groups and adventurous itineraries, of course, or else the industry niche wouldn't be filled, so to speak. But ASL has done pretty well that way, and I'd say we have ninety percent of the business now. It's kept the environment cleaner, and it adds a bit to the operating budget down here as well, so it's a winner both ways. Of course there are those who object to bringing so many people down here at all, but the truth is it's no more people than would have come anyway, and this way we have a chance to control the conditions of their visit.'

'Interesting.'

'It is, isn't it?'

Of course it was government muscling out private business in a way that the current Congress would probably hate. But Senator Chase was now part of the opposition, so probably would not mind. Hard to say. It occurred to Sylvia that she could use a political officer, like any other governor of a large province. But no such luck.

Perhaps this man could temporarily fill the role. In any case he did not appear offended by the trekking arrangement; on the contrary, he seemed to approve. He was a civil servant himself, after all.

Now he said, 'What about these disappearances – the South Pole overland vehicle, I mean, and the other irregularities we've been hearing about?'

Sylvia sighed, and pulled from her desk's in-tray a sheet of paper detailing all the incidents from the previous two years. 'As you see by the chronology, there has been a fairly sharp increase in incidents of theft.'

'Indeed,' Norton said, glancing through the list.

'We have ASL looking into it, of course, and the National Transport and Safety Board has been called in for this last case, as well as the FBI.'

'What do you think is happening?' He looked at her closely.

She shrugged. 'There are a lot of people down here. Civilians of various sorts. ASL itself has subcontractors. And despite our efforts with adventure travel, there are still private groups down here as well. So . . .'

'You're saying it could be just ordinary theft.'

'Yes.'

'It seems weird to steal things down here, though. Impractical.'

'Yes.'

A long silence. There was more to be said, but it seemed to Sylvia that some of it had better wait until he had seen some of the DV tour.

'Well,' he said, apparently reaching similar conclusions himself. 'What do I need to do to get ready for the Dry Valleys?'

After the meeting Wade was led by a young man who introduced himself as Paxman to a building nearby, a grubby old two-storey box sporting a painted sign declaring it 'Hotel California'. Paxman showed Wade in to one of the rooms on the ground floor, and Wade threw his two orange bags on a single bed. The room reminded him strongly of his college freshman dorm – small, institutional, a sink and mirror in one corner, the bathroom shared with the room on the other side of it. Curtains permanently pulled, it appeared, no doubt to provide darkness to sleep in.

Paxman said, 'Sorry, there are some great rooms up in the Holiday Inn, but they're all full on such short notice.'

'No problem.'

Not a place to hang out, however. So after Paxman left, Wade went down the stairs in the big freezing stairwell on the end of the building, and walked out into a frigid breeze. The sun was hanging in the west over white-and-black mountains that were as vertical as cardboard cut-outs. Wade wandered the unpaved lava-rubble streets of the settlement – not so much streets, actually, as mere open spaces between clusters of buildings. The buildings were a mix: new flying-wing shapes, covered entirely in metallic blue photovoltaic film; worn functional wooden or cinderblock warehouses and dorms; military barracks or Quonset huts from the Navy years, or perhaps even from the town's founding during the International Geophysical Year of 1956–57.

His wristphone beeped.

'Hi Wade! It's Phil. Where are you now?'

'I'm in McMurdo Station, Antarctica.'

'Are you! Is it cold?'

'It's cold.'

'What does it look like?'

'Well–' Wade looked around. 'It's what people mean when they say adhocitecture.'

'Hockey texture?'

'It's a real mix. All kinds of buildings.'

'Just tell me what you see, Wade. You're my eyes.'

'Well, I'm walking by the Crary Lab now. It's quite small, composed of three small buildings on a slope, with a passageway connecting them. There's a street sign saying that I'm on Beeker Street, but it's not much of a street. There are a lot of pipelines right on the ground.'

'Much traffic?'

'Not much traffic. Now I'm passing a building like a giant yellow cube, with a bunch of antennas on the roof. Must be the radio building. Now I'm passing a little chapel.'

'A church?'

'Yes. Our Lady of the Snows. Now I'm on a road going out to the docks.

Right now the docks are empty, because the bay is iced over. In fact there are trucks and snowmobiles out on the ice. There's a kind of mini-mall behind the docks, one of the newer buildings. A restaurant on the second storey, with windows. Looks like it would have a good view of town. Here's a sign that tells me I'm on the way to the Discovery Hut, built by Robert Scott's party in 1902.'

'It's still there?'

'Yes. A small square building.'

'Amazing. So did you meet with the NSF rep? How did it go?'

'It was interesting. She's a Brit, she's very polite. She was pretty much in damage-control mode, I'm afraid. Playing it cautiously. But I wouldn't expect anything else right now. I tried to lay the groundwork. The thing is, I don't know how much she knows. If she's just an annual appointment rotated in here, I can imagine she might be temporary enough, and formidable enough in person I might add, not to be told about some things.'

'Yeah sure.'

'So, I'm off to see a Professor Michelson, an old veteran down here. He's big in the Scientific Committee on Antarctic Research, apparently one of the major players.'

'Okay, good. Get the view from the top and then proceed. Give me a call if you need any help, and I'll call again to get the news myself soon.'

'Where are you again, sir?'

'I'm in Turkestan right now, but I'm off to Kirghiz tomorrow. I'll be in touch. Stay warm!'

'I'll try.'

It would not be easy. Out on Discovery Point the breeze was really cutting; so cold by Wade's standards that it was beyond cold really and down into some new kinetic sensation entirely. If it weren't for the very warm clothing encasing him he would have been, he didn't know – petrified perhaps. Instantaneously.

The historic hut proved to be locked. A bronze plaque declared it a World Heritage Site. Beyond it stood a memorial to a man named Vince, drowned nearby in 1902. Across the town stood a tall dark cinder cone, topped by another little cross. Wade found it hard to imagine what it had been like here in 1902. Walking back into the centre of town took only ten minutes, and though his nose and ears were cold, the rest of him was warming up just from walking around in his many layers of clothing. Before he knew it, he was at the other side of town; it was only a few hundred yards wide. He started climbing the volcanic cone. Paxman had pointed up at it from Hotel Californina, and mentioned that it had a good view, and that the cross was a memorial to Scott. And he was in Antarctica, after all. Had to get out and around.

A rough trail led over pipelines running behind the last row of buildings, then up the brown volcanic rubble of the hillside, following the spine of a ridge directly to the peak. It was a braided trail with lots of alternatives, the rubble tramped to sand by hundreds of pairs of feet making their way up the cone, including the feet of Scott and Shackleton, Wade supposed. Though the air was still cold he heated up inside his parka, and soon had it entirely unzipped and pulled open. Hands in pockets, climbing up a hill in Antarctica. He was on the lee side of the cone, and it began to feel as if he was in a skin-tight envelope of hot air, on which the cold air still pressed tangibly.

Near the top the rock became a single mass of cooled cracked lava, twisted and gnarly. The wind whistled over the peak and blew his envelope of hot air away. He zipped up the parka, impressed at how quickly the cold bit.

He reached the top. He could see a long way in every direction. A knee-high bronze panorama plaque named the various features one could see. At the foot of the other side of the hill lay the Kiwi's Scott Base, a dozen green buildings clustered on the shore of the smooth white plain of the Ross Ice Shelf. Ross Island broke steeply out of this smooth plain, and rose in the distance to the stupendous broad white volcano that was Mount Erebus, looking somewhat like the cone Wade stood on, only white and ten million times bigger.

In all directions the sea was frozen white, the ice either permanent or annual. Far out on the sea ice Wade could make out the faint lines that marked the airport where his Herc had landed. The airport's trailer buildings were the merest black specks on the ice, which gave Wade a sudden sense of how vast everything was. Far beyond the airport lay what the panorama informed him were Black Island and White Island, appropriately named, and beyond them Mount Discovery, a black cone maypoled with white glaciers, and the Royal Society Range of the Transantarctic Mountains, jumping out of the white sea. Buttery shafts of yellow sunlight lanced down the valleys of these far mountains.

Struck by the views, Wade only in a final dizzy turn noticed that there was already someone else on the peak. A man, sitting on the rocks just under the wooden cross, protected from the wind. 'Hi,' Wade exclaimed, startled.

A big man, massive in a dirty dark-green parka, broad face brooding behind sunglasses and the fur fringe around his parka's hood. Tan overalls, knees dark with accumulated oil and grease. One of the ASL employees, evidently.

He grunted something at Wade and continued to survey the scene. Wade manoeuvred past him to the big wooden cross he had seen from the town below. It was about ten feet tall, a thick squared-off beam. The letters they had carved into it in 1913 had been painted white, and the

75

paint had withstood the flensing of the wind so much better than the bare wood that though the letters had been carved in to begin with, they now stood out a little from the surface. The grain of the wood also stood out. *To strive, to seek, to find, and not to yield.* And then five names, with military ranks included. Wade stared at it for a while, at a loss. Tennyson was not a poet that postpostmodernism had managed to convert to its own purposes. And the Scott expedition had been a bit of a mess, as far as Wade recalled. He had never studied the matter.

The man sitting on the peak stirred, and Wade glanced down at him, again at a loss. Finally he said, 'Do you come here often?'

The man stared at him, impassive behind mirrored sunglasses. 'Often?'

'You've been up here before?'

'Yeah.'

'Nice view.'

'Great view.'

'Yes. A great view.'

They looked down on McMurdo together. The buildings' roofs were all metal of one sort or another: ancient corrugated tin, the latest photovoltaic blue gloss, everything in between. Except for a row of six brown dormitories, no two buildings were alike: gleaming blue spaceships, ramshackle wooden shacks, black Quonset huts, open fields of lumber, the Holiday Inn, the docks, the tourist mall, the row of brown dorms, the little Crary Lab, the even littler Chalet next to it, down by the helicopter pad and the shore . . .

'Have you lived here long?' Wade asked.

'No.'

'What do you do?'

'GFA.'

'GFA?'

The man turned to look at him; Wade saw that the question branded him a newcomer. 'General Field Assistant.'

'I see.'

'And you?'

'I work in Washington, for a member of the Senate.'

'Which one?'

'Chase.'

'The one that's never there?'

'That's right.'

The man nodded. 'You must be here to look into the ice pirates.'

'Yes,' Wade said, surprised. 'I am.'

'I'm the one who was in the SPOT train that lost a vehicle.'

'I see . . . There seems to be a lot of stuff like that happening.'

'Yes.'

'Do you have any idea what might be going on?'

'Me?' The man was amused.

They sat there looking down at McMurdo. 'Not a particularly attractive town,' Wade ventured.

'It grows on you.'

'Really?'

The man shrugged. 'It's ugly, but . . . you can see everything about it. Right there before your eyes.'

As he finished this statement a figure appeared below them: a woman, coming around a rocky knob as she climbed the same trail Wade had. Thick gloss of dark blonde hair, long thighs in sky-blue ski-tights, rising rhythmically under a black parka, covering broad shoulders. The two men watched her climb. Wade's companion had hunched forward. She was taking big steps up, in iridescent blue mountaineer's boots. She looked up and they caught a brief glimpse of blue mirrored sunglasses, broad cheekbones, fine nose, broad mouth. Wade's eyebrows shot up; a beauty, it seemed, with the shoulders of a rower or weightlifter. Wordlessly the two men stared. And then she was there, stepping easily, breathing easily; 'Hi,' she said easily. She had the breezy insouciance that Wade thought of as a cheerleader's cheeriness; the confidence of an attractive woman, brought up in the American West somewhere. An outdoorswoman.

'Hi,' the two men replied.

Startled, the woman looked again at Wade's companion. 'Oh hi, X. I didn't see you.'

'Uh huh.'

Uh oh, Wade thought, looking at the two of them. The man was hunched into a kind of boulder.

'Valerie Kenning,' the woman said to Wade, and extended a hand.

'Wade Norton.'

'Nice to meet you. What brings you down here?'

'Looking around,' he said, explaining again about Chase as he rubbed his mittens together.

'Are you cold?' she asked. 'Let's move down just a bit and get out of the wind.'

They all moved down into the lee of the gnarly brown peak. When the man she had called X stood, Wade realized that he was really tall, almost seven feet it seemed. Taller than the woman, but not by a great deal; and the woman was a good bit taller than Wade. X sat down again heavily.

'Aren't you cold?' Wade asked the woman, noting her relatively thin parka, tights and gloves.

'Why no. Can't say I am.' She laughed: 'A good fat layer I guess.'

77

'Uh huh,' Wade said doubtfully, glancing at the impassive X. A good fat layer indeed. 'What about you?' Wade asked him.

'I'm always cold,' X said shortly.

Wade tried to draw him back out. 'You were saying something about how everything in the town is visible?'

X nodded once. 'Nothing's buried. The whole town is right there where you can see it. There's its power supply, see the fuel tanks up in the gap, and the main generators there under us. There's the power lines, and the sewer lines, and the sewage treatment facility. Down there you see the raw materials for building, and then all the working shops, the warehouses, the vehicle parking lots. Then all the people stuff takes up just a small part of the space, around the galley and Crary.'

'The stomach and the brains,' Valerie said. 'It's like one of those transparent bodies with all the organs on view.'

X nodded but said nothing. He didn't want to have a pleasant conversation with her, Wade saw; he was resisting her attempts to be pleasant. She continued to point out features to Wade: the helicopter pad as airport, the harbour and docks still iced over, the mall behind the docks as entertainment district, also in deep freeze until the tour ships arrived. Then the radio building as communications industry, and even a historical district, in the single dot of the Discovery Hut on the point opposite them.

'Can you guess what's missing?' she asked.

'Police station?' Wade ventured. 'Jail?'

'That's true, very good. But that's not it.'

'The Navy would come in and be police, if they needed them,' X said darkly. 'And they don't need a jail because they take you away.'

'Hmm,' Wade said. 'So there's no law enforcement here at all?'

'Sylvia is a US Marshall,' X said. 'She could deputize people if she needed help locking someone up.'

'There used to be a town gun,' Valerie said, smiling at the memory, 'but they were afraid of some winterover going postal, so they had it disassembled and the pieces distributed around town in three or four offices. And now some of the offices have lost their piece.'

She and Wade laughed; X continued to brood. He would not be pleased by her, Wade saw.

'So what's missing, then?'

'People,' X said.

Val nodded. 'Nobody in sight, see?'

Wade saw. 'Too cold.'

'That's right. No one hangs out outdoors. McMurdo looks like that twenty-four hours a day. Occasionally you see people going from one building to the next, but other than that, it always looks like a ghost town from up here.'

'Interesting,' Wade said.

They sat and looked down at the empty-seeming town, which nevertheless hummed and clanked with a variety of mechanical noises. Some vehicles moved, up among the acres of lumber and container boxes.

'Where do you go next?' Wade asked Val.

'I've got a "Footsteps of Amundsen" to guide next week. But first I'm taking a DV out to the Dry Valleys.'

'Oh, that must be me.'

'Really! Well – nice to meet you. It should be a good trip. I'm glad to get the chance to see Barwick Valley, people don't get to go there very much.'

'So I was told. I still don't know exactly where it is.'

She pointed at the mountains across the flat sea of ice to the west. 'Over there.'

Wade nodded doubtfully. X was now staring at him, and though it was hard to tell with the sunglasses and hood and scarf and all, it seemed he was glaring at him. Perhaps because of this trip with Val. Though of course that was not exactly Wade's doing. 'Where will you go next?' he asked, trying to defuse the look.

X snorted. 'GFAs go where they're told. Although I might be quitting, now that you mention it.' Looking now at Val: 'I might be resigning from ASL, so I can take an offer to go out and work for the African oil people.'

'No!' Val exclaimed. 'X, are you really?'

'Yes,' he said. 'I—really.'

'Oh X.' She frowned, shook her head. Wade saw that she didn't want to talk about it in front of him. X was looking glumly down at the town.

Finally she turned to Wade: 'You're still cold, aren't you.'

'Yes.' He was shivering hard enough to give his voice a vibrato, almost a trill.

'Well, we should get down. I'll show you where we're going on the maps. Also, have you gotten your gear yet?'

'No.'

'I'll see that you get the good stuff.'

'Great, thanks.'

They stood up. X remained seated, staring at Val with that impenetrable look. Val returned the gaze: 'See you around, X.'

He nodded. 'See you around.'

'Nice meeting you,' Wade said awkwardly, aware that he was being used to get out of a confrontation of some sort.

'Nice meeting you too.'

And the big man sat watching them as they descended. Wade took one glance back and saw him there under the big wooden cross, hunched over and brooding.

X slouched down the ridge to Mac Town, his feet like two frozen turkeys attached to the end of his legs. His fingers were cold, his pulse sluggish, his heart numb. He went to the galley and caught mid rats. The night crowd was heavy, mostly the old iceheads finished with the swing shift, plus some beakers finished with their e-mail. X took two reuben sandwiches and a mug of coffee and sat at one of the empty round tables. First he downed the coffee, holding the cup in his fingers till they burned. Then while he was devouring the second sandwich Ron sat down beside him.

'So what do you say?' Ron said, leaning in toward X with an exaggerated conspiratorial leer.

X swallowed. 'I'll go for it.'

'Good man!' Ron nodded, first in surprise, then satisfaction: 'I knew you would.'

'I didn't.'

Ron grinned his pirate grin.

Abruptly X stood and grabbed his tray. 'When do I go?'

'Day after tomorrow. They'll drop by the Windless Bight station.' This was a private airstrip set beyond Scott Base, a kind of parasite on the two government bases, barely functioning these days. 'Get yourself out there, and they'll pick you up and take you out to their camp in the Mohn Basin.'

X nodded. 'I'm gonna go resign.'

He left the galley and walked by Crary to the Chalet. Inside he told Paxman that he was resigning, and Paxman got him the forms to sign with no surprise or objection. It looked as if he would not have to explain himself to Jan or Sylvia, as he had feared he would have to. Ever since Helen had resigned mid-season and ASL had sued her for breach of contract and lost, it had become one of the options available to disaffected ASL employees. It was burning your bridges, because ASL would never hire you again, that was for sure. But they couldn't stop you from doing it.

So he put his signature on the form, powerfully tempted to sign it 'X'. But he signed his full name, to make sure everything was legal, and gave the form back to Paxman.

'What are you going to do?' Paxman asked.

'Work for the African oil people.'

'I've been thinking of doing that myself. Good luck out there.'

'Thanks.'

Then he turned, and there was Sylvia in the doorway, looking at him with a calm, hard, evaluative expression. She was NSF of course, and what an ASL employee did was in theory not her concern. But it was all connected down here. And the oil exploration camps were the most visible sign that the Antarctic Treaty was in limbo, and in danger of falling apart for ever. So X tried not to cringe under her sharp eye.

'Didn't like general field assistance, I see,' she said.

'No.' He met her look and held it. 'ASL doesn't do right by its employees. We're treated like it's such a privilege to be in Antarctica that we can always be replaced. The hours are longer than is legal back in the world, there's no security season to season, no retirement, no benefits beyond the bare minimum. Nothing that real jobs have, or used to have. And NSF sets the conditions, you let them do it. You could tell them what they can do and can't do, and create better working conditions down here.' He kept his voice soft and calm; no fits here, just stating the facts.

Sylvia said, 'There are legal limits to how much NSF can interfere with the contractors they hire.' She shook her head, turned toward her office. 'Good luck, X.'

Back out into the wind, dismissed. He trudged up the torn snow and mud to the Berg Field Centre warehouse. Ob Hill loomed behind the old building. There were things about Mac Town that he was going to miss. Joyce was in the BFC lounge, an area of the upper floor which had a few couches, a magazine rack, a table and a coffee machine.

'I came to say goodbye,' X said. 'I'm off to one of the oil camps.'

'Oh, X,' Joyce said, looking annoyed. 'Not really.'

'It's all right,' he said. 'I'm looking forward to it.'

She didn't believe him. He wasn't sure he did either.

'Anyway I'm off,' he said.

'Does Val know?'

'Yeah. I ran into her up on Ob Hill.'

'What did she say?'

'Nothing.'

'Oh X. She misses you, you know.'

'Right.'

'No really. I think she's done her trolling, you know, and found out that she made a mistake. That guy Mike was a jerk. She likes you better than the rest of the guys down here.'

X shrugged. 'Too late now,' he said, trying to squash a tiny little hummingbird of hope that was now zooming around in his chest. Irritated, he held a poker face. Joyce stood up awkwardly, and came around her desk to give him a hug, her head just higher than his belly button. He accepted the hug gratefully, feeling like a beggar.

'What a mess,' she said.

'Yeah.'

She pulled back to look up at him. 'You shouldn't go, X. Not just

81

because of Val. We're working on trying to improve things here.'

'Uh huh.'

'No really. Listen X, the service contract comes up for renewal at the end of this season, and ASL very well might lose it.'

'I'll believe that when I see it.'

'No, really!'

But Joyce had educated X on the history of the companies hired by NSF to run its Antarctic bases, so she was in large part responsible for X's scepticism. The first company, Holmes and Narver, had won its bid during the height of the cold war, and was rumoured to have been a CIA front company. The second server, ITT, had just finished helping the CIA overthrow the Allende government in Chile, so there was no question about its CIA connection; and it had close ties with oil companies too.

The third company, Antarctic Support Associates, had been a great improvement over the previous two, Joyce had said. An ordinary and even good company – certainly the good people in it had made it as much of a home as they could, and they had been in the majority. Joyce and many other office heads still in McMurdo had started with ASA and still remembered it fondly. Its contract had been the usual ten-year deal, however, and NSF had required it to give potential competitors some subcontracts so that the competitors could learn enough to make truly competitive bids at contract time. ASA had dutifully done this, and in its third ten-year stint given a subcontract to a subsidiary of a multinational conglomerate, one of the most hardball in the new global economy. There were rumours that this subcontractor had conducted some cuckoo-in-the-nest type activities, subtly messing up ASA where it could; but in truth its aggressive downsizing had resulted in such low labour costs that it was able to make a very low bid simply by sweatshopping its McMurdo labour force, and counting on the attractions of the place and the tough times up north to keep positions filled. And as NSF was constrained by Congress to accept the lowest bid without judging labour practices for anything more than legal compliance, the new company had won easily, and ASA was gone. As they took over McMurdo the owners of the new company had rechristened it Antarctic Supply and Logistics, either because they had not looked closely at the resulting acronym or because they had and wanted to make it clear right away just what kind of tough lean nononsense twenty-first century corporation they really were.

This of course had been a disaster for all the old ASA hands who wanted to stay on, who had had to reapply for the same jobs at a fraction of the old salary and benefits package, with all their seniority lost. And it had been a déjà vu disaster for Joyce, who had seen it all before in her first profession, nursing; there she had been downsized to 'census-dependent full-time employment' early on, meaning that she was full time unless not enough beds in the hospital were filled, when she would be called and told to stay home without pay. She had got pissed off and decided that if taking care of sick people was going to be sweatshopped like everything else then she was going to quit and light out for the territory, in her case the white south.

So X's scepticism concerning her hope for change only reflected what she had taught him. But now she held off all that bad history with an outstretched hand: 'No, listen,' she said seriously. 'We've got some plans, we're really working on it. And you'd fit right in. People like you, and you're a good talker. You could explain to people what we're trying to do.'

'I've already resigned.'

'Shit.' She shook her head, disgusted. 'Damn it, X, you should have talked to me first!'

'I want to go.'

She gave him a very hard look. He was taking things too far, the look said; he was being oversensitive, romanticizing the whole Val thing. Miserably he stared back at her, refusing to concede the point.

She shrugged, dismissed him with a wave of the hand. 'Okay. But you remember what I said. It's the truth you know! We're going to change things!'

He nodded and clumped down the stairs. There at the turn in the stairwell was the big photo of Thomas Berg in the middle of a polar dip, grinning and wet, chest-deep in the subzero water of McMurdo Sound, in a hole hacked in the sea ice like a seal hole, the man like a big seal. It had always struck X as a poignant memorial, as Berg had soon after that died in a helicopter crash in the Dry Valleys. Now it struck him harder than ever, as some sort of general comment on what one's happy moments really meant, on how long they lasted. He walked out into the slap of the wind feeling worse than ever.

So he was in no shape to talk to anybody, much less Val herself, and when she came out of the galley door and saw him and approached, he groaned. This town was just too damn small. And yet there was that little hummingbird whirring around inside him now, trying to flit out of one of his pupils with his look at her – a very close inspection indeed – trying to judge the possible truth of what Joyce had told him, looking for signs of regret, or friendliness, or anything but the dismissive non-looks he had got from her since she ended their friendship.

And indeed she had such a look on her face, and no sunglasses to hide it; there was no mistaking it, she was distressed. Or else mad at him. 'Are you really going?' she said.

'Yes. I just finished resigning.'

'Oh X,' she said. 'God damn it, those folks are breaking the Treaty, you don't know what's going to happen down here if the Treaty doesn't hold, they'll wreck everything!'

Of course he wouldn't be doing this if they had stayed a couple. They both knew it, but they wouldn't talk about it. And here she was ragging on him while they were standing alone out in the wasteland of pipelines and telephone wires; but up on Ob Hill she had pretended not to care in the slightest, unwilling to show anything in front of the DV, that politico with his fancy haircut and his parka worn like a camelhair overcoat, talking on the wrist to Washington and to wherever his roving senator was now, a handsome guy with money and prospects and a career, onto whom Val had immediately glommed. Women were drawn to power like iron to a magnet; it was sociobiology in action, the gals looking to protect their little babies no doubt; but still it made X sick to see it.

So he glared at her and did not reply. He could not think what to say when he was so mad at her and yet at the same time that humming-bird was zipping around in him like an attack of angina.

'People have been breaking the Treaty for years,' he said finally. 'Your tour groups are breaking the Treaty as they used to interpret it. The southern countries doing this exploration are using really safe technology. And it's exploration only. It won't be a problem. I'm looking forward to doing some real work for a change.'

She waved a hand angrily, swatting him without actually swatting him. 'You'll end up doing the same kind of thing you do here.'

'They're going to train me to do more.'

'Right.'

He looked down at her. Not very far down, it was true; this was one of the things he had loved about her, she was a woman his size. And not just physically, but in her mind and spirit. He had loved her, and sure, he loved her still. But this was too much. If she wanted to ask him to stay, or berate him for not staying for personal reasons having to do with them, if she wanted to apologize for dumping him so brutally after their arrival, she could do it; here he was, this was her chance, her last chance for months at least, maybe her last chance ever; and here she was nattering on about the goddamned Antarctic Treaty, as if that mattered any more or was the real point between them.

Maybe some of that got across to her in his look. She pursed her mouth and looked off to the side unhappily. Unhappy cheerleader; it was a sorry sight. But she was too stubborn to apologize, and by God he deserved an apology. They had been partners, they had been sleeping together, making love; they had been in love. Or so he had thought. Then they had gone off to do their business in the world and come back here, just a couple of months apart, and as usual on her return (just three days before him!) there had been a bunch of guys coming on to her – big deal, it was no excuse, when had it been any different for a woman who looked like her? No, McMurdo was no excuse. They had been an ice romance only – she had wanted to break it off for reasons of her own, and the great number of men in McMurdo was just an excuse and a damned lame excuse at that.

And she wasn't going to apologize.

'I've got to pack,' X said, struggling to keep his voice level. He turned and walked away before he started to shout at her, or cry.

And the next day he was out at the little air station that the private tour companies had established in the Windless Bight – nothing more than two Jamesways and a fuel bladder next to the snowploughed landing strip, one of the smallest, barest camps X had ever seen. The plane didn't show, and he spent the night in a Jamesway named 'The Random House', sleeping uneasily on an ancient, dead mattress, listening to the Preway roar like the ghost boos of a ghost audience, watching his life movie from inside his head: a remake of *The Man Without A Country*, starring The Man With No Name.

CHAPTER FIVE

A Site of Special Scientific Interest

Hello again, my friends. As you can see, I am now out on the surface of the Ross Ice Shelf, a few kilometres south of Ross Island. I have come out here to spend a day at the Americans' Happy Camper Camp, where visitors are trained in ice skills to better prepare themselves for their time in Antarctica. The camp is well-named; I am happy indeed. The mountaineers have shown us how to light the stoves, to put up the tents and to use the radios. I have learned how to tie several knots. I know now that if you need to get a badly injured person inside a tent but are afraid to move them for fear of injuring them more, you are to slit the bottom of the tent open and erect the tent directly over the unfortunate person. Antarctica is a dangerous place. It is easy, looking around as we are now, to think that I stand on a broad snowy plain; in fact I am standing on cracked ice, with deep fissures all around, and the Antarctic Ocean below me.

Captain Cook, one of the greatest *feng shui* masters of all time, sailed the circumference of this Antarctic Ocean in the 1770s, trying to get as far south as he could. His wooden sailing ships ran into the pack ice at seventy degrees south, and as far as they could see to the south was only more ice. With the technology of his time they could go no farther. Later Cook wrote, 'I can be bold to say, that no man will ever venture farther than I have done and that the lands which may lie to the South will never be explored.'

This sounds odd to us, short-sighted and even a bit foolish. But we must remember that the man who said it was extremely intelligent and capable, accomplishing much more in his life than any of us have. His short-sightedness as exhibited in this remark has to be understood then not as a personal attribute, but as an attribute of his age generally. For Cook lived just before the great accelerations of the industrial age; his time was as it were the foothills of a mountain range so precipitous that the heights could not be guessed. Thus the radical foreshortening of the *kao-yuan* perspective. Cook sailed in wooden ships, which in their materials much resembled those used in ships for the previous two thousand years; only improvements in design had made them more seaworthy, and Cook rightly judged that these improvements, wrested slowly over the centuries out of human experience, had gone about as far with the materials as they could go. Thus he could not foresee the immense changes that would come so rapidly in the industrial decades to follow.

We, however, have no such excuse as Cook. We live on the heights of that mountain range, in a culture changing so rapidly that it is hard to gauge it. We look back on two centuries of continuous acceleration into this unstable moment, so we should be able to foresee that much the same will occur in the time after us. Who can deny that the future will quickly become something very different than our time, quickly become one of any number of possible worlds?

And yet by and large I think we still do no better than Captain Cook. We assume that the conditions that exist now will be permanent, even though every year the laws are amended, and even the ice shelf I am standing on now, that has been here for three million years, is melting away. Even the rocks melt away in time. This moment is like a dragonfly, hovering over a peach blossom; then off and gone.

Look then at this ocean I am camped on in this moment. A white immensity; nothing to say about it. Erebus stands in the air like a powerful deity. Before you can read a landscape, it has to become a part of your inmost heart. When I came before to Antarctica, as a proud young man, I saw the land and it baffled me, and I could not paint it in my poems. Nothing came to me. As the British explorer Cherry-Garrard said, 'This journey had beggared our language.'

Only later, as I dreamed of it, did I grow to love it. What words I could find were the oldest words, in their simplest combinations. Blue sky; white snow. That is all language can say of this place; all else is footnotes, and the human stories.

Now I am back, and those of you who care to share my voyage, watching and listening in China, or wherever else you may be; I welcome you, because I feel now, all these years later, with the love of these stories in me, that I am ready to film the land I see, and talk to you, my friends, about it; not to reproduce the effects of light, but to tap this light at its source.

For Scott's party in their first stay here, in 1902, this edge of this ice shelf was as far south as anyone had ever been, and no one knew what lay farther over the horizon. Except of course they knew for sure that that way lay the South Pole, the axis of the Earth's rotation. On Ross

Island they were still twelve hundred kilometres away, as they knew by geometrical calculation; but they had no idea what the land in between would look like; whether these Western Mountains across the bay would extend all the way south, as a great wall blocking them, or whether there would be an easy ramp up to the great plateau of ice, which short trips through the nearest Western Mountains suggested might guard the Pole. They could only tell by trying to walk there. It resembled the attempts on the North Pole, and the search for the Northwest Passage, which had been a major feature of British culture since Elizabethan times. As long as England had been a maritime power, as long as it had been an empire, it had been sending out brave men to explore the polar ends of the Earth, first the northern one, and now, with the invention of canned food and metal-reinforced steam-powered ships, they had been able to penetrate the pack ice surrounding the southern one – the ice that Captain Cook said would never be penetrated – and been able to establish a good base of supplies as close as they had, here on Ross Island. Directly south lay this broad featureless white plain of an ice shelf. And so they had to give it a try.

On their first trip south, Scott took along his friend and confidant, Edward 'Bill' Wilson, and Ernest Shackleton. Shackleton was chosen for his physical strength and for his drive, his will, his spirit to achieve and to cross this land.

But the snow of the ice shelf was soft, and pulling a sledge through it proved difficult, like pulling it through sand; very slow, and very strenuous. Shackleton had a heart defect that he hid from others all his life, and in the rigour of this forced march south, making five miles a day only after fourteen hours of badly designed manhauling, he succumbed to scurvy faster than the other two.

Within days of starting they could see by the slowness of their progress that they were not going to make it to the Pole, so the push south continued to no very great purpose, even though they were killing themselves to do it. This made them irritable. They never even got off the ice shelf, but only managed to make it to the tidal cracks separating the ice from the shore. They confirmed that the Western Mountains extended far enough south that they stood across any very direct route from Ross Island to the Pole; a rather ominous and discouraging discovery, and yet the only one they had made when they had to turn back.

And even so Scott had almost left it too late. The moment of return was his call to make, and despite warnings from Wilson in early December that Shackleton was developing scurvy, and the other two not far behind, Scott pushed on until the day after New Year's. At that point they had a desperate struggle to get back to Ross Island alive. On the return, Shackleton collapsed from the scurvy, and could no longer help haul the sledge; at most he could ski along freely next to the other two, at what cost to the will we cannot well imagine, as sick as he was – so sick that on some days he was forced to lie on the sledge and let the other two haul him.

And Scott, not knowing about the heart defect, had no sympathy for Shackleton. Here was a younger man, who had been so much more dynamic back on Ross Island; his breakdown Scott regarded as a moral defect, and as it endangered all three of their lives, and therefore Scott's own reputation for competence, he grew angry at Shackleton. He made contemptuous comments about 'the baggage' within Shackleton's hearing, often enough that Wilson had to pull him aside and tell him to stop.

And in the end Scott and Shackleton fought. Shackleton and Wilson were packing the sledges when Scott shouted at them, 'Come here, you bloody fool!' Wilson said, 'Were you speaking to me?' And Scott said 'No'. Shackleton then said, 'Then it must have been me. But you're the worst bloody fool of the lot, and every time you dare to speak to me like that, you'll get it back'.

Shackleton was an officer junior to Scott, on a British Navy expedition. This statement was therefore very like mutiny. It took Wilson to patch things up and insist that the two men calm down and continue. The incident was so traumatic that not one of the three men wrote about it in the journals they were keeping on the trek; it was too dangerous to mention. How then do we know about it? Because Wilson, who was the father confessor figure for everyone on the expedition, finally felt the need to speak of it himself, and at some point afterward told the geologist Armitage what had happened. Later still Armitage wrote down what he had heard. How accurate Armitage's account was, and Wilson's too for that matter, we have no way to tell. But certainly by the time they staggered back across this ice to the Discovery Hut at McMurdo, Scott and Shackleton were enemies for life. They could not stand each other. Scott used his command to invalid Shackleton out of Antarctica, sending him home on the supply ship that visited after their first year there, while the rest of them stayed on for another year and made more sledge journeys, testing routes to the polar cap and looking around.

And so Ernest Shackleton became determined to come back.

Val and Wade were given a ride in a pick-up truck down the two hundred yards from Hotel California to the helo pad, even though they were carrying only rucksacks for their walk up the Barwick Valley to the S–375 camp. Val watched Wade as they stood around waiting for the loadmaster to wave them over; he was observing the scene with great interest, and listened impassively to the loadie's unconvinced and unconvincing intro to the helo's safety features, basically a cranial that was no more protection than a bike helmet, and was mainly there to get an intercom on one's head. But no smirks or rolled eyes or blanched dismay from Wade; no doubt he had done a lot of helo travel before in his line of work. He stepped up into the pax seats and took the throne, the seat just behind and slightly above the two pilot seats. Val sat behind him, and after that she only had a view of the back of his head, his cranial actually; but as they took off she could see him looking down at McMurdo, then out at Erebus, then down at the sea ice as they crossed over the frozen surface of McMurdo Sound. He got on twice to ask questions, first about the trash ice, which Val explained was caused by windblown grit from Black Island landing on the ice and melting in, causing a ghastly dark-grey pitted badlands, impassable on vehicle or foot; then another about the giant greenish, tabular bergs sticking out of the sea ice, which Val explained were pieces of the Ross Ice Shelf that had broken off the previous summer, and were on their way out to sea. The sea ice was studded with these big chunks, even though the ice shelf between Hut Point and White Island was not breaking away at anything like the same speed it was along its broad exposed front east of Ross Island. Wade nodded to indicate that he had heard Val's explanations over the roar of the engine, and that was it. No excited commentary, no further questions.

They flew over the piedmont glacier lining the coast, and then between the rocky mountain points of Mount Newell and Mount Doorly, the last two peaks of the Asgaard and Olympus Ranges respectively. Then up the broad bare-walled valley between these ranges; this was Wright Valley, one of the biggest and most famous of the Dry Valleys. The co-pilot said, 'They'll be calling them the Wet Valleys soon – see how much snow there is on the ground these days? Later in the summer that'll all melt and run down the Onyx River, that white line there, into Lake Vanda.' Vanda was several feet higher than it had been in years past, its blue, cracked surface ringed with a broad band of whiter ice. The co-pilot fell into his tour-guide mode for the still-silent Wade, naming the peaks they passed and the hanging glaciers spilling out of the gaps between the peaks of the Asgaard Range to their left. Wade's head whipped from left to right to take it all in. Then the pilot cut in on the commentary to tell Val they were picking up a couple of scientists at Don Juan Pond before taking them on to their drop point. The helicopter veered to the left of the flat-topped island ridge called The Dais, up a side-valley to land beside Don Juan Pond, which was small, shallow, brown, and liquid. The pond was liquid because its water was too salty to freeze, the co-pilot told Wade. The scientists to be picked up were nowhere in sight, so they killed the engine and got out and wandered around the narrow brown valley. The ground around the pond was crusted white with salt crystals. Wade walked right out into the middle of the pond, as it was nowhere more than a few inches deep. Val followed him out, partly to make sure he did not step in a pothole.

'Now, why doesn't it freeze, again?' He was looking at everything very curiously, as if in an art gallery to view an exhibit by an artist he didn't quite trust.

'It's too salty.'

'Really?' He reached down and scooped up a handful – the water was perfectly clear and transparent in his hand, as thin as ordinary water – then before Val could say anything he put the handful to his mouth and drank it.

Only to spit it out in an explosive spray. 'Acck!' he choked, and began turning red-faced as he hacked away, spitting over and over again.

Val took her water bottle from her belt, opened it and handed it to him. 'Drink?'

He nodded, still hacking away. He pointed down at the pond: 'Poison?' he gasped.

'No. Just salty.'

'Wow.' He drank and spat, drank and spat. '*Really* salty. Like battery acid.'

'I know. I touched a finger of it to my tongue once.'

He nodded, spat out again. 'That would be the way. I had no idea.'

The two scientists appeared on the rock-covered glacier up the valley from the pond, and soon they had hiked down to the helicopter. They said hello and apologized for keeping the helo waiting.

'That's all right,' Val said, 'it gave Wade here a chance to drink the water.'

Wade gave Val a quick look, and she grinned at him. The scientists regarded him with raised eyebrows. 'Wow,' one said. 'What did it taste like?'

'It was salty,' Wade confirmed. His mouth was still puckered into a little knot.

'I'll say,' the other remarked as they climbed up into the silent helo. 'There's 126 grams of salt per litre in that water. As compared to three point seven for sea water.'

'It tasted saltier than that,' Wade said.

'It makes for a kind of minimum temperature thermometer. The pond won't freeze until it reaches −54°, and then if it does the ice itself is fresh water and won't melt until it gets above zero. So we can come out here in the spring and tell whether it got below −54° the previous winter. Hardly ever does, these days.'

Then they were strapped in and the loadie had unsheathed the blades, and they were off in the helo's whacking roar again, going up the Don Juan Pond's valley rather than back down. The co-pilot explained that they wanted to fly over the Labyrinth. Wade asked what that was, and one of the scientists got on to explain that the maze of intersecting canyons they were now over was probably carved by streams on the underside of a big glacier. 'See, the glacier itself is still there, only not as big now.'

And then they were over Wright Upper Glacier, a broad, smooth field of bluish ice covering the entire head of the valley, which was a kind of immense box canyon, walled by a huge, shattered semi-circle of cliffs. All the walls and promontories of this curved escarpment were layered light and dark, like a cake of alternating vanilla and chocolate layers. The same scientist explained that these were bands of light sandstone and dark dolerite, the dolerite harder and so nearly vertical in the cliffs, the sandstone softer and so sloping down at an angle. Above the cliffs loomed the ice of the great Antarctic polar plateau itself, extending off to the distant southern horizon; and in one place it spilled over the cliffs, like a Niagara Falls frozen in a second to perfect stillness. This was Airdevronsix Icefalls, the co-pilot said, named after the Navy helo division that had discovered it. The pilot took the helo right up next to the icefall, so that they were looking down just a couple of hundred feet at holes in the ice where the banded rock was visible; then they shot up into the clear air over the cliffs, where the vast ice expanse of the plateau ran off to the southerly horizon.

The ice fall was an amazing sight, one that Val never got used to no matter how many times she saw it; and it was a staple of all the Dry Valley treks, of course, so that she had seen it a lot. If it had been back in the world it would have been as famous as Monument Valley or Yosemite or the Matterhorn – a cliché, seen countless times in films and advertisements. But as it was down here it was still, even with the big surge in adventure tourism, the least-known of the great wonders of the natural world. And all the more thrilling for that, as far as Val was concerned. One of the glories of Ice Planet.

And indeed Wade was leaning down over the pilots' shoulders to see more out of the front, and looking left and right like a puppet head on a spring. But he did not get on the intercom to tell everyone how amazed he was, like the client who had shouted 'WOW' perhaps fifty times during a similar flight; nor did he become obsessed with photography like so many other clients did, fussing with rolls and exposures until they did not seem to be seeing anything outside at all. On the contrary, Wade seemed thoroughly absorbed. Which was only appropriate; but Val had judged him on their first meeting to be a typical Washington politician, not really interested in the ice itself. She liked it that he seemed impressed. And had tried to drink from Don Juan Pond!

The pilots could have flown up and over the peaks of the Olympus Range directly to their destination, but as the destination was a Site of Special Scientific Interest and a no-fly zone, the whole complex of Balham Valley, McKelvey Valley, the Insel Ridge (another Daislike mid-valley ridge) and Barwick Valley, were off-limits to normal scientific investigation, all fly-overs, and all adventure treks. This was to try to keep a part of the Dry Valleys as uncontaminated as possible, for baseline comparisons with the other more intensively studied and therefore polluted valleys. The team they were visiting had had to show compelling need to get permission to set a small tent camp in the Barwick Valley for a couple of weeks, and they had been required to walk in carrying a minimum of gear.

So the helo flew back down Wright Valley, over the turquoise and lapis sheet of Lake Vanda, up the white line of the Onyx River, and up more steeply into the windy defile of Bull Pass, a hanging valley connecting Wright to McKelvey Valley. Then they were through the pass and out over the broad barren floor of Victoria Valley, and landing on the sandy dunes upvalley from Lake Vida. This was another cracked frozen lake, looking like something tucked at about twenty-five thousand feet in mountains anywhere else; in fact they were just over a thousand feet above sea level. But high latitude was the equivalent of high altitude in its effect on landscape, and so Val and Wade climbed out of the helo and moved out from under the loudly spinning main rotor blades, and straightened to stand upright on what seemed the Tibetan plateau, if not the moon itself.

Then the bright red helo was off, loud and fast, downvalley and away, disappearing quickly into Bull Pass, the noise of it receding from their pounding ears much more slowly, until finally they were left alone in the windy but still silence of a vast rockscape, a valley that seemed cut off from – well, from everything. Wade stared around, looking stunned.

'Pretty, isn't it?' Val remarked out of habit, as if addressing a client.

'I don't think that's quite the word I'd choose.'

*   *   *

The gear they were carrying was minimal, and Wade's rucksack in particular was not very heavy; Val had kept it to perhaps fifteen kilos. Still he grunted as he hefted it onto his back, and remarked on the load.

'When I started working down here,' Val said, 'your personal kit weighed around a hundred pounds and was too bulky to be carried anywhere. That's why that pick-up truck took us down to the helo pad this morning; they're still not used to bag drag being something you can carry yourself.'

'Hmm,' Wade said, as if not convinced they had reached that point even yet.

Val shrugged into her pack (she was carrying about twenty-five kilos), and took off. After walking up Victoria Valley for several minutes she pointed past the prow of Mount Insel, up Barwick Valley. 'They're up there, see, under that glacier at the head of the valley.'

Wade glanced up and nodded. 'There by dinner.'

Val laughed, and Wade stopped and tipped down his sunglasses to have another look. 'Longer?'

'Longer. That's about twenty-five kilometres.'

'Oh wow. I would have guessed about five.'

'That happens a lot down here. There aren't any trees or buildings to give you a sense of scale, and the mountains are big. And the air is clearer than you're used to.'

'That's for sure.'

They walked side by side, as no one way over the sand and rubble underfoot was easier than another. 'People make big mistakes in perspective down here,' Val said. 'Thinking a snowmobile is a mountain, or a pack of cigarettes a building. Or vice versa.'

'Everything looks big to me.'

'But you thought we were just a short walk from their camp.'

'True.'

The afternoon passed as they walked up and down over low waves of rock. Although in the distance their way looked nearly level, the immediate vicinity was always up and down – twenty feet up a ridge, thirty feet down a saddle crossing an even deeper bowl – forty feet up to get out of the bowl, then twenty down, then a steep staircase – and so on. That local unevenness, and the rough rubble covering the valley floor everywhere, made it hard walking. But Wade slipped through it like a dancer, Val noted, with small neat graceful steps; no complaints; and he kept up a good pace. Val liked this kind of walking very much, but usually she toured these valleys leading trekking groups of up to twenty people, with the tail of the group always stumble-blistering along and requiring delicate care. So she enjoyed this empty afternoon a good deal; and after a few hours, declared it time to stop and cook a meal.

She found them a nook between two big boulders, in the sunlight and out of the wind, and sat down and broke out the food bag and the stove. Wade sat watching her as she cooked up some soup. She gestured at his pack; 'There's hot chocolate in your thermos.'

He helped himself, but didn't eat much soup or trail mix. Appetite a bit suppressed, as often happened to people when they started trekking out here. He would be ravenous by the time they reached the Hourglass Lakes, she judged. Although he was not a big man. But walking in the cold burned a lot of calories.

'So this is forbidden ground,' he noted as she cleaned up the site and packed her bag.

'Yes. It's kind of nice to be able to see it.'

'They must be doing important work to be allowed to come in here.'

'Yes. Actually I've heard they're controversial.'

'Letting them in here?'

'That, and also their work as a whole. If they're right, then the ice caps might be fairly sensitive to climate changes like the one we're in. Something like that. You'll have to ask them about it.'

They hiked on into the evening. Some small stumbles and a slowing pace made it clear that Wade was tiring. But he made no complaint, nor any requests for rests. Val was impressed; for a slender city boy he was pretty tough. She had had many a client who had come out here wild for the mountains and not done anywhere near as well.

Then they topped a short wall of crushed rock, formed in a polygonal frost heave, and the white splay of the glacier filling the upper end of the valley stood there unexpectedly over the rusty rock. 'Almost there,' Wade said.

'Actually it'll be a couple more hours,' Val said. 'Do you want to set camp for the night?'

'No. I think I can make it there.'

'Okay. How about another dinner, though?'

'Fine. Sounds good.'

And this time he wolfed down a whole pot of stew. A very quick adjustment, Val thought as she repacked the gear.

The S–375 camp consisted of four colourful small dome tents surrounding two Scott tents, which were tall four-sided pyramids of heavy canvas, looking archaic in the early twilight; one was lit from within like a yellow lantern, and wisps of steam escaped the tubular vent at its top. As they approached this one Val called out, 'Hello in there!'

They were expected, so the shouts from inside were not surprised:
'Come in!' 'Come in!'

'But take your boots off first, it'll be crowded in here!'

It was. Even with their boots off they were bulky in their parkas,
but the men inside were shifting around while they pulled them off,
and Wade wedged into a corner while Val dropped into the gap between
Misha, the group's mountaineer, and the Coleman stove. Both burners
were alight under big pots of water, and the heat felt good against her
side. Wade would be crushed in his corner, bent forward like a tailor,
but that would be his first lesson in the ergonomics of a Scott tent.
One of the main reasons Scott's group had perished, in Val's opinion,
was that their Scott tent was designed for four people and a stove, and
not five. This one was bigger, but six was still more than it could
accommodate comfortably, and it was crowded, stuffy, even hot; still,
after the frigid barren expanse of the darkening valley, a very welcome
refuge.

'Leave the door open for a bit,' the man on the other side of the
stove said. He was bearded, and perhaps twenty years the senior of
the other men in the tent; no doubt the PI that Wade had come to see:
Dr Geoffrey Michelson, a British veteran of over forty years of Antarctic geology, who had taught in the States for almost that long. Introductions were made: Michelson's team consisted of a younger colleague
from UCLA, Harry Stanton; a Kiwi glaciologist named Graham Forbes;
and Misha Kaminski, with whom Val had worked on some memorable
SARs. It was quite a mélange of accents, and Val noticed for the first
time the tinge of Virginia in Wade's speech as he said hi to the others.
He and Val were offered mugs of Drambuie, the traditional liquor of
the Antarctic Kiwis, and they both accepted gratefully. Val's feet were
throbbing, and she imagined Wade's were worse, though he had never
complained about anything. And the day's hike had totalled almost
thirty kilometres.

'Where are you off to next?' Misha asked Val.

'Footsteps of Amundsen,' she said.

'Dogtracks of Amundsen, you should say!'

'True. But we'll pull a sledge, as usual.'

'That's so crazy. These people come down here and pull a sledge
across the ice cap for a month–'

'Six weeks.'

'–when they could be climbing in the Asgaards, or wherever, somewhere really spectacular. And all because someone did it a century
ago.'

'History buffs,' Michelson suggested.

'Fools! People who are in love with ideas rather than real places.'

Misha was an Australian who had grown up in Switzerland with Polish parents, and his accent was an odd mix of Aussie and Central Europe.

'It's a fun trip,' Val said. But they only laughed.

'What about you?' Michelson asked Wade. 'What brings you to our special Site of Special Scientific Interest?'

'Well,' Wade said. 'I'm down to look into this situation with the African oil exploration that's going on, among other things. I work for Senator Phil Chase from California, and he's gotten interested. So, I'm curious to know just how – how realistic these people's expectations of hitting oil are.'

'Not my field,' Michelson said.

'No,' Wade conceded.

Val saw that he was thinking hard how to gain the older man's confidence.

'But I was told by Sylvia that you know more about the Transantarctics than, than most people, and that you might be able to tell me something about the geological situation.'

'Yes, I know the Transantarctics, but there's no oil there. That's not where they're drilling. They're out on the polar plateau, from what I understand.'

'Yes, but near the mountains?'

'Two hundred kilometres away.'

'Yes . . . but I thought you might be able to, to extrapolate – to tell me what you think about the likelihood of oil. Your contention is that East Antarctica had no ice sheet in the past, isn't that right?'

'Well, but we are studying the Pliocene, about three million years ago. The oil, if there is any, would have been formed a couple hundred million years before that.'

'Ah. So it was warmer down here then?'

'Indeed it was, although at that time Antarctica was not down here, but up nearer the equator. Part of Gondwana.'

'Ah!'

Wade was being toyed with, and he knew it, Val judged. But he was keeping his cool, going along with it, playing the game. A quick learning curve must have been a necessary job skill, after all. 'So oil deposits might have been established then, when it was up near the equator?'

'Possibly. Yes, almost certainly. One sees coal deposits right on the surface in parts of the Prince Charles Mountains–'

'*Giant* coal deposits,' Misha interjected.

'And so oil is quite likely. The Wilkes Basin, under the ice cap on the other side of the Transantarctics, is a possibility, certainly.'

'Out where this southern group is looking?'

'Well, up until now there has been no one looking out there, because it is forbidden by the Antarctic Treaty. Most of the oil assessment for the continental has been done by matching up the Antarctic craton with the continents it abutted when it was part of Gondwana, and going by analogy to those places. But there have been seismic tests done to try to determine other things, and no doubt some tests might have given people clues about where to look harder.'

'Why have they started now, do you think?'

Under his moustache a little smile tugged up the corners of Michelson's mouth. 'That's for you to explain to us, right?'

'They want oil,' Misha said with a grin, and the others laughed.

Wade nodded, smiling easily. 'So it may be there.'

'It may very well be. I don't think they know yet.'

'But it's not, you know – unlikely.'

'No, no. Given the coal deposits, and the continent's position in the Triassic, it's more likely than not to be somewhere down here.'

'What about recovering it from under the ice cap?'

'It should be like ocean drilling, eh?'

'Except the ice cap is moving,' Graham said. He was washing dishes in a big bowl of steaming water and listening to the conversation; but he was not the kind to add much to it, except when a point being overlooked forced him to say something.

'True. Their drilling holes would have to become slots over time, I suppose. Or they might be drilling in stable areas of the ice sheet.'

'In the lee of nunataks,' Graham suggested.

'What about transporting the oil out?' Wade asked.

They all looked at each other. 'Pipeline, eh?' Michelson said.

'So there would be the danger of a spill.'

'Yes. As in Alaska. Which didn't stop people there, as I recall.'

'No. But a spill on the ice plateau . . .'

'Messy. But perhaps they could use these bacteria that have been developed for cleaning spills on water. They eat the oil, die and are blown away. Or so the drilling cartel will claim, I'm sure.'

Michelson leaned over and picked up the Drambuie bottle, offered it to them. 'More Drambers? You've had a long walk. How about a midnight snack? Chocolate?' He indicated a box which held perhaps a gross of wrapped chocolate bars. 'Camp crackers?'

'Just the Drambers, thanks,' Val said. Wade nodded his agreement; then tried one of the camp crackers.

'What about shipping the oil out?' Wade asked.

'Tankers.'

'Dangerous?'

'They ship a big load of oil down to McMurdo every summer.'

'But if there was an accident, like the *Exxon Valdez* . . .'

'Very messy. The *Bahia* dumped a big load of oil off the Peninsula some decades back, and it was years and years before the coast cleaned itself. It did, however, eventually. The environment is pretty good with oil, if you take the long view.'

'And add bacteria,' Misha said.

'Yes, those bacteria.'

Wade said, 'We've heard rumours that the next generation of tankers might be submarines. Remotely operated submarines, with no crew on board.'

'Probably safer than staying on the surface, at least in this ocean.'

'Probably safer than sailing with sailors,' Misha noted.

Wade nodded, watching them all closely. Val felt herself getting drowsy in the warmth of the tent, but Wade showed no signs of it. 'What about your work here?' he asked.

The geologists looked at each other.

'Let's talk about it tomorrow,' Michelson suggested. 'It's after midnight, and everyone is tired. Come out with us tomorrow to one of our field sites, and we'll show you what we're up to out here in this bitter wilderness.' And he sipped his Drambuie with a little smile.

Outside the Scott tent the midnight sun was blinding, and the cold like a hard pinch all over. Wade's eyes spilled tears, and the details of getting on his sunglasses while wearing mittens occupied him through the first gasps of adjustment to the cold. He followed Val to their packs, his stiff legs aching with every move, and watched as she pulled a tent and tent poles from her backpack. 'Help me get this up,' she said. So he crouched and held down a corner of the tent while she clipped a maze of poles to its exterior. 'Nice tent,' he offered, beginning to shiver. It felt like the tears were freezing to his cheeks.

'Not bad. Light, anyway. One of the monster winds off the plateau will tear it to pieces, though.'

'Really?'

'Oh yeah. I've been in them when they come apart. Very loud. Here, tie the ties around rocks. Big rocks, no, like this one.'

'What did you do?'

'When? Oh. Well, once when it happened we had a helo. Those are really cold though, the metal sucks the heat right out of you. Then the other times there have been Scott tents to retreat into.'

'Those are stronger?'

'Oh yeah. Bombproof, as long as you set them right. Here, throw the sleeping bags in to me.'

Wade pulled bulky but light sleeping bags out of their stuff-sacks, and tossed them in to her, realizing for the first time that they would be sharing a tent.

'Now the pads.'

'The what?'

'The sleeping pads. In the long red sacks.'

'Ah.' These too were very light. 'All this gear is so light.'

'Yes. The new aerogels are fantastic. Here, blow it up.'

'It's an air mattress?'

'Not exactly, it's like a Thermarest. An air and foam combination, but in these the foam is incredibly light.'

'Why not just an air mattress, wouldn't that be even lighter?'

'Yeah, but air mattresses are as cold as helicopters. They're always just as cold as if you were sleeping on the ground, or even colder – the ground you could maybe warm up a little with your body, but the air in an air mattress keeps moving around and sucking the warmth away from you. The coldest I've ever been was on an air mattress my dad bought for us when I was a girl. I ended up sleeping on my pillow. Okay, all ready in here, come on in.'

'Ah, I guess I'll use my pee bottle one last time first.'

'Good idea. I'll do the same in here.'

Wade thought about that for a bit as he walked a few feet away and tried to pee; those images and the cold impeded him a bit. To distract himself he looked at the brilliant white glacier pouring down from the head of the valley. It was the middle of the night, and yet the mass of ice was glowing in the sunlight like an intrusion from some brighter dimension.

When he had finished he regarded dubiously the yellow fluid in the plastic bottle. Apparently he was dehydrated. Then he got on his knees at the tent entrance and crawled inside. Val was already in her bag, and appeared to be fully clothed except for her parka, which rested on her boots and served as a pillow. It was brilliantly lit inside the tent, everything tinted the yellow of the nylon: Val's blue eyes looked green, and her blonde hair was as luminous as the glacier outside. Wade hauled off his bunny boots, feeling the white rubber flex in his hands. They had been surprisingly comfortable on the hike in, and quite warm. It was too cold for his socks to be smelly; nothing smelled at all down here, except the steaming food in the Scott tent. He lay down in his bag and closed his eyes. It was like trying to sleep with your face six inches from the headlights of a car. 'How do you sleep when it's this bright?'

'You get used to it.'

'Nobody uses those black sleep goggles that people wear on planes?'

'I've never seen anyone do it. Not a bad idea, though. Especially if you're on ice or snow. Then it's a lot brighter than this.'

Her voice was drowsy. The idea of sharing a tent with a strange man was obviously not of concern to her. Done it a thousand times. Already asleep, it appeared.

And soon after that, so was he.

He woke and it was still light. He had no idea what time it was. He checked his watch: 7:04am. Val was not in her bag; it lay pulled down toward the door, a suggestively Val-shaped hole still in it.

He took his boots from under his head and put them on; then, as he was quickly chilling, his parka. He rolled forward with a stiff groan, and crawled out into the brilliant frigid morning. The sun was standing over a different ridge, no doubt the east ridge; he had given up trying to orient himself in McMurdo, but out here it might be possible, if you stayed put long enough. He needed to use his pee bottle again, and there was a rock outhouse up the hill, away from the white surface of the lake. Yellow hair shone over its top rocks. He looked away, down at the lake. It was cold, but in his parka he felt comfortable. Hungry, however. Very hungry.

He joined the group, which had already reconvened in the Scott tent, and they ate oatmeal and crackers and chocolate bars hastily, as if oppressed by the very same crowded tent that twelve hours earlier had been such a comfy refuge. Then it was outside again, where they occupied themselves filling backpacks, and taking turns up at the rock outhouse.

'Can I carry anything?' Wade asked Professor Michelson.

'No, thank you. But bring your pack, and you can help carry samples on the way back.'

Val and Misha took off ahead of the scientists, who followed them up the valley. Distant red dots, bobbing in the rock rubble under the white mass of the glacier.

'Why are the Dry Valleys dry?' Wade asked Michelson as they hiked along.

'It's not entirely understood. But people usually agree that the mountains at the heads of these valleys are so high that they choke off the ice sliding down from the polar cap. In places some ice spills over, but the winds ablate the ice faster than it pours through the passes, and so you have the hanging glaciers you see–' gesturing ahead– 'steep-sided because of the ablation, and fairly static in position. At least they have been since their discovery. Now, however . . .'

'The global warming?'

'Well, yes. There's no doubt the climate has warmed in the last century, because of carbon dioxide that we've put in the atmosphere.'

Wade nodded sharply, intending to say that this was a fact known even to Washington bureaucrats.

'Yes yes,' Michelson acknowledged, 'you know about that. But the effects of this warming on Antarctica aren't entirely clear. At first, you see, the warming increases precipitation down here, in the form of more snow, it not being so warm as to rain. And so the ice caps and the glaciers and the sea ice actually tend to grow. At least that is one force involved. So the Dry Valleys could be iced over again, as they have been before, if that were the only thing going on. In fact this snow you see on the ground here – this would have been very unusual at this time of year, thirty years ago. Now the valleys are snowy more often than they're bare, and they're never less than piebald, if you see what I mean. Which is no help at all to people trying to study them.'

'What about the big ice shelves breaking off?'

'Well, those turned out to be very sensitive to slight temperature increases. They've broken off because of their own dynamic with the ocean temperatures and currents, or so we think. Then as they detach and float off north, the ice coming down from the polar cap has nothing to slow it down, and so there are the immense ice tongues that we're seeing, and very fast ice streams and glaciers, and even a slight sinking of the polar cap itself, if the Ohio State people's results are correct.

But with more snow up there as well, it's hard to know what the upshot will be.'

Wade nodded again, more agreeably. Establishing the ground of understanding with experts who were explaining things to him was his responsibility; nod too often and the expert was likely to give up entirely; but in the absence of any sign of response, some of them would begin to explain everything. Michelson appeared to have a tendency in the latter direction, so Wade said, 'But if global warming takes things up to the point where it's above freezing down here for periods every summer?'

'Well, then things start melting.'

'Uh huh . . .'

'And with the ice shelves already substantially gone, and the ice streams, which are like ice rivers within the West Antarctic ice sheet, speeding up – then the ice sheets themselves will begin to detach. The western Antarctic ice sheet is grounded on land that is well below sea level, so it comes off very quickly. The eastern sheet is much larger, and more of it is grounded above sea level, so it will hold longer, but still, the warmer it gets the faster it will go, more precipitation or not. And if the eastern sheet goes, then sea level will be some sixty to seventy metres higher than it is now.'

'You'd think that would be enough of a threat to get everyone's attention.'

'Yes, but it's so inconvenient. If we have to take global warming seriously, then everything changes. CO_2 levels have to drop, industrial society can't keep burning fossil fuels – we would have to live differently. It's so much easier to find some scientist somewhere who would be ever so happy to appear before a congressional committee and declare that there is no such thing as global warming, or if there is that it isn't really a problem, or that burning fossil fuels has nothing to do with it. Then the problem can be declared non-existent by law and everyone can go back to business as usual.'

'You mean Professor Warren?'

'Yes,' Michelson said, nodding in approval at Wade's recognition.

In fact Professor Warren's appearance before the Senate Foreign Relations Committee had caused quite a stir, as Wade well knew, having been put in charge of substantiating Phil Chase's rebuttal to the professor. It was slightly possible Michelson was aware of Chase's opposition to the renegade professor, rather than knowing only that the committee as a whole had endorsed Warren's views enthusiastically, and used them to justify the blockage of the CO_2 joint implentation treaty with China which would have meant American money used to improve Chinese factories. But it was hard to tell; between beard, sunglasses and the black leather nose-protector attached to the sunglasses, Michelson's was a hard face to read. A face from a Brueghel painting, really. Best to make no assumptions.

'Is this where we're going?' Wade asked, pointing up a side valley where Graham Forbes was just in view.

'Yes. Follow Graham. Up into the Apocalypse Peaks,' he announced with some satisfaction.

Hiking uphill on the brown pebbly snow-crusted rubble was hard work, and Wade started to heat up. He unzipped his parka and let the cold air cool him a bit. Unfortunately no matter how hot his torso became, his ears and nose continued to freeze.

As they climbed higher they could see farther up the hanging valley. A glacier ran down its middle, reaching almost to the frozen lakes on the floor of Barwick Valley. Higher still and they could see the source of the glacier, a big tongue of ice pouring through the gap between two black rock ridges. Above and beyond that tongue the whole world was white. The edge of the polar cap, as Michelson confirmed; enough ice to cover the United States and Mexico. 'These Dry Valleys are very unusual, you must remember that. It will be a shame if they get overrun by the ice.' Michelson ascended at a steady relaxed pace, and appeared neither too hot nor too cold. 'That's Shapeless Mountain. Beyond it is Mistake Peak. Over there, Mount Bastion and the Gibson Spur. These are all peaks of the Willett Range, and the ice cap is running up against their southern flanks, and through the passes between them, as here.'

'You like the names.'

'Yes,' surprised, 'I do.'

He led Wade under the side of the glacier, right up to the faceted cliff of its sidewall, which gleamed pale blue in the bright sun. Spills of broken ice splayed out from the wall here and there, as if ice machines had churned out a vast oversupply of ice cubes. 'See how rounded all the chunks are,' Michelson pointed out. 'They're subliming away in the arid winds, and they'll be gone before there's another calving in the same spot. That's why there's no build-up of ice, and the glacier's sides are sheer like this. They break off as a result of slow pressure from behind, and then the wind cleans up the mess at the bottom.'

Eventually they climbed onto a section of rubble bordering the glacier that ramped up until it was level with the baord surface of the glacier, then just above it, so that they could see beyond the glacier, and a long way up the ice plain of the polar cap, rising gently to the south. It was not perfectly smooth, but had broad undulations that formed very low hills and valleys, Wade saw; subtle contours of up and down, all very smooth except in certain zones, where it was completely shattered. A kind of white, frozen ocean pouring through a break in the shore and down to a lower world. Also curving down in places to stand right over the shore, like waves that would never break. Puffing, sweat stinging one eye, Wade was nevertheless fascinated by the sight, glaring even through his polarized sunglasses; it was surreal, a kind of Dali landscape, with all its features made impossible and subtly ominous, as the ocean bulked higher than the land, and one surge of the immense white wave would sweep them all away.

But of course it stayed put. Michelson had hiked ahead, and joined Graham Forbes between the glacier and a broken cliff of reddish stone facing it. There at the foot of the red stone was a band of lighter sandstone, freckled with pebbles embedded in it. Graham Forbes was already kneeling before this sandstone, tapping away with a geologist's hammer.

'Now this is a very nice example of the Sirius group,' Michelson said as Wade approached them. 'Almost a textbook example of it, in that it would make a good photo in a textbook. See how it's laminated against the dolerite? Like the dirty ring of a bathtub. It's a sedimentary rock, called tillite or diamictite, depending. Glacial till, from an ancient glacier.'

'Not from this one?' Wade said, gesturing at the ice mass looming behind them.

'No, from a predecessor. It's been here a while.'

'How long?'

A snort from Forbes.

Michelson's moustache lifted at the corners. 'That's the question, isn't it? We maintain that some Sirius group sandstones date from around three million years ago.'

'Other people don't agree?'

'That's right. There are those who say that the eastern ice cap has been very stable, and has been here for fourteen million years at least. So. . .' He shrugged. 'We look at Sirius sandstone wherever we can find it, and see what we can see.'

'How have you established the three million year date?'

'There are microfossils buried in the rock, the fossil remnants of marine diatoms and foraminifera. These creatures have evolved over time, so that different kinds have lived in different eras, and the diatom record on the ocean floor is very well stratified and preserved. So when you find certain kinds of diatom fossils, you can match them with the record and say with fair confidence that the rock they are in is of a certain age.'

'And this is a real method – I mean, an accepted method?'

The little smile. 'Oh yes, very real. It's called biostratification, and it's very well established.'

'I see.'

'We've also found evidence of a fuller biological community than just marine diatoms – members of a beech tree forest biome. Which suggests it was so warm that the ice cap would have been substantially gone, with western Antarctica an archipelago, and even eastern Antarctic covered in parts by shallow seas.'

'You carbon–14 dated the beech trees?'

'No no, carbon–14 dating only works for a short distance back in time. These are much older. And beech trees have remained stable evolutionarily for many millions of years, so we can't date them by their type. There are some beetle fragments among the beech remains, however, and some other plants, lichens and mosses, and some of these can be dated using various methods, uranium-lead, argon-argon, amino acid . . . every little bit of biological material in Sirius tends to add its part to the puzzle.'

'Look,' Forbes said to Michelson, pointing with a geologist's hammer to the rock of the slope at about his knee level. 'A dropstone of diamictite, within the massive diamicton here.'

Wade saw that a round boulder of sandstone, the same colour as the rest but with more pebbles in it, was embedded in the rest of the sandstone.

'Interesting!' Michelson said, going to one knee to have a closer look. 'So this boulder must be very much older than the matrix.'

'Older, anyway,' Forbes allowed.

They continued to discuss the band of sandstone, pointing out features invisible to Wade. 'Do you think this could be our D–7 disconformity again, cropping up here?'

'It looks as if that could be some crude stratification below it, see that.'

'And above, massive clast-rich diamictite, with dolerite boulders, and more water-lain gravels.'

Back and forth they went, in a flurry of terms, as they wandered up and down the slope: deformed laminites, clast-poor muddy diamictite, rudimentary paleosols, lonestones, meta-sediments; 'And then at the bottom the Dominion erosion surface again, perhaps. See how scoured this dolerite is, with north-south striations.'

'Very nice,' Michelson said.

They were seeing much more in this rock than Wade had ever realized could be there, much as he might hear more than them if confronted with an unfamiliar piece by Poulenc. They were reading the landscape like a text, even like a work of art in some senses: 'See here!' Michelson exclaimed to Forbes, pointing at a patch of whitish rock at one end of the sandstone band, laminated very finely. 'Silt layers, calcite crystals perhaps, and deposited here certainly – these couldn't have been moved here, they're much too delicate, see? You can break the layers with a finger.' He demonstrated. 'Beautiful.'

'I'll take some samples,' Forbes said, getting a flat rectangular white canvas bag out of his day-sack.

'Is this the first time you've found this kind of thing?' Wade asked, feeling pleased: a scientific discovery!

'The first time here, anyway.'

'And what does this indicate?'

'Well, these silt or clay layers suggest the bottom of a lake, and as you can see, boulders have dropped onto the layers while they were still wet and could be bowed down under the weight, see that? One explanation of that could be that this was a lake in a glacier's margin, and icebergs calving would melt, and drop the boulders in them onto the silt on the bottom of the lake. We certainly see results just like these around living glaciers. So we may be looking at the bottom or shore of a lake.'

Michelson and Forbes got on their knees and began dismantling some of the precious layered deposit, putting chunks of it into sample bags, discussing more invisible features in their highly technical language. 'Here,' Michelson said to Wade. 'If you care to help, you can count the number of vertical layers this deposit has.'

Wade got on his knees and went at it, getting colder by the minute. The other two continued inspecting the sandstone inch by inch, apparently oblivious to the biting chill air, even though they were wearing less than Wade was.

Michelson looked back at Wade. 'Try counting how many fit against your fingernail, then measuring how many fingernails high the stack is, and multiply,' he suggested.

Wade, shocked at the idea of that sort of approximation entering the pure realm of science, continued to count the layers one by one.

Eventually they all stood up. Wade was cold, and very stiff from the previous day's hike, and his hands were numb inside their mittens. 'Six hundred and six,' he reported. 'So there was liquid water down here for six hundred years!'

'Or six hundred tidal cycles,' Forbes said. 'Which would be about one year.'

Wade saw the little smile reappear under Michelson's moustache. 'Liquid water, in any case,' Michelson said. 'And very possibly this disconformity in the succession represents the transition from a marine environment to a subaerial one. What we called D–7 over on the Cloudmaker.' At the end of his black noseguard an icicle curved down almost to his chin, turning his face from a Brueghel into something out of Bosch.

107

'Let's get back to camp,' he said, glancing up at the sun as if consulting a clock. 'I'm famished, and we mustn't be late for dinner. It's Misha's turn to cook, and he's planning something special, I can tell.'

Indeed he was. After a long walk back weighted down by many sample bags filled with rocks, they crawled into the Scott tent and the sharp smell of cooking garlic butter raked down their nostrils directly to their empty stomachs. They oohed and ahhed and knocked around against the sloping canvas of the tent until they were properly arranged, Wade back in his corner, which was very hard on his back – harder work physically than the whole rest of the day. But on this night Val was seated next to him, in fact jammed against him leg to leg, so that the entire evening he had the more-than-just-somatic warmth of that contact pouring into him. 'Just in time,' Misha told them, handing out *hors d'oeuvres*: mugs of cold Scotch and melted brie on camp crackers, followed quickly by the main course: lobster tails sautéed in the garlic butter, with a side of corn beef hash, followed eventually by a dessert of chocolate bars and Drambuie.

It was heavenly. Wade sawed away at the flesh of his lobster tails with a big Swiss Army knife, marvelling that food could taste so good. 'Four star,' someone muttered, and there were various hums and purrs and clattering as they all gulped down their meals. Near the end of the main course Michelson leaned on one elbow next to the radio and stretched out like a Roman emperor, the little V of a smile lifting his moustache. 'Remember,' he said to Wade, 'you must tell them what hell it was down here.'

'Ninth circle,' Wade agreed, wiping melted butter off his chin and licking it from his fingers.

'You liked the lobster?' Misha asked him.

'Kind of salty,' Wade said, which caused Val to choke.

'Don't worry,' she said to the frowning Misha when she had recovered, 'things are going to taste salty to Wade here for the rest of his life.' She explained what he had done at Don Juan Pond and the scientists laughed at him.

Then as they slowly downed dessert, and Misha heated water on the Coleman stove to wash dishes, the talk turned to the day's work. Wade asked them to tell him more about the Sirius group controversy, and Val seconded the request, and the scientists were happy to oblige. All four of them contributed to the telling, even Misha, who to Wade's surprise took the lead; he had had training in geology, that was clear. 'The old view,' he explained, 'was that the East Antarctic ice cap is an old and stable feature. The west sheet comes and goes, but the east sheet was established after Antarctic detached from South America, forty or fifty million years ago. Then it was here in place, and growing ever after, except for some warming periods, maybe, but those all long ago; most recently fourteen million years, at the latest.

'Then in the 1980s Webb and Harwood and their group found diatoms in the Sirius sandstone, and dated the diatoms at three million years old. When they published those data and their conclusion, that the eastern ice sheet hadn't been there three million years ago, the battle was on.'

'Battle,' Wade said around a final salty mouthful of lobster.

'Well, you know. Scientific controversy.'

'Battle,' Harry Stanton confirmed.

'The two sides wouldn't shoot each other on sight,' Michelson objected.

'No no,' Misha said, 'it's not like people after a divorce or something, you know, totally personal and vindictive. But still, they were both convinced that the other side weren't being . . .'

'Scientific,' Michelson supplied with his little smile.

'They both thought the other side was being a blockhead,' Harry said. 'Scientifically speaking of course.'

'Yes,' Misha said. 'They didn't like each other, after a while.'

'Suggesting lab contamination didn't help,' Michelson said.

'Lab contamination?' Wade asked Misha.

'Well, when Harwood and Webb first said they had found these diatoms in the Sirius sandstone, some of the stabilists suggested the diatoms had come from other studies in the same lab. That went over very poorly in Ohio, as you can imagine.'

'Indeed. Stabilists?'

'The old ice group. This is the battle of the stabilists and the dynamacists.'

'So we won the name battle at least,' Michelson murmured.

'Then next, when it was established that the diatoms were actually inside Sirius rocks, the stabilists suggested there were so few diatoms that they had probably just blown in on the wind from the coast.'

'That infamous coast-to-plateau wind,' Harry noted.

'Which blows so hard that it shoves the diatoms right under the ice cap that the stabilists claim has always been there,' Michelson said.

'Yes, of course,' Misha said. 'Blown over from Australia, perhaps. But they did find some diatoms in the ice at the South Pole, so the stabilists had some support for this idea.'

'And how did the Ohio group deal with that?'

Misha grinned. 'With *quantity*. Sometimes you have quality results, and sometimes you need *quantity* results. They blew up tons and tons of the Transantarctic Mountains. They went to every Sirius site they could find with a great big dynamite licence from NSF, and they blew up great masses of Sirius and took them back home and dumped them on the stabilists' desks, metaphorically speaking of course. Diatoms by the *ton*.'

'Not tons,' Michelson objected. 'Nothing in excess.'

'*Tons*. Whole nunataks you see on the map, now entirely gone and removed to labs at Ohio State.'

'No no—'

'Yes yes,' laughing, 'I was the mountaineer for one of those expeditions, I set the charges myself! It was awesome. There should be an Ohio State Glacier named up there, we tore a brand new pass in the Transantarctics.'

Much laughter in the tent at Michelson's expense, who clearly had been involved with this project. Wade saw that the younger scientists were fond of him. 'And they found good evidence?' Wade said.

'Quite good,' Misha judged. 'No doubt there were beech forests here when the Sirius group was laid down.'

'Parts of the Sirius group,' Michelson qualified. 'It could easily be that the Sirius group is fossil till from several different glacial periods.'

'And so the stabilists were convinced, and they recanted,' Wade said, to more hoots of laughter.

'Of course not,' Misha said, grinning and refilling their mugs with Drambuie. 'That isn't how it works, not really. No one is ever convinced of anything.'

'So how do new ideas take hold?'

'The old scientists die,' Misha said, kicking Michelson as an example.

The corners of the moustache lifted. 'That's the point,' he said to Wade. 'It's careers, you see. Whole careers have been given over to the stabilist position. Grad students are getting PhDs, assistant professors are getting tenure, all on the strength of papers advocating the stabilist position. They can't just admit they were wrong all along. But biostratification is a very solid dating method. So the diatoms are a problem for them. Not to mention the beetles and moss and beech trees.'

'But what do they say about those?' Wade asked.

'They say the beech forests are older than fourteen million years, perhaps even Cretaceous. They say the diatoms blew in from elsewhere. They ignore the beetles entirely.'

'The beetles flew in too,' Misha suggested. 'Flew down from Lemuria.'

Michelson chortled, then raised a finger. 'Mostly they ignore us now,' he said. 'They concentrate on finding areas that have been dry or covered with ice for more than three million years, which is certainly possible. Even at its warmest there would certainly have been glaciers down here. All we're saying when we call it warm is that there was liquid water possible for a minimum of five months of the year, which is all that *Nothofagus* need to survive.'

'And you're also saying that the east ice cap was gone,' Wade added.

'Yes, but there would certainly have been glaciers in the higher or more southerly places, probably big glaciers. But the diatoms are sea bottom diatoms, so there must have been seas. The cap was melted in the Pliocene! It's the only explanation that works for all the evidence we have. Glaciers in the mountains, and in the permanent shade, sure. And sea ice in the winters, of course. But water, nevertheless, over much of this area. Fjords filling the big glacier basins.'

'They have kind of a hard case to prove,' Val noted. 'They have to try to show that it stayed iced over everywhere.'

'Very true,' Michelson said. 'And a hard thing to do.'

'They could find climate data showing it stayed cold throughout,' Val said.

'Yes, and the oxygen isotope ratio in the offshore sediments even seems to support them in that idea, I must admit. But there are a lot of other climate data from the north that show that the early Pliocene was quite warm. It was a high CO_2 era, just like today.'

'Can't you date the ice cap outright?' Wade asked. 'Drill right to the bottom and count layers of ice, like I counted the layers today?'

'There are no layers below a certain level. They get crushed together. After that the ice has certain chemical signatures revealing a bit about the atmosphere that the snow fell out of, but it isn't useful for precise dating.'

'Ah.' Wade thought about it. 'So if the Pliocene climate was CO_2 high, like today, and Antarctica was an open sea with islands and some glaciers, then why isn't it like that today?'

'Well,' Michelson said, 'maybe it's on its way. The ice shelves are going, the ice streams are speeding up, the grounding line under the west sheet is receding fast. The east sheet is higher and thicker, so it will take longer. But it could happen.'

'How quickly could it go?'

'Very quickly indeed!'

'Meaning . . .'

'A few hundred years, perhaps.'

Wade and Val laughed, but Michelson waved a finger at them: 'No, that's very fast. A blink of the eye!'

'I'll tell Senator Chase that,' Wade said.

'No no,' Michelson protested, 'what you have to tell him is that nobody knows. No one can say. The Laurentian ice sheets went in just such a short time, a few thousand years perhaps, and they didn't have humans around pumping CO_2 into the air. There's some powerful positive feedback loops involved. Things can change rapidly. These methane hydrate deposits on the sea bottom are likely to stay put at first, because that's a matter of water pressure holding them in. But if the methane hydrates under the ice caps are substantial and that methane is released, then the greenhouse effect will be pushed even harder.'

They sipped Drambuie as Misha washed and Val dried the dishes. It was steamy warm in the tent. Wade's neck was killing him. The Drambuie was salty.

'There must be people who don't want to believe your scenario,' Wade said. 'I mean people besides the stabilists.'

'Oh yes. The same people who found Professor Warren, eh? You can always find a potted professor to back your claim.'

'So the stabilists are like Professor Warren then.'

'Oh no. Not at all. Warren is saying there is no human effect on global warming, when the entire scientific community outside of conservative think tanks believes the evidence is obvious that there is. Warren is a charlatan, or delusional. The stabilists on the other hand are serious scientists. They are trying to prove a hypothesis; they are down here gathering data every season; they're publishing results in peer-reviewed journals. They're wrong, I think, but they are still scientists. Many scientists are wrong, perhaps most. They end up serving as devil's advocates for the ones lucky enough to be right. Even we may be wrong.'

'No!' the others cried.

'No,' Michelson agreed. 'Those are Pliocene diatoms, and they grew here.' He raised a mug to toast them. 'Here in this cold, frozen hell.'

The conversation shifted to the day's work in the field, and a long discussion of what they would do the following day. Wade and Val would be hiking out in the afternoon, to make their rendezvous with a helicopter on the edge of the no-fly zone. The scientists would hike downvalley partway with them. Harry said, 'We'll either find some Sirius above Lake Vashka, or else just have a day of shits and giggles.'

'Shits and giggles?' Wade said.

'Recreation,' Misha explained.

'I hate that expression,' Val announced firmly. 'As if when you're not doing science you're not doing anything. It's offensive.'

'Sorry,' Harry said, looking surprised. 'It's something the grad students say.'

'I know.'

'The grad students who never get to leave their one research site,' Michelson added. 'It's no doubt compensatory.'

'No doubt.'

The Coleman stove roared airily in the awkward silence.

'I suppose there are people in Washington who think that all activities down here are nothing but shits and giggles,' Wade said. 'Science as much as anything.'

Val gave him a grateful look, but the awkward silence persisted.

'So that east ice sheet,' Wade went on. 'If it wasn't here three million years ago, then it grew back pretty fast, didn't it?'

Michelson raised an eyebrow. 'The three sounds small, but you have to remember the millions. Snow accumulation at the South Pole was ten centimetres a year before these so-called superstorms became a regular thing, and at that rate you get the three kilometres of the ice sheet in three hundred thousand years.'

'Compaction,' Forbes pointed out.

'Yes, but it's already almost firn, so the compaction rate may not be as great as with snow. Even if it is, a centimetre of ice for every ten of snow, that's what . . .'

'Three million years,' Forbes said.

'Well, you see,' the V under the moustache, 'there you have it! Just as thick as expected.'

Much later they crawled out into the blaze and bite of the frigid brilliant midnight, and Val and Wade went to their tent. Already they had a little domestic routine, he noted; he peed outside, she peed inside; when he crawled in she was already in her bag, on her side of the tent. Their second night together; and in the weird yellow overexposure she was as beautiful as before. It was ridiculous what a little pitter-patter of the heart he got from lying next to her. Even as exhausted as he was – from the day's fight with the cold, he assumed – it still kept him awake for a while; at least ten minutes; then he followed her into slumber.

Sometime in the bright yellow night, however, Wade woke to find that he was on his side, and wedged against Val's backside. And something about the pressure of the contact, or the warmth, or the contents of a dream, or simply the physiology of the REM state, had given him an erection. If it were not for their thick sleeping bags it would be pressed firmly against her bottom.

This comfortable snug was a position he and his girlfriend Andrea had often taken. She too had been a big woman, taller than him. She had hated Washington DC, however, and their relationship had not long survived the move there. And after that Wade had been too busy to start any other relationship, or so he told himself; it had been a hard thing, having Andrea leave.

Now that was not what he was thinking about. He felt he should move; he did not want to be misunderstood. The sleeping bags were extremely thick, however, so that nothing could be felt through them. And the tent was quite small. And bitterly cold; though the sky was still bright, the sun seemed to have dipped behind the Apocalypse Peaks. So it made sense to snuggle for warmth. In any case Val was asleep, breathing deeply. He couldn't see anything of her face from where he lay, but he could remember it. She had been really good in the Scott tent, very easy in the company of those men, trading banter with Misha, pressed unselfconsciously against people, joining the conversation when she felt like it, listening when she didn't. Everyone at ease, even with this big beauty in their midst. The men might have been even happier than on an ordinary evening, more alive and on their toes, as if the Drambers had an extra fire in it; but nothing more than that, nothing to draw any notice. It was skilful; as a diplomat Wade admired it. Not everyone could have ensured that the situation be so *normal*.

And the same with sleeping with a strange man in a small tent. Except now she was stirring. Quickly Wade rolled over in his bag.

But now it was she who was pressed up against his back. Hard against him, in fact, from his head to his heels; and she was so much taller than he that she enfolded him entirely, the back of his head down against her chest. More than ever before he realized he liked being smaller than the woman he was with. It was ravishing. No chance of that REM erection going away. He turned his head ever so slightly, and there was her face, inches from his; again the surgical glare of tent light; again her disconcerting beauty. The weathering of an outdoor life made her face look fiftyish, though asleep of course she also looked like a child, as everyone did. Mouth open, deeply asleep, breathing smoothly, pressed against him hard. He turned his head back and snuggled it into his parka hood, and after a long while his heartrate returned to something like normal, and after another while he fell asleep again.

The next day, after breakfast and taking down their tent and packing their rucksacks, Wade followed Val down the piebald snow-and-rock valley toward Lake Vida, which from certain high points along the way was visible as a white line on the valley floor. Again, it looked only an hour's walk away, but now Wade knew better. Professor Michelson was accompanying Harry and Graham down to look at the striated cliffs above Lake Vashka, and so for the first part of the walk they kept Wade and Val company. Wade and Michelson lagged behind to talk.

As they conversed, a red fly appeared in the distance over Lake Vida.

No sound; but it was a helicopter. It descended on Lake Vida, and then flew up again and away, toward Wright Valley.

'Were we late, or they early?' Wade called down to Val.

'Not for us,' Val called back.

'That was one of the NSF trekking groups,' Michelson said. 'Starting an expedition, or ending one, or both.'

'I'm surprised NSF has gotten into that.'

'Are you?' Michelson glanced at him, once again in his Breughel noseguard. 'They need money like anyone else.'

'But here they are, in charge of this whole continent . . .'

'On a budget smaller than that of most universities. Besides, they are not really in charge. I mean they control the American presence here, which is in itself amazing, I agree. I'm astonished some of your State Department colleagues haven't taken it over.'

Wade gestured at the brown-and-white desolation around them. 'They probably don't see the point.'

Michelson laughed. 'Well, so NSF keeps control. But with an ever-shrinking budget. It's Mars that is the hot place these days, scientifically speaking at least, and that's where all the money is going. This is a kind of backwater now, scientifically. Anyway, your NSF is just one player down here. There are about thirty national groups in the Scientific Committee for Antarctic Research, and that's the group that decides how things are run down here. NSF generally just goes along with SCAR. And within SCAR there's the old boys' club, of the countries who were down here from the beginning in the IGY, and then the new countries that have joined since, to make sure they have a say in case resource extraction ever starts. There used to be conflicts between those two groups, but all that has been forgotten because of the conflicts between SCAR and the UN, and SCAR and the non-Treaty nations. And now that the Treaty renewal is being held up – by people in the American government, as you know, though there are others who are not unhappy about that – it's more uncertain than ever. There are people in the UN who would like to be running Antarctica, because then the votes in the General Assembly could overwhelm any scientific advice, and the UN bureaucrats involved would be in charge here.'

'Complicated.'

Michelson laughed. 'Very complicated. Land without sovereignty! That's too odd not to be complicated, in this world. The Antarctic Treaty held in its time, but now it's a new world.'

'The Treaty always seemed fragile.'

'Fragile, idealistic – all those things. And even when it was in effect the Treaty nations broke its rules all the time. France, Russia, they did what they wanted, more or less. Now that the stakes are getting higher, the Treaty is revealed as the house of cards it always was.'

'I see.'

'So the NSF running trekking expeditions down here is actually a very small matter. It pre-empts the private companies, so that NSF can keep control of the visitors – keep them from coming up here, for instance. Keep them clean and neat, and so on. It's a good idea, I think.'

'Interesting.'

'Yes. The conflicts are endless. Not unlike your turf battles back in the Senate, I would guess.'

'Yes,' Wade said absently, watching Val's backside as she hiked down the valley with Graham and Harry. She walked like someone who had hiked a million miles, and no doubt she had. Now it was a kind of boulder ballet, a very graceful flow. He pulled back out of his distraction: 'Very much the same. In fact it's the same battle, I'm afraid. Different parts of the same battle, everywhere. This is only the outermost edge.'

The geologists said their farewells and took off around the other side of Lake Vashka. Wade and Val continued on down Barwick Valley together.

blue sky
brown valley

'Did you enjoy your visit?' Val asked when they were some way down the valley, and out of earshot of the scientists.

'It was very interesting.' So interesting that he could think of nothing further to say about it. He was still sorting out his impressions of the final conversation with Professor Michelson. Which was too bad, as he would have liked very much to say more to her. He didn't want to seem to be holding his cards close to the vest, when he had no cards at all. 'I don't know quite what to make of them,' he confessed.

She nodded. 'Beakers are funny people.'

'You must find it interesting, the way they look at mountains.'

'Yeah, that's pretty amazing. The things they notice. And the time spans . . .'

'Only three hundred years! Blink of the eye!'

They laughed. She waved a hand at the abrupt ridges walling the valley on both sides: 'As if rock were toothpaste, flowing from one position to the next.'

'Strange. Do any of them climb?'

'Oh sure. Bob, over in Taylor Valley, he climbs a lot. And vice versa

– some of the mountaineers have degrees in geology. Misha back there is a geomorphologist, for instance.'

'I knew he was into it somehow.'

'Oh yeah, he tries to fit his research in when he can, although it's hard to do – they're never in the right place for him, and he has a lot of work to do just to take care of them.'

He looked at her. 'You talk about it like it's babysitting.'

'Well, you know. This place can kill you in a matter of hours if you blow it. And a mountaineer's profession is keeping people from blowing it, and then also knowing how to stay alive even when you have blown it. You wait till your first storm, then you'll be happy you have me along.'

'I'm already happy to have you along.'

'Thanks,' she said, dismissing the comment. 'Anyway, a lot of these beakers are not thinking very much about survival, to say the least. The mountains are just data for their papers. For some of them, if they could get the data while sitting back home, they would be perfectly happy. I hiked with a group of them around a nunatak up on the ice after a helo didn't make skeds, and it was incredibly beautiful, the ice pouring around the rock, you know, and they complained the whole way home because the nunatak was nothing but dolerite. They hiked along singing "Dolerite, dolerite, dolerite, dolerite".'

Wade grinned. 'They were teasing you.'

'Sure. But the beauty of it, for them, it was only – whatever.'

'Data.'

'Yeah. And data can be beautiful, but still.'

'Beakers.'

'Right. Still, you gotta love 'em. For one thing they're really what gets the rest of us down here.'

'The continent of science.'

'Right. Science, and some really incredible shits and giggles.' She shook her head, disgusted again at the phrase.

'Expensive.'

'You aren't kidding. Once Bob told me he and a friend had calculated how much it costs to do science down here, just by taking the total Antarctic budget and dividing it by the number of scientist days – you know, it was the usual kind of beaker calculation – and it came out to something like ten thousand dollars a day per scientist.'

'You're kidding!'

'That's what he said. But hey, don't tell your boss that. I don't want to be responsible for NSF getting yanked out of here. I'm pretty much toast myself, but my friends would never forgive me.'

Wade laughed. 'I promise not to tell.'

Much of the rest of the morning they hiked on in silence. Then Val called a lunch break, and they sat in the sunny lee of a boulder eating trail mix and drinking hot chocolate from thermoses.

'How did you get into guiding?' Wade asked.

'Just fell into it, ha ha.' She thought it over. 'It was a long time ago now. A boyfriend, I guess. We climbed together and he was making money guiding, and that sounded good to me. At the time. I've actually tried to quit several times, because there's a lot of things about it I don't like, but one thing about it, it keeps you in the mountains, and making some money. So I keep getting back into it.'

'You've actually quit?'

'Not down here – that would be it – but a couple times before, yeah. I was guiding in the Tetons for a few seasons, and I had this client . . . Well, have you heard the three rules of mountain guiding?'

'No.'

'First rule is, the client is trying to kill you. Second rule, the client is trying to kill himself. Third rule, the client is trying to kill the rest of the clients.'

'Ouch.'

'Yeah. I told you there were parts of the job I didn't like, and one of them is that it makes you cynical about people.'

'Many jobs do.'

'I suppose so. Anyway, I was leading this guy up the Grand Teton, and we were on the ridge above the emergency hut, on a cloudy day, with a cloud smack against the east face, so that there was a slot of air there we could look down, like a crevasse five thousand feet deep. And I don't know, he had a thing about the Grand Teton I guess, and suddenly rules one and two came into play both at once, literally.'

'He tried to kill you?'

'He tried to kill both of us. It was a suicide thing. We were roped together, and when we were climbing a section of the ridge overlooking the east face, he let out this kind of funny yelp and threw himself off the ridge and down the face.'

'On purpose!'

'Yeah.'

'So what happened?'

'Well, I arrested us, obviously – threw myself the other way and got a hold, and luckily I was a lot heavier than him, and we held. Broke a couple of fingers,' she added, holding out her right hand for inspection.

'Ouch!'

'Oh, I've broken a lot of bones in the mountains, it's not so bad.'

'But what then!'

'Well, I had to talk him out of it, or at least I tried to – but when I had him calmed down and got up, he tried it again! So after that I throttled him, basically, and hauled him back down the ridge to the emergency hut and had us medevacked out of there. I don't know why I expected a suicide to be honest with me when he'd just tried to take me with him, but I did. That second try really shocked me. It made me mad.'

'I'll bet!' Wade tried to imagine it, shaking his head. 'So you quit.'

'Yeah. For a while. But–' she shrugged. 'I like to be out in places like this. All the time, basically. So . . . guiding is the best way to finance it.'

'All jobs have their downside,' Wade said.

'Yeah?' She shifted to look at him easier. 'Tell me about yours.'

'Well,' he said, and waved a hand. Actually, thinking it over, he realized he liked his job quite a lot. But he wanted to share her situation, her predicament one might even say, and so he said, 'Well, I have to live in Washington.'

'Don't you like it? I visited once and thought it was exciting.'

'It's a great town to visit, but living there is crowded – muggy – I don't know. There is no there there, you know.'

'Where did you grow up?'

'Oakland,' he said, grinning at his little joke. 'No, all over, really.'

'San Francisco is a great town too.'

'Yes. And so beautiful. After that, Washington is just a swamp.'

She nodded.

'And then I have to work with politicians all the time.'

'Are they bad?'

He laughed. 'Like your clients, I suppose. They think they're professionals, but a lot of them aren't.'

'Ah yeah. That can be hard.'

'Yeah.' But actually he liked it, and did not want to sound like a complainer; and so he said, 'Well, it's interesting anyway. A lot of the time I like it. I like Senator Chase. No, I like my job.'

She nodded her approval. 'It's like you said.'

'What?'

'All jobs have their downside.'

'Oh yeah.'

'Although right now I must admit mine doesn't seem so bad.' And she smiled at him. He suddenly remembered waking in the night, and his heart did a little tympani roll inside him. He smiled back, offered her a chunk of his chocolate bar. She took it from him and their gloved fingers touched.

'Salty chocolate?'

'Very.'

*   *   *

The rest of the afternoon he followed her across the great silent rock valley, watching her. Which was wonderful; like watching one of Chagall's long dancers come to life, flowing down the rock in her boulder ballet, total grace over the shattered fractal surface underfoot, and without looking at it at all, as far as he could tell. And she had such a tall, muscular body. Again he remembered lying next to her in their tent, and the impression he had had of being next to a bigger animal; that had been a thrill, a deep, ravished, erotic thrill, just in the idea of it. He was six foot tall almost exactly, and had not spent enough time with women distinctly taller than him to know for sure that he had this – this predeliction. He supposed there was some bit of a reversal in that, something feminine perhaps; but not enough to frighten him; one component of the thrill, perhaps. He liked her. He had figured her for a jock, but clearly there was a lot of thinking going on in there; an intellectual. He had heard that climbing included an intellectual element, that it was the intellectual's sport, a kind of physical chess played against nature. Whatever; he liked her; he was attracted to her; and not just in that simple attraction that no doubt most men felt on seeing her, but more than that; her specifically, the thinker inside the amazon body. And what a body. In that yellow tent – oh what could have been – fantasy images of her on top of him, inside a single sleeping bag–

Then he was surprised to find that they were dropping down the final scree to the flat white surface of Lake Vida. There was a cluster of bright mountain tents at one end of the lake, and Val headed for that. As they approached she turned to Wade with a smile. 'Well,' she said, 'back to work.' And his heart melted a little; and he felt the kind of smile that was on his face, and knew it was giving him away, if she was watching.

Then they were in the camp. It was, Val pointed out, the NSF regulated campsite for Lake Vida, occupied by every group that came through, on a bench just above the lake, under the broken face of Schist Peak, marked by cairns and another stacked-rock outhouse; all very unobtrusive in the grand landscape, there in the intersection of the Victoria and McKelvey Valleys, where everything seemed so vast. The few rock markers were as nothing to the vibrant neon colours of the tents. There were half a dozen dome tents for sleeping, and then a green walk-in dining tent, very much larger than the Scott tents at the scientific camp. As with everywhere else Wade had been, the campsite looked deserted as they approached. An incongruous collection of colourful children's blocks, scattered in the immensity of rock. Val walked up to the communal tent, and calling out a hello stuck her head in the door.

They were welcomed inside without delay, to meet another guide named Karl and his group of ten trekkers. They were backpacking around the Dry Valleys from camp to camp, and had already been out for ten days, with just a few more to go: a whiskery bunch, for the most part – only three women in this group – and with the slick, oily hair Wade had noted in the scientists, and more and more in himself. Over hot drinks and salty *hors d'oeuvres* they enthusiastically described their trip: dropped in by helicopter on Wright Upper Glacier just below Airdevronsix Icefalls, then on foot down through the Labyrinth, past the Dais and Lake Vanda and up the course of the Onyx River to Lake Brownworth; then up and over the Clark Glacier, wearing crampons, and past Clark Lake, over the Saharan dunes of Victoria Valley, to their current camp. From here they were going to hike down the McKelvey Valley on the edge of the forbidden zone, through Bull Pass and down to Vanda again. Longer treks would then cross the Asgaard Range, a difficult crossing no matter which route one took, and then descend the Taylor Valley to the Lake Hoare camp, or even New Harbour for a snowmobile or hovercraft trip across the sound to McMurdo, depending on the season; but this was a shorter expedition, and would be heloed out from Lake Vanda.

Most of this was explained to them by two men pointing here and there on a big well-used map, with the guide and the others sitting back and letting them at it. The larger of the two men was a dark blond, handsome American, who was directing his description to Val, who had to know these treks all too well, Wade judged. And all in an ironic style that was charming in a way, but had little true wit in it. Val listened politely, and smiled in the designated places, but Wade could see she wasn't interested in the same way she had been in the scientists' conversation back in the Barwick.

'And that will be the end of the Great Dry Valley Circle,' the man said.

'I'll be ready,' one of the other trekkers said. 'I'm going to take my next trip in New Guinea.'

'No, Tahiti.'

They laughed.

'It's so cold,' one of them said.

'And the same everywhere,' another added.

'And so much bigger than it looks – you hike along a valley expecting it to take an hour and it takes all day. It's like the reverse of the Himalayas. Wright Valley goes on forever.'

'It's the lack of haze.'

'It's the cold.'

'The lack of trees.'

'The fact that we flew over it in ten minutes on the way in.'

'Whatever. Anyway this is it for me. Been there, done that.'

Others pooh-poohed this sentiment. 'It's beautiful!' 'It's so big.' 'And beautiful!'

Which it wasn't, not by any definition of beauty Wade had ever heard. But this was what one said when impressed by a landscape, this was how attenuated the language had become for some people. Depauperate, as Forbes had said to Michelson yesterday about some section of the rock. But if Wade had spoken up and said It's not beautiful, it's sublime, the distinction would not be understood. So he kept his mouth shut and listened to these stock responses, back in the soup of American speech, in all its basic talkshow mindlessness–

'It's boring is what it is.'

And perhaps, Wade thought, without the science, without the politics, just walking around out here – maybe it was boring. Nothing but shits and giggles.

The other guide was smiling dutifully at all the criticisms, which were stated cheerfully, and in part just to tease him. These people would rave about the trek when they got back home, no doubt about that. So the guide nodded and shrugged as if he had heard it all before, and had already made his best attempt to counter them. It was all banter for the new folks.

'So, Val,' he said when he got a chance. 'Where next for you?'

'Amundsen,' she said.

'Hey, that's where we're going too!' the tall, handsome man exclaimed, with a quick glance at Val and then at his friend. 'You must be Valerie Kenning?'

'That's me,' Val said, showing nothing one way or another. 'Yeah, it should be a good expedition.'

The other guide said, 'I've heard the Axel Heiberg has become quite a challenge.'

Val shrugged. 'There's a steep section at the headwall, yeah. But if it's bad this year,' with a lightning glance at the other guide that Wade took to refer to the *it*, 'we'll take the descent route and save some energy for it.'

'Oh we'll manage the real route,' the tall client said confidently.

'Uh huhn,' Val said, with an encouraging smile at him. Wade remembered the three rules of mountain guiding and winced inside. Happy chance that he had met her not as a trekking client, but in some slightly different capacity! Although Distinguished Visitor, ouch; but still, better than this. He watched her continue to converse cheerfully with the group, and it occurred to him that in a couple of hours their helo would arrive and take them back to McMurdo, and that might very well be the last he ever saw of Valerie Kenning. And then he winced in earnest.

Val sat in the trekkers' dining tent, doing her best to conceal her irritation with the men who were going to be joining her Amundsen trip. Or man, to be specific; the other one, Jim McFeriss, was your typical sidekick and enabler; it was the main talker, Jack Michaels, who was going to be the real bummer. The way he looked at her, the way he talked to the others, complacent and assured and oh so certain he was the star of the movie: Val hated that manner with a fine passion. She had become so sick of the stink of bad testosterone that even the slightest whiff of it made her want to heave. And so she sat in one of the ultralight but unstable camp chairs at the end of the camp table, and became more bright and cheery than ever, an old technique she had picked up in high school when dealing with tremendous amounts of anger, anger often mysterious in origin but sometimes perfectly clear; and as it was inappropriate to scream at people, she had found that she could satisfy her need to lash out at them simply by lying to them so grossly, with the happy cheerleader routine. Hiding her real self and bearing down on people with a very aggressive happy face had always worked strangely well, in several different ways.

So now she was fine among this group of trekkers, though they looked to be a pretty lame bunch, as Karl's private glance confirmed. And the prospect of leading a reproduction of Amundsen's difficult *dirretissima*, with this Jack and Jim among other no doubt problematical clients, was in fact pretty dismal. There Jack sat, ostensibly telling a couple of his comrades from this trip about kayaking down the Dudh Khosi – oh no, now it was climbing the Matterhorn – and by their looks they had heard it before, and also they could see as well as Val could that he was not really telling the story to them but to her, looking left at them then right at her, pulling her into his audience. Men like him were seals, encased in a thick blubber of their own self-regard. Interested in her, however; looking at her, charming her, impressing her with his wilderness adventure credentials, which sounded extensive. They always did. Evaluating her as well; deciding that she was a simple cheerleader jock, a straightforward proposition, not as well-informed as he, but interested in learning more about the big wide world of which he had seen so much.

All so much crap. And all because of the way she looked. If she had been short and plain and unobtrusive, the wattage of his attention would have been so much lower that she might have had a chance to see something of him; as it was the dazzle had reduced her pupils to pinpoints, and she stared out at a chiaroscuro shadow-tent, inflicting the cheerleader routine on its occupants full force, until soon they would be pinned to the floor by it and admitting that they too wished they all could be California girls, in four-part harmony.

Which caused Wade to look at her a bit oddly, no doubt nonplussed. But how different it had been up in the cramped Scott tent, sitting around the hissing stove talking about geology and politics, and the Antarctica below the ice and the f-stops. To those men she had been just a person, and so she had been able to relax and be just a person; which was such a relief that it made her much more pleasant and therefore more attractive, she was sure. Which was what they deserved for being so normal themselves. That was something she liked very much about Wade; he had been no more interested in her than any of the beakers he was meeting, no more and no less; and growing more interested in her the more he knew about her, and the more they talked about things in general. Which was how she liked it; indeed how she demanded it. No doubt about it, she was pretty demanding and intolerant when it came to men's behaviour toward her; she knew that; it had been that way for a long time. And was only getting worse.

Because beauty was a curse. It's always getting worse, because beauty is a curse . . . in four-part harmony. She didn't recall the Beach Boys singing that one, but the girls on the beach (who are all within reach) could have told Brian, if he had been able to listen from within his own layer of toxic blubber. Beauty is a curse. Of course it brought attention to you, that was not the issue. Val's good looks had brought her attention all her life; but by now she hated it. She did not like attention. That was why she had taken off into the mountains every weekend of high school, and then permanently the moment high school had ended and she had been released from four years' solitary in the prisonhouse of the American dream.

And it was silly anyway, silly at best. She was not *that* good-looking when it came right down to it, no fashion model – her face as she saw it in the mirror was utterly plain, and filled with irritations. Men were wrong about that, as they were about so much else. It was just that she was tall, and blonde, and big, and athletic, with what in the end was fundamentally a friendly face – regular, pleasant, somewhat cheerleaderesque, she had to admit. And that was enough to have men lying to her her whole life long. They got in traffic accidents driving past her. One time one had braked his Toyota pick-up to a screeching halt in a parking lot and stuck his head out of the window and yelled at her 'Will you marry me!' at the top of his lungs. This incident in particular had made her laugh, as it had at least had the virtue of straightforward honesty; but later it had come to stand in her mind as the purest image of what that particular kind of attention from men had really been. It didn't matter what she was like, that had nothing to do with it; her looks alone were enough to justify men slamming on the brakes and spontaneously pitching their whole self at her. And what was she supposed to say to that? What was she supposed to do with all these strangers hitting on her, crashing in crying *me me me, be mine, love always, will you marry me?* It was so obvious they were coming on for the wrong reasons. And so from the very start they revealed themselves to Val as people with bad principles, fools, jerks, pathetos, sometimes as insecure as she was about the worth of their characters, sometimes idiotically certain that they were the greatest thing around, but either way worthless to her, their attentions useless, stupid, irritating, sometimes dangerous, often maddening. They made her mad.

And of course the ones who had laid her and left her, as they said, had made her frightened and uncertain as well as mad. Some of those guys she had really loved, or thought she had; they hadn't come on in the usual idiot way, and she had thought they were different; and still it hadn't worked out. How could that be, if she was so attractive? Was she too much of a bitch to live with? Or too boring? She didn't think so. But then again she had always had trouble articulating her thoughts; somehow what she said aloud was always a platitude approximating the original thought, which had been far more interesting. She had never learned the trick of catching those hard thoughts on the fly, and indeed when she had caught them and expressed them properly, those were often the times that got her into biggest trouble, convincing people (men) that she was mean, or just weird. So it was either vanilla or bile, or staying silent. Or going climbing, free solo, the best way.

Or later, to make a living, leading tour groups of strangers and spending the whole time on automatic pilot, playing the role of the Happy Mountain Woman, earth mother, nature spirit, athlete philosopher, wild woman – which role actually seeped back into her, to an extent, as she became what she was playing at, like during her cheerleader days; inflicting a role, like spiking a volleyball right in their face; and this one felt good; a relief from the usual cynicism and distrust. Clients could very legitimately be held at a proper client distance, a professional relationship, and from there some fairly decent interactions could be had, with some nice men willing to treat her as the guide and no more. It was enough anyway, the client/guide relationship – it had a certain student/teacher or even child/parent aspect to it, depending on how the people in the roles played them. Taking care of people. So, many fairly pleasant human interactions. But the big man/woman thing; no luck. Lots of bummers, enough to disturb the whole thing. She wanted a big time-out.

Unfortunately Antarctica was not the place for that. The man-to-woman ratio was still about seventy to thirty, and that made a lot of them even crazier than they were in the world. The women too sometimes went hectic with glee, women in some cases who had never had enough attention in the world and so revelled in it now, trolling around and having some hard fun, breaking hearts like gutting little fish they'd caught. She'd done a bit of that herself. Bit of revenge in it, no doubt. Other women went catatonic under the testosterone assault, or burst out laughing and said *No* to the whole fool lot. Others tried to keep their eyes open and their wits about them, to see if they could find a man they liked. After all, there were a lot of men there. As the Mac women said, The odds were good, but the goods were odd. So that took a little sorting out, usually – trying a few men to find the one you liked. Which could look like trolling. And this caused problems. In fact when it came to their love lives most of the women on the ice were like walking soap operas. Many went through one ice romance after another. Some did seasonal contracts, like ASL. Certainly nine out of ten ice romances ended badly.

Among them, unfortunately, her relationship with X. He was a lot of the things she liked, too – he was big, gentle, smart; as Steve had used to say, teasing her even in his last year, just her type: trustworthy, loyal, helpful, friendly, courteous, kind, obedient, cheerful, thrifty, brave, clean and reverent. As Steve had been. No, not really. Anyway X had been many good things, but also over-idealistic and moody, over-intellectual, naïve, indoorsy, inactive, unathletic, curiously passive; and even though she was sick of men's aggressiveness she had to admit that she did like a certain dash in a man, a certain fire and style, which X had lacked. He railed against the system all the time, and yet slouched around without doing much physical out in the world, which was her usual solution to frustration. He was just too mellow. And he was younger than Val too, four years younger, so that he often seemed like a kid to her, a sophomoric college kid, even though strictly speaking he was older than that.

So she had chafed a bit during their vacation in New Zealand. And it hadn't helped to have him break into the I'm-being-tortured-by-a-Nazi-mountain-guide routine as they hiked up the utterly easy Bealey Spur, a routine that she had got so sick of that she could not even express it. Every time someone said anything to that effect, or even suggested it with a look, it made her so mad that it ruined the whole trip for her. And it happened every trip. Even walking up a green escalator into alpine mountain glory.

So they had said goodbye and she had flown back to the States, and arrived there with no plan, and just kind of wandered that whole off-season, from one climbing hole to the next. In the past she had spent her off-seasons with her grandmother on the old family farm, taking care of the old woman and being taken care of by her, and that had been pleasant, a real anchor in her life; but Annie had died two years before while Val was in Antarctica, and now Val had no pattern to fall into when back in the world. It had been a strange few months. And by the time she went back down to the ice for the new season, she had lost any interest she had had in X. The on-ice/off-ice format of the McMurdo lifestyle was hard on even the good relationships, and if one was troubled, the big breaks made it very easy to end them. So when she got back to Mac Town she had had her eye out for an excuse to disengage from X, as she realized consciously only later. And a new mountaineer named Mike had served as about the perfect excuse, or so she had thought at first; she had been smitten, she had to admit it. Now it was clear that Mike had a bad case of what Val called climber's syndrome, consisting of a self-absorption so deep that it could not be plumbed; compared to it the usual male blubber was no more than the subcutaneous layer with which everyone had to cope. Mike had been quite happy to sleep with her, of course, but in a month he had not learned a thing about her; it would probably be dangerous to ask him to recall her last name. In only two days this Wade Norton had learned a thousand times more about her. So it was bye-bye to Mike; and now X was gone from Mac Town, and she hadn't even apologized. So it was back to trolling. Or not. In any case, yet another bad experience to add to all the rest. She had been the one to screw up this time, she had to admit it.

On the helicopter ride back to Mac Town, Wade sat next to her in one of the side compartments of the Huey, where they were alone together in their own sonic space; they were just barely able to hear each other, but could if they spoke directly in each other's ears. Looking down at the sea ice flashing under them, they traded comments. When she thought about how nice he had been on this trip, it made her wince; to go from this smart, polite, interesting, somehow subtle, even with-drawn man, to Jack and Jim and the rest of the clients on the Amund-sen! It was painful. She liked this man a lot; he had just the mellowness that she liked, but that extra dash she admired as well – a Washington operator – a sly sense of humour; paying attention to those beakers with what seemed his total interest; and then to her too, but as a guide, a person with career problems, an equal in the world; not to be instructed in Washington politics or the global situation or whatever, but just talked with, in mutual interest. Now of course leaving, and soon no doubt. It always happened that way.

'Do you have brothers and sisters?' he exclaimed in her ear, surpris-ing her.

'No,' she said in his.

'Only child?' Sounding surprised.

He was looking down at the trash ice. 'No,' she said in his ear, surprising herself. She never talked about this. 'No, I had a brother. But he died.'

He nodded; looked at her briefly. Looked back down at the ice. All the way back to Mac Town he sat beside her, looking down at the ice, his arm pressed against hers, his hip against hers, his leg against hers. The pressure was saying, I'm sorry. It was saying, there's nothing can be said about that. Which was true. This was how Steve himself had comforted her in his last year, sitting beside her with an arm over her shoulder, not saying anything. At sixteen and twelve, neither of them had been able to figure out much to say about it. Val stared down at the trash ice flowing underneath them. She liked this man who was leaving.

Back in Mac. She walked up to her room, lost in her thoughts.

She had been eleven when she first learned something was wrong. They told her that Steve was sick, that he had mononucleosis and it would take a while to recover. He was in the hospital, and then in Houston, to go to a special hospital. That's when they told her it was leukaemia. He was gone for months, but came home for visits. In later years she didn't remember much about those visits; but she did remember being shocked at how much thinner he was, and that he moved so slowly. All his muscles seemed stiff, including eventually his lips, so that it was hard for him to talk the same.

Most of their time together in that period they played a board game he had liked when they were younger. She couldn't recall the details of the rules, but the board was a map of the world, and the game had to do with weather, and your piece was on a clear square that was a quadrant of the world map, and if you rolled a twelve the clear square had to be shifted to another quadrant of the map. Something like that. They had played it for hours, in near silence. Val had the impression that Steve had grown up very rapidly in Houston, and was a kind of grown-up now because of what was happening to him. He looked at her as from a great distance away. Once he rolled boxcars twice in a row, then three times; four times; five times. Moving the quadrant around the world every time. Then six times in a row, double sixes every time. They had stared at each other across the board, then looked down at the dice again, acutely uncomfortable, aware together that something very strange was happening. 'Guess I'm going on a trip,' he said, and Val had interrupted his turn and picked up the dice and rolled them herself.

That little memory was all she had, for hours and hours of time –

that and a few more fragments, like him walking slowly down the hall, bowlegged, to put the game away. Or when he left for Houston for the last time, and said to her, 'See you later,' and she had said 'See you later.'

Then horsing around in history class and Mr. Sanders coming in near the end of the period and taking her outside, very serious, to tell her her brother had died, he was very sorry, she had to go home. She remembered looking down from the second storey balcony at the parking lot, the scatter of teachers' cars, the tennis courts in their line off to the left.

So her brother Steve had died. He had been bigger than her, and stronger than her, and more full of life; he had taught her to love the outdoors, and had taken her along when a lot of older brothers wouldn't have. He had been trustworthy, loyal, helpful, friendly, courteous, kind, etc. Her hero.

And after that no one else had seemed quite as good. She had in him a standard for behaviour that was no doubt very high. She had also a fuse that was no doubt very short. No doubt a lot of what had happened to her since then had followed from those characteristics. It is eerie sometimes to contemplate how much we create our own reality. The life of the mind is an imaginary relationship to a real situation; but then the real situation keeps happening, event after event, and many of those events are out of our control, but many others are the direct result of the imagination's take on things. So she was aware that her problems were not just because men were so often screwed up; because sometimes they weren't, and still she botched her relationships with them, sometimes with men she had liked a lot. But they hadn't been as good as her Steve. Sooner or later they let her down, and she blew up. And on she went, getting more and more skittish. The shorter her fuse got, the shorter it got. She was a case of walking burnt toast; mountain guiding was the last thing she should have been trying. It was like trying to be an open air therapist when she was the one that needed the therapy. She needed a big time-out from people in general. She needed to find a man she really and truly liked. But the goods were odd, and the odds were not good. And not just in Mac Town.

CHAPTER SIX

In the Footsteps of Amundsen

Flying over the Ross Sea in a helicopter, I cannot help remembering Shackleton's expedition of 1908, one of the greatest in Antarctic history, though little remembered now. The sea ice below us is now filled with the broken fragments of the old ice shelf, the big white islands all cliff-sided and atilt; no language can speak them – I am happy you have these images to see so that I do not have to try. We fly at a hundred kilometres per hour, perhaps two hundred metres over the bergs: like gods we flit over the surface of this world! But for Shackleton and his companions it was not so easy.

When Shackleton decided to try to return to the Antarctic after Scott had sent him home, he did not have any very enthusiastic backing from either the British Navy or the Royal Geographical Society. He managed to raise the money through his own efforts, gaining grants from rich patrons in English society; and he returned south with a private crew, in 1908. Now Scott at that time was himself organizing a return to the south, through official naval and Royal Society channels, and he was outraged at the existence of Shackleton's expedition. He felt that even the very chance to try for the Pole was his; as if he were St George, and had all rights to the dragon until it or he be dead. Anyone who challenged that idea was betraying him.

Shackleton wrote to him, however, and asked him if he could use the Discovery Hut that we recently visited in McMurdo. Scott refused this permission! Moreover, he claimed explicitly that all attempts on the Pole from Ross Island were his to make, and that Shackleton must stay east of a certain longitude line which put him far on the other side of the Ross Sea.

And Shackleton agreed to this arrangement! These British are so strange. They were playing a game left over from the Middle Ages. But we should not be too surprised at this, because all stories are immortal and alive at all times, and these men had been told all their lives the tales of medieval chivalry. And we should consider also how many times we ourselves have jousted with a rival for love or fame.

So Shackleton gave Scott his word not to go to Ross Island, unless it was necessary for survival. Scott understood this to mean 'survival of their lives', of course.

But Shackleton could not find a suitable base on the other side of the Ross Sea. Over there, where I am looking now, there are no islands like Ross Island – for there are no mountains like mighty Erebus anywhere else on Earth – it is a singularity, a bolide of dense *ch'i*. Over there on the other side of the bay the coastline is drowned in ice, and only the edge of the Great Ice Barrier, as Ross so accurately named it, presented itself to those who arrived by sea in tiny ships. And Shackleton did not trust the edge of the Ice Barrier the way Amundsen later did. Amundsen climbed onto the ice shelf at what seemed a permanent indentation, and he read the snowscape to the south, and postulated the existence of a very low island, much later confirmed and named Roosevelt Island; a fine bit of *feng shui*, that. And it caused Amundsen to trust that the ice at this Bay of Whales would hold for the six months he would live on it. It was a risk, for even that stable ice calves from time to time into the sea; but a calculated risk. Shackleton, however, did not know enough to make the calculation. And yet at the same time he was a cautious man, a good planner. Only this allowed him to get so far south with so little snowcraft.

And so he returned to Ross Island! Unhappy man! To break his promise to Scott racked him; he did not sleep for a week, writing a anguished letter to his wife in which he explained that he was going to twist his promise to Scott to mean that he would not visit Ross Island, unless it was necessary for survival of the expedition. But he was not really satisfied with this formulation. And neither was Scott.

Shackleton built a new hut of his own, twenty miles down the coast of Ross Island from Scott's hut. He did not use the Discovery Hut except under duress, and generally even then slept in tents outside it, claiming that it was colder inside than outside, an uncanny phenomenon that many others have noted since. In time he forgot about his medieval promise, and carried on with his expedition. And in the Antarctic spring of October 1908, he and his group took off for the Pole.

And he was a better leader of men than Scott had been, and had learned some things about sledging. He failed to use skis at all, a strange lapse in equipment even if you are determined to manhaul. But he did take along ponies, which they marched to depots and shot and deposited as food, just as Amundsen would do later with his dogs.

So Shackleton and his men and the ponies pulled a sledge across the ice you see below us now, much thicker then of course, and uniform, and flat. But we have been flying at a hundred kilometres an hour now for nearly an hour, and there is no end in sight; even the tall Transantarctics are still under the horizon ahead of us, and will not appear for a couple of hours more. It took those men weeks to haul their sledges across this space below us, as you can imagine.

Then when they made their landfall they discovered the Beardmore Glacier, the Great Glacier as they first called it so much more finely, pouring out of the mountains for as far uphill as they could see. Up the Great Glacier the four men hauled their sledge, going tremendously better than Scott and Wilson and Shackleton had gone in 1902.

But they were cutting every aspect of things right to the bone. And up on the high polar plateau they began to break down. They were starving to the point of illness, and to save weight they had left behind a great deal of their clothes, so that they were wearing only long underwear, overtrousers, sweaters, and jackets; this left them so cold that when Eric Marshall, the doctor, tried to take their temperatures, no one but him registered higher than the thermometer's minimum of 94° Fahrenheit. They were cold!

Yet they hauled their sledge over the polar cap until they were only one more week's walk away from the South Pole. After two months of hauling, and two years of preparation, only a week more to go.

But they had run too low on food. The amount they had been able to haul was not enough to sustain them at the pace they were keeping. They fell short by about five percent of what they needed. If they had started from the Bay of Whales; if they had learned to ski; who knows. But not on this trip.

Shackleton recognized this, up there on the polar cap; he did the calculations, and saw clearly what they meant. And yet he was wild for the Pole: he did not want to turn back. He knew Scott would get the next chance, with the route found, and a large group of men to make the try. He knew this would be his only chance.

But it became clear they could not reach the Pole and survive. As a consolation, in the last week Shackleton fixed on reaching to within a hundred miles of the Pole. The clever Marshall did what he had to as navigator to convince Shackleton that they had done this. But still, in the end it was Shackleton who decided to turn back, when he was ninety-seven miles away. His men's lives were in his hands, as his life had been in Scott's six years before. In the tent he wrote in his diary, 'I must look at the matter sensibly and consider the lives of those who are with me.'

And so they turned back. They took a final day trip to get as far south as they could before the return, then turned back. What latitude did they reach? I don't remember.

But for sure the return journey was a close enough thing to prove that Shackleton had needed to turn back. Half a dozen times on that return they missed death by a hair, and in the end Wild and Shackleton had to make a dash for the Discovery Hut and a hasty return to save Marshall and Adams, an effort that lasted for Shackleton some hundred consecutive hours, this after suffering a complete collapse just two weeks before at the upper end of the Great Glacier. Marshall had saved them during that collapse, and Adams and Wild had carried on throughout, complaining vociferously in their coded diaries about all the others, but persisting, enduring all – growl and go, grin and bear it. And on one of their last desperate nights, as Huntford points out to us, the failing Wild wrote in his diary that Shackleton had that morning 'privately forced upon me his one breakfast biscuit, and would have given me another tonight had I allowed him. I do not suppose that anyone else in the world can thoroughly realize how much generosity and sympathy was shown by this: I DO by GOD I shall never forget it. Thousands of pounds would not have bought that one biscuit.' And every word of the entry was underlined.

And in the end they lived. But they could not have added two more weeks to their trip, no, not two more days, not two hours! It was cut very fine indeed.

Shackleton returned to England a hero. Some people made note of the presence of mind and sense of values involved in turning back when so close to one's goal, and they commended the *shen-yun* of such an act. Most applauded the achievement itself, of ascending the polar ice plateau and getting so far south. At that time it was the closest anyone had been to either of the Poles. As for Shackleton himself, when he got home he said to his wife, 'Better a live donkey than a live lion'. And she agreed.

Later, in his own final tent, it is possible that Scott reversed this formulation, and decided that it was better to be a dead lion than a dead donkey. Certainly the world at large often seems to think so. Of course it is impossible to say for sure if Scott ever thought anything like this. The British mind is an inscrutable thing.

black white
rock ice

The Transantarctic Range is unique – not in its rock, which is the
same sort of igneous array found in other mountains – but in its ice.
In effect the entire range serves as a dam or a dyke, holding back the
polar cap. Flying over the range X could see this just as clearly as if
looking down at a diorama designed to illustrate the situation. It was
a Dutchman's nightmare: against the south side of the range pressed
a sea of white ice, submerging the range nearly to its full height;
directly on the other side of the range lay the Ross Sea, ten thousand
feet lower; and at every dip in the range the ice was pouring down to
the sea, ripping away rock like water tearing open breaks in a levee,
until some of the gaps in the range were huge floods of ice, rivers ten
and twenty and thirty miles wide. The half dozen biggest glaciers in
the world were all down there one after the next, slicing through the
shaved black rock walls and spires that remained above the flood. And
as they flew farther south, X saw that sections of the range in the
distance were entirely submerged, the ice pouring over and down in a
smooth white drop that extended for scores of miles, the dyke entirely
overwhelmed. Ice Planet at its iciest.

Their little Twin Otter flew into the gap torn by one of the great
ice rivers, and flew up it. This one was the Shackleton Glacier – not
as big as the Byrd or the Beardmore or the Nimrod, but very substantial
nevertheless. One of the dozen largest glaciers on Earth, and no doubt
it would have torn its channel even wider and rivalled the Byrd and
the Beardmore for size, were it not for the presence of a rock island
blocking the head of the glacier, like a cork sucked into place by the
flow and nearly plugging it entirely.

This rock island was Roberts Massif. As they flew over it X looked
out of his little side window, fascinated by the rusty, bumpy wasteland,
a pocked humpty-dumpty shatter of dolerite, dominated by a single
transverse ridge that stood above the scraped red rock and smooth
bluish ice surrounding it. The massif was about twenty kilometres wide
and twenty kilometres long, and on its polar side the ice came rolling
in like a high tide, creating several ice bays in the shoreline.

As their plane descended, the smooth curves of the ice ravished X's
eye, as did its bluish tint, which glowed as if the sky's colour had
seeped into the white ice and stained it all through. And as the plane
landed on a narrow snowploughed airstrip like a long strip of carpet,
he suddenly felt happy, for the first time in a long time. Aesthetics as
ethics; that was X's new motto. Whatever was beautiful had to be good.

From the airstrip the plane taxied bumpily toward an ice bay indenting the shore of the massif, under a fluted red-and-white peak named Fluted Peak. One side of the bay sported a small dock, standing on squat pylons. On the rock shore above this dock clustered a small settlement of solar habitats, like metallic blue mobile homes – no more than a dozen buildings all told. The settlement was no bigger than some of the beaker outposts X had helped to open during Winfly, which was a comfort to him. Surely such a small operation could not be doing any great harm.

The little Twin Otter stopped next to an oblong fuel bladder, lying on the ice at the end of the dock. When the props had stopped spinning X followed the pilot out of the little door and down the steps. Out from under the wing he straightened up, and was greeted by a bearded man in a plaid shirt and Carhartt overalls, approaching hand out, smiling.

They shook hands. 'I am Carlos,' the man said. 'Welcome to Roberts Massif.'

'Thanks,' X said. It was frigid out, and breezy, but the man's bare hands were warm. He led X to one of the buildings, and in through the meat-locker door. 'Pretty windy to be out in shirtsleeves,' X remarked.

'Oh, yes, Roberts is a windy place. Even when it's not windy it's windy.'

'That's too bad,' X said with feeling. Wind was the hard part of the cold.

'Yes, well, you know, the katabatic. Air is always falling off the polar cap just from its own weight, and we are right on the edge of the cap. So it can be perfectly still out on the ice, or down on Shackleton, but never here. We have entered it in the Windiest Town On Earth contest, but so far no reply.'

'That's an environmentalist contest though, isn't it?'

'Precisely. A great one to win when they finally admit we are the windiest.'

Carlos, as he told X while heating soup for their lunch, was Chilean. His father had been an officer in the Chilean Air Force, and during one of the periods when Chile and Argentina had been actively trying to sub-stantiate their overlapping claims to the Antarctic, he had been stationed on the Antarctic Peninsula. So Carlos had spent the first ten years of his life as a resident of the Chilean stations Arturo Prat and General Bernardo O'Higgins, up in the Banana Belt as he put it, which was somewhat warmer than most of the continent, but notorious for storms.

'It was a wonderful childhood,' he told X cheerfully. 'Wonderful! I can bicycle on ice, I can pilot a Zodiac through anything, I can talk to penguins and skuas. Not to mention the more usual skills. I'm a true Antarctican, one of the few. Most of them are Chileans like me, although there are some Argentinians as well, not as good at it of course. One of my first memories is of the time that their Almirante Brown station burned down, and the old *Hero* brought its people by on their way out. They were sad, and the *commandante* had fallen into a *loco antartida*. Later we found out he had set the fire himself. Now both countries have given up on the occupation programme, so there are no Antarctic children growing up any more, which is also sad, I think. Because it was a great, great childhood. The happiest time of my whole life.'

'And now you're out on Roberts Massif.'

'Yes.' A quick glance from the stove, to see what X meant. 'There is opposition to this project, admittedly. But from people ignorant of what we are doing and how we are doing it. This is a clean project, a very clean project, the latest in everything, you will see. Everything has been engineered with massive redundancies at the criticalities. Because of the latest advances in extraction technology, that means it is very safe indeed. A sure thing. Here, there is some of our new stuff out the window now, look.'

He pointed out of the little building's one window, and X saw a vehicle like a ferry glide down from the high horizon and float across the slope of blue ice into the bay, then slowly up to the dock.

'A hovercraft. The latest thing, a Hake 1500A.' Something in his grin made it clear he was joking, but X didn't get it.

'Wow.'

Carlos stroked his black beard, which was as dense and fine as seal fur. 'Okay, let's eat quick and go load it, and then we can go out to the drilling site itself. Your work will take you back and forth, but mostly you will be out there, on the ice.'

The hovercraft was not quite as smooth to ride as it was to watch, but once the pilot and co-pilot got it up and running, it was at least as smooth as flying a plane; and faster than a boat; and not quite so loud as a helicopter. One set of fans blew air down into the space under the skirts of the craft, lifting the body of it, which they called the tub, off the ice and onto the air cushion; then a big fan set in a tall housing at the back of the craft propelled it forward, rather like an Everglades boat. Little stripped-down snowmobiles had been attached to outrigger booms on each side of the craft, and usually these machines hung in the air from the booms, but they could be let down and the snowmobile treads run in order to give the floating hovercraft some traction against a sidewind, or a steeper undulation than usual on the ice. These outrigger booms, as they called them, were late additions to the craft, and the pilots were proud of them. It was an older vehicle than X had expected, functional on the inside, well-worn, even battered, which was perhaps the explanation for the joke Carlos had made back at Roberts. X inquired over the roar, and Carlos nodded. 'A product of Corrosion Corner,' he replied loudly. 'Miami Beach, Florida. Three Hakes cannibalized and rebuilt as one. With improvements.' He grinned.

The ice flowing past them on either side was a rolling white sea, broken by ferocious-looking shear zones, where for some reason the ice was broken to shards; perhaps a submerged rock reef, or a clash of two ice currents; Carlos shrugged when X asked him. Red flags flying on poles set at kilometre intervals marked their way, and at the base of the poles were round radio transponders, guiding the hovercraft's automatic pilot; at this point the human pilot and co-pilot, Geraldo and German, were up and about, refilling their coffee mugs. Previous passes of the hovercraft had blown down the sastrugi en route, so that the craft travelled over a distinct road, dull white through bright white and vice versa, running from flag to flag. As the hovercraft floated along it tilted gently up and down, and sometimes side to side, as they hummed over the big shallow waves of the polar cap, its extremely slight hills and valleys, basins and mounds.

'There is our camp, straight ahead.'

A black dot on the sunburnt white horizon.

'Another ten kilometres, but we'll be there in a few minutes.'

'We're going that fast?'

'Yes, look – a hundred kilometres an hour! It is the fastest vehicle on the ice, by a long way. Not quite so fast as helicopters, but it hauls a lot more. And helicopters, you know . . .'

'Yes,' X said. He had seen the wrecks on Erebus and in Wright Valley: burnt skeletons.

'The flying refrigerator, as they say. You talk about criticalities! But this thing, even if it fails you can get out and walk. No crash and burn. Now you can see the main building, just showing. It's a very little camp, you see.'

Geraldo and German took over the controls and brought the hovercraft slower and slower into its parking lot, next to a fuel bladder and a warehouse. Carlos saw the look on X's face, and laughed. 'Ah good, I see you're going to like this place, eh? Good man.'

The drilling station was even smaller than the supply depot on Roberts Massif. It was manned for the moment by Carlos, Geraldo and German, two Malaysians, a Namibian and a Zimbabwean. All of them greeted X in a friendly way, looking up at him from their seats in the station's common room and grinning as one of the Malays said, 'We can get you to do the work on the top of the derrick!'

After a ceremonial hot chocolate, Carlos took X around the facility to show him what they had. Carlos now wore a thick parka over his Carhartts, X noticed; it was really cold out here, even though the wind was not as stiff as at Roberts. As soon as they got back outside X asked, 'Where's Ron?'

'Oh,' Carlos said, looking at him. As always with people outdoors in Antarctica, sunglasses kept him basically expressionless. 'You have not heard? Ron was let go.'

'Let go?'

'Yes. We had to fire him. I don't know how well you knew Ron, but, well . . .' He shrugged. 'He had ideas about how things would work out here that were not right.'

'Hmph. Well . . . I can't say I'm surprised.'

Ron, the emperor of Antarctica. He had been so pleased to be quitting ASL and coming out here, and no doubt he had thought he would be secret boss of the system here as in Mac Town. X had no doubt he had done things that justified firing him. Still, to actually do it . . . It was hard to believe that anyone had had the guts. ASL had been trying to ignore Ron's abuses for years, simply to avoid the confrontation that these folks had taken on within weeks of hiring him. Which must have made Ron even angrier. He'd burnt his bridges to make this move, and now he was fired and presumably back home in Florida somewhere, stewing with rum and resentment. It was a creepy thought.

X turned his attention to Carlos again, who was leading him to the derrick and the drilling rig underneath it. Everything in the camp constellated around this derrick, a tall, spindly structure much like the classic configuration of oil derricks from the very beginning, although this one had a substantial gantry standing next to it, a tall heated chamber, Carlos said, where the coupling of drills and pipeline units was accomplished. The technology incorporated powerful new ice borers with oil extraction techniques learned in the North Sea. Much of the work was automated, of course. X would be learning a variety of the jobs that remained for humans to do; not because he was to be a general field assistant, Carlos was quick to add, but because everyone on station was a generalist, by necessity. 'It's the best way – there are a lot of jobs to be done, and not very many people to do them.' This looked right to X; the station was very small, the galley a single stove and a sink without running water, in an old blue beaker box that also served as meeting room and coms centre. A Jamesway next door was the dorm, and for those who disliked the dry heat and noise of its Preway heater there were some tents staked out on the hard snow. Those, and a few heated and unheated warehouses, and a yellow bull-dozer and a crane, and some forklifts in a shed, and a machine and carpentry shop, and a dozen big solar and piezoelectric panels in an array to the north – and that was it.

'This is just an exploratory station, you understand,' Carlos said. He took X into one of the heated sheds while they were talking, and opened a small freezer and took out a chunk of ice. He flicked on a cigarette lighter taken from one of his inner pockets, and applied the flame to the chunk of ice; after a moment blue flames flickered off the top of it.

'Whoah,' X said.

'This is methane hydrate. There is a lot of it under us, at the bottom of the ice cap. If we find there is enough of it, then they may decide to expand, and drill for extraction. We are also evaluating the possibility of oil, of course, but that is secondary. The methane hydrates are the thing.'

'And what are they, again?'

'They are single molecules of methane – natural gas, you know – trapped in crystalline ice cages. They only form under high pressure, but when they do form there is a lot of gas there, as much as thirty litres of gas per litre of sediment. Of course there is a great deal of natural gas in the world, but for the southern countries that have no oil, and are crippled by debts to the North, if they could find even gas supplies of their own it would be very helpful.'

'But can gas be transported by tankers?'

'It isn't how they do it. But there are new pipelines now, flexible and unbreakably strong, designed to lie under the surface of the ocean. It's possible to run pipelines directly from here to South America and southern Africa. The materials are fantastic, they're made of meshes like kevlar, and include plastics grown in soy plants. The pipes have laser pigs, insulation, everything. Fantastic pipe. And so deep underwater nothing will disturb them. So these new technologies make methane a more useful fuel. And burning these methane hydrates could actually help the global climate situation. You see, if the polar caps melt, like we see them starting to, then this methane below us will be released into the atmosphere, and kick off a greenhouse warming that makes the one we have now look like nothing. We think now that some of the great rapid climate warmings of the past were caused by the release of methane hydrate deposits. So it's possible we can capture this gas, and burn it for our own power, and reduce greenhouse gases at the same time. It's very elegant in that way.'

X nodded, wandering the shop and looking at equipment. 'What about the sliding of the ice?' He pointed in the direction of the derrick. 'It must be moving a little, anyway. How do you deal with that?'

'The movement is not so big here as to be a problem,' Carlos said.

'Here it moves only five metres a year, and does not seem to be speeding up, like so many places on the cap are. So we can simply add length to the pipe, and by the time the methane here is extracted the station will only be a few hundred metres to the north.'

'What about ice surges?'

'Don't say that word! No such thing as ice surges on the polar cap!'

But ever since the Ross Ice Shelf had detached, and Ice Stream C come unstuck from the position it had been frozen in for the last few centuries, surges had been common all over the place. The possibility couldn't be denied that ice anywhere in Antarctica might move with startling speed, as Carlos now admitted: 'If it surges, we are done here. But the hole will be capped by the surge, so that there would be no spill, even if we were pumping oil. Maybe the top part of the pipe, but we clean that up, and, I don't know – go home, probably. We are underfunded as it is, as you probably have noticed. It would be hard to recover from the loss of that much pipe, and if there is one surge, there might be more. No, there can be no surges! They are forbidden here! Come on, let's go in and get warm. It's Geraldo's turn to cook supper, and he is very good.'

Inside the steamy fragrant beakerbox the others were talking about glaciology, and Punta Arenas, and laughing a lot; and X felt another glow of happiness. Carlos and Geraldo explained what X's first jobs would entail; the ongoing exploratory efforts were still pretty wide-ranging, and though they were sure enough of this deposit to start drilling, they had not yet established the size of the deposit, or the location of others suspected to be nearby. So they were taking trips out from the station on snowmobiles, to do what they called '3-D seismics', which involved setting out a grid of geophones, to record the shocks from explosions set off in the ice, and in the rock of nunataks to the north. Geologists working for the group would then look for 'bright spots' in the record, and map the rock and the stratigraphy of the subsurface. Their well was therefore an early 'cost well', and just one in a giant X pattern of them out on this sector of the cap. Down their well they would send tools to measure the gamma radiation, and take actual looks around with fibreoptics, among other new detection methods. 'We're definitely on top of a big methane hydrate deposit,' Carlos said, 'and under that is a seal rock, which is a lithologic seal over sedimentary rock that often contains oil. The drill is cutting through the seal rock now, which is a very hard old lava field.'

X nodded over and over again, happy to hear the confident beakerspeak; and feeling more and more pleased at the growing conviction that no matter what happened here, he would not be contributing to the despoilation of the pure Antarctic. The Man Without A Name, yes, The Man Without A Country, sure; but not The Man Without Environmental Ethics. Which meant he could face Val in his mind. And he would be working, he saw, with people who were sort of a mix of beaker and ASL – something seldom if ever seen in McMurdo, where the two roles were so strictly separated for the sake of 'efficiency' – even though the set-up here was obviously the way it should be, everyone doing part of the support work, everyone participating also in the science involved, and benefiting from both. No, this was great. He would never run into Val and have the rest of his day ruined; he would spend his season out here under the vast low dark blue sky, with real work to do, surrounded by Spanish and African voices and laughter, with a tent of his own to sleep in. It was a GFA's paradise. It was X heaven.

Beep beep. 'Hey Wade, are you awake?'

'No.'

'Where are you.'

'. . . I'm not sure.'

'That happens to me sometimes too.'

'Oh yeah. Hotel California.'

'You're in California?'

'Hotel California. McMurdo Station, Antarctica. Wow. I couldn't remember there for a minute where I was.'

'That happens to me a lot.'

'What's up?'

'I couldn't sleep. You know Wade, sometimes I don't see why half the people in America don't just walk off their jobs and start up their own companies. I say that right on the floor of the Senate.'

'Yes Phil. We read it in the *Post* and we gnash our teeth. We can't believe our eyes. Only in California would you have even the slightest chance of getting elected.'

'I get elected by seventy percent majorities, Wade.'

'That shows what California can do.'

'I get almost a hundred percent of the Hispanic vote.'

'That's because you're a Democrat, plus you speak Spanish like a barrio textile worker.'

'That's because I was a barrio textile worker. And those girls work hard let me tell you. My fingers are still all scarred from that.'

Phil had spent three months working in a legal sweatshop with legal aliens, part of his Ongoing Working Education as he called it, the OWE programme (pronounced Ow in the office) that he had instituted for himself, in which he spent three months working full time at a great number and variety of Californian occupations, so many that the list was beginning to look like the jacket copy for a new novelist.

'I know,' Wade said. He got out of bed and went to the room's sink and began to clean up. 'It's great what you've done. You're very popular and you deserve it. But only in California. And even there you have high negatives.'

'How high can they be when I get seventy percent of the vote?'

'They can be thirty percent, and that's what they are. A record high negative.'

'Any time you create a high positive you're going to get a high negative. Even in California.'

'Especially in California.'

'God bless our state.'

'The most volatile in the nation. Pendulum swings that defy all laws of physics and political science. You're one of the big left swings, up there with the Browns or Warren or Boxer, but shuffled in with you guys are people like Reagan and Nixon, with no rhyme or reason to it. You're all way off the charts anywhere else in America.'

'So now you're comparing me to Richard Nixon. You're waking me up in the middle of the night to compare me to Richard Nixon.'

'He was great at foreign policy.'

'Please, Wade. I get elected because people like what I stand for. It's populism come back again. In California that's important.'

'Used to be populism anyway. Now, Phil? A leader in the Democratic Party? Having changed your tune over the years from calling for the complete revamping of everything to advocating legislation to encourage co-operatives?'

'I've grown up in fifteen years, better have or else.'

'Everyone in the middle of the road says that, it must be like a chorale there on the painted line, you really sing well together.'

'Hey. Gorz is even worse than me, he went from demanding the impossible to suggesting a thirty-hour work week.'

'You've called for a thirty-hour work week too.'

'It's a good idea. Reform by increments, Wade, it's the only way. You demand the impossible you get nothing. In co-ops people own their work, that's a very big step right there. After we get that, we can think about further steps.'

'If you can even get that far. Maybe these days asking for co-ops and a thirty-hour work week is demanding the impossible.'

'Maybe so. We'll find out when we try for it, Wade. You can only learn useful lessons by trying things out. I like things you can try, rather than big systems that you can't figure out how to move toward or test out.'

'You're a true Democrat, Phil.'

'Yes I am. So what's next for you down there?'

'I'm flying to the South Pole today.' It was a sentence that felt odd in the mouth.

'You be careful. How was your trip to the Dry Valleys?'

'It was interesting. Good background.'

'How was your mountain guide?'

'She was very competent.'

'Ooh.'

'Please Phil.'

'Well, you have fun out there Wade. I'll be calling you again to get a report from the Pole.'

'Yes you will.'

It's a dog eat dog world, especially if you shoot half your huskies and feed them to the rest. This had been the Amundsen expedition's method of operation; they had started out with fifty-two dogs, and most of those had not only pulled the sledges but somewhere along the way been turned into food, for both dogs and men. Each dog eaten provided about fifty pounds of meat, and therefore saved that much from the sledge loads. It was a classic case of pulling your own weight, or of what the American weapons industry called 'dual-use efficiency' when pointing out that their high-heat laser weapons would also make very nice ice borers (which they did). Amundsen however lost a lot of style points for this particular dual use; he was criticized for it ever afterward, especially in Britain.

Obviously Val's 'In the Footsteps of Amundsen' expedition, the thirteenth to trace Amundsen's route to the Pole, was not going to be using the same methods the Norwegians had used. For one thing dogs were now banned from Antarctica; for another, the Ross Ice Shelf, the crossing of which had comprised about half of Amundsen's trek, was no longer there. The ice shelf had been an amazing feature in its time: a stable floating cake of ice nearly a thousand feet thick, covering an area about the same size as California or France, and at its outer edge towering a couple of hundred feet over the open sea. As it turned out, however, it had been highly sensitive to small changes in air and ocean temperatures, and the global warming had been enough to break most of it up and carry it off to sea. It had been replaced by a jumble of thinning annual sea ice, remnant iceberg chunks of the shelf, and enormous ice tongues pushing out from the Transantarctic glaciers and the West Antarctic ice streams; with the brake of the shelf gone these outpourings had greatly accelerated, and they slid out onto the sea and floated there, long white peninsulas that occasionally broke off and joined the iceberg armada.

As a result of all this the Ross Sea was no longer a viable proposition for foot travel. And Val was among those who considered this a great blessing, for to start a trek with three hundred miles of hauling over soft snow, entirely flat but frequently crevassed, was not really how modern wilderness adventure travellers wanted to spend their vacation time. In truth it had been the kind of miserable travel no one would do unless they had to. But of course there had been purists who had insisted on doing it because the early explorers had, and so their guides had had to oblige and lead them across it, bored out of their minds and working to keep the rapidly disillusioned clients from getting surly. Now that option was gone, and no one was happier about it than Val.

So this Footsteps of Amundsen expedition, like the twelve before it, was taking turns hauling a single ultralight sledge full of their gear, and therefore travelling more like Scott's party than Amundsen's. And they started their trip, as had become traditional, a day's haul out from land, on the sea ice between the ice tongues from the Strom and Axel Heiberg glaciers. This gave everyone a taste of what it had been like to cross the level white waste of the ice shelf, and then without further ado they made landfall where Amundsen and his men had, on the gentle northern slopes of Mount Betty, named after Amundsen's childhood nurse. After crossing the tidal cracks in the sea ice at the shoreline, and setting a camp a couple of hundred metres up the slope, they were also able to visit the cairn that Amundsen and his men had built, on the exposed ridge of Mount Betty called Bigend Saddle. This cairn had marked the only depot Amundsen had made during his trek to the Pole, and now the chest-high stack of big flat stones was also the sole remaining object left by Amundsen's team anywhere on the continent, their base camp having calved into the sea soon after their departure.

So this stack of stones was it. Nothing in the century since had disturbed it, for no wind was going to knock it over, and Antarctica had very little in the way of earthquakes. Val's group stood around it reverently, almost afraid to touch it for fear of accidentally tipping it over. But it had been stacked with the kind of neat skill that marked all Amundsen's operations, and it would not fall unless someone deliberately dismantled it. And no one who cared enough to visit the site would do that.

It had first been relocated, Val told her group, by members of Admiral Byrd's expedition, in 1929. In a hollow in the stack of stones they had found a tiny can containing pages torn from Amundsen's notebook, informing the world, in case they did not survive the return crossing of the ice shelf, that they had in fact reached the Pole.

The five clients shook their heads at this bit of information. Incredible that this little stack of stones, in all the empty thousands of square miles of ice and rock, had been relocated at all, much less by men flying around in a little Fokker aircraft just seventeen years after it had been built. The wreckage of the Fokker could still be visited as well, Val told them; it had been destroyed on the ground in a blizzard in March of 1929, and its crew rescued by men in the plane that a few weeks later made the first flight over the Pole.

All amazing. But it was cold on that exposed ridge, and after a few minutes standing around, the group was ready to get back into the dining tent and eat dinner. It had been a hard day's haul. No one advocated visiting the wreckage of the Fokker, which was nearly ten kilometres away, and was, when all was said and done, still a plane wreck, never anyone's favourite subject for archaeological tours.

So they headed down for the tent. But as they were leaving the rock of the ridge and stepping onto the snowy slope of Mount Betty, Elspeth exclaimed, 'Look there!'

She was pointing at another rock cairn, lower and smaller than Amundsen's. The others followed her over to look at it. It was a little ring of rock, surrounding a snow-plastered black box and a satellite dish wired to it. Scientific instrumentation.

'One of the science teams must be doing an experiment of some kind,' Val said. 'They're probably using the Amundsen cairn as a locater.'

'That's stupid,' Jim said. 'I'm surprised they let them disturb a historical site like this.'

The others looked noncommittal. Presumably this ring of stones would be dismantled when the experiment was over; and given the vast view they had of the coastal range and the berg-choked frozen sea, it was hard to argue that the site was *too* disturbed. Still, Jim continued to complain as they hiked back down to their campsite, and Val promised to look into the matter and see whose experiment it was, and what they were doing so close to the Amundsen cairn.

Then they were at the camp. The big dining tent was still clear on its north side, maximizing its own little greenhouse effect; the fabric would go blue when the temperature inside got to about forty, so that the discrepancy of inner and outer temperatures didn't get too large. The little sleeping tents were all colourful nylon domes, with snowblock walls protecting them from the possibility of strong downslope winds. The snow here was classic Antarctic styrofoam; they had cut it with a big saw into perfect blocks, and lifted them easily for stacking, as the snow was very light, and yet cohered perfectly.

Now they all took off their crampons and hustled into the dining tent, enthusiastically declaring their starvation. And Val followed them in, taking a last look over the jumbled sea ice thinking, So much for the Ross Ice Shelf. A day's haul. Amundsen's group had taken three weeks to get here from their base on the Bay of Whales. So nice to have an excuse to pass on that. The old guys had done stuff that was just too hard, no matter how into it you were. You had to tailor the past a little to make it bearable.

Not that she meant to be unfair to her clients. They were skiing or walking three hundred miles across Antarctica, after all, and taking turns hauling the sledge, and hauling it from sea level up to nine thousand feet as well, which was a big up. So a few hundred miles of ice shelf subtracted from the total was not that important, nor were the exact details of the route. It was the spirit that counted.

Except to some people, who came down with the idea of retracing the historic routes precisely. A particular character type, and one of Val's least favourite. But even that type had to make allowances when it came to Amundsen's trip. And really, no matter how closely they tried to reproduce the experience – some expeditions had tried wearing the same clothing and using the same gear, with spectacularly unhappy results – it could not truly be done. Because Amundsen and his group had approached a section of the Transantarctics that no one had ever seen before. It was an unknown mountain range that they had to cross somehow, with food supplies so tight that they had not had the luxury of scouting out alternative routes to find the easiest way to the polar cap, which they only knew was there because of Shackleton's trek three years before. So as they approached the mountains in their crossing of the ice shelf, watching them rear up day after day into a range as big and ferocious as the Alps, Amundsen had not been amused. He made a sketch in his notebook naming the big peaks Mounts A, B, C, D, E and F. Between the peaks the big glaciers that characterized the range spilled down from the polar cap; but which one should they take? In the end Amundsen thought he saw a rampway next to one of the big glacial openings, a ramp that appeared to rise straight up and straight south to the foot of one of the biggest of the inland peaks, where he hoped he would be deposited on the polar cap with little trouble. There was no way of telling until they tried it; and so up the ramp they had climbed, ignoring the broad glacial opening just a few kilometres to their left.

The ramp, however, had turned out not to be a ramp. It had been a big shoulder, around which the broad glacier to the left had curved on its way down. So after intense efforts to climb the rugged shoulder and cross it, they had been left looking down onto the glacier they could have walked right up, and they had had to descend to this glacier and then restart their climb. It had been one of Amundsen's biggest mistakes; it had cost them days, and a great deal of backbreaking effort; and in retrospect it seemed obvious that the broad curving glacier had been the way. In fact they had had to beat their dogs to get them to start up the shoulder, as the dogs had been all for taking the glacier road to the left. Even the dogs had known better.

But that was the kind of thing that happened when exploring unknown territory, when struggling through the mountains of terra incognita for the first time. It was the kind of experience that humanity would never have again, not even on other planets. Of course there were wilderness adventure tours these days being dropped in Alaska or Mongolia or the Himalayas without maps or compasses or GPS or radio, to try to reproduce that experience. But no matter how they tried, Val did not believe what they were doing was really the same.

147

It was impossible to regain that mental state, of wanting to know and not knowing.

In Amundsen's case, the mistaken route had been only the beginning of their troubles. By an unhappy twist of fate, the glacier they had chosen to climb, the Axel Heiberg, turned out to be one of the steepest and most broken glacial ramps to the polar plateau in all the Transantarctics. Its upper section rose eight thousand feet in less than twenty miles, in a series of ice cataracts that fell across the glacier from sidewall to sidewall, making them unavoidable. Only the champion skiing of Amundsen's lead skier Bjaaland – one of the best skiers alive at that time – and the generally superb ice skills of all the Norwegians, had got them (and their surefooted dogs!) up the thing.

So repeating the Amundsen route was hard enough even if you decided to pass on the mistake at the beginning, and stuck to the Axel Heiberg throughout. Most of the previous Footsteps expeditions had taken the glacier route, which had been the Amundsen descent route as well, and so still following in the footsteps (reversed) while saving strength for the difficulties that lay above. It made sense.

And Val's group this time was not made up of Norwegian champion skiers and hardened polar explorers. On the contrary, it was a somewhat less skilful group than usual. Not that all five didn't have many adventure expeditions under their belt; indeed as they wolfed down *hors d'oeuvres* and cooked their main meal, they were hearing story after story from Jack and Jim about climbing the Seven Summits (meaning the tallest one on each continent), kayaking down the Baltoro, completing the ice hat-trick (meaning North Pole, Greenland and South Pole), and so forth. The adventures were endless. But their expertise still seemed thin to Val. The husband and wife team, Jorge and Elspeth Royce-Paulo, took photographs and wrote articles for the outdoor magazines and onlines; they were well-known. Jack Michaels and Jim McFeriss were friends from the Bay Area, both lawyers, and had climbed and gone on treks together a few times before. And Ta Shu, although he had spent many years wandering in the Himalayas, was around sixty. He was one of the Woos, a *feng shui* guru. During the days he wore heavy black sunglasses which contained fibreop cameras and a phone to transmit his narration and 3-D video back to a facemask TV audience in China. While hiking, his head swivelled about and he talked to this audience almost continuously, but in the tent he kept the glasses off, thankfully. Val's impression of *feng shui* was that it was one of those ancient modes of knowledge that was so deep and profound that no one alive could actually explain it, and indeed when she asked him what he made of the landscapes Ta Shu had said very little, usually 'This is a good place.' Although it could have been that his English kept him from offering the long version of his analyses; it was limited enough to make Val wonder why he didn't just give up and use a computer translation program.

In any case, all these clients were taking on something a little bit harder than most of what they had done before. And so Val was not sure that they should be tacking on the mistaken traverse.

But Jack was. 'I think we should follow the original route,' he said as Jorge and Elspeth ladled beef stroganoff into their bowls. 'Let's do it just like they did it, I mean that's what we came here for.'

'We already skipped the ice shelf,' Elspeth pointed out.

'That's because it's gone! If it were here we would do it. But this part of the route is just like it was when they came through, and so we should follow them, or else what's the point?'

The others sat on their sleeping bags and ground pads, eating and looking at Jack or Val, as if this was going to turn into some kind of confrontation between them. That was the last thing Val wanted, however. She said to them, 'It's your trek. You can do what you want.'

Jack nodded, lips pursed, as if he had won an argument. Val ignored that and focused on the others. They looked uncertain to her, even Jim, and so she unfolded the USGS topo of the area and traced with a finger the two alternative routes, and then only ate her stroganoff and listened to them debate the pros and cons. Slowly they began to come down on the side of following the exact route. Either they couldn't conceptualize the amount of sheer work it would add to the trek, or else they were just into the idea of it. Or else Jack was intimidating them. Group dynamics were such a mess.

Jack and Jim argued for the mistake; the Royce-Paulos did not seem to care, or were perhaps not enthusiastic, but not willing to say so. Ta Shu was becoming a kind of tie-breaker, unless Val herself got involved. He looked at her, perhaps for guidance. She said, 'It's no worse than the icefalls above. I suppose doing it might get us tuned for the icefalls.'

He said, 'We come to see what Amundsen saw.'

'Good man,' Jack said with a wink to Jim.

So the next morning they broke camp and loaded the sledge, and started up the shoulder of Mount Betty, onto the false ramp benching up the side of the Herbert Range.

Immediately the steepness of the slope began to give them trouble. It was windless, the sun right in their faces, and the snow on the slope pretty soft for Antarctica. Val had everyone switch from skis to snowshoes to gain traction, but even in the cold air, it was hot work. And it did not help that the snow concealed frequent crevasses in the ice below. The air was on average ten degrees Fahrenheit warmer than

149

in Amundsen's time, and as a result all Antarctic ice was moving downhill a bit more quickly. For the most part this was noticeable only to beakers, but on steeper slopes one saw evidence of fresh ice spills much more often than when Val had first come down.

As here and now: a fan of blue shatter-ice splayed out over the smooth white tilt they were climbing, the broken ice still sharp-edged. The hyperarid winds would quickly round all exposed edges, and indeed blow away chunks this size in a year or two, so this was clearly a recent spill. Which meant they had to be extra-careful when crossing snowbridges over crevasses, or moving under séracs. And on this day they were having to do a lot of both.

Val's GPS gave her a detailed map of the slope, which pinpointed their location and all the crevasses out of sight above them. So she did not have to climb ahead of the rest to find a way, as Bjaaland had done continuously for Amundsen. Which meant she was available to help haul their sledge. This was the latest German lightweight wonder, built by the same firm that made the winning sledges and luges in the Olympics, and the gear and food for all six of them fitted into its sleek blue body and yet weighed less than three hundred pounds (most of that food); a miracle of all the latest in materials science; but still damned hard to pull up a slope this steep and soft.

So Val stayed in the lead harness and hauled the sledge, teamed with Jack, then Jim, then Elspeth, then Ta Shu, then Jorge. Up left, then right, then left, switchbacking up steep ramps of snow-covered ice, looking down into cobalt crevasses. Hard work indeed, which on Amundsen's trek had been done mostly by the dogs. Really the problems for the two groups were almost reversed; Val's group knew the way but had to pull their load, while the Norwegians had had their dogs to pull, but had not known where they were going. Val much preferred her group's problem; it was hot work, but relatively safe. Heading into unmapped territory with limited food and no chance of rescue; that was a situation she did not envy. Now the problems were more mundane: 'Try not to sweat,' Val reminded them after one especially aerobic stomp up a hard snow ramp. 'Thermostat yourselves. Even your smartfabrics can't do it all.'

'You'd have to be naked not to sweat on a pitch this hard,' Jack called up cheerfully. With a small smirk. His glacier glasses were a glossy gold colour, which made him look like a bug. All their sunglasses were at full power, and their solar earbands were the usual prisming metallic blue. Aliens on ice.

'A naked head is usually enough,' Val advised.

The sun blazed off the snow. Even with sunglasses at full power, one's pupils shrank so far down that the brilliant world appeared somehow dark underneath it all. A steepening bluewhite hillside, rising shattered above them. They were traversing now across the great shoulder of the Herbert Range, so that their right boots always hit higher and dug deeper than their left boots, which quickly grew tiresome. Traverses were tough.

Val was enjoying herself. This was where the years of making her living as a professional beast of burden paid off. Oh of course she hadn't been a pure beast of burden, like the porters in the Himalaya; but a good mountain guide usually ended up carrying a load as heavy as a porter's, to try to make things easier on the clients. Just a Sherpa with software, as the guide saying went. So no matter how many trips these clients took in a year, or how much they worked out at home, they were still not on their feet humping loads as often as she was, not by miles and miles. Probably they spent an hour a day doing some stairmasters and thinking that meant they were in good shape. But now, Val thought with a hard little grin, they were on the stairmaster from hell. They had come up about the height of two World Trade Towers at this point, and had about two Empire State Buildings to go. And they were beginning to suffer. Even Jack was huffing and puffing. Which was one of the many reasons Val had not tried to talk him out of taking this route; she was hauling the sledge by herself now and still pulling ahead, waiting for them to catch up, then taking off again; not a bad lesson for Mr Jack Michaels to contemplate, she tried not to think consciously. And meanwhile she was able to stomp uphill and look around as she did, relaxed, continuing to enjoy the views in a way that the tiring clients couldn't.

And it was easy to take the icescapes down here for granted anyway, because they were so ubiquitous and so spectacular, but in a fractal way, self-similar at all scales, so that one lost perspective. It was like becoming an ant and hiking through the ice tray in your refrigerator; there are scores of beautiful ice formations in every refrigerator, but how many people notice? You had to be a connoisseur of ice. And you had to be in good enough shape to be able to pay attention; for you did pay; work hard enough and you would stop paying attention, and it would get easier. It was a very physical aesthetics. But Val was more than up to it, and now she hauled the sledge up step after step, deep in her own rhythms, enjoying the dense cross-cut textures of the dry snow underfoot, and the ice dolmens rearing out of the snow to left and right, each windsculpted blue block a work of art, a pulsing and it seemed almost living thing. The squeak of her snowshoes and her breath in her ears were the only sounds, all in rhythm together, like music. She was a dromomaniac, in love with this walking uphill. It was movement as pleasure, movement as the rhythm of her thoughts, movement as meditation. Looking down at the bright microtextures of the snow underfoot, there was a lot of time to think; this kind of walking was measured in hours. Her mind wandered, out of her control. She thought of Steve again, touching each wind-rounded shard of memory without pain. She thought of her grandmother, for the first time without pain there either. They had lived together in her off-seasons for the last five years of her grandmother's life, from ninety to ninety-five, in the old family house in Wyoming. Annie Kenning, a tough woman with a bright laugh. *I was a wild one, Val, you better believe it. I was taller than you before I shrivelled up like this! That strength of yours didn't come from nowhere!* One morning in what turned out to be their last summer together Val had walked out of the old house and found Annie standing on top of a stepladder, reaching up into one of the old apple trees to pick a high apple – this just three months after a broken hip sustained in a fall off the front porch, and Annie still unsteady on stairs or even on level ground. Frightened, Val had run over yelling at her, almost scaring her off the ladder, and had helped her down, scolding her, *what could you be thinking, you could kill yourself,* and her lower lip had stuck out and suddenly at the bottom of the ladder she said, *Shut up! Shut up! I used to climb all over these trees! Don't you tell me what to do! Once when I was fifteen I jumped from one tree to the next one over! And that was just a couple weeks ago.* She had sat down on the grass and Val had sat next to her, an arm around her. *Just a couple weeks ago,* she insisted. *And now I'm ninety-four.*

Beep beep beep! A break in the bright dark snow ahead. Val came back to the present with a start, looked around. The others were behind and below. Val inspected the slope above, whistled, checked her GPS. They had reached a section where knowing the location of the crevasses was no great help, as they were everywhere. That meant crossing snowbridges, which was always chancy, and never more so than in an icefall, where the ice forming the two sides of the crevasse was offset vertically – in this case, the uphill side about ten metres higher than the side she now stood on. And the only snowbridge filling the crevasse had a gap at its upper end. Crouched on the snowbridge, looking down into the depths of the crack, Val sighed. It would be an operation to get up and over it, and there wasn't a good alternative as far as she could see, by eye or on her GPS. Well, that was ascending an icefall for you. Endless delay, hassle, precaution, despite which a gnawing sensation of danger, as the deep icy cracks underfoot could not be ignored. Also, there was too little to do for those not dealing with the problem directly. So she worked as fast as she could to set a deadman belay, digging the anchor deep in the snow while being sure not to degrade the structural integrity of the bridge. By the time all the others had caught up she was prepared mentally, and she got Jack and Ta Shu to belay her.

She jumped across the narrow gap and hit the wall of ice with crampon tips and two ice axes, and stuck like a fly. Like Spiderwoman, yes! Then up, one move at a time, always three points stuck in the ice, axe axe, toe toe, axe axe, and quickly up and over the top, onto thin hard snow. Quickly she pounded in a long snow stake, which left her free to walk about and pound in a couple more. Despite her admonitions to the clients, she was sweating. She unzipped her parka and took it off, and as she was now standing in a windless bowl of ice like a big reflecting solar cooker, she took off her sweater and shirt as well, right down to a sky-blue jogging top. The insectile stares of the clients below seemed to convey notions that she was indulging in some Antarctic cold-macho; no doubt they were still cold; but they would learn. Now Jack was clipped to the line and jumping across and climbing up, making it look like a lark – as indeed it was, on a top-rope.

Against her bare sweaty skin the air was frigid, but she didn't stay wet for long. She could actually feel the sweat wafting away. Against that evaporative cooling the radiant heat of the sun was a palpable hit, as from an open fire, so distinct that she turned to get the sunlight on her back as well, doing a little rotisserie. The side of her exposed to the sun was hot, the side in the shade of her own body was cold; it felt as if there were about sixty degrees difference between the two.

She got the clients up and over the wall one by one. Then they all pulled the sledge up to them through a jumar, which allowed the rope up but would not let it slip back down–'one, two, three, haul!' After that they sat beside the sledge; everyone was now following Val's example with the thermostatting, and it looked like beach-blanket south, for a few minutes anyway. But they were only ten metres higher, and twenty farther on, with several crevasses to go before they could simply slog uphill again. 'It's going to take all day to go the next hundred yards!' Jorge exclaimed.

'Oh it shouldn't take quite that long,' Val said cheerfully. 'But I guess we'd better get to it.'

'Oh God.'

'Not again.'

'You slavedriver.'

'Yeah yeah, yeah yeah.' Val put on the sledge harness, then her sungloves. 'Come on, let's go.'

So they did. Up here the ice proved to be broken in a series of broad ledges, like a giant's steps. The crevasses were frequent, and the tortured ice gleamed in the wild shear zones walling them in on left and right. The work was unrelenting, and it took careful thermostatting to keep from sweating, then to keep from getting overchilled after the hot spots. The view changed slowly. While waiting for the others Val looked back and down and out – two thousand feet down, thirty or forty miles out – over the jumbled, frozen surface of the Ross Sea, in this month of the year white all the way to the horizon, the big icebergs scattered like a great fleet of torpedoed aircraft carriers. Mount Betty was now below them; the rest of the Herbert Range still loomed to their right, with a spur running off the range blocking the way ahead of them. To get to that spur they had to cross the bowl at the head of the Sargent Glacier, a little glacier high in its own basin, falling down to the Axel Heiberg on their left.

On they climbed. The sun wheeled around in the blueblack sky, until when Val looked back the glare off the sea ice was blinding. She checked her watch: though it was still sunny mid-afternoon, it was 9pm. She had wanted to reach the saddle in the spur ahead of them, to give them a view of the Axel Heiberg below, but it was too late to continue. 'Time to camp.'

So they pitched the dining tent and their little sleeping domes, and then in the nylon blue incandescence of the diner they got three pots of ice on the stove. In the violent blue light of the team tent everyone tended to look like morgue photos of themselves, but Jack did not seem to mind this effect, as he kept glancing at Val while they wolfed down the *hors d'oeuvres*: taste of smoked oysters, sip of tea, glance at Val, three little taste treats, repeated over and over. And a bit of a come-on too. But Val had had a lifetime's experience of ignoring such looks; she could ignore men across a whole broadband of registers, from outrageous flirtation to demure appreciation to neutral obliviousness to cold warning to gross insult. Back in the world she would have ignored him in a really dismissive way, the back of her hand to him; but as he was a client, she kept it oblivious.

Besides, it was hers and Ta Shu's night to cook, and cooking made one generous. The two of them sat by the stove tending the rehydrating spaghetti sauce, cooking the pasta, frying hard bread in garlic butter, and passing out cup after cup of hot tea. Val did not always enjoy cooking for even as small a group as this, but Ta Shu with his fractured English and his unusual ideas about food (he wanted to put ginger in the spaghetti sauce) made it entertaining. It was a pleasant couple of hours, one of the unsung attractions of mountain expeditions: getting off one's tired feet, getting warmed up, getting food in the stomach, food which because of the extreme states of hunger involved often tasted wildly delicious even if it was very plain fare; and all the while lounging around on soft sleeping bags in colourful silky clothes like

Oriental pashas, and talking a mile a minute. In these conditions cooking for others was a solicitous, avuncular activity; taking care of people; which meant that the cooks got a little taste of how the guide felt all the time. Even Jack was not as much of a jerk on the nights when he and Jim cooked.

On this night, however, he was not cooking, and so free to look, and to talk. And the day's exertions had made all of them talkative to tell the truth.

'That was so hard!'

'I can't believe they got fifty-two dogs up that!'

'Three thousand vertical feet, and a lot of it gnarly indeed.'

'And then to find out it was all wasted effort!'

'And with the big icefalls still to come!'

But the Norwegians hadn't known that, Val thought. Perhaps not knowing what lay ahead had made them less apprehensive rather than more. Ignorance as bliss. At least sometimes. 'It's a good thing we came this way,' she said. 'It's nice to see what they saw.'

Jack nodded complacently. 'That's what it's all about.'

After more food intake Jorge said, 'You know, it gives you an interesting new angle on the myth of Scott as total bungler and Amundsen as hyper-efficient genius. I mean unless you've done today you don't realize what huge risks Amundsen took. There were sections today that were worse than when we went up the Khumbu Icefall.'

To the same kind of goal, Val thought – Everest, the South Pole – the tallest, the bottommost; something only had to be the most and suddenly it was the holy grail, worth taking fatal risks for. For a certain type of person.

'But the Norwegians were good on ice,' Jack told Jorge. 'They were experienced polar travellers.'

'Yes,' Jorge said, 'but that wouldn't have helped if a snowbridge had collapsed at the wrong time, or if a sérac had fallen on them. That easily could have happened.'

'You can imagine them disappearing without trace,' Elspeth added. 'Then Scott's group would have gotten there first, and had the extra psychological push to make it back home, and the whole story would have been reversed.'

'The rash, presumptuous Norwegians,' Jorge declaimed, 'and the amateur but tough, steady Brits. It's the story everyone wants, really.'

'Not me,' Jack said. 'Scott was an idiot. If it had turned out that way it would be the genius punished and the idiot rewarded.'

'Very realistic,' Val murmured, but no one heard her, as Elspeth was crying 'Oh come on!' and waving a finger at Jack. 'Scott was *not* an idiot!'

155

'But he was!' Jim said. 'He did everything wrong!'

'*Everything*,' Jack said, with a knowing smile at Val.

And then he and Jim were off and running, playing riffs they had obviously played many times before, variations on the theme 'Scott and His Stupidities'. He had become a torpedo lieutenant in the late Victorian Royal Navy, a ridiculously dead-end post in a ridiculously moribund service. He had acquired the polar assignment through personal connections even though he had no knowledge of polar regions. He had not bothered to learn a thing from previous polar explorers, nor had he bothered to study the Arctic indigenous peoples – perish the thought. In fact he took exactly the wrong lessons from those who had gone before, disdaining Eskimo furs in favour of naval canvas clothing, disdaining dog sledge travel in favour of manhauling. Actually he had tried to use dogs, as well as ponies, motor tractors, and skis; but as he and his men could not manage to master any of these modes of transport over snow, they had had to fall back on walking as a last resort. Only at that point had Scott proclaimed to the world that manhauling was really the only honest and noble way to go.

'It wasn't a matter of style,' Jim said, 'or consideration for animals. They killed their ponies and dogs too, only without ever admitting they were going to have to do it, so that sometimes they didn't have pistols there for the job. Wilson had to knife some of them to death, while Scott sat in the tent wringing his hands about how bad he felt. It was sheer incompetence.'

He had also been a bad judge of character, Jack added. He had been the sycophantic disciple of bad men; he had chosen bad men to work for him; he had led them badly. He had had bad friends.

'Oh come on,' Elspeth objected. 'Wilson cannot be called a bad friend. He was a wonderful man.'

'He was too good to be good,' Jack said, which cracked Jim up. 'A passive Christlike martyr in the making. And the rest of them were buffoons.'

Except for the ones who had ripped Scott privately in their diaries, of course, who all turned out to have been wise men. But the rest – buffoons.

'He also seems to have gotten in trouble with a girl in America,' Jack said, with another suggestive glance at Val. 'And his marriage . . .'

He had married a woman too beautiful for him, it seemed, too ambitious and smart. An Edwardian Lady Macbeth, who had pushed him south 'and then had an affair with Nansen at the very same time Scott was dying on the ice,' Jack said, shaking his head woefully.

He had been a scientific dilettante as well, Jim went on, only using the sciences as a cover for his desire to get to the Pole. He had had sulks and depressions lasting up to a month. He had sent Wilson, Bowers and Cherry-Garrard into needless danger and exhaustion on the Winter Journey, while the rest of his men sat around the hut writing a newspaper and putting on skits, rather than learning to ski or control their dogs. As for ponies, he had obtained glue-factory nags from Siberia in the first place, then killed half of them during pointless excursions during the winter, little trips which read like rehearsals for Keystone Kops Icecapades.

Then during the trek south he had overworked his men, demanding that they keep up with his unhealthily strong strength. He had got into a race mentality with the second sledge team, thus breaking Lieutenant Evans. He had seriously underestimated the provisions needed to feed four people to the Pole and back; then at the last depot he had decided to take five people instead of four, sealing their fate.

'Now that was a mistake,' Val admitted in her murmur at the stove. She had heard all this before, of course. It was a frequent topic of conversation on these expeditions. Everyone who joined a Footsteps expedition was an expert; it only took half a dozen books to fill you in on the entire history of Antarctica, and after that everyone had an opinion. Including her. But she had learned to stay out of the discussions, having become tired of the faintly condescending responses she got if she joined, responses all the more irritating because even though these were outdoor people, they still seemed to share the desk-jockey notion that anyone doing physical work for a living must have had all thoughts fly for ever out of their head. She knew this was only the defensiveness of the couch potato, but it still annoyed her. And it was always the same discussion anyway.

Jim and Jack were by no means finished with the litany of Scott's mistakes. Jim focused on technical errors of competence, Val noted, Jack on moral turpitude. Jim pointed out that Scott had failed to notice that the canisters they were using allowed their stove fuel to evaporate out of the cap screws. He had also ignored all signs of scurvy. He had hiked facing into the sun on the return from the Pole, when they could just as well have reversed their schedule and hiked with the sun to their backs, as Amundsen had done. Jack took over and insinuated that Scott had probably pressured Oates into committing suicide, and then probably invented Oates's famous last words, 'I am just stepping outside and may be a little while.' It was certain that he had altered other diary entries when publishing them in his books. ('Oh heaven forbid,' Elspeth interjected.) In general he had been too good a writer; and in the end he had written his way out of responsibility for the fiasco — out of responsibility and into legend. In fact, Jack said, he had probably preferred to die heroically, rather than return to England as the second man to the Pole. And so he had no doubt coerced Bowers and Wilson into staying in their final campsite, rather than brave a storm to try to reach their next supply cache only ten miles away, a storm that Amundsen would have waltzed through with barely a note for it in his journal, except perhaps 'some wind today'.

No. Scott was an idiot. He had read Tennyson; he had *believed* Tennyson; he had been the disastrous end product of a decaying empire, whose subjects had told themselves any number of comforting delusional stories about amateurs muddling through to glory, as at Waterloo or in the Crimea. This was the crux, even Jim maintained it: Scott had believed in bad stories. JM Barrie, the author of *Peter Pan*, had been one of his best friends. And so he and his men had never grown up. They had been Peter Pans, they had been Slaves to Duty like Frederick in *The Pirates of Penzance*; they had not had the sense to notice that *The Pirates of Penzance* was a satire. No, it was Browning and Tennyson and GA Henty and the *Boys' Own Weekly* for them, all the stupidities of the Victorian age turned into cast-iron virtues by the stories the boys were told. Into the valley of death rode the six hundred; onto the plateau of death manhauled the five.

'PG Wodehouse made fun of that stuff all the time,' Jim mentioned as they started dessert, which consisted of immense chocolate bars and brandy. 'That's why he was so funny.'

'They were Woosters!' Jack exclaimed. 'They were a bunch of Bertie Woosters on ice, without their Jeeves along to help them out.'

'It's worse than that,' Jim said. 'The Jeeves were right there at hand being ignored – men like Bowers or Crean or Lashly – the able seamen from the working classes. Those guys were very, very tough, and they almost managed to haul the toffs out of there despite everything. In fact that's what Crean and Lashly did with Lieutenant Evans, on their retreat from the last depot.'

After Scott had taken five men to the Pole, as Jim now reminded them, there had only been three to return from the last depot, and for these three it had been a very close thing indeed. Lieutenant Evans had collapsed, a victim of scurvy, and seamen Crean and Lashly had had to haul him on their sledge five hundred miles back to Cape Evans, an ordeal that included emotional moments such as sticking the Lieutenant's frozen feet onto their exposed stomachs, right through clothing and the membrane of class itself, to save him from a fatal frostbite. Finally Crean, at the end of four months of a manhauling regime so intense that it killed everyone else who tried it except Lashly, hurried ahead for help, covering forty miles of the ice shelf and getting down its edge to Hut Point, in a push of thirty-four straight hours of walking.

'And in the end Bowers almost managed to do the same for Wilson and Scott,' Jim added, 'like he did for Wilson and Cherry-Garrard on the Winter Journey.'

Little Birdie Bowers, Val thought, remembering the spring trip to Cape Crozier. Henry Robert Bowers – never cold, never tired, never discouraged. But even he hadn't been able to Jeeves his way out of that last trip. Worked into the ground like the poor knackered ponies, until he had died in his traces.

'No,' Jim insisted. 'Bertie Woosters. And Scott the worst of them – the one who killed them. He's the one who had the authority. He could have studied the problem, and figured out solutions. It's not like the solutions weren't there, because they were. But he couldn't be bothered. And so he tipped the balance, from life to death.'

All through this conversation, this dissing duet, everyone had been eating, powering their spaghetti down and enjoying the rant for the tent entertainment it was, laughing even when they were waving chunks of garlic bread or shaking heads to mark their objections. And when Jack and Jim had finished, and were into their second mugs of brandy, Elspeth wiped their whole case away with a single sweep of a chocolate bar. 'This is all just Huntford,' she said firmly. 'You can't take him seriously.'

Ta Shu looked interested in this; he had been following the whole conversation as if watching a sport he didn't know, head swivelling this way and that, entertained but mystified. 'What do you mean?' he asked Elspeth.

'All this anti-Scott stuff they've been giving us. It all comes from the Roland Huntford biography of Scott and Amundsen. It's a good book in some ways, but it should really have been called *Scott Was An Idiot*. It's a five-hundred-page list of stupidities. But a lot of them are crazy.'

'What do you mean?' Jack challenged.

'I mean Huntford went overboard,' Elspeth said, with a steady look at Jack. Val saw that she didn't like him either. 'Sometimes he was right, but other times he was just making a case. He was the first writer to debunk the Scott myth, and he got so into it he turned into a prosecutor rather than a judge. Complaining that Scott had ambitions to be more than a torpedo lieutenant! I mean really. Or pretending it was Scott's fault that he was given a bad ship. Or pretending that his men weren't loyal to him. Or that England was so bad, and Norway such a virtuous little country, when at that time the Norwegians were out slaughtering the world's whales to make their fortune and build their pretty towns.' She shook her head. 'Huntford made everything black and white, and that's not the way it was.'

159

Jim gulped a mouthful of brandy and choked a little, waving a hand at her. 'Even if you discount Huntford – and I take your point about his book being extreme – you still have to admit that Scott was pretty comprehensively incompetent. That part is simply true.'

'Nothing is simply true,' Elspeth said. She liked Jim better than Jack, Val saw. 'Cherry-Garrard didn't think Scott was incompetent, and Cherry-Garrard was there.'

'He was biased.'

'So was Huntford.'

'But Cherry-Garrard was an apologist. He tied himself in knots to try to tell the truth and still protect Scott's memory.'

Elspeth nodded. 'His is a complicated book that way. It has some of the greys in it, you see. That's what makes it a great book. He tried to be honest. And all his best friends died in it, remember. And he was in the group that found their bodies the following spring. They were only eleven miles from the next depot, and it was Cherry-Garrard who had laid that depot the previous fall. He had had orders from Atkinson to lay it in that spot and turn back, and he was wrecked himself by then, so he obeyed the orders. But if he had gone on a little farther, and set the depot another fifteen miles farther out, the return party might have found it and gotten home okay. It was a possibility that haunted him all the rest of his life. He was a haunted man. The night they found the bodies he wrote in his journal, "I am afraid to go to sleep." And when he got back to England he was sent right into the trenches of World War One. He drove an ambulance and he saw it all. And then he got colitis and was sent home. And after that he wrote his book, and it took him years and years. It was the book of his life. And struggling with mental illness a lot of the time.'

Val, remembering the Ponting photo encased in the new display at Cape Crozier, said, 'You can see that in the picture of the three of them after the Winter Journey.'

'Yes you can, can't you? He looks quite mad. And in his later years, when he looked back on his time in the Antarctic, it was like looking back into another age. Into the time before the fall.'

Back when your friends were alive, Val thought. Back when your big brothers were alive. Bowers had been twenty-eight, Wilson forty-five; Cherry had been twenty-two.

'But even he says Scott was moody,' Jim pointed out, 'and a bad judge of character. Even when he was idealizing the whole experience, he had to say that.'

'That's right. And I believe him when he says it, because he was there. But he was still intensely loyal to Scott, he still admired him despite the mistakes. And even more so did he admire Wilson and

Bowers, and they were Scott-loyalists as well. You can't take that away from Scott, no matter what Huntford said.'

Ta Shu turned from the stove, where he had started washing the dishes in a basin of steaming water. 'Like Huxley,' he said.

They looked at him, nonplussed.

'Thomas Huxley?' Jim ventured.

'Al-dous Huxley. English explorer. Explorer of higher states of consciousness. Mescalin, LSD. He take LSD in last hours of his life, to see what would happen. Very brave! One of your great British explorers, like Scott or Shackleton. And in one of his books there is very profound scene. A man and a woman are in a hotel room, making love. Out their window there is a neon sign that changes colours, from red to green to red to green. Over and over. And that light comes in their window and falls on them. And when the red light is shining on them, all is rosy. Full of life. Mysterious and beautiful. And then the light change, and the green light shine on them, and all becomes ghastly and pale. Mechanical. Like a nightmare of insects. And the lights keep changing, back and forth, back and forth. Red to green to red. Lovers don't know what to think.'

'Like Huntford and Cherry-Garrard,' Val said.

Ta Shu nodded.

Jack yukked: 'Cherry red and Hunt green!'

'But it isn't just a matter of interpretation,' Jim objected. 'Some things happened and some things didn't. And the point of history is first to try to determine what really happened, and not just tell lies about it. The heroic Scott is a lie, for the most part. When you really look at what really happened – that's when you get away from black and white and into the greys. And then when you find something admirable, as Huntford did with Amundsen, and later with Shackleton, then it's really worth your admiration. It's a real accomplishment, rather than just lies and wishes.'

'Yes,' Elspeth said, 'but Huntford went too far. I mean, to say that Scott made up Oates's last words – how could he possibly know? He wasn't in the tent.'

'No, but we have Oates's diary. He was totally disgusted with Scott.'

'So? Do you think Scott would have lied about something like that? Say that Oates got up and said, "You bloody fool, you've doomed us all with your stupidity, and now I'm going to go out and kill myself because it's obvious you want me out of the way." Would Scott then have written down in his diary, "Oates said, *I am just going out and will be a little while*"? What if the three men remaining had made it back, what then? Wilson and Bowers would have known it was a lie!'

'Neither of them mentioned the incident in their diaries,' Jim pointed out.

'That proves nothing. Wilson wasn't even keeping his diary any more at that point, as I recall. No, I'm sure Oates said something just like that – probably those precise words. These were men at the end of their tethers, you have to remember. They were starving and frost-bitten and gangrenous. They were in desperate straits. Oates was only the worst of them. Scott would probably have lost his feet as well, if they had gotten home. In times like that it's the old stories you were talking about that kick in more than ever, the public school ethos and the military code. You don't break down and shout accusations at each other – you live out the deepest scripts in you.'

'Maybe,' Val said, remembering South Georgia Island.

'No, you see it time after time,' Elspeth insisted. 'Men going to their deaths for some idea or other. Following a script, living out an ideology – there are a lot of ways of putting it.'

'Some people break under stress,' Val said despite herself.

'Yes they do. But that's another story – that's *Lord Jim*, a story that all these men knew very well. It was a cautionary tale to them – break down once, and your honour is lost for ever. That's why so many of them died in the trenches, going to certain death to make sure that they didn't look like a shirker.'

Jim shook his head. 'World War One killed that story for good.'

'I know what you mean by that,' Elspeth said. 'But I'm not so sure it did.'

Ta Shu spoke again. 'All stories are still alive,' he said. 'All stories have colours in them.' He looked around at them, an older man from a different culture, weathered and strange, incongruous in his red parka. 'This present moment – this is clear.' Although actually the light in the tent was its usual virulent blue; but they took his point. 'The past – all stories. Nothing but stories. All coloured. So we choose our colours. We choose what colours we see.'

Soon after that the big loads of food in them and the exhaustion of the day's climb hit both at once, and they groaned through the icy brilliant air to their tents, to fall in their bags and sleep deeply, no matter the incandescent brightness lasting through the night. And the next morning they got up and ate breakfast in silence, contemplating no doubt the day ahead of them. They broke camp and got it stuffed into its bags and into the sledge, and then they were off again. Val hauled the sledge by herself, starting slow so that people could get warmed up gradually. The hard field of firn covering the head of the Sargent Glacier was pretty easy going.

Then they had to climb into the saddle between Bell Peak and the high ridge of the Herbert Range to their right, and this proved to be a mean little wall; it took three hours of hard hauling to get the sledge up it.

Finally they made it, however, and Val took the sledge and pulled it across the saddle until she reached the far side, where they had a full view of the Axel Heiberg. It would make a dramatic lunch spot.

She pulled up the final slope to a little snow-covered knob she had camped on during a previous expedition, and gestured to the others as they straggled up after her, waving at the view ahead. 'Lunch time!' she cried.

While she waited for them she goggled at the view. A good two thousand feet below them, down the steep snow-blanketed slope of the glacier's sidewall, lay the great ice river itself, the Axel Heiberg, pouring down from the polar cap in truly frightening icefalls, like an immense waterfall that had frozen to stillness and broken to shards. Then below them it flattened out and curved around the shoulder they stood on. It was easy to see that they could have taken the flat, broad, curving road of the lower Heiberg glacier in from where it poured onto the Ross Sea, and avoided every difficulty they had overcome in the previous two days, also the tricky work of successfully descending the slope leading back down to the glacier.

What also became suddenly clear to the understanding was just how huge and strange the Transantarctic Mountains were. This stupendous ice stream had torn a trench in the range so clean in its lines that it was hard to grasp how big it was; but it was almost as deep as the Grand Canyon, and considerably wider, and when one's sense of scale came into focus, so to speak, it was hard not to feel a bit frightened, like a speck on the side of the abyss. It was clear also from this vantage point that the mountain range was a dam holding back the polar ice, the ice pouring down these giant spillways ten thousand feet to the sea. There was nothing like it anywhere else in the world, and standing there it was easy to feel the truth of that.

Ta Shu, the first one to join Val on the knob, needed no time to make his *feng shui* analysis. 'This a very big place,' he declared, puffing and grinning at Val.

Jorge and Elspeth arrived and just stared at the scene, looking appalled. Jim arrived and was stunned. Jack arrived and said 'God damn!' and hooted a few times. 'Wow! Will you look at that!'

'God damn is right,' Jim said, checking out the precipitous slope they now had to descend. 'Why didn't Amundsen just follow the dogs!'

CHAPTER SEVEN

Down the Rabbit Hole

blue sky
white snow

The South Pole was cold. At first when Wade climbed out of the Herc and saw the white glare and the dark-blue sky, it was familiar enough to make him think it was going to be like McMurdo or the Dry Valleys. Then the cold shot up his nostrils into his head and his snot froze, with a tickling sensation that was only a little painful. After that there were icicles inside his nose. This seemed to stabilize the nasal situation, and after that his nose stayed relatively warm – warm, with icicles inside it! – and the sensation of cold shifted elsewhere, to the various joints in his clothing: between boots and trousers, and at his wrists, neck and eyes. Cold!

By this time he had rounded the nose of the Herc, and was walking across the smashed snow of the runway. He passed a little glass-walled booth topped by a big sign: 'South Pole Pax Terminal.'

Beyond it stood the new Pole Station, gleaming in the sun like a blue spaceliner stranded on the snow. Actually like three spaceliners, all standing on thick blue pylons, and linked by blue passage tubes. At the end of the leftmost module a cylindrical blue control tower stood overlooking the scene. Farther across the glittering white plain, past heaped mounds of snow and a line of yellow bulldozers, he could see just the tops of a little sunken village of antique Jamesways. Farther still, a pale-blue geodesic dome stuck out of snow that appeared to be in the process of burying it entirely; the old station, apparently.

A man approached Wade and introduced himself: Keri Hull, NSF rep for the Pole. He led Wade to the spaceliner and up metal grid stairs like those Wade had seen in ski resorts. From here the new station looked like a segmented flying wing, aerodynamic in the polar winds. They went through the usual meat-locker doors, inset into the curved blue wall.

Keri led Wade down a hall to a bright warm galley. They sat down at a long table with a few other people; one of them got him a mug of hot chocolate, and he held the mug in both hands gratefully. The inside of his nose began to defrost. The room was full of people eating and talking. It was steamy.

'First a few words about the station,' Keri said. 'We're supposed to do this for everyone. We're at nine thousand three hundred feet here, and because of the Earth's spin the atmosphere is thinner at the poles than at the equator, so our nine three is the equivalent of about ten thousand five hundred feet at the equator. It's a hard ten thousand, too, because of the cold and the dryness. So stay hydrated and don't run around too much in the first days of your stay. And if you have a persistent headache or loss of appetite, see the station doctor and she'll fix you up. Officially we recommend avoiding caffeine and alcohol, but, you know – moderation in all things.' He grinned and sipped from a giant coffee mug with his name painted on it. 'Just pay attention to your body signals and behave accordingly. Okay? Good. Now – how can we help you down here at ninety degrees south, Mr Norton?'

'I'd like to have a look at the whole station, with the idea of going through the various, um, incidents that have been reported, kind of step by step.'

Keri frowned. 'You mean going into the old station?'

'Yes?'

'Oh. That's against regulations, I'm afraid.'

'Of course. But it seems that it will be necessary, given that some of the, the removals, have been happening there.'

Keri raised his eyebrows. 'Necessary?'

'I'm down here to investigate the incidents,' Wade said firmly.

The other man's look made it clear he thought this was a waste of time. 'It's potentially dangerous,' he warned. 'The snow accumulation is crushing down the dome.'

'But the archway next to the dome is still in use, as I understand it?'

'Yes.'

'So the approach is safe.'

'Yes, but–'

'So we could go down the archway, and just have a quick pop in to see under the old dome, and hope that it won't collapse at that very moment.'

Keri didn't appreciate that way of putting it. 'You've talked to Sylvia about this?'

Wade nodded.

'All right. We'll take you in tomorrow, okay? We'll have to get some gear and people together to do it safely.'

'Fine.'

So he had a day to kill. Keri appeared to have finished with his orientation, and for some reason seemed miffed at him. A young woman named Lydia took him down the hall and showed him what would be his room – like a nice hotel room, greatly miniaturized – and gave him his room key. He was free to do what he wanted.

But it quickly became clear that the South Pole was not a place where there was much to do. He went back outside to snap some photos of the station. There were not many places he was allowed to walk, as the snowy plain surrounding the station to all horizons was forbidden ground in three of four quadrants: the dark sector for astronomy, the quiet sector for seismography, and the clean sector for incoming air from the prevailing wind, which almost always came from that particular north. He was left with the area between the station and the runway, where a short barber pole with a mirror ball on its top stood inside a curve of flags. This was the ceremonial South Pole, there for photo purposes. He walked over to the mirror ball and looked at the bulbous reflection of his hooded face. In the tiny reflected image of his mirrored sunglasses he could make out two little mirror ball-topped poles, marked by even tinier reflections of himself. An infinite regress of person and place. He tried to take a photo, but nothing happened; it seemed his camera battery had frozen.

Well. This was not the actual geographical Pole anyway, which was located somewhere inside the forbidden old station, Keri had said; it would be moving through the station for another couple of years, until the station had been carried over it by the ice cap as it made its slow flow north to the sea.

There seemed little else to do outdoors but freeze. Wade gave Phil Chase a call on the wrist, and was a bit surprised when he answered. 'Phil, it's Wade! I'm at the South Pole!'

'That's good, Wade. Is it cold? Is it bright?'

'It's cold. It's bright.'

'That's good. Here it's warm, and dark. I'm asleep, Wade. Call me back when it's daytime there. I want to hear more about it.'

So much for outdoors. Wade retreated inside, grateful for the space-liner's sudden warmth. He looked out of a tinted window at the view: a snowy plain in all directions, to a horizon which was about six miles away, Keri had said; Wade found it hard to tell. The surface snow was marked by sastrugi; these were hundreds of small waves, and they and the chiselled, sandlike snow that lay between them must make skiing hard work indeed. He tried to imagine what it would be like to ski across such a plain plane of a plain, day after day for hundreds of miles, a whole continent, like walking from New York to LA, all the while pulling a heavy sledge, and often against the grain of the sastrugi, no doubt. And yet there were people out there doing it at that very minute, the Herc pilot had said, crossing the continent for fun, some of them following the SPOT route from the Pole to McMurdo. It must have been a disheartening sight to see a train of giant yellow tractors clumping past them on autopilot. But presumably their motivations had nothing to do with practicality.

It was not for him. And as he walked down the hall to his cubicle, to rest from his half-hour trip outside, he thought, what if there was no indoors? What if one had to stay out in this cold all the time, day and night, fresh in the morning or sweat-soaked (if one could sweat) in the afternoon? He didn't think he'd last more than a few hours.

Although indoors required a different sort of fortitude. How long could one stand to stay locked up in a motel? Wade did not think of himself as an outdoor person, but he did like to be able to go places. Here there was no there there, and scarcely a here here. He went to the galley and had a leisurely lunch, and watched the inhabitants of the station come in and go through the food line, and sit down and eat in small groups, talking busily, not paying too much attention to the other people in the room. When he had finished he cleared his plate and went down the main hall of the southernmost module to the library; then the games room; then the gym; then the coms rooms: first the official use room, filled with big radios and other machinery, then the personal use room, filled with computers and video screens. Most of the terminals in the room were occupied, by off-duty personnel making contact with the world.

The second module of the station was mostly private quarters and bathrooms, with some lounges, mostly empty. Every hall window had the same view, of course. And the third module was locked. Wade retreated to the first module to ask about that, and Keri looked up from his computer screen (distracted) and said, 'Oh, it's empty, didn't you know?' In the fluctuating vagaries of Congressional funding, he went on, keeping his face carefully blank, the money to complete all of the station had been cut, and NSF had decided to use what they had to build the outer shell of the third module, leaving the completion of the insides to some flusher or more southerly-thinking Congress. The Japanese were willing to contribute the money to complete it if part of it were turned into a small hotel, but so far NSF was resisting the temptation.

'Interesting,' Wade said. 'I'd like to see that too.'

Keri held his eyebrows in position, and merely rooted in a drawer and handed Wade a large key. 'Be sure to lock it when you leave,' he said, and went back to his screen.

Wade looked at him curiously, then shrugged and went back down the halls to the closed door of the third module. The door was heavy. Inside, he saw the empty shell of a building; vertical struts were all that broke the expanse of a room which looked both larger and smaller than he would have expected. The view out of the windows was the same as everywhere else.

He went back to the first module and returned the key, then sat down in the library, which had two walls covered with books, most looking very well-read indeed. A captive audience. It was all very interesting; but not. Only the idea that all these rooms were at the South Pole made them other than a weird cross of military base, airport lounge, lab lounge, and motel. It was, to his surprise, extremely boring; boring in a way that contrasted very strongly to his experience in Antarctica so far.

So the next morning, when Wade put on his heavy clothing and clumped down the hall after Keri and another man named George, he was greatly relieved, so anxious was he to do something. He followed the other men watchfully.

Outside on the landing the cold gave him its pop on the nose. They descended to the snow and walked past the little sunken village of Jame. ways, and a small blue dorm on stilts that looked like a model for the big station, and then down a long slope in the snow, like one half of a funnel placed on its side. Tracks in the dry snow made it clear that the depression had been cut by bulldozers. At the thin end of the funnel was a dark corrugated-metal arch, the opening of a tunnel that was about ten metres below the surface of the plain.

This was the archway, essentially a long, metal-covered tunnel. When erected, it had stood on the surface of the snow in front of the dome, which had been much taller then. As they walked inside, Keri explained that this station had been built in the early 1970s, and had been sinking under the accumulated snow ever since. The tall inner curve of the archway above them was completely covered by a fuzz of hoarfrost, the ice crystals large and flaky and arranged in big chrysanthemum shapes, all mashed together. To their right as they walked the tunnel was jammed with one big box after another, like meatlockers again, or containers from a container ship. The passageway was squeezed against the white wall to the left. They walked on hard-packed snow. It got darker fast. They passed a short pole with a knob on top, stuck in the floor; this was the current geographical South Pole, the thing itself, such as it was.

They came to a crossroads of tunnels. To the left a short tunnel led to two large doors that met imperfectly, revealing snow behind. 'The old entrance to the station,' George said. To the right an ice-bearded low tunnel led in to the darkness under the old dome.

They followed their flashlight beams down the tunnel into the centre of this chamber. At the high point of the dome a round circle of open air let in some light. The underside of the dome was coated with a fur of ice crystals so thick that the hexagonal strut system of the old fullerdome was only suggested, as if it were a feature of the crystallization process. The effect for Wade was of some kind of immense igloo cathedral, the filtered light pouring down onto three or four large red-walled boxes, buildings that looked like two-storey mobile homes, with exterior metal staircases like the new station's, and metal landings outside their second-storey entrances.

Keri and George led Wade through each of these buildings in turn. They were all much the same; narrow halls connecting tiny rooms, all packed with boxes, or empty chairs, or filing cabinets. One upstairs room had a pool table in it. 'Come on to the galley,' Keri said as Wade stared at this lugubrious sight. 'That was the real place to hang out.'

They went out onto a metal landing and downstairs, then across to another refrigerator door, and in through a coat room to the darkened galley. In the flashlight beams long shadows barred the walls. The narrow room looked much too small to feed a whole station. One side was open to the old kitchen, where stoves and ovens and refrigerators were still there. Only a few holes in the cabinetry marked where scavenged items had been taken away, to the new station or elsewhere.

'They just left all this?' Wade asked.

'As you see. By the time they built the new station, this was all old stuff, breaking down. Or it wouldn't fit, or wouldn't match the energy requirements. It was too much trouble to integrate it. And too expensive to haul away. Actually they were going to dismantle this whole station and dome, but it was too expensive. So here it is. Someday we'll break it all down and SPOT it to Mac Town and they can use it there, or put it in the dump ship and landfill it.'

'Or put it in a museum,' George said.

'But meanwhile,' Wade said, 'someone else appears to be taking things.'

The two men were silent.

'Right?'

'Well,' Keri said. 'We don't know what's happening. Some items have disappeared from here, it's true. But it may be a kind of, I don't know, a kind of game being played.'

'A prank, you mean?' Wade asked.

'Something like that. We're not sure. But it doesn't make sense any other way. The stuff being taken is not that useful. Old refrigerators. Stoves. Boxes of files.'

'Hmm,' Wade said.

'It just doesn't make sense. Unless it's a game.'

'Would people play games like that?'

'Well . . .'

'Most of this stuff happened during winterover,' George explained.

Keri nodded. 'During the winters there are only seventy people here. They're all evaluated by ASL and NSF ahead of time, of course, and they spend two weeks together to see how they'll do. But naturally there are some times when people get down here who are not exactly, ah, normal. Or maybe they start normal, but during the winters here they, uh . . .'

Wade nodded. Next to a restroom door was a shelf of condiments, still filled with boxes and bottles of sugar, salt and pepper, creamer, hot chocolate powder, tea bags, mustard. Heinz ketchup. A strawberry syrup bottle with a round *Haz-Mat* sticker on it. All the contents frozen for sure, as it was bitterly cold.

'I was at the last Thanksgiving dinner they had in this galley,' George said, 'and it was about a twelve-course meal, the complete Thanksgiving feast, with all the trimmings. We smoked the turkey in an old fifty-five gallon steel drum, right outside that door. Best Thanksgiving I ever had.'

On this nostalgic note they left the dark freezer of a building, and tramped over ice flowers back out to the archway and the blaze of light at its end. As they walked toward this light at the end of the tunnel it grew brighter and brighter.

After all the black little rooms, the infinite white plain of the polar cap was too bright to see properly – shockingly sunny, windy, vast, all under a low blue sky. Like a geometrical plane. Like the frozen bottom of a world. It was hard to reconcile the two places, in and out. 'They built themselves a cave,' Wade said. To comfort themselves on Ice Planet.

'More an igloo,' George said. 'It was brighter then.'

Still – something to hunker down into, to make the place habitable. Now replaced by the long, blue, metallic flying wing of the current station, like any postmodern hotel anywhere. We are here!

And that was that. The old station, the empty spaces in it where some unremarkable things had disappeared. Nothing more to see. Obviously Keri and George and the others here did not think there was any purpose to his visit. Professional investigators from the NSF and the National Transport Safety Board and the FBI had already been down to investigate the hijacked SPOT vehicle. It stood to reason a Senate aide couldn't do anything they hadn't already. So Keri's looks said, and George's too, to an extent; and Wade did not know exactly how he would argue the point, if he had cared to. Phil Chase had sent him, and that was reason enough; and more power, perhaps, than these men suspected. But he had to do more than be Phil's roving eyes if he wanted to exert the power.

But what? This damned place was balking him; it was a kind of no-place, a blank on the map. No reason to be here except for the abstract fact of the spin axis of the planet, which was a pretty strange reason once one thought about it. Ridiculous in fact. He glanced out of a window at the ubiquitous view. It was like a minimum security prison for affluent white-collar criminals, or a spaceship for real. But even if it had been on a trip to a paradise planet Wade would have had to refuse the trip, to avoid dying of boredom en route. There was no interest to it at all, except perhaps for the human factor.

But the scientists rushed by, obviously very busy, and, from what Keri had said, involved in subjects too esoteric to explain to mere mortals. And the support crew were working, or sitting in the galley in small groups, talking among themselves. Insular.

Wade went to the coms room. Two young women were looking at screens; one looked up at him. 'Keri said I could get an e-mail line?' Wade asked.

'You sure can,' one said, standing up. Strong southern accent, short, quick in her movements. 'I'm Andrea,' she said. 'How long are you gonna be here?'

'I'm not sure.'

'You're on a DV tour?'

'Kind of,' Wade said. 'I'm down from Washington.'

'That makes it a DV tour.'

Wade nodded, and as she led him down the hall to a terminal in the personal coms room, he told her a bit about his visit.

'Oh, the old dome, yeah. Good idea.' Meaning not a good idea; meaning there were better ideas. 'Did they show you the utilidor?'

'No.'

She shook her head. She looked at him curiously; she wanted to help him, he thought. Either just to show him their place, or something more, he couldn't tell. She had been noticeably blank-faced about Keri. 'We'll have to show you the utilidor, at least.'

Then the door to the coms room burst open and the other woman said, 'Viktor's here, Viktor's here,' pronouncing the name in a way that somehow made the spelling clear.

'Who's Viktor?' Wade asked.

'Oh, he's our Russian friend,' Andrea said. 'He lives out here and comes by occasionally, he's great.'

'He lives out here?'

'Yeah, come on,' and as she headed down to the rec room Wade followed. She explained over her shoulder: 'He skis around the polar cap between Vostok and Dome C and the Point of Inaccessibility, and here and the oil stations. Wherever. He's got his sledge filled with everything he needs and just skis around, or puts up his sail and sails.'

'Where does he resupply?' Wade asked, thinking of the disappearances.

'Well, there are ways. You know Vostok is closed now, but they left everything behind, and so he drops in occasionally and takes things.'

'Ah ha! I'd like to meet this Viktor.'

'Yes you would.' She leaned her head into the rec room and shouted, 'Viktor is here!' and there was a cheer from inside. 'Come on, he'll be down at Spiff's place.'

She led him to the outer door of the first module, and Wade followed her outside with his parka barely zippered and his hood still on his back; the cold's snap to his head almost knocked him down the stairs. Andrea was running ahead of him toward the quiet zone, and Wade saw she wasn't wearing a parka at all, but was in the same light clothes she wore in the office. 'Aren't you cold?' he cried out as he followed her.

'Why?'

She led him to a pick-up truck, unplugged it from its battery warmer and drove him across the runway to the Dark Sector, where little rectangular buildings stood on stilts in the midst of a network of poles and lines. They went up stairs and into one of these buildings, Andrea shouting, 'Is he here yet?'

'I am here!' boomed a voice from inside the room.

'Viktor!'

In the room, walled everywhere with big machines, a group of people stood around a tall, bulky man, dressed in blue photovoltaic clothing the same colour as the new station's exterior. Several conversations were going on at once, but most were listening to Viktor give his news:

'Yes, I have big new project going! Hello Andrea! Hello! And here is the senator we have visiting, I see! Hello Wade! Yes, a new project with the Sahara mitigation people. You know they have a very great problem with spread of the Sahara, and I have designed a plan to help, and have just gotten a grant to start. You know,' he said to Wade, 'how there is Lake Vostok underneath Vostok Station – a freshwater lake at the bottom of the ice with as much water in it as your Lake Ontario.'

Wade said, 'No, I didn't know that.'

'Yes, it is one of the biggest bodies of fresh water in the world. And under four kilometres of ice, so the water down there is under most enormous pressure. Drilling through the ice cap is of course no problem these days, and now the materials scientists at Chevron are making flexible pipelines, a kevlar and soy plastic mesh, very strong, very light, and very cheap! And so we are going to drill down to Lake Vostok, and pipe the water in a direct pipeline to Sub-Sahara desert border!'

'No!' several exclaimed. 'You're kidding!'

'Impossible!' one of them declared, with a grin that said he was only egging Viktor on.

'No, Spiff! Is possible! Is quite possible! The height of the ice cap and its pressure on the water will be such to drive it all the way to the equator. Just a few pumps near the end to keep the flow going. The pipe will sink to a few hundred feet under the sea, and come up in Gabon. After that, fresh water for free! The Saharan mitigation group is very excited.'

'Then when the lake is drained the weight of the ice will melt more water,' Spiff suggested, again egging him on.

'No, no. Is not possible, I'm afraid. Not possible. But it will take years to spread Lake Vostok over the Sahara, years.'

Spiff extricated little tumblers from a cabinet of scientific equipment. Viktor pulled a large glass bottle of vodka from his rucksack and poured shots all around. Everyone gulped down a toast, except for Wade, who sipped his. Viktor explained the details of his new project to Spiff, who was saying things that would force Viktor to say either 'Is possible' or 'Is not possible'. Wade had heard other people around the station using these two phrases earlier, and now he heard someone else insisting to a man sitting on the desk, 'Is possible, is very possible'.

Viktor came over to Wade. 'So you work for Senator Chase. That is good, I admire him very much. The nomads will inherit the Earth, this is what I say.'

Wade nodded. 'Sometimes it seems so.'

'What is it like to work for him? Do you ever see him?'

'I very rarely see him,' Wade admitted. 'Perhaps twice a year.'

'Twice a year! Very good! This is like an equinox.'

'More like the solstices,' Wade said, which caused Viktor to grin and nod very rapidly. No doubt he was more aware of the difference between solstice and equinox than anybody on the planet.

Spiff came over and joined them, and Viktor gave him a hug with one arm. 'My crazy astronomer friend. You are jealous because finally there is a project on the ice crazier than yours!'

'I think I still win,' Spiff said, smiling.

Viktor laughed: 'Indeed so.' He looked at Wade: 'Do you know Spiff's work?'

'No.'

'He is the greatest astronomer in the world.'

Spiff rolled his eyes.

'Is not possible,' someone else around them said.

'Exactly,' Spiff said.

'From here Spiff studies the *northern sky*,' Viktor told Wade. 'He is part of famous AMANDA Project. They use the whole body of Earth to catch neutrinos. The neutrinos that fly through Earth from the north mostly miss everything completely and fly right through without obstruction, am I right, Spiff? Weakly interacting particles, like me. But sometimes they hit atoms from Earth and knock off muons, and muons fly into this ice cap from underneath and cause a particular blue light, Cherenkov light, yes? So they use the planet for their filter, and the ice cap for their lens, and they record the blue lights with strings of photomultiplier tubes extending one, two kilometres down. These tubes are like lightbulbs in reverse – they take in light and put out electricity – but what lightbulbs! They amplify incoming signals by a hundred million times – isn't that what you said, Spiff? And from that they determine how many neutrinos, and even where in the sky they came from.'

'You're kidding,' Wade said. 'Impossible.'

'No, no! Is possible, is quite possible!'

Spiff was laughing at Wade. 'Andrea,' he said across the heads in the room, 'isn't the dance starting soon?'

'Yeah!'

'You know me,' Viktor said to Spiff, 'I always arrive in time to take a shower.'

'Oh yeah, of course. Here, here's my key. I'll see you at the dance.'

Viktor took the key and left. The party in Spiff's office went on without him; people were getting ready for the dance, Spiff explained to Wade.

'The dance?' Wade asked.

'Hadn't you heard?' He shook his head. 'Keri probably didn't think to tell you. It's October twelfth, you know.'

'A Columbus Day dance?'

'No, no, this is the day Lake Bonney camp was first established.' He cracked up at the look on Wade's face. 'Not really. The Polecats, the band here, just want to try to convince NSF to make ASL send them to Icestock, and so they're putting on a dance every Saturday night for a while. This one's a special one because Viktor's here.'

He asked what Wade was doing at the Pole, and Wade tried to explain. Spiff nodded and took him to his desk for a vodka refill. 'They took you into the old Pole station, did they?'

'That's right. Very interesting place.'

'Uh huh. Did they take you into the utilidor?'

'No, what's that?'

Spiff nodded. 'Did they tell you about how the Rodwell works?'

'No.'

'Lake Patterson?'

'No.'

'The buried Herc?'

'Buried Herc?'

'They didn't take you anyplace else, did they?'

'No.'

'Is not possible.' Spiff shook his head, thinking it over. 'They're afraid of fingies like you. They're paranoid after all these years.'

'Fingies?'

'Fucking new guys. Tell you what, talk to Andrea after the dance, and we'll see what we can do. The truth is, the people down here are going to need some help pretty soon. Someone who isn't in NSF or ASL who might take their side. Talk to Andrea.'

'Okay. I will.'

'We'll go over in a second, let me close down here.'

While he was working at a boxy, unidentifiable machine that filled half the room, Wade read a small flow-chart diagram that had been taped to the wall.

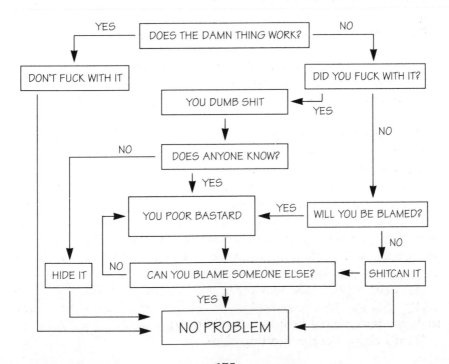

175

'It's like a map of Washington DC,' Wade observed.

'What – oh, that? It's a map of the world, man. Here I'm done, come on, the band is supposed to start now, and even with the Antarctic factor thrown in they might be starting soon.'

'The Antarctic factor?'

'Murphy's law to the power of ten. Things fall apart. The centre cannot hold. Nor the spin axis. Come on.'

Out they went, down the stairs in the blaze of day. The pick-up truck was gone, however, and Spiff led Wade back over chewed snow toward the station; it looked close, but ten minutes later it was as far away as it had been when they had started, and they were walking fast. 'How far is it?' Wade puffed.

'Two k. It's good for you.' Spiff upped the pace.

'How'd you get the name Spiff?' Hoping to slow him down.

'Well, the original name was Spliff, but I was going through New Zealand so often I had to change it.' He grinned over his shoulder at Wade.

'The dogs, you mean?'

'Yeah. Insane. It's an alcoholic nation, basically, so they do the dog thing to convince themselves that they're really all right. But it can be damned inconvenient. Once I flew down straight after a going-away party without changing my clothes, and the dogs in Auckland went off like a smoke alarm.'

'Scary.'

'Oh yeah. It took hours to get through customs after that, I missed my flight to Christchurch and everything. And I was sweating it anyway, because I had three big spliffs inside sealed pipettes floating in the shampoo in my shampoo bottles, and I couldn't be sure the damned dogs wouldn't smell them even so. They're *very* good. It would have ruined my thesis. After that I gave it up. Too stressful. Now I just knock back two shots of Scotch and try to imagine it's a decent buzz. So much noise to signal though. Terrible drug, alcohol. So now I'm Spiff.'

'I see. Was it you thought up this AMANDA experiment?'

'Oh no, no. It's an old idea. Pretty neat, but I'd rather be doing the cosmic background stuff. Phase change vortices in the first second of the universe. That's what we are, man. Flaws in the fabric. Eddies in the whirlpool. Pattern dustdevils.'

'Hey, aren't we here?'

Spiff was walking past the big blue station.

'No, the dance is in the old summer camp. They tried doing it in the empty module, you know, and it's a good space, but the windows meant you could never really get away, if you know what I mean. It's

176

a lot more fun out here.' He led Wade through rows of low mounds, the tops of buried Jamesways, and then down a slope cut by bulldozers into an area like a sunken plaza, where a dozen Jamesways and some blockhouses were still sitting on top of the ice. 'This is the old summer camp, where they kept the summer overflow crowd before the new station was built.'

'They meant to pull it out but never got around to it.'

'Right. Besides, there's always a use here for sheltered space. Nothing ever gets pulled out, you'll see. It's like hermit crabs moving from one shell to the next.'

The Jamesways they passed had names over their doors: Larry, Curly, Moe, Shemp. 'Just say Moe!' Spiff exclaimed, heading for a somewhat larger Jamesway. 'Sounds like they've started. Yow!'

He stopped outside the door of a longer Jamesway, pulled a flask from his parka, unscrewed the top and handed it to Wade. Wade took a swallow of cold, fiery whisky and gave it back to Spiff, who did the same. Then Spiff opened the door – a simple metal handle, Wade noted, on an ordinary wooden door – and walked into loud darkness.

Wade followed him in, through a second door. Inside it was dark and hot. The whole Jamesway was a single long space – half a cylinder, just like a Quonset hut. A band at the far end was playing loud rock and roll. Red stage lights and some strings of ancient Christmas tree lights were the only illumination. A cloth sign spread behind the band said 'The Polecats'.

Wade took off his parka and hung it on a rack crowded with them, watching the band as he did. The lead guitarist was good, that was instantly obvious; the rest of the band was like that in any other garage band, or worse. One of the astronomers Wade had seen in the Dark Sector was being urged onto stage to play sax. He had sheet music in hand, and the bass player clipped it to a mike stand, and then as they began to play, paused to stick the mike right down into the sax bell, after which Wade could just hear a few strangled honks cutting across the grain of 'Louie Louie'. Wade himself could have done better; anyone in the room could have done better. The astronomer's eyes bugged out as he tried to read his music.

But the bass player, after replacing the mike on the stand, was solid; the drummer was solid; the rhythm guitarist was inaudible; and the lead guitarist was great. He was a balding man wearing wire-rims which windowed an intense, abstracted expression. Wade waded into the thick press of dancers to see the man's hands better, then jounced up and down with everyone else, and found that near the front it cleared out a bit for some real dancing. Here the women of the station were performing a very complicated dance indeed, like that of high

schoolers or bees, the social tangle of their minority numbers prob-
lematizing matters pretty severely, so that they were dancing with
each other a lot, and also with any number of the men around them,
but seldom with any one man, except for Viktor. Everyone knew everyone, Wade saw; and even in pantomime he could see example after
example of rude or bumptious invitations to dance, the shy awkward
men trying to get one of their female friends from daily life to turn
into something else, for one dance or even part of one. It probably did
not help the awkward interactions going on all over the floor when
Spiff and Andrea broke into some very blatant dirty dancing, and both
very good at it, having a lot of fun, Spiff making exaggerated pelvic
thrusts and holds, Andrea straddling his outstretched thigh and wig-
gling over it, all without touch or eye contact, all in time to the music,
in their own private world but very public too, of course, and peculiar
when the music was 'Summertime Blues', but perfect for 'Wild Thing'.

Wade got into the rhythm at the edge of the crowd, enjoying the
lead guitarist's work, which kept getting better and better as the band
warmed, playing solo after solo that stung, ripped, howled, soared. The
crowd became one big group creature as it followed him outward,
singing all the lyrics for the hapless singer/rhythm guitarist, whose
guitar was completely inaudible in every song no matter how fast he
strummed; he might as well have been unplugged, and possibly was.
So it was lead guitar, bass and drums, and the bassist and drummer
were rising to the task of laying a groundwork for their leader on his
explorations.

Spiff drifted over at one point to shout in Wade's ear: '–used to play
in five bands at once! Club bands – never recorded – every night of
the week – New Hampshire, Vermont!' He gestured at the guitarist,
shaking his head in awe. 'Not possible!'

Wade nodded to show he had heard. He took another couple of
swallows from Spiff's flask. They danced and danced. Someone turned
on black lights, and even a strobe, apparently damaged, so that it
changed frequency rapidly. Whenever the mass of dancing bodies
overheated the room someone would open the door at the back and in
about twenty seconds the room would chill so far that all the sweaty
moisture in the air fell to the floor and lay there, a white dust that
never melted. At floor level it was always below freezing, Wade realized
as he watched the swirls underfoot. '*Great* air conditioning!' he shouted
at Spiff.

Time passed in its own uneven strobe, with some long patches of
timeless dancing thrown into the mix of quick, choppy impressions.
The band finished everything in their repertoire and threatened to quit,
but the crowd wouldn't let them; Andrea and Lydia and two or three

other women knelt at the lead guitarist's feet as if begging him to continue, though it also seemed clear that if he refused they might tear him to pieces. Briefly he smiled, his only expression of the night as far as Wade saw, and looked back at the band and started up again. In the interval the bass player had taped his right fingers with duct tape, and he played on with a happy expression.

Then they started up 'Little Wing', which Wade had not heard in the first set, and after a strangled vocal from the singer, the lead guitarist hammered out the powerful succession of minor chords that Hendrix had laid down, and slowly but surely cast loose from the rest of the band, and, from the look in his eye, from the rest of the universe as well – away from the song, away from the hut, out into some private space of his own, drawing the entire Jamesway along with him, out to that distant place of pain and suffering that was the world – all those nights playing to people who did not understand he was playing about the ice, his blues and the South Pole Blues become one and the same, the blues of someone who had come back down to the ice for the *nth* time after swearing he never would again – drawn down here away from the bars and bands and women and friends, seduced away again by the ice and then stuck down here in its cold boredom. First you fall in love with Antarctica and then it wrecks your life, breaks it in half year after year, every year the same, going north and not knowing where you are or where your home is or what you're going to do next, swearing never to return and then returning anyway, over and over again, to work all day in the frigid sub-biological chill, talking a mile a minute until people actually would say *No Robbie no be quiet* don't say a *word* for at least *ten minutes*, Okay but I'm only saying one millionth of what I'm thinking and then shutting up, zooming in silence, working in solitude – until suddenly here a chance to play the guitar and speak all those thoughts, no matter that it was all in music, better that way, for this was the language that meant more than any other even though no one could quite understand it. The awestruck Wade, who had not known until now how much he had been missing music, stopped dancing just to listen to it and watch those two hands fly about speaking such beautiful, untranslatable sentences. Many other dancers had already done the same, standing stock still as if hearing the national anthem or some great hymn; they all shared this guy's situation, they all knew what he was feeling, they felt it themselves, and this 'Little Wing' was deep, better than Jimi's or Eric's or Duane's or Stevie Ray's – bigger, darker, more profound. Wade found himself next to Spiff, and tried to convey to the astronomer this perception that had struck him again so forcefully, that music was the language simultaneously the deepest and the most incomprehensible, and the

179

swaying Spiff nodded and cried back in Wade's ear, 'It means the whole project of science is *backwards*, the more you *understand* something the less it *moves* you, my goal now is to reverse that, to do anti-science, to *know less* to *understand less* and thus *feel it all more*, I want *less* understanding. Come with us after this and I'll show you what I mean.' Wade nodded, fell back into the guitarist's infinite travelling. Far away from Earth, far away from Ice Planet, out to the far reaches of their shared inescapable predicament . . .

At the end of this great solo the guitarist bowed his head, crushing the last brutal chords, shoving the guitar next to the amp for some shrieking feedback. It seemed to Wade that he had finished not only for the night, but could justifiably hang his guitar up for ever. He would never play better than that; no one could.

But then the women were on him again, like sirens or succubi, laughing as they tugged his arms and wrapped around his knees, begging him to play another one, demanding it; which, after a big sigh, and a single shake of the head at their greed and lack of understanding, he did. He played 'Gloria', singing the words himself this time, and he led the hoarse crowd through a singalong that lasted many, many, many choruses, clearly intending to bludgeon them all into insensibility so that they would let the band stop before they died. During this eternal 'Gloria' Wade was pulled by Andrea into the middle of the network of women and was passed from one sort-of partner to another for a few score choruses, soaking in what he could of these women, who were so obviously tough, strong people, wearing greasy Carhartts, sweaty and wild-eyed, a lot of them big and tall and so reminding him of Val, fluid in their stocking feet, working-class Americans with a lot of bar hours in their dance moves and their dangerous, sharklike smiles, their sidelong glinting private expressions which told Wade they were wild people who had done wild things, so wild that the South Pole was a terrible confinement to them. Watching them Wade could not stop thinking of Val, and he wished like anything she were there; he would have danced with her, not diffusely as he was with these sirens spelling G-l-o-r-i-a over and over again, but directly and, in some much less blatant way, like Spiff and Andrea had been dancing before. If only she were here!

As 'Gloria' ended the lead guitarist hurried around pulling all the plugs out of the amps. Abruptly the music halted. The grinning bassist held up his bleeding right hand, the duct tape long gone. Someone turned off the strobe and black lights, leaving them in a dim Christmas-tree glow.

Wade was surprised to see that Spiff and Andrea were still there; he had reckoned they would be hustling off to one of their rooms given the incendiary nature of their dancing, but here they were coming over to him, and Andrea took his arm. 'Come on,' she said under the noise of the applause, 'get your coat.' Struggling into his parka Wade followed them out of the door.

Brilliant sunlight exploded in his head. The cold slammed into him like a great side of frozen beef, nearly knocking him down. He was wet under his parka, and the cold hurt right to the bone. It was a relief when the others started running and he could run too, blinded by a flood of cold-induced tears. Running brought freezing sweat into contact with various parts of him as he moved.

He followed Spiff and Andrea and some others down the ramp into the archway of the old station. In the tunnel it was black as the pit, and by the time his sight returned he was past the geographical Pole's pole and being led into the centre of the domed area. Next to the box that had held the old galley there was a round railing and a round trapdoor, like the cover of a giant sewer hole. 'This is the old utilidor,' Spiff said up to Wade. 'Follow me.'

Wade climbed down a metal ladder so cold he had to yank on his mittens to get them to detach from the rungs. At the bottom of the ladder a flashlight beam revealed that ice crystal flowers had covered everything to the point that it was impossible to tell what was under them. It was like caving in a white grotto. Spiff brushed off a handful of crystals, and jammed it in his mouth after a swallow from his flask. 'Scotch snow-cone,' he mumbled. 'Real good. This is the utilidor.'

'Which is?' Wade said, watching their breath freeze and fall to the floor.

'It was the passageway they used to work on the guts of the old station. Cold down here.'

'Yes it is.'

'Sixty-six below, all the time.'

'Sixty-six below?'

'Fahrenheit. That's right. You can imagine the guys working down here on some busted plumbing or broken wiring or the like. And this was before heated gloves.' Now they were moving along at a good speed, crouched under a ceiling of ice chrysanthemums, and when Wade slowed down Andrea pinched his bottom. 'Now here's the start of the tunnel to the rest of the underground complex.'

'Complex?'

'That's right. Did they tell you about old old station?'

'No.'

'Not possible! Those guys. The old station above us here is not the oldest station. The old old station is the one they built back in the IGY, in 1956. It's about thirty metres under the surface now. The buildings are all getting squished, but there's a fair amount of space down there still, and a lot of stuff.'

They ducked through a hole at the end of the utilidor, and stepped into a tunnel walled by crystal-coated plywood, which was bowed in at the sides, and down from the ceiling, and up from the floor, and in places even shattered. 'It's okay,' Spiff said. 'It's a slow motion process. Now we don't even mess with plywood, because we can remelt the holes so easily with the new laser melters.'

'So you cut this tunnel?'

'Parts of it were cut by a number of different people. Here, look here.' He gestured in a side door at what looked like a closet, with a mattress on the floor and some boxes next to it. 'This is really old. There was a winterover when one guy started only showing up for dinners, and no one knew where he was the rest of the time. Then several seasons later the seismograph crew came through and found this place. He must have brought in a lamp, and maybe a space heater. But when they found it there was only a single page from a *Playboy*, and this stuff here.'

'Wow,' Wade said, peering into this memorial to mental illness.

'They keep it on the route to remind people to be more active in their resistance. See, NSF and ASL think they own this station, they think it's here for beakers like me, but the people who work here, they know better. They know a lot that NSF doesn't know about this place.'

They moved on in the frigid tunnel, past a side tunnel that ran, Spiff said, to a crashed Herc buried at the end of the landing strip; then down a branch tunnel that led into the quiet zone, where Spiff shouted out, 'Hey Ed, come on, we're going to go sliding!'

No response, so they went down and pounded on the door. It opened, and a pony-tailed head stuck out. 'Six of you, three in bunny boots, three in tennis shoes.'

'Right again. This is Wade. Ed can identify the number and footwear of his visitors by reading his seismographs.'

'As well as Chinese nuclear tests, oil exploration blasts anywhere in the southern hemisphere, rocket launches from Canaveral, arguments my ex gets into with her new victims, and dropped bowling balls in Iowa.'

'Sensitive instrumentation,' Wade ventured.

'You bet.'

Ed scribbled an explanation for the sudden explosion of squiggles on the paper rolls slowly emerging from his machines, and followed them down the tunnel.

Another half hour's freezing walk, and then they climbed down a ladder set in a crack, into another station. Wade looked around, amazed.

This station was crystallized entirely. The walls were buckled, the ceiling in some places only waist-high. In the flashlight gleams it looked like a museum exhibit of artefacts from the 1950s, shattered and crystallized. Thick wires looped down like strings of jewels, or the long-sunken rigging of a shipwreck. 'Don't worry, there's no power here any more.'

'So you say.'

'No electricity, then. Here, let's go to the galley. See, look in here.'

Wade noticed that no one was behind them any longer. 'Where are the others?'

'Oh, they're setting up the slide. Here, take a look.'

Wade followed the astronomer into the next broken-walled white cave. Here tables were still covered with china plates and styrofoam cups, and the walls had shelves of condiments and galley equipment – just like the old station he had already visited, in fact, except more iced-over. A pair of dirty bunny boots on a table. A big coffee pot. Heinz ketchup. Over in the corner on the floor lay a spill of rib-eye steaks, badly freezer-burned and topped by what looked like a human turd.

'This was the first permanent settlement,' Spiff said. 'They lived here about twenty years. It was mostly Jamesways buried in the snow, and some bigger plywood boxes, and the connecting archways.'

'Incredible.'

'Yeah. But listen to this: there was a lot of stuff down here just a few years ago, that isn't here any more. Most significantly, a big generator. They even considered pulling it when they built the current station and putting it back to work, because there was nothing wrong with it. But it wouldn't meet the safety codes and so on. In the end they just left it here. But two seasons ago we came down here, and it was gone.'

'Gone from down here?'

'Exactly. So how did it get out of here, you ask?'

'I do.'

'So did we. We went to every corner of this station that hadn't been crushed, to try and find out. And on the far side of the station, near where the generator was, we found a snow wall that had been repacked. We cut through it, and there was a tunnel like ours, going off in the other direction. There were wheel marks in the floor. And that tunnel went on for *ten kilometres*.'

'Not possible.'

'I agree, but there it was! And then it came up to the surface, where there was a little trapdoor covered by snow. And outside that, the polar cap. Nothing else. We were over the horizon from the station. We had gone under the snow the whole way. And no sign of where they went.'

'None?'

'No tracks of any kind!'

'How could that be?'

'I don't know. I thought maybe a helo had dropped people, but there are no helos on the polar cap. Ed thought a hovercraft might have come in, but I thought the sastrugi weren't disturbed enough.'

'Are there any hovercraft on the polar cap?'

'Yes, there's an old Hake at the oil camp on Roberts Massif.'

'So you think *they* took the generator?'

Spiff shook his head. 'It doesn't make sense. They would have the same trouble with the old dog as the people here.'

'So who?'

Spiff shrugged. 'Who knows? But we wanted you to have the full complement of mystery before you left here. I'm afraid the people who work here, the locals, the people you just saw at the dance, are going to get blamed for all this stuff. They need someone outside ASL to help. So I wanted you to know.'

'I appreciate it,' Wade said sincerely. A convulsive shiver vibrated through him, head to foot. 'I'm cold.'

'I know. Let's go take a slide down the rabbit hole, that'll warm you up.'

'A slide?'

'Yeah. Have you ever been in a waterslide?'

'Yes,' Wade said, thinking of a park in Virginia, a hotel in Vancouver. 'But–'

'I know. Come on, I'll show you.'

This walk was shorter than the others. Up and out of the eerie crushed ghost town, then along a snow tunnel, into a snow-walled chamber, bigger than anything left in the buried station. There were a lot of parkas and clothes piled inside what looked like a giant dumb-waiter, next to a round opening nowhere near as big as the tunnels they had been walking through.

'You made this too?' Wade asked.

'A group of us. The new heating elements can cut through the ice very efficiently. Did they tell you about the Rodwell?'

'No.'

'Of course not. Did you ever wonder where the station gets its water? Well, it all comes from an underground lake, a chamber down in the ice that is heated until there is a big pod of liquid water. They just keep going deeper and deeper with it as the water is used. The sewage dump is the same; it's just another underground pod of liquid, good old Lake Patterson, and when it fills they move the heating element to another spot, and the old stuff freezes and heads off in the ice cap, moving north ten metres a year.'

'Lake Patterson?'

Spiff pulled his head out of the hole. 'Named after Patterson. Okay, it's ready. Take off your clothes and down you go.' Spiff was already unzipping.

'You're kidding.'

'No. The tube is ice, but we're running some hot water down it now, hear that? And the air is warmed too, it's almost up to freezing. So it's like any other waterslide, only darker. The ride only lasts a couple of minutes. It goes down about say five storeys in about three hundred metres, and then you land in a warm bath. Be ready for that, it's a shock when you hit if you're not forewarned.' He pulled off his trousers, stood before Wade naked. 'Hurry up, you go first and I'll shut down here and follow. Hurry, I'm getting cold.'

'I'm already cold,' Wade protested. In fact he had never been colder in his life. But he did as he was told. By the time he had all his clothes off he was shivering violently.

'Okay, jump in and go for it. You can go head first or feet first, but you shouldn't try changing from one to the other midway, or knee-riding. Not the first time anyway.'

'I won't. Will it be dark all the way?' Wade said, peering down the hole.

'Black as the pit. Have a good ride.'

Wade took a step up and sat his bare bottom on the ice. 'Jesus.'

'Have fun!' Spiff shouted, and gave him a push and he was off, sliding on his bottom. Then the tube dropped away in the blackness and he was on his back, like a luge rider. In fact it had all the qualities of luge – insane speed, rapid turns left and right, up and down, but mostly down, down down down in gut-floating no-g drops, sliding in a stream of warm water over cold, slick ice, and all in pitch-blackness so there was no way of telling where he would go next. He yowled. The cold of the ice seemed less severe as he sped up, but the air rushing over him was freezing. He shouted again at a heartstopping drop and right turn, you could crack your skull! Except he didn't.

Three or four more dramatic turns and he began to enjoy himself. Then he was flying through free space, and he shrieked just as he plunged into boiling water. His skin went nova, especially along his bottom and back.

He shot up spluttering and took several gasping breaths, shouting once or twice between them, treading water desperately. It was pitch-black; he could see nothing.

'Must be the senator.'

'Just stand up, man.'

'Jesus!' he said, finding his feet. 'Hi!' He found he could stand, on an ice floor. The pool of hot water was chest deep. The air was steam. In the blackness he could hear several people talking, including Viktor. His skin was still blazing, but less painfully. 'You guys are nuts.'

They laughed happily. No one contradicted him.

With a shout Spiff fired into the pool and rammed Wade, sending him under again. He was pulled to the surface and set on his feet. The person who had pulled him up was a woman. One of the big women from the dance. There were several of them in the pool, in the blackness and clatter of watery noise and voices, everyone moving about. 'Ice is such a great insulator.' As his eyes adjusted Wade saw that the chamber was not pitch-black, but black with just a touch of blue in it. He still could see nothing whatsoever, not even the basic shapes of the people around him. Under the general clatter he did hear lower voices, and right next to him a quick urgent low exchange: 'Ah come on.' 'Don't or I'll break it off.' 'All right! Okay.' Wild laughter.

Wade sloshed around gingerly, wishing Val were in the pool with the rest of these unseen Amazons. If you had a thing for jock women, he thought, the South Pole was definitely the place to be. The ice on the bottom of the pool was covered in some places with what felt like big rubber shower-mats. Against the unseen walls there was a narrow bench, similarly matted. After a while Wade was thoroughly warmed up and his skin stopped burning. He began to see black shapes in the indigo blackness of the cave. He ran into Spiff, who told him more about the waterslide, with Andrea or someone else her size limpeted to his side, or so it seemed to Wade; it was too dark really to tell. Several years ago, Spiff told him over the noise, Viktor had come by and described a waterslide complex cut under Vostok Station. The local PICO crew, meaning the Polar Ice Coring Office, had included some folks very prominent in the Why Be Normal Club, and they were just beginning to use the new ice-cutting technology, which used hot laser melting elements and steam removal, 'real Stars Wars stuff, I mean it was developed by the space beam people at Livermore and Los Alamos, and turned out to be good for nothing at all except it turns ice to steam no problem, which is very useful down here of course – the old ice-coring tech used three thousand gallons of diesel for every kilometre cut through the ice, at ten dollars a gallon, and slow. Basically like melting it with your shower head. But with these lasers you could cut a whole city into the ice, man, and so these PICO freakos helped some winterovers cut this slide here, just to pass the time and keep up with those Vostok Ruskies. Although later Viktor confessed that he had made that whole thing up, and Vostok had no such thing. He just thought it would be a good idea.'

Wade heard Viktor's booming laugh across the chamber. 'A good idea!'

'A great idea,' Spiff said. 'People here need to resist. It's been hard here for a long time. I mean ASA wasn't bad, and yet even then people snuck down and explored old old station, stuff like that. And now, no one likes ASL at all. They treat people like shit, and NSF lets them get away with it. So people resist. It's a way of staying sane. You can only spend a few weeks here before you begin to go nuts.'

'It was only a few hours for me,' Wade confessed.

They laughed, and someone kissed his cheek; although it was someone with a beard. Viktor no doubt. 'Sounds like Viktor is having quite an impact on polar cap society,' Wade said.

Spiff laughed. 'Yes, yes. But it's mostly talk,' he said louder.

A volley of splashes struck them.

'It is! You say so yourself, Viktor. The great idea man. Is very possible! He comes up with a lot of ideas, but he's undercapitalized. This water pipe to the Sahara–'

More splashes.

'It's not happening?'

'Well, I'm sure it's technically feasible, but that doesn't mean it will ever get done. Hey, stop that! And if it does, it probably won't be by Viktor.'

'I have grant in hand. Is very possible.'

Then one of the women called out, 'Whirlpool, whirlpool!' People began to move by Wade around the perimeter of the pool, all in the same direction; and soon enough he was pulled along as well, in the whirlpool growing because of their movement. 'At the North Pole we'd go the other direction, right?' No one replied.

Floating in blue-black darkness. Spinning down a maelstrom, blind. Wade struggled to keep his head above water, then deduced from the splashing, and from people's breathing patterns, that the others were mostly submerged. He took a deep breath and went under himself, the water very hot on his face, and reached down to the floor and pushed along in the flow. Banging into the icy walls of the bench. Bumping into the bodies of other people, their limbs slick and muscular. Men or women, there was usually no way to tell. His dives got longer and longer. While submerged he turned and tumbled, upside down, right-side up; it got hard to tell, it did not matter, except when it was time to breathe. He let the water tumble him however it wanted to. He was flotsam.

'Look for the Cherenkov light,' he heard Spiff gasp at one point.

'Look down at the northern sky, see the muons coming up at us. This ice is as transparent as pure diamond, you can see the light from three hundred metres away, the PMTs see a neutrino every second, blue light,' and then Wade was swept under again, and looking down. Then he was seeing blue streaks from far, far below. The light of distant supernovas. The ice was clear. He did not want this rolling tumble ever to stop. Apparently no one else did either, for it went on and on and on and on and on and on and on. Eventually it achieved a sort of no-time, a limbic limbo, such that afterward Wade could not have said how long it went on; perhaps an hour, perhaps two. What in the world could possibly tempt them back from such amniotic bliss?

Finally Spiff hauled him up. 'Come on, man, we don't want to drown a senator.'

'Oh go ahead.'

They laughed and pulled him up again. 'Come on, we're going to miss breakfast.'

Food; that was what would bring them back. Bare necessity.

Now they were all getting out, climbing up a rubber mat and into a passageway Wade couldn't see. Blind and freezing, though they assured him it was heated air. Flashlights were turned on, and towels and clothes lay piled in the same dumb-waiter, which was open on two sides; there were two changing rooms, it appeared, one for men one for women, it seemed. In any case there were only men in this room, which was walled by ice rather than the compacted snow in all the tunnels and chambers above: Spiff, Ed, Viktor and the bass player, who appeared utterly blissed-out, though he whimpered as he tried to dress, using fingers that were like Polish sausages. 'Snackbar gave his hands so we might live.' They had to zip up his fly and his parka for him. Then they were dressed, thank God, and walking along a crystalline tunnel, the women and the men, all of them steaming like horses, and the steam falling to the floor as white dust.

'If we didn't heat the air you couldn't dry off fast enough. You can take a pot of boiling water and sling it up in the air and it hits the ground as dust and pebbles,' Spiff said to Wade. 'Crackles like mad.' Wade's snot was already refrozen, in fact; but his body core was warm, and he felt fine, just fine.

They came to a vertical shaft with a wooden ladder extending up one side. Above they could see nothing. Wade began to climb. It went on till his hands hurt. Then they were climbing snow stairs in a snow-walled passage on a slant, taking a turn on a snow landing, going up stairs again.

Finally they banged up through a trapdoor. They were in the little glassed South Pole Pax Terminal, out by the runway, crowding into it.

Wade stumbled back up into the stupendous light. He couldn't stop blinking, and the cold-shocked flood of tears froze on his cheeks. He had been struck blind for sure this time, going from pure black to pure white. Out of the door of the shelter and the wind hit like another smack from the invisible side of beef. Wade felt his body ringing like a bell from the blow. It still looked to be the very same time of day it had been when Viktor had arrived, so many aeons ago. In an earlier incarnation.

Wade staggered up the metal stairs of the new station, into the stuffy warmth of the blue flying wing. He was reeling, he could barely stand. He could barely pull off his mittens.

He was headed for his room, one pruned hand propping him against the wall, when he ran into Keri.

'So how did you like old station?'

Wade jumped, composed himself. 'Very interesting,' he said. 'Kind of like a, a cave.'

'Indeed. Now look, there's a Herc coming in tonight, do you want to take it back to McMurdo?'

'Um, ah.' Wade tried to think. He gaped, and Keri stared at him curiously. 'You know, I'd like to visit Roberts Massif, actually.'

'Roberts? The oil folks?'

'Yes.'

'I see. Well, there's no direct transport there, of course. You'll have to go back to McMurdo, and then fly out to Shackleton Glacier camp, and then helo up to Roberts.'

'Fine,' Wade said. 'Whatever it takes.' He floated past the man into his room.

Sylvia stood before her wall map of Antarctica, marked now with a variety of red, orange and yellow numbered dots. There were only a few reds and oranges, though each one was individually troubling, of course. But there were a lot of yellows, especially along the coast of Victoria Land, and down the long spine of the Transantarctics. Some of these could be explained by the recent influx of oil exploration groups, and the few remaining private adventure firms. Others couldn't.

She took the orange marker from her desk and carefully entered a '14' next to the Amundsen cairn on Mount Betty. Another USO, an Unidentified Sitting Object; some kind of radio with satellite dish, apparently, placed much too close to the historic site; owner unknown; discovered by T–023, Val Kenning's Amundsen trek. She wrote all this down on a sheet of paper numbered '14' in orange, and put it in a file. Helo pilots had seen two other such objects when flying S–046 around the Beardmore Glacier, and another had been stumbled upon near Ice Stream C, by one of the ASL team working out of Byrd Station. That one had been brought back in by the worker, and proved to be a satellite dish and radio transmitter of unknown provenance. She had had it sent out to Cheech and then Washington for analysis, but no word had come back yet. Geoff often spoke of black boxes in science; here were the ultimate black boxes.

She was still staring at the map, trying to see a pattern in the dots, feeling balked and apprehensive, when she heard Paxman's light tap-tap-tap at her door. 'Come in.'

He stuck his head in. 'Wade Norton's back from the Pole, and he wants to talk with you.'

'Certainly, send him in.'

She moved behind her desk, and Wade entered the room. He presented quite a different appearance to what he had on arrival, all very predictable of course: sunburned except around the eyes, which had an unfocused, somewhat stunned expression; hair slicked down into the characteristic Antarctic bad-hair mat.

'How did you like the Pole?'

'It was very interesting.'

A long pause, as he appeared to be lost in reminiscence. 'In what way?' Sylvia prompted at last.

'Ah, well. Lots of ways. Tell me – are you aware of any other, ah, incidents at the Pole like the ones we discussed when I arrived?'

She stared at him. 'None except the ones I told you about.'

'Ah.' Another pause. 'And the NSF rep at the Pole, and the ASL station manager; they're in your full confidence?'

'Why yes. Did they seem not to be?'

'I don't know.'

Now his gaze was focused, and he was staring at her. Their gazes met for a matter of seconds.

'They weren't particularly helpful,' he said. 'The NSF rep in particular appeared to think I might represent a threat to the Pole station, somehow.'

'I'm sorry to hear that.'

He waved a hand. 'It's not really important. But . . .' He thought for a moment, appeared to change tack. 'I'm thinking of trying to visit the oil exploration camp on Roberts Massif, at the head of Shackleton Glacier.'

'I see,' Sylvia said, taken aback. 'And why that one, in particular?'

'Well . . .' He drifted over to her wall map, found the Shackleton and put his fingertip on Roberts. 'See, it's not so far from the Pole. And it's not so far from the place where the SPOT train was hijacked or whatever.'

'Here's the actual site of their current cost well,' Sylvia said, pointing to another red dot. 'That's even closer to the Pole and the SPOT incident site.'

'Ah ha. And they use a hovercraft to get around on the cap?'

'Why yes, I've heard they do.'

'Do you know anything about this hovercraft?'

'Yes,' she said, looking at him closely. 'It's an old Antarctic veteran, actually. Or part of one. It was based here at McMurdo long ago, then shipped out to Christchurch when it was found not to be very useful.' Actually the rumour Sylvia had heard was that the pilots had been a pair of wild women who had hotdogged around in the thing until the ASA brass in charge at that time had become annoyed and taken it away from them. But that was the kind of rumour one heard when out in the field. Transmission error in gossip was a phenomenal thing, and there was no way to know now what had really happened. 'Anyway, when these people put together their programme they tracked the Hake down in a warehouse in New Zealand, bought it, had it modified and flew it back down. But why are you interested?'

He shrugged. 'There were indications at the Pole that a hovercraft might be involved in some of the thefts from old station.'

'Really? What were the indications?'

'It was something some people said. Just a matter of seeing tracks, you know. Or not seeing tracks. They didn't want me to break confidentiality, so I shouldn't say more. I guess because they didn't tell the NTSB investigators about it. Something about seeing the tracks only because they were out where they weren't supposed to be, in one of the proscribed zones.'

'I see.'

'Anyway, I thought I'd visit Roberts and see what I could find out there. Keri at Pole said I had to come back here and fly out to Shackleton field camp, and then get heloed up to Roberts.'

'Yes, that's right. And we can certainly do that for you. There's a flight to Shackleton leaving in, let's see . . .' She consulted the schedule: 'Oh my. In three hours. Think you can make it?'

He blew out a breath. 'Ah, why not? I can sleep in the Herc.'

'That's right. First law of Antarctic travel; go when you can.'

'Yes.'

'But what about the people at Roberts, and out at this drill site? What makes you think they will talk to you, or even take you in? They haven't acknowledged a single one of our messages.'

'I've got Senator Chase talking to them directly, and to the home offices in the consortium. It sounds like they're willing to have me visit.'

'Really! Well, that's good. That's progress. I'll be very interested to hear what you learn there.'

He nodded, looking at her oddly. Another pause. He was not laying all his cards on the table, she saw; and he suspected that she wasn't either. Well, that was life: NSF and Congress did not have identical interests. Of course NSF reported to Congress, and so in theory she should be telling him everything she knew, or else she would be getting in trouble. 'Let's meet again when you get back,' she said, 'and go over everything we don't have time for now. You'd better get out to the skiway, or else you'll miss your flight. I'll have Paxman call out and tell them you're coming.'

'Thanks.' Wearily he rose and went to the door. Two Herc flights in a single day; and already he looked wasted. He stopped in the doorway and allowed a flash of irritation to show, then shifted it into a wry smile. 'If we were to put together the pieces of the puzzle we each have, we might be able to make enough of the picture to recognize it.'

'Yes,' she said.

He stared at her, then continued out of the door.

When he was out of the Chalet, Sylvia checked her watch; 9pm. She sighed; she'd have to wait until mid rats to eat, and she was starving already. She pulled a box of camp crackers out of her desk and got on the phone and had Randi patch her on a radio link out to S–375.

'Geoffrey, it's Sylvia here, do you read me, over?'

Radio static, harsher than usual; then Geoff's voice: 'Yes, Sylvia, we read you, how are you? What's up, over?'

'I've just had the assistant to Senator Chase here, Geoff. He's just back from Pole, and he's off to visit the oil exploration camp in the Mohn Basin.'

'Ah yes. He visited us here, as you know.'

'What did you think of him?'

'Well, he seemed to have a good head on his shoulders. Interested in us, or so it seemed. He asked good questions. We enjoyed his visit, anyway.' Voices and laughter in the background. 'Although that may have been because of his mountaineer, or so my young libidinally-starved colleagues seem to be implying, yes.' More laughter. 'I myself am far above such things, as you know.'

'Oh of course, of course.'

'But do you think he means trouble for NSF?'

'No no, not necessarily. But I think he might have stumbled into the local culture at the Pole, and been told some things that he thinks we don't know.'

'Ah, I see.'

'Tell me, Geoff, did the discussions at SCAR last winter shed any light on what we were calling the unfunded experiments?'

'Not really, no. There were stories, of course. Everyone agrees that there is some of that going on, but no one really knows how much. That's the nature of the beast, isn't it?'

'Yes. Do you think Mai-lis is still part of it?'

'I would guess so, yes. I think it very likely.'

Sylvia stared at the wall map. The coloured dots on it were like the connect-dots of some foreign alphabet. 'Well, thanks, Geoff. How is your work going out there?'

'Oh fine, fine. Field work. You know how that is, Sylvia.'

'Yes,' she said with a pang. Compared to NSF administration in McMurdo, he meant to say, it was paradise. Beaker heaven, as the ASL staff put it. But it was after the fall for her. 'Let me know if you hear anything more.'

'I certainly will, although out here we are not in much of a position to hear anything. But some nights we surf the radio waves for enter- tainment, and if we hear anything interesting I'll let you know.'

'Thanks, Geoff. Good luck out there.'

'And the same to you, Sylvia. You need it more than we do.'

'I suppose so. It would certainly be nice to have some kind of serious regulatory ability for a change, that's for sure.'

'Well, you're a US Marshall yourself, right?' Sounds of laughter behind him.

'That's right,' she said. 'But it may be that we will end up needing a bit more firepower than that.'

CHAPTER EIGHT

The Sirius Group

Graham walked some distance behind Geoffrey and Harry and Misha, over broken dolerite. They were checking a beautiful long band of Sirius sandstone plastered above them against one of the dolerite cliffs of the Apocalypse Peaks. The band was a succession horizontally stratified at scales both large and small diamictons containing different mixes of boulders, cobbles and laminated silts, and bounded above and below by distinct disconformities, horizontal to slightly inclined. Planar to slightly undulating small-scale relief. One line was traceable for more than thirty metres as Graham walked it off. Certainly this succession had been deposited *in situ*, and then ploughed away by the next grounded glacier to pass over, leaving only this band against the rock, where the force of the passing ice was lessened just enough to leave a trace against the wall.

He leaned down and tapped at white diamictite with his geological hammer, then scratched at it. The D–7 disconformity, about a centimetre wide. Below it all the diamictons were marine; above it they were subaerial. Which did not mean that this line had been sea level, but that the rise of the Transantarctics had lifted this region out of the seas for good at about the time this disconformity had been laid. As they were now at some fifteen hundred metres above sea level, it implied an uplift rate of about five hundred metres per million years, if you accepted the Pliocene dating of the Sirius, as Graham did. That was a fairly rapid uplift rate, and one of the ways that the stabilists criticized the dynamicists' conclusions; but faster rates were certainly known, and it was hard to argue the evidence, displayed here on the cliffside like a classroom diagram. Graham would have very much liked to take his first thesis adviser by the scruff of the neck and haul him to this very point and shove his face into such a display, clearer even than the Cloudmaker Formation. See that! he would have said. How can you deny the facts!

But of course it was not actually a cliff of facts, but of sandstone. Interpretations were open to argument, at least until the matter was firmly pinned down and black-boxed, as Geoffrey put it, meaning become something that all the scientists working in that field took for granted, going on to further questions. Some scientific controversies resolved themselves fairly quickly, and others didn't; and this was proving to be one of the slow ones. As they had not black-boxed this particular question, it was still sandstone only and not yet fact.

This process was something that Graham had not understood early in his career, and it had got him into considerable trouble. He had started his graduate work in geology at Cambridge, working with Professor Martin, unaware of the fact that Martin's own work dating ash deposits in the Transantarctics allied him with the stabilists in the Sirius controversy. Graham had merely wanted to work in the Antarctic and knew that that was Martin's area of research. He had been very naïve, having been educated mostly in physics, with only a late switch to geology because of the fieldwork, and the tangibility of rock – a switch begun by his entry into graduate level work in Martin's group. Then he had been so immersed in catching up on the basics of geology that he had not been fully aware of the Sirius controversy and how Martin fitted into it, and so he had not understood why Martin had been so cool to his geomorphological research into the question of why the Transantarctics were there at all. As part of that study Graham had examined the question of how quickly the range was uplifting, and had come to the conclusion that although the range was quite old, dating from about eighty million years ago, when the east Antarctic craton began to show intracraton rifting, still it looked as if it had been rising at a fairly rapid clip in the most recent period, perhaps (he had ventured rashly) because of the lithostatic pressure of the ice cap pushing the other side of the craton down. And Martin had been cool, and had never devoted any of his time to critiquing Graham's papers on the subject, or contributing any of what he needed to contribute, as second author and principle investigator, to make the papers publishable. In a fit of angry frustration Graham had sent one paper to a journal without Martin's approval, as the approval seemed likely never to come; and the paper had been rejected, Martin informed of the submission, and Graham basically dismissed from the course, as he was not invited to return to Antarctica in Martin's group the following season.

This experience had made him bitter. He had gone back to New Zealand, and there one night in a pub one of his old teachers from the university in Christchurch had shaken his head and explained some things to him. Martin had cast his lot in with the stabilists in the Sirius controversy because his findings in volcanic ash convinced him that the Transantarctics and Antarctica generally had been in the deep-freeze for at least twelve million years. One of the many other aspects of the controversy had to do with the rate of uplift of the Transantarctics, with the stabilists maintaining that there was no reason for the range to be rising anywhere near as fast as the dynamicists claimed, so that the Sirius formations had to be older than they claimed in order to be found now at such high elevations. And so naturally, his old teacher told him, Graham's conclusions had not been welcome.

This had outraged Graham. A perversion of science! he cried. But his old professor had chided him. No no, he had said, it's your own fault; you should have known better. Perhaps it's even my fault; I should have taught you better than I did how science works, obviously.

There was nothing particularly untoward in Martin's response, Graham's teacher explained to him, with no outrage or indignation whatsoever. Indeed, he said, if Graham had joined the course of one of the dynamicists, and begun to produce work indicating that the ice had lain heavy on Antarctica for millions and millions of years, he would not have prospered there either. It was not a matter of evil-doing either way; the simple truth was that science was a matter of making alliances to help you to show what you wanted to show, and to make clear also that what you were showing was important. And your own graduate students and post-docs were necessarily your closest allies in that struggle to pull together all the strings of an argument. All this became even more true when there was a controversy ongoing, when there were people on the other side publishing articles with titles like 'Unstable Ice or Unstable Ideas?' and so on, so that the animus had grown a bit higher than normal.

So, Graham had been forced to conclude, thinking over his talk with his old teacher in the days after: it was not that Martin was evil, but that he Graham had been naïve, and, yes, even stupid. Thick, anyway. Bitterness was not really appropriate. Science was not a matter of automatons seeking Truth, but of people struggling to black-box some facts.

So his education began again, in effect, after two years wasted in Cambridge. Which was not so very great a length of time in scientific terms. Many scientists had taken far longer to learn how their disciplines worked. And so Graham had become reconciled to the experience and had shelved it, and got into a course on glaciology at University of Sydney, and gone on from there.

That had all happened a long time ago. And yet still the Sirius controversy raged on, with both sides finding new allies and students, and producing papers published in peer-reviewed journals. Graham thought he began to see a tilt on the part of outsiders toward the dynamicist interpretation; but as he was a dynamicist himself now, he supposed he could not really tell for sure. Anyway, the case was beginning to look stronger to him as the years passed and evidence from other parts of Antarctica was collected. Over in the Prince Charles Mountains, for instance, on the other side of Antarctica, the Aussies were making a good case that there had been Pliocene-era seas as far as five hundred kilometres inland from the current shore. The Beardmore Glacier had been pretty conclusively shown to be a paleofjord, and there were unallied scientists referring to a 'Beardmore paleofjord' in other contexts, also to *Nothofagus beardmorensis*, the beech type found in the Cloudmaker Formation and named by dynamicists to underline its location of discovery. And evidence of beech forests was appearing elsewhere in Sirius formations, with seeds and beetles and other plant material all pointing to the Pliocene or late Miocene. No, the case was coming together at last, after all these long years; all of Geoff Michelson's career, effectively, and passed on to him from his adviser, Brown, who had also spent a career working away at it; and now, come to think of it, a good fair fraction of Graham's career had been devoted to it as well. All to build the walls that would box this part of the story up for good, building it brick by brick over years and generations. Because the stones did not speak, not really. They had to be translated.

The sun wheeled and the steep wall of dolerite overhead now cast them in the shade, and it became markedly colder. They were truly much younger-looking mountains than any other eighty million year-old range, still as steep and jagged as the Himalayas or the Alps, both only a quarter as old; saved by the cold from the ravages of water erosion, and so aged by the winds only, and rising so fast that the rise more than compensated for that abrasion. Cryopreserved, so to speak.

To keep warm Graham went to work taking some samples from the disconformity just above head level. The diamictite would rub away with a gloved fingertip, but hacking out a good sample was work to warm one up. Certainly water had been here, and seafloor diatoms, the paleobotanists told him, benthic genera that indicated brackish to near-normal marine conditions. A shallow sea-bottom, a fjord probably, perhaps later a lake that slowly dried out. Shoreline of a fjord. Above the shore, a low, hardy beech forest. The Pliocene had without a doubt had temperatures high enough to support *Nothofagus*; this was agreed upon by everyone, having been an earlier case that some other group had already black-boxed: warm Pliocene, no questions asked. And now a fact basic to the dynamicist case; that was the crux of their whole argument, really – that if you got global temperatures

197

as high as the Pliocene, the Antarctic ice sheets melted both east and west, leaving glaciated archipelagoes and an embayed craton, in a sea covered every winter by substantial amounts of sea ice. That would account for the clear varving here, now that he thought of it; it need not be just the tidal marks on a seashore, but annual sediment fall on a sea-floor that in winters was covered by a roof of sea ice. 'Hmmm . . .' Graham said, glancing up at Michelson.

Beech trees had not evolved greatly, and any fossil fragments of them found here could have been much older than the Pliocene. Indeed when they had first found beech wood in the Sirius they had assumed it was Triassic wood picked up by a glacier much later. Only when they had come on thousands of beech leaves as well did they realize the wood had been alive when Sirius was laid down. And beech forests supported an array of smaller plants as part of their ecology, of course, mostly mosses and lichens, but also weevils and other beetles, fresh-water snails, and perhaps even some amphibians. Some of these would be specifically Pliocene species, or could be dated by chemical tests that worked specifically for them. So that looking into the rock of this ancient sea-floor (granting for the moment that that was what it was), it was quite possible that one might find fossils larger than the micro-scopic foraminifera and diatoms. Michelson often mentioned the possi-bility at the beginning of the day when they set out, or when the helos arrived to carry part of the team to a distant site; cheerily and with no expectations he would call out in farewell, 'Keep an eye out for scallop shells!' A kind of joke. Actually the foraminifera and diatoms, although too small to be seen by the naked eye, were enough to prove their contention that the Sirius group was the remnant of a sea-floor, and date it as well. But certainly a fossil clam shell would be welcome.

And so when Graham's finger took a big flake of the diamictite off, revealing a band of yellow-red rusty, clayey material, he said, 'What have we here!'

It was not a clam shell, of course. But it was unusual.

He climbed up the strata to have a closer look at it. He pulled a lens from his pocket and took a glance at 30x power. Crushed plant material.

He called out to Harry, who was worrying at a round block of tillite up the slope. Harry heard him, and called back, 'I think I'm in an old estuary here!'

'Very like!' Graham said. 'Come here and look at this!'

Harry came around the corner and saw the rusty strata in the grey sandstone. 'Hey!'

'Yes. Look at where it is, too. Rudimentary paleosol, at the upper surface of a fluvial diamicton, and see here, root structures going down here vertically, and then spreading out farther laterally.'

'Beech forest,' Harry said, his eyes round. 'Oh, my God – this looks like it'll be as big as Oliver Bluffs or Bennett Platform.'

'Yes.' Carefully they worked the diamictite off the yellow-rust leaf-litter mat. 'Look, it's especially well-preserved where it's compressed under these boulders.' Graham tapped away some more. Harry got on his wristphone and called Michelson. 'Geoff, it looks as if we've found another beech-leaf mat, a good one. Moss cushions too, but mostly beech. Preservation looks good.'

'I'll be right up. I'm downvalley from you still, right?'

'That's right. We're up against the cliff wall, site three.'

'I'll be right there.'

Harry was their paleobotanist, and so now grinning ecstatically. At that moment it was like a treasure hunt, Graham realized; or like prospecting for gold. A find like this would result in a paper that would help make a case that would help make a career that would help pay the bills. Gold nuggets right there in the ground, if you wanted to think of it that way. The philosopher's stone. Or another brick in the wall.

Although Harry was not thinking in such prosaic terms. 'Look at that, oh my God. Can you imagine a beech forest growing down here, what it would have looked like! So *beautiful*. This is a beautiful fjord shoreline, Graham, it's like a holy place. Really fine mineralization too.'

Another flake of diamictite came off. The yellowy stuff was bowed under the boulders resting on the disconformity. A tiny oil-bearing deposit in the making.

'Leaves up to six or seven centimetres, it looks like. That's big.'

'So mild temperatures.'

'And maybe cloudy a lot. Check this out, veins in the leaf. Incredible venation.'

'Very nice.'

Of course this would only be another case of disputed age of biological material. Still, it seemed very clear that at the times when the Sirius group was being deposited, this region had been much more than lifeless sand occasionally catching windblown diatoms from afar; if nothing else, this helped to make that very clear, so the main counter-explanation given by the stabilists for the presence of the diatoms was obviously wrong. And if it was clear that there were beech forests here during Sirius, on a cold coast that looked more like the coast of southern Chile than like the current inhospitable icy shore, then one had to admit that Antarctica had certainly had some mild times. And then the diatoms that absolutely permeated the Sirius sandstones, to the point where some diamictites were simply pulverized diatoms and foraminifera and nothing else, could be quite definitively dated to the Pliocene by solid biostratification dating; and so where was the flaw? How could the interpretation of a liquid marine era be faulted at that point? You would have to simply ignore evidence to do it; pretend certain papers didn't exist; pretend that certain rocks in the field didn't exist either. And unbiased scientists, without their careers committed to one view or the other, would not do that.

Then another flake of grey rock came off under the pointy end of his hammer, and he and Harry both saw the rounded double bump and the shard behind it. When Michelson hiked up to join them he found them both flat on their chests, their faces centimetres from the stone, their sunglasses pulled off to enable them to see the object better. 'What's this I see?' Michelson cried.

'I'm not sure,' Harry said. 'But I think it may be the leg bone of a frog. Oh my God.'

'Call it your famous scallop shell,' Graham, sitting back and grinning crookedly up at Michelson. He felt the sun lance through the chill and drive into his face, a very pleasurable sensation.

The world is a body. Rocks are the skeleton, watercourses are the arteries, trees are the muscles, clouds are the respiration. We are the thoughts. Here, then, we can say that the body has been stripped to the skeleton, for there are no muscles, or veins, or arteries. Yet still the breath of clouds. A skeleton that breathes under its white cloak, and from time to time wakes, and thinks.

We walk up the ice road to the inner highland, the inner self. Morning in sunwashed camp: exercises in *chih-fa*, the method for the fingers. Valerie, our *roshi*, the shepherd of this pilgrimage, is purest form in the art of *chih-fa*. No tea ceremony could have cleaner lines than her breaking camp zazen. The way she cares for us is a joy to behold. And now here we are again, walking. Walking for hours, in the footsteps of Amundsen.

What can we make of Amundsen? His story is a knot. All his life he had been a man of the north, all his career had been an exploration of the north. He had found a Northwest Passage; he had desired for years to reach the North Pole. Then came news of Cook's and Peary's claims to have reached it, in the midst of his preparations for his own trip there. But he had no desire to be the third man to the North Pole, nor even the second. This casts his desire in a different light. What he wanted then was not the North Pole, centre of his life's work and placement. He wanted to be first. It is not at all the same thing. Not a hunger for place, but for position. A concentration on time rather than space; a desire to write one's name on history, rather than to occupy a place on Earth.

Thus when Amundsen wrote of the strangeness of standing at the South Pole, after all his life trying to get to the North Pole, he was only partly correct. In a deeper sense he was standing exactly where he wanted to be: first. And indeed he has been remembered, especially on this continent, where there has been so little human history that what happened at the start still overshadows all. So he made his mark on time. First to the Pole. When did he reach it? I can't remember.

The method Amundsen used to reach the Pole is also a knot, and difficult for us to come to terms with. On the one hand he had a genius for contemplating his polar experience and analysing his methods, and making continual innovations in equipment and technique to improve them. His trip used the finest combination of modern and archaic technology possible in his time, much of it custom designed by Amundsen and manufactured under his direction.

But his change of destination, from one end of the Earth to the other, he hid from all, for fear of losing his financial support. This is one of the strange things about his trip that have puzzled people ever after. Even his men did not know where they were going; he did not tell them until after they left Norway. At that point he also sent a telegram to Scott, which said 'Going South'. This shows he too was aware of reaching the Poles as a kind of medieval joust, with certain rules of fair play. Amundsen obviously did not agree with Scott's notion that no one else should get to try until Scott either won or died. But he did agree they were running a race. So he sent Scott his notice.

And then he used dogs, and ate them. Of course many of us eat animal flesh, and in any market in China you can see more cruelty to animals in a single day than anything Amundsen and his men did to their dogs in their entire polar careers. We cannot judge him. But there is something about planning to use dogs to pull you to the Pole, while eating them as you go, that strikes the British mind at least as somewhat cold and over-efficient. The British are both unsentimental and highly sentimental at one and the same time – like the Chinese. And dogs are our comrade-helpers, and intelligent, so there seems to be a touch of murder in killing these sentient beings, especially shooting and eating them to facilitate a trip to a first.

And then there is simply the question of being taken there by other beings, rather than under your own power. Scott by his inability to master dogs in effect raised the stakes to a higher level, where it was not just a matter of getting there, but how you did it. By accident Scott and his men fell in love with walking on Earth, and after that Scott asserted that doing it on your own mattered; and what has happened since tends to reinforce his values rather than Amundsen's. The first climbers of Everest, for instance, used oxygen, and were the apex of a giant logistical pyramid; later Messner and Habler climbed the mountain without oxygen, and then Messner climbed it alone and without oxygen. Messner's beautiful act of *feng shui* made the first climbs look over-reliant on aid. In Antarctica it was much the same. People drove tractors to the South Pole, then flew, and everyone recognized that this represented no great personal achievement for the people using the transport. And standing on the back of a sledge pulled by dogs is not that different from sitting in the cab of a tractor, as my friend Elspeth pointed out recently. In short, we can be taken anywhere now, but going alone is still hard. When Børge Ousland walked across the continent alone and unaided, it was an amazing achievement; and it hearkened back to Scott rather than to Amundsen, even though Ousland was another Norwegian.

But Amundsen's goal was simple; get to the Pole first. No scientific research, no scruples about dogs. He engineered a beautifully efficient trip to an idea. He was first to the axis of rotation, to a spot of planetary power in the landscape of our imagination; a gathering of all the dragon arteries into a single tight knot. Very much an act of *feng shui*.

Thus for me his expedition is a bundle of contradictions. As we follow their route, I feel confused about what they did, and about what we are doing. The land they crossed is superb, and the crossing of it was a work of art. But an art that included dog murder; and all for an idea of firstness that in the end I don't find very interesting. North, south, east, west and all the other attributes of *feng shui* – these are parts of the landscape of the imagination, which is a crucial part of all landscape, of course; crucial to our placement in the real world, on the Earth as we find it. But if the reality of Earth is perceived merely as material to be passed through, then it is not really there for you, and so the imagination becomes impoverished. The Earth is the imagination's home and body. Unless you inhabit a place – not stay in one spot, but inhabit a place, as the paleolithic peoples inhabited their places, with every bush known and every rock named – then it becomes too decentred and metaphysical; you live in the imagination of an idea. True *feng shui* springs forth as an organic part of the landscape itself, which we perceive rather than invent, after learning the land down to each grain of sand.

So Amundsen was the first to the spin axis. But the Americans who started living in that place in 1956 were the first to be there in the full sense of being.

Ahead of us the headwall of the glacier, the crux of our climb, the heart-knot of our pilgrimage. A most serious case of *kao-yuan* perspective. I'll practise silence now, and keep the cameras on and let you see it newly. We'll talk again at the top, on the ice cap.

Once they had got down onto it, the lower stretch of the Axel Heiberg Glacier turned out to be such a broad river of ice that Val's group ascended long stretches where the ice was bare and crevasse-free. It was like walking on the surface of a pour of unbroken water, the flush surface of a smooth torrent, everything frozen in an instant, even the ripples. Hard work cramponing up this smooth slope, and they traded off the sledge – pulling every half hour, first Val and Ta Shu, then Jack and Jim, then Jorge and Elspeth; but it was quite straightforward compared to the steep, broken ice of the mistaken traverse, and they made good time. It would have been a lark, in fact, except that every time they looked forward and up they saw the glacier rising ever more steeply before them, until it leaped right up in a gigantic headwall, the section of the glacier now called the Amundsen Icefalls, towering over them in a broad curve from black sidewall to black sidewall, the great broken crackle of the glacier's ice gleaming like shattered mirrors in the sun. A thousand vertical metres in less than five kilometres. And they were going to have to get up that, if they wanted to continue.

As they hiked on toward it, hour after hour, crevasse fields began to appear on the ice, like rapids in the current. Here the GPS system helped tremendously, because when they looked up the great white flow the steeper sections beetled down at them, but the flatter sections were telescoped to near nothing, making their way seem steeper (but also shorter) than it really was; and making it hard to see enough to choose a way. One of Amundsen's many talents had been an ability to read the unseen glacier above well enough to avoid impassable crevasse fields, and the shear-zones where the ice was not so much fissured as pulverized.

For Val, whose wristscreen was giving her information from satellite visuals, radar and a GPS location to within two centimetres, not to mention the pulse-radar on her shoulder constantly searching for crevasses ahead, the skill consisted in correlating all that data to the actual icescape facing them, and then choosing from the alternative routes it suggested, where there were alternatives. Usually there were; it was a kind of multiple-path maze they were threading, and at no point in this lower stretch did they run into a set of crevasses and shear-zones that was continuous across the front of the glacier. Although once or twice it was close; they had to twist and wind their way, and walked perhaps two or three kilometres for every kilometre of the glacier climbed; so that it was slow, slow work. But they made progress.

And the hours passed. Val looked at the dim little screen strapped to her right wrist, and then up at the blazing white jumble, and pointed out the way to the string of clients behind. Off they would go again. She had begun to haul the sledge by herself most of the time, and no one objected. Sometimes the glacier was covered with the hardpacked white snow called firn, and they could tramp along at a good clip. Their sunglasses were all at max power, polarizing so heavily that the cobalt sky had a blackish tint to it.

In some sections the glacier was clean blue ice, pitted or smooth, so that they had to stop and put on crampons, and chip-chip-chip on up. Often the blue ice was pitted with regular cusps that resembled suncups in snow, though not so deep; it was like walking across the surface of an enormous golf ball, their ankles twisted to a different resting angle with every step. It was very hard not to sweat, even with the smart-fabrics open wide and the ambient temperature well below zero. The sledge clitter-clattered behind Val, tugging hard as if trying to escape and shoot back down the length of the glacier, on a mad luge run into the Ross Sea. Looking around during rest-breaks, it was so obvious that the glacier was a stupendous flood streaming down an enormous break in the mountain wall; the curve of the fluid obvious in the many rubble lines marking the surface, or just in the creasing of the ice itself, parallel creases like the lines in a whale's white belly, all turning together with each sweep down the valley. The trench the glacier had carved was deep; the ranges walling it in were both nearly four thousand metres above sea level, and three thousand metres above where they were now, so that it felt like being in the bottom of an enormous slot. Sometimes it seemed it would take weeks to climb out of a box canyon as huge as this one. In their rest stops they exclaimed over it:

'Stupendous!'

'Awesome!'

'Gnarly.'

'Sublime.'

'Big.'

That was Ta Shu. He spent the rests standing off to one side, rotating like a whirling dervish in extreme slow motion, either to give his distant audience a complete three-sixty or simply because he could not take enough in. His low Chinese commentary was like the chirping of invisible birds.

Val kept the rests short, and the hours passed, hour after hour, each one full of effort. They made progress. It was surprising how hot you could get in Antarctica – walking on a kind of mirror, sunblasted from above and below, working very hard. And yet still the potential for chill was always tangible, in the tip of the nose and the ears, and sometimes, if the going was easy, in the fingertips and toes. At one point she checked; it was fifteen degrees below zero Fahrenheit, and most of the group were still wearing ear bands, so that they could keep their ears from frostbite while still exposing the rest of their heads, which meant they would not sweat profusely in their suits. The head was the key to thermostatting. Most of them on this day were down to shirts and windtrousers over the smartfabric longjohns, with the heating elements in their photovoltaic windpants turned all the way off. The gleaming blue-purple fabric complemented nicely the glarey turquoise of the ice and the dark cobalt of the cloudless sky. The sky appeared to pulse over the blaze of ice and snow, as if breathing lightly – a phenomenon that Val had long ago learned to attribute to her own pulse, pounding in her vision somehow. She was working hard, and her clients even harder, but still keeping up. This was the kind of hour she loved; little to worry about with the clients, taxing, basic work to do, the mind absorbed in the work and the feelings in her feet and legs and the rest of her body, and in the landscape towering around her as they slowly got higher and higher, with the views corresponding- ingly larger. Sweating, breathing hard, mouth dry; thoughts ricochet- ing all over the canyon, flying out of it all over the cosmos; but also, for long stretches of time, merged with the ice underfoot and in the ten metres ahead of her, and so happy. The dromomaniac at full stretch.

Her screen data and the view above made it clear they were reaching the foot of the icefall proper. Up there out of sight, sixteen hundred metres higher than they now stood, the ice fell off the polar cap, down a funnel-like head section, channelled between the triangular mass of Mount Don Pedro Christophersen – Amundsen's financial saviour – and the high southern end of the Herbert Range, called Mount Fridtjof Nansen – Amundsen's patron and friend. With a rock bump in the middle of the funnel, which Amundsen's group had christened Mount Ole Englestad, after the Norwegian naval officer who had been Amundsen's second-in-command until killed by lightning while still back in Norway. Being a friend of Amundsen had meant getting some quite amazing peaks named after you, Val thought as she studied the map on the screen.

The Norwegians had been pushed ever rightward in their ascent by the crevasse fields of their time, until they had been forced to climb the funnel on the right side of Mount Englestad, and only then turn left and south. But Val could see on the screen that the glacier had changed in the last century; there was a makeable route leading off to the left, straight up the more southerly slope. If they went that way it would save them several kilometres, and also save them the ascent of the right side of the funnel, which appeared to be quite a bit more broken up than it had been a century before.

So she waited for everyone to catch up to her, and declared a rest-stop. While they were drinking the meltwater out of their arm-flasks – which were on the outside of their upper arms, and wired to the photovoltaic elements in their suits so that they melted a pint of water per hour in good sunlight – she showed them what she had seen on her screen. 'Maybe we should go left here, directly to Butcher's Spur.'

'Oh come on,' Jack said, panting, a little red-faced, dried sweat streaking his cheeks, grinning handsomely at her. 'We've been sticking to their route through all the other really hard parts, and once we get up to the plateau it'll be easy from there on to the Pole. Why wimp out now with just this last stretch to go?'

The others shrugged uneasily, looking at the cracked ice above. Both ways looked bad, to tell the truth. Elspeth muttered something. No one seemed to care that much one way or another.

It was Val's call, she knew. If conditions in the icefall had changed enough to make the righthand route too dangerous, they should go left, and that was it. No one tried to repeat any particular route up an icefall, that would be absurd; icefalls changed every month, and one had to react to that.

Irritated, she looked at the screen again. Hard to tell what it would be like on either side, really, until they tried it. 'Let's set camp for today,' she said finally. 'This might be the last flat spot in a long time, and it's too late to take on another hard pitch. And I'll need to think about the route a bit more.'

'Why?' Jack said.

'To see if it will go,' Val said shortly, and went to the sledge and started the work of making camp.

That night in the dining tent they ate for the most part in silence. They were tired, and the crux of their entire trek would be in tomorrow's climb; and camped right under the slope the foreshortening made the icefalls seem very steep indeed, so that every time they looked outside they were confronted with what they had taken on. Even inside the tent the great broken white wall seemed to be visible to them. It reminded Jack, he said, of the night he had spent at the Hornlihutte on the side of the Matterhorn, looking up at that great spike overhanging them and wondering what he had got himself into. 'And then we started while it was still dark, and we couldn't see a thing. I climbed the first hour with my flashlight hanging from my teeth so I could use both hands. But in the end it turned out to be a piece of cake.'

People nodded. It was curious anyone ever boasted, Val thought, considering that no one was ever taken in by it.

'Have you climbed the Matterhorn?' Jack asked her.

'Uh, yeah. Long time ago.'

'The Normalweg?'

'What – the ridge from the hut? No no. We did a traverse that time.'

'Oh yeah – up the Zmutt and down the Lion? I've heard that's great.'

'No, that time we went up the north face and down the south face.'

Jack was taken aback, and he coloured a little. 'Whoa,' he said. 'That must have been radical!'

'Yeah. My partner was five months pregnant at the time, so it was kind of nerve-racking.'

People laughed, and Jack did too, colouring some more as he watched her.

'Like Alison Hargreaves!' Elspeth exclaimed, eyes smiling wickedly.

'That's right. In fact Meg called it doing her Hargreaves.'

Like many women climbers Val honoured the memory of Hargreaves, a Brit who had climbed the north face of the Eiger in a single day while five months pregnant. Later on she had been killed on K2 when her kids were four and six years old, which was a shame. But certainly after that it was hard to do anything as a woman climber that seemed unmaternal in comparison.

Jack abandoned the Matterhorn, and the conversation wandered as they shifted from chilli to chocolate, and began to wash the dishes. At one point Elspeth said to Ta Shu, 'Butcher's Spur is where they shot half their dogs, you see.'

'Ah! I see.'

The Norwegians had of course become fond of their dogs by the time they reached this point: each one a hardworking, eager enthusiast, like a furry Birdie Bowers. So it had made them melancholy to shoot so many of them. Each man had shot the weaker half of his team, meaning two or three dogs apiece. And so despite the incredible accomplishment of climbing the icefall, the accomplishment that Val's party still faced – despite making it from sea level to the polar cap in only four days, taking a difficult route never seen before by humankind – they had still had a very, very melancholy evening of it. Not that that had kept them (or the surviving dogs) from feasting on steaks carved out of their late companions.

'Kind of like cannibalism,' Elspeth said.

'The British killed dogs too,' Jack reminded her. 'They wanted to use dogs, they just couldn't figure out how.'

'And all the while hammering Amundsen for it,' Jim said, shaking his head ruefully. 'You know the British Royal Geographical Society finally held a dinner in Amundsen's honour, years afterward, and the man introducing him ended the introduction by saying, "I propose three cheers for the dogs"!'

'You're kidding!' Elspeth said.

'I am not kidding. Lord Curzon, as Amundsen recalled when he wrote about it in his autobiography. He was really pissed off.'

'What did he do?'

'He left after the dinner and went to his hotel, and asked for an apology but never got one. And so he quit the Royal Geographical Society, and never went back to England again.'

'Incredible.'

'There's no one ruder than the British when they want to be.'

They ate in silence for a while, thinking about it. Val tried to imagine it: the roar of laughter from the British audience, Amundsen furious and humiliated, sitting on the stage unable to move. Quite a scene.

Ta Shu finished a chocolate bar. 'These dogs deserved three cheers,' he observed.

'But it was Amundsen who should have toasted them,' Elspeth said.

'He did not get chance, not then. But other times he always told their importance.'

They sat eating, resting, thinking it over. It was strange, Val thought, how heavy a mark those first expeditions had left on the people in Antarctica; they composed the continent's only shared culture, really. No one knew what had happened here in the International Geophysical Year, no one knew what the US Navy years had been like, no one knew the history of the Australian sector, or the Kiwis up at Lake Vanda, or the steady trickle of solo crossings and the like. Nothing remembered but the beginning.

Now Jim said to Ta Shu, 'I've been thinking about what you said last night, about how all our stories have coloured lights on them. I know what you mean, and to a certain extent it's true, of course. But what good historians are trying to do, I think, is to see things in a clear light – see what really happened, first, to the extent possible, and then see how the stories about the events distorted the reality, and why. And when you've got all those alternative stories together, then you can compare them, and make judgements that aren't just a matter of your own coloured lights. Not just a matter of temperament. They can be justified as having some kind of objectivity.'

Ta Shu nodded, thinking it over as he jammed down a second helping of chilli and camp crackers. He ate, Val thought, like a man who had been seriously hungry at some time in his life.

'A worthy goal,' he remarked between gulps. He got up and went over to the faintly roaring stove to refill his bowl. The others looked at each other.

Under his breath Jack announced, 'And there's your fortune cookie for the day.'

*　　*　　*

The next morning Val decided to agree to follow the Norwegians' route. She could see, on both her screen and when looking up at the ice fall, a makeable route to the very far right of the funnel, up and under a small nunatak on the edge of the polar cap called Helland Hansen Shoulder. So she told the others, and Jack nodded complacently, and they packed the camp into the sledge and took off.

It should have been easier than it was. It was the least steep part of the funnel, after all; Val could see why the Norwegians had trended to this side. But something – perhaps the slight lowering in the height of the polar cap, reducing the thickness of the glacier's upper section – had caused the ice across the whole chute to break up. Possibly it was crossing an under-ice rock ridge between Mount Englestad and the Hansen Shoulder, for it looked on the map as if they might be two exposed parts of a curved saddle overrun by ice.

In any case, it was very hard going. They zigged and zagged, from one narrow ramp or block of ice up to the next, sometimes crossing snowbridges over narrow crevasses, other times physically hauling the sledge over even narrower breaks in the ice, all of them pulling together. In sections like these the Norwegians had each dealt with their own sledges and dogs, and reported in their journals that they had become quite inured to the incessant danger below; they photographed each other straddling crevasses to look down into them, or eating lunch with their feet hanging over the edges of them. But the NSF would not of course sanction any such cavalier approach, and in zones as fractured as these Val's group had to rope up and treat it like any other serious climb, which was only appropriate. So Val went ahead and screwed in ice-screws, and belayed the others up and over any serious exposure; then they hauled up the sledge; then she went back down to remove the ice-screws, and climbed back up again and carried on. It was slow work, and hot and cold in turns, depending on whether they were making adrenalated climbing moves or standing around stamping their feet waiting for the others to do the same. Even the smartfabrics were not up to that kind of alternation, and as the sun wheeled over and stood right at the top of their route, blazing down at them in a photon deluge, the temperature differentials became more and more extreme and uncomfortable; a hundred degrees of subjective difference between sun and shade, one's face and one's back; and nearly two hundred degrees difference between work and rest. Even Val was uncomfortable, and this was really what she loved doing above all else. If she had been without clients, alone or with other climbers, she would have been in that state of hyper-alert attuned-to-landscape no-mind that was the Zen of climbing, the great joy of it, the source of the addiction. As it was, however, the objective dangers underfoot were great enough to put her in a high state of apprehension for her clients' sake. A guide was only as happy as her least happy client, and right now she was surrounded by a bunch of frost-flocked, insect-eyed, mute people; Ta Shu and Jack enjoying themselves, the rest really eager for this part to be over.

And yet as it got higher it got steeper, and they had to go slower. It was as if they were trapped in Zeno's paradox, and halving the distance to the top in increments of time that remained the same. Burning and freezing; waiting for Val to screw in ice-screws, or screw them out; looking or not looking at the blue gaping fissures in the ice underfoot, each one a potential death-trap.

Thus it was nearly three in the afternoon when they finally came under the Hansen Shoulder, where a narrow ramp of ice led them right under its exposed rock, up toward the polar plateau. There was a wide bergschrund gap between their ice ramp and the dolerite of the shoulder, smoothed into a vertical wall by the ablation of the wind. There was also, unfortunately, a tumble of big broken seracs to the left of the ramp as they climbed, cleft with deep crevasses that ran out across the first great drop of the icefall. So they had no room for manoeuvring on either side, and could only press onward up the ramp, their crampons sticking in the blue ice as they laboured up the slope. But the screen image showed that it would go all the way.

Before they topped out, however, they had to pass a single tall block of ice filling the bergschrund to the right and overhanging their ramp – a smooth, bluish fang of ice, a chunk of a serac which must have fallen from higher on the Hansen Shoulder, or across the ramp from the serac field to their left. The width of the ramp as it curved under this serac was just a bit wider than the sledge itself, because a crevasse curved out of the serac field and ran parallel to the ramp on the left. Val saw that this crevasse was a deep one. So they were on an icebridge, in effect, running up the slope between bergschrund and crevasse. Where the crevasse ran out across the icefall, it was soon filled at its top by a snowbridge, leaving an opening under the snowbridge that was a very considerable ice tunnel. Not an unusual sight, but it added a certain frisson to the narrowness of the ramp, suggesting as it did the depths on each side of them.

Val stopped her group. It looked as if the ramp ran all the way around the overhanging block without obstruction, after which it widened again. Very workable, but narrow enough that a fixed line would be appropriate. So she uncoiled one of the ropes, flaking it out neatly so that it would come up after her without knotting. From her gear sling she took an ice-screw – a hollow metal tube, screw-threaded on the outside, with a sharp point on the driving end, and holes in the other end to insert an ice axe for easier turning – and chipped a hole about a quarter of an inch deep with the sharp end of the screw, then got it set and rotated it in squeaking at every turn, the first half by hand, the second half with the leverage of her ice axe, until it was almost completely buried. A bombproof belay. She asked Jack to clip onto the screw with a runner, which was a looped piece of webbing, and belay her as she went on up. Then she took off up the ramp, Jack feeding out just enough rope that Val could feel it tugging back on her a bit. Jack somehow always ending up doing this job, and it was true he was good at it; a tight belay, with just the right slack in it, so that the middle of the rope scarcely touched the ice.

Around the corner and above the ice block, Val stopped and screwed in two more ice-screws, connecting them by a sling attached to each through carabiners, so that any force that came on them would be equalized. She tied a figure of eight in the end of the belay rope, and attached it to the sling with another carabiner.

Before returning to the others she reattached herself to the belay rope with a prussik loop. This was a small loop of rope, tied to the belay rope in a simple knot that tightened and held position when you put weight on the loop, but could be loosened and slid up or down the belay rope by hand when there wasn't weight on it.

She got back to the others. 'Okay, up we go.' She lined the clients along the rope, made sure they were attached to both the rope and their harness, and sent them ahead. They cramponed up the ramp, hunched over a bit. Jack stayed behind to help her haul the sledge up.

The others had all gone around the ice block to the higher belay and got off the rope, and Val and Jack had clipped their harnesses onto the belay rope and were just beginning to pull the sledge into line, when the ice block above them leaned over with a groan and fell. Val leapt into the crevasse to the left, her only escape from being crushed under falling ice. She hit the inner wall of the crevasse with her forearms up to protect her. The rope finally caught her fall and yanked her up by her harness; then she was pulled down again hard as Jack was arrested by the same rope below her. For a second or two she was yanked all over the place, up and down like a puppet, slammed hard into the wall. The rope was stretching almost like a bungee cord, as designed – it was very necessary to decelerate with some give – but it was a violent ride, totally out of her control.

But the belay above held, and the belayers too. As soon as she stopped bouncing, however, she twisted and kicked into the ice wall with both front-point crampons, then grabbed her ice axe and smacked the ice above her with the sharp end to place another tool.

A moment's stillness. Nothing hurt too badly. She was well down in the crevasse, the blue wall right in front of her nose. Ice axe in to the second notch, but she wanted more. Below her Jack was hanging freely from the same rope she was, holding onto it above his head with one hand. No sign of the sledge.

Voices from above. 'We're okay!' she shouted up. 'Hold the belay! Don't move it!' Don't do a thing! she wanted to add.

'Jack!' she called down. 'Are you okay?'

'Mostly.'

'Can you swing into the wall and get your tools in?'

'Trying.'

He appeared to be below a slight overhang, and she above it. A very pure crevasse hang, in fact, with the rest of the group on the surface several metres above them, belaying them, hopefully listening to her shouts and tying off, rather than trying to haul them up by main strength; it couldn't be done, and might very well end in disaster. Val didn't even want to shout up to tell them to tie off: who knew what they would do? Not wanting to trust them, she took another ice-screw from her gear-rack, chipped out a hole in the wall in front of her, set the screw in it, then gave it little twists to screw it into the ice. Its ice coring shaved out of the aluminium cylinder. A long time passed while she did this, and it became obvious that they were underdressed for the situation; it was probably twenty below down here, and no sun or exertion now to warm them; and sweaty from adrenalin. They were chilling fast, and it added urgency to her operation. She had to perform a variation of the operation called Escaping the Situation – a standard crevasse technique, in fact, but one of those ingenious mountaineering manoeuvres that worked better in theory than in practice, and better in practice than in a true emergency.

The screw was in, and she clipped onto it with a carabiner and sling attached to her harness, then eased back down a bit. Now both she and Jack had the insurance belay of the screw.

From the surface came more shouts.

'We're okay!' she shouted up. 'Are the belay-screws holding well?'

Jim shouted down that they were. 'What should we do?'

'Just hold the belay!' she shouted up anxiously. 'Tie it off as tight as you can!' More times than she cared to remember she had found herself in the hole with the clients up top, and they had often proved more dangerous than the crevasse.

She tied another prussik loop to the belay rope, then reached up and put her right boot into it. Then she stood in that loop, jack-knifing to the side, and unclipped her harness from the ice-screw, then straightened out slowly as she slid the prussik attached to her harness as high on the rope as it would go. When she was standing straight in the lower loop, she tightened the upper prussik, then hung by the waist from it, and reached down and pulled the lower one up the rope, keeping her boot

213

in the loop all the while. There was the temptation to pull the lower loop almost all the way up to the higher one, but that resulted in a really awkward jack-knife, and made it hard to put weight on her foot so she could move the higher one up. So it was a little bit up on each loop, over and over; tedious hard work, but not so hard if you had had a lot of practice, as Val had, and didn't get greedy for height.

'Jack, can you prussik up?'

'Just waiting for you to get off-rope,' he said tightly.

'Go ahead and start!' she said sharply. 'A little flopping around isn't going to hurt me now.'

Soon enough she reached the edge of the crevasse, and the others on top helped haul her over the edge, where she was blinded by the harsh sunlight. She unclipped from the rope and went over to check the belay. It was holding as if nothing had ever tugged on it. Bombproof indeed.

Then it was Jack's turn to huff and puff. Prussiking was both hard and meticulous, accomplished in awkward acrobatic positions while swinging in space all the while, unless you managed to balance against the ice wall of the crevasse. Jack appeared to be making the classic mistake of trying for too much height with each move of the loops, and he wasn't propping himself against the wall either. It took him a long, long time to get up the rope, and when he finally pulled up to the point where the others could haul him over, he was steaming and looked grim.

'Good,' she said when he was sitting safely on the ramp. 'Are you all right?'

'I will be when I catch my breath. I've cut my hand somehow.' He showed them the bloody back of his right glove, a shocking red. The blood was flowing pretty heavily.

'Shit,' she said, and hacked some firn off the ramp to give to him. 'Pack this onto it for a while until the bleeding slows.'

'A sledge runner caught me on its way down.'

'Wow. That was close!'

'Very close.'

'Where is the sledge?' Jorge said.

'Down there!' said Jack, pointing into the crevasse. 'But it got knocked in and past us, rather than crushed outright by the block. I gave it a last big tug when I jumped in.'

'Good work.' Val looked around. 'I'll go back down and have a look for it.'

'I'll come along,' said Jack, and Jim, and Jorge.

'You can all help, but I'll go down and check it out first.'

So she took from her gear-rack a metal descending device known as an Air Traffic Controller, and attached it to the rope, then to her harness using a big locking carabiner. She leaned back to take the slack out of the rope between her and the anchor, then started feeding rope through the Air Traffic Controller as she walked backward toward the crevasse, putting her weight hard on the rope. Getting over the edge was the tricky part; she had to lean back right at the edge and hop over it and get her crampon bottoms flat against the wall, legs straight out from it and body at a forty-five degree angle. But it was a move she had done many times before, and in the heat of the moment she did it almost without thinking. After that she paid the rope slowly up through the descender, one hand above it and one running the rope behind her back for some extra friction. Down down down in recliner position, past the ice-screw she had placed, down and down into the blue cold. She was keeping her focus on the immediate situation, of course, but her pulse was hammering harder than her exertion justified, and she found herself distracted by an inventory that part of her mind was taking of the emergency contents of everyone's clothing. This was no help at the moment, and as she got deeper in the crevasse she banished all distracting thoughts.

Just past the tilt in the crevasse that blocked the view from above, there was a kind of floor. Her rope was almost entirely paid out, and she had not tied a figure of eight stopper-knot in the end of the line, which was stupid, a sign that she wasn't thinking. But it got her down to a floor, and it was possible to walk on this floor, she saw, still going down fairly steeply; and as she saw no sight of the sledge, but a lot of chunks of the broken ice block leading still onward, she called up that she was going off-rope, then unclipped, and moved cautiously over the drifted snow and ice filling the intersection of the walls underfoot – a floor by no means flat, but rather a matter of Vs and Us and Ws, the tilts all partly covered by drift. There was also no assurance at all that it was not a false floor, a kind of snowbridge in a narrow section, with more open crevasse below it; she would have stayed on-rope if there had been enough of it. As it was she crabbed along smack against the crevasse wall, hooking the pick of her axe into it as she went, testing each step as thoroughly as she could and hoping the bottom didn't drop out from under her.

She moved under the snowbridge she had noted from above, and the crevasse therefore became a tall blue tunnel. She moved farther down into it. Sometimes ice roofed the tunnel, at other times snowbridges, their white undersides great cauliflowers of ice crystal, glowing with white light. The view from below made it clear why snowbridges over crevasses were such dangerous things, so tenuous were they and so fatally deep the pits below them. But that was why people roped up.

215

The tunnel turned at an angle, and then opened downward into a much larger chamber. Val kept going.

This new space within the ice was really big, and a much deeper blue than what she had come through so far, the Rayleigh scattering of sunlight so far advanced that only the very bluest light made it down here, glowing from out of the ice in an intense creamy-translucent turquoise, or actually an unnamed blue unlike any other she had seen. The interior of the space was a magnificent shambles. Entire columns of pale-blue ice had peeled off the walls and fallen across the chamber intact, like broken pillars in a shattered temple. The walls were fractured in immense translucent planes, everything elongated and spacious – as if God had looked into Carlsbad Caverns and the other limestone caverns of the world and said *No no, too dark, too squat, too bulbous, I want something lighter in every way,* and so had tapped His fingernail against the great glacier and got these airy bubbles in the ice, which made limestone caves look oafish and troglo-dytic. Of course ice chambers like these were short-lived by comparison to regular caves, but this one appeared to have been here for a while, perhaps years, it was hard to tell. Certainly all the glassy, broken edges had long since sublimed away in the hyperarid air, so that the shatter was rounded and polished like blue driftglass, so polished that it gleamed as though melting, though it was far below freezing.

Val moved farther into the room, enchanted. A shattered cathedral, made of titanic columns of driftglass; a room of a thousand shapes; and all of it a blue that could not be described and could scarcely be apprehended, as it seemed to flood and then to overflood the eye. Val stared at it, rapt, trying to take it all in, realizing that it was likely to be one of the loveliest sights she would ever see in her life – unearthly, surreal – her breath caught, her cheeks burned, her spine tingled, and all just from seeing such a sight.

But no sledge. And back at the entrance to the blue chamber, there was a narrow crack running the other way, not much wider than the sledge itself; and looking down it, into an ever darkening blue, Val saw a smear of pale snow and ice shards, and below that, what appeared to be the sledge, wedged between the ice walls a hundred feet or more below; it was hard to judge, because the crevasse continued far down into the midnight blue depths below. There was no way she could get down there and get back up again; and even if she could have, the sledge was corked, as they said. Stuck and irretrievable. In this case crushed between the walls, it looked like, and broken open so that its contents were spilled even farther down. A very thorough corking. No – the sledge was gone.

CHAPTER NINE

Big Trouble

Wade slept through the flight to Shackleton Glacier Camp, and sleepwalked his way through the transition from Herc to helo, then fell asleep again. The next time he woke he found himself suspended above the upper reaches of Shackleton Glacier, in the clear plastic bubble of a little Squirrel helicopter. The ice curved down to the sea in a broad sweep, with long lines of rubble marking very clearly the direction of the flow, and tributary glaciers pouring in and merging in just the way the water of rivers would, although here the eddies and cross-currents were indicated by rippled blue crevasse patches, or even in some places gnashed into fields of turquoise blades.

The Kiwi helo pilot pointed down at one such field. 'Ever seen one of those close up?'

'No.'

They dropped like a shot bird, tilting forward and to the left as they spiralled tightly downward. Wade gritted his teeth. Kiwi pilots were scary, as he had begun to learn on his flight down from Christchurch. The young American pilots working for ASL moved their big beasts around the air like trucks, and like good truck drivers they were impressive; but the Kiwis, older and wiser, flew as if their helos were extensions of their bodies, like dragonflies. This man looked unconcerned as he brought the helo swooping down to hover, in dragonfly style, well down inside an avenue of serac skyscrapers. Wade was shocked at their size, as from a thousand feet up they had looked like waist-high ripples. 'Wow.'

The pilot pulled back up and continued without comment. Back at cruising height, the crevasse patches again looked like ice-cubes; but now, knowing how big they really were, Wade's sense of scale popped like one's ears did, and he realized that the glacier and the mountains flanking it were all huge, huge, huge. The helo buzzed along like a bee up a winter canyon. It was a big planet.

Ahead, a rusty rock-island grew. A spill of glacier poured over a low point in its outermost ridge and fell down into a bowl of rock that it never even reached, much less filled. As they passed the island Wade could now see the polar cap, extending to the south for ever. On the southernmost point of the island clustered a tiny knot of green, square roofs, like Monopoly houses. Vertigo of scale: it was as a gnat or a microbe that he watched the tiny structures recede behind them, and the nunatak get lower and smaller, until they were out over the ice of the polar cap, and it was ice as far as they could see, on a world grown as big as Jupiter, or the sun itself. Then the helo began to drop again. They were landing on the ice.

The complex of buildings they descended on was of course bigger than it had appeared from above. As Wade got out of the helicopter the complex looked entirely deserted, in the usual Antarctic way; everyone indoors. The empty continent indeed.

Then one of the doors opened, and out of it appeared the big man Wade had met back in McMurdo, on Ob Hill. It seemed a very long time ago; in actuality, less than two weeks.

'Hi!' Wade said.

X looked closer, then recognized him as well. 'Hi. Welcome to the ice.'

Wade nodded, looking around at the brilliantly-lit scene. Flat white to the horizon in all directions; much like the Pole in that regard. A gentle breeze cut deep into him. The main building of the complex was a small meat-locker/mobile home, behind it a gleaming oil derrick or something like, resting on broad pontoons that were only slightly snowdrifted on their south sides. Metal grid stairs led up to the usual locker door, and after a brief look around they went inside.

The interior of the room was like the bridge of an invisible ship, the walls banked with the consoles of anonymous machinery. From this height expansive shallow basins and low hills were discernible on the ice plain.

'Nice,' Wade said.

'Yes,' said X, and called into the next room. A man entered. 'This is Carlos, the leader of the group here.'

'Good to meet you,' Wade said to the bearded man. They shook hands.

'And you too,' Carlos said. 'Nice to have you here. Here, let's have some lunch, and then we'll take you out and show you around.'

'That would be nice.'

Lunch was a spicy Chilean prawn and scallop stew. There were other men in the room, Latinos and Africans, eating the stew and talking in

218

Spanish or English. Then they left in a group for the machine shop, and Carlos and X and Wade sat at a lab table under one of the end windows, and talked, looking out at the view. Wade described his mission to Antarctica, and told them some of what he had discovered at the South Pole and back at McMurdo. Carlos nodded, then expressed his admiration for Phil Chase. 'He is very important now, very important.'

Wade said, 'Do you mind if I try to transmit our conversation to him? He'd like to hear this, I'm sure.'

'Oh no problem, no problem.'

Wade tapped the Congressman's button on his wristphone, hoping it was not the middle of the night wherever Chase was now; or if so, that he was feeling insomniac again. Voices in the night: that was how Phil spent many a sleepless hour.

'First,' Wade said, 'can you tell me if your hovercraft has ever been out to the South Pole, either with you, or piloted by someone else?'

Carlos looked surprised. 'To the Pole? It's more than two hundred kilometres away.'

'Couldn't the hovercraft get there?'

'Not without refuelling.'

'Couldn't fuel caches be out there?'

'Well, yes, I suppose so. I mean there are, at our field stations. But they are all located over this basin under the ice that we are investigating, the Pothole as we call it. We don't go toward the Pole much.'

'And no one else could have used the hovercraft?'

'No way.'

Wade nodded, thinking it over. 'Tell me more about this place.'

Carlos described the nature of the work going on at the station, emphasizing its exploratory nature, the new fail-safe technologies being employed in the hunt, and the fact that the main quarry at this point was methane hydrate, which if burned as fuel rather than released into the atmosphere would actually help the overall picture concerning global warming. He listed the points of the suspended Antarctic Treaty, and described how they were in fact conforming to all of them: 'especially at this point, when the drilling is being done for science only'.

Wade nodded throughout this description, then said, 'It's very interesting, but you must agree that there is a lot of criticism and opposition to your project.'

'This is political in nature.'

'Well, some from Antarctic scientists too. If the project is as harmless or as beneficial as you say it is, then why are they making these objections?'

Carlos rolled his eyes. 'Unfortunately there are a fairly large number of scientists who are not completely scientific. Not good scientists when it comes to life outside their own field of study. It's part of a more general crisis ongoing among scientists worldwide, concerning how to behave in the world outside their field. You have been down here long enough to notice, I hope, that this continent is run by scientists, and mostly for their own benefit. They are funded by governments to come down here, and they generate the only export of the continent so far, which is scientific papers. Knowledge, you can say, but say also papers, careers, livings.'

X was nodding deeply as Carlos said this, and Wade looked to him to invite him to explain why.

'That's the way it looked in McMurdo,' X said. 'Beaker utopia. And the rest of the people down here making things nice for them, freeing up their time, but just making wages for themselves. It's a caste system.'

'Exactly,' Carlos said. 'Most scientists have analysed life scientifically, and realized that sufficiency is all that you really need, and that pursuing money beyond the point of sufficiency only degrades life. So that it is no coincidence that very rich people are often fools or crazed, while scientists are smart people who have carved their little utopia out of the world-system, by extending their efforts after knowledge rather than money. They know that knowledge can become power, and with the power that science wields in this world, they control things. Control even the political realm, but without the hassle of politics per se. They just advise the decision-makers what is possible and what is advisable, and ask for money, and go out and do what they want.'

Wade said, 'So you're saying scientists control not just Antarctica, but the whole rest of the world?'

Carlos got up and took their bowls to the stove for refills. 'Exactly true! And this illustrates a very important principle of mine, which is that whatever is true in Antarctica is also true everywhere else in the world. But in Antarctica there are no, no,' he waved at the blank, featureless white plain outside the window, 'no distractions. No trees or billboards. You can see what really is true, naked out here. So if you come down here and see a continent ruled by scientists for their own convenience, it is true also then on all the other continents as well.'

Wade said, 'Well, but, I don't know . . . I'm not used to thinking of scientists actually being the ones in control. I don't think most of them would agree that's the case. I doubt they would even want it to be.'

'Oh no, not explicitly! Of course not! Who would want that, it is obviously such a hassle! Politicians–' he looked at Wade, raised a palm

220

to say, What can you say? 'No sane person would want that, apologies to Senator Chase. It violates the principle of sufficiency. But tell me, who do you think rules the world?'

'Governments,' Wade said.

'Okay, but not politicians per se. The whole government.'

'Yes.'

'Meaning you. I mean, in that the politicians get elected, and they have staff people who actually know how to work the system. And so when they want to get something done, they ask their staff how they can do it, and if the staff like the project they tell the politician how, and if they don't like it, they subvert it.'

'*Yes, Minister,*' X said. 'Great show.'

Wade had to agree. 'I certainly am in complete control of my politician,' he said distinctly toward his wristphone. 'Sir Humphrey has nothing on me.'

'So,' Carlos said, 'but when you make your decisions, who do you consult? Do you call yourself a bureaucrat?'

'No, no really.'

'Because they are just functionaries, they do not set policy?'

'That's right.'

'But what about technocrats? What about scientific staff, who tell the politicians what is physically possible and what isn't? Are you a technocrat?'

'Perhaps,' Wade said. 'But not usually. I have an expertise, I suppose, but I'm no scientist.'

'A bureaucrat then! Or staff assistant, or political aide. Whatever you call it. Let's just say government, like you said at first. But you make your decisions by consulting with a technical staff, the technocrats, and they make their decisions by consulting with the scientific bodies, the scientists. And so the scientists call the shots!'

Wade and X stared at each other in consternation.

'And now we have overshot the Earth's carrying capacity,' Carlos went on as he gave them full bowls. 'We have maybe two, maybe three billion more people than we can support. And this global warming, the bad weather. It's an emergency situation. Governments have to guide us through the tight spot in history, if we are going to get through it without super-catastrophes. But how will they do that? Who will tell them how to do it?'

'Beakers,' X said.

Carlos nodded.

'But they're not even trying!' X objected. 'They're got their island utopia, like you said, and so they just come down here or wherever else and hang out in the field or the lab and do their thing, and they're not doing anything to save the world, as far as I can tell. They're just part of the capitalist machinery.'

'Yes and no,' Carlos said. 'Capitalism is the dominant economic order, and it tends to subsume everything else, it wants to subsume everything else. But the great outsider, the system that capitalism cannot conquer, is science. The two are actually at odds with each other, the one trying to defeat the other. This is the great war of our time!'

'Capitalism versus science?' Wade said, sceptical.

'Sure. First it was capitalism versus socialism, and then capitalism versus democracy, and now science is the only thing left! And science itself is part of the battlefield, and can be corrupted. But in essence, in my heart as a scientist, I say to you that it is a utopian project. It tries to make a utopia within itself, in the rules of scientific conduct and organization, and it also tries to influence the world at large in a utopian direction. No, it is true!' he cried, noting the looks on both Wade's and X's faces. 'Here, have you seen this book?' He leaned over the lab bench and pulled a book from under a stack of dirty dishes. 'Do you know it? This is the Spanish version, it was written by Chileans. *Los Elementos Eticos, Políticos y Utópicos Incorporados en la Estructura de la Ciencia Moderna*. Recently it has been translated into English, of course, for that is the language of science. In English it is called something like *The Ethical, Political, and Utopian Elements Embodied in the Structure of Modern Science*. And this book is really having an impact, it is quite a revolution in scientific circles. Because what it demonstrates very clearly is that what we think of as neutral objective science is actually a utopian politics and worldview already. There is a big historical section describing the rise of science, showing that science is self-organizing and self-actualizing, and always trying to get better, to be more scientific, as one of its rules. And there is a big middle section showing how various features of normal scientific practice, the methodology and so on, are in fact ethical positions. Things like reproducibility, or Occam's razor, or peer review – almost everything in science that makes it specifically scientific, the authors show, is utopian. Then the final section tells what the ramifications of this fact are, how scientists should behave now, once they realize this truth. And the book is a kind of underground bestseller! It goes from lab to lab, the graduate students are all reading it, the senior scientists who are still thinking – everyone! This is the cause of the recent explosion in appropriate technologies, if you ask me, the so-called materials revolution, the ecological efficiency movement, all these scientific movements and strands, all networked together of course, and all vibrating now with the philosophy of this book!'

222

'I'd like to read that,' X said, tapping madly at his paperback's console to see if it was in there already.

'Me too,' Wade said.

Carlos nodded. 'It should be in most of the e-books like X's here, unless you have an old one that isn't getting supplemented. The translation is about five years old now. Anyway, you know, what I have been saying to you is the utopian description of the situation. In reality, there are a great number of scientists who are not interested in the reasons they do what they do. This makes them bad scientists in that way, but there you are. Bad work is done in every field. So, you know, there are some scientists used to the old ways down here, when the technology being deployed was not safe for the environment. Consider the nuclear reactor that American scientists brought down to McMurdo, for instance.'

'Nuclear reactor?' Wade said.

'It's gone now. Along with a big chunk of Observation Hill, which had been contaminated. A hundred thousand tons of earth, shipped north to the nuclear dump in South Carolina. Nukey Poo, they called it.'

'You can still set a dosimeter ringing if you stick it in the dirt in the right places,' X confirmed. 'Some people used to do that for fun.'

'For fun?' Wade said.

'McMurdo,' X explained.

'Anyway,' Carlos said, taking their emptied bowls over to a narrow shelf on the wall and stacking them, 'when more people realize what we are doing out here – the high safety factor, the need to capture as much methane as we can before it is released as a greenhouse gas – the desperate need for energy in the countries of the consortium – then there will no longer be this ignorant outcry. Meanwhile–' he grinned at Wade, waving at the door– 'let us show you something.'

Hey you, do you read?

We read.

Everything ready?

Everything's ready. The hardware's in place, and we have made contact with the friends who are going to clear all personnel from active sites. They're in position, so we can go on the prearranged schedule.

Great. They've got track of everyone?

Yes. Everyone's in their site camps.

Cool. Okay, we go on schedule then, very good. Everyone have a nice trip home, and remember, no talk ever. Eco-radical not ego-radical. This is probably the last time most of us will communicate, so for all of us, let me say it's been nice working with you.

You too.

You too.

Over and out.

Outside, the other two men prepped three snowmobiles. While Wade watched he called Phil Chase back again; 'Did you hear any of that, Phil?'

'Yes I did. I was asleep when you called, and I may have slipped back under from time to time, but I kept the phone to my ear, and it was very interesting. Sir Humphrey indeed. And I want to read that book. It would be good if what this man said was true. But I don't think he's taking into account the true power of power. There's guns under the table, Wade. There's a cancer in the social body, and the tumour cells are the brains of these goddamned executives, guiding the traffic over the cliff and then flying off to their Caribbean isle. I'd like to figure out a new kind of chemotherapy . . . it'd look kind of like *Eraserhead* I guess . . .' Either the connection broke or Phil had gone back to sleep.

Then Carlos and X were ready, and Wade was given a one-minute tutorial in operating a Skidoo, which was a little snowmobile with a single broad ski for a front wheel. Then they were off, buzzing over the white surface in a line of three, with Wade in the middle. He had never ridden a snowmobile before, but with a thumb-squeeze accelerator, no brakes at all and handlebars for the front ski like a bicycle, it was no great problem to handle. It was like being astride a giant, clumsy, extra-wide Harley Davidson, he supposed, having never been on a motorcycle either. Certainly balancing the thing was no problem, except for occasional lurches into dips he did not see, for which he grossly overcompensated, with anxious leans and turns in the other direction.

But by and large the ride was very close to effortless, especially after he relaxed the vicelike grip he had taken on the handlebars, which were heated to keep his hands warm. Both his hands and wrists were inside giant, borrowed mitts called 'bear claws', but without the heat from the handlebars they still would have been cold.

After several more minutes of roaring over the white firn, he felt free to unlock his gaze from Carlos's back and look around a bit. Off to their left a black, serrated rock ridge broke the horizon. Carlos was following a barely discernible line of green flags, waving limply on top of bamboo poles. At one of these he slowed down, turned to the left and sped on, toward a new manifestation of the black mountains on the horizon, this time straight ahead of them. As they closed on it Wade saw it in more detail, looming up over the white plain: a brown-black spur of rock, lined horizontally. A mountain buried to the neck in ice. Nearer to it he saw that the rock disrupted the ice around it into rings of frozen eddies, and even what looked like frozen breakers, for ever almost about to break against the lower slopes of the rock cliff.

When they stopped, outside the turbulence, Wade pulled off one bear claw to check his wrist GPS. They were in the Mohn Basin, it seemed; the spur of rock appeared to be D'Angelo Bluff; beyond it the black spike of Mount Howe. The ice between these nunataks was lined and cracked with entire cities of blue shatter. Carlos started up again and headed straight for one of these broken zones, finally manoeuvring in broad turns until he appeared to be riding right into the open end of a broad ice ravine. Blue, gleaming séracs overhung one wall; above those black rock towered high in the sky.

> blue sky
> black rock
> blue ice

Happily Carlos stopped at this point in the growing chasm, and turned off his snowmobile engine. X and Wade did the same. Suddenly they were out there, in a silence so complete it seemed noisy.

Except there; a breeze, soughing over the ice. It was Debussy should have been the composer for this continent, Wade thought. Debussy or Satie, or Sibelius, mystic spirit of snowy Finland. Sibelius the composer and Dali the artist. Or Escher. Or Rockwell Kent, or Canada's Group of Seven, or Nisbet of the Antarctic. Only a few could have caught it. Empty blue sky. It was a strange place to be.

Carlos and X converged on Wade, and Carlos pointed at a big snow block. 'See it?'

Wade stared at the white snow. 'See what?'

They laughed at him. 'Come on.'

Over firn they crunched. It did not give underfoot, and they left no tracks. Quite close to the ice wall, Carlos pointed again. 'There, see it?'

Wade peered. Against the white was a white shape. Then it jumped out at him, like one of those 3-D mashes suddenly revealing its pattern: a white metal box on tracks, somewhat like the old Hagglunds he had seen at McMurdo, but smaller; only seven or eight feet tall. One would have to crouch to get in its door.

'Wow,' Wade said.

They approached it. The sides were covered by hoarfrost or wind-plastered snow, but under that appeared to be painted white as well. The metal tracks ran over small sprocketed metal wheels. All painted as white as the cab. The three men stood before it. X could look right into one of the wind-drifted windows.

'What is it?'

Carlos and X looked at him.

'It took a long time to answer that question,' Carlos said. 'We found it here by accident, while putting out a geophone grid last year. This is nowhere near where anyone has been, you see. And the Americans didn't have any vehicles missing, not then anyway. In any case, it's a Weasel, made in England in the 1950s. There was a Weasel used by Edmund Hillary's group when they drove tractors to the Pole in 1958. Most of their tractors were Fergusons, but they had one Weasel that they ran until it fell apart, and then they left it out on the polar cap.'

'But . . .'

'It must have been completely buried. Perhaps as much as ten metres down in the ice, and out there on the cap, with nothing for hundreds of kilometres in any direction.'

'Wow. Who could have found it?'

An expressive shrug from Carlos.

'Someone with a metal detector,' X said.

'And a bulldozer,' Carlos added.

'And the new ice borers.'

'And familiarity with Hillary's route,' Wade suggested.

'That would be easy enough,' Carlos said. 'Hillary wrote a book about his trip.'

'I never heard of this expedition,' Wade confessed.

'Who has? Driving tractors to the South Pole?'

'That would be hard,' X noted.

'Yes, but what is the point? You sit in the driver seat, you try to stay warm, you look for crevasses.'

'That would be hard.'

'I suppose. But it is not the right kind of method to make people notice. We could drive these snowmobiles to the Pole, eh? But so what?'

Wade said, 'Can we look inside?'

'Sure, sure.' Carlos went to the door of the cab, and turned a handle – no lock – and pulled open a thin metal door. Clearly the Weasel had not been a warm experience. A box of thin metal, primitive controls for the driver, benches against the side. The heat of the engine would be all that made it possible.

'Whoever dug it out doesn't seem to have refurbished,' Wade remarked, running his hand over a wooden bench.

'No. Except for the white paint, I think. But there's no clue to their identity. As if they used it for something and then abandoned it.'

'Or stored it,' X said.

'Maybe so. Anyway, here it is.'

'Does it run?'

'Yes. Half a tank of gas.'

'It evaporates through the cap,' X said. 'It could have been full not too long ago.'

They walked out of the shade of the chasm, back into the blazing light. Wade's sunglasses shifted back to full strength. He looked around; still the empty icescape, the pure blue sky. The Hillary Weasel sat against its ice wall – a white oddity, incongruous, something like the prehistoric man found in the ice in Austria. Thrown up by the ice. Or excavated. Someone was out here doing things, Wade thought. Someone who liked rescuing bits of the past. Salvaging useful tools, giving them a try. Perhaps giving up on them if they didn't work out, and leaving them around, as exhibits in a kind of open-air museum, or art gallery. Or whatever. He shook his head, climbed back on his Skidoo.

They were running the snowmobiles back over their outgoing tracks, and at a certain point Wade's Skidoo tilted and veered and he pulled it back on track with accidental ease, and realized that the vehicle was not going to tip over no matter what he did. All of a sudden he forgot all his cares and all the mysteries, and was just riding a big motorcycle-thing, a wonderful bit of Antarctic technology, fit for a museum or an art gallery itself, over the snow at the bottom of the world. He hummed some Wagner and christened this 'The Ride of the Valeries', because he was thinking of her again. This is what she liked, and perhaps this was how she felt when she was out here. This was what she lived for. Exuberance is beauty! And those distant, low black mountains on the white horizon, that sky! An exaltation came over him: Wade on ice, humming Wagner through the mesh of his ski-mask.

Such moments are transitory. Wade was already considering how much the roaring power of the Skidoo was implicated in his euphoria, how much it was the technological sublime he was feeling rather than the glory of Antarctica per se – when from ahead of Carlos came a flash, as from a mirror reflecting the sun. Immediately after that a black plume of smoke lofted into the air, narrow and dark, and suddenly choked off. A big puff, wafting off on the breeze.

Carlos's Skidoo took off. Apparently he had been holding back as a courtesy to Wade's inexperience, and now he was hellbent on getting back to the station as fast as possible, leaving Wade and X quickly behind. Wade pressed his tired thumb even harder on the accelerator, and his Skidoo shot over the snow faster than before. Despite this acceleration X drew up beside him, barrelling over the untracked sastrugi, seeming unaware of the bumps, his whole being focused on the smoke puff ahead. He passed Wade and slammed his Skidoo into the tracks ahead so that he could go even faster.

Then both Carlos and X were stopped, and Wade let his cramping thumb relax, and his Skidoo quickly slid to a halt. He stood astride his snowmobile, looking at the station ahead of them. The main building was knocked flat and scattered all over the ice. One propane tank still burned, the fitful blue-orange flames pale in the sunlight. Otherwise there was no movement. The tents were flattened. The Jamesway and the machine shops were ripped to shreds. The drilling platform was on its side, its base shattered. There was no one to be seen.

Hesitantly they walked toward the wreckage. Thankfully, there were no bodies in sight; strange but true; the main building and machine shops were smashed open to their inspection, and it appeared they must have been empty when they were blown apart, for there was no sign of anyone.

Despite this good news Carlos hopped in a rage beside what remained of the main building, literally shaking his fist, cursing violently, 'Hijo de puta!' and so forth – the most sulphurous Spanish Wade had ever heard. X walked around saying, 'Where is everybody? Where is everybody? There's no one here. That's very weird. How could there be no one here? Where did they all go? Oh God, I hope they're not under the wall–' He went to his knees, looked under one of the larger fragments of the main building.

He stood again. The three of them looked at each other. There was no one there. It seemed to Wade that the buildings must have been deserted at the moment of impact. Perhaps people had had time to run? But then where were they now?

'It's very weird there's no one here,' X said to Wade. 'It's like when I was ripped off on the SPOT train. Some kind of, I dunno. Some kind of group out here.'

'The ones who dug out Hillary's Weasel?' Wade wondered. 'Or the ones salvaging the old Pole station?'

X stopped pacing. 'There are people salvaging the old Pole station?'

'Yes.'

'I thought they still used that for storage.'

'Not the old Pole station. The old old Pole station.'

X stared at him. 'Wow,' he said.

The three of them wandered together to the downed drilling rig, none of them willing to get very far from the other two. At the foot of the collapsed structure was a mass of blasted and melted metal, distorted shapes under the fallen superstructure. No sign of methane hydrate leakage, of course. No doubt the explosion had capped the hole down there somewhere. Carlos cursed again. 'This *never* would have happened, never never never, it was safe, we made it safe, everything was backed up, nothing could go wrong, they had to *blow it up* to make this happen, those *hijos de putas*,' hopping in place, weeping, shouting, roaring. 'I *live* here, I *born* here, this is *my country*. I know how to take care of it, I *kill* these people these terrorists, I kill them kill them kill them!'

Wade and X nodded, neutral but sympathetic.

'How are we going to get home?' X asked.

'Home?' Wade said.

'McMurdo. Or even Roberts.'

'Call in a helo,' Wade said. 'Or that hovercraft you mentioned.'

X nodded. 'But what if the same thing happened to Roberts?'

Wade felt himself blinking in the frigid cold. He hadn't thought of that.

X shrugged. 'Could have happened.'

Wade tapped Chase's phone number on his wrist. Might as well get help from the top.

But there was no connection. Quickly he tapped through his other regular numbers, the operator, everything. All connections were down. He felt a little shiver that had nothing to do with the cold, that was not corporeal at all. A metaphysical shudder, an informational shudder. The shutdown of one of his senses.

'The phones aren't working,' he said to the others.

Carlos ended his muttering abruptly. 'Really?'

He hurried to his Skidoo and took a briefcase-sized radio from the box behind the seat. He set it on the seat and strung out the antenna lines in a broad V, then plugged together several of the miniature coloured plugs that appeared every couple of feet in the antenna wire. He turned on the control console and began calling out.

First Roberts; static only. Then McMurdo directly.

Again, nothing but static.

'*Madre.*' Carlos looked at X and Wade. 'They seem to have put out Mac Town radio. And the satellites.'

He moved the antenna lines so that the broad V they made faced a different direction, changed some plugs, tried again on a different channel. 'Ah. At least that sounds like the usual static. But the Peninsula is too far for this thing. I can almost hear them, but they will not hear us.' Nevertheless he tried transmitting again, in Spanish then English. No response.

The three men looked at each other, their ski-masks and sunglasses hiding their expressions. To Wade the snowmobiles now looked like fat motorbikes, their spare fuel canisters like gallon milk containers from the supermarket. Really inadequate to the task. Carlos was doing calculations on his wrist. 'If we load the Skidoos to their maximum,

230

we will have enough fuel to get to Roberts. Or if we run out we'll be just a few kilometres away, and we can walk on in.'

He looked at the other two.

X shrugged. 'Let's get going.'

He and Carlos took short shovels from their Skidoo boxes and went to a spot in the snow at some distance from the camp. Here Carlos had a cache of emergency gear, buried for use in case of a station fire. 'I was in a Jamesway once that caught fire and burned to the ice in seven minutes. Seven minutes! If we hadn't had kitchen knives under our beds to cut through the wall, we wouldn't have made it. But once you get out, you need something else to replace the shelter, or you die of cold rather than hot. I guess that's an improvement, fucking bastards.'

In the wreckage X found one of the little hand-pumps they used to transfer fuel from fifty-five-gallon steel drums into the vehicles and Skidoos. He brought it over and stuck one hose in a fuel canister Carlos had pulled from the buried cache, the other into the tanks of the snowmobiles, and cranked the pump handle until the canister was empty. Meanwhile Carlos strapped onto the Skidoos tent, stove, food bags, skis, crampons and so on.

'Nice to have this stuff,' Wade observed.

Carlos nodded. 'This is the fourth time I've had to use an emergency bag. Every time it reminds you never to forget.'

Before they left Carlos tried the radio one last time. Again no answers, on any band. Lots of static. *What* is going *on?*' he exclaimed.

The other two took this as a rhetorical question and pulled on their bear claws, Wade checking his watch one last time before he did. It was three hours since they had seen the explosion; Wade would have guessed forty-five minutes. They pull-started the Skidoos, and took one last look back at the camp; but behind masks and sunglasses Wade could see nothing of the others' expressions.

Off they went on the snowmobiles.

Back in the sunlight Val had everyone follow her up the rest of the ramp, which – of course – widened and levelled off and became as easy as anyone could have asked, until they were up on the white mass of firn-covered ice just to the south of the Hansen Shoulder; on the polar cap, in other words. Yes, but under very different circumstances to those expected.

She had the others sit down on rocks that had fallen off the Shoulder onto the ice, and walked a few metres away and got on the wrist to call Mac Town and get an SAR started. It was embarrassing, but there was no way out of it.

She punched the channel codes and waited, angry, worried, and ashamed. She ought not to have let it come to this. Accidents happened, of course. But it was her job to make sure no accident could hurt them very much. She ought not to have let Jack coerce her into taking the Amundsen route, given the changed nature of the glacier's head. She ought not to have ventured under that ice block. Both had been stupid; now it, along with the South Georgia disaster, would be what got her into the thin history of Antarctica, which like the history of climbing was just a list of expeditions, with special attention given to firsts and fiascoes. Stupid!

In this blaze of self-recrimination it took her a while to notice that Mac Town was not answering. Sometimes Randi was slow, but not this slow. Val pushed the button again and repeated her message. 'Hello, McMurdo, this is T–023, do you read me, over?'

Hiss of radio space; white noise. No McMurdo! She checked the wrist-radio for status. It appeared to still be working, but there were no connections at all, all across the usual band. This was unprecedented, and she switched quickly to the emergency band, and then back around the dial. No answers anywhere. No radio.

'Shit,' she said, staring at the little display screen. She pushed the function button and checked around. GPS was down too.

'Hey folks,' she said. 'Will you all try your wristphones, and Ta Shu your radio glasses? I'm not getting through, and I want to see if it's my phone that's the problem.'

One by one they tried calling out, with no success. Ta Shu whipped off his heavy video glasses and squinted at them.

'Someone's messed with the satellites,' Val concluded, staring at her wrist-screen. Of course she knew their present location all too well, but still. All satellite connections appeared to be severed, which was amazing, because there were a lot of satellites up there. The GPS system alone relied on making contact with up to eight satellites per fix. She tried the radio again. No more luck than before. Sunspots, perhaps? But the satellites were supposed to have alleviated the problems that sunspots gave Antarctic radio communication.

It was possible the big radio in the sledge would have done better; their little wrist-radios didn't have the power to reach geosynchronous satellites, and sometimes there was trouble with the system of lower satellites. But there was no way to test that now. The sledge was corked and no two ways about it.

'Hmm.' She thought it over. Single sledge travel was based on the idea that if you lost your sledge down a crevasse (it had happened before, at least three times that Val knew of), you had personal radios and helicopter rescue to back you up. Without coms to alert the rescue system, however, they were on their own.

It was an ugly situation. Essentially they needed to get to the nearest shelter as fast as they could. In that regard at least they were much better off than the old guys would have been; there were a fair number of camps and stations in the Transantarctics. The closest one to them, Val decided after looking at the paper map she kept in her parka pocket for just such an eventuality as this, was the SCAG oil base camp on Roberts Massif, just across the Mohn Basin to the west. But that was about a hundred kilometres away.

She sat down on a rock in the middle of the others, and got them all to stop trying their phones. 'Come on, we've proved it. All satellite coms are down as far as we're concerned, and we're not getting GPS either. It means we have to get ourselves to the nearest station. But that's okay, I know where that is, and we only have to cross a bit of the ice cap. We're going to be all right.'

'Where's the nearest station?' Elspeth asked calmly.

'It's to the west, there across the Mohn Basin.' She pointed. 'It's one of those African oil camps, on the south side of Roberts Massif. It's on the side we'll be approaching, so all we have to do is cross the ice plateau. Level easy walking all the way.'

'How far away?' Jorge asked.

'Well, it's about a hundred kilometres,' Val said, looking at each of them in turn. 'Maybe a bit more. A long way, for sure, but not too long. We can do it. We'll just pace ourselves, take rests when we need to, and keep walking till we get there.'

'No problem,' Jack said. 'I ran a fifty-miler once.'

Val nodded, suppressing all irritation. 'That's right. And we won't be in any special hurry. Our suits are like little walking emergency huts. They're warmer than we'll need, and they've got emergency food sewn into them, and the arm-flasks for melting snow to water.' She patted her upper arm. 'It's too bad we don't have our skis, but we have our crampons and ski poles, and we'll be fine. Walking is easier than skiing anyway.'

Which was only true in certain conditions. But they were likely to run into sastrugi and blue ice on the Mohn Basin, also the snow dunes called supersastrugi that were building on the ice as a result of the increase in precipitation; and in all those areas the skis wouldn't have helped them. So it was partly true. Anyway they needed the encouragement, Val judged. Not that anyone looked particularly frightened; they were serious but resolute. Jack was nursing his hurt hand, and he had his lips pursed in a scowl of determination, but he certainly did not look worried.

In any case, there was no reason to delay. In fact the sooner they were off, the better. 'Let's get going,' Val said. 'We'll keep trying the wrist-radios at every rest stop, and probably they'll click back in soon, and we'll have an SAR team out before we get very far. But even if we don't, we'll still be fine.' She stood. 'Hey, a real adventure this time.'

No great laughs at that. The situation was too much felt in the body to be made light of; it was very cold, sitting there in the wind falling off the cap down the glacier. So they stood up stiffly, and followed her as she led them around the shore of Hansen Shoulder. This was a hard part, actually; the ice was beginning its fall into the glacier, and as it deformed around the little nunatak there were many crevasse fields and shear-zones to be avoided. But Val found flat ice all the way through, and soon enough they were on the broad plain of firn to the west of the nunatak – on the ice plateau of the great polar cap. Nothing before them but white snow and ice, and the dark blue sky.

Six people, alone in such an immensity; a strange sight; a strange sensation. White snow, blue sky; in the polar cap's extreme simplicity, the black cliffs of the Transantarctics behind them and to the right were somehow comforting, bleak and jagged though they were. Compared to the ice plateau they were familiar, even homely. But there was no help to be had among them, only broken ice and empty glaciers falling to the sea. And they would be hiking out until the mountains passed under the horizon and there would be no land in sight, as if they were far out on a white ocean.

Val started walking over the ice.

Snowmobiling across the polar cap felt different now. Wade was aware that the change was psychological in origin, but that did not lessen the sensation, which was as distinct as the difference between a sunny day and a cloudy one. Speaking of which, a few cirrus clouds now scythed the pure blue overhead, located distinctly lower in the sky than cirrus clouds usually appeared, indicating the great altitude of the ice plateau, or the altered physics of Ice Planet itself; the effect somehow made the world seem huge. And he could not make it shrink back to its previous size.

A bigger world, and emptier. The surface of the plateau was rougher. The snowmobile was less stable, and louder, its racket that of a motor grinding away, filled with skips and irregularities, as if always on the edge of stalling. Tipping the thing could be a fatal mistake, and it was rocking violently from side to side. The sun stood overhead at its usual angle, a blinding chip in a dark immensity. It seemed he was catching brief glimpses of space itself, up there behind the dark blue sky. And it was colder as well, the wind in his face a bitter, numbing blast. The Skidoo tilted and he overcorrected every time, his pulse racing.

He had to admit it; he was afraid. Cold fear. There was nothing ahead, and nothing behind. A white plain of snow in all directions. No other kind of exposure could match it. As if they were alone in the world, under the blinding eye of a cold god. Alone on the blank white roof of the universe.

And nothing to do but follow Carlos, and try to ignore the fatigue in his thumb. He wondered about the two men he was with, men he scarcely knew. Everything out here depended on the support of one's companions. Without them there was only the cold, and it could kill you in a matter of hours – he could feel that in his face, feel the stiff numbness that led to frostbite and then fatality. Hypothermia straining to get in and do its work. Any tilt of the snowmobile could start the sequence that ended in hypothermia; broken ski, broken knee, anything would do it. So haul left! No right! No left!

On he drove.

Three very long hours later – it felt to Wade more like eight – Carlos waved an arm, and his Skidoo quickly halted. All along he had been following the road in the snow blasted by the hovercraft – the sastrugi that so impressed Wade were actually much flattened – and now the three of them stomped around on the road's crust, trying to get the circulation going in their extremities. Carlos and X taught Wade to windmill his arms rapidly to speed the return of blood and warmth to his hands. For a while they stood around spinning their arms like a bunch of Pete Townshends. Then Carlos took a shovel and an ordinary carpenter's saw from his Skidoo's back-box. He stuck the saw in the snow and began cutting.

'Shouldn't we keep going?' Wade asked.

Carlos shook his head. 'We need food to stay warm. Roberts isn't going anywhere.'

So he sawed blocks of snow, and Wade shovelled them up to X, who carried them over to a curving wall built around the south side of the Skidoos, protecting them from the breeze. The big blocks had the consistency and feel of styrofoam, and were not much heavier.

Then they sat in the lee of the wall while Carlos set up the primus stove, a skeletal little piece of equipment that obviously came from the dawn of the industrial age. Wade watched in appalled fascination as the physics of Ice Planet were again revealed: Carlos applied the flame of a lighter to a pool of stove fuel under the cooker, a move that should have caused a small explosion, and the fuel lay there under the flame, inert, until after a time it flickered bluely, like the burning brandy on a Crêpe Suzette. 'Incredible,' Wade said. 'Not possible.'

Carlos glanced at him. 'Yes. A cold day.' He had recovered from the first shock of his station's destruction, and was now calm and unhurried, even somewhat cheerful; certainly he did not appear to be feeling the dread that chilled Wade's gut. He jammed snow into a pot, and began melting it over the growing flames of the stove, and got packets of lemonade powder and soup ready. A pot of snow melted down to only a third of a pot of water, and when that was boiling Carlos made mugs of hot lemonade and soup. Several pots of snow were transformed over time into dehydrated stew, hot chocolate, and finally mud-thick coffee. The chunks in the stew did not fully rehydrate, so that they tasted like bits of chalk, but Wade did not complain; he had discovered with the first mouthful that he was ravenous, and the stew tasted fine. The chalky bits just gave it some needed texture.

After the meal they packed up. Wade felt considerably warmer, from the stomach outward. Carlos checked the radio and GPS again, and though the radios were still out, apparently some of the GPS satellites were coming back online, for he got a brief fix before the system crashed again. 'About three hours more,' he declared. 'Not long.' They started the Skidoos – a moment of great fear to Wade, followed by relief – and took off again. Wade followed Carlos as always, impressed by the man's calmness at lunch. It was comforting to be out here with a local.

And there they were again in their row, Carlos, Wade, then X, chuntering across the hard-packed firn. Occasionally they passed some of the new snow dunes people talked about, areas with fields of crescent dunes marring the smoothness of the cap, the snow looking just like sand, and the dunes like a very pure part of White Sands in New Mexico. Up close these dunes were much more textured and sastrugi-like than any sand would be, like Georgia O'Keefe stylized dunes, Wade thought, or some kind of fractalized hyperrealist hallucination. But the hovercraft road avoided going directly through any of these.

All too soon the cold began to gnaw again at Wade's knees and face and hands. He felt more clearly than he ever had the struggle between heat and cold in his body, a kind of war fought on many fronts, with differing success depending on exposure. His core heat was definitely there, still radiating as a result of the hot food and drink, sending out reinforcements to fight the encroachment of cold on the distant fronts of the extremities. Out there the battles were being fought capillary by capillary.

And lost, at least on the farthest fronts. Away from the torso's furnace it was a matter of slow ache, loss of feeling, numbness. Carlos called a short stop to help them fight the fight, and with the engines still running they stamped around and danced and did jumping jacks and Pete Townshends, and kneaded their sore buttocks and excruciated right thumbs. New heat was sent out from stomachs to the distant fronts. Then they were off again.

The next time they stopped it was to refill their fuel tanks, a very cold operation in itself. Then off again, and another long interval of snowmobiling and thumb pain and getting cold. The cold penetrated everywhere, until Wade could not drive as well as he had at the start, awkward though he had been then, because of the stiffness of his cold arms.

He was considering speeding up to Carlos and waving him down for another session of warm-up exercises, and perhaps a hot drink, when stopping became a moot point. His engine sputtered, ran, sputtered, ran, sputtered, died. The Skidoo skidded to a halt. Carlos looked back, hearing or otherwise sensing that something had changed, and as he turned, his vehicle also slowed and stopped. X coasted up next to Wade, shaking his head. They were out of fuel.

'We're close,' Carlos said to Wade. The green flags marking the hovercraft route were numbered, apparently, and the last one had been number ten, so they were only ten kilometres out. The rusty mountains marking the horizon ahead were Roberts Massif. Very soon the station would appear over the horizon. They could ski, or, if Wade did not want to ski, walk on crampons.

'I'll try skiing,' he said. Ten k was not too bad; just over six miles. Before his arrival in Antarctica he would have laughed at such a

237

distance, perhaps five minutes on the highway; how bad could it be? But now he had the memory of his walk with Val up Barwick Valley to tell him just how long ten k would feel. In fact the knowledge still tweaked a little in his left knee. It was a significant distance. But he could do it.

And they were beyond choices now. So he changed his bunny boots for heavy cross-country ski-shoes, chilling his feet and hands thoroughly in the process. 'Damn.' It was difficult if not impossible to hurry any of these operations, no matter how much he tried. In fact it took an effort to manage them at any speed.

He had tried cross-country skiing a few times before, and had fallen a lot. He would have to get better fast. X's skis look like popsicle sticks at the bottom of his massive tree-trunk legs. It was hard to believe they would support him. X did not look convinced either; he shook his head at the sight. Curious how with their faces behind ski-masks and sunglasses, so much was yet communicated. Body language indeed.

When they were all ready they stood on their skis, Wade and X propped on their poles. Like a trio of bank robbers on ice, anonymous and insect-eyed. The sunlight prismed on their photovoltaic gloves and overalls and parkas, and Wade was grateful for their warmth, but still his fingertips, nose, ears and feet were cold, and getting colder.

But as Carlos pointed out, the work of skiing would cure that. He took off, wearing a rucksack that contained much of what was detachable from the snowmobiles. Wade followed.

X hit a bump and fell like a tree. As if struck by his bow wave, Wade fell too. The snow was hard and his elbow hurt. Uneasily he got up again, faster than X, who was very awkward on his too-short skis. Carlos was skiing ahead effortlessly. When he looked back and saw his fallen comrades, he made a swooping turn and came back to them. 'Follow me, I'll find the flattest part of the track and it will be easier.'

So they followed him and it was easier, although sometimes Wade's skis got caught on two sides of a little sastrugi ridge and drifted apart no matter what he tried. He fell often, and so did X. The sheer work of getting back to his feet tired him. He began to sweat, overheated everywhere except for at his frozen tips, which stubbornly continued to freeze. He remembered encountering the phrase 'penile frostbite' in an article on runners' problems in wintertime. Hopefully the hot blood in his body core would warm that and all other chilled extremities, while the cold blood in the extremities would cool the hot core of him, like water from a radiator. But it didn't seem to be working; he was too hot and too cold at one and the same time. He struggled on.

It was some comfort to see X falling as often or more often than he did. The two of them went down like bowling pins. After one fall, as they were both getting up and pushing off again, X said, 'Too bad we don't have those spacesuits the trekker groups wear.'

'What do you mean?' Wade said. 'There's better gear than this?'

'Yes.'

'There's better gear than this and I'm not wearing it?'

'Ha.'

'Are there super DVs that get better stuff?'

'You tell me. Probably so. But what we've got is normal government issue, and you can buy gear that's better. This stuff can't convert piezoelectric energy from your walking into heat, it can't melt you water, it can't feed you–'

Wade fell again. 'Can't ski for you.'

'Can't ski, that's right. Nothing.'

'Why not?'

'Why not what?'

'Why don't we have the best stuff?'

'Expensive! And what we have is adequate for what we're supposed to be doing out here. We're not supposed to be out here skiing around. This is trekker stuff.'

'So if Val were here we'd be okay.'

'Probably so.'

They skied on side by side. The snow got smoother, and they glided along without mishap for a while. Carlos was a black mark on the horizon ahead of them; Roberts Massif was bigger, and they could see right to the ice shoreline at the foot of the rock, where the station would soon be visible to them, though they hadn't spotted it yet. Then X said to Wade, 'If that's blue ice then we're fucked.'

'How so?'

'It's as hard as rock, and slick. Bumpy but slick.'

'Oh.' Wade's heart sank. His only attempt at ice skating had broken his tailbone. He had had to sit on an inflated doughnut for three months.

'Shit. That's blue ice all right.'

They came up to Carlos, who was on the last peninsula of white snow, sticking into a sea of blue ice.

'I can't ski ice,' X said.

'Few people can,' Carlos replied. 'We'll have to put on crampons and walk.'

So they sat down and took off their skis, got their boots and crampons out of their day-sacks, changed shoes for boots, strapped on crampons, repacked the daypacks, stood up, and walked on with skis and one ski pole over one shoulder – one hand for them, the other hand poling the ice with a ski pole. All parts of this operation were bitterly, numbingly cold.

But walking with crampons was absurdly secure after skiing, like walking on fly paper. The crunch of the ice underfoot reminded Wade of twisting ice trays back home, and for an instant he was desperately homesick for a world where ice came in one-inch cubes. The change of footgear had chilled him so deeply that his legs were shaking. His thighs felt like jelly. And the crampons quickly tired his feet and ankles, for they made him *too* secure on the ice. From too little traction to too much; nothing comfortable.

'We're almost there,' Carlos called back to them.

'He starts saying that at around the halfway point of any trip,' X warned Wade. 'He's just like Val that way.'

'Ah.'

X was narrating his journey to himself; from the snatches Wade heard it sounded as if an unseen sports commentator of great cynicism was peering out from inside X's ski-mask. Past a gentle rise, snow returned to cover the bare, blue ice. After a short conference they sat down and changed back into skis, which was welcome in one sense, as the weight of the skis over his shoulder was becoming oppressive to Wade; but the gear change chilled him even further. His hands would barely work. Carlos had them eat chocolate bars. Feeling famished, Wade bit into a frozen bar and what felt like a rock in the chocolate jolted a tooth filling with pain: 'Ow ow shit ow!'

'Watch out for the frozen raisins!' X and Carlos warned together.

'Oh thank you very much!'

'Sorry. They're like pebbles when they freeze.'

'Now you tell me.'

'I hate this kind of chocolate, for that very reason.'

Gloves back on, hands numb and clumsy. Frigid air, cutting right to the bone. Up and on. It seemed to Wade that he could feel parts of his mind begin to numb like his fingers; the outer layers of the cortex, the delicate lobes behind the nose, all chilling and shutting down. A pure white plain in a clear blue sky. Ups and downs, thankfully mild. Skiing as bad as ever, or worse. Over them the lowering sky. Looking toward the sun, off to his left, made it like noon, and the snow blazed in a mirrorflake fan. Looking straight ahead across the sunlight made it dawn, the sastrugi thrown in high relief by countless small shadows. Looking away from the sun made it midnight, the layered, grainy bedding of the snow darkly lustrous. The angle of light the only landscape. Or rather the landscapes were all boot-high, so that they Brobdignagged over them, left, right, left, right, in the cold one could never adapt to, the frozen air spiking up the nose like a dangerous drug directly into the brain, a drug needed but feared, the inescapable addiction to oxygen now something like a fatal necessity. Colder and colder, no matter the skiing. More parts of the brain regressing, losing the ability to talk or even to think, all the words fading out like stars at dawn. Ahead the rock seemed closer, and he saw gleams of colour at the shoreline; the station, presumably. The sight made Wade feel dully better. They were going to make it.

Then the snow tilted down toward the massif, and he could pole along without moving his legs, a blessed relief. But then the snow turned to white ice, and he was sliding down without pushing at all – downhill skiing, in other words, and faster and faster, as if on a bike without brakes. His skis chattered, and he bent his knees and crouched, poles tucked under his arms and head down in a grim parody of real skiers, until an unseen bump upended him and he landed on his bottom again, and slid down the slope almost as fast as before, spinning on his back like a cartwheel. His skis had detached and disappeared, but his ski poles were still flailing around him, so he grabbed the end of the left one with his right mitten as it bounced over him, and twisted on his side and jammed the point against the ice. It barely cut a line but it did slow him down a little, scraping like chalk on a blackboard, and by and by he was sliding slowly enough to jam his boot-edges onto the ice without immediately breaking his legs. Eventually he bobbled to a halt, perhaps a hundred metres out from the hovercraft and a little wharf sticking out from the rock onto the ice. After that, little shoves of his mittens slid him down a gentle incline, ten metres at a shove. Behind him, Carlos and X were tromping down the slope upright, having stopped to take off their skis for the final descent. Wade waved at them weakly, and they cheered his survival.

Their pleasure was short-lived, however, because Roberts Station was destroyed – knocked apart and burned. They stepped onto rock and climbed up to the edge of the wreck, Carlos shouting curses in Spanish again but almost absently now, as he began to probe the ruins in search of the equipment it would take to keep them from freezing. A hard wind keened over the rock and they tottered like wooden men, finding nothing, the ruins revealing how small the buildings had been, like trailers in a trailer park, and now all black sticks and lumps. 'Where is everyone?' X croaked over and over again. Wade stumbled with every step; his boots would not rise high enough.

'They're gone,' Carlos said. 'Come on, let's get in the hovercraft.'

The hovercraft was out on the ice some six or eight feet from the wharf, pushed out there apparently by the blast that had levelled the station. X found a piece of singed panelling and carried it over and dropped it on the gap as a gangplank. They staggered across it onto the deck of the craft and fell through the door into the cabin. It was as cold inside as out. Wade could barely move. Carlos banged open a cabinet and lifted out a green Coleman stove, and dropped it on the shelf under the windows and slapped it open. Painstakingly he screwed a gas canister onto the coupling at the side of the stove, then fumbled in his parka for his lighter and applied it to a burner, turning a dial on the stove and flicking the lighter repeatedly; the scraping flint was a primeval sound. Then with a whoosh they had fire.

CHAPTER TEN

Roberts Massif

It was Misha's night to cook again, and the heavenly smells of corned beef hash filled the yellow Scott tent. They wolfed down the food and then slowed down, moving easefully into the dish-washing and Drambers phase of the evening. Graham Forbes sat back, taking wet dishes from Harry and drying them, while a recumbent Geoffrey Michelson tapped the McMurdo code on his wristphone to make their nightly scheduled coms with Randi.

No Randi, however, on this night. No Mac Town at all. Static all up and down the dial, in fact.

'What's this?' Michelson said, looking at his phone.

'Try the box,' Misha suggested, indicating the big old radio in the corner of the tent.

'A clever idea.' Michelson turned on the radio, clicked the dial to the McMurdo frequency, tried a call. Again, nothing but static. Graham put down his teatowel and leaned over to inspect the radio.

'Something odd going on,' Michelson said.

'More than something,' Misha noted with a puzzled expression. 'They're different systems. For both of them to malfunction at once–' He shook his head, sipped his Drambers.

'You're suggesting something more than an accident?' Michelson asked.

'It doesn't look like an accident to me.'

'But what?'

'Don't know. Sabotage?'

The four of them thought it over, looking at each other.

'The satellite links are vulnerable,' Misha said. 'You only have to train a tracking dish on a satellite and send a stronger signal at it than the one it's supposed to be getting, and you've captured it.'

'But there are so many satellites up there,' Michelson objected. 'The system is massively redundant, I would have thought.'

Harry and Misha were both shaking their heads.

'There's a lot of satellites because there's a lot of traffic,' Misha said. 'And they all are part of various overlapping networks, with a lot of carriers and hub satellites transferring messages before they're sent back down to Earth. So if you had your dishes down here, and targeted the right hubs as they came over this area, you could knock down a lot of the system.'

'Especially down here,' Harry said. 'There aren't that many fully polar satellites.'

'But if one satellite failed wouldn't they switch to another?'

'Sure,' Misha said. 'But it might be possible to track that and redirect the disruption as well. Just find the new hub and point the dish that way. It could all be done by a single program, I bet.'

'The hard part isn't making it break down,' Graham said, remembering pub talk with a friend in the coms business. 'The hard part is making it work at all.'

Michelson looked at his three companions. 'Well,' he said. 'I'll thank you gentlemen to stay out of Greenpeace, please. And I'm shocked to learn we live in such a vulnerable system.'

'The satellites are up there,' Misha said, waving up. 'Easy to see, easy to disrupt. Anyone with a transmitter at fourteen gigahertz can do it.'

'But it doesn't explain McMurdo,' Graham pointed out.

They considered it in silence. 'Disable the radio building,' Misha suggested finally.

'But the town is full of radios like this one,' Harry said. 'They should be back on the air pretty soon, no matter what.'

Michelson nodded. 'And we should still be able to contact Burt right now. Let's try that.'

He clicked the tuning dial over two stops, and pressed the transmit button on the handheld mouthpiece. 'S–374, this is S–375, are you there Burt and crew, do you read me? Over.'

A pause, the faint hiss of a radio connection: 'We read you, Geoff! But we haven't been able to contact Mac Town or make calls out, and our GPS isn't working!'

'That's our situation here too, Burt, although we didn't know about the GPS.'

'That's even more satellites,' Misha said.

'It's not just that, Geoff, our helo pick-up didn't show tonight either! We had to walk back to camp, it was pretty hairy!'

'They must have had to cross some ice,' Misha joked.

Michelson waved him quiet and pressed the transmit button: 'Something's gone wrong in Mac Town, I'm afraid. But they're sure to be back on the air soon, so I suggest we sit tight out here until we find out more about what's happened.'

'That's fine by us, Geoff. No way do we want to walk all the way back home. Besides, we're finding some great stuff over here. What about you, have you found anything?'

'We're plugging away, Burt. Nothing extraordinary so far.' With a warning glance at Misha not to guffaw while he was transmitting. 'Let's keep in close contact while this situation continues, Burt. Talk again at nine tomorrow morning, all right? And let us know immediately if you hear from Randi or anyone else.'

'Sure thing, Geoff! I'll bet you anything it's Greenpeace again, gone after those oil camps!'

'Mac Town would seem to have little to do with that. But we'll find out. Have a good night, you fellows, and over and out.'

'Same to you, over and out.'

Michelson put down the radio transmitter. They sat in the hiss of the Coleman stove, sipping their Drambuie.

Misha said, 'So you didn't want to tell your co-PI about your find, eh?'

'Misha.' Michelson sipped. 'Not on the radio. Anyone could be listening.'

'All those people out here,' Graham said, needling Michelson like Misha always did. It was a bit catching.

'There *are* other field camps out here,' Michelson said. 'Besides, even if it was just Burt, he might be tempted to crow about it to people in Mac Town, or in the north.'

Graham nodded. He liked Michelson's caution in this respect, because he thought he understood what caused it. A premature announcement, indulged in before all the work was done and the results accepted for publication, could actively endanger the results themselves. Internet science and press release science were both potentially dangerous in that respect. The beech-litter mat they had found in the Apocalypse Sirius was a crucial find, Graham was sure; but only when properly fitted into their case, and supported. Then it would be a very solid brick in the wall, maybe even one of the things that tipped the balance to general acceptance of the dynamicist view of things. But they were very far from that at this point. Right now what they had was just some rusty yellow organic matter, no more; it could be two hundred years old, it could be two hundred million years old. The stabilists would certainly challenge them on that basis, and on every other basis they could think of. So they had to build a framework for these fragments, and forestall all possible objections to their interpretation of what they meant; for objects remained objects until the objections were countered. One had to locate them in dense meshes of history to turn them into facts, facts that would then support a theory. This part of the process was crucial to doing any lasting, influential work. And so Michelson would be enlisting an array of paleobotanists, paleobiologists, geomorphologists, geophysicists, paleoclimatologists, and glaciologists like Graham himself, all bringing their speciality to bear on the subject at hand, all of whose own careers, if they took part in this effort, would then become at least somewhat connected to the success or failure of the dynamicist view.

As was certainly true for Graham, working on questions of glacial sedimentology. He was already fully committed, of course; and now his fate was somewhat intertwined with Michelson's. So he was reassured by Geoff's style, which he admired enough to try to emulate in his own work – that reticence, that sense of the history of the geosciences. The fairly consistent attempts to keep things low-keyed and playful; certainly things had happened in the course of this controversy that would have made Graham furious if he had been in Michelson's position, and he could only presume that Geoff had indeed been angry back when those things had happened. Yet now he spoke of the stabilists not as enemies to be crushed, but with great, almost exaggerated, politeness, expressing underneath that a basic respect for them as scientists, especially for the ones whose work he thought was the most well-done and therefore challenging. Perhaps this merely reflected his sense of the most certain, one might even say most scientific, method of crushing them as flat as a leaf-mat; in any case it was a position he held to all the time, even here in his own camp. Possibly he was different in private, at home. But after a few weeks in the field in Antarctica one began to feel that one knew one's companions pretty well. In the end it was very much like the privacy of home.

So before talking to anyone outside their group about their fine discovery, the lab-work on the samples would have to be done, and the literature would have to be researched, and other scientists asked to make contributions, possibly; and the papers would have to be written, revised and submitted to the most prominent appropriate journals, where anonymous reviewers would no doubt suggest further revisions, which, as they often strengthened one's case, were usually incorporated; and only then would the papers be published. By that time the inferences made from the physical objects taken out of the field would be tied down the way Misha tied down their sleeping tents, in a redundant-looking network of stakes and lines: bombproof. And in that state they would be read, and would add to the dialogue among the small groups of people who had the expertise to judge the arguments, to probe them for weaknesses; people who would indeed make judgements and criticisms; and later their own scientific assumptions about the field would take this new set of facts into account, and engage the theory, and they would design their own next projects accordingly; and see different things than they would have otherwise, out in the world; and the dialogue would go on, as it had ever since Lyell, or Newton or Aristotle or the first talking primates, depending on how broad a view of science one wanted to take. In the most fundamental sense, Graham decided, science had begun a very long time ago.

So it might be three or four years before these papers were published, and the effects felt only in the years after that. This was the pace of discourse which had kept the Sirius story going for more than thirty years now. Like the glaciers at the centre of the story, it moved slowly but ground fine.

So now Michelson, keeping his cards close to his chest, quickly shifted the talk to what they could do there in the field in the next few days to help their situation later in the lab. Because back in the north it would do no good to wish for one more sample rock; one had to get it now.

After that part of things was all worked out, however, Harry flipped open his laptop and called up the Pliocene Antarctic map that he had been working on for some time now, entering all the data that had been collected in the decades of the dynamicist effort. Now he reworked the line describing the little inlet of the fjord they had been investigating. Michelson regarded it over the top of his glasses with a little smile. 'Whatever happens in the end,' he remarked contentedly, 'the Sirius question has certainly been good for Cenozoic geology in Antarctica.'

Harry finished redrawing the fjords and hills. The whole stretch of what was now the Transantarctic Mountains was much lower in his map, and deeply cut by fjords – like the current coastline of Labrador, or Norway, or for that matter southern Chile. Elsewhere on the map, western Antarctica was an archipelago somewhat resembling the Philippines. Michelson was always encouraging Harry to look for possible land bridges connecting the Peninsula to the Transantarctics, as *Nothofagus* did not migrate across water well, and it seemed to him that there had to be dispersal routes over land to make Pliocene beech forests as far south as eighty-five degrees comprehensible. Either the trees had had routes to come and go with the fluctuating climate, or else there had been places on the craton proper that had remained refugia for the biome during even the coldest parts of the last fourteen million years. 'The Peninsular refuge seems more likely, if the trees could get back south when it warmed.'

Behind the Transantarctics, where the great ice cap now covered all, the Pliocene map showed a continental mainland like a violently chewed Australia. The craton had begun to come apart like the basin and range territory of North America, leaving basins running all over east of the Transantarctics, from the Weddell Sea all the way across to the Indian Ocean, which intruded south in a bay bigger even than the Ross Sea. Those ancient inland seas contained many of the regions that the oil teams were interested in, for if they had been seas for long enough, they very possibly would have been floored by enough organic material to create oil.

The paleofjord they had been studying today ran through the Transantarctic Hills all the way to this Pliocene Wilkes Bay; or at least this was the way Harry had it drawn. It was not something that they could easily confirm, because the relevant region was deep under the ice cap. But the uplift rates they were establishing, and the depth of the subglacial basin on the other side of the range, made it very likely to be true. Or perhaps there had been a saddle peninsula there dividing the two seas, a saddle from which one could look down into the head of both fjords. Thus keeping one of Geoff's precious land bridges.

After they had played with the map a while, talking things over, Harry switched to a photo of a krummholz beech forest, taken on the slopes above a bay in southern Chile. Ceaseless winds had swept the tops of the little trees back in a permanent curve. They had all grown together into a single mat, like a lichen-mat seen in a microscope. Bright-green and dark-green mosses covered the understorey of the miniature forest. Moss carpets still served as surrogate soils in the Antarctic Peninsula, and the microenvironments in these little biomes were several degrees warmer than the outer air. 'This photo was taken just north of Tierra del Fuego,' Harry said. 'The Magellanic moorland biome matches the species list we've found down here almost perfectly.'

'That's probably very much what it looked like here in the Pliocene,' Michelson said, staring over his glasses again. 'Odd to think that temperatures have risen now to the point where such a forest could survive here again. People would have to plant it, but after that . . .'

Harry was shaking his head. 'The Treaty forbids bringing in exotic plants.'

'But this wouldn't be an exotic, would it? Merely native vegetation, returned home after a period of exile. The Chileans and Argentinians already tried growing beeches up in the Peninsula. It didn't work then, but it's considerably warmer now than when they tried.'

The other three let this pass. It was not the kind of thing they would consider doing, and it was hard even to know if Michelson was serious or not.

After staring at the laptop photo for a time, lost in their own thoughts, they stirred themselves, and prepared to make the cold transfer to their sleeping tents. 'I wonder what's happening in McMurdo,' Harry said.

'We'll find out soon,' Michelson said. 'Randi will call us the moment she gets back on the air, we can be sure of that. Meanwhile, we're self-sufficient here for longer than it will take to sort things out. So we can continue to work while we wait.'

Wade sat in the passenger compartment of the hovercraft, clutching the warmed ceramic of a mug of hot chocolate, gulping at it and scalding the roof of his mouth, and slowly, slowly coming back up out of the depths of hypothermia. Back from the deepest cold he had ever felt in his life; back to the point where he could shiver; then through violent shivering, to the point where he could stop all but a residual quiver.

Carlos was out on another exploration of the burned station. X sat across from Wade, hunched over the stove to catch as much of its warmth as possible, sucking down his own hot chocolate.

'This is turning into quite a trip for you,' X observed.

'Yeah.' Wade glanced at X. 'I wish I still had Val assigned to me as a guide. I'd feel better.'

X grunted. 'This'd be nothing to her.'

'Is that right?'

'You should hear some of the stories she tells.'

'So she's an exceptional mountaineer.'

'Well, I don't know about that. I think a lot of mountaineers are like her. It's just that they all have lots of really scary stories to tell. They go out close to the edge, I'm telling you. It's scary.'

'It seems decadent to me.'

'Decadent?'

'Well, you know. I hear a good version of *La Mer* and I'm thrilled, I mean really thrilled. So, you know, if you need to risk your life to get your thrills, I don't know. It seems jaded to me.'

'Maybe. I'm not sure it's the same kind of thrill you're talking about. I'm not sure it's the risk itself these people are hooked on. It's something else, I don't know. I never understood it. I've been thinking about it a lot, trying to understand it. One time Val told me about getting avalanched on the side of Mount Cook and carried down the mountainside toward the bergschrund at the bottom of the slope, you know the crack at the bottom? Certain death. But the avalanche carried them right over it. They were left waist-deep in the snow on the flats, unharmed, except Val had busted a rib. And she said it hurt like hell, but they had to walk ten miles to get to a roadhead, and somewhere on the way they started laughing so hard that she almost died of the pain, but she couldn't stop laughing. It was so great, she said. She says it with this little Aussie accent sometimes – it was *grayte*. Like an Aussie gal. Totally scary.'

'So you two were some kind of a–?'

'Yeah yeah. We had an affair, an ice-romance you know, end of last season.'

'Wow.'

'I know.' Brooding. 'But this season when we got back to Mac Town she wasn't interested.'

'What?'

'Yeah. It was over.'

'No.'

'Yeah.'

'Oh man. I hate that kind of thing.'

'Yeah well.' X sipped his hot chocolate. 'Better for your chances with her anyway, right?'

'What!'

'Come on.'

'Come on yourself!' Wade shook his head. 'Why would she even consider me? A Washington bureaucrat, a functionary.'

'She liked you.'

'I can't even ski.'

'That's true.'

'Hey now. Neither can you, and I notice she went with you.'

'See?'

'Oh, so maybe there's hope. Maybe I can be so lucky as to get the same treatment you got.'

They cackled briefly.

'We can dream,' X said.

Carlos slammed in and made for the stove. 'Not good,' he told them. Apparently the blast had knocked apart all the buildings and set the fuel bladders on fire, and almost everything had burned after that. The force of the explosion appeared to have broken the hovercraft's mooring ropes and skidded it across the ice a few feet, saving it from further harm. Carlos rooted in his bag of finds, cursing again in Spanish, but almost absentmindedly now.

'But where did everyone go?' X asked again, as he had out at the station on the ice cap. It seemed to Wade that they had made the crossing of the polar plateau only to find themselves in the same situation they had been in before, except now much more tired, sore, cold and hungry. His legs lay there before him like jelly held in long balloons, and his tailbone was aching, though he did not think his spectacular fall had broken it again.

Carlos poured himself some hot water from the pot on the stove into a mug of powdered chocolate. For a moment Wade smelled the sweet, dark smell. He felt intense relief at being indoors. They were still on their own, in the interior of Antarctica, in the midst of what appeared to be a general terrorist attack; but at least they were indoors.

'First another meal,' Carlos said, as he put more ice in the pot to melt. 'And warm up some more. Then we'll try the radio again and see if we can make coms with Shackleton or McMurdo. Or anybody.'

The other two nodded, staring hard at the pots on the stove. They were all now sitting encased in thick sleeping bags Carlos had pulled out of the hovercraft's cabinets, the red nylon bunching around them to the chest. With their ski-masks rolled up into thick-rimmed caps, they looked almost human.

'Is there much food?' Wade asked. 'If we have to wait to be rescued?'

Carlos frowned. 'The galley burned. There's some scattered around in other buildings, in emergency bags. And some here on board. Enough to feed us for a week or two, certainly.'

'Surely it won't take that long to get to us.'

'One would think so. Hopefully we can find out by radio.'

'Could we drive this thing down the glacier to Shackleton Camp?'

Carlos and X looked at each other.

'I was thinking about it,' Carlos said. 'I've driven it a few times, I know how to do it, but it takes two . . .' He looked at X.

'I've watched,' X said, hand up. 'I could do the co-pilot, I guess. We could try if we had to.'

'Maybe we could figure it out,' Wade said. 'How hard could it be?'

The other two shared another look.

'Maybe,' Carlos said. 'We'll see what Mac Town says first. If we can get them.'

Then they heard shouts outside.

Ice like white paper before the first brush stroke. The original emptiness from which all begins. A fifth element beyond space and time, emptiness in its supreme degree.

Ice and rock. Consciousness of white, capacity of black.

Perpetual winter. The planet Winter. One day, one night. The yin and yang of dark and light. Camera, please save these images and voice-over for later transmission.

A white ocean. In the far distance a dragon's back, buried in ice. We walk in a straight line, yet it is a movement that simultaneously turns on itself and opens to the infinite. Spiral development. We have come into a strange situation, as you will learn when this transmission reaches you. In many ways it is a clarification of our purpose. We have to reach a refuge and food, or we will die. All other tasks are set aside, as this one of survival takes precedence.

It is a situation strangely like that reached by Shackleton's *Endurance* expedition, begun in 1914 after Amundsen and Scott had finished their fateful race to the Pole. The Pole having been reached, subsequent expeditions had to find different rationales for going, and at that time this was not so easy. Shackleton called his voyage the British Imperial Transantarctic Expedition, but this grand title only partly concealed the fact that the trip had no real point. Crossing the continent was merely a goal invented to replace reaching the Pole; no one had thought of it before. It was the excuse of someone who wanted to be here just for the sake of being here. Exploration, science, neither really mattered to Shackleton; what mattered was living in Antarctica. There he had first experienced that being-in-the-world which is our fundamental reality, our one true home; and rather than try to find that experience also in the wilderness that is England, he kept returning south.

So he and his men embarked on a new kind of enterprise, similar in many ways to the wilderness adventure trips we see today. Like the trip we are sharing at this moment.

Each expedition has a different character, you see, fulfilling different karmic fates. In fact many expeditions encompass entire karmic lifetimes all in themselves. For karmic lives are shorter than human lives, and each of us passes through many different karmic existences during the course of a single biological span. This is a fact that is not well known in the West, I have found, even though the demonstration of it is there for all to see in the history of their own lives.

In any case, Shackleton and his men sailed the *Endurance* into the Weddell Sea, on the side of Antarctica opposite the Ross Sea. The Weddell Sea is covered with pack ice far more than the Ross Sea, and Shackleton's ship was caught in this ice, and they were forced to live on the ship for ten months while the ship was carried in the ice's slow dance around the great bay; and then the ice crushed their ship and sank it, and they lived in camps on the ice for five more months, still drifting north and west.

The trip Shackleton had planned to make was gone for good. They could only camp on the ice as it drifted out to sea, waiting for the ice to break up, when they could try to sail in three very small lifeboats to some solid land. At that point they would be cast into one of the greatest voyages in history. But the waiting, for month after month; this was a very difficult thing. Other expeditions were driven to madness by such enforced inactivity.

Yet all Shackleton's men attest to the fact that he was calm in waiting, even jovial, and that his unfailing good spirits, and the close regard he had for his men, helped them to endure the wait. He created a community of trust. In spiritual terms it may be that these months of waiting were the greatest achievement of that group – an extraordinary experience of being-in-the-world, which changed them fundamentally and for ever: living on ice, using the collective unconscious of their palaeolithic minds. 'We realized that our present existence was only a phase,' as Worsley put it. And as this is always true, everywhere, they had realized a very valuable thing. And it was Shackleton who made it possible. He never faltered.

But we need not wonder at Shackleton's ability to keep his spirits high during this time. Marooned though they were, he was just where he wanted to be. He was living in Antarctica, having a difficult adventure – it was just what he wanted! So he was able to keep his men cheered up because the joy of life was in him. He was in his place. This is a big part of the greatness of Shackleton: he found his place, he went there, he enjoyed it. He shared that joy in a way others could feel.

This is particularly important for us to remember now. We started in the footsteps of Amundsen, but we must end in the mind of Shackleton. So far our leader Valerie has exhibited that Shackletonian optimism which will be so important to the success of our endeavour, and I trust completely that she will stay that way and see us through. How I admire her calm, happy spirit, her strength in leading us. And we are lucky; walking across the ice is not as hard as living on it and waiting. We have a goal to travel toward, just beyond the horizon.

We live an hour and it is always the same. No distractions to the spirit. A white plain to infinity. Not sensory deprivation exactly, but rather a kind of sensory overload, within just a very few massive elements: sun, sky, ice, light, cold; all intense to the point of overwhelming the mind. But then time passes and here we are still. On we walk. The micro-forms of snow under my feet are a true infinity of worlds. The sky is several different tints of blue. The sun is a star.

Everything is so clear in this moment. No past, no future. Messner's mantra: We have come a long way, we have a long way to go. In between we are somewhere.

Only this moment, always. We never get to change the past. We never get to know the future. No reason to wish for one place rather than another; no reason to say I wish I were home, or I wish I were in an exotic new place that is not my home. They will all be the same as this place. Here the experience of existing comes clear. This world is our body.

Now we must walk over it a certain distance. We like Shackleton's men have had our supplies crushed in the ice. And though our hour's wait was nothing like their fifteen months, in the long run we end up in the same boat. We have to cross this white immensity now. We have to make our way to food and refuge. We make our brush stroke on the empty paper. We are like they were once the ice under them broke up, and the truly dangerous part of their adventure began.

At first they walked over firn, which took their weight like a pavement. There were sastrugi of course, but they could easily step over them, and the different angles of hardpack that their boots landed on actually gave their feet and ankles and legs some variety in their work, so that no one set of muscles and ligaments got tired, as when pounding the pavement in cities or in the endless corridors of a museum. So in these sections it was good walking.

They spread out in little clumps: Jack and Jim up with Val, Jack going very strong, even pushing the pace a bit; Jorge and Elspeth behind them; Ta Shu back farther still, rubbernecking just as he had before their accident. Val set the pace and did not allow Jack to rush them. 'Save it,' she said to him once a little sharply, when she felt him right in her tracks. 'Pace yourself for the long haul.'

'I am.'

But he dropped back a little, and on they walked. They were doing fine. As she always did on long hikes, Val stopped the group to rest for about fifteen minutes after every ninety of walking, in a system somewhat similar to Shackleton's. In ninety minutes their arm-flasks had melted the snow and ice chips stuffed into them, and so everybody had two big cups of water to drink. They could also eat a few inches of their belts, as Elspeth put it; their suits' emergency food supplies were sewn into an inner pocket wrapped all the way around the waist. The food was something like a triathlete's power bar, flattened and stretched into something very like a wide belt, in fact. It was good food for their situation. At some stops they chewed ravenously; during others their appetites seemed to Val suppressed, by altitude or exertion no doubt. She made sure they didn't force it. In truth it was water that was crucial to this walk; they were breathing away gallons of it in the frigid hyperarid air, and they were sweating off a little bit as well. Two flasks every ninety minutes was by no means enough, but it certainly staved off the worst of the dehydration effects, which could devastate a person faster even than the cold, and made one more susceptible to the cold as well.

So between the walks and the breaks they made steady progress. But after several of these had passed, they came upon swales of softer snow, which had been pushed by the winds into sastrugi like crosshatched dunefields. These snowdrifts were new, the result of unusually heavy snowfalls on the edges of the polar cap in recent years, generally assumed to be an effect of the global warming generally, and of the shorter sea ice season in particular. Climatologists were still arguing what caused all the different kinds of superstorms, aside from the overall increase in the atmosphere's thermal energy. In any case the snow was here, one more manifestation of the changes in weather.

Val stopped for a meeting. 'Follow me and step right in my footsteps, folks, and it will be a lot easier.'

'We should trade the lead, so everyone saves the same amount of energy,' Jack said.

'No no, I'll lead.'

'Come on. I know we've got a long walk, but there's no reason to get macho on us.'

Val looked at him for a while, counting on her ski-mask and shades to keep her expression hidden. When her teeth had unclenched she said, 'I've got the crevasse detector.'

'We could all carry that when it was our turn.'

'I want to be the one using it, thanks. I know all its little quirks. It wouldn't do to have any falls now.'

'You having the radar didn't keep it from happening last time.'

They stood there under the low, dark sky.

'Go second, and make her steps better for us,' Ta Shu suggested to Jack.

'We shouldn't have anyone lose more energy than anyone else.'

'I have more energy than anyone else to start with,' Val said. 'Everyone except maybe you, but you're hurt. You cut your hand. You hit the wall of the crevasse. Let's not waste any more energy arguing about it. It'll work out.'

It was very hard to be civil to him. She couldn't think of anything else to say, and so took off before she said something unpleasant.

He stayed right on her heels, like some kind of stalker. She could hear his breathing, and the dry squeak of his boots on the snow. Untrustworthy, disloyal, unhelpful, unfriendly, discourteous, unkind . . .

They followed her through the soft snow dunes in single file. She kept the pace easy, resisting the pressure from Jack. Never was the snow as soft as Rockies powder, of course, but it was extremely dry, and already had been tumbled by the winds until it was on its way to firn. It was more like loose sand than any snow back in the world, loose sand that gave underfoot, thus much more work than the firn. Then in the areas where it adhered, she had to pull her boots out of their holes after every step, and lift higher for the next one, which was also hard work. But she had put in her trail time – a lifetime's worth – and it would take many many hours of such walking to tire her. No, she would be fine; she could walk for ever. It was the clients she was worried about. She was responsible for them, and she had got them into trouble, as Jack had pointed out; but she couldn't carry them, they had to walk on their own. So it had to be made as easy for them as possible.

So she did what she could. But as they walked on, and hour after hour passed, under the sun that wheeled around them in a perpetual mid-afternoon slant, they began to lose speed and trail behind. Jack no longer trod in her bootprints the second she left them unoccupied, nor during the breaks did he again mention leading the way. In fact he spent the rest periods in silence now, a mute figure under his parka hood, behind his ski-mask and shades. He wasn't eating much of his belt, either. That worried Val, and she tried to inquire about it by asking the group generally how they were feeling, and getting a status report from everyone; Elspeth was developing blisters on her heels, she thought; Jorge's bad knee was tweaking; Jim and Ta Shu reported no problems in particular, but like everyone said they were tired, their quads in particular getting a little rubbery with all the loose, soft snow. Jack, however, only said, 'Doing fine. "Pacing myself for the long haul".'

So, okay. End of that break. On they walked.

Her GPS was still out of commission, but occasionally when she turned it on it flickered and gave a reading, then blinked out again. The last one that had come through indicated that they were averaging about three kilometres an hour, which was normal on the plateau; a bit slower in the soft snow no doubt, hopefully a bit faster on the hardpack.

Then they came to a patch of blue ice, and Val groaned to herself. They had to stop and put on crampons, then scritch cautiously across the ice, which here was pocked and dimpled by big, polished suncups. The nobbly surface gave their ankles a hard workout indeed, as their crampon points forced them to step flush on the terrain underfoot no matter its angle. It was best to step right on the cusps and ridges between the little hollows, crampons sticking into the slopes on both sides and keeping the foot level; but that took a lot of attention and precise footwork. So *scritch, scritch, scritch*, they stepped along, making perhaps two kilometres an hour at best. Val headed directly for the nearest stretch of snow in the distance, so that as soon as possible they reached the far side of the blue ice, groaning with relief, and could sit down and take the crampons back off, and drink what water had melted at the bottom of their flasks, then restuff the flasks with hacked chips of the blue ice, which would yield more water when melted than snow. Then they were up and off again, on what felt like land, after a precarious crossing over water.

Jorge and Elspeth were clearly tiring now, though they did not complain. Jim too was getting tired, and Jack stuck with him, arms crossed over his chest. Jack still wasn't eating very much compared to the others, but he still wasn't responding to her questions about it, either.

'Aren't you hungry?'

'I'm fine.'

'We're probably burning three or four hundred calories an hour doing this.'

'I'm fine.' Don't bother me.

So she shrugged and took off again. They were back on good firn again, and could make decent time with minimum effort. Just walking, a great relief after what had preceded it.

But now when she looked back, she saw that Jim and Jack were behind Ta Shu, bringing up the rear, and losing a couple of hundred yards per hour on all the rest of them. It didn't seem like much, but it added up. And it worried her. But there was nothing to do but carry on, and ratchet down the pace a bit so that no one pushed too hard, especially those bringing up the rear.

They had been hiking for ten hours when Val got another GPS fix. They had come some thirty kilometres, a good pace; but she had aimed them out to the south to avoid the crevasses at the top of the Hump Passage, at the head of the Liv Glacier. So they still had at least seventy kilometres to go, she reckoned, depending on how far south they would have to detour to get around the ice ridge extending southward from Last Cache Nunatak. Beyond that ice ridge lay the head of the Zaneveld Glacier, which was heavily crevassed; they would have to stay south of that; and then on the far side of the Zaneveld was Roberts Massif. All those features lay below the horizon, of course; they could see only about ten kilometres in all directions, which meant that they could see nothing but the ice plain, except for occasional glimpses of the peaks of the Queen Maud Range, poking over the horizon to their right.

Into her rhythm, taking it slow. So far of all the clients Ta Shu seemed the least affected by their long march. He spent all his rest time contemplating the distant peaks of the Queen Maud Range, deciphering their *feng shui* message no doubt. While walking he stumped along steadily, and at times caught up with her and walked by her side. 'We are doing well!'

'Yes.'

He pointed at the mountains, the only thing marring a perfect white/ blue circle of a horizon. 'This is a good place,' he said. He was pointing at what Val hoped was Barnum Peak, standing over the west side of the Hump Passage. 'Open to the south. Protected on the north by mountains. This is good. At least in northern hemisphere.'

'Doesn't all that reverse in the southern hemisphere?'

'No. Constant everywhere. A dragon spine range, that. Fire over water. Sometimes bad health. I would have to do more study.'

'No time for that,' Val said politely. 'Anyway, it looks like your health is fine. You're really going strong.'

259

'Thank you,' he said. He was hiking with his face uncovered, and now as he smiled some of the icicles in his grey moustache broke off and fell away. 'No problem so far. I can walk; one of the few things I can do. I spent my childhood harvesting rice. Walking to town. Walking to school, when I went. A peasant life. Then given a place at university, very lucky. Then, just after I got there – re-education!' He laughed. 'So back to the fields for some more years.'

'Good way to get in shape.'

'Oh, there are better ways, I assure you.' Laughing at her. 'Better ways indeed. Not enough to eat, you see. But it made me strong. Now I am old, but that kind of strength, ha – you must sit many years before it is all gone.'

Val nodded. She knew what he meant; she had often seen that kind of strength in Nepal, where people had an endurance that no Westerner could touch. A couple of Sherpas she knew had walked from Everest Base Camp to Kathmandu in three days, just to see how fast they could do it – a trek that even the best Western mountaineers took two weeks to do, back when they had walked it at all. No, Val had walked many miles with the Sherpa and Rawang porters, and she had seen that although they had mostly been very cheerful people, they were pack animals, really, like draught horses or donkeys – that was how they made their living, as beasts of burden, working hard, tired in the afternoons, eating like starved dogs every evening. Val had admired a lot of those guys for the way they worked, loved them dearly even though she had towered over them, and hadn't spoken their language. It hadn't been the kind of love that had any real connection in it. But sometimes watching them she had wanted a big Western man to have that kind of spirit, that cheery toughness, something like Ta Shu's. These were the kind of people she wanted to walk with.

Instead this little group of clients, with only one Ta Shu in it, and the rest slowly losing steam. In fact Jack and Jim were falling behind faster than ever. Puzzled, Val stopped and watched them closely for a while. It was not Jim who was slowing them down: it looked as if Jack had hit the wall. 'Fuck,' she said. He had gone out too fast, perhaps, and burnt out. Or was feeling the loss of blood from the cut in his hand. Or both. Anyway he was slowing down markedly.

Val called an early break, and waited for the two men to catch up, cursing to herself. They joined the group twenty minutes after Jorge and Elspeth came in, and during that time the others had eaten and drunk their flasks and refilled them, and were beginning to freeze. This was a serious problem, and she couldn't help thinking that it was Jack's fault. So often it happened that men like him took off too fast, on an adrenalin rush, thinking their emergency energy would be inexhaustible, and then they were the first to hit the wall. Pacing took a lot of self-discipline. And big, muscular men were generally not so good in ultralong-distance events: they had too many muscles to feed, and when they ran out of the day's carbo-load, they had too little body fat to throw on the fire.

So when Jim and Jack clumped into the group, Val suggested that they have a bite of their belts to give themselves more energy. Jim nodded, and pulled out some of his belt and tore it off and stuffed it under his ski-mask into his mouth before it froze.

Jack just shook his head irritably. 'I'm just pacing myself,' he snapped. 'Like you said to do. Don't get neurotic about it, that's the last thing we need. Let people go what pace they want.'

'Sure, sure. Try eating some food, though. We need the group to stay more or less together, or the people in front will freeze waiting for the ones behind.'

'Don't wait then!'

She stared at him. 'You should eat,' she said finally. 'And drink your arm-flasks and refill them, for God's sake.'

And after a little while more she had taken off again, and was soon leading the way. No beeps, thank God; they were out on the big ice-cube itself now, a solid mass with very little cracking. Just a matter of walking. Pacing oneself, yes, and walking. Hour after hour. She shifted them to a ten-minute break every hour, which was exactly Shackleton's pattern. Frequently she glanced back over her shoulder. Jack was still falling behind, perhaps even more rapidly than before; and Jim was sticking with him.

At some time when she was not looking the sun was touched by a thin film of cloud which had appeared out of nowhere. A white film, but heavily polarized by her sunglasses, so that it was banded prismatically.

As usual, it only took the slightest cloud cover for the day to go from blinding and hot to ominous and chill. Already they were pulling their ski-masks down over their faces, and zipping up their parkas; and as they did so the cloud thickened further, into a thin rippled patch thrown right over the sun, as if someone had tried to place it there. So often it happened that way; the cloud could have appeared anywhere in the sky, but ended up right between Val and the sun. It happened so frequently that she reckoned it must be some trick of perspective rather than a real phenomenon. In any case, there it was again.

Which was bad, bad news. The immediate effects were that their suits wouldn't be as warm, and worse, their arm-flasks would be much less efficient at melting snow and ice. It would take twice as long to melt snow now, maybe three times. So they were going to get thirsty.

The mental effect of the cloud was also bad. What had been a blazing plain was now shadowed and malign. Underfoot the beautifully elaborate crosshatching in the snow was revealed better than ever, a granulated fractal infinity of sharply cut micro-terracing. This complex world underfoot was as prismatic as any cloud whenever it flattened enough, and now when she looked in the direction of the sun Val saw diaphanous icebows, curving both in the cloud and across the snow itself. They walked forward into a geometry of rainbows. Val looked back at Ta Shu, and he raised a ski pole briefly, to let her know he had noticed the phenomenon, and appreciated her thinking to bring it to his attention.

A beautiful sight; and yet still the world seemed dim and malignant. Clouds of any kind on the polar cap often presaged even worse weather, of course, which perhaps was part of the mood it cast. With luck her clients did not know that and so wouldn't be affected as much. They were still many hours' walk out from Roberts, and a lot could happen to Antarctic weather in that amount of time.

Nothing to do but forge on, of course, into a landscape turned alien; the awesome become awful, and all in the few minutes it had taken for a thin cloud to form. After which they were mere specks on a high plateau on Ice Planet, a place in which humans could not live except in spacesuits. And they could feel that palpably, in the penetrating cold.

At the next rest-stop they drank and ate in silence. There was no point, Val judged, in trying to cheer them on. She could have pointed out to them again that they were having an adventure at last, after trying so many times and paying so much money. But she doubted that would go over very well now. One of the distinguishing marks of true adventures, she had found, is that they were often not fun at all while they were actually happening. And in one of their camp conversations Jim had quoted Amundsen to the effect that adventure was just bad planning. So that if she called it that, they might blame her for it. Jack was certainly ready to.

And she blamed herself. It had been a mistake to take the righthand route, as it turned out. Although still – as she walked on thinking about it, trying to cheer herself up – it seemed that what had happened showed that Amundsen was wrong, and that adventures could also be a matter of bad luck as well as bad planning. You could plan everything adequately, and still get struck down by sheer bad luck. It happened all the time. That was what made these kinds of activities dangerous. That was what made all life dangerous. You couldn't plan your way out of some things. You had to walk your way out, if you could.

In any case, while there was no obvious way to cheer them up during the rests, there was also no great need to urge or cajole them along.

The situation was plain; they either walked on or died. The intense cold they were living in reminded them of that at every moment.

She tried her GPS and it gave her a reading, showing them on the 172nd longitude. About the halfway mark of their hike. Not bad at all, except that they were getting very tired. They had hiked around thirty miles, after all, and were beginning to run out of steam; she could see it in the way they moved. Jorge was limping slightly. Elspeth was letting her ski poles drag from time to time, no doubt to give her arms a rest. Jack was doing the same, and moving like a pall-bearer. Jim was trying to keep to his friend's slow pace, though often he pulled ahead and then stopped and waited, not a good technique. Only Ta Shu still had the contained efficiency of someone with some strength left in his legs, placing each step precisely into her bootprints, using his ski poles in easy short strokes. He looked as if he could stump along for a long time.

Val herself was feeling the work, but was well into her long-distance rhythm, a feeling of perpetual motion that was not exactly effortless but a kind of contained low-level effort, one that she could sustain for ever; or so it felt. Obviously there would come a time when that feeling would wear away. But she had seldom reached it, especially when guiding clients, and right now it was still a long way off.

Her endurance, however, was not the point. They could only go at the speed of the weakest members of the team, and there was nothing she could do for them. Well; she could give them her meltwater. And so at the next break she did that, giving one cup to Jack and another to Elspeth, over their objections. 'Drink it,' she ordered, her tone peremptory in a way she had not let it be until now. 'I'm not thirsty.'

But of course after that she was. The parching in her mouth and throat reminded her of multi-day wall climbs back in the world, when they had only carried a quart or two a day for days on end, and spent the last couple of days hanging on sunny granite faces sick with thirst, hauling themselves up despite that, their sweat white. Dry mouth, dry throat, the tongue thickening until it became a foreign object lodged in the mouth, obstructing the breathing; the physical reality of being a water-creature drying out, therefore losing substance; getting thin. One could dry up and die, parch to death. It was a feeling more painful than cold by far, though down here it often combined with the cold, allowing it to penetrate more quickly, so that one ended up freeze-dried, like the mummified seals in the Dry Valleys.

Well, fine. But just as she had done on the big walls, she gritted her teeth, bit the inside of her cheek lightly, and powered on. She would drink one arm of her next melt, and then alternate after that. She was fine. She could walk for ever. But the clients couldn't.

The little cloud was thickening, a white blanket thrown right over the sun, holding its position with maddening fixity. You could laugh at the Victorians for talking about a battle with Nature, but when you saw a cloud hold its position like that, in the freshening wind now striking them, it was hard not to feel there was some malignant perversity at work there, a Puckish delight in tormenting humans. It might be the pathetic fallacy, but when you were as thirsty as Val was it felt tragic.

She slowed down to hike with each of the others in turn, inquiring after them. Except for Ta Shu, and perhaps Jim, they were hurting; nearly on their last legs, it appeared, with more than thirty kilometres to go. Well, she would shepherd them there. Bring them on home. Give them her water, give them her mental energy. There was something about taking care of clients in such a way that felt so good. Others before self. The sherpas' business Buddhism, their ethic of service. Being a shepherd, or a sheepdog. Husbanding them along.

At the next stop, however, she tried again to give Jack her water, and suggested that he eat, and he refused the water and yanked the power bar out of his belt and tore off a piece savagely, muttering, 'Lay off, for Christ's sake. We're doing the best we can.'

Jim and Elspeth and Jorge all nodded. 'This is hard for us,' Elspeth said to Val wearily.

'Of course,' Val said. 'I know. Hard for anyone. You're doing great. We're making a very long walk, in excellent time. No problem. Let's just keep taking it easy, we'll get there.'

And as soon as possible she had them moving again, despite Elspeth's suggestion that they take a longer break. That would only allow muscles to stiffen up; besides, the sheer impact of the cold made it impossible. They had to move to stay warm.

So she took off, trying to tread the fine line between going too fast and tiring them or going too slow and freezing them. She lost the glow she had felt during the previous march about the ethic of service and all that; in fact another part of her was taking over, and getting angry at these people for getting so tired so fast. Sure, she should have kept anything like this from happening. But they had no business coming down here to trek if they were not in shape. Even these so-called outdoorspeople were still very little more than brains in bottles – weekend warriors at best, exercising nothing but their fingertips in their work hours, the rest of their bodies turning as soft as sofa cushions. Watching computer screens, sitting in cars, watching TV, it was all the same thing – watching. Big-eyed brains in bottles. These clients of hers were actually among the fittest of the lot, they were the best the world had to offer! The best of the affluent Western world, anyway. And even they were falling apart after walking a mere seventy kilometres. And thinking they were doing something really hard.

But in their spacesuit gear the level of raw suffering was not that great, if they could just learn to thermostat properly. Indeed the whole idea of Antarctic travel as terrible suffering which required tremendous courage to attempt struck Val as bullshit, now more than ever. It was all wrapped up with this Footsteps phenomenon – people going out ill-prepared to repeat the earlier expeditions of people who had gone out ill-prepared, and thinking therefore that you were doing something difficult and courageous, when it was simply stupid, that was all. Dangerous, yes; courageous, no. Because there was no correlation between doing something dangerous and being courageous, just as there was no correlation between suffering and virtue. Of course if you went at it with Boy Scout equipment like Scott had, then you suffered. But that wasn't virtue, nor was it courage.

In fact, Val decided as she stamped along, most of the people who came to Antarctica to seek adventure and do something hard, came precisely because it was so much *easier* than staying at home and facing whatever they had to face there. Compared to life in the world it took no courage at all to walk across the polar cap; it was simple, it was safe, it was exhilarating. No, what took courage was staying at home and facing things, things like talking your grandma out of a tree, or reading the wanted ads when you know nothing is there, or running around the corner of the house when you hear the crash. Or waiting for test results to come back from the hospital. Or taking a dog to the vet to have it put down. Or taking a group of leukemic kids to a game. Or waiting to see if your partner will come home drunk that night or not. Or helping a fallen parent off the bathroom floor at four in the morning. Or telling a couple that their child has been killed. Or just sitting on the floor and playing a board game through the whole of a long afternoon. No, on the list could go, endlessly: the world was stuffed with things harder than walking in Antarctica. Compared to those kinds of things, walking for your life's sake across the polar ice cap was *nothing*. It was *fun*. It could kill you and it would *still be fun*, it would be a *fun death*. There were scores of ways to die that were immeasurably worse than getting killed by exposure to cold; in fact, freezing was one of the easiest ways to go. No, the whole game of adventure travel was essentially an escape from the hard things. Not necessarily bad because of that; a coping mechanism that Val herself had used heavily all her life; but not something that should ever be mistaken for being hard or heroic. It was daily life that was hard, and sticking it out that was heroic.

Val shuddered at this dark train of thought, stopped in her tracks. She looked back; she had been going too fast, and the people she was caring for had fallen far behind. 'Come on, goddamn it!' she said at them. 'You are *so* fucking slow. This is fun! This is your adventure! Are we having fun yet?' Almost shouting at them. But they were so far back there was no chance they would hear her.

They had too little energy and she had too much. And one thing about walking for hours and hours like this; it gave one an awful lot of time to think. Sometimes that was good, sometimes bad. When it was bad, it took a bit of an effort to remain the cheerful optimistic person that one was.

She checked her watch, and found that half an hour had passed; her arm-flask was almost melted. She walked back to the others, pulling herself together to do the cheerleader thing, very hard now. My God, was she toast! No one could have been less in guide-mode than she was at that moment, feeling parched but strong, well into her long-haul groove, and immensely irritated that these people had no long-haul groove to fall into. The back of her throat was so dry that it hurt to talk; but if she was that thirsty, then it was certain the clients were in worse shape; in need of her help; and in this situation that meant her words, as there was little else she could do. So she pulled up her ski-mask so they could see her smile, and said, 'Roberts Massif, coming over the horizon any minute now! We're almost there!' Which, as they were still at least twenty-five kilometres from the oil camp, no doubt took the long distance record for saying *We're almost there* even in her own notorious career of misuse of the phrase. But it needed to be said, she judged; and so she said it. And it helped them to keep moving.

Except it wasn't working for Jack. When he dragged up to the rest he only stared at Val and her good news, and after they started off he quickly fell behind again.

Then Val looked back and saw him squatting on his haunches, a terrible position for rest, as it trapped so much blood below the knees. It looked as if he had gone faint. Jim was hurrying forward, trying to get her attention.

She met Jim on the way back to Jack, and gave him the crevasse detector and told him to keep walking with the others. It might very well have come time to do the fascist guide number on Jack, she judged, and drive him on by snapping him with the whip of his own machismo, for his own sake and the sake of the whole group; and serve him right. But she didn't want any witnesses.

She reached Jack and stood over him. He glanced up, looked back down.

'Well,' she said, 'how's it going?'

He waved a hand: go away. Leave me alone.

'Come on,' she said sharply. 'We can't go away. We can't leave you behind. We're with you, and you're with us, so let's get together. Otherwise everyone's in trouble. Tell me what you need to feel better. Are you hurt?'

He looked down and away. 'I'm okay. I'll be okay in a while. I just need to rest.'

'Did you hit very hard when we fell in the crevasse? Do you think you're concussed?'

'I don't know.'

'Do you remember the fall?'

'Yes.'

'Do you feel nauseous?'

No reply.

'Do you think you're concussed, or in shock?'

'I don't know! Just let me rest, will you? You're always pushing us. I just need some rest.'

'Okay, we'll rest.' She sat down.

'No, no! Get going. You've got the radar, you should be out there, what are you doing?'

'I'm waiting for you. I gave the radar to Jim. We can't go on any farther without you, or else we'll get separated.'

'I'll follow your tracks,' he said. 'Leave me alone.'

Val stared at him, irritated but also worried. He sounded pretty irrational to her. But something was needed to get him going. 'Oh come on,' she said again, standing. 'We can't go on without you! You're endangering everyone right now, do you understand? Goddamn it – why is it always the macho guys that wimp out first?'

'You're the macho guy here!' he cried. 'Always pushing it! Always making us look bad!'

'Right,' she said. 'Like insisting on taking Amundsen's route even though the ice had changed. Come on! And for God's sake either stand up or sit down, Jesus, you're only trapping a bunch of blood below your knees by squatting like that. You don't have to be stupid along with everything else.'

He sat heavily. 'Just go on. I'll catch up.'

'We can't go on. What is wrong with you! You lost blood, you took a hit, okay! You sound kind of in shock to me, and you certainly have hit the wall somehow or other. But we need for you to walk. Just stand up and put one foot in front of the other. Give it a try at least! We can't carry you, and we can't go on without you. So you just have to do it. Reach down and show some guts for once.'

And she turned and walked off a few metres, mouth pursed into a tight line of disgust. High-school-coach bullshit, no doubt about it; but she could remember going into a berserker state as the result of her high school volleyball coach's ballistic exhortations, and Jack was certainly the type if anyone was to still fall for that routine.

She turned around and looked back. He was struggling to his feet. Something was definitely wrong; concussed, perhaps? He was like Seaman Evans, she thought uneasily, the first member of Scott's team to die on their march back from the Pole – a big man who took a fall and afterwards just fell apart. Big men didn't do well down here. Macho men often did, she had to admit; but machismo itself was a weakness and could be stripped away in such a situation as this, where you had to pace yourself for the long haul. Maybe that was all it was; he preferred the blaze of the adrenalin rush and had burnt out fast, and then looked for someone or something else to blame.

She caught up to Jim, who was waiting for the two of them. The others were strung out ahead, struggling along, well in front of the crevasse detector, which was not good even if they were on the Big Ice-Cube. It was cloudier than ever, and bitterly, bitterly cold.

'You're supposed to be out in front.'

'Hey look, he's hurt,' Jim said angrily. 'He's lost blood.'

'I know. He still has to walk. We can't carry him.'

Jim stared at her, clearly angry, balked, frustrated. Mask to mask in the whistling wind.

Val looked back. Jack was coming on now, slowly but steadily, using his ski poles to push forward. He was favouring his cut hand. 'Here he comes. Do what you can to help him keep going. Give me the radar.'

She took back the crevasse detector and walked ahead of them, trying to keep herself down to their pace, though she needed to be out in front with the radar, safe ice or not. As she plodded on she felt worse and worse. There had been a certain amount of pleasure in tongue-lashing Jack into action, of course, after biting back so many remarks in the previous week. Perhaps too much pleasure. In any case it left a bad taste in her mouth. Shackleton would have done it better. Although once after the *Endurance* had sunk, McNeish had refused to haul the boats over the ice any farther, and Shackleton had taken him aside and given him a choice; go on hauling or Shackleton would shoot him dead. McNeish had gone on.

Nice if you could do it. And in some ways cleaner than sticking a knife into a man's sense of himself. But not a choice Val had had. They needed Jack moving; and now he was moving. But she had a foul taste in her dry mouth – the sick, salty taste of South Georgia Island – and she did not want to look back at those particular clients any more.

On they walked. She kept to the stragglers' pace. They came to a long, low hogback hill in the ice, an extension of the ridge running south from Last Cache Nunatak, and she hurried to the front of the group. It was good that they had got this far, but crevasses here were a real possibility, and the snow was deep on the side of the slope, and cut by the winds into high sastrugi. Val stamped out as deep a trail as she could, and reminded everyone to stay in single file and in her steps. The ice was flowing over a buried rock ridge, so she kept the pulse radar sweeping the ice ahead, and watched the ice itself closely for telltale dips or changes in snow texture. None appeared, and they were able to walk over the ridge without incident. But even that slight uphill made it clear to Val that her legs were getting tired. Which meant the clients must be wasted. She checked her watch, calculated back; they had been walking for twenty-six hours. She figured they had about twenty kilometres left to go.

Then she heard a faint shout, and looked back quickly. Jack was collapsed on the snow, the others standing or crouched in a knot over him. Val ran back down the slope to them. Jack was semi-conscious at best; he was trying to get up, and the others were holding him down.

'Keep down!' Val said to him sharply, almost pleading. She took his pulse, checked him out as best she could. It looked like hypothermia to her, along with whatever else had slowed him down; shock was her best guess, shock from the loss of blood and the fall generally.

She stood and thought it over. Then she took Ta Shu's ski poles and her own, and with their rope lashed the poles to Jack's back in a double X pattern. It was a lousy stretcher, but with the rope tied to her harness she could pull him along on his bottom and boot-heels, his neck and head supported. It was harder than pulling the sledge had been, but only Jack's bottom and heels were in occasional contact with the snow, and his head was supported by ski poles and a net of rope. Now that he wasn't walking he would chill down fast, of course, but there was nothing she could do about that, except dial his suit's photovoltaic system to max and hurry to Roberts as fast as she could. 'Keep up with me if you can,' she ordered the others when the arrangement was finished. 'And stay in my tracks for sure.' She took off.

And then she really began to work. It was particularly hard without her ski poles, for those helped walking in snow a great deal. But there was nothing for it. As long as they did not encounter bare ice, she intended to go as fast as she could without stopping, all the way to the Roberts camp. The others would have her bootprints to show the way if they fell too far behind, and Jack's heels would knock down the largest of the sastrugi, leaving even more of a trail. With luck the others would, like her, feel a new surge of energy at this emergency, and keep her in sight. And once she got to Roberts she could drop Jack off and go back for them.

So off she went, pushing it as hard as she could given the distance left. She had a lot in reserve, and it felt good finally to stop holding herself to the clients' pace and just *take off*. This, she thought blackly, was the only part of guiding she was good at.

white sky
rust rock
white ice

A few hours later the closest client was on the horizon behind her, perhaps six to eight kilometres back. She stopped and watched them as she drank her meltwater and took a breather; she thought it was Ta Shu and Jim leading the way. Jack was still semi-conscious, but he seemed aware enough of his predicament to stay still in his traces. On reflection it seemed to Val that he might have suffered a concussion when they fell. Although he had been gung ho for a while after that. Or else he had gone into shock from loss of blood – mild shock at first, followed by serious shock. Hard to say. Now cold would be the major factor; serious hypothermia could not be far away. Only the photo-voltaic elements in his suit were protecting him from it, and with the sun obscured by clouds they were much less powerful.

But Roberts Massif was now revealed right to its base; so they were less than ten k out. The oil camp was right around the southernmost point of the massif. So they had done most of it. When the others got closer she pointed at Roberts, hoping to give them the little surge of adrenalin they were sure to get when they saw the goal. Then she was off again, faster than ever. No truly long haul is ever done with much of a kick kept in reserve for the end, but she had gone out extremely slowly in the first half, so a good negative split was a distinct possibility. Anyway she was going to give it her best shot; the others could follow at whatever pace they could manage. Although they had looked shat-tered, they also seemed as though they could carry on to the end. Ta Shu had even spun around once to do his filming or his geomancy, or both. Val liked his imperturbability.

The red dolerite of Roberts reared before her. Then she was stomping down the bare ice dropping to the massif, and she had to pull Jack around and let him down ahead of her. She leaned forward to look at his face; he appeared to be asleep. 'We're almost there,' she said. 'We'll get you some help.'

Then she turned the last corner and saw that the little station had burned down. Completely destroyed. A new kind of fear spiked into her. Her shouts brought no one out of the ruins. Then a figure appeared on the hovercraft still lying next to the dock.

CHAPTER ELEVEN

Extreme Weather Event

red
rock white ice

X opened the door and shouted back at the approaching stranger. A tall woman hauling an injured man on a kind of travois, lashed together from ski poles and climbing rope. Feeling amazed without knowing why, X looked closer. It was Val. His heart leapt: 'Hey!' he cried. She looked over at him, saw he was on the hovercraft, and pulled wearily over to the dock. X crossed the broad section of panelling he had made into a gangplank, and helped her to get the stricken man on board. Trouble on her trek, and without helo support from Mac.

'X, is that you?' she said, staring at him from behind ski-mask and sunglasses.

'Yeah.'

He helped her lift the casualty over the side of the hovercraft and inside. They got the man on his back on the floor. She croaked, 'Water,' and pulled off her mask; she looked grimmer than he had ever seen her, by many magnitudes. 'Any doctors with you?'

'No.' He went back to the stove and poured her a mug of warm water. 'We're barely here ourselves.'

'Uh.' She looked out of a window at the station. 'What happened?'

'We're not sure. We're the only ones here.' He gave her the mug and she gulped some of the hot water down. 'We just got here ourselves a little while ago, and found the place like this.'

'It was blown up,' Wade said from stoveside, somewhat unnecessarily in X's opinion, as there were not any competing explanations.

Val looked in at Wade, again surprised. 'Wade! Jeez, what is this? I thought you were at the Pole.'

'I was.'

'Uh huh,' she said. She held the mug to the stricken man's lips.

271

Distracted by him, on conversational automatic pilot, she said, 'And how was that?'

'It was interesting.'

Val didn't hear him. She couldn't get water into the man; he was out. She looked up at X. 'But then you both ended up here?'

'The drilling camp we were at was also blown up,' X explained. 'And when we got here we found this one as you see it. We presume there's been a terrorist attack on the oil camps.'

'You presume?' Val said.

'We haven't been able to establish radio contact with anyone.'

'Oh really! We haven't either.'

'What happened to you?' Wade asked.

'We lost our sledge. An ice block fell on it. So we came here. I would have waited for search and rescue if I could have made coms, but I couldn't. It was weird.'

'Where were you again?' Wade asked.

'Top of the Axel Heiberg.'

'How far away is that?'

'Hundred k or so.'

The men stared at her.

'I've got four more clients out there following me,' she said.

'I'll go help them in,' X said.

'Thanks.'

As X put on his boots and outdoor gear, Wade explained in his deadpan style what had happened to the three of them since their trip out to see the Hillary Weasel; that felt to X as if it had happened a few weeks ago, though in reality it had been the previous day. 'We assume the people in these two camps got warned somehow, and managed to get out. Or were taken out. Or whatever, because there was no one at either place – you know, no bodies, no one wandering around.'

'What about the radios here?' Val asked, her face serious as she digested the implications of Wade's story.

'There's only the one here, I think. We haven't tried it yet.'

'What about emergency bags?'

'I've found a couple,' Carlos said as he came in the room, dragging one across the floor behind him. 'And there's a radio on board. But I don't think it's the radios.'

'I know. But we only had our phones, and I wanted to try something stronger.'

'Me too.'

He and Val started discussing the base and its resources. With the main complex destroyed, these were limited indeed; so far, two emergency bags, for nine people. That would feed them for a few days, and

Carlos said there was some food in the hovercraft. In the ordinary course of things that would be enough to hold them until they were rescued by Mac Town; but obviously they were not in the ordinary course of things.

X left them discussing it and went out into the cold. He cramponed up the ice slope to the plateau proper, then waved at the four stragglers coming in. The first of them, a small Oriental man not wearing a ski-mask, smiled and waved at X, then frowned as he saw the station. 'Oh my! More trouble I see!'

'Yes. We're in the hovercraft there, it's still okay.'

'Hovercraft, okay. Hot chocolate?'

'Sure, go on in. I'll wait for the others.'

'I also. They will soon join us. Doing very well.'

Actually they looked wasted to X, but they were happy to have made it, and though shocked at the sight of the burned station, they got down the slope to the hovercraft without difficulties. Over the gangplank, into the hovercraft's interior, which felt nice and cosy after the outside, though it was probably only ten or twenty degrees warmer, at the most. But it was shelter.

Inside it was loud for a while as introductions and explanations filled the air. Only slowly did the new arrivals grasp that their troubles were not yet over; and even then their main feeling was pleasure at having successfully crossed seventy miles of the polar cap in a single push. X went back to the stove, and mixed mug after mug of hot cocoa for the new arrivals, observing as he did that this session alone would use up nearly half the hot chocolate they had. Val said thanks as he handed her the last mug, but other than that she was focused on the hurt man. Carlos was checking him out with a perhaps illusory paramedic competence; it wasn't something X knew anything about. He resolved to take a first aid course the next chance he got. He wanted to comfort Val somehow (impress her somehow), but could not think what he might do; there was nothing he could do for the stricken man, who, he suddenly realized, was probably Val's latest romantic interest. Oh well.

He went down the passageway behind the passenger compartment, and started rummaging through the cabinets in the wall, which were packed with boxes, mostly containing machine parts and the like. 'I think this guy is just cold now,' he heard Carlos say to Val. 'Even a bad concussion shouldn't leave him comatose like this, and you say it wasn't a bad concussion anyway.'

'I didn't think so,' Val said.

'Well, hypothermia will do this to you. How long were you pulling him?'

'Four hours or so, I guess. I had his suit on full heat.'

'But it's been cloudy. That's a long time to be doing nothing out here. Let's get a core temperature and start warming him up.'

'How?'

'The hovercraft should have a body bag in it.'

X had just found this item in one of the passageway cabinets, and now brought it into the passenger compartment. He had only seen one deployed once, in an ASL demonstration in Christchurch, but Carlos said, 'Yeah, here we go,' and took the package from X and pulled it apart quickly, unfolding what looked like a sleeping bag made of bubblewrap. It worked, as X recalled, in a manner similar to the anti-quated handwarmers that some old iceheads still carried around in their Carhartts in Mac Town; the act of getting a person inside the bag twisted it enough to break all the internal pockets in the bubblewrap fabric, and that mixed some chemicals contained in separate pockets, starting chemical reactions that generated heat. After that the person was inside a sleeping bag that emanated heat like a lukewarm bath, focusing especially on torso and jugular. 'Here, cut his clothes off first,' Carlos ordered, working with a massive pair of scissors he found in one of the e-bags. As he worked he said, 'It's very dangerous to reheat a hypothermic person too fast, they get what is called rewarming shock. All their closed capillaries reopen at once, and the sudden drop in blood pressure causes the heart to fail.' With what X regarded as questionable gusto he went on to tell them a story about being on a ship in his youth which had rescued six Argentinian sailors out of the sea off Tierra del Fuego; the crew had dried them off, fed them hot food and drinks in the cabin, and watched all six keel over dead. But he trailed off as he stared at the little computerdoc console embedded in the bag. 'Eighty-six degrees? What is this, Fahrenheit?' He pushed buttons. 'Ah yes. Thirty degrees. Well, that is hypothermia all right. But I have seen worse.' The man in the bag looked like a sleeping film star. Playing Lazarus, hopefully. Carlos was pointing out the sophisticated thermostatting that the bag was capable of, with its array of thermom-eters, rheostats, dampers and supplementary heaters, when he interrup-ted himself and said, 'Oh, my. Look at this. He was injured, eh?'

'Well, his hand was cut,' Val said. 'And he banged his head, I think. He seemed okay right after the accident, but later he lost it.'

'Yes, but look at his collarbone. See that bend? I think he must have broken his collarbone too.'

X glanced at Val; her eyes were round.

'He didn't say anything about that,' she said. 'I didn't know.'

'He must not have been using ski poles?'

'Well, no, mostly he was. Other times he was letting them hang at his sides. I thought he was just tired. Goddamn it – why didn't he say anything?'

Carlos shrugged. 'Well, hopefully he'll be okay. A broken collarbone isn't so bad, and if he was doing okay for a while after he hit the ice, it couldn't be that bad. We'll see. Looks like he's just sleeping now. We'll try to give him some hot liquids as soon as we can.'

After that there was little they could do for the man, and Val and Carlos took charge of ransacking the hovercraft, to inventory what they had. X resisted the tendency to sink into client status with the rest of the group, and joined them in the search. He had only spent a few days at the station, but he remembered it well enough to go back out into the cold, on a quick search for anything that might have survived the blast and fire in the main complex.

No luck. The fire had been comprehensive. He returned gratefully to the protection of the hovercraft, blowing into his fists to reheat his hands. It was still nearly as cold inside as out, but shelter from the wind made all the difference, and the hovercraft's cabin was warming a bit. Inside it, Val's clients were still sitting on the benches, eating and drinking without pause. Val and Carlos were fiddling with the hovercraft's radio. 'Misery Peak is right in the way,' Carlos was saying. 'No way we get a good connection.'

'Misery Peak, Dismal Bluff,' Val said, reading a map. 'The people who named this area sound like they were as bad off as us.'

'No, those were just the names of their dogs.'

'Ah.'

'Can't radio-waves bounce off the, the ionosphere?' X asked.

'Not down here. We're at the end of the magnet, so to say. The radio-waves just shoot right up the lines.'

'Uh huh.'

'But we might hit a repeater. Worth a try, that's for sure. This is a lot more powerful radio than the one we tried before.'

The radio had a handset like a telephone's, connected to the big console by a typical handset cord. Carlos picked up this handset and pushed the button on it that would allow him to transmit, and a piercing high buzz filled the air. Carlos let off on the button and the noise ceased; tried it again, and got the same result. 'Shit. There's something wrong with the radio.'

He pushed in the handset cord's clips at both ends, banged the handset against the console, slapped the dashboard containing it. Still the earshattering buzz when he tried to transmit. 'Ouch. I suppose the force of the explosion might have damaged something. Well, let's see if it transmits anyway.' He pushed the button while covering the earpiece with his other hand, which muffled the high buzz somewhat, and said loudly into the transmitter, 'Mac Coms, this is Roberts Station, Mac Coms, this is Roberts Station, do you read me, over?'

After a few seconds of loud static, they heard a faint voice under the noise, a sound which brought them all on point like bird dogs: '*Kkkkk* Roberts Station this is Mac Coms *kkkkkkkk* very broken *kkkkkkkkkkkk* repeat, can you *kkkkkkkkkkkk*.'

'That's Randi,' Val said. 'Tell her that T–023 is here too.'

'Okay.' Carlos pushed the button again, and through the muffled whine shouted, 'Mac Coms, we read you, this is Roberts Station and T–023, over!'

More static. Then: '*Kkkkk* you say T–023 *kkkkkkkkkkkk* thought you said you were Roberts Station, over.'

Carlos shouted 'Yes, Mac Coms, this *is* Roberts Station, and we have T–023 with us! We need a medevac for T–023 at Roberts Station!'

'*Kkkkkkkkkkkkkkkkk* do you need a medevac, over?'

Carlos spared time to roll his eyes. He was in a better mood, X saw, now that they had established contact; and so was Val.

'*Yes*, Mac Coms, we need a medevac. Repeat, we need a medevac, over!'

'*Kkkkkkk* most of Antarctica needs a medevac, Roberts!' Even through the static X could tell Randi, too, was glad to have made contact. 'What's the nature of your problem? Where's Val? What's T–023 doing at Roberts anyway? Over.'

Carlos shouted, 'T–023 walked here, Mac Coms. Roberts Station is wrecked, it burned down. Same with Mohn Basin Camp. They were both bombed. We have nine people, one suffering hypothermia, and very little food. Can you help us, over?'

'*Kkkkkkkkk* lost helo and we are arranging evacuation. Many camps have been damaged, repea *kkkkkkkkkkkkkkk* SAR is booked and we do not have full helo or coms *kkkkkkkkkkkk* get down to Shackleton on your own, over?'

'Randi, repeat, we have a hypothermia case here, over.'

'Well warm him up for Christ's sake! Over.'

'He's injured as well, Randi. When can you get us a medevac, over?'

'*Kkkkkkk* yourself to Shackleton Camp, over?'

Carlos and Val stared at each other. Finally Val took the handset and pressed the button, and through the howl said loudly, 'Randi, this is Val! I don't think we can make our way on foot to Shackleton Camp! We've already had to walk from the Axel Heiberg, and people are walked out. We need a lift, over!'

'Didn't read that, Val. You are very broken up, can you *kkkkkkkkk*.'

Val clicked in, shouted, 'We need a lift out! Over!'

'Lots of people feel left out right now, Val, but the SAR is over-whelmed! We've had twenty-two calls for help, and everyone else is calling in trying to find out what happened to coms *kkkkkkkkkkk* six or seven parties. We're only just now back on the air, and still waiting for fuel resupply! We're glad to hear from you, but if you can't get to Shackleton Camp you're going to have to sit tight for a few days, maybe more, over!'

Val and Carlos looked at each other. Val shouted, 'Okay, Randi, we read you! What happened to McMurdo, over?'

'*Kkkkkk* trouble reading you, Val, and I've got a call in from *kkkkk* schedule next coms for nineteen hundred hours, do you *kkkkkkkkk*.'

'We read you, Randi, sched coms nineteen hundred, we'll talk to you then, over!'

'Nineteen hundred, over and out.'

Carlos turned off the radio, took a deep breath and let it out. 'What a noise that thing makes!'

But despite the frustration and the earsplitting noise, the call had done them all a lot of good. Even bad news was better than no news at all; the absence of contact had been oppressive, even frightening. Now they were back in contact, with another scheduled coms to look forward to. And the idea that they were not the only ones in Antarctica suffering problems was comforting too, X saw. Misery loves miserable company; and there they were, right under Misery Peak.

So when Jim said, 'What are we going to do? How are we going to get to Shackleton Camp?' Carlos just waved a hand and said, 'Let's not worry about that yet. First let's get a big hot meal inside us, and I'll finish finding out exactly what we have here. Then we can decide what comes next. Also we might learn more from our next coms, although,' he glanced at the radio and frowned, 'we will see.'

Wade and Ta Shu and Elspeth dug into the e-bags and got two more Coleman stoves set up on the broad shelf running down the side of the cabin, boiling water for stew and more hot drinks. 'We will eat hoosh,' Carlos declared. 'We will eat hoosh, like Shackleton and Scott!'

'Like Amundsen,' Ta Shu corrected. 'We are Footsteps of Amundsen expedition.'

'Fine. Norwegian hoosh. Chunks of reindeer,' cackling as he inspected the antique package labels of the food in the e-bags. Watching him it occurred to X that Carlos was happy not only to be back in contact with McMurdo, but also to have heard that his had not been the only operation in Antarctica targeted for attack. Now he didn't have to take it so personally. Although even when he had been taking it personally, at no point had he seemed to feel that they themselves were in terrible trouble being out here alone. For X, and he suspected for most of the rest of them, it was like being marooned, a kind of protracted death sentence. But for Carlos this was home – dangerous, but not terrifying. It was nice to have him there.

Val had gone into the little storeroom behind the passenger compartment to check on her hurt client, and X followed her to see if there was anything he could do. When he got to the doorway she was leaning over the man's handsome head, her own tilted to listen to his breathing, a look of deep concern on her face. She looked up at X and he stopped, raised a hand: 'Sorry,' he said softly, 'didn't mean to intrude.'

'You aren't,' she said quietly.

'So,' X said. 'He, he means a lot to you,' gesturing at the man.

'What?' she said. Then she understood him, and looked so surprised that X knew immediately that his suppositions had been wrong. And indeed she was staring at him now as if he were completely insane. X raised his other hand so that both were up, palms out, as if to ward off a blow.

'Sorry,' he said quickly. 'I didn't mean . . .'

'Oh X,' she said, shaking her head. 'You're such a . . .' She couldn't find the word.

X ducked his head, sighed. It was true.

'How's he doing?' he said, to change the subject.

She looked back down at the man. 'It looks like he's just sleeping now. The thermometers show his core temperature is about ninety-four. Anyway the bag is just barely heating him now.'

Carlos appeared behind X. 'How is he?' He came in and looked at the console's numbers. 'That's good. Slow and steady rise. Pulse and blood pressure okay.' He stared at the man's face. 'Hello! Hello!' He shook his head. 'Still out. Well, come on,' gesturing at the other room, 'hot drinks, and dinner is on the table soon.'

After their meal Carlos and X geared up again, went out and made a really thorough search through the wrecked station. They found no further food supplies. 'Hmm, hmm,' Carlos muttered as they returned to the hovercraft. 'At Bernardo O'Higgins we always kept a big cache of food and supplies buried out in the snow, in case of fires in the winter. Here I should have done the same. I was thinking more about Mohn Basin, I must admit. And it is hard to believe that the transport system could break down this badly for so long, in this day and age. In the future we will have to remember.'

'What about now?' X asked.

'Well, what do we have. Four, no five e-bags . . . nine people . . .' He thought about it while they hurried across the gangplank to the shelter of the hovercraft. 'We should probably get ourselves down to Shackleton Camp.'

'That's a long walk.'

'Beats starving. Besides, we may not have to walk.'

'What do you mean?'

Carlos pounded the side of the hovercraft.

'Do you really know how to drive it?'

'Yeah sure. I think so.' A broad grin for X, a slap on the shoulder; then they were back inside, which, though it was around zero Fahrenheit, still felt distinctly warm and comfy. It would be nice to get to Shackleton Camp without having to leave such a refuge, that was for sure.

'I think we should try the hovercraft,' Carlos said to the others when they were settled back in the cabin, downing another mug of hot lemonade. 'It's fully fuelled, and that's more than enough to get us down to Shackleton.'

'Do you know how to pilot it?' Val asked.

'Yes. I have watched them pilot it many times, and co-piloted, and it is not difficult. It does take two people, but I can tell X how to do the co-piloting, and do the main piloting myself.'

'X?'

'X has seen it piloted too, so he has the most familiarity with how it works. Right?'

X nodded. 'The co-pilot just operates the lifters and the outriggers. Most of the trip he doesn't do anything at all.'

Val looked dubious; the rest of her group looked hopeful. 'How much food do we have here?' she asked.

'We have five e-bags,' Carlos said. 'With nine people, that's enough for a week, maybe ten days if we go hungry. It's not bad, but it sounds like we are not high priority in McMurdo. It might not be enough.'

'We could wait and see,' Wade said, 'and when we only had a day or two left, go on down.'

'Yes, we could. But by that time Shackleton Camp may have been evacuated. Then we would be low priority again. I would rather do something now. And also, you have this man who is warmed up but not really conscious yet. I don't know what that means, but . . .'

Val nodded to herself.

'It would be good to get him to McMurdo soon,' Jim said.

'Yes it would,' Val agreed.

Jorge and Elspeth seemed willing. Ta Shu merely watched them, as if it were not his call to make.

'We should get down there,' Val finally told her group.

'I don't think we can walk it,' Elspeth said.

'No. But we have the hovercraft.'

She looked at each of them in turn, and they nodded their comprehension. They had already been through a lot, X saw, and they trusted Val.

'Tell you what,' Carlos said, 'I'll start up the hovercraft, and we'll take it for a trial run right here outside the dock, make sure we know what we're doing. If it looks good to you, we can go for it.'

So X and Carlos went forward to the controls, and sat in the two pilots' seats, and looked around at the intimidating banks of control consoles. At that moment it looked to X like the inside of a plane's cockpit. He had watched Geraldo and German pilot the craft to Mohn and back, but that, he saw now, was not enough.

As they went over the controls together it became clear to X that they had an unspoken agreement not to discuss the many banks of toggles, switches, gauges and dials of which they were completely ignorant. They focused instead on the few things they knew which were crucial for running the thing: ignition, steering wheel, thrust throttles, lifter controls, outrigger deployment toggles. X nodded as Carlos named everything. The lifters and outriggers were the co-pilot's only responsibilities. They seemed manageable.

The two men grinned nervously at each other. 'No problem,' Carlos declared.

'Let's see,' X said.

Carlos turned on the engines. Muffled roar from behind and below, vibration all through the metal of the craft. They waited while the engines warmed up. This hovercraft was old, X saw, looking at the finger-polished tops of the toggles. A Hake 1500A. At some time in its life, no doubt its stint at Corrosion Corners, the outriggers had been added to give the craft more resistance to side winds and small inclines. By and large the craft was intended for flat surfaces only, like water or sea ice; in strong winds, or traversing any kind of slope, it tended to sideslip pretty badly, floating as it was on its own air cushion, with little or no contact with the ground. The enterprising engineers who had reworked the craft had therefore welded and bolted booms onto the sides, with a hydraulic system to lower them down onto the ice or raise them again. At the ends of the booms hung what looked to be snowmobiles stripped to their functional essence; when the booms were lowered and the snowmobiles' engines turned on, their tracks would engage the ice and do their best to haul the whole craft in that direction, which gave the hovercraft some traction to that side. X had seen them deployed, and the system worked pretty well, helping the hovercraft to glide up and down the gentle undulations of the polar ice without sideslipping into basins on the side.

Carlos had travelled with Geraldo and German on a route they had worked out down the steeper sections of the Zaneveld Glacier's descent to Shackleton Camp, and now he found their maps marking the route in the craft's computer, which X saw was a later addition, stuck on the dashboard and plugged in.

'Okay, try the lift fans.'

X found that the levers controlling these were extremely stiff, and had to be shoved up by main force; but when he did that the air intakes in the roof aft of them buzzed, the fan engines whined, the skirts that held in the air bellied out to their full extension, and the body of the hovercraft rose up off the ice, with only a single thump of the metal tub.

When they were fully lifted, Carlos gave the thruster of the propeller fan a push forward. That engine proved to run several thousand rpm faster for every centimetre he moved the thruster, so that the craft jerked and slid forward over the ice, tilting down a tiny bit.

'Jeez,' X said, 'who did the ergonomics on these controls?'

'An idiot,' Carlos said. '*Where* are Geraldo and German? Goddamned Argentinians . . .'

'I thought they were Chilean.'

'Well, now they are Argentinians.'

Carlos turned the steering wheel gently. In this case the control was less sensitive; it took nearly a full revolution of the wheel to get the craft to change direction even slightly.

'A total idiot. Still, we can do it. See, we are going in a circle. Here, better slow down,' knocking the thruster level back down to idle.

'What about brakes?' X asked.

'No brakes. If you really want to brake, you turn the craft around and hit the thrusters, and that slows it down.'

'Great.'

'Well, how are you going to have brakes when you aren't touching the ground? I suppose deploying both the outriggers would slow you down.'

X shook his head.

'It's all right,' Carlos said. 'We can turn around and go down the steepest sections backwards.'

'Uh huh.'

It was sounding pretty tenuous to X, but on the other hand Carlos was now driving them around the ice offshore from Roberts in big swooping glides, just as if he knew exactly what he was doing.

Val came up behind them. 'Looks like you have this thing in hand.'

'No problem,' Carlos and X said in concert.

'It looks like Jack is coming to a bit.'

'Good, good! And it's almost time for sked coms with McMurdo. We can tell them what we're doing. And remind me to ask about German and Geraldo and the rest of them.'

They brought the craft back in to the dock, and X muscled down the lift fan lever, and the tub thumped hard down onto the ice.

Carlos stood. 'Let's get ready quick, and get going while the engines are still warm.'

They went to the back of the cabin. The injured trekker, Jack, had been awakened by the sounds of the hovercraft's test run. Ta Shu and Jim were crouched at his sides, getting hot liquids into him; the others crowded in the doorway to see how he was, X at the back. Between sips Val and Carlos asked him questions. He was a bit groggy, and could not remember the accident in which he had been hurt; but he did remember much of the walk here, he said, with a brief glance at Val that X could not interpret. His shoulder hurt, he said, but otherwise he was fine. X got the impression that he was pissed off, but unwilling to talk about it. Something had happened out there on the ice. Val did not seem at all comfortable with him, which was in marked contrast to her behaviour with her other clients.

'Okay,' Carlos said when Jack had finished drinking. 'Time to try Randi again.'

He went to the radio and turned it on, then wrapped a fist around the shrieking earpiece and started the call. 'McMurdo, this is Roberts Station! Roberts Station at nineteen hundred *scheduled coms*, over!'

Reception was if anything worse than last time. But then Randi's voice was cutting through. '*Kkkkkkkkkkkk* got you, Roberts! How's it *kkkkkkkkk* ver?'

Carlos managed to make most of a status report, and Randi told them a bit more about what had happened. As far as they could gather through the static, one or all of McMurdo's big fuel tanks had been contaminated somehow. 'The Navy's flying in some fuel and there's a tanker on the way, but meanwhile the guys are filtering the shit out of what's left, and we're burning it as fast as they clean it. Really too bad Ron isn't still here to work on the filtering. So search and rescue activities are still being conducted on a need basis, over.'

'Triage,' Wade commented.

Carlos waved him quiet. 'Randi, does that mean you will not be able to collect us by helo, over?'

'No helo ops at Shackleton Camp at this time, T–023! Their fuel is wrecked. Do you still need a medevac?'

'Well, he has a broken collarbone.'

'*Kkkkkkkk* down the list. You should get down to Shackleton Camp if you can. We plan to fly a Herc there tomorrow and evacuate everyone there. Apparently a lot of the Roberts crew ended up there, did you know that Roberts? Roberts Station and the Mohn station too.'

'Hey!' X and Carlos said, giving each other a brief hug.

'—to Shackleton, or hang tight at Roberts, and wait for us to get to you.'

'We don't have the food to wait long,' Carlos said into the screeching, reaching over Jorge to shake hands with Wade as well.

'Then get yourselves to Shack*kkkkkkkkkkkkkkk.*'

'Okay, okay,' Carlos said, 'but who did all this, do you know, over?'

'Did not read you, Roberts, can you repeat, over?'

'Who did all this!'

'*Kkkkkkkkkkkkkkkkk.*'

'Mac Coms, this is Roberts, do you read me?'

'Roberts, are you there, repeat, Roberts, do you read me, over?'

'*Yes*, Mac Coms, roger, roger, we read you!'

'We read you too, Roberts, over!'

'Repeat – who did all this?'

'No information on that, Roberts. We assume saboteurs of some sort, but *kkkkkkkkkkkkkk.*'

'How illuminating,' Carlos said, shaking his head and staring at the handset. 'Randi, listen! We are planning to take the hovercraft to Shackleton! Can you give us weather forecasting please, over!'

'*Kkkkkkkkk* would you like weather forecasting, Roberts?'

'Yes, Randi, yes! Affirmative, roger, over!'

'Roberts, repeat message, I say, would you like weather forecasting here, over!'

'*Yes*, Mac Coms! Yes! Yes! Roger! Affirmative! Ro-ger ro-ger ro-ger!'

'I can't read you guys any more, but I'm gonna switch you over to weather forecasting, Roberts. Listen, are you aware that there is something wrong with your radio, over?'

Carlos waved the handset in the air over his head, eyes bugging out. Then he shouted into it, 'Roger, Mac Coms, we are aware of that! Over!'

'Listen Roberts, can you call back in half an hour? Weather is out to lunch right now, and I'm getting a *kkkkkkkkkkk.*'

'Roger, Mac Coms! We will try to call back in half an hour, but we are going to leave for Shackleton now! Over!'

'Excuse me Roberts, what did you say, over?'

'We will STAND BY and call back in HALF AN HOUR. Over.'

'Roberts, I'm not reading you any more. Please stand by, over.'

'Okay, goddamn it! Roger! We will stand by!' Carlos began to laugh maniacally.

'*Kkkkkkkkkkkk* what?'

'No, what's on second!' Carlos shouted. '*Who's* on first!'

'What?'

'No! *What's* on *second*! *Who's* on first!'

'*What?* Oh! Oh ha ha ha! Very funny, Roberts! Tell you what, you keep on doing your Abbott and Costello by yourself, I gotta go attend to the Three Stooges now! Call back in half an hour, goddamn it, over and out!'

Carlos slammed the radio off and shook the handpiece like he wanted to smash it to pieces, still laughing. 'Ah, ha ha ha! We used to laugh ourselves sick at that when we were kids. It was the best English lesson we ever had. I don't know's on third!' he shouted at the handset.

He looked around at the others. 'Come on, let's go. Shackleton Camp here we come.'

Wade was helping Carlos and X and the others to secure everything in the hovercraft for the trip down to Shackleton Camp when his wrist phone beeped. He jumped as if shot, and ran up the short set of stairs to the aft cabin to get some quiet and reduce interference, then clicked the receive button.

'Hello!'

'Wade, Wade, is that you?'

'It's me, Phil! Where are you?'

'Never mind where I am Wade, where are you! What's going on down there?'

'Well, let's see, there's been an attack on the oil camp I was visiting, and we're now at the oil group's base camp on Roberts Massif, top of the Shackleton Glacier, and that base has also been destroyed, so we're about to take a hovercraft down to NSF's Shackleton Glacier Camp, to be flown back to McMurdo.'

'You're kidding.'

'No Phil, listen, what have you heard, what's happening?'

'Well I don't have the full story yet, I got a call from John and he told me that satellite communications to Antarctica had been interrupted and there were no reports coming out, but clearly something was wrong, and at that point I started calling you and got no reply! I got no reply!'

'I know.'

'But now I'm calling you using a Pentagon code I got, they must have some satellites of their own up there that are a little bit more reliable, but they don't like to share them. I had to get John to contact Andy right in the Pentagon to get the codes, but it seems like they're working pretty well.'

'Better than our radio contact with McMurdo, that's for sure. Could you patch me in to McMurdo, do you think?'

'Sure, I can try. Just a second.'

The line went dead.

'Hey!' Wade said, punching Phil's button on his phone. No answer. The same blank he had got since the moment they saw the smoke rise over Mohn Station. 'God*damn* it.'

'What's wrong?' It was Val, up to see what had happened.

'I just had a talk on the phone with Phil Chase. He was using a military satellite link, and said he would patch me to McMurdo.'

'Must not have worked. We're almost ready to go here.' She leaned against the seat back next to him, let out a deep breath.

'You must be tired,' Wade said.

'No, not tired exactly.'

'Worried about your group. That guy who's sick.'

She nodded, then shook her head. 'I knew there was something wrong with him, but he wouldn't tell me. He had a broken collarbone and he didn't tell me.'

'Some people are like that. He may not have known exactly what was wrong, anyway. If he was stunned.'

'Maybe not,' she said sombrely, thinking it over.

'Over in the Dry Valleys, it looked like he was going to be a–'

She nodded. 'Yeah.'

'So did it come to anything, I mean get difficult? Was he mad at you?'

'Maybe.'

'Well. So he might have been punishing you. But that's his problem, really. Nothing you can do about that.'

'No, I know. But I don't want him to die on me.'

Wade risked putting a hand to her arm, very gently. 'Carlos seemed to think he was just shook up, and cold. We'll get him down to Shackleton Camp and back to McMurdo, and he'll be okay. Besides he's too convinced of his own importance to let himself die, right?'

A small smile. She glanced at him. They went downstairs to the passenger compartment. 'Keep trying to get your senator,' Val reminded him.

'Oh yeah,' Wade said, staring at his wrist phone. 'I'll set it on repeat call. It'll try for me once a minute.'

They got the hovercraft off with only that same minor thump of the tub; X suspected a weak lift fan at the left rear, though Carlos gave him a dubious glance, as if he might be doing something wrong with the lifters. Whatever; they were up and moving over the ice, and there was no reason to look back.

At first the hovercraft was dreamlike in its smoothness, and X and Carlos grinned at each other. Then they left the flattened road out to Mohn camp and ventured onto the sastrugi-covered white firn of the virgin glacier. Out here the craft rocked a little, this way then that, as air blew out from under the skirt at different points depending on what kind of deformations they were floating over. Nevertheless it was a pretty smooth ride compared to, say, a snowmobile, and as Carlos cautiously notched up the prop throttle they found that the faster they went, the smoother it got. Soon they roared smoothly over the ice, first outward from Fluted Peak, then around Roberts Massif on its east side.

As X had noted from the air on his journey in, the massif stuck in the head of the Shackleton Glacier and nearly plugged it; it was like a rock island in the midst of rapids falling out of a lake into a river. The narrow gap on the west side, between Misery Peak and Dismal Buttress, was shattered blue ice from wall to wall, entirely impassable. So their only choice was to go around the eastern side of Roberts, where a wider ice stream called the Zaneveld Glacier made a smooth, curving drop into a confluence with the western stream and the Shackleton proper. The Zaneveld was also crevassed pretty heavily in places, but there were unbroken ramps that descended from one level section to the next, and Carlos said Geraldo and German had taken the hovercraft up and down the route they had worked out several times.

As they moved away from Roberts, out to a kind of ice causeway running smoothly between two crevassed sinks, they noted that the hovercraft moved somewhat like a plane in flight, in that it was frequently struck on the side by the wind, so that the bow of the craft yawed and was not always pointed exactly the same way that the craft was moving, skidding along at a bit of an angle. And as usual the wind was strong out here, beginning its katabatic drop down the glacier to the sea. The leeway they were sustaining from the force of this wind was blowing them into a crevasse sink on their right, not to any great extent, but Carlos turned left a bit more to counteract it. This did little but increase their yaw to that side.

'Try the left outrigger,' he said, stroking his beard.

'Okay.'

X pushed down the toggle. When the little snowmobile hit the ice and X squeezed its throttle, shredded ice shot out from its back end toward the hovercraft, and immediately they could see that they had some resistance to their leeway.

'That's enough,' Carlos said, and X held the throttle at that point. After a bit: 'Okay, we're past that one. Wind should be directly behind us now. Pull the outrigger.'

'Left outrigger up,' X said, enjoying their imitation of co-pilot procedures.

Then the craft's pulse-radar began to ping, loud and fast. Carlos looked over at the radar screen: crevasses ahead, on the last section of their ramp between the sinks. 'Damn.' He looked at Geraldo's map again. 'Ah yes. That's why they made this turn, see here? We have to go down right against the shoreline of the massif. That's blue ice without a break. At its side it curves down to the rock, so we can't get too close and slide over that curve. We ride down on the flat stuff.'

So he slowed the craft, and brought it back in toward Roberts. X saw what he meant; there against the shore was a broad band of turquoise ice, very smooth and unbroken, as if these were calm shallows where the glacier did not move as quickly as it did out in the middle of the stream. The only complication was that the mass of the glacier was considerably higher than the rock of the shoreline, bulking over it in a way that added to the surreal quality of the view: the drop from the glacier to the shore was a smooth blue curve, like a wave bulging up ready to crest. Wind ablation of the grounded ice, Carlos said. If they got onto that slope they would slip sideways and crash down onto the rock.

But as Carlos had said, the level, creamy-blue ice above the curve was wide enough to travel on. And so they proceeded down the glacier, looking left and down at the shoreline of Roberts, the red of the shattered dolerite very pronounced against the blue of the ice. On their right a nasty shear-zone broke the ice into a million glittering blue shards. So they could not shade far either right or left; but they had their road down.

They hummed along. On their left appeared a little side stream of ice separating Roberts Massif proper from an outlying island of rock called Everett Nunatak. After that they came to an overlook and could see down the broad expanse of the Zaneveld. From above their route was clear; they could glide down between two of the many parallel rubble lines marking the surface of the glacier, the rubble composed of boulders and pebbles that had fallen off or been ripped away from Roberts, and conveyed out gradually to the centre of the ice, revealing the slow-motion currents by the way they were lined along the surface.

Val came up to the bridge. 'This manual I found says the hovercraft should not be taken onto slopes more than three degrees off horizontal.'

Carlos shook his head. 'The manual was not written for Antarctica.'

'This hovercraft wasn't made for Antarctica.'

'True. But it does fine. We go down backwards, we have the outriggers. We take a line and cleave to it.'

'Uh huh,' Val said dubiously.

Yet it seemed to X that Carlos was right to be sanguine. Majestically they floated down the Zaneveld, over flat ice next to one of the main rubble lines, shooting over small cracks and rocks that would have eaten a snowmobile, floating down a slight incline, effortless and smooth. Carlos and X were sitting back, feeling quite pleased with themselves as Val peered suspiciously over their shoulders.

Then the ice tilted downward just slightly more than it had been before, and suddenly the hovercraft was like a ball in a gravity-well demonstration, speeding up distinctly, and what was worse, sliding off to the right. With a brief clatter the craft ran directly over the nearest rubble line, and then it was flying downslope – the true downslope – right toward a gnarly shear-zone underlying Wiest Bluff, on the other shore of the Zaneveld.

Carlos sat forward and turned the craft to the left, and it responded, swivelling on its axis; but they merely continued sideways in the same direction they had been going before. 'Left outrigger,' he said tersely.

X brought it down onto the ice and squeezed the snowmobile accelerator to full throttle. 'How about going down backwards, like you said?' he suggested.

'Yes yes,' Carlos snapped, spinning the steering wheel.

'What about brakes?' Val asked.

'No brakes.'

'No brakes!'

'It's like a boat. You cut the engines and it slows.'

'Except on a slope like this!'

'We have to turn around. Bring the outrigger up.'

Carlos spun the steering wheel harder left, and the craft came around so they were going backwards, more or less, but still sliding down toward Wiest Bluff, never changing the overall direction of the craft's movement at all. 'Right outrigger now.'

X dropped the right outrigger. Then for a moment the craft was facing true uphill, and they were sliding down backwards, and Carlos shoved up the prop fan's speed; but X's outrigger tracks caught the ice at that same moment, and the craft swung around and began sliding sideways again. Carlos cursed and turned the steering wheel the other way, but it took a while to stop their spin momentum, and when he got it going the other way it spun right past the backwards position again.

'I'm going to try bringing the tub down into contact,' X said nervously, thinking it would act as a brake. He put his weight on the stiff lifters.

'Don't,' Carlos said. 'The ice is too rough.' As he spoke the craft began to chatter and jounce horribly underneath them.

X hastily yanked the lifter back up.

'What about in a smooth patch?' he asked.

'That was a smooth patch.'

'Oh. Well, what about when we're over snow?'

'Sure.'

But the glacier was gleaming blue ice for as far as they could see in all directions, like a giant racing spillway, with all its waves and turbulence frozen in place for them to observe as they slid farther down into it.

'When I get it straight backwards put both outriggers down,' Carlos said. 'Then if we turn left accelerate the left one, right if we drift right. I'll do the same with the steering.'

'Okay.'

'Then if we slow down enough, bring the tub down fast.'

'Okay.'

'Goddamn, you guys,' Val said, looking downslope. 'You're headed for a crevasse field.'

'We know that.'

Carlos began to spin the steering wheel again. He was getting the hang of it, and after a bit he held the craft going directly backwards down the slope, long enough for X to engage both outriggers on the ice and set them running, which gave them a bit more stability. Unfortunately the slope of the ice grew even steeper at this point, and they crunched over a set of rubble lines and the right outrigger snowmobile snapped off and went spinning out of sight, boom and all. The hovercraft too was spinning again, dropping from time to time as they flew over crevasses at terrifying angles, hitting the tub then billowing up again on the skirts; if they hit one of those lengthwise they would shoot right down into it and be swallowed. Carlos struggled to get them oriented backwards again. Out of the front window they could see back up the glittering blue flood they had so far descended, all completely still and yet receding away from them at great speed. It was a steep slope. 'We're still headed for that crevasse field,' Val said. Behind them the whoops and shouts from the passenger cabin had been replaced by dead silence.

Carlos looked over his shoulder and then spun the steering wheel to the right. 'Full left outrigger,' he said to X. 'We need to go hard left.' He shoved the prop fan throttle to full power and took the steering wheel in both hands, standing before it with his head swivelling around in an attempt to see all directions at once. And then they were jetting sideways across the slope of the ice, sliding downhill still but making tremendous progress across the slope as well. If they went into a spin now they would be doomed to slip down into the crevasse field and crash. X ran the left outrigger motor faster or slower depending on the craft's yaw, and Carlos did the same with the steering wheel, and suddenly it seemed as if they were two parts of a mind that actually knew what it was doing, shooting a traverse across the Zaneveld Glacier like an Everglades fan boat going full speed, jiggling their controls minutely, absolutely locked onto the scene rushing at them, the glacier surface here a smoothly curving drop, with some small crevasses straight ahead; they flew right over them; to their right and below, a veritable Manhattan of blue seracs was flashing by. They were rounding Wiest Bluff at about ninety miles an hour.

But then as they rounded the great turn, another chaos of blue ice reared up directly before them, across all the glacier they could see. Without a word Carlos brought the hovercraft around so that it was facing uphill again, and X stabilized as much as he could with just a single outrigger; they were still working together with perfect co-ordination, and the craft held its rear to their destination and with the fan at full power slowed, slowed, slowed; but the shear-zone was coming up at them so fast that Val hissed. X leapt onto the lift fan throttles and muscled them down with all his strength, and the skirts puffed out and collapsed and the tub slammed down onto the ice, and they were all thrown about as in a giant earthquake, Carlos and X holding on hard to try to keep the craft pointed uphill. They slowed, slowed, slowed. Then with a huge metallic crash the craft fell backwards into the first crevasse of the shear-zone and smashed to a halt, tilted up at about forty-five degrees.

X pushed himself off the floor. Carlos had already leapt back to the controls to kill the engines. The craft remained tilted up at the sky. The rear of the hovercraft was stuck down in a crevasse, which fortunately for them was both narrow and shallow. Not that they would ever get the craft out; but at least they had not fallen all the way into an abyss. Carlos and X and Val looked at each other, white-faced and round-eyed.

'Everyone all right back there?' Val called to the others.

Moans, curses. 'What in the *fuck* was that?' Jack said.

'Glad to hear you're feeling better,' Val said.

'We are fine!' Ta Shu called up. 'This is a good place!'

More curses.

'Let's get off this thing before it falls all the way in,' Val said. 'It's back to walking for us.'

No one could object. The hovercraft was obviously out of commission. And it had, as Val pointed out when they staggered back to the cabin door, got them down the steepest section of the glacier. 'We're only about twenty miles from Shackleton Camp, and it's only a few hundred metres lower than we are here. Easy sailing all the way! It's going to be fine! We're almost there.'

'If you had missed this crack we would have been there in about half an hour,' Jack said.

Val's jaw clenched so hard that X could see all the muscles on that side of her face bulge out. Carlos and X merely looked at each other. They shook hands. 'Let's get going,' Carlos said.

Val ran around at full speed until they all stood on the ice beside the tilted hovercraft: nine people encased in full extreme weather gear, crampons on their boots, two of them pulling banana sledges piled with equipment and bags. They had skis and ski poles tied to the sledges, but they were on bare ice here, and crampons were mandatory. High, thin clouds covered the sky, and down the broad glacier, between its cliff-sided mountain walls, a bloom of thick cumulus cloud sat right on the ice. It was windy, although fortunately the wind was from above, and so would be behind them as they walked. It was cold. No one looked happy.

Val surveyed the group one more time before starting out. 'We'll walk down to Shackleton Camp and take breaks every hour on the way,' she said. 'It'll be fine.'

No response. Jack had not said a word since they had climbed off the hovercraft back into the frigid blast. Probably they should have been hauling him in one of the banana sledges right from the start, but he had refused to co-operate, and the sledge was there if needed; and anyway it was a good sign that he was still well enough to be himself. All the clients looked weary and tense, she thought, except for Ta Shu, who was wandering away from the rest and turning in slow circles, talking rapidly in Chinese. The others were huddled around her. Wade and X stood beside each other, watching her like a little Greek chorus. Wade had not received any further calls. He seemed resigned to whatever happened next, pinched by the wind but resolute. X stoical as always. As least those two were fresh compared to her clients, who had already walked farther than their ordinary strength would have taken them. To tack on twenty more miles was a hard thing. But they needed to get Jack to the med clinic in McMurdo, and they were still very short on food. So there was no choice but to walk the remainder of the way.

Val took off, hauling the banana sledge and keeping her pace down so that she would not get too far ahead of the rest. Carlos pulled the other sledge; between the two of them they had everything they thought they might use on the hike.

Despite the sledges, the other seven were much slower than she and Carlos. Her clients were stiff and exhausted; and Wade and X not very good on the nobbled blue ice. Jim walked next to Jack, giving him something to grab onto if he slipped. A man who had hidden the fact that he had a broken collarbone, the fool. If he had known. Val sighed and shook her head. Lots of climbers were heavily psyched to do the hero thing, they knew all the great injury stories, Doug Scott getting off the Ogre with two broken legs, Joe Simpson smashed like a doll and crawling back to his partner in Patagonia; the stories were endless; but why not tell your companions you were hurt? What did that accomplish, except perhaps to make them feel guilty afterward for wondering why you were going so slow? Which was stupid. She was not going to feel guilty. It was so stupid that, combined with his periods of unconsciousness, she had to worry again about how hard he had been hit in the crevasse. Get stunned and go silent, like a hurt animal. It happened. Sad in a way.

But she was pulling too far ahead again, even ahead of Carlos. She waited while the others staggered to her. The worst part was the wind. Back in the world they said (way too often), *It's not the heat it's the humidity*. And in Antarctica they said, just as frequently, *It's not the cold it's the wind*. And it was just as true. On a windless day the proper clothing made it possible to withstand the coldest temperatures Antarctica had to offer – even to overheat in them. But with even the slightest breeze that warmth was ripped out and flung away. Even the best of the new spacesuit gear was not much shield against its bitter power. And if a wind rose to gale force, it became unbearable. You simply couldn't face it.

Unfortunately, she could see that that kind of a wind was very possibly approaching them from downglacier. It was like being in a train crash in slow motion; the wind was behind them, strong but at their backs, so that they could hunch over and endure it, and in some ways it even helped a little, pushing their legs forward as they lifted them; a wind at one's back was not such a bad thing, no matter how cold. But despite this katabatic wind, the cumulus cloud lying on the glacier down near the NSF camp was coming their way, in what appeared to be utter defiance of the laws of physics. 'Goddamn it,' Val said to herself as she watched it come. Something different was going on down there, of course; the cloud was impelled by some other wind, a northerly coming off the Ross Sea it looked like, pushing up and under the katabatic. Or whatever. Storms in Antarctica could do almost anything. In the ordinary course of things she would have been checking satellite photos on her wrist to see what was up, maybe calling Mac Coms for a detailed weather report, and if the forecast was bad she would probably be ordering her group to stop and put up their tents. As it was, she continued to watch the cloud come at them, hoping it would slow down, swearing at its apparent ability to move against the wind. 'Goddamn it. There is a curse on this trip.'

She took a look back. Getting too far ahead again. Carlos was behind her, hauling the other banana sledge. Then X and Wade. Behind them

Ta Shu, still looking around every few steps, still talking to his distant audience, or presumably taping a talk. Then Jorge and Elspeth, obviously wasted; and Jim hanging back with Jack, who was holding his right elbow with his left hand. All eight moving in slow motion, as far as Val was concerned. The wind was getting gusty, hard buffets interspersed with dead air. She found it hard not to feel for Jack, who was certainly a jerk, but whose collarbone must have hurt with every misstep on the ice. He was definitely angry at Val for spurring him on, back on Mohn Basin. And X was angry at her too, for that matter, for the Mac Town stuff. Of course. There really was a curse on this trip.

Wade was holding his wrist to his mouth and shouting into it, in yet another fruitless attempt to reach the world; or maybe he had heard a ring and was trying to respond. Then he slipped, and hastily started using that ski pole again. Anyway there would be no help for them from the outside now, no matter if he made contact or not. Val took off again, very chilled, happy to stop facing the wind. The glacier here was nearly flat, only a slight tilt downhill. The blue ice was dimpled as usual, but other than that easy going. A rubble line of black and rust-coloured rocks paralleled them to the left. The black cliffs walling the glacier on both sides had clearly been shaved smooth by earlier versions of the glacier, which must have run a thousand feet higher by the look of it, for the cliffs were shaved that high, right to the feet of ramparts which then jumped up, scaling to peaks in the sky far above them. It was not as tight and deep a canyon as the Axel Heiberg's, but something about the vast breadth of it was even more impressive; as if they were ants. Everything was enormous. Shackleton Field Camp was about seventeen miles ahead of them, down where the McGregor Glacier poured into the Shackleton, in a giant confluence under Mount Wade. But all that was invisible under the massed clouds rolling up the canyon, except for Mount Wade lofting high over all—white snow over white cloud. Storm coming.

This group was not going to be able to hike in a storm of any severity. Despite herself, Val recalled Krakauer's searing account of the notorious Everest débâcle, ten people killed in a single day, and mostly because the guides had got a bit overconfident; they had been taking complete amateurs to the top of Everest for hefty fees, and had dealt with all kinds of problems shepherding them up and down, including hauling comatose ones from the peak all the way back down the mountain, so that they thought they had all possible situations in hand; but had never been on the summit ridge in a storm. And so when the inevitable happened and a storm struck on summit day most of the clients had died, and the lead guide had stayed high on the peak trying to save one of them and had died too. Near the end, his base camp had patched his radio link into their satellite phone so that he had been able to have a final talk with his pregnant wife back in New Zealand. An early example of the total com age's mixed blessings.

When Val had read Krakauer's account, early in her guiding career, she had vowed never to make the same sort of mistakes. And she hadn't, at least so far. She had never guided on the eight thousand metre peaks, or on any other radically dangerous climbs or tours. Other guides were still taking amateur clients up Everest, of course, and people were still dying up there on a regular basis; these days the southeast ridge resembled a cemetery cracked down the middle and thrust into the stratosphere, the bodies (a couple of hundred now) spilling down both sides of the slope. But she had refused all such work. She had only taken on competent clients, she had never pushed the outside of the envelope when she was with clients, she had paid very respectful attention to the weather. In Antarctica you had to. She had sat out storms many many times, sometimes for up to two weeks straight, resisting all pleas to forge on from the (mostly bored) clients. And so on. She had been a safe guide!

But here she was. There really did seem to be a curse on this trip, a malignant combination of problems. Well, that was what had struck down Hall's group on Everest too. But here there was the added factor, unprecedented as far as she knew, of human sabotage. From what Carlos and X and Wade had said, it sounded as if the saboteurs had tried to destroy the oil camps without causing any loss of life. But if anything went even slightly wrong down here, then the danger from the cold was immediate.

The wind stopped. Val stopped too. It shifted onto her left cheek, like a slap to the head; went dead, though the howl of it was all around them; then hit her again from the right. Then it struck her full in the face, the hardest blow of all. And suddenly they were hiking into the wind instead of away from it.

Val cursed into her ski-mask. Already her sunglasses were icing up, and even at their lightest coloration their polarization dimmed the world to various shades of brilliant or dull grey. Still she could see quite clearly that the cloud that had been coming up the glacier was now upon them.

She took a sharp turn to the left, toward the rubble line, looking back and waving to make sure that everyone was following. She had almost left it too late, she saw, in her desire to get down to Shackleton Camp before the storm hit. Carlos had grasped the situation, and was actually running for the rubble. Bad weather changed everything. On a windless, sunny day they could have marched down to Shackleton in style. But not today.

Then they were fully in the cloud. The wind shrieked. Visibility dropped to a few score yards – not a classic whiteout by any means, but a blizzard. The ice dust that composed the cloud was driven horizontally into them: it was like having an industrial sandblaster shot into one's face. Val's clothes plastered against her, the wind penetrating right through the fabric. What she could see in the cloud was a kind of rapidly fluctuating bubble which appeared lit from below, as the glacier seemed brighter than the dark cloud rushing by. Her face hurt, and she had to drive each leg forward to take steps. Buffets of wind struck like blows from an invisible heavyweight. The noise of the shriek was incredibly loud, *krkrkrkrkrkrkrkrkr krkrkrkrkrkrkrkrr.*

But she reached the rubble line. She turned and waved to the others. They staggered in one by one. She went back to help Jim help Jack over the remaining fifty yards or so, fighting to keep her balance. Jack was hunched, and couldn't throw his right arm over her shoulder. She walked on the windward side of him with an arm around his waist, trying to protect him from the blasts. Any injury would be bound to hurt in this frigid wind, and a collarbone was much too close to the centre of things. The noise was like a fleet of jet engines, it was too loud to talk.

They reached the rubble line and Val got Jack sitting down in the lee of a boulder that was a foot or two taller than she was. As good a start for their shelter as any she could see at a quick glance, and so she made her way around to the others, and using hand signals got them all to move to the huddled Jack. The rubble line was a big collection of rocks, from chunky boulders to pebbles and sand, all piled in a surprisingly well-defined line on the ice, resting in a shallow depression. Startling features at first sight, they were often found many kilometres away from the rock banks that fed them; they were something like the lines of debris that collected around the eddies in a stream. Val wasn't clear on the dynamics, but she seemed to recall they marked the quickest-moving parts of the ice. And as befitted one of the largest glaciers on Earth, this rubble line was big too, a kind of pebble road studded with boulders and dolmens.

Val bent over and picked up the biggest boulder she thought she could lift, given the body-blows from the wind, and gestured at X to do the same. She started filling a gap between the tall boulder and a chest-high one nearby, while at the same time clearing all large rocks out of the space on the lee side of them. Carlos saw the plan and pulled his banana sledge over to the gap, tipping it on its side to form a windscreen at the bottom of the wall. X hopped around propping it in position with rocks, moving fast, in X-overdrive. He could lift rocks none of the others would even think to try. As they lifted and set rocks he and Val banged into each other hard, and they grabbed each other to keep from going down. He looked at her as if asking a question, but masked by sunglasses and clothing they could see nothing of each other's face, and the roar of the wind made it impossible to talk. They might as well have been on opposite sides of the glacier. She felt stuffed with energy, and went for another rock, mute in the howl of the storm, which if anything was louder here than it had been out on the glacier; shrieking over the rocks, no doubt. They were all cut off from each other. Nine strangers in a storm. Wind-chill factor must have been a hundred below; it dropped exponentially with the speed of the wind. Too windy to put up any tents. But the rock wall was growing. Had to be careful, though, as the wind would quickly throw any loosely-placed rocks down on their heads. The stacking had to be right. It was something to concentrate on, something with which to distract herself; and it was the only thing she could do at this moment to improve the situation. So she set about building the best rock wall she could. X was a big help; it was amazing what heavy rocks he could lift. Carlos and Wade too were helping, as was Ta Shu. Jorge and Elspeth and Jim were getting sleeping bags off the banana sledge and out of their stuff-sacks, dropping big, slabby rocks on them as they pulled them out so that they wouldn't blow away. The wall was thigh-high now, and beginning to help; though it was still insanely loud, behind Jack's rock there was some shelter from the blast, and more with each row they managed to stack on the one below, and each foot of curving extension to the sides. The work kept them not warm but at least functional, and there was an endless supply of rocks to choose from. A U-shaped wall to start with, then perhaps a full oval later, to ensure that any more reversals of wind didn't take them from the rear. After that they might be able to set up one of the tents inside the rock wall and get even more shelter, enough to light a stove. It was actually looking pretty good, Val thought; if it hadn't been for Jack, huddled at the foot of the largest boulder, she would have considered the situation to be somewhat in hand, given the circumstances. Jim and Jorge were pulling a sleeping bag up over Jack's legs and torso. When the wall was finished they would all be able to get into bags. They would be all right. Except they didn't have enough food or stove fuel to wait out a storm of any great length. Hopefully coms would come back and they could get a report on the weather. So odd to have all this happen in the mute solitude of the storm's roar. And the light was odd too, fluctuating rapidly as thinner or thicker clouds shot overhead; despite all it was a well-lit scene, the sun wheeling about somewhere overhead though it was the middle of the night, Val thought; but it didn't matter. The flickering made it like being inside an antique film. X put his face against her ear: 'It's good shelter!'

She nodded to show she had heard. She appreciated the gesture. The others were now sitting in the lee of the rock wall, clustered around Jack to give him more warmth; he looked as if he was sinking into hypothermia again, and she wouldn't be surprised if he was, lying there with a broken collarbone, cut hand, lost blood; in shock, and maybe concussed as well. He was in trouble.

Which meant she could not rest. The shelter didn't matter; she had to get to Shackleton Camp, bring back a snowmobile and sledge to carry Jack to real shelter, and at least the first aid that the people at Shackleton Camp would be able to provide. Something. To do it she needed a bit of a break in the storm, she judged. And she would need a GPS position to come back to. And perhaps a companion, for safety's sake; Carlos, though Carlos should probably stay here to take care of the others. X, then. The truth was she didn't know what to do. The obvious thing was to stay put, but with a failing client on her hands, she wasn't going to do that. And they were short of food and fuel anyway. Storms here could last over a week. Something more would have to be done. And she had walked in storms like this before, she had climbed in storms like this for that matter; tough work, but not impossible if you kept your head.

She crouched down to have a shouted consultation with the others. She got X's attention and he crouched next to her. Ta Shu was still moving about the others, adding rocks to the wall; and suddenly they looked to Val like a little huddled pile of bodies, with Ta Shu building a memorial cairn.

X kept adding rocks to their rock wall until he could find no good candidates for stable stacking in the immediate area. The work had warmed him, although the rocks themselves had been cold, and heavy enough to crush his gloves' insulation, so that his hands were frozen insensible, and tired. Val gestured him to her and he crouched next to her. She was getting into a sleeping bag next to Wade, and gestured for X to do the same. He struggled into a sleeping bag much too small for him, lay against the rock wall next to Val.

Down on the pebbles it was remarkably calm. Given the insulating power of their clothing, the warm, red masses of their sleeping bags, and the shelter of this nifty windbreak they had built, X supposed he should have been as comfortable as if he were at home in bed; in actuality it was nothing like that, as each howling buffet of wind jolted through him in a kind of mental electrocution. He couldn't get used to these slaps of wind; they were so hard and distinct they seemed not like wind but the concussions from great explosions, any one of which could knock their wall over. Little lulls, moments of relative calm, and then WHAM, another shock to the system.

Val was crawling around in her bag, having shouted conversations with Carlos, then Wade. She seemed calm and deliberate, her posture relaxed; she did not seem appalled at the power of the wind, just dealing with it. X however was appalled. He had never been in any Condition One in Mac Town that had been anything like as strong as this wind. He hadn't known they got this strong.

Val crawled over to him and sat beside him, leaned into him, one arm around him, and shouted in his ear. 'I may have to go down to Shackleton Camp! To get help for Jack!' She gestured at Jack. 'I'm worried about him!'

'What about the storm!' X shouted in her ear.

She shook her head, shouted, 'It might last a long time! Too long!'

'But can you walk in this!' X shouted, amazed at the very idea.

'If you wear crampons – and lie flat during the worst parts – you can do it! No problem! This stuff we're wearing is like a spacesuit!'

X pulled his head away and stared at her. No problem? Was she kidding?

She was not kidding. She was a mountaineer, and what they thought to do out in the wild boggled the imagination. His heart began to pound hard in his chest. Carlos was the best candidate to accompany her on such a hike. But no doubt she wanted Carlos to stay and care for the people left behind. He leaned over and got her ear. 'I'll go with you!'

Now it was her turn to pull back and look at him. Sunglasses, mask;

who knew what she was thinking? She caught his ear: 'I'll be going fast!'

He nodded that he understood.

She said: 'Carlos is cooking us a meal.'

So he was. Against and partly under the banana sledge the stove was burning, the blue flames wavering somewhat, but burning fiercely nevertheless. That they had in this stupendous howl and rush created a pocket of air still enough to allow the stove to burn was amazing to him.

'Wade got a GPS fix! He says the system is coming back. His senator has reached him on a military satellite system we can use too. So as soon as we're done eating we should go!'

He nodded that he understood. He realized he was going to do it. His heart was still pounding hard.

Then flickering dark shapes appeared overhead, like killer whales flying horizontally through the storm. X leapt to his feet, astonished, and the wind blew him right out of their shelter and down onto the ground. He pushed up to his knees; yes; blimps were flashing by overhead, coloured like the clouds but still undeniably there, sweeping past over them. Harpoons on lines shot down and stuck the ice in little explosions. The blimps swung around on these anchorlines and were pulled right down onto the glacier next to the rubble line, at which point more harpoons shot down, holding the blimps fast to the ice. Three in a row, vibrating in the wind. They had big tail sections at the backs of the bags, containing fans in round housings. Stubby wings protruded from the taut sides of the bags, and underneath the bags narrow gondolas rested right on the ice. Doors in the gondola were shoved open against the wind, and out jumped three people on tethers, dressed in photovoltaic bodysuits much like the trekkers'.

'Want a lift?' the first person to reach them shouted. Sounded like a Southern accent. A short young woman.

Everyone in the rock shelter was standing; even Jack had lifted his head up to stare. Clearly the woman's question was rhetorical. Val and Jim got Jack onto the free banana sledge and carried him to the nearest blimp and got him into the gondola. Jim followed him in, then Ta Shu.

'Three in each blimp!' the woman shouted. 'We'll meet up there!' She gestured beyond the rubble line and said something else X couldn't make out.

Val looked at X, as if to ask him what they should do, and despite everything his heart warmed. He gestured in reply; what other choice did they have? She nodded and went back to retrieve some of their gear. X joined her, and as they leaned over the banana sledge in their wall she shouted, 'Who are they?'

'I don't know!' X shouted. 'But it reminds me of when my SPOT train was robbed!'

She stared at him, taken aback. 'That's not good!'

'No, but–' He didn't know what else to say. 'They seem to be rescuing us!'

'True!'

They stared at each other.

They returned to their visitors and helped Carlos and Jorge and Elspeth into the second blimp. Then Wade and Val wedged into the back seats of the third blimp's gondola compartment, which reminded X of a Squirrel helicopter's insides, the two front seats looking out of big, curved windows, the back seats jammed against the back wall of the cabin, with storage underneath for their stuff. X sat in the front seat next to the pilot. She was checking dials and flicking toggles, talking into a headset intercom. She pushed a button and the blimp began to vibrate madly as they rose off the ice on its anchorlines; then she pushed another button and the harpoons must have exploded free or been cut away, because all of a sudden they were off on the wind, spinning up and away, inside the cloud itself, the light flickering from dark grey to spun glass whiteness and everything in between, changing instant by instant. The noise was terrific at first; then it got a bit quieter, and the ride smoother.

Their pilot watched screens before her, giving her data in various false colour images that X couldn't interpret. Powerful motors whirred behind them, and between their noise and the howl of the wind it was still too loud to say anything. The pilot indicated headsets hanging from hooks in the ceiling of the gondola, however, just like in a Squirrel, and X put on his set, and over the now-muffled roar heard Val saying, '–you taking us?'

The pilot pointed forward. 'Bennett's Other Platform.' Her voice was clear over the headset, and she definitely had a Southern accent. X pulled a folded topographic map out of the open compartment before him and studied it. Bennett Platform was a triangular plateau of bare rock overlooking Shackleton Glacier, across the ice from the Shackleton Camp, underneath a Mount Black. But Bennett's Other Platform? The pilot did not elucidate, and neither Val nor Wade nor X wanted to bother her any more, as she suddenly seemed completely absorbed in the workings of the blimp, which was tossing wildly in some extra turbulence of the storm. She muttered to herself as she flew with both hands and both feet, looking out of the windows more than at her screens, though they could see nothing but mist.

'Isn't this dangerous?' X inquired.

The pilot looked at him briefly. 'What, this? What could happen?' A high sweet laugh. Then she was talking to the blimp again, or the

clouds: 'Ah come on. Y'all stop it. This is ridiculous. Quit it. No way.'
And so on.

'Where are you from?' X asked during a lull in this monologue.

'Mobile, Alabama.'

'No,' X said. 'I mean down here.'

The pilot shrugged. Then she became preoccupied by another hard smack of wind. 'Give me a break. I mean to tell you. No way.' After a prolonged struggle with the controls she said, 'Okay. Here we are. Come on, you beast. Behave yourself for our guests here.'

'Can you give medical attention to the man in the other blimp?' Val asked.

'Sure. That's why we came out in this kind of wind. It looked like you needed help.'

Below them black rock appeared through the rushing clouds, startling X so much that he jumped back in his seat.

'Don't worry!' the pilot said, and laughed again.

white white
black
white white

X worried. It was frightening to be so close to rock in such a volatile craft. But their pilot merely coaxed the blimp around into the wind, and then began to wrestle the controls to force the thing downward, or so it seemed. Suddenly an orange pole poked up out of the cloud at them, and the pilot broke into the same muttered argument she had had before as she dropped the blimp down behind this mooring mast. She manipulated controls right in front of X, a metal arm appeared under them, and a claw like an artificial hand clamped on the mast. 'Gotcha!'

After that they descended slowly. The rear of the blimp attached to something else, it seemed to X by the reduced bouncing of the craft; and then they were suspended tautly some ten feet off the flat black rock, frozen mist shooting past on all sides. The pilot reached across X and opened the door. 'Out we go!' she shouted, and X unbuckled his seat belt and took off his headset, and made his way down a swinging ladder, the metal rods cold through his mitts and gloves. When he stood on the ground again he found his knees were trembling. He helped Wade and Val down, then the pilot climbed down halfway and let the door slam above her. She jumped down beside them and gestured forward. 'Come on in!'

CHAPTER TWELVE

Transantarctica

Val followed their pilot through the wind, X and Wade on each side
of her. Ahead of them a low escarpment of rust-coloured rock loomed
out of the frozen mist shooting past. They were on a nunatak, or
perhaps one of the larger rock ranges. What Val could see actually
resembled Bennett's Platform, as far as she could recall; she had visited
the plateau once, with a team of paleontologists who had been using
helicopters to pull fossil trees out by the stumps. The rock underfoot
was like a rough parquet floor, part rock, part ice.

Ahead there was a kind of embayment in the rock, about the volume
of two Jamesways set side by side. In the embayment the air was clear,
and spindrift was bouncing over it and collecting at its foot; the empty
space was covered by some kind of clear fabric, very taut and obviously
very strong. Tented.

Inside this clear space, this room in the side of the storm, a
number of people were seated on rocks placed like benches against the
sidewalls. They were dressed in a great variety of styles, from the
glossiest of client chic to thick fur jackets to ratty long underwear that
reminded Val of Sherpa yak wool. She wondered again if these were
the saboteurs.

Then she saw the rest of her group emerge out of the flying cloud,
and she hurried over to see how Jack was doing. He was flat out in
the banana sledge, but conscious; trying to crane his neck around to
see where they were going, a move which obviously hurt him; he
looked cold and miserable. 'They say there's a doctor here,' Val told
him, but he just stared at her.

Their pilot reached the tent, unzipped a zipper in the clear fabric
next to the rock wall, and waved them into the gap. Inside there was
a clear inner wall; they were in a lock or vestibule. Their pilots were
taking off their parkas and then their boots; two women and a man.
Val's sunglasses were fogging up; she took them off, pulled off her

304

ski-mask, then her parka, then her boots. Everyone jostling in the vestibule's little space. Then one of the other pilots zipped the outer wall, unzipped the inner wall, and they went inside.

Their arrival was greeted with indifference by most of the occupants. A glance only and then they were back to whatever they had been doing before: eating, working on clothing at a table covered with scraps of cloth and fur, reading, talking around a radio set that appeared to be turned off. The conversation by the radio sounded to Val like German.

'The doctor?' she said to their pilot.

'That's May Lee,' she said. (Later Val learned it was spelled Mai-lis.) 'Mai, we got a patient for you.'

'I know,' said a short, elderly woman. Her round face was remarkably leathered and wrinkly, and Val took her to be an Eskimo. 'Bring him over here.'

They followed the old woman, Jim and Jorge carrying the banana sledge. They laid it down on a rough rock bench against the dolerite wall, and Mai-lis pulled over a wooden deck chair and sat down next to Jack. 'How are you?' she asked him as she opened a large long bag and attached a monitor to his arm.

'Broke my collarbone,' Jack said.

'Ah. So you have. Are you hypothermic?'

'I'm cold. Not as cold as before. My lungs hurt.'

'I will check them.' She was getting his clothes away from his upper body; Jim helped her. It was warm in the tented chamber, so that would not be a problem. The wind was still loud, but it was muffled inside just enough so that they could hear each other talk. 'I will inject anaesthetics around the clavicle,' the old woman said, 'then reset the bone. After that you cannot move that arm. We will get you a sling for it.' As she spoke she was unwrapping a hypodermic needle, and after gently swabbing the skin over the broken bone she injected a syringe's contents into him. Then another one. Val was so happy to see this evidence of bona fide medicine that she could hardly stand.

After that the woman checked the readings on the monitor, and listened to Jack's lungs with a stethoscope. 'Your right lung is a little full. Have you coughed up any blood?'

'I don't think so.'

'We'll keep an eye on it. It may be a touch of pneumonia. Your temperature is low, but you're not badly hypothermic any longer.'

'I'm cold.'

'No doubt. Let's check your feet. Hmm . . . perhaps a little frostbite in the toes. We can help that.' She worked on his feet for a while, applying patches from her kit. 'Now, can you feel your clavicle?'

'No.'

'Okay. I'm going to reset it. You will feel the contact for sure, but tell me if it hurts and we'll give you another shot.'

'It's okay,' Jack said. He stared at her face impassively as she put both hands to his shoulder. 'Addie,' she said to Val's pilot, 'help me here.'

'Sure thing, Mai.'

'Hold his shoulder down, right there. Don't look, young man. Head the other way. Twist your left shoulder to the left. That's it. Okay. Now I'm going to inject some muscle relaxants. You will have a bump for good in your clavicle, but if you can keep it in this position, it will heal all right. Ah good, here is hot chocolate, for all of you. Now you should rest, young man. We will keep a watch on your lungs. If you have some pneumonia we will give you antibiotics. But we should wait and make sure. Sleep now, but stay flat on your back. Addie and Elka will help you into a sleeping bag. Be careful,' she said to the two women attending. Then she led Val and Jim to the back of the chamber, where delicious smells were steaming out of a big pot on an ordinary green Coleman stove. 'Let's eat,' she said.

They sat on doubled-up sleeping pads on the ground, staring up at the cook. The smells of cooking food struck Val and she realized she was ravenous. 'We appreciate what you're doing for us,' she said to Mai-lis.

'Oh, Addie and Lars and Elke, they enjoyed the opportunity. They like to do crazy things like flying the blimps in storms, but it's a bit too dangerous, so in the ordinary course of things they don't get to. So a rescue situation is just an opportunity to them. They loved it.'

'And you knew we were in trouble?'

'Well, we heard your radio, and looked and saw you coming down the glacier. And then the storm hit, and it didn't seem like you had much in the way of shelter. So they went to get you.'

The cook, a big man with tattooed arms, tossed slabs of white fish steak into a giant frying pan. As they sizzled Addie came over and laughed at Val and her companions' intent expressions. 'You got an appreciative audience, Claude!'

'I can see.'

'What's cooking?' Ta Shu asked, coming over to look into the frying pan. He appeared happy and comfortable, as if he had met these people before and was feeling at home already.

'Mawsoni,' Claude said. 'Mawsoni fried in seal fat, and seasoned with herbs grown in local greenhouses. An all-indigenous main course, see? And local krill-cakes too. Then vegetable stew, that's not so local,' indicating the pot.

Killing fish and seals was illegal under the Antarctic Treaty, as Val recalled. But she decided it was not a good time to mention it.

'Mawsoni?' she said instead. She had heard of the big Antarctic fish, but never seen one. Now Addie opened a box and hauled out the head of a big, gutted fish.

'Oh don't show them that, it'll spoil their appetite.' Claude laughed. And indeed the fish face was a monstrously spiked, big-eyed, misshapen thing. 'Antarctic cod!' Claude said facetiously. 'That's what they call it in the grocery stores, even though it has no relation at all to real cod. They call all the real ugly fishes cod so they can sell them. No one will buy *Dissotichus mawsoni* or *Pagotenia borchgrevinki*, but Antarctic cod! Yum yum!'

'Long as they keep the heads hidden,' Addie said.

'Tastes just like chicken,' someone else said.

'It tastes like fish, actually, but not as fishy as penguin eggs. And big. Catch one and it'll feed this group for a week.'

'So that's what you eat?' Val asked, looking around again at the people. Seal fur, perhaps, in that parka. Local fish . . .

'It's one of the protein staples, sure. Mawsoni, penguin egg whites – the yolks are vile, like rotten fish – sometimes seal steak. Then cereals and vegetables from the greenhouses and terraria, though there isn't enough. We ship in a lot still.'

'From where?'

'New Zealand, just like anyone else.'

Claude wielded spatula and fork like a short-order chef, and soon everyone was eating speechlessly, stuffing it in. Many of their hosts appeared to be as hungry as Val and her group. The fried Mawsoni was good, the meat firm and flaky; better than cod, despite the kraken face of the creature. Cod weren't that good-looking either, now that she thought of it.

When they had eaten she sat slumped next to Wade against the rock wall. Over on the bench Jack was lying in his sledge. 'He's going to be all right?' she asked the doctor.

The woman nodded, swallowed. 'He is in no danger, as far as I can tell.'

'He was acting really strange. In shock, or concussed, I thought.'

'He might well have been. But his vital signs are strong.'

Val felt a wave of relief pass through her, as warm and tangible as the burn of the food. Jack was going to live; they were all going to live; she was going to get home with all her clients alive, and at that moment she cared not at all that it was not her doing, nor that the expedition was still a fuck-up. Neither their accident nor the rescue had been her doing, really; but if one of her clients had died she never would have forgiven herself. For she should not have let them go up toward the Hansen Shoulder.

But now it looked like it was not going to be a fatal error, and for that she was so relieved she could barely think about it. She began the process of forgetting what it had felt like; she let her head loll against the rock, feeling the exhaustion in every muscle of her body. Wade looked similarly relaxed, staring around him bright-eyed with interest.

Then Mai-lis sat down before them with her plate full, and without moving his head Wade said, 'So who are you people?'

'I am Mai-lis,' the old woman said. 'That's Addie, that's Lars . . .'

'Yes. But what are you doing out here?'

'Why do you ask?' Lars said aggressively from across the tent. 'We rescue you from the storm, you think you can interrogate us?'

'Just asking.'

'Be quiet,' Mai-lis said to Lars. 'This is a new situation now, because of these attacks.' To Wade and Val she said, 'We are a long-term research group.'

'And what do you study?'

'We study how to live here.'

Val said, 'On your own?'

'We have some help from the north, of course, like everyone down here.'

'But you live here. In the Transantarctics.'

'Yes. We are nomadic, actually. We move around.'

Wade said, 'How many of you are there?'

'It varies year to year. About a thousand, this year.'

'A thousand!' Val exclaimed.

'Yes. Not so many for a continent.'

'No, but . . . A lot for no one to know about. People in McMurdo don't know you're out here?'

'A few do. We have some helpers there. But most, no.'

'Aren't you seen from the air? From satellite photos?'

'Yes, we are visible if you look very closely at photos. But there are many scientific camps and oil groups and trekking groups. Very few photo analysts are looking for groups where we are, and we hide as much as we can. We have some analyst friends, too. And we move around with the seasons, sometimes at night, when there is night, or under cloud cover, like today. So there is little to see.'

'Where are you from?' Wade asked.

'Where from? In the north? We come from all over. I am from Samiland.' Seeing Val and Wade stare at her, she explained: 'Lapland, you perhaps call it. The north of Scandinavia.' She gestured at the others. 'Addie is American, as you know. She used to work for ASL. Lars is Swedish, Elke German. Anna is Inuit, from Canada. There are other Eskimos as well. John is a Kiwi. We have lots of Aussies and Kiwis. And so forth.'

'And you live down here,' Wade repeated.

'That's right. Some call it going feral. I don't like that word. I say we are studying how to become indigenous to this place. Antarcticans. It's a new thing. Like the Arctic cultures, but not. Not all of us agree what we are doing.' Her face darkened as she said this, and she looked to the lock door, where another group was coming in. 'Excuse me,' she said, and went over to them.

Val sat in the centre of her group. Wade on one side, X on the other. The clients were looking well-fed, warm, sleepy – except for Ta Shu, who was conversing with another Asian man. And Carlos was talking animatedly in Spanish to a small group of ferals. Jack was asleep on his sledge bed. Val was feeling so relieved, so pleased, really, that she could scarcely keep a smile from her face.

But when Mai-lis came back, she still had that dark look on her face. 'These saboteurs have changed everything,' she said, half to herself. 'Endangered everything.' She looked at Val. 'I must ask you to prepare to leave.'

'Now?' Val asked, surprised.

'Soon. We are going to deliver justice. I want you to witness this, so you can tell the people in McMurdo what is happening up here.'

She sat down on her pad, picked up her plate, continued eating. Between bites she explained. 'You see, there are many divisions among us down here. Some of them are normal. We have what we call the fundies and the prags, fundies meaning fundamentalists, who want to live down here with no help from the north, using Eskimo and Sami methods to make our food and clothing and shelter. The prags are pragmaticals, and willing to try out all the latest things from the north, to see if they can be useful down here. As you can see we are mostly prags here, but like most of the feral groups we are a mix of the two. Most of us are individually a mix of the two. This is normal, as I say. Part of inventing the Antarctican way of life.'

She paused to eat a bite or two, shaking her head as she thought things over. 'Other divisions are more dangerous. There are some among us who despise all the other people in Antarctica – the oil teams, the adventure trekkers, even the scientists. They never help these people. Sometimes they impede their work. And they feel no objections to steal from them.'

'My SPOT train,' X said.

She nodded. 'Yes, a SPOT vehicle was taken by one of these groups, the most extreme of them all.'

'Did they take the old generator from the buried South Pole station?' Wade asked.

'No.' She looked at Wade, somewhat surprised. 'That was us. We make a distinction between salvage and theft. A lot of perfectly good equipment has been abandoned in Antarctica, and if it is never going to be used by anyone else, and we can use it, then we excavate it from the ice and make use of it. The old Pole generator is now heating a greenhouse farm on one of the nunataks near here.'

'And the Hillary expedition's Weasel,' Wade said, nodding with satisfaction, as at a mystery solved.

'That's right. We used it to haul things, and may use it again, in situations in that area where blimps wouldn't be better.'

'You took away the generator with a blimp?'

'Yes. We have salvaged equipment from Siple Dome, Vostok, the Byrd stations, the Point of Inaccessibility station, and so on. All abandoned and buried in the ice. But the new ice borers are very powerful. Also the new remote sensing devices. We even know where the tent is that Amundsen left at the Pole. That we have left in place. Other things, more useful and less — less historical — we have dug.'

She took another bite, swallowed. 'But all of this is salvage. And salvage is not theft. Theft we do not like. The people down here who steal say it is all the same. They call everything we salvage and they steal "obtainium". But this is just their insolence. They defy us all.' She scowled, looking ferocious for a moment. 'And so they endanger us all. Because it very well might happen that some military come down here to clear up this matter of the ecotage, and kick us all off the ice because of these people. And we cannot allow that to happen.'

'But how can you stop them?' Wade asked.

'Well, this is the question. We have very little political organization down here. This is what they have endangered also. To the extent that we have any at all, we are a pure democracy.'

'Mai-lis thinks it's a democracy,' Lars interjected from behind her with a jagged grin. 'Actually it's a matriarchy, and she is the high priestess.'

'And Lars is court jester,' Mai-lis said, without looking at him. 'Actually I am just the doctor, but that is enough power out here. Anyway, we try to agree on everything. And a few seasons ago, we agreed together that if any feral hurt any other feral, or anyone else in Antarctica, then they could be judged in absentia by the rest of us.'

'So these are the people who sabotaged my camp?' Carlos asked.

Several of the ferals sitting around listening shook their heads, and Mai-lis said 'No,' though she looked uncertain. 'We don't know who did the ecotage. I wish we did, but we don't. Oil camps took most of the attacks, and the communications system was disrupted. And McMurdo's fuel tanks were contaminated. But who did this, we do not know. We know it was not the anarchist ferals we are quarrelling with, because we have informants among them. So we know this was not their idea. But some of them were in contact with these ecoteurs, apparently, and they did help the ecoteurs to empty the oil camps of people before they were destroyed. They think we do not know this. They think that they are free to do what they want. But we know, and we know where they are. And we have judged them and voted, and agreed that they are to be punished, to the maximum in our system.'

'Which is?' Wade asked, in a serious silence; this was the first some of the ferals had heard about the decision, Val could see.

'Exile from Antarctica.'

Mai-lis looked around at all the members of her group, as if to defy any challenge to this judgment.

'About time,' Addie opined. 'They'll kick us all out if we don't get rid of these jokers soon.'

Mai-lis nodded. 'We have been listening to McMurdo, and from what we have heard, we know the US Navy is coming. We want them and the NSF to be clear about what has happened up here. That we are not the ecoteurs nor the thieves. And that the thieves among us are gone.'

'Who do you think the ecoteurs are?' Val asked.

Mai-lis shrugged. 'I suppose some radical environmentalist group from the north. People who have gone beyond Greenpeace-style protests to direct resistance, like Earthfirst! or Sea Shepherds. People who think Antarctica should be a pure wilderness, with no people at all. Many world park advocates don't even like scientists down here.'

'So your group would not be something these people approve of,' Val said.

'Not at all. We have very little in common with them.'

'Deep ecologists,' Lars said scornfully. 'Very deep! And we are so shallow!'

Mai-lis shrugged. 'Their philosophy is good. There should be fewer humans on Earth, using fewer resources. We try to do that ourselves. But to make some parts of the Earth precious wilderness, while the parts we live on can be trashed as usual – no. There is not sacred land and profane land. It is all just land. All equally valuable.'

Ta Shu, watching Mai-lis closely (to Val they looked like cousins) nodded at this. 'All sacred,' he said.

Mai-lis shrugged. 'We try to find a different way here,' looking at Ta Shu. 'We say the land is sacred, yes. Then we live on that sacred land. And theft is no part of that.'

Lars shook his head vehemently. 'To glorify property like this, to kick people off the ice just because of property–'

'Their thieving will get us all kicked off the ice,' Mai-lis said sharply. Lars got up and stalked away, drawing some supporters in his wake.

'And the Antarctic Treaty?' Wade said.

'Yes?'

'Aren't you breaking it by being here?'

Some rude noises from the ferals still listening.

Mai-lis shrugged again. 'Aren't you too breaking it by being here?' She stood up. 'We don't bother anyone, and we live very lightly on the land. We don't change Antarctica even one tenth as much as McMurdo Station alone. So we will argue the particulars of the Treaty before the World Court, if you like. But now we have to clean our own house.' She glanced after Lars: 'Because I am a pragmatical, and I want to be allowed to stay here.' She scowled. 'So I want you to witness this.'

Sometimes life gives us such opportunities. In moments of pressure things flow quickly in a new direction. Through a mountain opening, and here we are in a new land. Source of the peach-blossom stream, green valley in an ice world, like our pale blue dot in space. My friends, I hope I am reaching you now, but cannot be sure. I am saving often just in case. If you are with me, note please how quickly we leave this little refuge notched in the rock, where people were making a home in the ice. It seemed to me a cave from the paleolithic. The minds in there were fully engaged. They were no longer sleepwalking. I could have stayed there a long time, and never wanted for anything else. And yet my companions have agreed to leave, and I am going with them. Perhaps there was no other choice.

Cloud-mountains, mountain-clouds. It is the gift of the world to offer such winds, it is a gift to travel in such a storm. How the blood races! How the mind awakes! Sometimes it seems that only in storms am I truly alive, as if the winds indeed carried my spirit, and filled my body with joy.

Onward we move, cast on the wind. How eerily this voyage resembles the experience of the *Endurance* expedition. I think of those men so often now. Like them we have had a leader who has held true through all. Like them we have been lucky; taken all in all, circumstances have been kind to us. They have allowed us our opportunity!

For Shackleton's men, when the pack ice under their camp finally began to break up, they were forced into their three boats, as we into three blimps. But they were in seas crowded with ice, sailing in narrow leads, and hauling the boats back onto floes when it seemed they would be crushed between colliding bergs. Frantic days of insane effort, with never a moment's sleep; inspired seamanship, and always do or die. Sometimes life is like that!

And at the end of that week's sail, they landed on Elephant Island. Better than drowning, for sure; but it was an uninhabited ice-covered rock at the end of the Antarctic Peninsula, rarely visited by anyone. No one would look for them there, and in the winter they would likely die of starvation. So after some time to rest, and do carpentry on their biggest boat, Shackleton and Worsley and four other men sailed for South Georgia Island, where the Norwegians manned a year-round whaling station. It was twelve hundred kilometres away, roughly downwind, and in the direction of the prevailing currents – but across the ocean in the high fifties of southern latitude, where there is only water the whole world round, and the great rollers of the perpetual groundswell are gnawed and chopped by the windiest storms on the planet.

Their boat journey across this sea was a superb achievement of being-in-the-world. The man whose skill at sea made it possible was Frank Arthur Worsley. Shackleton had never made a small boat journey of any length. On the second day out he said to Worsley, 'Do you know I know nothing about boat sailing?' And Worsley said, 'All right, Boss. I do, this is my third boat journey.' And Shackleton was ruffled and said, 'I'm telling you that I don't.' He was saying that even though he was the boss, it was Worsley who was now responsible for their success or failure; Shackleton was now the student, Worsley the teacher, and Shackleton wanted Worsley to know that he knew it.

And Worsley rose to the challenge. He navigated them across twelve hundred kilometres of empty ocean to a small, solitary island less than a hundred kilometres long: British *feng shui* in its highest manifestation.

Not because of the technical aspects of navigation, you understand, which involve mathematical formulas that can be mastered by anyone; a child's first wristwatch could do the calculations now. But before the calculations have to come the data, and this involves taking a reading with a sextant to determine how far above the horizon the sun is at a particular time of day. With that knowledge one can then calculate one's latitude and longitude. But the calculations rely crucially on getting accurate data in the first place. The sextant has to be level with the circle of the horizon; tangent to a point on a giant sphere. One has to see and feel the world, and one's body in it, with exquisite accuracy! And Worsley had nowhere to make his readings but on his knees, on the bucking canvas deck of their wave-tossed boat, held upright in the grasp of his companions, as both his hands were needed for the sextant. All this in the very few moments of the journey when the sun was shining through the clouds, and in continuously wild seas. What is level when dancing on a cork that is shooting up and down such a violent sea? I might as well be asked to do it here, spinning about in the clouds like a bird! This is the aspect of Worsley's navigation that is so astonishing and beautiful. He had to feel his place on the planet, he had to make himself sensitive to the gravitational pull to the point where he could tell, with only a bucketing horizon to help him, when he was upright and the sextant level. At that moment he 'shot a reading' as they put it, with a quick glance at the device's curved scale. This number then went through the elementary formulas, along with the precise time of day – note that their clock was a life-or-death item for them, essential for locating themselves in the flow of timespace – and the figures were matched with a book of tables to produce a latitude and longitude. All this in mist and fog and cloud and rain and sleet, flying up and down on the coiled surface of the water.

And yet they made landfall. Worsley wrote, 'Wonderful to say, the landfall was quite correct, though we were a little astern through imperfect rating of my chronometer at Elephant Island.' Ha! Because of the chronometer! But happily we must grant him this one touch of pride, so well-earned. Wonderful to say 'wonderful to say' in these circumstances, where the achievement saved their lives. Sometimes we are given opportunities, and we take them and make something fine, and the story of that will live forever; and so we have our bodhisattva moment.

After their wonderful landfall, then, and the incredible crossing of South Georgia Island, the Norwegians there took the six men to the Falklands, and Shackleton went into a rage of negotiations, there in the middle of the First World War when few people cared what happened to twenty men; he obtained the aid of no fewer than four ships before one was finally able to penetrate the pack ice, and save the marooned men before winter came down on them. And so the greatest engagement with Antarctica in all of history came to a close.

And then these men returned to a world tearing itself apart. They never made it back to their lost paradise. Where we go next we never know; plans are only plans. I remember vaguely a story I seem always to have known, encountered perhaps in the heavy coloured pages of some old children's book – about a party of travellers lost in polar regions, who after struggling over icy passes stumble on a valley green amid glaciers, warmed by a hot springs; and they find the oasis is home to people descended from Eskimo and Norse, living in peace cut off from the world; and they leave the valley, why I can't recall, perhaps to bring back family and friends – but can never afterward retrace their lost steps. And only the story survives.

Now we in this moment are off through space, whirled by the wind to our next landfall, so soon having left that bubble of peace; so sure that a path thus traversed would never be lost to us. But glaciers and peaks are never the same glaciers and peaks. Even if we look and look all the rest of our lives, bubble of peace, how to tell? Where to find?

'**Wade! Are you there,** Wade?'

'I'm here, Phil. Speak up if you can, it's kind of loud here.'

'Where are you?'

'I'm in a blimp.'

'A blimp! Whose blimp?'

'Addie's blimp. We're in a cloud right now, Phil, it's kind of windy. You'll have to really speak up if you want me to hear you.'

'What's that?'

'Speak up!'

'Where are you, Wade? Where is this blimp?'

'We're somewhere in Antarctica, Phil. More than that I can't say. We tried to take the hovercraft down to Shackleton Camp, but it fell into a crevasse. Then we tried to walk to Shackleton Camp, but we were overtaken by a storm. A very windy storm. You can hear what that's like. Then we took refuge in a rubble line, and after that we got rescued by some people who are living out here in the Transantarctic Mountains, living on their own.'

'Jesus, Wade, it sounds great! Are these the people who did the ecotage and took all the stuff that's been missing?'

'They say not. Apparently there are factions out here—'

'Not there too!'

'—yes, inevitably, and the group that rescued us claims another faction has been stealing stuff, and they claim ignorance of the ecotage, though apparently the other faction helped the ecoteurs somehow. We still don't know what's really happened.'

'Well you're big news, Wade, let me tell you that. I've been calling you every five minutes for the past day!'

'Sorry I've been out of touch.'

'Not your fault! So where are you headed now? What are you going to do?'

'I don't know where we're headed, but I think we are being taken to witness the exiling of this rogue faction from Antarctica.'

'Uh oh. That sounds like it could be trouble, Wade. You watch out.'

'I will.'

'Tell me what you're seeing now, then, if you don't know where you are.'

'Well, we're in Addie's blimp, and right now we're above the clouds. It's very sunny up here. We're looking down on cloudtops that cover the land as far as I can see. It's windy. There are some peaks sticking out of the clouds to our right.'

'All right!' Addie said over the intercom. 'Let's go get 'em.'

Wade stuck his wristphone under the right side of his headset. 'How are you going to kick people out of Antarctica?' he asked Addie.

'Oh we have our ways.'

'Which are?'

'We find them and ambush them.'

'Is this going to be dangerous?' Val asked from beside Addie, sounding surprised.

'Dangerous? Oh no, not dangerous at all!' Again Addie's sweet laugh. 'Nothing we do down here is dangerous, oh my no!'

Val said sharply, 'I don't want my group taken into a fight.'

'No no. It'll all be over by the time we get there. Mai-lis just wants you to see the results, so you can be her witnesses if it comes to that in McMurdo. She's a very practical lady that way.'

'She seems to be an authority,' Wade ventured.

'Yeah, she's the local chief, no matter what she says about democracy. Lars is pretty much right about that.'

'How did she reach that status?'

'Well, she's been down here the longest, and she knows how to do more things than anyone else. She knows how to survive down here. The Sami know about snow and weather. And she's very up to date technically. She's good with the photovoltaics and the batteries and the hydroponics. All of it. Better than most of us, anyway. We all have our specialities, but you know, it's a work in progress sort of thing. An experiment, like she said. So nobody's all that good at everything. It can be a little dangerous, actually.'

Wade said, 'Like flying these blimps in a storm?'

'Oh no. No danger there at all.' She grinned. 'Actually it's not bad. These things float really well, it's hard to drive them down. So it's almost the opposite of a helo in that respect.'

'What about getting blown into mountainsides?'

'Well, you have to look out for that, but if you stay above them you're fine. These are great machines. Top speed of three hundred k an hour, so even if you have to go straight into a full-force gale you can make progress, usually. Turbulent, as you saw, but not impossible. No, blimps are the only way to go down here. Getting around on foot is just too hard, as you must know. The air is the way. But planes and helos are too much of a hassle. Much more dangerous than these.'

'Who makes them?' X asked.

'A Japanese company.'

'How do you pay for them?' Wade asked.

'Money.'

'But how do you make the money? You're not selling mawsoni cutlets and seal fur coats.'

'No. Some of us winter in the world and make money there. Some of us do northern jobs from here, just like any other telecommuter.'

'Is that what you do?' Wade asked.

'Me? No, no way. I'm no telecommuter. I'm all right here. Real time real space, twenty-four hours a day.'

Then she tilted the blimp down. Wade saw out of the windows that there were other blimps ahead and behind, dropping just as fast as they were. He sat back in his seat and extricated his wristphone from his headset.

'Did you catch any of that, Phil?'

'Some of it – I couldn't hear you, but I heard some of the others. But it's pretty windy there, hey? There's quite a background noise.'

'Yes. Hey Phil, we're back in the cloud, on our way down. Do you want to stay on the air or not?'

'Oh on, on! Just keep the line open, this is great! What I want to know is why these folks have factionalized, I mean that's really the problem, isn't it, you have people of like mind and they still end up at each other's throats, I can never understand that–'

'Hey Phil, sorry, we're, it's getting kind of busy here, I can't really focus–'

'Oh hey you do what you need to, I'm just thinking out loud here!'

The blimp was being driven down by its big fan, and it jounced up and down on gusts. Addie began arguing with the wind again. Wade was starting to feel a bit airsick when suddenly the blimp was rushing down at a blue glacial slope, firing its harpoon anchors into it and then reeling itself down in a final convulsion. As soon as they were secured Addie took off her headset and opened her door and leapt down. 'Wait here a minute!' she shouted at them, and was off running toward a big clear-roofed gap, cut into a giant lobe of glacial ice – no doubt a refuge like the one they had left earlier. Several other blimps were already anchored, and their crews were out standing in front of this refuge, pointing some kind of instrument at it. 'What are they doing to them?' Val exclaimed, and she was opening her door when X grabbed her arm.

'Look,' he said, pointing to the side. 'Whatever they're doing they haven't got all of them in there, see?'

'Wade, you watch out,' Phil's tinny voice said from his wrist, 'you keep your eye peeled, I don't like the sound of this, watch out all directions, that's what I always say . . .'

White slips of movement; tiny black dots against a field of blue seracs; those were darkened sunglasses, Wade saw, and realized that their ferals were being ambushed, perhaps by people from the refuge who had slipped outside.

'Come on,' Val said, and opened her door and jumped down. X followed, and after a split second's scared hesitation, Wade too jumped out of the blimp.

Val ran to one of the blimp's anchors and picked up two big chunks of ice lying beside it. She tossed one of them at the ferals outside the refuge entrance, to get their attention; the other she fired at the white figures coming up on them. This drew the attention of the white figures, and one of them pointed their way – aiming guns at them, Wade saw with a jolt. In a panic he ran forward and dived into Val and X at the ankles, knocking their feet out so that they fell on him. Little snapping sounds in the wind caused his stomach to shrink to the size of a walnut; gunshots! He hugged the ice, looked up in time to see the ferals at the refuge entrance turn their odd-looking weapon on their ambushers. The figures in white staggered spastically, fell like marionettes whose strings have been cut.

For a moment nothing moved but the wind. Phil's voice chirped from Wade's wrist like a cricket. Only a few moments had passed but to Wade time had distended, ballooned by his panic; he could have given a long and detailed account for every second that had just passed. His heart was pounding like the fastest tympani roll in the Maestro basic sounds set. Val and X were getting off him. They were both big people.

Finally there was movement in front of the refuge's clear tent. Mai-lis and Addie emerged and walked over to the latecomers. Wade put his wrist to his mouth. 'Listen to this, Phil.'

By the time Mai-lis and Addie got to them everyone was standing again. Angrily Val exclaimed, 'You said this wouldn't be dangerous! What the fuck were you doing?'

'Sorry,' Mai-lis said shortly, with a glance at Addie that Addie ignored. 'You weren't supposed to get here until the operation was over. Thanks for helping us.'

Others from her group were collecting the fallen figures, hauling them unceremoniously across the ice to the largest blimp. More people, unconscious or paralysed, were dragged out of the refuge itself. Perhaps a dozen or fifteen all told. The blimp they were being loaded into was considerably bigger than the others, but still, it would be stuffed.

Addie's face was flushed bright pink. 'That's a lockable gondola,' she explained to Wade and Val and X. 'There's nothing they can do in there. It's a remotely operated vehicle, and this one's programmed to fly to a base in the Peninsula, refuel, then fly across the Drake Strait to Chile.'

'What did you do to them?' Val said.

'We shot 'em with a thing made for Japanese banks that get robbed or whatever. It messes up muscle control, with ultrasound or taser, I don't know. A stun gun.'

'That's not what they were using,' X pointed out.

'No, those were real guns they were shooting! Glad they didn't get you! Nice move there on the senator's part. Here, come on over: Mai-lis is going to pronounce the verdict and send them on their way.'

Around the big blimp the whole group had gathered. Carlos was shouting abuse at the people locked behind the gondola's windows, shaking a finger at them. As they walked over Wade said into his wrist, 'Getting this, Phil?'

He put the phone to his ear. 'Hard to hear, Wade, but stay on the air.'

Some of the captured outlaws had recovered from their neuro-muscular incapacitation, and were standing at the windows shouting down at Carlos and the others, red-faced and furious; one crying; one screaming; one pounding the window as hard as she could – she would have put her fist right through the glass if she could have, and damn the consequences. And all unheard through the glass, in the wind and the sound of the blimps' fans.

'That's Ron!' X exclaimed, pointing at the gondola window. 'That's Ron Jasper in there! He joined the ice pirates!'

Mai-lis was now using a handset walkie-talkie, presumably to speak to those inside on their radio. Wade hurried to her and put his wristphone right up next to her walkie-talkie's mouthpiece. Mai-lis nodded at him as she continued to speak.

'—ninety percent voted on exile, and exile it is. You are not to return on pain of death. Remember this lesson in your new life in the north.' She stared up at them. The look in her little Sami eyes was cold. She made a gesture, and one of her group manipulated another handset, and the big blimp cut away from its anchors and shot up on the wind, spinning its prisoners into the clouds.

After that Val and X and Wade and Carlos were led inside the pirates' lair, as Addie called it. It was much deeper than the refuge they had been taken to, extending far back into the ice, in a gigantic tunnel of the purest blue. There they found box after box stacked against the walls, and gear of all kinds. At the rear of the tunnel squatted a big yellow vehicle that reminded Wade of a road construction earthmover.

'That's it!' X yelled. 'That's my SPOT train's caboose!'

'Told you,' Addie said. 'Come on, let's get out of here. We'll give you the GPS co-ordinates for this place, so Mac Town can recover this stuff.'

When they were airborne again she said over the intercom, 'Whew! I'm glad that's over! Thanks for helping us out. Sorry to get you there early, but I wanted to be in on it to tell you the truth. I hate those bastards, them and their obtainium. As if they could do whatever they wanted.'

'So will you kill them if they return?' Wade asked.

'Nah. Unlikely. I suppose it could happen, but in reality we'd probably just try to zap them and ship them out again. The truth is they probably won't come back. They wouldn't get any help from anyone else, and you need to be part of the whole feral scene down here to make a real go of it. So even if they did come back they'd just be like those trekker guys, out wandering on their own. It's not the same as making your living down here.'

'But I don't see how you do it,' Wade insisted. 'The gear you have here must cost a lot more money than you can make.'

A long pause, filled by the sounds of the wind and the fan's buzz. 'Well, you know,' Addie said. 'We have our audiences, just like most of the groups down here. Sponsor audiences I mean. Weren't any of your clients sending out reports on their trek?' she asked Val.

'Yeah sure,' Val said. 'Ta Shu was. Still is, I suppose, if he can transmit.'

'Well, we do a bit of that too. And some of the companies that make this stuff like the prototypes tested hard. So we have some alliances.'

'But the Antarctic Treaty,' Wade said again. Once again he had his wristphone wedged between his right ear and the headset, and he was trying to imagine what Phil would want to ask. He supposed Phil could even have asked his own questions, but he was keeping quiet, and Wade could see how that might be the easiest way to do things.

'Yeah yeah, the Treaty. In suspension now, right? And even when it was active it was only paper. Its values were so pure because the stakes were so small! As soon as oil exploration's become economical, non-Treaty nations are down here sniffing around, and the Treaty governments are jockeying for position above them. There was never any enforcement to the Treaty, see? No one was going to come down here and zap offenders and ship them out like we just did. The French, they signed the Treaty and then bulldozed a big airstrip right through a penguin rookery near their station. Greenpeace went down there and stood right at the bottom of the slope where the bulldozers were pushing rocks, and the bulldozer drivers just kept on driving. Nearly killed a few Greenpeacers. That was the most dangerous thing they did, I think, worse than driving Zodiacs in front of those Japanese mama whalers. Greenpeace did some great things down here if you ask me, they really made a difference. And without blowing people up, like these whoevers we're dealing with now. But they couldn't do it all, because everyone was breaking the Treaty. The Russians broke the treaty, the Poles broke the Treaty, the Americans broke the Treaty: you should see the bottom of the bay off McMurdo! We were as bad as anybody until Greenpeace went down there and poured trash from the dump onto the floor of the Chalet right in the middle of a big meeting. That was so great. The NSF rep went nuts and forbade any of us from talking to any Greenpeacer, and retired end of that season. But it got NSF to think things over. And at the same time the Environmental Defense Fund was suing them back in Washington for breaking NEPA. It was a pincer attack, really. So NSF got religion then, but it was Greenpeace that did it, Greenpeace and EDF. No, the Treaty's been abused, you take my word for it! There was too much else going on in the world for anyone to risk making anyone mad over a little thing like Antarctica. So the Treaty was there, but no one paid much attention to it except for when it suited them. So, you know. Mai-lis keeps us in compliance with the Treaty like a kindergarten teacher, better than most countries when you actually look at what the thing says. We register all the animals we kill for food and do science on them so we're no different than the scientists really, except we eat the data when we're done with it. And Art Devries does that too. So, you know. You can't expect us to take the Treaty too seriously.'

'Unless it gets you kicked off the continent.'

'Ain't that the truth.' She shook her head. 'That's why these bastards we shipped out, and whoever it was blowing up the oil stations and messing with coms ...' A gust of wind swirled the blimp around, and Addie wrestled with the controls and did not finish the thought. 'Come on.'

'What brought you down here?' Wade asked her.

'Airplane.' Another laugh. 'No no, I know. I'm from Alabama, right? I never had a thought about Antarctica in my life. If you'd of asked me I'd have said it was some kind of radiator fluid. But I was selling some land, and a man who came to look at it, we talked for a while. I've been a plumber since I was ten, and a carpenter, electrician – my daddy was a contractor, and I did it all. And then after my Army days I was flying helos for Louisiana Pacific. So I was telling this man about all that, and showing him a well and pumphouse we built, and telling him about us, and he said, Did you ever think of working in Antarctica? And I said, Why no – I never did.' Laugh. 'It turned out he was from ASL, and he thought I'd make a good Carhartt. Which I did, for a while.'

'In McMurdo?' X asked.

'And the Pole. Five summers and two winterovers. Then my second winter at the Pole, I was shown some things ...'

'Like the waterslide?' Wade asked.

'Yeah, how do you know about that? Who are you again? Oh yeah, the senator.'

'I'm not actually the senator.'

'Waterslide?' X said. He and Val were looking around at Wade.

'So you went feral,' Wade prompted Addie.

'Yeah. One day I was out emptying a Herc, completely toast, and I looked up and there was a skua flying around. They get blown in to the Pole occasionally, but I didn't know that then, and when I saw it I thought it was, I don't know. God. And that very night Herb asked me if I was interested in lighting out for the territory, and I thought of that skua and said you bet, and never looked back.'

'You don't regret losing . . .' A loud gust of wind drowned him out.

'Losing what?'

'The world!'

That sweet laugh. 'What's to miss? The world's just a big ASL, you know that. Driving in boxes to go sit in other boxes, and look at little boxes – that's no way to live. Even building the boxes is no great thrill after the first fifty or so. No, I don't miss anything about the world. Except Tahiti of course!' Laugh. 'And I go there every winter.'

'You don't winterover?'

'No way. I've done it twice, and that's at least once too many. Life is too short. Of course I'm committed to wintering over one year every seven, to help keep things going. But I haven't hit seven yet, and when I do I'll have to think it over. See if I can buy out. Even quit maybe. Nah, but I'll think of something. Maybe I'll take a paired assignment if I find the right guy, that's the only way to do it, just hibernate and spend the whole winter in bed staying warm.'

'So most of you don't winterover,' Val said.

'No. Just a maintenance crew, like Mac Town or Pole. We're Antarcticans, okay, but we aren't masochists, except for some I could name. We do it 'cause it's fun. The whole point is to stay flexible. Nomads, you know. That's how the Eskimos and the Sami do it too. So it's Tahiti in the winter for most of us, or New Zealand or Alaska or wherever. But hell, I'll winter here again if I have to, to help things along.'

Below them a rift in the clouds appeared, and they could see parts of a vast, broad glacier, flanked by black peaks. 'That looks like the Beardmore,' Val said.

'Well, let's not talk about that. And if you would pass on checking your GPS I would appreciate it,' she added, glancing back at Wade.

'Where are you taking us?' Wade asked.

'Your final destination is Mac Town, of course. But first we're going to Quviannikumut, to refuel. And I think Mai-lis wants you to see something other than our dark side, so to speak. Dirty-laundry law enforcement.' She shook her head. 'Those bastards.'

'It sounds like Mai-lis is really quite an authority,' Wade noted.

'Well, someone's gotta do it. She's the big mama, no doubt about that. The democracy stuff can only go so far before it becomes chaos. Someone's got to have the final word, or the first word anyway, and that's Mai-lis.'

'I wonder what brought her down here.'

'You'll have to ask her that. But I think I remember her saying she had gotten mighty sick of Norwegians. They treat the Sami like we treat Indians, you know? Ah – there's Quviannikumut, see?'

Wade saw nothing but white clouds.

'Means to feel deeply happy. Nice name, eh? Okay, down we go. Come on, you dog. Down boy! Down!'

white white white
white green white
white white white

Val walked into Quviannikumut, amazed. It was a big shelter, much bigger than the first refuge they had been taken to: a modular assemblage of clear tenting covering several ragged embayments of a dolerite slope, which ran down gently into an ice surface that then rose up over the shore, so that fingers of rock and ice intertwined. The rock had the mazelike quality of the Labyrinth in Wright Valley, so that little canyons crossed higher on the slope and became sunken rooms. The smooth blue ice peninsulas bulking into the embayments were part of a larger glacier, or the polar cap itself – in the flying mist of the storm it was impossible to say – and the ice too had been incorporated into the shelter, honeycombed with tunnels and open-roofed chambers and long blue galleries. And all under the keening flight of the flying white cloud, so that it seemed a village under glass. It was beautiful.

All Val's clients from the other blimps were already gathered in what appeared to be a dining hall; so that was okay, and she relaxed. Or began to relax; it was going to take some time to unwind. They were having another big meal, it seemed, dipping krill-cakes in salsa, and talking with other diners around them. Jack appeared to be recovering; he was wearing a sling and regaling one of the feral women, a tall Scandinavian blonde, with the story of their crossing of Mohn Basin. 'A matter of pacing yourself.' Jim and Jorge and Elspeth were interrogating the cook. Carlos was talking to another Latino contingent in Spanish; Ta Shu was looking out at the icescape beyond the refuge, nodding enthusiastically. 'A very good place!' X and Wade were behind her, crowding in, still chatting with Addie. It was loud; things were turning raucous as they celebrated the exile of the ice pirates.

'Pretty hard,' Val remarked to Mai-lis. 'Presumably they liked being down here.'

Mai-lis shrugged. 'They brought it on themselves. And it's not as if we've thrown them in prison.'

She took Val and Wade and X around the shelter, and Ta Shu joined them. Several of the little ravines upslope from the ice were in effect greenhouses, sealed off from the rest of the camp by triple-lock doors. Inside these canyonettes vegetables and grains covered the floors and walls, most growing hydroponically, some in soil boxes and big glass terraria. The roofs were clear. 'On sunny days the fabric goes white. From above no one can see,' Mai-lis said. 'We shift this work from place to place to follow the sun. We try to grow as much as we can.

325

Of course it is not enough, but we are getting closer. It's wonderful how productive modern greenhouses can be.'

Wade asked a lot of questions, as he had with Addie; he was clearly fascinated by the whole phenomenon. 'What are the staples of your diet, then?'

'Fish, of course. And krill-cakes. Being indigenous in Antarctica means being coastal and living off the sea most of the time, because there is nothing inland to live on. Fortunately with the Ross Ice Shelf gone the Transantarctics are themselves coastal, which is good. So we can live here as well as around the rest of the coastline. And up on the cap too, in the summer, to cross to the far coasts. Or just to be up there.'

'But why?' Wade said.

'Well, because we like it.' She smiled, for the first time that Val had seen. 'You gain a lot by being out in the world. And at this point technology has advanced to the point at which we are allowed to practise a very sophisticated form of nomadic existence. Not hunting and gathering, but hunting and doing mobile agriculture. And clothing is so advanced that in most ways it functions as your house. That's a good thing. It means you can travel very lightly on the land and still be sheltered. It isn't like being truly exposed. As you found out, yes?'

'It still felt pretty exposed to me,' X said.

'Yes, but it's partly a matter of getting used to how well it works. Of learning to trust it. Think what it used to be like! Occasionally we remind ourselves of that by going out in the old gear, just so we know what we have now. Also it's a way of doing honour to the first explorers, to remind us what they endured. They were the first Antarcticans, you see. They loved it too.'

Val said, 'You have some of their outfits here?'

'Facsimiles of their outfits, made for adventure travel groups reproducing the old expeditions in every detail.'

'Ah yes,' Val said. 'I know that stuff. I did a couple of those trips.'

'We bought it heavily discounted.'

'I'll bet.'

Mai-lis led them into the next module of the shelter, rock-walled under a rock-coloured tent roof. This was the bedroom; the sleeping chambers were little individual cubicles, curtained off from each other and the hallway down the middle.

'It looks pretty cramped,' Wade noted.

'When we are indoors things are tight,' Mai-lis said. 'An exercise in efficiency. But we don't spend that much time in any one place, so it doesn't bother us. And it's a pleasure to design a new way of living. All kinds of possibilities are opening up. These are important to explore in such a world as ours. Lars talks about a Plimsoll line. Do you know this term? It's the line on a ship's hull marking the maximum load possible. He says the world has sunk below its Plimsoll line, weighted down by people. He has worked out how much total energy each person alive today could burn and yet the world altogether still remain above its Plimsoll line. It's not very much. Less than you would think.'

'Is that why you live down here?' Wade asked. 'To ease population pressures up north?'

'Oh no. Antarctica can never do that, its carrying capacity is magnitudes smaller than the scale of the problem. People everywhere have to reduce their numbers, that is the only solution at this point. Population reduction and climate stabilization are the same thing now. No, we live here because we like it. And it may also be a way to think about how people should live everywhere. But we do it because it gives us pleasure.'

'You must burn some fuel to keep this place going,' X said. 'I can hear a generator.'

Mai-lis smiled. 'You sound like a fundie. What if we fuelled it with whale oil, would that make you happy? A local renewable resource?'

X shrugged.

'We have a better way still in some places,' Mai-lis said. 'Where they exist we have drilled down into geothermal areas, and we heat those refugia with hot springs. They are the best of all.'

Wade said, 'Is that generator we hear the one from old old Pole station?'

Mai-lis nodded. 'It is. And it's a problem, because its fuel is an antique mixture we have to brew specially. But serviceable, as you hear.'

At the far end of that ravine corridor, the tenting closed to the ground in a vestibule door. Beyond it the rooms continued out into the blue bulk of the glacier, the ice carved into elaborate pillars and ceilings. Their blimp pilot, Lars, was out there, and when he saw them he waved for them to come out. 'Yes, let's take a look,' Mai-lis said. 'We're dressed warmly enough, it's kept just below freezing out there, you'll see.'

They went through the vestibule and out into the ice gallery, and indeed it was not very much colder than the rock-walled rooms had been. As they moved farther out they could see how much of the ice had been carved into rooms and chambers; it looked like an entire lobe of the glacier had been honeycombed, some of it tented, the rest open to the air, and all of it sculpted like one of the great festival ice villages of Scandinavia, but on a truly vast scale, with one immense courtyard entirely devoted to smooth-sided blue ice statuary.

'This is amazing!' Wade exclaimed, pressing up against a clear wall to look out at the untented sculpture garden. 'Who – how–'

Lars joined Wade at the wall, more friendly than he had yet been. 'This was not just us fooling around. This is the work of one of the artists from McMurdo. He applied to NSF to use the new ice borers to do this to the end of the Canada Glacier in the Dry Valleys, and they refused him. So he spent all his time in McMurdo making snowmen and pretending that that was all he was doing, but in the meantime he made three trips out here to do this. No one pays much attention to what those Woos do once they get in the field, and somehow he found us, and we brought him here when we were building this refuge. I was with him when he did this, and I felt like Rilke with Rodin, I tell you.'

'I can see why,' Wade said, nose pressed into the clear fabric. 'What a sense of form.'

'Yes. He was a true artist. The ice borer was like his fingers. And you must understand, the ice did not look like this when he finished with it. He was planning on the ice to sublime away, so that the sculptures would change in time as they ablated. There was no way to be sure exactly how they would diminish, so there is an aleatory element to it. But he wanted to know the prevailing winds, to try to shape what would happen. And this is how it looks now. A few more years and the wind will blow it all away.'

'Wow.'

'He changed the way we thought about ice borers. About what we should be doing out here with the refugia.'

Ta Shu, grinning, thumped himself on the chest. 'I too am a Woo.'

'Is that so?' Lars asked, interested.

X pointed across the glacier to the next tented embayment, which appeared stuffed with mist. 'What's that?'

'That's the sauna,' Mai-lis said. 'A way to relax and get warm after a day outside. My next destination, if you don't mind. Feel free to join me if you want.'

She led them back around and past the sleeping tent, to the door of a big, damp changing room, where piles of clothes were stacked neatly or otherwise on a rock bench against a rock wall. She went inside and stripped down to blue smartfabric long underwear, then stepped through a zipdoor in a clear wall, down into a long room stuffed with mist, a steaming pool at its bottom. Most of the people in the shelter appeared already to be down there. The pool floored one long room of the tent, where the rock embayment dipped in a basin that had been filled waist-high with hot water. The clear tent wall came down beyond the pool, just before the ice of the glacier, which curved down like a blue wave about to crash onto them.

Val stripped down to her underwear and jogger top, not looking at X or Wade, who were studiously not looking at her, staggering and crashing into each other as they got out of their clothes too. She went through the inner door into the pool room. Inside it was shockingly hot and wet. Here one could not really see the blue glacier overhanging the far end of the room; that side of the room was simply bluer mist than the mist around her. She walked into the pool and sank to her neck, then sat on a rock bench set a little higher. Hot! Hot! And oh so luxurious. Suddenly it seemed she had been cold for months.

The sauna was above the pool, its benches in a little tent around a steamer. All the air was steam; in there it must have been simply hotter steam. Voices were confined by the rock walls, and the watery clangour was loud. Val sat and watched the faces. She had not slept in three days, or four – for so long that it was too much trouble to work out just exactly how long – and so she was deep into the exhausted, buzzed insomnia that all Antarcticans experienced from time to time, when for one reason or another you stayed awake for so long that it felt as if you would never sleep again. Stunned, detached, disembodied; although there were bodies everywhere in the water and the mist, pink and brown shapes against the blurry blue ice; including her own body, relaxing at last, her hand pulsing pinkly there in front of her face, every detail of it microscopically distinct, the skin very obviously semi-transparent. But her consciousness was well detached from that pink thing. Many of the ferals were naked; others were in bathing suits or underwear or longjohns, the smartfabrics so smart that they would dry on the body almost as soon as one got out; even immersed in the pool Val felt a layer of warm dry fabric against her skin, where she was clothed. Looking down at her pink skin from a point of view that seemed distinctly higher than her own head, Val was glad to be some-what covered; even so she was a shocking sight, she felt, as she had been torn up badly in her two falls, and had had other accidents and surgeries; scars everywhere, so that it seemed to her a very Bride of Frankenstein sort of body, stitched together from various parts that did not match very well. Oh well. X was sitting beside her in his longjohns, making the perfect Frankenstein to her Bride; big, massive, graceless. It was a comfort to have him there. They made a kind of pair, like a couple of football players, linebacker and noseguard, soaking away their bruises after a hard game.

Wade on the other hand was very slim and lithe. Now swimming around the hot bath like an otter. A good-looking man. Lars too was very attractive, in Norse god style; a face that reminded her of Sting. No fat on him. The ferals' bodies showed they worked hard out here, which did not surprise Val in the least.

Mai-lis stood in the centre of the bath, round and wrinkled, listening to Carlos and Ta Shu. The big mama. The three of them were circulating slowly, and coming toward Val and X through other knots of conversation. Living out here. Making their living out here. X leaned into Val, gestured at the three approaching them. 'We're so damn lucky. Here's a Chilean and a Chinese and a Laplander talking, and they use English to do it.'

'You can thank the Brits for that.'

'I guess so.'

'It's true,' Carlos was insisting to Ta Shu and Mai-lis, 'and if it is true in Antarctica then it is true everywhere, this is what I say!'

Ta Shu squinted, uncertain. 'Colder here. People cannot so easily live off land.'

'True,' Carlos said, 'but people can't easily live off the land anywhere! So true here, true there, just like I said! Where in the world could a person be put outdoors and find an easy time living off the land? It's not so easy!'

'I suppose not,' Ta Shu said, thinking it over. 'Savannah, maybe.'

'But if we can do it here,' Mai-lis said, 'then everywhere else it can only be easier. That's why I don't agree with the fundies that we should use only things we can make down here. There is no reason for an artificial exercise like that. It's the latest technologies that make what we do here possible. When your clothes are your house, and your tent is your farm, then you can go where you please. Even Antarctica can be inhabited, as you see.'

Higher voices cut through the clangour, and Carlos looked at the door. 'Are those kids I hear? Hey, look! Some boys and girls!'

Indeed it was true; a pack of kids like wild animals crashed down into the water and started splashing each other, oblivious to the adults in the bath.

'I did not know this!' Carlos said. 'You didn't tell us about this!'

'Oh yes,' Mai-lis said. 'We have quite a few families down here, and they tend to clump together so the kids will have company. This refuge is a big family camp.'

'Now this is what you need!' Carlos exclaimed. 'These are Antarcticans, you see? This is all they know. This is how I was brought up – we didn't have a spa like this of course, I wish we had, but there were fifteen kids in Bernardo O'Higgins when I grew up there, I could name them all to you and tell you everything about them, right up to this very day! They are my brothers and sisters, I tell you. X, X, this is how I grew up, look at them!'

'I am,' X assured him.

'You must have many memories of that place,' Ta Shu said.

'Oh my God. My God, yes. One time in Bernardo,' Carlos said, talking to them all now, including Jim, who had joined them and was regarding him very closely: 'One time I was four years old, and I was fascinated by the bulldozer we had for snowploughing – I liked to sit with the driver and drive it, you know. And one day I went out there by myself and climbed up into it, just to pretend, and you know how a bulldozer will start with just a push of the ignition when the key is left in – well, I pushed the button and the engine started, and it had been left in low gear, and it took off. I didn't know what to do, I was too scared to move. And the bulldozer had been parked pointed toward a cliff that fell directly down into the sea ice, which was thin. So the bulldozer ran toward that cliff, and I could see it coming but I couldn't figure out what to do, and someone inside the dining hall saw me out the window and they all came running out, and they were running for me as hard as they could, my father in front, I saw his face so clearly, I can still see it. And yet they would not have reached me in time, because the bulldozer was very close to the cliff. But then the bulldozer stopped. The engine conked out, you know, it misfired and died. They looked at it later, and it had fuel and ran smoothly and everything. But it stopped at the edge of the cliff! And everyone carried me back inside. It's practically the first thing I can remember.'

'You are a true Antarctican,' Ta Shu declared.

'Yes, yes yes yes yes. Antarctica said to me, Okay, you can live, Carlos. But you must remember. You must serve me.'

Then a bunch of people from the sauna were rushing through the pool toward the lock at the end of the tent, the lock leading outside. 'Come on!' Addie said to them as she passed (stuffed in a flowery swimsuit, pink, sexy), 'come on y'all, it's a hundred fifty Fahrenheit in the sauna and fifty below outside if you count wind-chill! You can join the Two Hundred Club with an asterisk, not quite the Three Hundred Club but very exclusive nevertheless!'

'Oh God,' X said, not moving.

'I've heard of this,' Val said. 'It's like the polar dip at Mac Town.'

'A heart attack waiting to happen.' He glanced at her. 'You want to try it?'

'No . . . Ah hell, why not? I'm so spaced, it might wake me up.'

He grinned. 'If it doesn't then nothing's going to.'

They stood, and in that movement Val saw suddenly that he was relaxed. As they sloshed down the pool she thought disjointedly about this. It had been true pretty much since she had run into him and the others at Roberts. Not hangdog and accusatory as in McMurdo. Not that he hadn't had cause! Because he had. And still did. But he seemed to have forgiven her. And she hadn't even apologized. She clutched his arm for balance as they kicked into cold tennis shoes next to the lock, clutched it hard as they crowded into the lock with others. 'Keep

331

a hand on the safety line,' Val said to him. 'It could be extra windy in the slot between the tent and the ice.'

'Do you think they'll have a safety line?'

'Shit.'

They crowded out of the door with the others.

Instant cold, a brutal slam of it everywhere at once. The wind poured right through her and her skin snap-froze. Everyone was shouting, and she realized she was too. Steam was erupting off them and flying downwind; they were pink firecrackers, exploding steam! The cold was astonishing. Val felt a moment of pure fear, as it occurred to her that this is what the end would feel like in Antarctica; this was death; then she was laughing at the insanity of it, people trying to dig snowballs out of a snowbank hard as concrete, screaming, all the steaming pink skin glowing in the dim omnidirectional light; seeing it all without sunglasses, through a torrent of tears freezing on her cheeks; her underwear and jogger top freezing solid. Brass bra like an amazon. Amazed laughter.

Then all at once they were jostling back into the lock, then crashing desperately down into the water and shrieking even louder at the heat. Val's skin was blasted all over again by the hot/cold assault on her stunned capillary system, the two sensations of freezing and boiling merged into a single burn. Shrieks and shouts all around. She had to laugh. 'What a rush.'

After that sensory detonation everything was rendered hyperlucid. Her skin needled and burned; she saw everything in a kind of twenty-ten vision. Sleepiness had vanished utterly: she felt as if she would never sleep again. All her muscles were melting inside her but her mind remained alert, as hypersensitive as her skin.

And so a very strange state indeed, as she observed the ferals and their refuge. She got out of the pool before she melted entirely, and put on undershirt and leggings, and wandered around just looking, free from all responsibility. All the rooms were warmer now, and people were dressed in various degrees of clothing, many still in their drying long underwear. Some rooms looked like they were shooting a special Antarctic issue of the Victoria's Secret catalogue, and Jack had found one of these and was telling a couple of the Scandinavian women about something. Jim was at the dining room table conversing with Ta Shu and Carlos, intent about something or other: I do social law, but that's where you can see that unless the system itself changes . . . Jorge and Elspeth were back talking to the cook, Jorge taking notes on a little pad of paper. Recipes for an article. The ferals were not going to be hidden very much longer.

There were about as many women as men among them, Val noted

as she walked around. If that were true generally then it would be a first in Antarctic history. So there were some firsts left after all.

And the women there were a capable-looking crowd, reminding her in many ways of her lunch group in Mac Town. Scandinavians, Japanese, Eskimo, Kiwi, whatever. Muscled or round, tall, short, scarred and weathered, underfed or nicely blubbered; very few classic beauties in this crowd, though there were a few analogues to Lars there too. All of them looked good to Val. They liked to spend their time out in the wilderness, working hard. And they were doing that without being part of the tourism industry. Some kind of high-tech polar hunter and farmer life. What do you do for a living? I hunt and farm. I farm the ice. She had to laugh.

And when she stopped and asked one of the women about it, about the way they lived, the woman was instantly friendly. She had a German accent; she said, 'Come with us now, we're going to empty traps in the bay.' Val was still sloshing around inside her skin, her muscles turned to jelly; but this was her chance to do this, and another might never come.

So she told Ta Shu and Jim where she was going, geared back up, and left the tent with a group of five women. Back into the rush of frozen mist; but in her clothes it was not so bad, the spacesuit effect very distinctly felt after their exposed, wet foray outside; she was in the wind but protected, warm, disconnected. Geared up! It was pretty remarkable how protected they were. And it was by no means as windy as it had been on the Shackleton Glacier.

They followed a rope line, an Ariadne thread the woman called it, down the glacier to a very broad ice staircase, cut into the side of an ice slope with one of the laser borers. They were on a piedmont glacier, Val saw, or a remnant of the Ross Ice Shelf itself. So this camp was located where the Transantarctics dropped into the Ross Sea, tucked into some rock outcrop like Mount Betty. Iceberg fragments of the old shelf dotted the misty sea ice offshore, like a vast city of white buildings slowly dispersing into the distance. Visibility fluctuated in the cloud; sometimes she could see a few metres, at other times a few kilometres, but all within the rushing cloud.

Down on the cracked surface of the sea ice there was a little fishing hut, beside a round hole that had refrozen. They took turns breaking the new ice with a crowbar, Val taking a single whack and then passing the bar along, as she judged she was a danger to them all. Then she helped haul up on a chain, her mitted hands chilling swiftly, first throbbing with dull, cold pain, then numbing to the point they became only big, fat, gloved things at the ends of her arms. She did windmills to return feeling to them, then helped the other women lift up the metal trap at the end of the chain. Out of the hole it came, splashing water that froze on the ice in seconds. Inside was a big mawsoni, and they stood back and watched as it thrashed out its life, everyone silent and intent. 'What a dragon,' one said emphatically after it was dead. They opened the trap; it was like an elongated lobster trap, with a door people could unhook. They hauled out the dead monster and laid it on a banana sledge. Val took one end of the sledge, and helped the Germanic woman who had invited her out to carry the sledge up the steps cut into the broken slope of the ice shelf. She could feel the exhaustion of the long walk across Mohn Basin in her legs; she was tired, very tired.

Then they hauled the fish over the ice, tramping back up to the camp slow step after slow step. In harness and pulling a sledge again. It felt like a long way, going uphill and into the wind. The cloud flew right at them over the ice; everything white; not a classic white-out, in the sense of losing all horizon and distance, but a blustery frozen mist flowing right on the white glacier. Val was beat, her legs quivering and tweaking, on the edge of cramps. But her mind was sharp, needling inside her like her thawing hands. She felt full. The haul through the white wind suddenly ballooned: it took for ever, it was the whole world, and she there in it completely, seeing it all in exquisite detail, the surface of the glacier as textured and semi-transparent as her skin in the pool, everything flowing but still, everything in its place. She hit her stride and pulled for ever.

Back in the refuge she sat again in the dining room, warming up by the stove, listening to the people around her talk. 'All the Eskimos I've seen have had to learn snowcraft all over again, they've been living in pick-up trucks or off their government grants. Either too poor or too rich. But what stayed with them was their values. Eskimos think it's important to be happy. You're supposed to react to difficult situations cheerfully. A happy person is considered a capable person, a good person. Unhappy people are thought to be deficient in some significant respect. It isn't acknowledged to be an appropriate response. You have to face up to Naartsuk, that was their storm spirit, the biggest god in their pantheon. They don't seem religious any more, but they definitely still believe in Naartsuk.'

Carlos was telling people at Val's table about arrowheads found on the Peninsula, indicating visits by prehistoric peoples in boats, no doubt from Chile. Also ancient maps which showed a surprisingly accurate Antarctic coastline, some of them even accurate to the point of appearing to map what the deglaciated coastline would be, as if the civilization had been ancient beyond knowledge. Ta Shu was shaking his head at this, murmuring, 'No, no. Von Daniken, very bad. We are first here, we have that obligation.' Wade too seemed dubious about the possibility of previous Antarctic humans: 'Is not possible,' he repeated more than once. 'Is not possible.'

Many of the ferals, however, seemed to disagree. 'There were beech forests here for millions of years,' one of the German women said. She had pulled a foot-powered sewing machine over to the table, and with Lars's help was sewing together pieces of what looked like seal fur. 'Who knows what else might had lived here?'

'We will bring the beech forests back,' Lars said. 'The climate is just right for them again. It only needs planting them. Prehistoric and posthistoric. Our children will take refuge in these forests. They can harvest the wood, and make what they need, and set terraria in the protection of each grove. The fjords will come back too.'

Then the cook set a plate of fish cutlets and rice before Val, and a big salad of mixed lettuce and cut cabbage, and after she had wolfed it down Mai-lis came in and said to her, 'We would like to move you on toward McMurdo now.'

'Now?' She was surprised; it was still storming outside, the clouds right on the ice and very windy. Of course that hadn't stopped them so far.

'Yes, now, please. It's best for us if our involvement in your affairs is over before McMurdo is back to normal. The ecotage has caused them to call in the US Navy. Right now this storm is still keeping flights from Christchurch from coming down, but when they arrive we want to be gone.'

'Does it matter, now that people know you're here? Once they start looking they'll be able to find you for sure.'

Mai-lis nodded. 'We haven't decided what to do yet. Saving people was more important than staying hidden, that was clear. We don't think anyone will actually try to evict us, so . . . well, we will see. But we want to start this next phase with some distance. So if you and your group will suit up, we will fly you to Ross Island.'

'Sure, sure. Whatever you say.' In fact Val would have loved nothing more than to try to sleep; the idea had come back, which was a sign that if she could just get under the blanket, so to speak, she would stay under for an entire day, maybe two. Not at all a comfortable feeling. But she didn't want to argue with their hosts.

She went around the chambers of the refuge, rounding up her group and Carlos, Wade and X. Many of them appeared to be as exhausted as she was; she had to rouse them from the classic Antarctic ten-foot stare, saying, 'Come on, come on, they're flying us to McMurdo.'

Half an hour later, they and their few possessions were on board two big blimps, Addie again piloting the one Val was in. And then they were off once again, into the clouds on a rush of wind.

335

After that Val lost focus a bit. Despite the booming and whistling of the wind, the bouncing of the blimp and the sheer fact of their situation, she was seriously winding down, falling asleep as if making a cliff dive; sooner or later – sooner – she would hit and be gone instantly. Because of their situation she tried to fight this dive, and the strangeness of what was happening helped her, so that eventually what she fell into was a peculiar, struggling, sandy-eyed half-sleep, a kind of waking dream or conscious sleep; the direct contact of reality and her unconscious. In this state she was aware of X and Wade and Ta Shu and Addie talking on the headsets, and aware that they were flying over the Transantarctics in a marvellous blimp; but it was all jumbled together and incoherent. Brief visions of steep mountains, appearing through rents in the cloud as in Chinese landscape painting. Nunataks in a sea of white meringue. Another glimpse of green below. Addie saying, 'Yeah that's Shangri-la, we won't be stopping there.'

'Why not fly straight to Mac?' That was X. Her friend.

'Well, you know, if the ice shelf was still there we might. But now the sea ice is breaking up and there's lots of open water in the bay, and I still don't like to fly over open water, even in the blimps. In case a skua pecks a hole in the bag or whatever. So we'll fly down the range, see the sights. The most beautiful mountains on Earth, anyway. If you could see 'em.'

'Wake up, Val, there's another one of their camps.'

That was Wade. Nice man. She liked him. He was thinking of her. 'Uhh.'

She tried to wake. Like struggling under the surface of a syrup sea. She even slapped herself in the face. X regarded this with a curious expression, as if he wouldn't mind helping out. Part of him. Of course. Though he was fond of her. Shouldn't have dumped him like that, that was mean. Trolling was mean. The blimp dropped hard and she reswallowed her stomach, looked down blurrily: flying clouds, then a patch of green in spun glass; another refuge. Green valley in the ice. Then white clouds again, and Val shook her head, too groggy to remember properly what she had just seen. A waking dream.

'That's Norumbega.'

'How many live there?' Wade asked.

'Well, it's more a crossroads than a town. Johan and Friedrich hold things together there, maybe a dozen others.'

'Do you mind if I have us on the phone to Senator Chase?'

'Oh, yeah, not usually, but don't do it now, okay? I don't want anyone overhearing us during the approach. Besides you're the senator, don't you know that?'

X and Wade looking at each other round-eyed, in faked alarm at this news. They were friends. Val leaned her forehead against the cold window, looked down without quite seeing. Until she got some real sleep she would not be all there no matter how hard she tried. She closed her eyes and dropped into light sleep and dreams, without being aware of the phase change. The Room of a Thousand Shapes, the corked sledge. Rushing clouds, flying down the Zaneveld, a pile of bodies in the snow. She surfaced briefly, groaning. Then back under.

There's Shambala.

There's Ultima Thule.

There's Happy Valley.

There's the Byrd Glacier, the biggest glacier in the world, look at that mama. That glacier is wider than the longest glacier in Europe is long. *What* a mighty river.

A wild interval, swirling around, tossing on a downdraught. That's Skelton Glacier, sucking down a katabatic as usual. Come on, you dog.

Skelton? That's the way I came up on the SPOT train.

Yeah. A hell of a drop.

So we're almost there.

Yeah. But listen, we're not taking you folks right to Mac Town, understand. We don't like to go there. Not at the best of times, and especially not now that the Marines have landed.

So where will you leave us?

Well, I said Black Island, but Mai-lis is a romantic.

Through the clouds, a stark black-and-white landscape. The sea black, dotted with brilliant white bergs. An island like a black castle, rising out of black water.

Then Addie was chivvying the blimp down, down, down, and Val pushed with all her might, and broke back up through the membrane of sleep, groggy and disoriented. Naps were not going to do the job at this point, and she needed to be awake. Addie was clipping the blimp onto a big rust anchor, half-buried in black sand.

'Okay!' she said. 'Your radios ought to get Mac Town no problem now.'

She popped the gondola door, then handed them a key. 'This'll get you inside the hut. Nice to meet y'all.'

They climbed down onto the black sand of the beach. The other blimp was anchored to rocks up on Windvane Hill. Val's group stood around as if they had just got off a train together. Then the blimps detached and sailed off downwind, rising quickly into the clouds and disappearing. 'Where is this?' Wade asked.

'Cape Evans,' Val said. 'Let's get inside, out of the wind.'

Before you, my friends, you see the Cape Evans hut. This is the hut that Scott's expedition built in the summer of 1910–11. They lived in this hut through the autumn and winter of 1911. Wilson, Bowers and Cherry-Garrard left from here on their winter journey, and returned. Scott and his men left the following spring for the Pole. Sixteen men started out; five men did not come back. That autumn and the next winter, the men surviving lived still in this hut, through the long months of perpetual darkness, knowing their comrades would never return. When spring and the sun came back, they went south once more, hoping only to find the bodies of their friends. And they found them – the last three anyway, frozen in their tent, with their gear, and their twenty kilos of geological specimens, and the diaries and letters containing their stories. They had reached the Pole, and found there a tent and a Norwegian flag; Amundsen's group had got there some time before. And on the way back Evans, Oates, Wilson, Scott and Bowers all died.

The survivors left the three bodies they had found in the tent on the ice shelf, and came back to this hut. The relief ship returned at last, and they sailed away for ever.

Now this hut. See inside. They are dead; their stories live. Yet so many questions remain. Why did they come here? How can we live here? How should we live anywhere on this Earth?

Our places speak for us. Our spaces speak through us. This hut still speaks their story. I will go inside now and be silent, so you can hear it.

The nine members of the group gathered before Scott's grey, weathered hut. X took the key Addie had given him and unlocked the massive padlock on the door. They filed in one by one, all but Ta Shu, who wandered up the slope of Windvane Hill, presumably to get an exterior shot. Val waved to him and he waved back; he would be in soon. She followed the others in.

She passed through the dark vestibule. The inner door was opened onto the dim main room; the others already inside. This hallway was their version of a lock. Also a storeroom: slabs of seal blubber stacked on the floor. Butchered sheep hanging in a nook. Horse harnesses on the wall.

Into the big room. The nearer half of it was walled with stacks of boxes, supplies for that fateful expedition of 1911, never used. The further half narrowed, as wooden bunkbeds stuck out from the walls on both sides. Beyond the big central table were workbenches under the southern window, and on the other side, in the far corner, Scott and Wilson's nook. Against the far wall, the black closet of Ponting's darkroom. All dim in the grey light.

Jack and Jim and Carlos had sat down wearily at the far end of the big table, and seeing them Val was reminded sharply of Ponting's photo of Wilson, Bowers and Cherry-Garrard after their return from the Worst Journey. They had been seated in the same places, at this very same table. After thirty-six days out, in midwinter. Val shivered. It was cold in here, as cold as outside, or colder. They had judged in ignorance.

'Anyone for some Heinz ketchup?' Jorge asked, standing before one of the stacks of boxes.

Wade joined him. 'So strange,' he said, touching one of the bottles arrayed on top of the highest box. 'I saw the same ketchup bottles at old Pole station, and the old old station too. The only difference is this one has a cork instead of a screw top.' He left a finger touching the bottle, bemused. These things of ours that carry on, Val thought. Small objects we use. And so the people to come will know we were real too. Because we used Heinz ketchup.

'I'll radio McMurdo,' she said. She went out into the hall; Ta Shu was coming in, and she waved him past her. Then she tried her wristphone. 'McMurdo, this is T–023, this is T–023, do you read? Over.'

To her surprise an answer came quick and clear. 'T–023, this is McMurdo, once again in touch with all the world. Hey Val, where are you?'

'Hi Randi. We're at the Cape Evans hut.'

'Cape Evans! How you'd get there?'

'We had some help.'

'Oh I see! Well you're not the only ones, let me tell you. You got a lift from our back-country residents?'

'Yeah. Listen, can you send a boat over to collect us? I'm not sure we can walk home.'

'Oh sure, sure, no problem there. How many of you are there now?'

'Nine.'

'How's that collarbone?'

'He's okay.'

'Good. Okay, I'll get them to send a Zodiac over right away.'

Back in the hut Jim was holding a bottle of marmalade up to the light. 'I read that once the Kiwis at Scott Base ran out of jam and one of them got on a snowmobile and rode over here and took some of this marmalade back with him. They ate it on their scones.' He smiled at Ta Shu, standing next to him. 'Frozen for fifty years or so.'

'Very tasty.'

'I don't suppose it's any different now.'

Nevertheless they left the food alone. Jim went on telling Ta Shu and the others about the place: how Scott had had a wall of boxes set across the hut to divide officers from able seamen; how they had had a player piano on which to make music; how the hut had been plundered for souvenirs during the IGY years, and been filled to the roof with drift snow and ice before its restoration.

Val wandered around restlessly, only half listening. The bench under the south window looked like an alchemist's laboratory. Little dark bottles, white powders, retorts, all the proud paraphernalia of Victorian science: antique, primitive, handmade. It was the same on the shelf above Wilson's cot, and in the darkroom. All kinds of things. And everything immaculate; no spiderwebs, no dust. Scott's bookshelves, actually the framing of the wall over his bed, were empty. There was a dead Emperor penguin lying on its back across his desk table. The space looked like Scott's, somehow. Blank, private, austere; an empty stuffed-shirt; but something more than that.

Around the corner the bunkbeds seemed to her much more human. Here one over the other had slept her favourites, Birdie Bowers and Apsley Cherry-Garrard. Their magazine pin-ups were still stuck to the wooden wall over their beds: Cherry's were portraits of Edwardian young ladies, dreamy, impeccably dressed, lace at the throat; not people who were ever going to come to Antarctica. Bowers' pin-ups were of dogs.

340

In the dim light it began to seem to Val as if she had never woken up, but was walking in the dim spacetime of dreams, so that these men might stamp into the outer hallway at any second. But they had died out there. Scott had taken five men on the last leg instead of four, and they had died. If he had sent Seaman Evans back with Lieutenant Evans, all might have been well. That close to survival; one decision; eleven miles out of sixteen hundred. And yet they scorned Scott for his incompetence, they made fun of him. He who had hauled a sledge all that way, and almost made it. One bad call was all it took. No one to fly in to the rescue.

Now her group sat or stood wandering the room, chilling down in the grey light. The matted reindeer hair of the sleeping bags looked woefully inadequate. Val went back around the corner and sat on Wilson's cot. She stared at Scott's empty bed. She had misjudged these men; she had taken other people's casual, superior judgements and accepted them. As if the people who had lived before them in time were somehow smaller because they had lived earlier. Looking through the wrong end of a telescope and saying, *But they're all so small.* Following their footsteps and then thinking that what they had done was as pointless as following in people's footsteps. As if they had not been as intelligent and cultured as any living human, and in many ways far more capable. Walk sixteen hundred miles in Antarctica and then judge them, she thought drowsily, head resting back against the wooden wall. She heard the voices of her group as the conversation of those odd Brits, those strait-laced young men, strong animals, complex simplicities, running away from Edwardian reality to create their own. Say it was an escape, say it was Peter Pan; why not? Why not? Why conform to Edwardian reality, why march into the trenches to die without a whimper? In this little room they had made their world. The first Antarctic chapter of the Why Be Normal Club. Happy at the return of some distant party which had been out of touch for weeks or months, out there on one crazed journey after another, pointless and absurd – the pure existentialism of Antarctica, where they made reality, or at least its every meaning. The pathetic fallacy of the Edwardians or the pathetic accuracy of the postmoderns; nothing much to choose between them; certainly no priority, either of heroic precedence or omniscient subsequence. Just people down here, doing things. Flinging themselves out into the spaces they breathed, to live, to really live, in this their one brief life in the world. They had been in no one's footsteps.

CHAPTER THIRTEEN

The McMurdo Convergence

blue sky
black water

The clouds broke up and blew off to the north. Between the last low, white stragglers the sun shone brightly, burnishing the grey interior of the hut. Wade followed the others outdoors into the sun, and blinked up at Erebus. Offshore the sea ice was gone, and waves lined the water. Hungrily Wade gazed at the open sea, at movement in the landscape, such a relief after all the days of snow and ice. The ocean here was black even though the sky overhead was blue; he had never seen anything like it.

A while later a fast fat-rimmed rubber motorboat came slushing out of the sun-blasted water to the south, and beached below them in a surge of floating ice chunks. The three-person crew of the boat did not appear surprised at Val's group; their manner made it clear that in the last week they had picked up so many groups in trouble around the shores of the Ross Sea that search and rescue was nothing to them any more; they were worldly now, and jaded. No one had died, they said, as far as they knew. But there had been a lot of close calls.

So the nine said quick goodbyes to Scott and his men, locked up the Cape Evans hut, piled into the boat with their nearly-empty day-sacks, and off they went purring over the black water. Through the steep riven Dellbridge Islands, past the broken stub of the Erebus Ice Tongue. To the left soared steaming Erebus. To the right, across the black water, the Western Mountains stood two or three times their usual height, raised by a *fata morgana* into a kind of fantasy range, the super-Himalaya of Ice Planet.

Wade sat in the bow of the Zodiac, looking around. He was tired, vibrated, spaced out. A bitter wind blew splinters of sunshine. Antarctica had never looked so surreal to him, so sublime; whether this was because he was on the last leg of his adventure or because of the intrinsic beauty of the scene was hard to say. He felt both detached and absorbed at the same time; happy in some Buddhist sense: desiring nothing. Clarified. The buzz of the craft's engine was loud enough to allow him to hum at full volume without anyone else hearing him, and so without thought or choice he happily hummed his soundtrack to the scene, the music buzzing in him as if transmitted by the landscape, as if he were a mere radio receiver – the end of Beethoven's 131 quartet, then the bass phrase from the Ghost Trio and the Ninth that Berlioz had termed the work of a madman, Wade humming it over and over again and feeling more glorious the more glorious he felt, the muscular tunes bouncing along with the boat over the low waves, melodies so stuffed with meaning that they were landscapes in themselves, landscapes very like the one they hummed through now, vast and clear and clean of line. Could they live up to the greatness of these tunes, to the greatness of this planet, so vast and beautiful?

As they skimmed in toward the hollow end of Hut Point, overrun with McMurdo's clutter of buildings, Wade found himself uncertain. The court was still out, no doubt about it. But the tunes kept fountaining out of him. A sort of plan was beginning to take shape in his mind.

They passed a big chunk of broken sea ice, a flat iceberg almost awash in the waves. A crowd of Adélie penguins was standing on it watching the Zodiac pass, some waving their flippers. Wade waved back at them. He saw that other penguins were shooting up out of the water and landing on their stomachs on the ice, sliding over it like big hockey pucks and sometimes colliding with other penguins already up there. Sudden explosions of sundrenched water, and then a slick, gleaming penguin suspended in the air over the ice; yet another Escher moment to add to the rest, fish-to-bird, metamorphosis. Wade laughed to see it.

McMurdo now looked like a big town to him, a metropolis, as big and tawdry as any freeway strip in the United States. No; hard to feel the glory there. Hard not to feel a sense of diminution, looking back at the *fata morgana* to the west, and then forward to Mac Town. He would have to work out how to hold to this moment of grace.

The pilot idled in to the dock, the crew tied the Zodiac to the clews. The members of the expedition stepped back into Little America.

Each reality is followed by one stranger than the last. After this trip away, which had lasted only – well – Wade was too tired to calculate it, but it couldn't have been more than a week or so – the sheer weirdness of McMurdo shot in his eyes like the over-exposed sunlight, image after image knocking him back on his heels. Scott's Discovery hut, looking much like the Cape Evans hut, dwarfed and empty out on its point beyond the docks and the mall. The buildings of the little town scattered over the volcanic rubble, all of it snow-plastered by the recent storm; but the snow was thawing at this very moment, and all the streets were filled with frozen runnels of ice-crusted mud.

The Zodiac crew led the nine travellers into a big building at the back of the docks, next to the mini-mall. Inside, a group of US Navy officers greeted them with paper cups of hot chocolate and coffee, asked them to sit down on folding chairs, and with tape recorders and clipboards ran through their story, asking question after question. The travellers answered everything as clearly as they could, told them the whole story, though it was clear from the inconsistencies, repetitions and confusions that they were tired. But the Navy men were business-like and friendly, and soon they were hustling Jack into a pick-up truck for a ride up to the medical clinic for a check-up on his shoulder and general condition. The others they asked apologetically to check in at the Chalet, where Sylvia and her team would ask them many of the same questions before they could go to their rooms and get some rest. Those of them who had given up their room on leaving for their trip were given keys to new rooms, and off they went.

Beeker Street, Crary Lab, the Chalet. The eight remaining travellers slowed, then bunched in the muddy open area above the Chalet.

Wade turned to Val, who was looking around at the town as spaced as any of them, or more so. 'Why don't I go check in at the Chalet for us, and tell them the rest of you will come down after you've had a chance to clean up.'

'Sure,' Val said.

Ta Shu was circling slowly, baffled. 'This place,' he said. Jorge and Elspeth headed toward Hotel California. X led Carlos off to the BFC. Jim took off for the Holiday Inn. Wade drifted over to the Chalet, climbed laboriously the steps onto the porch. He looked back; without further ado the group that had travelled together so far, the group that had huddled on Shackleton Glacier bare to the storm, had dissipated in all directions.

Wade pulled back the heavy door of the Chalet. Inside things looked just as they had when he had last seen them, and he realized ruefully that he had expected everything everywhere to be changed.

But of course not. Paxman led him across the main room to Sylvia's office. She was standing behind her desk, listening to a short man speak to her in a low voice. She saw Wade and waved him into the office without ever taking her attention from this man, who talked on in a low monotone, not acknowledging Wade's appearance with even a glance. Something in Sylvia's look told Wade that she had been listening to him for quite some time.

'My clients are not associated with Earthfirst! or the Sea Shepherds or the Arctic Peoples' Defence League, or the Antarctic World Park Emergency Rescue Action, or the Voluntary Human Extinction Movement, or any of the mainstream environmental groups, or any of the underground groups.'

'Okay,' Sylvia said. 'Who are they then?'

'They don't tell me,' the man replied levelly. 'They've given me to know that they are private individuals, of no affiliation, who have decided to practise civil disobedience and direct action in the form of targeted non-lethal ecotage, to resist and hopefully bring to an end all transgressions of the Antarctic Treaty, which was until its expiration the only law this continent had. They feel that the other environmentalist groups allied with their cause can provide the arguments, the legalities, the publicity, and all the rest of the apparatus of resistance, and their function is to take direct action, and then to stay out of sight and remain undiscovered. In this particular case only, they've gone so far as to hire me to speak for them here to you, because none of the other groups they contacted would agree to do that.'

Sylvia looked at him closely; Wade would not have wanted to be on the receiving end of that flinty gaze. She could not have been at all happy that the Navy was back in town, Wade thought. And this man was representing the people who had got them there.

The man did not seem to notice her gaze. Sylvia said, 'Mr Smith, this is Wade Norton, an assistant to Senator Chase from California.'

'Hello,' Mr Smith said, shaking Wade's hand. 'I admire many of the things Senator Chase has done.'

Sylvia nodded, as if to say, Of course. 'Wade, this is Mr Smith. He has shown up here in McMurdo by sea, unannounced.'

'I came privately,' Mr Smith explained. 'I'm from Smith, Jones and Robinson, environmental law.'

'I see,' Wade said.

'Wade has been out in the field, and I believe he has witnessed the impact of your clients' actions. Is that right, Wade?'

Wade nodded. 'We survived,' he said.

Mr Smith was dressed in standard trekker's garb, which meant he was too warm in the Chalet. In spite of the prisming blue photovoltaic suit he looked innocuous, like a small-town lawyer; he had so well practised the semiotics of the non-confrontational that he had become nearly invisible. A puppet only, his appearance said; a spokesman for

345

his clients and that was all; no views of his own, no thinking, nothing but a medium of transmission, like a walking telephone, or a microwave signal repeater.

Of course that had to be a front, and a front Wade was quite familiar with; in fact it was a popular style in Washington these days, usually practised by very sharp lawyers indeed. He said, 'How do you communicate with your clients?'

'I'm not at liberty to say. I can say I have never met any of them in person.'

'So some of them might be down here among us, and you wouldn't know.'

'That's correct.'

'I might be one of them, and you wouldn't know.'

'That's correct.'

The bland little man looked closely at Wade for the first time, as if trying to ascertain whether this were the case.

Wade thought it over. He said to Sylvia, 'Senator Chase has suggested to me that since we have all the players involved in the recent events here at hand, you might consider meeting to discuss the issues involved openly, with the idea of making a report to the investigators who no doubt are on their way to join us, or already here.'

'Most of them will get here tomorrow, weather permitting,' Sylvia said. 'The storms have held them up in Christchurch.'

'The Senator wonders if we could even make some recommendations for future policy which would help to avoid any repetitions of incidents like this one. And I think Mr Smith's presence here means this meeting could have even wider representation than Senator Chase imagined. I could also invite some friends into town to participate as well – the people who helped us get back here.'

'Ferals?' Sylvia asked sharply.

'Why yes,' Wade said. 'So you do know about them.'

She met his gaze calmly. 'I've heard rumours. I'd be interested to hear what they had to say. I've tried to make contact with them before. But never any reply.'

'No. But now they may be willing to come in. Given what has happened.'

Sylvia nodded, thinking it over.

'If anything positive is to come out of all this,' Wade said, 'it will have to happen here, I think. Up north it will sink into the mass of everything else.'

'Possibly,' Sylvia said. 'Although SCAR, and the Treaty negotiating committee, and now it looks like a UN committee, will all be considering the matter, along with our Congress and other governments.'

'No doubt. But the fuller our report, the more they'll have to work with.'

'My clients would welcome such a meeting,' Mr Smith said.

'How do you know?' Wade and Sylvia said together.

Mr Smith returned their stares blandly. The role of the spokesperson was an ambiguous one, as Wade very well knew, having just put words into Phil Chase's mouth. Walking telephone or mastermind? There was no way to tell.

'Have you gotten all stranded parties back to safety?' Wade asked Sylvia. 'I mean, is it appropriate to start holding such a meeting?'

Sylvia nodded. 'S–375 have been heloed back from the Dry Valleys, and I've just heard from Palmer and Patriot Hills that all the affected oil personnel have been recovered. Everyone's in.'

'Nobody was hurt by my clients' actions,' Mr Smith noted.

'That was luck,' Wade said. 'That was sheer luck, I can tell you that personally. If it weren't for the help of people your clients don't even know about, a good number of us would have died. Destroying life-support systems on the polar cap is very, very dangerous. Reckless endangerment at the very least.'

'Nevertheless,' Mr Smith said. 'The fact remains.'

'Let's not get into that now,' Sylvia said. 'The fact is that Mr Smith's clients committed serious criminal acts, very dangerous to people down here, and that will be taken into account I'm sure.' She looked at the man. 'I hope you're prepared to answer for what these clients of yours have done, Mr Smith. It could come to contempt of court and more, I imagine, if you choose to shield them from the law.'

'I've never been cited for contempt, and don't plan to be now,' Mr Smith said. 'Of course I'm prepared for anything. I brought my toothbrush.'

Sylvia and Wade looked at each other.

'I have to get cleaned up,' Wade said. 'Get some food, and see if I can contact the ferals. And talk to the Senator.' Or not. He too was a spokesperson. You're the senator, as they kept saying at the Pole. Or wherever it had been.

Sylvia said, 'I'll talk to some of the others. Let's meet again after dinner with whomever is available, for starters. As you say, there's no time to lose.'

Val kicked the muddy snow off her boots and stamped up the stairs of dorm 308, then dragged down the hall to her room on the top floor. She opened the door and went inside, and sat down heavily on the bed. Everything in its place, same as always. A functional little space, like a ship's cabin. It appeared that Georgia, her roommate for the season, was out on a trip of her own; her bags were gone, her wardrobe doors shut. They had barely even met.

She felt utterly drained. Hollow. McMurdo looked terrible. Her trekking group had dispersed with barely a word, off to dorm or hotel, no plans for a final dinner together that night, nothing. She had got them all home after losing the sledge in the crevasse, but it hadn't really been her doing. If it weren't for the ferals Jack very possibly would have died on Shackleton Glacier, and none of them could be sure they would have survived that storm; weather said it was still going strong out there. Besides, *back home without anyone dead* wasn't exactly how you wanted to characterize a trip, given that it had been an expedition undertaken for pleasure. There needed to be more than 'Got home alive'.

Better luck next time, she always said to herself after the bad trips. There were bad ones and good ones. There had been good trips too. And there would be more of them in the future. No doubt about it.

Still she couldn't shake the low feeling. Post-expedition blues, sleep deprivation, polar T–3 syndrome, whatever; she felt bad. Just on the edge of tears. It was a mood she hated. Whenever she saw it coming she fought it tooth and claw, she would not allow it. The antidote was action. She stood up and left the room, which at this moment seemed a black trap. She pulled on her parka and stumped back down the metal stairs at the end of the dorm, went back outside into the bitter wind.

Funky old Mac Town. There was nowhere to go. She was weary to the bone, her muscles stiff and sore – a feeling she usually liked, but not now. It had gone beyond that. She was hungry but the galley was closed. She went to the Chalet but it was after hours, and Sylvia and Wade had already left. There would be friends to talk to at the BFC, although they would no doubt still be busy sorting out the mess caused by the ecoteurs.

But by now the Erebus View would be open. She walked past the Holiday Inn and up the stairs to the private restaurant, stomach growling, almost faint with hunger. She walked through the door, into an ambrosia of food smells. Looked around for an empty table.

And there were Jim and Jack and Jorge and Elspeth, having dinner. Jack saw her and quickly looked away, scowling. Elspeth saw him turn his head, and glanced over her shoulder: 'Oh hi Val,' riding over any awkwardness, 'come join us.'

But Jack was glowering still, and after glancing at him, Jim would not meet her eye. Elspeth and Jorge, necks craned to look at Val over their booth back, didn't see the other two.

Val waved a hand: 'I'm looking for Joyce right now, I've got to talk to her. I'll come back and catch you for dessert maybe.' And she retreated out of the restaurant.

Standing outside in the chill of McMurdo. Cloud shadows flitting through town. Blindly she stamped down the street behind the docks, helplessly thinking of all the bad expeditions she had ever been on, the ones people had walked away from furious or ashamed or sick at heart. It happened, oh yes it happened; under the stress of some of these radical endeavours people cracked, and the truth came out. And sometimes it was ugly. That ugly scowl on Jack's face – Val had seen it before. One time she had been on the receiving end of that look for a whole week, on the ship returning them to the Falklands from South Georgia Island, after the worst ever *In the Wake of Shackleton* expedition.

It had been one of the groups that had worn period clothing, a particularly crazy idea when repeating the boat journey, as the stuff the old guys had worn was ridiculously inadequate, and the re-enactors could not have been more soaked, cold and miserable. If they had been in a boat like the *James Caird* they would have died many times over; and even though their twenty-two foot, ultra-modern boat had resembled a floating submarine more than Shackleton's little lifeboat of the same length, and thus kept them afloat even in horrifying seas, it had still been a complete nightmare: everyone seasick, always lost unless they turned on the emergency GPS, cold and wet in the terrible gear, hurting with an accumulation of injuries as the result of being hammered relentlessly by huge waves. By the time they made their GPS-aided landfall on South Georgia Island, they were all wasted.

With the hardest part yet to go. For Shackleton and his men had been forced to land on the west side of the island, when all the Norwegian whaling stations were on the east side. And the island was a mountain range sticking up out of the South Atlantic.

Shackleton and Worsley and Crean had made it over, however, and Val's three clients were stubbornly determined to do the same. So they had set off from King Haakon Bay to make the thirty-six-mile crossing of the island's spine in a single push. It was a long way given the shape they were in, and over a steep range five thousand feet high, no small height when both ends of the trip were at sea level, and the island right in the Furious Fifties storm track. And they were minimally equipped for the hike, carrying only what Shackleton and Worsley and Crean had carried in 1916. It was a radical trip; a real test.

As they ascended and began to cross the island's high, empty glaciers, however, struggling through deep snow, Eve had begun to tire fast. She had been the most seasick on the boat journey, and it became clear that she just didn't have any fuel left in the tank. The two men were almost as weak, and even Val was not feeling the usual dynamo effect that a hard hike had on her; it really hurt to give it her usual push. So they were in bad shape as they approached the crux of the journey, a ridge called the Trident directly blocking their way. There were four high passes to choose from, between the five tines, so to speak. Shackleton and Worsley and Crean had started at the right and climbed up to each of the passes in turn, looking down the other side of each and finding them cliffs too steep to descend; then traversing under the towers to the next pass, each time with a terrible effort.

Without discussion Val's group gave up on following this precise route and went straight for the fourth pass, the one Shackleton and his men had finally forced their way over. By the time they got close, the weather was degenerating. They had no tent or sleeping bags with them, and little food or clothing. And darkness was coming on fast, with the strong possibility of losing the moonlight to cloud cover, and perhaps even being stormed in. And then on the final approach to the pass, very steep even on that side, Eve had slipped and had to be arrested by Val, and in the jolt Eve somehow twisted her ankle pretty badly.

So when they finally reached the fourth pass, it had been a horrible shock to look over the other side and find that the slope there was insanely steep. The drop fell away so sharply that there was a big section in the middle they couldn't see at all, which could have been a sheer cliff for all they could tell. The precipice only levelled off a full two thousand feet below them.

Shackleton, a careful man, had only decided to risk descending this slope because at that point they had no other choice. The three had therefore sat down in a line on their rope, legs around the man in front, and fired down the slope on their bottoms; two thousand feet in a matter of seconds, a drop that certainly could have killed them, as they had no idea what the hidden section below them would bring. Worsley said later he had never been more scared in his life, and he had done a lot of scary things. But they had lived.

Now, looking down this cliff, Eve had lost it. She refused to try the jump. This is crazy, she cried, this is *crazy*. Snow conditions might be different now, it might be icier! This must not be the right pass, we must have read the map wrong! We'll be killed going down this!

Entirely possible. But this was the right pass, and it was getting dark, and a storm was coming. And they had gone so far that the only way out was forward – an all-too-common mountaineers' dilemma. And Eve was shivering as well as crying, going into shock perhaps from her fall and the twisted ankle. And they had no tent, nor much food – yes, they were in the same fix as Shackleton – this was the plan after all, to put themselves in the same fix! They had engineered it this way! They too had no choice.

But Eve refused. Her boyfriend Mike begged her to try, he yelled at her; she yelled back at him, crying harder; their friend Brett tried to reason with her, but got nowhere. Whimpering in straightforward animal fear of death, she refused to make the leap. And while they sat there arguing it got darker and darker, and they were chilling down in a truly dangerous way.

Finally Val had snapped. She said, 'Look we've *got* to do this,' and grabbed up Eve, who kicked and screamed like a child in a tantrum, and pulled her around in front of her and jumped over the cornice, shouting back at Mike and Brett to do the same.

The slide quickly accelerated to something like free fall. Val crushed Eve to her hard, and they skidded down on Val's backside, airborne at times, going faster and faster until Val was sure they were doomed; it would only take one rock in their path. But they never caught on a rock, never lost balance and tumbled into a bone-shattered bloody mass . . . And some timeless interval later, probably less than a minute, they skidded out onto flat, thick snow at the bottom of the slope and came to a halt. Mike and Brett arrived seconds later. Val's pants were shredded, her legs and bottom bloodied.

After that they had had to help Eve, who was crying helplessly all the while; one on each side of her taking turns, though mostly it was Mike and Brett who did that, while Val found the way in the dark, through most of that night. And they reached Stromness just before a giant storm hammered the island.

Great adventure. But Eve never spoke to her again.

Now Val looked around McMurdo, remembering Jack's quick look away at the restaurant table, his scowl. Or that wounded look, when he was hunched out on the ice. She had done it again.

'I am not a good guide,' she told the empty town. 'I am toast.'

Even though she was very near tears, the word *toast* reminded her of how hungry she still was. She moved off shakily toward the BFC. She could break into a box of camp crackers there, and hear stories of the other SARs of the last week, and huddle over the space heater to try to get herself warm. 'I am the coldest burnt toast in town,' she said, and stopped and let herself cry for a minute before going on.

'Hello, Phil?'

'Yeah, who is it? Wade is that you? Where are you?'

'It's me, Phil. I'm in Antarctica.'

'*Where?* Oh yeah. I was asleep, Wade.'

'Good.'

'What's that you say?'

'Were you dreaming, Phil? What were you dreaming about?'

'What? What's this, you call me up to wake me to ask me what I'm dreaming about?'

'You've had me do that a lot, remember?'

'Yes – no – I'm not having you do that now, am I?'

'You don't remember what you were dreaming about?'

'Well, let's see. Let me think. No, I guess it's gone. Wait, something about bicycling. No, it was a unicycle. I was riding a unicycle down the Capitol steps, that was it – no, the Lincoln Memorial, because I could see the Capitol down the Mall. People were there like I was giving a speech, a big crowd, giant, but actually I wasn't giving a speech, I was unicycling up and down the steps, making the hops in both directions and getting a lot of applause. It was great. No one could figure out how I was hopping back up the steps, and I couldn't either. It was mystifying but fun. All the Republicans I like were there going *Shit, Phil, how are we gonna beat that when you can hop up steps on a unicycle?*'

'Mark and Colin?'

'Yeah, they were pissed. Then all the Republicans I hate were down there getting tossed in the reflecting pools.'

'A crowd scene.'

'Like the guppie tank at the pet store. I was planning to ride the unicycle right across their backs once they were all in, keeping my balance no matter what they did. Then you woke me up. Bummer, that was going to be fun.'

'You enjoy your dreams, don't you Phil?'

'I do, yeah. Unless I don't. But most dreams are wish-fulfilment fantasies, I think you'll find.'

'Maybe for you. Mine are usually terribly complex problems I can't possibly solve.'

'That's too bad, Wade. I'm sorry to hear that.'

'Thanks. So where are you now?'

'I'm in Kirghiz, I think. Yes. I'm seeing the Kirghiz light.'

'Very nice. Well. I should let you go back to sleep.'

'I'd like that, Wade.'

'All right. Thanks for calling, Phil.'

'You're welcome.'

'Oh, and by the way, just one thing?'

'. . . yeah?'

'I'm going to make some suggestions and the like down here in your name in the next day or two, Phil, I'm just going to go into ambassador mode because things are moving so fast here and I'm not sure I'm going to have time to check with you but I want to use your name as if everything I suggest is coming from you okay? Is that okay?'

'How is this different from the way we usually operate?'

'It isn't, I just wanted to confirm.'

'Confirmed. Night night.'

'Night Phil.'

The Antarctic Treaty had always been a fragile thing, a complex of gossamer and blown glass which had spun in the light of history like a beautiful mobile – a utopian project actually enacted in the real world, a model for how people ought to be treating the land everywhere – until it got caught in the pressures of the new century, and at the first good torque shattered into a thousand pieces.

Now Sylvia presided over the wreckage, hoping still to patch it back together. She was operating on as big a sleep deficit as anyone in town, perhaps even the largest of all; she had spent almost every hour of the crisis in her office or up at Search and Rescue, trying to deal with the multiple emergencies. It had been a troubleshooter's nightmare. But at the same time, a part of her began to think (no doubt the part most affected by sleep deprivation) that it was also the ultimate troubleshooter's challenge, or even an opportunity: not just to keep plugging away at the succession of little stopgaps that formed her ordinary work, but actually to consider the rehaul of everything.

She stood at the front of the big central room of the Chalet, watching people file in. A lot of people wanted to talk to her, and she had told them all to come on over to the Chalet. She was curious to hear them, in part to help her to clarify her own thinking about the situation. What would happen next, what should happen next? Without laws, without sovereignty, without a military, without police, without economy, without autonomy, without sufficiency – without any of the properties needed in the world to make life real ... It was as if they were a small group of travellers in space, marooned on Ice Planet and now forced to invent everything from scratch.

Except that the world was still there, of course. Sylvia had been juggling calls from all over the place, now that communications were restored; most importantly from NSF's head offices in Virginia, asking for a quick accounting of the last week, identification of the ecoteurs if possible, and, luckily for her, any recommendations she might have for avoiding such events in the future. Also, the home office clearly wanted to contain the problem as much as she did, to minimize it and declare it an isolated anomaly, a sport in biological terms, so that the military was not called back in for good, and the Antarctic taken out of NSF's hands. All perfectly appropriate in Sylvia's opinion; but one Navy plane had made it down already, at great risk, and a big task force would soon follow to investigate the ecotage, naturally; and what would happen then was anyone's guess. The big storm (inevitably termed a superstorm in the US popular press) had stalled all these outsiders in Christchurch, however, and so she had this little window of opportunity to conduct her own investigation.

Now here they were, filing into the big room. The ASL managers;

Geoff Michelson and some of his colleagues, just returned from the Dry Valleys; several Kiwis from Scott Base; Ta Shu; Mr Smith; Wade Norton; Carlos and X, and some of Carlos's colleagues from the SCAG consortium; Val and some of her clients. Others were standing in the loft or in the offices off the main room. The Chalet had seldom seen such a crowd.

'Thanks for coming,' Sylvia said. 'We're here to discuss what's happened in the past week, to see if we can make any recommendations to our various contacts in the north concerning where we might go from here, and how we can avoid any repetitions of this kind of thing. My notion is to conduct it like a small and informal scientific conference, with short presentations followed by questions and discussion, with the hope that at the end we could perhaps collaborate on a general statement. This of course will all be merely an addendum to the full official investigations, but I hope it will be useful. Ta Shu has suggested that for a meeting like this we should move our chairs into a circle formation, so that we can all see each other when we're talking – among other no doubt valid reasons,' waving Ta Shu down, 'and I think that's a good idea, it will save us craning our necks to see who's talking. So why don't we do that first, and then begin.'

When they were rearranged in a rough circle, chairs all the way back to the walls, everyone able to see everyone else, Sylvia went on. 'Mr Smith here has arrived privately by boat, and he says he represents the, the ecoteurs who disrupted operations here and in various outlying camps. Without granting him priority, or in any way legitimating those attacks – in fact I condemn them here and now as criminal, dangerous and useless – still I think we might start by hearing what Mr Smith has to say concerning their actions.'

Mr Smith nodded and rose to his feet. 'My clients are private individuals, allied in some senses with the Antarctic World Park Emergency Rescue Action, and with more than a hundred other mainstream and grassroots environmental groups concerned at the non-renewal of the Antarctic Treaty and the flagrant violations of its principles in the last two years. Other than that my clients wish to remain anonymous. They undertook to temporarily impair certain of the most egregious examples of Treaty breaking, to protest these operations and draw the world's attention to them. They wish no harm to anyone, they took great pains to insure that no one would be injured or killed, and they were successful in that goal, for which they are thankful, aware that in Antarctic the destruction of property will always bring some risk to life.'

'That's for damn sure,' someone said, among other various mutterings. There were a lot of fierce looks directed at Mr Smith from Carlos's

355

contingent especially, but Sylvia kept her focus on him, and he looked at her as he continued, oblivious to the others.

'Now of course they are aware that they are the subjects of a vast manhunt on the part of governmental authorities, and this does not surprise them, but they would like to point out that this is typical of law enforcement, to pursue very vigorously individuals performing civil disobedience or other protest actions, while allowing hundreds or even thousands of corporate executives to comprehensively break the laws without obstruction, or even with so-called law enforcement's help and protection. Corporations and governments from many countries have been despoiling this last wilderness continent in complete contempt for international law, and so for the US Navy and the FBI now to come here searching for my clients is a travesty, the equivalent of arresting the protesters of a crime while the criminals stand right at hand. It makes them not a police but rather a private security force, which might as well take its pay directly from the foreign governments and transnational corporations it is serving. As private security for corporations it makes sense to overlook gross malfeasance while brutally pursuing small individual protest actions, which to corporations are indeed the more dangerous of the two. The small spontaneous protests of individuals suggests after all that democracy might be a real thing, rather than just a cover story told to people to keep them in their places in the economic hierarchy. And of course the idea that democracy might be real is much too dangerous a notion to allow it to spread very far, for if it did, and if everyone acted on truly democratic principles, including protesting obvious crimes against the law, then social control would be impossible and the gross inequities of the current economic order, in which five percent of the world's population own ninety percent of the world's wealth, would be revealed for the hypocritical environment-devastating injustice that it is. Democracy in the United States and most of the rest of the industrial West is therefore a false front on a rich man's mansion, a sham in which people are given a political vote but then clock in each day to an economic system in which their entire lives are regimented by a small group of executives busily downsizing whatever workplace rights people had gained in centuries of struggle. So people can vote, yes, but for politicians all funded by the corporations in control of the system, meaning you can either vote for the part of the owner class that believes in treating its employees well, or for the part that believes in taking as much as possible from its employees, but in any case you have to vote for the continuation of the system and therefore of the owner class. So the right to vote is meaningless. And in such a situation, a non-democratic situation, civil disobedience and direct non-lethal resistance are the only true options to co-optation within the owner system. And thus as the only true options for resistance these are of course ruthlessly extirpated by the authorities wherever they appear, with the idea of discouraging the spread of protest by rank intimidation. And in the past this has usually worked, for very few want their lives shattered in order to protest an injustice that is massively entrenched and made to appear the natural order of things, and unlikely to fall to any individual act.

'So the only answer at this point is to use modern technology to act at a distance, and with perfect anonymity. And that is the course my clients have taken. The way they have structured their action makes it impossible for them to be identified, and you can be sure that I will keep their confidentiality, not only as a matter of legal ethics but also from the practical consideration that I myself do not know who they are. I only know that they wish to announce to you that in the current state of materials science, and the balkanization of communication technology, the means now exist to act in ways that encrypt and sequester the identity of the actors so watertightly that no one will ever know who they were. And this will be true in future protest actions as well, if they happen. That being the case, the views of the disenfranchised are going to have to be listened to again, and the environment and the world's disenfranchised people are going to have to be re-enfranchised by the dominant order, which is going to have to change, or else anonymous and untraceable non-violent protests and ecotage will crash the system. The last week in Antarctica is an announcement and demonstration of this fact.'

He paused to take a breath and Sylvia held up a hand. 'Thank you Mr Smith! Perhaps we can give someone else a chance to speak now, in response perhaps for a moment or two, and then we'll get back to you.'

'Fine,' Mr Smith said, unperturbed. He sat down.

'Carlos? You and your colleagues in the Southern Club Antarctic Group were the people most affected by Mr Smith's clients' ecotage. Would you like to make a response to Mr Smith's, um, remarks?'

Carlos popped to his feet. 'My pleasure to speak! Contrary to what Mr Smith has been saying, although there are some of his general remarks that I can agree with, there is no question that our oil and gas exploration, and the extraction of oil and methane hydrates from the polar cap, is both legal and environmentally safe!'

He waved a finger at Mr Smith, who was a most unlikely-looking object of anyone's scorn. 'The Antarctic Treaty forbade mineral exploration, yes, but Japan and Russia never ratified the 1991 environmental protocol, and oil companies based in Treaty countries have looked for oil anyway. And now the Antarctic Treaty has expired and renewal has been held up, as everyone knows, mostly because of opposition to the Treaty from corporations based in the United States, using their allies in the American government to hold off approval of the Treaty until it has been altered to allow some exploration rights to *them*. So for the last two years we have been operating in a vacuum. And the Southern Club Antarctic Group, a group composed of nations in the southern hemisphere who never signed the Antarctic Treaty, and were never invited to join the Treaty conferences – they decided unanimously to pursue the path of clean extraction of important resources, especially methane hydrates, whenever this was deemed technically possible without harming the Antarctic environment in any way. There has been some protest from environmentalist groups in the North about this policy, but these protests come from nations who are using up the world's resources at five to twenty times the rate of the members of the Southern Club Antarctic Group, so I personally feel that it is very presumptuous for these people of the North to protest when in effect the North has historically conquered the South, taken everything portable back to the North with them, destroyed the Southern landscape and left the people of the South in misery, thus prospering so greatly that they can afford to have an upper class at leisure to order the environmental ethics of the countries that they have so shattered and left behind! The hypocrisy of the North, on this as on so many other issues, is *endless*, and beyond defence. It has beggared our language. It is the major fact in the history of the world in the last five centuries, colonialism that has never really ended, but merely changed formats.'

Mr Smith said, 'The risk of oil extraction–'

'No no no no no! The risk has been made *so small*,' Carlos exclaimed, squeezing his finger and thumb together till they went white, 'so *very* small, as to be completely insignificant in the real world! This is what modern extraction technology allows, as we have explained to anyone prepared to listen. If we had not been *bombed* nothing bad ever would have *happened*. This isn't the twentieth century after all. There has not been a significant oil spill in the last thirty years, and this is not because of chance, but because the technology and procedures employed by the oil industry have made them a thing of the past.'

'Panama Canal,' Mr Smith said. 'San Francisco. Djakarta.'

'Those were all *sabotage*!' Carlos cried, hopping up and down a little to try to contain himself. 'These were spills because of your clients, not because of us!'

'My clients were involved in none of these incidents,' Mr Smith said quickly.

'How can you be sure,' Wade asked, 'if you don't know who they are?'

'I asked them.'

'People like your clients,' Carlos went on, grimacing, 'are people driving around the industrial North in their BMWs dreaming of killing tigers with their teeth and eating them raw and then telling the rest of us what to do, it is the most *ridiculous fantasy possible*: there are ten billion people on this Earth and half of them are starving, and it is not some rich well-fed aristocrat son-of-a-bitch hunter-gatherer Disneyland wilderness advocate that is going to feed those people or their children! We have to provide them with food and the energy to make food and shelter and clothing and schools and hospitals and *you cannot do it* with your deep ecology wilderness dream. I hate you hypocrites for this holier-than-thou anti-human nonsense!'

Mr Smith replied calmly, 'Oil men always hate environmentalists. It means nothing except that your own brain has been overdetermined by your structured position in the global hierarchy. In fact you can't sustainably provide energy and food and clothing, and the other means of existence, without the Earth. It is not the values of deep ecology that are causing the problem, but the exploitative economy of a world system in which a tiny aristocracy-of-the-wealthy stripmines the world's natural and human resources, and retreats with the loot to its fortress mansions and islands, leaving the rest to survive as we may in the wreckage they have escaped. This is Götterdämmerung capitalism, this is our moment, and just as you say colonialism never ended, this feudalism has never ended, and it has nothing whatever to do with the so-called democratic values used to palliate the masses. Indeed all the armies of the world are now employed in enforcing this system against any group that takes the idea of democracy seriously.'

'There was nothing democratic about this sabotage,' Carlos said. 'There are just a few of these ecoteurs, and most people condemn what they do, but they do it anyway. If they were for democracy they would have abided by the majority view on the matter, and people want electricity, they want light at night, they want refrigeration so their children don't get sick from bad food.'

Mr Smith pursed his lips, his most violent expression so far. 'If sufficiency were the true goal then the world's needs could be met and more, using current and emerging technologies. It's economic growth and the enrichment of the feudalist-capitalist aristocracy that are the true goals of this society, and the masses do not truly go along with these goals which are against their own interests, but are rather intimidated to accept what they can in an unjust system, or else be fired or jailed or shot. Thus my clients encourage widespread democratic resistance to the current destruction of the Earth, in which a few hundred thousand people benefit excessively while billions suffer, and the coming generations handed a scorched and plundered world.'

'Speaking more particularly,' Sylvia suggested.

'Antarctica is the last clean wilderness,' Mr Smith pounced. 'As such it stands for what we could do if we lived in a right balance with nature.'

'Antarctica is clean because no one lives here!' Carlos said. 'It's easy to be pure when there are no people around. For the rest of the world, the best possible strategies have to be followed to keep people alive.'

'Gentlemen,' Sylvia said, looking hard at Carlos and Mr Smith. 'We could perhaps debate general principles for ever. I'd like to hear what happens if we keep our discussion focused on Antarctica in particular.' She glanced at Geoff, hoping for some help there; but he was staring into infinity, deep in the Pliocene no doubt.

'But they are discussing Antarctica,' Ta Shu said. He had been watching the argument as if at a tennis match, head swivelling from side to side, nodding at both speakers with what looked like complete and total approval. Now he said, 'People here talk about the ice and the world. As if here we are not in the world. But this is not so. To speak of this place truly, we must bring in everything else. And so these gentlemen are not wrong to speak generally. What they say is simply the basic problem of our time – that the Earth must be allowed to live, while at the same time people must be fed. One emphasizes one, another emphasizes the other. But both must be done.'

'My clients are not just advocating park status for Antarctica,' said Mr Smith. 'The whole world must be treated as a wilderness in which we have to live, with minimum impact everywhere.'

'Like in Manhattan,' Carlos said.

'Even Manhattan can be made a wilderness of a certain kind.'

'And even Antarctica can be inhabited,' said a short old woman by the door.

'Mai-lis!' Sylvia said, surprised. 'You've come to join us.'

Mai-lis walked into the room, into the circle of chairs. 'Yes. I am Mai-lis,' she said. 'My colleagues and I live in the Transantarctic Mountains.'

The people in the room stared at her, and she gathered their gazes calmly, like a story-teller readying her start by the fire at night. Sylvia extended a hand, as if to say Speak; and Mai-lis nodded.

'I am here to speak for my colleagues and friends, a group of Antarcticans who have decided to become indigenous to this place. Some call it going feral. It is a mixed-ideology project, in that we do it for different reasons, rising out of different value systems, and we do not always agree among ourselves. But in general terms, I can say that we take Antarctica to be a beautiful, sacred landscape, worthy of sacred-inhabitation, which is our word for a joyful or worshipful living in a land – to be the land's human expression and part of its consciousness, along with the rest of its animal and plant consciousnesses.

'To do this in such a harsh climate, it is necessary to use techniques and technologies from many times and places, from the Sami and Inuit and other Arctic indigenous peoples, to the best of communal social theory, to the latest appropriate technologies. We take what seems right to us, from the paleolithic to the postmodern, and most of us do not worry too much about purity. We live democratically. We think it's important to live off the land as much as possible, but sustainably, without harm to the land. In Antarctica this means keeping our numbers small, and helping the parts of the northern economies which we need to help us in turn. We regard our way of life as an experiment under extreme conditions. If it works here, it should work anywhere, as long as the number of people trying it is not too large for the land being lived on.'

'So you don't believe in the Antarctic Treaty either,' Wade suggested.

'We do. We live by the Treaty very specifically. We kill some animals for food, but we study them scientifically before we eat them, and thus we are in technical compliance with the Treaty. We agree with the goals of the Treaty. But most of us have no intrinsic objection to oil and gas extraction, if it is done with no impact to the environment. This is the question; how cleanly can these extractions be made? Can accidents be treated as criticalities? Can the engineering be made redundant to the point where the risks are negligible? And if that kind of engineering is applied, is the extraction still worth it to the extractors? These are questions that need to be answered. It is a matter of doing a true-cost true-benefit analysis, which is to say that all costs and benefits are included, including the so-called exterior costs, while the unpriceable aspects of the situation are also acknowledged and included. We are trying to do this in our own subsistence here, and we often talk about the feasibility of such accounting in the world generally. Environmentally safe technologies, green technologies, applied according to a humane green analysis of the costs and benefits of our various activities – calculating needs and wants, methods and technologies – this is necessary work for people everywhere. It occupies many an evening in our camps, around the table and at the computer. And most of us believe it can be done everywhere, if – and these are big ifs – if human populations were to decline, and if people were everywhere to go feral on the land.'

Sylvia sighed, and made a small steering gesture. 'Let's try to keep the focus on Antarctica in particular now. Just as an exercise, if nothing else. Perhaps it can serve as a kind of experiment, as you called it. In any case, it's all we can concern ourselves with for now. It's an open question whether we can even deal with that, obviously.'

In fact small muttered discussions or arguments were breaking out all around the circle, neighbours jabbering emphatically about perma-culture or survival or whatnot, and for a moment it looked to Sylvia like some sad, red-eyed debate society in a mental ward, going nowhere.

She clapped her hands hard, and they went silent. 'Let's take a break,' she said. 'We need to organize what we're doing here a little more, I think. Go get something to eat, and we'll reconvene in a while. What I want to do then is work out some *specific protocols*,' very heavy emphasis, 'governing our conduct in Antarctica, that everyone rep-resented here could abide by. Whether that's possible I don't know yet, but I want us to try, or this meeting becomes nothing but talk. And I want more than talk. I want a report–' glancing quickly at Wade, who was nodding– 'and I want us to come up with a list of suggestions, perhaps even a full protocol. Do you understand me? Mr Smith, can you speak for your clients here?'

'I can.'

'Please go have a meal with Carlos then, and let him describe for you the engineering of the oil and methane exploration technology. I'd like to have a few of our people at that meeting as well. The rest of you can perhaps meet with Mai-lis, and hear more about how they conduct their settlements. We'll reconvene when we're ready, but in any case by tomorrow morning. I'll keep you informed on all phones and beepers.'

CHAPTER FOURTEEN

From the Bottom Up

X observed Sylvia's meeting with a growing sense of alarm. He could see a potential settlement coming in which the oil consortium altered its practices to conform to standards set by Mr Smith's ecoteurs, who became a kind of conscience to the project; and all would continue as it had been before; and no one would ever notice that in their debate both men had been attacking the practices of Götterdämmerung capitalism without seeming to notice the complementarity, and thinking instead that they were attacking each other. And X would be x'ed out of ASL for ever, and therefore out of McMurdo, and no doubt he could get back on with Carlos and the oil crews, but then he would be an exile for good, truly A Man Without A Country, and all the hierarchies would remain, and he would never see Val again. After all that he had been through, he might as well have been right back on the floor of the heavy shop. Exiled without having ever been anywhere – nowhere but Antarctica and America, and Antarctica was another planet, while America was a dream. He had no home; he had no country. If he didn't want to become the Man Without A Country permanently, wandering the Earth for ever exiled, he was going to have to do something about it. He would have to make his home.

So as people poured out of the Chalet into the brisk bright light, most heading over to Crary or the Everest View, he wandered the muddy streets of McMurdo, balked, frustrated, perplexed, at a loss.

Deep in thought, hiking up past the BFC, he ran into the beaker he had worked for in the Dry Valleys. Graham Forbes. X had seen Forbes's older colleague in the meeting at the Chalet, so now he wasn't entirely surprised. He remembered the day with Forbes vividly; in all his adventures since he had never been colder. 'Hey,' he said, 'how are you?'

'Fine. And you?'

'I'm okay. How did your research go out there?'

'It went well, thanks.'

'Make any big discoveries?'

'Well–' Forbes hesitated, looking puzzled as to what to say. 'Yes, as a matter of fact.' He held up a hand quickly: 'Not anything too definitive, of course.'

'No brass plate saying Pliocene Fjord Slept Here.'

'No.' Small smile. 'But we did find a mat of beech-tree litter – leaves and twigs and other organic matter. It's similar to mats found elsewhere, but new to this area, and very well preserved.'

'So even the weirdo Dry Valleys were part of your story.'

'Yes, so it appears.'

'That'll be big news, I guess. Will one of you do a Crary lecture about it?'

'Oh no. Not this season, no. That would be premature.'

X nodded, thinking it over.

Forbes excused himself; he needed to get over to Crary for a meeting. As he was turning away he stopped suddenly, and said, 'Thanks for your help that day, by the way. That was an awfully cold day.'

'Oh hey,' said X, startled. 'My pleasure.'

Forbes veered off toward Crary.

X continued to walk around the streets, thinking harder than ever, but also taking the time to stop and look at what he was walking past. This had been his town, for a while. And in a lot of ways he had liked it. Right there at the mail building the Kiwis came over from Scott Base and held a *hungi* and *haaka* for Mac Town, barbecuing whole pigs and doing a ceremonial Maori war dance – twenty white Kiwi men stripped to the waist and dancing martially to the harsh, shouted commands of a Maori woman Kiwi air force officer. That was the kind of thing you saw in Mac Town.

But he had burned his bridges, and now he felt the immense nostalgia of the exile seeing his old home again, briefly. Nostalgia, pain of the lost home; and physically painful, yes. A heartache.

He ran into Randi. 'Jesus, Randi, you're not in the radio shack.'

'They let me out for an hour now that we got everyone home.' Her voice was hoarse, and she had the same wild-eyed, red-rimmed insomniac look as everyone else in town. 'You look lost, X.'

'I am lost.' It was strange seeing her face again; he was so used to her as nothing but a voice on the radio. Nice. One of Val's galley gang. You could see how much she laughed right there in the look on her face. 'I don't know what to do,' he said. 'I know ASL will never rehire me, and so – I'm fucked, I guess.'

She nodded. 'You sure are if you have to depend on ASL. But listen, their contract is up for renewal, right? And some of us have been talking about making a bid ourselves.'

'What's this?'

'Go talk to Joyce, she'll tell you all about it.'

She shooed him off to the BFC and he hurried over there, remembering as he went that Joyce had mentioned something about this when he had dropped by to say goodbye before leaving for Mohn Basin. He had been so distracted by his distress over Val that he hadn't really listened; and at that point he was committed anyway, and didn't want to listen. But now he did. Joyce would give him another tongue-lashing for sure, but he didn't care. Whatever it took.

Up into the BFC offices.

'Hi Joyce. I'm back.'

'Yeah, I saw you at the meeting at the Chalet.'

'Oh, yeah. What did you think of that?'

'Interesting.' She was staring at him hard. 'You want back in, don't you?'

He dropped onto a chair, held up a palm to forestall her. 'Yes, I do, and I know I'm fucked.'

'Yes you are.'

'But Randi reminded me of this bid thing you tried to tell me about last time. I know I wasn't listening that time. I'm sorry about that. This time I am, though, so tell me again.'

She nodded, accepting his apology. 'NSF makes ASL give subcontracts to some potential competitors, so they'll know enough to be able to make competitive bids when the contract comes up for renewal. It's the same system ASL used to beat out ASA last time. And they'll be getting strong challenges from PetHelo and GE for the general contract, and I wouldn't be surprised if PetHelo beats them out, because you know ASL, they're so efficient that everyone hates their guts, even NSF if the truth be known. In fact there's a rumour that NSF is trying to get ASA to come back again for a bid, now they see what a good thing they had. Anyway a group of us thought we'd try to form a co-op and make a bid for the coms and BFC subcontract.'

'Really?' X said, feeling his heartbeat accelerate.

'Yes, really.' She laughed at his expression. 'I take it you're interested this time.'

'Oh God.'

She laughed again. 'Right. And you're our big social theory guy. So there are some people on the fence I think it might be safe to try you on. You can explain the theories behind what we're doing to some people I'll direct you to.'

'I sure the hell can! Just let me at 'em.'

'Okay, okay. But beyond them you should mellow out, X, I don't want you going too far, okay? Don't do a Mr Smith on people, please God. We don't want to scare anyone or it'll just reduce our chances to win the bid. But we've got a lot of people already, and in coms and field services it's really experience that matters. ASL has always threatened us by saying they can hire new people to take our place, which they can, but if we all walk at once and make a bid, then we're the ones with the on-site experience, and ASL will only have their Seattle experience and a bunch of fingies to show to the NSF. The actual people NSF has been working with the last few years will mostly be on our side. So it might work. And the more the better.'

'Oh sure, it makes sense,' X said. 'NSF is just hiring a group to run their own infrastructure. So it removes the problem of competing with the old company's capital, to an extent.'

'Right.'

'This is *great*,' X exclaimed. 'Why didn't I hear anything about this? Why didn't you tell me until I was already on my way out of here?'

'Well, you know. It's not the kind of thing that GFAs are usually let in on.' She shrugged. 'That's just the way it is. It's been kind of touchy talking about it, since we're all still ASL employees at this point. Mutiny, you know. Breach of contract. People were afraid of getting singled out and fired. So we only talked about it among people we trusted, which meant we had to know them real well. So, you were coming along, people were talking about asking you in on it, because we knew you were into that kind of thing. But then you were gone. We figured you'd gotten fed up with ASL too fast, and in bad with Val, and that was that.'

'But now I'm back.'

'Now you're back. So tell you what, why don't you go talk to Nancy, and Spec, and Harold, and George . . . I know there's a few more – oh yeah, Mac; see him first, he'll tell you what we've got worked up, and then you can talk to the others about joining. Tell them about co-ops and how great they are, and see if you can get them to commit. They say they're thinking it over, but I think they'll join if it's put to them right. And if we get all the people we want to get, I think we've got a really good chance.'

'Oh yeah, yeah, yeah. I'll try to think who else would be good to have.'

She nodded, patted his arm. 'Check with me first on that. Remember to stay calm, X. This is business. It's going to take a lot of planning and hard work, and it'll be a while before we know anything.'

'Oh yeah, sure. Very calm. Total business.'

He grinned at her and she had to laugh. And then he was off.

Sleep was forgotten, although in fact he hadn't tried to remember. They were all fried for that matter, firing around McMurdo like droplets of water on a hot griddle, insomniac to the point of insanity; but when had it ever been any different? Mac Town was a hyper place in the summers. X went to the galley to stuff himself yet again, to fuel himself for the next lap of wakefulness. While in there he spotted Spec and Harold, and he went over and ate with them, and at the end of the meal he brought up the co-op idea, which they had heard of. They had feelings both ways. So they talked it over for a while, X arguing for employee-ownership as a general principle, not bothering to talk about the particulars of their situation in McMurdo, which these two knew a lot better than he did. After that he was off to make his rounds, visiting all the offices that he had visited before as a Good For Anything, talking to the people Joyce had mentioned and others he had liked, asking them to think about joining.

A lot of people shook their heads as they listened to him, and he began to understand that because of his rants in the past, and his recent disappearance, he was regarded as a crank – or, more accurately, as an innocent. Of course what he said was true, the old iceheads' looks said, of course they're screwing us, but to think there could be a change in the system was silly. The current method of business, the hierarchy of employer and employees, was all part of the Bad Design of Reality, their looks said; it was unfixable, there would always be owners and workers, no matter how vehemently one denounced them. Certain people owned the businesses, the capital, the governments, the laws, the armies; and that was all it took to back the present system up, no matter how bad it was. This was what their looks said, X decided as he walked from office to shop, looks fond and indulgent or irritated and contemptuous though they otherwise might be. A lot of the old iceheads thought he was full of shit. Or, at best, a dreamer hopelessly out to lunch.

X nodded at this judgement and learned as he went. He tried to get more particular, to stick to the specifics of what they could change right there on Hut Point. He described the other co-op complexes he knew about, usually the Basque town of Mondragon, where everything was a co-op. He enjoyed these conversations more, but they were hard, too. He was fomenting revolution, and saving his chance at having a country, and a home, and it was incredibly exciting and all that, but the devil was in the details ... So. He had to describe the co-op that would come to be, a co-op of people who had had years and years of Antarctic experience and expertise, using that expertise to organize a better way of running things in field service; they could be competitive with ordinary companies; NSF would have to agree they were the best even according to NSF criteria; and then they would keep it among themselves, not go public with stock, arrange for profit-sharing without being greedy, thus allowing them to make a low bid and still make a living, because not paying a big profit to shareholders in the world would save money for them and their needs.

It made perfect sense. The basic sensibleness of the co-op system: it was more just, and therefore would increase employee motivation and loyalty, and thus make for better work, leading to more efficiency, even by the standards of the downsizers. X found it very easy to make a case for this. It meshed coherently with what most Americans were taught as children to be the basic values, fairness, justice, democracy – it was easy to defend using those base values. So he described to his old friends and acquaintances a McMurdo that had become a kind of miniature Mondragon, every business structured as an employee-owned co-op in an interlocking system of co-ops, including the banks. In a McMurdo like that, X would say, emphasizing this point very heavily, people would finally be able to take control of their careers in Antarctica, and not have their lives fatally split between their love of the place and the whim of the one boss in town.

That got them thinking. And though there were a lot of sceptics, a lot of other people nodded and said, 'Sounds good, count me in.'

Returning from the latest of these meetings he ran into Wade, and they stopped to confer without having to say a word about it, like two brothers crossing paths in a city. 'Listen,' X said, 'you ought to try talking to Professor Michelson about what they found out in the Dry Valleys this season. Graham Forbes told me they found something good – he wouldn't say more, but it seems to me that your Senator ought to be able to use this dynamicist scenario to make it clear just how dangerous global warming is, and then press his programme that much harder.'

'I've been thinking that myself,' Wade said. 'I'll ask Michelson as soon as I see him, thanks. How's it going otherwise?'

'Pretty good. I'm helping Joyce and Randi and some of the other folks here to mount a bid for the field services subcontract. We're forming a co-op of all the people in town that we think would do well, it's a lot of the best people here.'

'Phil will love that too, that's one of his current obsessions. Keep at it, and I'll see how I can help from my end.'

'Okay I will.'

A brief hand to shoulder and they were off, each in their own direction.

Wade for his own part was working the town almost as hard as X was. Soon after the first meeting was over he went back into the Chalet and found Sylvia on the phone in her office, and tapped on her open door. She gestured him in and he went to the big wall map of Antarctica, looking at Sylvia's system of dots. He had forgotten her code, and the patterns the coloured spots made still suggested nothing to him.

She got off the phone. 'That was Christchurch. The storm is finally clearing off Cape Adare, and so they should be sending down the whole crowd any time now.'

'So we have eight hours more on our own?'

'Yes.' She didn't look happy at the prospect of all the official investigators who would soon be descending on them.

He gestured at the map. 'So do the dots match with the ecotage events, as far as you can tell?'

'Some of them correlate with the satellite dishes that were disrupting communications,' she said, coming around the desk and pointing to some of the orange dots, all over the continent. 'Then others would appear to mark camps of the ferals whom you met.'

'Hard to see patterns when there's more than one thing going on.'

'True.'

'Are you confident that your satellite-photo analyst is giving you all the sightings that he's making?'

She looked surprised. 'Not confident, no. I suppose I was assuming as much, but I don't have the wherewithal to check him.'

'Would you mind if I gave him a call and asked him some questions? I'd like to discuss some ideas I've had with him, and if you give me a reference, perhaps he would agree to talk with me.'

She looked at him, making an unspoken question.

'I'd like to help if I can,' Wade explained. 'Help the Treaty process. Help keep NSF in control of the American Antarctic programme. And so on. It all fits with what Phil Chase is trying to do. With what I'm trying to do.'

She thought it over. 'I don't see how it could hurt. He's in the security agencies, some kind of split position, but he can always take a call and then make his own decision. I'll get you his phone number,' she said, going to her desk to look it up and write it down.

'And his name?'

'Ask for Sam.'

Wade nodded. 'Thanks. Now about the ecotage. Can you tell me the . . . ?'

'I have an overview from Search and Rescue here.' She plucked another piece of paper from her desk. 'Apparently everything was synchronized to start on October fifteenth – let's see, just six days ago, my. It feels like longer.'

'So true.'

'Whether they waited for a Condition One storm to hit or it was just a coincidence, I can't say. Automated satellite tracking dishes coupled with powerful radios – we've found seventeen of them, stretching from the Peninsula down the length of the Transantarctics to Cape Adare, with five more out on the polar cap beyond the Pole. The assumption is there are more we haven't found yet. They appear on initial investigation to be chop-shop compilates with east Asian source materials from the turn of the century. The dishes were pointed at carrier satellites, mostly Ku-band fourteen gigahertz, the report says, and some twenty gigahertz hub satellites; unmodulated signals were sent at frequencies that captured these satellites. When the captured satellites' traffic was rerouted, dishes then found and captured the new carriers. All that activity ended after forty-eight hours of disruption. At its start, however, seven of the SCAG consortium's test drilling sites were destroyed, as were the base camps at Roberts Massif and Pioneer Hills. The bombs appear on initial investigation to be home brewed and contain no taggants. Before they exploded all occupants of the oil stations were rounded up at gunpoint by masked teams carrying assault weapons, and they were taken by snowmobile or blimp,' raising her eyebrows, 'to the nearest scientific field camps. Most of them to Shackleton Glacier, some to Byrd, some to the Italian camp in the Ellsworth Range.'

'Except they missed us, because we were out on a trip,' Wade said.

'Yes. They appear to have gotten everyone else, however, and no casualties have been reported. No identification of the kidnappers made so far.'

Wade explained what he had seen with the ferals. 'So, you know, as far as I can tell, which isn't all that far, the ferals who are still out there didn't have anything to do with this, and the ones who did are somewhere in South America.'

'Hmm.'

'So do I take it that no NSF property was damaged, then?'

'No no, we took our share. Small hits but carefully placed, and quite debilitating. There are some lessons to be learned, no doubt. A small bomb on the roof of the radio building, and another at the repeater on Crater Hill, augmented the satellite failure. And lastly sixteen fuel tanks, including all the big ones up in the Gap, and several outlying helo fuel bladders, were contaminated with a variant of one of the oil-eating bacteria designed to clean up oil spills on water. This particular species grew into thousands of small clumps until it died, so that it was dangerous to use the fuel remaining in those tanks. That was a real nightmare – we had to figure out how to filter the fuel, and then test it for reliability.'

'It must have been quite the forty-eight hours here.'

'Yes.'

'The FBI's going to be here for a long time.'

'Yes. They'll have several avenues of investigation, of course. The satellite hardware, the bombs, the bacteria, these exiled ice pirates wandering around Chile, Mr Smith himself . . . I wonder if he's right to be so confident his clients will remain anonymous. It's clear they were being careful, but still . . .'

'Yeah. Depends how careful they were. I could imagine a group with experience and forethought making it difficult. And since no one got killed, and the FBI's plate is overfull with more violent and lethal terrorist activities back in the States, they may not put years of effort into this case.'

'Hmm.'

The two of them sat there, staring at the desk. The amount of sleep they had got between them in the last week wouldn't have covered a single night. Wade found himself blinking out unexpectedly and then coming to with a start; he stood up abruptly before he fell asleep in front of her. 'Thanks for all the information. I'll convey what I've learned to Senator Chase, and we'll do what we can to help.'

Sylvia nodded, still thinking things over.

Back outside, Wade cringed at the raw sting of the wind through the Gap, then stumbled over the muddy wasteland toward the galley and a few mugs of coffee. Just outside the big building he ran into Professor Michelson, going the same way.

'Professor! Hello!'

'Ah hello,' Michelson said, recognizing him. Then after a closer look he said, 'You've visited us during interesting times, I see.'

'Very interesting. What did you think of the meeting in the Chalet?'

'Well, obviously it's important to discuss these matters. There will be many such discussions in the wake of what happened this week.'

'Including within SCAR?'

'Oh, most definitely.'

'Yes. I suppose that makes sense. So . . . How did your work go in the Dry Valleys?'

'Well, we continued to work.'

They stood in the sun, protected from the wind by the galley itself. Michelson stared at him curiously. Finally Wade said, 'My friend X spent a day out with your team working for Graham – he tells me that Graham told him that you made a significant discovery out there.'

'Did he? Well, yes, I suppose. All discoveries are significant really, aren't they? When you consider the vast realm of non-discovery?'

'Yes, I'm sure. But–' Wade tried to figure out how to say it. 'But if you've made a discovery that will confirm the dynamicist position unequivocally, then that will demonstrate that the east Antarctic ice sheet is unstable, and wasn't there three million years ago, and possibly will go away again if global warming continues. Right? So it's important, and, you know. Maybe if you have a kind of smoking gun piece of evidence then you should share it immediately, so that policy can begin to take it into account?'

That little V of a smile, under the moustache. 'I don't think we need to be quite as dramatic as that.'

Maybe you don't, Wade thought.

'I'm not sure there is even the possibility of what you call a smoking gun. What we found has to be studied and interpreted, and fitted into a much larger pattern. It means nothing by itself. Its meaning can be disputed, and will be disputed, believe me. Dating Sirius is no easy thing. Particularly since different Sirius outcropping may in fact date from different warm periods. So we must proceed cautiously.'

'So it's not really a smoking gun.'

'No, it's a mat of beech leaves. Beech leaves and other associated litter, from a forest floor.' He shrugged. 'It's more evidence, we hope.'

'But you're becoming more convinced, yourself, that the ice sheet was gone in the Pliocene?'

'Oh yes, you can say that. What we're finding now in Sirius formations resembles the coastline biome of southern Chile. The beech forests, the insect life, the microscopic life, it all fits together. And it becomes clearer that it can be dated to around two to three million years ago. So we will toil on, and see what happens.'

'So no press conferences about this season's discoveries.'

Michelson laughed briefly. 'No, no press conferences. Not much drama, I'm afraid. Just evidence.'

'Which you will introduce when?'

'Oh, pretty quickly, pretty quickly.'

'Two hundred years?'

'Ha, no, not quite that long. Preliminary reports next year, then see how the lab work is going . . . full publication a year or two after that, perhaps.'

'It's so slow.'

'It is rather slow. The samples themselves are going north by ship, you know, and won't be available for study until next spring.'

The discipline itself was beginning to imitate geological time scales,

Wade thought irritably. While politics whizzed on ever faster, science was slowing down; making the two match was like trying to catch neutrinos with the Earth. Little sparks of blue light, that was all. 'But – but, you know – people *need* to know this stuff soon! It needs to be part of the policy debate that's ongoing right now.'

The professor gave him a kindly glance. 'But that's your job, right?'

Wade thought it over.

'Listen,' Michelson said, looking at his watch, 'I'm supposed to be meeting Mai-lis inside. I haven't seen her in about twenty years.'

'Oh, sorry. Of course. I'd like to talk with her too, actually. Her group saved us from the midst of all this, up there on Shackleton Glacier.'

'Is that right? You were in need of salvation?'

'Yes. We were pinned down by the superstorm, with one of our group sick. Mai-lis's people picked us up and took us in.'

'That sounds like her.'

'You knew her twenty years ago?'

'Yes. She was a doctor and biologist in the Norwegian programme. Unusual. Sylvia knew her too. Let's see if we can locate her.'

They went in the galley. The hallways and dining rooms were all crowded, people in a hurry but moving clumsily, like manic zombies. Mai-lis was at one of the round tables in the main galley. It took a long time for Wade to get a chance to talk to her, but at one point she got up to refill her bowl at the soft ice cream machine, and Wade followed her over. She greeted him pleasantly and handed him an empty bowl.

'Thanks,' he said.

'Thank you for calling me about this meeting. Out of habit I wanted to keep our distance, but on reflection I think it's a good idea to have come in, to make our own case for ourselves.'

'Oh good, good. I agree completely. We need your input here if we want to have more than some kind of stand-off, or a partial, what you might call technical solution.'

'Yes.' She looked at him closely. 'And so . . .'

'I've been thinking about the situation, and I think Senator Chase might be able to do some things for you, concerning the Treaty renewal and so on, making allowances for the kind of thing you are attempting. As part of that effort, to give him more leverage so to speak, I was wondering if you would put me in contact with the satellite-photo analyst you mentioned at your camp – you know, the one that was helping you.'

'Tell me what you want from him.'

He explained his reasons, encouraged to see that Mai-lis was nodding as he spoke. When he had finished she continued to nod, thinking it over.

'I'd especially like to talk to him if it's Sam,' Wade ventured. 'In that case he's doing analysis for Sylvia as well, and I could come to him with a double reference.'

'Really!' she said, surprised. 'Well. Our contact is confidential, you understand, and he'll want to keep it that way. But given what you want to do, I think he would be willing to talk to you. I'll give him a call to make sure first, if you don't mind. Then if he agrees, I can give you the number we use, and his encryption codes.'

'Thanks, thanks. I'm sure it will help.'

Mai-lis went back to her table, and Wade stared at the empty bowl in his hand, then put it back and went over to the line for hot food; he was starving, but he didn't think he'd ever again be warm enough to eat ice cream.

At the end of his meal Mai-lis walked by and gave him a phone chip. 'Sam says give him a call.'

'Thanks, Mai-lis. Thanks for everything.'

'No problem. We Antarcticans have to stick together.'

'Yes.'

Wade finished eating and walked over to his room in Hotel California. He inserted the chip into his wristphone, then pushed the call button.

'Hello.'

'Hello, I'm Wade Norton, a friend of Mai-lis? I'm an assistant to Phil Chase—'

'Down in Antarctica, yes. In the Hotel California I take it.'

'Yes, that's right,' Wade said, looking around at the ceiling. 'And you must be Sam. Hi. Listen, I've been talking to Mai-lis, and to Sylvia, and thinking about the situation down here, and I've got some questions for you.'

'I've got some questions for you too.'

'Oh good, good.'

Wade pulled a pad of paper out of his briefcase.

My friends, we are back in McMurdo, on Observation Hill, but our travels are not yet over. Now we have spaces to get through colder even than Antarctica; the timespace of human history, and our life together in these overshoot years. There are more people on this planet than the planet can hold, and how we act now will shape much of the next thousand years, for good or ill. It is a bottleneck in history; the age beyond carrying capacity; the overshoot years; the voyage in an open boat, weighted down beyond its Plimsoll line. There is the possibility for very great tragedy, the greatest ever known.

But tragedy is not our business. So now we must learn this Earth as closely and completely as our paleolithic ancestors knew it on the savannah; we must know it in the mode they knew it, as scientist and lover wrapped together in one. The loverknower. We must draw the paleolithic and the postmodern together in a single design. I sense the dragon arteries have knotted together on this promontory in such a way as to allow some early precursor glimpse of this knowerlover knot. Because people come to this place to study it, and in doing so they invariably fall in love with it.

But why, you may well ask, seeing only the cold images I have been sending you? Why fall in love with it, so stripped and bare as it is? I wish I could explain it more clearly. But truly this place beggars the language.

Still I must try one last time. You see, the air is so clean. Mountains so distant, yet still focused and detailed; as if your eye had become telescopic. Water lying there glossy and compact, like shot-silk in the sun. Never have you seen such clarity before, where the spiritual landscape stuffs the visible landscape until it bursts with luminous presence. Seeing things this clearly makes you wonder what the rest of the world would look like in such clean air. Not that more northerly air could ever be as clean as this, so cold and dry, so dustless – but on certain days, on certain mornings, all the world must once have had this clarity, and we the eyes to see it, and the desire to look. It must have been so beautiful.

And then also, as you see again from this glorious *p'ing-yan* vantage point on Observation Hill, it is all so big. Big, huge, vast, stupendous, gigantic – I have said these words many times, I know, and still I must say them over and over again, until they react in your heads like paper flowers dropped in water, expanding there to their original size. Really very big! Suggestive of the infinite. Immense simplicity and brio, as in the brush strokes of a bold wise painter. Everything in all five dimensions, all visible at once. This too is so lovely.

Then the mantle of ice provides such elaboration, on microscales you can barely see in my images, scales of vision you can only experience when you look down at your feet as you walk – visions of the infinitely bedded, planed, crosshatched, and contoured textures of snow and ice, prisming everywhere the colours of the rainbow, spiralling inward all the way to the crystalline patterns in snowflakes, spiralling outward to the massive sculptural bulks of the tabular bergs, each one a masterpiece. Beauty is fractal to infinity in both directions.

Clean, big, icy, prismatical – somehow I feel that I'm still not capturing it. Surely these are not the attributes that make this place so ravishing. Perhaps all beauty has a mystery in it that cannot be explained. For this place *is* beautiful; and once the whole world was beautiful just like this. Seeing the former, we realize the latter. We understand just how beautiful the whole Earth once was.

And we can make it that way again. On the far side of our hard time I see a returned clarity, as fewer of us get along ever more cleverly, our technologies and our social systems all meshed with each other and with this sacred Earth, in the growing clarity of a dynamic and ever-evolving permaculture. Clean air then, not just so that we will live longer, but so that we can see again. Big things and small things in their right place. It will come. We are the primitives of an unknown civilization. And here that becomes so clear. This primal icescape brims with *chi's* vital breathing, its winds blow clear every nook in our brains, balloons them as it did in the original co-evolution; and so when we're here love fills us, that's all.

Then this love for the landscape that is our collective unconscious, this knowerlover's apprehension of the land's divine resonance, blossoms outward and northward to encompass the rest of the planet. Love for the planet radiating from the bottom up, like revolution in the soul.

So it has always been, loving and knowing together; and thus from the moment humans first arrived on this continent, it was the scientists who stepped up and said, This is our place.

And now they have to decide again if that is really so.

It's part of a process that has been going on for a long time. For instance, see the town below us. An American town, as in Alaska. Inhabited for generations. A big part of the Antarctic story.

But only now is it becoming its own place. Because the Americans who founded the town in the International Geophysical Year, a very great *feng shui* event, were military men. They were there to support scientists, and they made Antarctic culture a military thing. The soldiers and sailors were young men, taken away from women, commanded by older men who for much of their lives had also been away from women, in a social structure that looked back to the hierarchies of an older time. To put it in its simplest terms, there was too much *yang*.

In most histories we think of that world dying in the First World War, and being replaced by our ferociously knowing and hermaphroditic modernity. But in Byrd's expeditions, and the early American stations, you find men living in a nineteenth century style, in the Peter Pan world that we saw Scott's men inhabiting some decades before, but now long after most of the rest of society had given it up.

And slowly this mode of life became harder to maintain. When Scott's men came back to the world and described what they had done, people said, Wonderful, marvellous. But when the United States Navy men returned to the north they were met with incomprehension, and a neglect like contempt. Why bother? people asked. And the men themselves, coming from the uprooted placeless culture of Cold War America, had no way to talk about their experience of this extraordinary continent. As I have said, in any language it is hard to know what to say. But these men were triply dislocated, in language, space and time; they were like the travellers in space stories who fly so fast that relativity effects come into play, and though they are only away for two years as they see it, return to a world several centuries farther on. They were refugees in time.

This effect, result of the complete but residual preponderance of *yang*, perhaps accounts for the coarsening of their culture as the years passed. The walls of all the American Antarctic stations were plastered with photos of naked women. The tabletops in the galleys where they ate were covered with pictures of naked women. The thoughts of the sailors stationed there, as far as one can judge by the few records they left, were somehow limited. Their traditions were simple and brutal. One custom had groups of men descending on newcomers, tearing off their clothes and depositing them in a hole in the snow. The Three Hundred Club, where people rush from a two hundred degree sauna into a hundred degree below zero night, also dates from this period, as do the ritual swims in holes cut in sea or lake ice. The best parts of this culture no doubt include these attempts to ritualize the experience of the cold; also to celebrate the experience of isolation, as when the winterover crew at the Pole lined up waving on the runway to welcome the first Herc of the spring, every one of them naked and stained bright purple from a bath of tincture of violet crystals. But for the most part the record of their lives is a sad litany of Peter Pans become Rip van Winkles.

Then came a bifurcation point, where the balance of the pattern tipped in a new direction. This moment began as a symbolic gesture of the Cold War. The Russians had sent one of their women into space, and we in China included six Tibetan women in our summit team on Chomolungma. In that geopolitical context, then, six American women were flown to the South Pole station, thus becoming the first women to go there. November 11, 1969. A day of peace in a year of conflict. For some a political gesture, yes – a symbolic gesture. But the meaning of the symbol bifurcated because of what the women did.

Recall the wrestling boatload of men who first made landfall on the continent. Farce – lovable in its way, but still farce. On Armistice Day of 1969, however, these six American women had a different solution; they joined hands and walked from the plane to the Pole together, so that no one of them could be called first. This struck them as the best way to do it. This was their new story. And thus they began the end of the *yang* dominance of Antarctica, so militarized and peterpanized; thus they began the start of Antarctica's entry into the fully human world, a balance of *yin* and *yang*, of men and of women, together surging dynamically this way and that, yes even at the very moment we speak.

Those six women were Lois Jones, Eileen McSaveney, Kay Lindsay, Terry Lee Tickhill and Pam Young. Wait, that's only five. What was the name of the sixth woman? I can't remember. It will come to me.

In any case, the continent then began to enter what some have called its golden age, the age of the 'continent for science', when Antarctica must be understood as one version of the scientific utopia – a golden age lasting from the arrival of women and the corresponding withdrawal of the military, until the recent non-renewal of the Antarctic Treaty, just two years ago. The Treaty was an attempt to describe a scientific and utopian relationship of humanity to land, a relationship in which there was no sovereignty but rather a *terra communis*, a return of the concept of the commons and of commonality, with scientists of all nations, including nations that were at each other's throats back in the north, co-operating in peace for the good of all. That was indeed a golden moment in history. And though it was very top-heavy in men at first, as was science itself, it became more balanced in men and women every year that passed.

Of course the balance is not yet here. Nor is there balance anywhere in human affairs, or in the universe at large. Indeed, if ever you are asked to choose between fixists and mobilists, as the two sides were called during the plate tectonics controversy – or between the stabilists and the dynamicists in the current Sirius debate – always choose the dynamicists. History is on your side.

And so here and now, in the relentless surge of time, we confront another bifurcation point in history. They come so often! The people gathered in the Chalet discuss what to suggest to the world, after the events of this unusual week. We will try to tell the world how better to live. An empty exercise, you say! Kick the world, break your foot! But everyone does it anyway, I notice. And this is little America, and America is very big. And as you have heard our new friend Carlos say, whatever is true in Antarctica is also true everywhere else. So we must attend very closely to what we do here now.

I think it is an open question whether Americans can learn the habits of co-operation and sufficiency quickly enough to avoid catastrophe. We in China, so crowded into our middle kingdom, have had to learn long ago that life is co-operation, that life is helping each other for the good of all, including oneself. We have the experience of thousands of years of history, coherently compiled, to guide us; and we have the direct experience of the last century, both good and bad, in making a communal society work. Much of this last century we owe to the example of Chairman Mao, great master of *feng shui* that he was. Now I know what everyone says – I say it myself – that what Mao did was sixty percent good, forty percent bad. And I have heard the recent joke of the wags in Beijing, that this slogan will keep juggling the figures downward until it reaches fifty point one percent good, forty-nine point nine percent bad. And I know the other saying too, that what is good in Mao all comes from Tao. We will tell this story in all its different ways forever. Whichever version you believe, it is still true that in part because of Mao we have started a bit earlier than the rest of the world in structured co-operation, and this has given us our great power in the twenty-first century. It has also prepared us to change ourselves for the sake of the Earth; we have lived through three one-child family campaigns already, and are slowly reaping the benefits of the resulting stable, even shrinking population. And we are working at making cleaner technologies; we are aware of the problem of the overshoot as few others can be, seeing it every day so clearly in our jammed streets. This is not to say that we never make mistakes. The dam at Three Gorges on the Yangtze, for instance, is a terrible mistake. We must take that dam down and allow the great Yellow River to flow again, or else the ecology as well as the *feng shui* of our country will never again be right. That dam poisons our land and clogs our thinking.

And of course we must give Tibet back to the Tibetans, and let them live on their high plateau in peace. That is worse than a mistake; that is a crime. As I have already told you during our walks together on that sacred roof of the world, we add a hundred karmic lives to our atonement every day that the occupation of Tibet continues; already it will take millions of karmic generations for us to atone for what we have done to them. The sooner started the better.

379

And of course there are many other disasters of lesser magnitude as well, some that face us specifically as Chinese, others that belong to all the world together. But we can face them. Everyone has at least part of the habit of co-operation; this too is part of lovingknowing; for science is above all else a community of trust. The true scientist has to be intent on co-operation in a communal enterprise, or it will not work at all. And to the extent that we know well, and love deeply, we are all true scientists. So we will keep inventing that community of trust.

CHAPTER FIFTEEN

Shackleton's Leap

When the next meeting convened in the Chalet, X still had not slept. A lot of the people there hadn't, he could tell as they trickled in. There were not as many people as before, and many were still hunched together discussing specific issues, but after Sylvia got them seated in the big circle, and went through a description of some of the smaller meetings that had occurred since the session the previous evening, X raised a hand (sudden schoolboy nervousness, engendered by just that gesture alone).

When Sylvia called on him in her strict school-teacher style, he said, 'Sylvia, I want to emphasize that what we're talking about here is not just a question of what technologies we use in Antarctica, or of whether we're abiding by the strict letter of the Treaty or not. The treatment of Antarctica will never be respectful and environmentally aware if the people living down here continue to be organized in the same way they always have been – that is to say, in hierarchies where the majority of the workers have no power or responsibility, and are merely doing what they're told to do, for wages and nothing else. As it stands now, we're hired and fired at the whim of people back in the world, and the people who love Antarctica the most end up suffering the most, because they keep coming back here when that wrecks the overall shape of their lives, back and forth with no continuity or security, no career advantage so to speak. So there's a feeling of helplessness that creates a carelessness, which a lot of us wouldn't have if we were more in control of our destinies down here. I know this because I was a General Field Assistant down here, and you can't be more powerless than that and still be here. I know very well from that experience that ASL uses us to make their profits – we're paid poorly and we have no job security, and if we don't like it they just hire someone else. And, excuse me, but those employee practices have led to a hell of a lot of employee abuse here, right under the NSF's nose, and to a certain extent with

NSF approval – the suspension of the forty-hour work-week, for instance, among many other things. NSF's attitude has been to turn its head and let the contractor do whatever it had to do to keep the beakers running smoothly, while still making a profit for the contractor's owners back in the world. And employees have taken the brunt of that kind of looking away for years. No way can people pay proper attention to Antarctica as a project or a life under those conditions. We can't call our jobs ours, or this place home, so naturally we treat it like strangers.'

Sylvia was watching him very closely now, X saw; it had not been a bad thing to implicate NSF in ASL's sweatshopping. 'What are you suggesting, specifically?' she asked.

'The service contract comes up for bid again soon,' X said. 'You could hire new contractors, either general or sub. Hire a company made up of ex-ASL employees reorganized as an employee-owned co-op, dedicated specifically to enacting a really rigorous environmental policy. As Mai-lis said about her group's efforts, it could be seen as an experiment – a scientific experiment in seeing how a co-op with no profit beyond salaries and so forth could compete with a standard company, in terms of the services provided down here, combined with environmental improvements and the like.'

'We already expect our Antarctic service contractors to conform to NEPA and all the specific regulations we've made,' Sylvia said. 'As to the type of company, it would be less clear that we could decide that ourselves – I mean one type of company compared to another. Congress directs us there, I'm afraid, and the budgetary constraints are very tight.'

X nodded. 'Sure, I understand that. But without the need to generate a profit for shareholders, an employee-owned co-op should be able to do the same job for less money. So Congress would have no objections there.'

Sylvia nodded doubtfully.

Wade said, 'Some relevant laws are up for review by the congressional ways and means committees, and by the administration. Government contract preferences for employee-owned co-ops is an idea that has been introduced by Senator Chase many times before, and while there is resistance to the idea, there is also considerable support. Growing support.'

Mr Smith said, 'Resistance from the owner class, support from the people. The idea that each corporation can be a feudal monarchy and yet behave in its corporate action like a democratic citizen concerned for the world we live in is one of the great absurdities of our time–'

'Yes yes,' Sylvia said, cutting him off before he got rolling. 'But in our situation here, specifically? With the contracts for service organizations coming up for renewal . . .'

Wade said, 'NSF might be able to make their decisions based on their current environmental regulations, so that it won't have to wait for the ultimate decisions Congress makes concerning private contractor preferences. Especially in situations in which the infrastructure is owned by NSF, as is the case here. This would be an area in which a new employee co-op might be able to avoid the problems of capitalization. And if they could include a solid plan for increased environmental sensitivity as part of their bid, at a lower price, I should think it would be easy for NSF to support the more socially responsible organization.'

'The two are the same,' X insisted, pounding his knee. 'Social justice is a *necessary part* of any working environmental programme.'

'Yes,' Sylvia said slowly. 'Well. At least we can include that as one of the recommendations in our little report here.'

X sat back in his folding chair. His heart was pounding fast; it felt as if a penguin was flapping its wings in there. Find those ruby slippers, put them on, click them three times together, and maybe then you'll get to go back, to the home that has never yet existed.

Val found herself proud of X, watching him make his pitch to the Chalet meeting; he was serious, intent; it was hard to ignore him or what he was saying.

Nevertheless, she could see how things would be. Sylvia would try to broker a settlement, no matter how absurd that goal appeared in the light of the world. Washington and the other capitals would call the shots. The hunt for oil and coal and methane hydrates and fresh water would go on, buffered by all the latest hardware science could offer, with Mr Smith's invisible clients hovering offstage, watching, judging, no doubt striking again if they were displeased. McMurdo would go on, perhaps with new companies running the services, perhaps some of them co-ops that treated their employees right; but always the same, even as everything changed; still tour groups coming in on ships and planes, and adventure trekkers packaged and taken out into the back country to see things, guided by their guides.

Guiding would never change.

And meanwhile the ferals would continue to move around out there in Transantarctica, living their lives. Trying to wrest a living from this bare land. Working toward a kind of self-sufficiency, even if it were backed by the invisible world beyond the horizon; self-sufficiency not of means but of meaning.

Val thought about this as the second meeting broke into several smaller groups working on specific issues, and she went back to her room, did some laundry, took a shower, and went to the galley and ate a big meal. Finally she flicked open her wristphone and got Joyce on the line. 'Joyce, where did you put the visiting ferals?'

'Nowhere. What, you think they're going to stay at Hotel California, or maybe the Holiday Inn?'

Of course not. 'Where are they then?'

'I think they've set up a couple tents on Ob Hill, just under the peak. Can you see them from where you are?'

Val looked up at the pointed cone standing over the town. Yes, there was the round curve of a tent. 'Thanks, Joyce. I see them.'

She walked up the road to the BFC building. As she neared it Wade joined her, huffing and puffing.

'Hi, Val.'

'Oh, hi.'

'What do you think of the meetings?'

'Very interesting.'

They stopped outside the BFC.

'What do you think of Mr Smith?'

Val raised her eyebrows. 'I think he's the one, myself.'

'The mastermind?'

'Yeah. Or for that matter even the whole operation. At least he could be. It only took a few bombs and radios and satellite dishes to do everything they did, after all. He could have done it from New Zealand, or his boat.'

'I don't know,' Wade said. 'It would be a lot of places to get to.'

'I suppose. Probably he has some friends working with him, sure. But he's not just a lawyer, I don't think.' She shrugged. 'Or maybe he is. I doubt we'll ever find out for sure.'

'No.'

He was looking up at her, intent and serious; considering whether to say something to her. He hesitated; gestured at Ob Hill. 'Going up to take a look around?'

'To see the ferals,' she said.

'Ah.'

He registered immediately that he wasn't invited. A lot of men would have taken a lot longer to see that. Oh well. She liked him; but he would be leaving any day now, and then he would be back in the world, where who knew what would happen. So now she watched his face framed in its furs, that owl look hiding all.

He said, 'You know, we're going to need to have people who know Antarctica well, back in Washington. To work out a protocol that stands a chance of being accepted by all the parties involved. No matter what happens here at the Chalet, there will still be a lot of work to do.'

'Yes. I'm sure you'll do very well for us on that.'

But that wasn't what he had meant, she saw immediately.

'Oh,' she said stupidly.

He saw that she understood him, and stared at her. Wind whistled through the gap and down onto them.

She shook her head. 'I couldn't,' she said. Then: 'I like you a lot.' He blinked, smiled just a little. 'But I wouldn't be happy in Washington, you know. And then, well . . .'

He frowned. 'It's no worse a bureaucracy than here. You could live outdoors – my boss already does.'

She shook her head. 'I'm going to ask the ferals if I can join them.'

'Ah.'

She said, somewhat mischievously, 'You could join them too! You could do your job from down here, telecommute like your boss does.'

He had to smile, just for a second. They both laughed, briefly.

'I take your point,' he said. Then: 'Can I walk up with you part of the way?'

'Sure. I'd like that.'

They hiked up the spine together, crisscrossing over the broken lava steps of the ridgeline. A couple of hundred feet below the summit Val stopped, and Wade caught up with her. She took a step down and around, so that he was on the spine just above her, where she did not have to lean down to give him a kiss. Two cold mouths and noses. He put an arm around her to steady himself. She had learned long ago that there were certain times when you knew it was only going to be a single kiss; and that knowing that made it different. He was a good kisser.

He let her go. His face was flushed. He looked at her as if it was the last chance he was ever going to have.

'That was nice,' she said. Ice around her hot heart.

'You'll have to come north sometimes,' he said, 'even if you do join the ferals.'

'Maybe. Sometimes.'

'You'll visit?'

'I don't know. I'll make it to New Zealand, I guess. I don't know.' Again she tried turning the tables. 'You'll be one of the Antarctic experts in Washington – you'll have to come down to DV things from time to time, right?'

'Right. Very true.'

She nodded. 'We'll stay in touch.'

He nodded, thinking it over. Looking wan. She shrugged. He nodded again. A last brief hug. Then he was off, back down the rough trail, heavy-footed, looking out at the Ross Sea and the Western Mountains: the perfect way to trip and go flying. But he managed not to. Val turned around and hiked up the final section, going hard. She nearly tripped herself.

She stood outside the ferals' little tent, a patched old North Face mountaineering dome, blue nylon faded almost to white. The familiarity of it brought her up short. Scavenging for one's means of subsistence: was she ready for that?

'Hello?' she said.

A head popped out. Lars.

'Is Mai-lis here?' Val asked.

'Moment.'

He moved aside, and Mai-lis appeared in the doorway.

Val said, 'I wondered if I could join you.'

Mai-lis saw what she meant. 'One moment,' she said, and the tent door closed. Rustles inside; she was getting dressed. Val looked down at McMurdo spread below her, feeling bleached. She realized that Mai-lis' face reminded her of her grandmother Annie. They looked nothing alike, but still.

Mai-lis unzipped the tent door and crawled out. She stood, gestured at the peak above them. They climbed together in silence, like pilgrims. On the peak they stood under the old wooden cross, in the wind.

'You have a great view here,' Mai-lis observed, looking across the sea at Mount Discovery and the Royal Society Range; Black Island, White Island; the giant bergs of the collapsing shelf.

'Yeah.'

They stood looking at it.

'It is no easy life,' Mai-lis said.

'I know. That's not what I'm looking for.'

'What are you looking for?'

Val tried to express it. She waved down at McMurdo. 'I want to be free of all that. All but my friends. I want to be in Antarctica, but not like that. I want to try it your way.'

'It is no easy life,' Mai-lis warned again. 'It's not like expeditioning. You would have a lot to learn, even with all you know already.'

'That's good.'

'It is not all good.'

'No, I know that. I'm ready for that.'

'It is no easy life.' Three times, as in some ritual, some rite of acceptance.

'I know,' Val said. 'I'm ready.'

Mai-lis nodded then. 'All right. We talked about you already. We hoped you might be interested. We were going to ask you.'

'Really?'

Mai-lis nodded. 'You're a mountaineer.'

'Yes.'

'We need more mountain people. There are never enough of them.'

Mai-lis took up Val's gloved hand, and put it against the post of the cross. 'They said, to strive, to seek, to find, and not to yield.'

'To strive, to seek, to find, and not to yield.'

Not to yield. Like Annie climbing her ladder. Val swallowed, tried to smile at Mai-lis. Off with strangers, into the icy wilderness: a strange fate to choose, really. She knew that.

'Go back down and arrange your affairs,' Mai-lis said. 'See if this feels right to you. No one will be angry if you decide this was a mistake. This is a hard road for a life to take.'

'I know. I want it. I've always wanted something like this, really. Guiding was just the closest thing I could find. I'll be ready in a day or two, I guess.'

'We'll be here still. There is a lot to talk about with the people in the Chalet.'

'True.'

And so Val started back down Observation Hill.

Energized by the possibility of return, of a home at last, X continued to make the rounds of his little town, talking to one acquaintance or friend after the other. He took breaks in the Coffee Hut, and downed quadruple espressos while talking at the bar with whomever was in there, even trying darts at the dart board when asked. He was declared the worst darts player who ever lived, a danger to people in the full three hundred and sixty degrees around him. No one minded this, however, except for the one that bled; rather it was cause for celebration. 'You know I'm the worst basketball player in the world too,' X said, happily tossing darts into the wall or the side of the espresso machine. 'A biathlete I guess you have to call me.' And the players talked on through all the games and the shift changes, fuelled by caffeine, and sleep deprivation, and frustrated hatred of ASL, and frustrated love for Antarctica, until it began to seem to the giddy and hoarsening X that they would certainly be able to count on the support of most of the caffeine addicts in town; and that was everybody, right? They might even consider making a bid for the whole contract and not just part of it. Although that would be a logistical nightmare. But he thought they could make a compelling case that they had the best people and the best system for the field ops, thus augmenting the pure economic rationality of their expertise and efficiency with what X was now calling the Antarctic factor – not the magnitude-order leap in Murphy's Law that people used to mean by the phrase, but rather the ecological issues that the new co-op could address better than ASL, because of increased worker tenure, involvement, satisfaction, awareness, esprit de corps, and so on. Treating people like free adult human beings: NSF could indeed consider it a kind of experiment.

Of course not everyone was interested, even after word got around about Sylvia's approval, and it became clearer that they were going to have a shot at it. Some had prospered in ASL and become part of its management, or at least they thought they were, though since they were in McMurdo rather than Seattle they were certainly mistaken about that. Others had their lives focused back in the world and were on the ice simply to make as much money as fast as they could, and they didn't want this project complicated by the responsibility and risk of any new-fangled non-profit system. And there were others still who had complained endlessly about ASL but were too chicken to try a co-op, as Joyce put it, or too cynical to think it would make any difference. And lastly there were those who did not want to see change of any kind, because they did not like change. Or else for no reason at all, at least as far as X could tell. Four months ago this attitude would have shocked him; but he had been young then, and had not fully grasped how completely people could act in contradiction to their own best interests.

Here in McMurdo, however, enough people had been burned by the one-company town syndrome to make for a huge pool of talent waiting for a chance to move. Enough had had enough. And Joyce and Debbie and Alan and Randi and Tom, who had been here for ever and seen it all, and had worked so hard to make little communities under the umbrella of their responsibility, humanizing their zones despite the pressure from above to downsize and rationalize – they were poised to act. And now was the time. X was just a messenger.

And how he enjoyed it. He seemed to have lost the need to sleep, or the ability, one or the other; as far as he recalled he had not slept since their return to McMurdo, and for a good long time before that; it must have been nearly a week all told, and all that time in the perpetual sunlight, hurtling sandy-eyed from one crisis to the next, spending the town's brief downtime around 3am on the phone to the States talking to the Co-op Aid Co-op, as well as to any other groups and agencies that could help them in the preparation for their bid, talking until the sunlight sprayed over Erebus and the galley was opened and X ravenous for breakfast, no different from the sleepless day before except that his eyes were twenty-four hours sandier and his mind twenty-four hours more sleep-deprived, in a hyperlucid derangement of high hopes and apprehension.

And that was the state he was in when he ran into Val as he left the galley, feeling the possibility of the return of sleep into his life: vastly tired; bone-tired; completely wasted. But there she was, staring at him with a funny expression. After the retreat down Shackleton Glacier and the time with the ferals, he felt he knew her much better than he had during the weeks they had gone out together – better than he knew the members of his own family, if the truth were known. As Cherry-Garrard had said, in Antarctica you get to know people so well that in comparison you do not seem to know the people in civilization at all. But X hadn't had much of a chance to speak with Val since their return, and now, he saw, there was something on her mind.

'How's it going?' she said unsteadily.

'Okay! I think we've got the people we need to make a good bid for the field services. How about you?'

'Oh, I'm all right.'

They stood looking at the mud of McMurdo under their feet.

'So you think there'll be a co-op?' she asked.

'I do! I sure hope so, anyway. It's my only chance of staying.'

She nodded.

'What about you, Val? Do you think you'll join?'

She shook her head. X felt it like a blow. He began to go blank inside, as he had when she had first broken up with him.

She put a hand to his arm. 'I'm going out with the ferals.'

'Oh Val.'

He didn't know what to say. To him the ferals had seemed alien.

'I can't stay here, X. Even if the co-op works, my job would still be guide. And I can't do that any more. Those trips always reduce to the level of the person having the worst time.'

'To the Jack level.'

'Yeah, exactly. But it isn't just him. It's always something. I'm a shitty guide.'

'You are not!'

'I *am*. I am *not* a good guide. You don't know.'

'I do know, I've seen you! You shouldn't let that guy get to you; he was a jerk. Hiding the fact that he was hurt, that was bullshit. He was setting you up.'

She shook her head. 'It's not him. I mean it is, but there are always people like him on these trips. Listen to me, X. I don't like the clients any more. I think the Footsteps thing is bullshit. I'm not even seeing Antarctica any more when I'm guiding. I might as well not be here! I could get the same hassles and live in Jackson Hole. I'm toast, X. Burnt toast. But I want to be in Antarctica. I want to want to be here. I want to live here and work, but not as a guide.'

'What about search and rescue, couldn't you do that?'

She shook her head, giving him a hard look. 'The rescues don't always work. A lot of times you're going out to collect bodies. Have you ever gone out to a crash site where everyone has burned to death?'

'No,' X said, shocked.

'I have. I don't want to do search and rescue, I don't want to lead expeditions, I don't want to be a guide. I just want to live in the mountains. And I liked the look of the ferals, I really did. I'd like to try what they do, try *living* here.'

'Ah.'

He thought it over. *Listen to me*, she had said, so sharply, as if he never had. She had always been one of the mountaineers, ever since he met her; crazy to be out in the frigid landscape, clambering around. He wasn't like that, but now he wanted to understand her, really understand her; and that meant understanding that wild urge, that craziness in her that he wasn't sure he even approved of. He had to get that or he wouldn't get her.

'What about you?' she asked, suddenly intent, squeezing his arm. 'You could come too, you know. You could join.'

'Join the ferals, or join you?'

'I don't know! Who knows how things will be out there! I don't know at all. But if we were both out there, then . . .'

390

Then they would have a chance. Or at least she would have company among all those strangers.

'Ah, Val,' he protested. 'I wouldn't know what to do out there. I barely know what to do here. And I'm – I'm interested in what's happening here now.' He waved around – muddy old Mac Town, raw cold under a lowering sky, and the usual wind through the Gap – it was a hard place to make a case for even at the best of times. And this morning was not the best of times.

They looked at each other. Wistful: full of wishes.

'I'll stay here,' he said finally. 'But, you know. Maybe you'll come in from time to time. If the ferals–' He saw it– 'If Sylvia makes a deal that includes the ferals, and if the ferals tell her that they would prefer to deal with a co-op here rather than ASL, then maybe it'll help us win a bid, and we'll be here, and we'll need to have a liaison with the ferals, at least, to discuss what they're doing out there. And so . . .'

She nodded. She smiled; there even seemed to be tears in her eyes, though that could have been the wind ripping by. She stepped into him, hugged him hard. Then they were kissing, just as they had on the Bealey Spur, the only woman he had ever kissed where he did not have to do his hunchback routine or lift her up bodily from the ground. Someone his size.

'I'll talk to Mai-lis,' she said when they broke it off. 'Oh X – it'll work. It'll work somehow.'

He nodded, too full for speech. They would make it work, they would take back the world from the overlords, they would make a decent permaculture from the bottom up. Well; or at least work on their moment, here, now, in McMurdo.

With a few more incoherencies they parted.

X walked away. He had forgotten where he had been going, if indeed he had had a destination. He was on another plane now, wasted but exhilarated. Mac Town was not enough at a moment like this. He could walk out to Discovery Point and sit in the old hut, as he had many times before, but that would not be right either. Those old ghosts and their Keystone Kop routines were not what this was about. To strive, to seek, to yield . . . something like that. But not now. He could see why Val wanted out of that whole Footsteps game, out and back onto the land as it had been before Scott arrived, Antarctica itself all bare of history, ready for a new start.

So. Wasted, happy, nowhere to go. His room was not his room, and this town was not his town. He tried to see what it might be if they did it right, all Hut Point inhabited by some new aesthetic, so that it mattered what it looked like and how they lived there. Not just re-cycling their junk, but making a place that looked like a home. Those towns in Greenland and Lapland were like little works of art, the houses painted bright primary colours, lined out in rows and diagonals . . . Make the town itself a work of art. NSF might be receptive. They had changed before as a result of activists, as for instance after Greenpeace dumped McMurdo's rubbish on the floor of the Chalet. NSF was a reasonable outfit; a group of scientists, bureaucrats, technocrats, whatever; reasonable people, committed to reason, trying to make a community of trust in the universal chaos. The scientific project; ethics, politics, all embedded in the same enterprise. Who knew what they might do next?

But meanwhile, in this very moment, here he was. And he wanted out somehow – to fly, to celebrate! Perhaps a trip up the coast. A trip to Cape Royds, to see how Val's hero Shackleton had done it. Snug little cabin up the coast–

Suddenly he saw it. A vision: he could do it too, like Shackleton or Val, only his own way. A McMurdo feral. An indigenous Ross Islander. With a job making things work for the beakers, sure, but living in his own place, just as clean and neat and low-impact as anyone could ask; a tent house somewhere, something really snug and small. Nothing but footprints. It would have to be closer to Mac than Cape Royds, for sure, closer to town and work. Perhaps around the corner of Hut Point, facing the north and thus the sun. Val could visit some time. Or he could go out with the ferals on vacations. Live like them, but help reorganize McMurdo as well.

He went to the BFC and said to Joyce, 'Can I take a Zodiac around to the Dellbridges?'

'No way, X. The penguin cowboys are using them. Why do you want to go?'

Then the phone rang, and she gestured at him to wait and picked it up. 'Oh hi, Ta Shu. Uh huh . . .' She glanced at X. 'Well, yeah, now that you mention it. I think we can do that. Sure, no problem. X will take you. He'll meet you down at the dock.'

She hung up. 'You're in luck. Ta Shu is in short-timer mode, and he wants to see Cape Evans and Cape Royds one more time before he leaves.'

'Great!'

'Must be meant to be.'

'Yes yes yes.'

> black
> rock black water

Meant to be. X grabbed his parka and boots and went down to the docks, downed another cup of terrible coffee, got a Zodiac ready. Ta

Shu showed up, and X called weather and got clearance, and they took off.

Over the puttering of the engine, and the slap of the windchopped black waves, X told Ta Shu about his plan, and Ta Shu listened impassively.

Finally Ta Shu said, 'Good idea. Let us look for a place for you now, shall we?'

'You really want to?'

Ta Shu squinted at him. 'My job, you know.'

'Of course.'

So now he had a world-famous geomancer situating his house according to ancient *feng shui* principles. Meant to be!

They turned the corner of Discovery Point, and began slowly to run down the long straight northern coast of the Hut Point Peninsula, toward the stub of the Erebus Ice Tongue. The entire peninsula jumped out of the water pretty steeply; the black peaks sticking out of the snow along its top were a couple of hundred metres above sea level. Looking back as they puttered along, they could see a shiny new radio sphere on top of the last peak, which overlooked McMurdo on its other side. The slopes dropping into the sea were about half black rock, half crusted snowfields.

They motored slowly past Arrival Heights, then Danger Slopes, where Scott's seaman, Vince, had slipped to his death during one of the icecapades in the first year there. Then they passed a rocky knob called Knob Point; beyond it there was a mostly rocky section of the peninsula, smoothbacked, its side like a giant berm sloping into the ice-fringed water. There appeared to be a couple of indented ledges halfway up this section of the slope, like raised beaches from ages when sea level had been higher, though X had no idea if that was really what had formed them. From the water they appeared to be very narrow, lines only, but Ta Shu was pointing at them; and indeed, they looked to be the only flat land on this whole side of the peninsula.

So they puttered in to the icy shore and landed on a steep, black pebble strand. 'You could keep boat here,' Ta Shu said as they got out over the bow. 'Row to town when it is water. Bicycle on ice when it is frozen. Or ski. Or walk.'

'True,' X said.

They climbed. The black rubble was steep and loose, but an inconspicuous path of stabilized steps in the rubble could eventually be tramped out.

When they reached the first ledge they found that it was much wider than it had looked from below; perhaps fifty yards wide; a long and level terrace in the steep slope; one could have fitted several big houses

393

on it, in fact. And something little and snug could be tucked at the back of the terrace and not even be visible from the water below. And out of the wind.

Looking over the sea to the north, they saw the ridgy little Dellbridge Islands, and beyond them the dark points of Cape Evans and Cape Royds. 'That was another volcanic cone,' Ta Shu said, pointing at the Dellbridges. 'See how the islands make the pieces of a circle?'

'Ah,' X said. 'Yeah.'

He wandered around, looking at the ground. Under the layer of rubble was cracked volcanic basalt, as solid as could be. Bedrock. He stood with his back to the slope and looked north again. To his left he could see over the black water of McMurdo Sound to the mountains of the Dry Valleys. To his right Erebus rose like a white castle, steaming from its top as usual. Behind him, if he went up onto the crest of the peninsula, he would be near Castle Peak, in the area called the Japanese rock garden. There was a flagged cross-country ski trail running from Castle Peak to McMurdo.

Ta Shu sat crosslegged on the edge of the great ledge, and appeared to be deep in meditation. Finally he came out of his trance and turned to X. 'This is a good place.'

After that they had a lovely day, puttering slowly through the Dellbridges up to Cape Evans and Cape Royds. Ta Shu like Val had a great admiration for Shackleton, and at Cape Royds he walked around Shackleton's hut exclaiming at its location, its size – everything about it was apparently perfection in the *feng shui* sense. Meanwhile X wandered out to take a look at the rookery of Adélie penguins at the end of the cape, and while he was there one of the males stuck his head at the sky and squawked wildly as he tried, it appeared, to fly straight up, without ever getting even an inch off the ground. Ecstatic display, as the beakers called it. X knew just how he felt.

And at the end of the day X coasted the Zodiac back into the docks at McMurdo, noticing that a big contingent of red-parkaed people was standing at the entrance to the mall; the investigators from the north, no doubt.

Ta Shu squinted up at the town:

grey sky
brown earth

'This could be a good place,' he said.

394

1. The Antarctic Treaty should be renewed as soon as possible, after whatever renegotiation is necessary to get all parties to agree to terms and sign. Some law needs to be in place. Paraphrasing the original proposal for an Antarctic Treaty, written by people in the American State Department in 1958: 'It would appear desirable to reach agreement on a program to assure the continuation of fruitful scientific co-operation in that continent, preventing unnecessary and undesirable political rivalries, the uneconomic expenditure of funds to defend individual interests, and the recurrent possibility of misunderstanding. If harmonious agreement can be reached in regard to friendly co-operation in Antarctica, there would be advantages to all other countries as well.'

2. In this renewed Treaty, and by a more general proclamation of the United Nations, Antarctica should be declared to be a world site of special scientific interest. Some may wish to interpret this to mean also that Antarctica is a sacred ritual space, in which human acts take on spiritual significance.

3. Oil, natural gas, methane hydrates, minerals and fresh water all exist in Antarctica, sometimes in concentrations that make their extraction and use a technical possibility. (Oil in particular, to be specific about the most controversial resource, is located in no supergiant fields but in three or four giant fields and many smaller ones, totalling approximately fifty billion barrels.) Given that this is so, and that world supplies of some of these non-renewable resources are being consumed at a rapid rate, the possibility of extraction needs to be explicitly considered by not only the Antarctic Treaty nations, but the United Nations as well.

Non-Treaty nations, in the Southern Hemisphere in particular, think of the possibility of oil extraction from Antarctica as one way of solving energy needs and dealing with ongoing debt crises. At the same time current oil extraction technology presents a small but not negligible risk of environmental contamination as the result of an accident. Technologies are likely to become safer in the future, and world oil supplies are decreasing so sharply that any remaining untapped supplies, left in reserve for future generations who may need oil for purposes other than fuel, are likely to be extremely valuable. These trends point to the idea of caching or sequestering certain oil fields for future use. Southern Hemisphere nations in need of short term help could perhaps make arrangements modelled on the debt-for-nature exchanges that have already been made; in this case, the World Bank or individual northern countries might buy future rights to Antarctic oil from southern nations, with the payments to start now, but the oil to be sequestered, with extraction to be delayed until the extraction technology's safety and the need for oil warrant it.

At the same time, demonstrably safe methane hydrate drilling could proceed, providing a less concentrated but still valuable source of fuel and income to the drillers, while serving also as a training ground for drilling technologies that could be considered for later use in oil extraction.

4. The Antarctic Treaty suspends all claims of sovereignty on the continent, at the same time that it specifies free access to all, and a ban on military presences for anything but unarmed logistical support. The continent is land without ownership, *terra communis*; it is not property but commons, in the stewardship of all humanity. It is also the largest remaining wilderness on this planet. As such it exists in an experimental legal state which cannot ban visitors. Therefore if people desire to live in Antarctica, and take that responsibility and that cost on themselves, this is their right, even if all governmental and other official organizations disapprove and withhold all support.

However, because Antarctica is such a delicate environment, individuals like countries should be required to adhere to the principles of the Antarctic Treaty in its current form, and to respect the continent's status as wilderness. This adherence and respect puts severe limits on the number of indigenous animals that can be legally killed under international convention and law; thus the natural carrying capacity of the continent for human beings is very low. People interested enough in Antarctica to consider living there should keep this in mind, and a scientifically established 'human carrying capacity' should be ascertained for Antarctica and for its local bioregions, and the human population of the continent and the bioregions should not exceed carrying capacity. Current preliminary calculations of the human carrying capacity of the continent suggest it is on the order of three to six thousand people, but human carrying capacity in general is a notoriously vexed topic, and estimates of capacities both local and global range over many orders of magnitude, depending on the methods used; for instance, for Antarctica figures have been cited ranging from zero to ten million. Possibly work on this issue in Antarctica could refine the concept of human carrying capacity itself.

5. If people do decide to try to become indigenous to Antarctica, special care will have to be taken to avoid polluting the environment, because the Antarctic serves as a benchmark of cleanliness for studies of the rest of the world, and in the cold arid environment many forms of pollution are very slow to break down. Some would wish to add

that as sacred space, cleanliness of treatment is our obligation to this place.

Again the entire continent must be considered a site of special scientific interest, in this case becoming an ongoing experiment in clean technologies and practices, including sufficiency minima, recycling, waste reduction and processing, etc. The goal should be a zero-impact lifestyle, and the reality cannot stray very far from that goal.

The Treaty's ban on the importation of exotic plants, animals and soils means that any local agriculture attempted by inhabitants will have to be conducted hydroponically or aquaculturally, in hermetically-sealed greenhouses and terraria or in well-controlled aquaculture pens containing only indigenous sea life. This constraint will be one aspect of the carrying capacity calculations, and suggests also that self-sufficiency for any indigenous Antarctic society or societies would be impractical and risky for the environment, and should not be considered a goal of such societies. The reliance on outside help should be acknowledged as a given.

Anthropogenic reintroduction of species that used to exist in Antarctica is an issue that we leave to further discussions elsewhere.

6. The achievement of clean, appropriate zero-impact lifestyles in Antarctica is not merely a matter of the technologies employed, but of the social structures which both use these technologies and call successor technologies into being, as a function of the society's desires for itself. This being the case, all inhabitants of Antarctica should abide by the various human rights documents generated by the United Nations, and special attention should be given to co-operative, non-exploitative economic models, which emphasize sustainable permaculture in a healthy biophysical context, abandoning growth models and inequitable hierarchies which in Antarctica not only degrade human existence but also very quickly impact upon the fragile environment.

7. In such a harsh environment all attacks against persons or equipment constitute a threat to life and cannot be allowed. All those interested enough in Antarctica to come here must forswear violence against humanity or their works, and interact in peaceable ways.

8. What is true in Antarctica is true everywhere else.

Back into the antique interior of a Herc, like something out of Jules Verne, rocketing them back in howling vibration to planet Earth, twenty-first century. Out of the bathyscape windows the endless blue sea and its scrim of white cloud, thirty thousand feet below and closing fast. A very big world. Wade slept through what he could.

As he slept he dreamed of his last conversation with Sylvia, the dream's day-residue in this case only a slightly skewed replay or continuation of their quiet talk, there in her office looking out at Beeker Street. He had told her about his conversation with Sam, and described his plan, and she had nodded thoughtfully. Two bureaucrats, deciding the fate of a continent. An empty continent of course, the least significant of the continents; but still. A continent ruled by scientists, Sylvia said. Bound not to last. Scientific government. Trying to catch neutrinos. We try to study things, she said. Do what's best for the long haul. The ferals, the oil people – both look to the scientists for their answers. Both use the scientists' mode of being in Antarctica as their ideal. A way of living on the land. Wanting nothing from it but questions to be asked. Maybe it will work, Wade said, again in his dream, maybe technocrats have taken over the world, maybe scientists have taken over the world. Maybe the highest, driest, coldest, least significant of the continents would show the way. We'll see, Sylvia said. The weather has cleared. The FBI is on its way, and past the point of safe return. We are all past the point of safe return.

Then an image of Val in her long underwear lighting a Coleman stove knocked him awake. Reluctantly he looked around at the other sleeping passengers in their heavy parkas, heads on strangers' shoulders, knees enjambed for balance, bunny boots thrust unceremoniously between other people's legs. Antarctica had crushed them together and made them all family, body-space abolished as a concept, all sleeping together in the Victorian roar like cubs in a litter.

Then the plane's crew were walking through, waking people, gesturing at seatbelts. They were landing. There was some kind of trouble again, someone shouted in Wade's earplugged ear: the wheels wouldn't come down, or the skis wouldn't come up, he couldn't hear which. In any case they were going to have to land on the skis.

Wade groaned. The passengers looked at each other, rolling their eyes. Landing on skis on a concrete runway did not sound good. But what could you do? They were in a Herc; anything could happen. Wade rose up a little to look out of the window above him one last time: still blue ocean, white cloud. Descending to Earth.

Presumably they were lubricating the runway with that emergency foam. Planes had bellied down on that stuff without problems; skis no doubt would be fine. Piece of cake. If they had been here the Kiwi helo crew would be cackling. They even had flaps this time. Could fly in like a stunt plane no doubt.

Touchdown, bounce, down again, run out. No taxiing afterward, but other than that, no different to any other landing. People grinned, made the thumbs up gesture. The family had survived another Herc trip. Wait your turn to get out.

Then out, into the shocking heat of a spring day in Christchurch. Maybe fifty degrees Fahrenheit, even sixty – incredible. Standing on the runway. They had indeed foamed it. A bus to take them over to the airport buildings. They had their own building, and no one was there to tell them what to do.

Wade followed the others as they hauled their orange bags through the building, then down the road to the Antarctic Centre. He was sweating as he walked. The smell of grass, so strong. The greens everywhere, so vivid. Low clouds which were clearly made of liquid water. Coming at him were children, laughing. A little girl in a blue dress, her older brother teasing her. Their high voices in the humid, grassy air.

Inside the clothing centre Wade stripped off his Antarctic gear, inspecting it item by item as he dropped it on the floor: the glove with the ripped finger-seam which had made that finger colder than the rest everywhere he went; the parka zipper that would not zip all the way up past the throat. Shimmery blue overalls, red parka, his springy white bunny boots. All piled on the concrete floor as he slowly pulled on the street clothes he had left behind, his limbs sticky with sweat. That life was over. A young Kiwi checked off all his gear and gave him a pink receipt. Back in the world.

NSF had him scheduled for a flight home the next day. So he checked into the airport hotel, and sat there vibrating on the bed for a while, thinking things over. Back to Washington; back to his life.

He got on the phone and called Phil Chase.

'Hello, Wade! Where are you now?'

'Christchurch.'

'Good flight back?'

'It was interesting.'

'Good. Hey I got the report you sent on the ecotage, also those protocols, I thought those were great. Those could be made into a more global programme very easily, I'm very excited, I'd like to try to do something further with those. I see your hand in that document, Wade.'

'Only in asking for it, and that was you. It was mostly Sylvia's doing. With input from everybody, of course. She got the most help from Ta Shu, I'd say.'

'Whatever. She may have made her mark with that, though, I'm telling you.'

'I think she just thinks of it as a report.'

'Doesn't matter what she thinks. It's out of her hands now.'

This struck Wade as a more general truth, and he did not reply.

'So, Wade, you sound tired. You're back from your big adventure.'

'Yes. But listen, Phil – I think it's your turn.'

'My turn for a big adventure? That's my whole life, Wade. It's just one big adventure after another.'

'I know that. But this time you've got to try something new. You've got to go to Washington.'

'Ha ha.'

'No I mean it. The time is right. Listen, you know the ferals in Antarctica had a helper in the American security community, right? A satellite-photo analyst who gave them information, and covered for them a bit up there, you know.'

'That's right, I think I remember you telling me that. You kept calling me when I was asleep.'

'Well I've been talking to him. He's a split position between NOAA and one of the security agencies, and a hard man to reach, but I had introductions from both Mai-lis and Sylvia, so he agreed to talk to me.'

'He knows Sylvia too?'

'He's the same photo analyst she was using.'

'Is this good?'

'Definitely good. I had a long talk with him, and he was very interesting. He has solid photographic evidence that he would be willing to forward to us, that the Southern Club's oil group has not been the only party down in Antarctica looking for oil this season. He says he can prove without a doubt that some of the big American-based companies have been down there as well. They've been using the southern cartel as a cover, basically, counting on them to distract attention and take the heat, while they're down there too, very unobtrusively, using a Nigerian operation as a front but organizing it and making quick spot-checks to look for the supergiant field rumoured to be in the Bransfield Strait or the Weddell Sea. And one of them is Texacon.'

'Uh huhn. Are we surprised at this, Wade?'

'No no, of course not, but it's not *known*, it's been hidden, and this guy is offering us proof. And you know Texacon is one of Winston's biggest campaign contributors.'

This had been a seven-hour wonder in Winston's last campaign; despite the latest campaign finance recomplication campaign, *The Washington Post* had managed to publish an exposé identifying overlarge contributions to Paul Winston from Texacon, among several other major corporations. It was true that the contributions had been laundered sufficiently to be in compliance with the recomplication, and

Winston's poll-ratings had climbed rather than dropped after the exposé, but the allegations were there, and Winston himself had never denied them.

'Hmmmm,' Phil was humming, 'hmmm, hmmmmm, and so you're saying?'

'Winston gets big campaign contributions from Texacon, only marginally legal. He blocks Antarctic Treaty re-ratification in committee. The Treaty's ban on mineral extraction goes into limbo. Then Texacon is found down in Antarctica drilling for oil!'

Phil started to laugh. He interrupted himself: 'You know there's no linkage there, Wade, you know that. They're totally innocent. Winston is blocking the Treaty because he wants to harrass the President, and Texacon contributed money to him because he's the kind of guy they like to support. And they're drilling in Antarctica because they drill everywhere. I'll bet no one on either side of that equation is explicitly working a *quid pro quo*. It's just business as usual, guys on the same team doing their thing.'

'But the appearance.'

'Yeah sure. Big favours for big money. Bribery, we'll call it. I'll say that right on the floor of the Senate. I can press that issue hard, being so clean myself. All my contributions come in coin rolls.'

It was true that Phil had once financed a campaign by asking all his supporters to send the coins piling up in their houses, a move that had brought in a lot of money as well as sparked a million jokes and political cartoons about spare change etc., all the more pointed in that Phil had indeed in one of his OWE stints spent three months living as a street beggar.

'It gives you a crowbar to pry at him with,' Wade said.

'Yes.' Silence as Phil thought it over. 'Bad timing, though, I must say, given how busy I am here.'

'You need to go to Washington with this,' Wade said firmly. 'You need to drop into town like a bomb and take it to Winston, see if you can use this oil stuff to put the heat on enough to get him to let the Treaty out of committee. Hell, maybe even drive him out of the chair. Maybe even out of the Senate!'

'Fat chance.'

'But it is a chance! The Ethics Committee might go chaotic and swerve and throw him out. The moment is here, Phil, and it's important.'

'What I do out on the road is important too.'

'Of course Phil, of course! But you wouldn't have to stay off the road for long. Depending. I mean if you picked up some momentum, then maybe you would want to stay. Things are riding in the balance here,' Wade finding it oh so easy to read back some of Phil's midnight rambling. 'We're at an unstable moment in history, the teeter-totter is wavering there in the middle, co-opification versus the Götterdämmerung, they've got the guns but we've got the numbers! The time is ripe, Phil, ripe for you to come falling down out of space onto our side of the teeter-totter and catapult them out of there!'

'Hmm, yes, well. It would be nice to stick a pin in Winston anyway, at least.'

'It sure would! That bastard. Pop him like a balloon.'

'Indeed. Hmm, yes – but I've got a lot of commitments out here. I don't know what I could do about that.'

'I'll represent you where I can, Phil. I'm thinking of staying in New Zealand a while longer, try to tie up some of the loose ends of this Antarctic business, see what I can do. After that I could cover for you out on the road, and of course keep track of this Antarctic situation for you, and I can keep making reports to you, be your eyes for you so to speak, like I've been doing here, while you kick their ass in Washington.'

'Hmm, yes . . . So you've got solid evidence Texacon has been drilling in Antarctica since the last campaign?'

'Photos in colour, Sam said. Photos from space that read their phone numbers off the screens on their wristphones.'

'Cool. Interesting. Drop back in like a bomb. Blow their minds. That would be fun, wouldn't it? Might even get the Antarctic Treaty ratified. That would be a coup. Although it's funny – if it works, then you've got to say it was those ecoteurs that did it – they found the right part of the system and gave it a whap, it's admirable in a way.'

'Don't say that on the floor of the Senate.'

'You don't think I should?'

'Lawmakers endorsing law-breaking? No. It's unseemly.'

'Obscene? Come on, Wade. It's lawmakers know better than anyone that laws are more a matter of practical compromise than any kind of moral imperative.'

'Just don't say that on the floor of the Senate.'

'We'll see. I never know for sure what I'll say when the moment comes. But just between you and me, I admire those ecoteur guys.'

'Because they took action.'

'Okay, Wade, okay. I'll go to Washington. I'll talk to Glen and Colleen here, and John back at the office, we'll try to set it up. Get those photos to me, and we'll work from there.'

'They're on their way. I sent them to the office.'

'I'm in Samarkand, Wade. Send them here too. And try to call during business hours. Call me tomorrow, and we'll continue this.'

'Sure thing.'

Wade sat on his hotel bed, feeling himself vibrate. He liked Phil Chase; he wanted to keep working for him. And co-opification was going to be a long, hard campaign. But if he could keep Phil convinced that he was on the edge of winning, or at least in the heart of the battle, then Phil would stay in Washington, and Wade would have to be out on the road, serving as his eyes. Which meant that Wade was going to have to keep finding things big enough to keep Phil in Washington in order to be able to stay out on the road, with the chance of occasionally coming to Christchurch. In short, making Phil save the world in order to create the off-chance of returning to Antarctica. It almost made sense.

After a while, feeling time suddenly heavy on his hands, he went out and took the shuttle bus into the centre of Christchurch. He looked out of the windows at the trees and the low clouds, stunned by the greens and the warm, wet air. Sixty degrees Fahrenheit, they said. He couldn't imagine what DC would feel like. Oh, but it was October. It would be cold in DC. Cold, well – it would be cool.

In Christchurch he wandered, overwhelmed at every turn. Smells of coffee, food cooking, Kiwi voices. The faces from Masterpiece Theatre. Next to the Avon River, a statue of Scott, in concrete for ever, wearing what Wade saw now was ridiculous gear. On the pedestal: to search, to seek, to find, and not to yield. Tennyson's immortal concrete. Ta Shu had told him that around the time Scott had died, his two-year-old son had rushed into his mother's bedroom in England and said, 'Daddy's not coming home.' You could be immortalized in concrete, or see your child grow up. Better a live donkey than a dead lion, Shackleton had said. Scott hadn't agreed. But which would the world choose? Which story did they like better?

Wade wandered in the huge botanical garden at the south end of the town. There were so many shades of green! And varieties of plants. All these species had evolved out of lichens and mosses, it was amazing what the warm world had generated. He was still vibrating with the props. He saw that there appeared to be people living in these gardens, under the big trees. Ferals here, too.

On a complex of soccer fields south of the botanical garden, crowds of people surrounded a group that were inflating enormous bright balloons – like hot-air balloons, only filled from gas canisters. Some of the balloons reminded Wade of the blimps they had flown in over the Transantarctics. Others were truly huge, their gondolas like three-storey Amsterdam houses. A festival atmosphere. People with picnic baskets, waving at the departing flyers.

'Where are they going?' Wade asked one of them.

Wherever the wind took them. Can't do much else in a balloon. Stocked to live aloft for up to a year, some of them. Take a sabbatical in the clouds, or work up there. Go around the world a few times. Off on a tramp. Sky-tramping, they called it.

'Going feral?'

That's what the Aussies call it.

'Much of that here?'

Yeah, sure. Most of the kids off in the wild. The balloons are more family. Like boating. Hook a bunch of them together once they get aloft. We've always been a bit like that here. Not very many people. A lot of land. Nothing new to us in these McMurdo Protocols you see in the paper. We redrew all our county lines to match the watershed boundaries, a long time ago.

Then the balloons and blimps were all inflated. One by one, up and up and off into the wind, mingling with the low, liquid clouds. It was surprising how clearly you could tell liquid clouds from frozen ones. These were as wet as a bath, and dropping a bit of rain on them all. No one noticed.

When the balloons were gone, Wade wandered off. He was aimless, and vibrating still. Christchurch looked like a California town.

That night in his hotel there was nothing on the TV news about the balloon departure. It had to have been a couple of hundred people taking off at least. But as far as the news was concerned it had not happened. Wade was puzzled. He channel-surfed trying to find mention of it. Good visuals, perfect story for TV. Nothing. It had not happened. But if you've seen something with your own eyes and then there is no mention of it on the news, who are you going to believe?

Suspended between worlds. Vibrating on a hotel bed like a Herc engine idling, in front of a muted TV, the images familiar but drained of all meaning. Looking at them Wade was reminded that as he had left McMurdo, Ta Shu had given him a TV chip that would allow him to hook into Ta Shu's show in China. Now he dug in his briefcase until he found the little plastic minidisk, and went to the TV and inserted the disk into the slot in the TV's control panel.

After some flickering the Kiwi images were replaced by a bright white landscape: the Royal Society Range, seen from across the Ross Sea. 'Hey!' Wade said, leaning forward from the edge of the bed, staring into the image. That was the view from Observation Hill!

Ta Shu's narration was in Chinese, of course, and very rapid and fluid, not at all like his English. Of course. After a minute or two of listening to his voice, Wade's curiosity grew. He wanted to know what Ta Shu was saying at such length and with such apparent urgency. He got up and went back to his briefcase, and pulled out his laptop, and called up the menu for the translation programs that the laptop contained in its hard drive. He had heard that Chinese-to-English programs were still the worst of all the major language programs, but still it would be better than nothing.

He put the laptop next to the TV and punched in the code for the translation program. After a short pause the laptop began to speak in English, almost as rapidly as Ta Shu himself, in a mechanical monotone.

'So my friends we are come to end of our adventure in Antarctica. Soon I will leave this land, I will fly north over the south ocean, to the New Zealand. It has been a true event time, I am sure you agree. Many interruptions, many discoveries. Full of lands so powerful, action so strange, you must wonder if I am transmitting you from another world. But I remind you, all this happens on Earth. This too is Earth. A world beyond all telling. For me it has been a profound being, a trip. For you at home in China, watching what I have looked at in facemasks or on television screens, not so there. Without space, without spaciousness, as it must be. Like a story told, or a dream you have had. Of course this must be so. Where then have we been together? In a vision we share a story. Lemon said stories are false solutions to real problems. Lamb added corollary, that stories from other planets hence are false solutions to false problems. What then have we done together? Look around you. Is it all a dream only? Or are all the worlds one world. Black said, dreams commence obligation to world. Seashells say poets are the unknown government of the world. And we are all poets. So now we tell the world what next to do.'

The image on the TV panned left, to an expanse of white ice; the screen was cut horizontally right across the middle, blue above, white below, like a powerful Rothko. The view directly south. Ta Shu spoke again, and after a pause the laptop translator picked it up. 'Ah yes. Very nice view. Now we come to the end of our time together, and I ask one thing of you, my friends who have stayed with me long and faithfully. When my transmission has ended, go outdoors. Go take a walk outside in the open air. Wherever you find yourself on the face of this planet, it is a good place. Breathe deeply the breath of the world. Look at the sky over our heads all together. Feel yourself walking; this too is thought. Feel the wind in your face. Feel the way you are animal, breathing in the spirit wind. If our time together gives you no more than this walk, then still yet it has done well. Farewell now, my friends, until our next voyage together.'

The view from Ob Hill disappeared. Cut to a Chinese commercial. 'Do you have trouble cleaning kitchen hardware?'

Wade turned off the TV. He went downstairs. He opened a glass door cautiously, but it was still warm. Out of the door, into the hotel's inner courtyard. It was night, the darkness like a caress to the eyes.

He could feel his pupils blooming. Air warm and humid against his skin – so warm, so benign. The caress of the breeze. Maybe it would work after all. He walked over to the lawn by the pool, sat down on the warm fragrant grass. He ran his hands over it. He lay down in it, on his back, and looked up at the stars.

The next spring X made all his preparations, and took off for a walk across Ross Island.

It had been a busy winter. The McMurdo Field Services Co-op, usually called Mac Co-op, won the bid for the field services subcontract. PetHelo won the general contract; ASL was gone. After the initial celebrations, there had been endless hours of organizational meetings and paperwork in Mac Town. In the meantime, friends had helped X to build a little hut on the ledge next to Knob Point, mostly out of parts scavenged from McMurdo's construction yard dumpsters: three arches of an old Jamesway frame, essentially, with new insulation, a triple-paned window with two panes cracked, and photovoltaic sheeting tacked to the outside for the coming sunny months. Inside there was a little propane stove for heating and cooking. A bed, a desk, a chair. It was very cosy, but X liked it that way. It was his place. Tucked back against the slope, out of the wind, invisible from below. Especially of course during these sunless months.

On every day the weather allowed, he skied up through the rock garden to the cross-country trail and down into town, and did some work at the co-op office, and either stayed a night in the BFC office on the sofa, or skied back home. Sometimes he went home on the sea ice, around Discovery Point. It depended on how much moonlight he had to work with. On dark nights it was best to go around on the sea ice; on moonlit nights it was fun to stay up on the ridge. He found that a full moon on the snowy land was bright enough to read by, much less ski. During these trips, and on his days off, he worked hard on his snow skills. He decided that he wanted to make a traverse of Ross Island, going over the three volcanoes and down to Cape Crozier, to see the 'Return of the Sun' ceremony which George Tremont was planning to stage out there. This would be a big trip for him, X knew that well, and he prepared for it all winter. He found that unlike a lot of sports, mountaineering was mostly a matter of walking. One only had to walk without falling and one was a successful mountaineer. More a matter of navigation than athletic skill – at least at the level he was trying, which was merely to get around Ross Island. And so he had been pleased at his progress. Countless times he had climbed the rock steps from the sea ice up to his hut and back down again, to build his strength and endurance. He had worked on walking up and down steeper and steeper snow slopes; he had practised with snowshoes on snow, and crampons on ice. He found he liked snowshoes better than skis, even if they were harder work; they were easier, indeed almost identical to walking in boots. He learned to use a GPS, and a crevasse detector. The crevasse detector was critical; without it X wouldn't have had the courage to attempt hiking around on his own. As it was, whenever it beeped he stopped like Lot's wife, and carefully worked out where he was, and where the crevasse was, and then he went around it. He would make extravagant detours, hiking miles out of his way, in order not to have to cross a crevasse, no matter how solid any snowbridges in it might appear. No crossing beep-beeps and he would be okay. And so he had gradually ranged farther and farther away, and spent nights out in a tent and sleeping bag, learning slowly to manipulate the gear and to trust in it to keep him alive and warm. The days – the endless succession of sunless hours – had passed quickly.

Back in his little hut the hours had also passed quickly. He had studied Heraclitus, and co-op economics. From time to time he heard from Carlos in Santiago. More often he heard from Wade, who e-mailed hellos from all over the world, having apparently switched roles with his senator (and X thought he knew why). The senator had returned to Washington, and got a rival in trouble with the Senate Ethics Committee about campaign donations, and as an indirect, fifty-dominoes-down-the-line result, it looked as if the Antarctic Treaty renewal was going to be ratified soon. Wade seemed cautiously optimistic. The two messages he sent when actually in Washington on visits were brief and ambivalent: 'We're kicking ass,' and 'This is not a good place.'

Along with his snippets of news, he sent X a lot of music that X had never heard before; it became clear that he was a rabid closet DJ and inflictor-of-music-on-friends; but tucked in the little hut for as many hours as X was, he did not complain; on the contrary, he listened to these gifts again and again. Often he listened to them while watching Ta Shu's latest transmission on his computer screen. These days Ta Shu was taking a boat trip down the Yangtze River. The translation program X used made him sound like a long succession of incoherent fortune cookies, but still it was interesting to see him take on the Chinese equivalent of the Bureau of Reclamation. And when this voyage was over, X was going to try to view a copy of Ta Shu's Antarctic adventure; that would be even more interesting than the Yangtze, and it seemed almost certain that there would be some film of Val in it, too. There was footage of her in the SAR's Happy Camper videos, X had found, and once he watched this footage over and over for most of one Sunday. Then he trashed the file and stopped looking for such things. But glimpses of her in Ta Shu's program would be okay.

Late in the winter, despite X's warnings and protests, the co-op hired Ron to come back down and run the heavy shop. X cursed when he heard the vote on this: 'Damn it, he's a pirate! He joined the ice pirates!'

'He was desperate,' Joyce said. 'It doesn't matter now. Get used to it.'

Later, thinking it over in his hut, X decided he could get used to it. After all, it had not made him comfortable to think of Ron either plotting revenge in Chile or holed up drinking in some Florida beachfront. Certainly he would come back down and try to take everything over, and then there would be a major jerk in their fine new co-op; but at least it would be a jerk that X knew and liked. And X would not have to answer to him. And Mac Co-op would survive him.

Twice X got e-mail messages from Val, just brief ones; once on his birthday, once on the solstice; but there they were, right there on his screen. Her winter was turning out not all that different to his. Like all the other animals wintering over down here, the ferals had to hunch down in the cold and dark, bunch together like the Emperor penguins. They made some expeditions out, apparently, but no one could stand the winter cold for long. The one interesting thing they had done was to carve a refuge in the ice cap itself, lighting it intensively for half the day, and living in this artificial oasis for several weeks without many trips outside. So Val was hibernating too.

X had replied to her messages carefully, and gone back to his Heraclitus. The same road goes both up and down. Knowledge is not wisdom. Wholeness arises from distinct particulars. All things come in seasons. Character is fate.

And now spring and George Tremont's celebration were almost here, and so he took off, waving fondly to his battened-down little hut. It was close enough to the year's first sunrise that there were a few hours of clear twilight bracketing noon every day, and he started in that clear, grey light. There was a full moon as well, and after the twilight darkened he could still see the snow underfoot perfectly well in the moonlight. Up onto the ridge of Hut Point, around Castle Rock, and on up the long flank of Erebus. Up and up and up, one step at a time. Higher on the volcano the slope got steeper, but it was always just a matter of walking, and circumventing the beep-beeps. A shield volcano, nowhere precipitous. One step after another. Up and up, one step after another. The end of a circle is also its beginning. Snowshoes were so wonderful.

He kept track of the time, and after six hours of hard climbing had passed, he stopped and took off his rucksack, and pulled out his sleeping bag and tiny bivvy tent, and got in them and cooked a dinner on his little stove. After that he tried to sleep for a while. He was too excited to sleep very well, but after an hour or two he fell into a doze, and when he woke up, face freezing, he started the stove and cooked up some hot chocolate, then porridge. He got his boots on, got his rucksack repacked, jumped out and repacked his tent. Then off he went again, poling methodically with his ski poles, his snowshoes clicking and squeaking. Left, right, left, right; up the great ghostly white mountain, luminous even in starlight only. Higher and higher.

Up on the highest slopes of the volcano it was very cold, and very still. No wind. He had checked with weather before setting off, and it was supposed to hold good for a week, but the air now was unusually still. In the lack of wind there was no sound; and only starlight illuminating the landscape, which nevertheless was clearly visible, white on black. Nothing moved for as far as the eye could see; as if time itself had frozen, and X the Golem impervious to that freezing and left wandering still, tramping through eternity.

Erebus was still steaming from its cratered summit, however; steaming more than ever, no doubt, in the cold, still air. X hiked quickly around the rim of the active crater, keeping well back from the edge, feeling very small, and obscurely frightened – as if it were simply *too bold* for a lone human to hike around the crest of Erebus in the dark before dawn. But there he was; and really it was just a matter of putting one foot in front of the other. Nothing more than that; and yet so strange! Could this really be him? On Earth? In this present moment of his life? He could scarcely believe it was happening. But there he was. When he reached the far side of the crater, he even turned and went right up to the rim's edge, to look down into the active caldera. The steam billowing up past him was pinkish orange, lit from below. Under that was burbling orange lava, scarcely glimpsed through the steam. The rising steam roared airily, and boomed in echoey booms. Beginning of the world.

He hurried on, feeling that he had tempted fate: gases, lava bombs, the spirit of the vasty deep, something ought to get him for taking such a chance for a glance. But he had done it! And now it was all downhill.

By the time he had descended to Mount Terra Nova, and stopped for another brace of meals and a nap, and gone up and over Mount Terror too, it was getting very near the time of the first sunrise. It was in the midday twilight that X glissaded down the last spine of Mount Terror to Cape Crozier, the sky lightening all the while, as if he were redescending from the dark peak into the world of light and motion and wind. He had traversed Ross Island, from Knob Point to Cape Crozier, over the tops of the three volcanoes! And so he felt marvellous as he glissaded down one of the long snowy chutes between lava ridges, left snowshoe, right, left, right, all the long way down to Igloo Spur.

He was happy as he came over a final bump, and saw the little knot of people surrounding the rock hut. He walked down and joined them, explaining briefly where he had come from. They congratulated him, then pointed out what they had just recently been surprised to discover, which was that the little museum shelter, built the year before, had disappeared. The structure itself was gone, that was; all the equipment that the three early explorers had left behind was still there, but now relocated in the rock hut itself; the things put back, evidently, where they had been left by the three explorers.

X went over to have a closer look. A narrow wooden sledge lay across the rock oval, and under it on the floor of the hut, coated with a rime of snow, all the objects lay scattered in the tumble they must have been in when the three had beat their hasty retreat.

'Good idea,' X opined.

'George didn't think so. He practically pulled out his beard.'

'But he's getting used to it now, see?'

'I wonder who did it.'

'Shh! They're about to start playing.'

As George had organized the ceremony, there was of course music to be played; and, of course, mikes and cameras to record it. Quite a lot of people, in fact, clustered on the lee side of the ridge under the rock hut.

X walked a short distance back up Igloo Spur, to get some distance from the fuss. Then they all waited. George was apparently timing the start of the music so that the piece would end during the arrival of the sun. X stood with his back to the wind, looking up the jagged coastline north of Cape Crozier. I live on this island, he thought. I just walked across my island. I live in this world. A gust of wind peeled over the ridge. The sky was getting lighter by the second. George raised his baton and jerked it down, and his little orchestra began to play what one of the celebrants had informed X was Jean Sibelius's 'Night Ride and Sun Rise'. Although it was clear immediately to X that the night ride referred to in the title had been a train ride, it was still easy to imagine the strings' rhythmic rise and fall to be a stylized version of the winds pouring over this place, rather than of a train crossing Finland; the wind and the music in fact fitted together very nicely; it was hard at times to tell which was which. Of course no matter what the musicians had tried in their attempt to keep warm, their instruments and fingers and lips had inevitably frozen, and the little ensemble had a windy, cracked, untuned sound, somewhat like an early music ensemble using period instruments; but music neverthe-less, with strings and brass and woodwinds pulsing up and down and up and down, just like the wind.

And George had timed things so well, conducting with many an anxious glance at his wristwatch, that the clarinet made its sudden flight up the stave at the exact moment when the sun cracked the horizon, a very beautiful synchrony, which had George hopping with triumph as he conducted the thawing orchestra through the final rich chords, the whole white world now ablaze with brassy light, beaming outward from the blinding chip of sun on the horizon; the celebrants on the ridge rapt, then cheering as the musicians finished the song. Then one of them pointed south and cried, 'Look! Look!'

Black dots in a pale, sunwashed sky. Could be a flock of distant skuas; could be blimps, even farther away. Could be Val, come to give him a ride back over the island, come to see his new home. X's heart leaped inside him. First you fall in love. Then anything could happen.

Acknowledgements

I went to Antarctica in 1995 courtesy of the National Science Foundation, as part of the US Antarctic Program's Artists and Writers' Program. My thanks to the members of the NSF and the US Antarctic Program who gave me the opportunity, and especially to Guy Guthridge of the US Antarctic Program for his help throughout the process.

Thanks also to Donald Blankenship, Christopher McKay, Bud Foote, John Clute, Fredric Jameson, Lou Aronica, and Arthur C. Clarke.

In McMurdo, thanks to Lisa Mastro, Kristen Larson, Robin Abbott, Mimi Fujino, Ethan Dicks, Tim Meehan, Steven Kottmeier, Tom Callahan, Cheryl Hallam, Kathy Young, Melissa Rider, George Blaisdell, Sridhar Anandakrishnan, and Jessie.

In the Dry Valleys, thanks to Paula Atkins, John Schindler, Karen Lewis, Robert Collier, Peter Doran, Ray Kepner and Jeffrey Schmok.

At the South Pole, thanks to Ellen Mosely-Thompson, John Pask-ievitch, Bjorn Johns, Frank Brier, Tim Coffey and Harry Mahar; also to Paula, Karl, Jaime, Gloria, Tim, Sparky, Mark, and all the rest of the 1995-96 Pole crew who welcomed me to a wonderful Thanksgiving.

In the Shackleton Glacier area, thanks to Allan Ashworth, Michael Hambrey, Derek Fabel, Lawrence Krissek and David Elliot.

Thanks to the wormherders Ross Virginia, Page Chamberlain, Melody Brown, Mary Kratz and Rich Alward, for a memorable trip to Cape Crozier. Thanks also to the Kiwi helo crew Jim Finlayson, Jon Moore and Lisa Frankel, for that trip and several others.

On Erebus thanks to Philip Kyle, Ray Dibble, Kurt Panter, and US Navy helo pilot Greg Robinson.

Thanks to my fellow Woos Jody Forster, Peter Nisbet, Anne Hawthorne and Sara Wheeler.

Back at home thanks to Charles Hess, Patsy Inouye, Steve Mallory, Nigel Worrall, Sharma Gaponoff, Ricardo Amon, Terry Baier, Victor Salerno, Peter Dileanis, Jennifer Hershey and Ralph Vicinanza.

Special thanks to Stephen Pyne, Robert Wharton, Tom Carver, Peter Webb, and Buck Tilley.

Also to Lisa Nowell, David and Tim Robinson, and Don and Gloria Robinson.

In the text Val mentions you only need to have read five books to know the whole history of Antarctica; this is an exaggeration, but if I were to limit myself to five, I would recommend starting with Stephen Pyne's wonderful *The Ice*; then Roland Huntford's riveting biographies, *Scott and Amundsen* and *Shackleton*; then, most of all, two of the primary sources, Frank Worsley's *Shackleton's Boat Journey*, and above all else Apsley Cherry-Garrard's *The Worst Journey In the World*.

Thanks once again to all the people listed above, without which this book wouldn't have been. If you've read this book already, however, you know how much I have rendered the information and experiences given to me by these generous people. As they say, what's right is from them; the mistakes are all mine.